Home as Found

James Fenimore Cooper

The Writings of
JAMES FENIMORE COOPER

HOME AS FOUND

JAMES FENIMORE COOPER

Edited with Historical Introduction and Explanatory Notes
by Stephen Carl Arch

"Thou art perfect."
Shakespeare, *Henry IV, Part 1* 2.4.35.

SUNY
PRESS

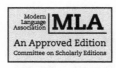

Modern Language Association | **MLA**
An Approved Edition
Committee on Scholarly Editions

The Emblem of the Committee on Scholarly Editions indicates that this volume is based on an examination of all available relevant textual sources, that it is edited according to principles articulated in the volume, that the source texts and any deviation of the edited texts from them are fully described, that the editorial principles, the text, and the apparatus have undergone a peer review, that a rigorous schedule of verification and proofreading was followed to insure a high degree of accuracy in the presentation of the edition, and that the text is accompanied by appropriate textual and historical contextual information.

Cover: Louis Remy Mignot, *Cooperstown from Three Mile Point, 1850–1860*. Oil on canvas. Fenimore Art Museum, Cooperstown, New York, Bequest of William Festus Morgan. N0146.1971. Photograph by Richard Walker.

Published by State University of New York Press, Albany

For information, contact State University of New York Press, Albany, NY
www.sunypress.edu

Library of Congress Cataloging-in-Publication Data

Names: James Fenimore Cooper, author | Stephen Carl Arch, historical
    introduction, notes, and text
Title: Home as Found / James Fenimore Cooper, author.
Description: Albany : State University of New York Press, [2022] | Series:
    The Writings of James Fenimore Cooper | Includes bibliographical references.
Identifiers: ISBN 9781438485379 (hardcover : alk. paper) | ISBN 9781438485386
    (ebook) | ISBN 9781438485362 (pbk. : alk. paper)

LC record available at https://lccn.loc.gov/2022931952

10 9 8 7 6 5 4 3 2 1

Contents

Acknowledgments

I thank Lance Schachterle and Jay Elliott for their painstaking care in reading drafts of this edition. Their suggestions improved this volume considerably. Their ongoing encouragement over many years is the main reason I completed my work on two volumes of this valuable project to edit the works of James Fenimore Cooper begun more than fifty years ago by James Beard. I did not know what I was getting into nearly twenty years ago, but the journey has been stimulating and enriching.

I thank the dozens of other editors and contributors to the multivolume Cooper Edition, whose dedicated work has done so much to improve our understanding of Cooper's artistry.

I thank the current editorial board of the Cooper Edition for their continued support of that good work. I specifically want to thank Wayne Franklin, Robert Durwood Madison, and Anna Scannavini for their feedback on an early draft of the historical introduction to this volume.

I thank Peter Berg in the Special Collections unit of the Michigan State University Library for his assistance in providing a copy of the first US edition of *Home as Found* for Hinman collation; the librarians at the Historical Society of Pennsylvania for assistance in accessing the (partial) amanuensis copy of the text and later for making a digitized copy of it; and the librarians at the Albert and Shirley Small Special Collections Library at the University of Virginia Library for assistance in accessing and later digitizing the (partial) author's manuscript.

This volume was generously supported by a Humanities and Arts Research Program grant from Michigan State University, administered by the Office of the Senior Vice President for Research and Innovation. It was also supported by three consecutive department chairs (Pat O'Donnell, David Stowe, and Cara Cilano), whose friendship I value highly.

In 2016 the grant from Michigan State University supported the research assistance of two graduate students from the Department of English, Christine Peffer Bennett and Cameron C. Clark. I thank them for helping me read the witnesses against the copy-text and for tracking down the sources of epigraphs. My good friend Marshall Olds, now Professor Emeritus of French at Michigan State, reviewed and corrected my translations of Cooper's French. (Any remaining errors are mine!) Thank you, Marshall.

And finally, I thank Nicole McCleese for her unwavering love and support. I am profoundly grateful for new beginnings.

Historical Introduction

Home as Found is a continuation of James Fenimore Cooper's *Homeward Bound* (1838), which he began to compose in July 1837. He worked steadily on *Homeward Bound* through the summer and fall, but by January 1838 he realized that the single novel would not be able to contain the plot as it had developed. On 21 January 1838, he wrote his British publisher, Richard Bentley, to say that he had determined "to continue the tale in another work to be put to press immediately."[1] True to his word, Cooper completed the first volume of the continuation in spring 1838; volume 2 was in the mail on 15 May and the third and final volume on 25 July.[2] *Homeward Bound* was first published in May in England and August in the United States; *Home as Found* was published on November 15 in the United States and on November 28 in England. From July 1837 to July 1838, Cooper wrote what is essentially a double novel, or a novel and its sequel. At the same time, he was completing and publishing *The American Democrat* (1838), proofing his fifth and final travel book (published as *Excursions in Italy* in England and *Gleanings in Europe: Italy* in the United States), publishing the slim historical volume *Chronicles of Cooperstown* (1838), and completing the research for an early draft of his two-volume *History of the Navy of the United States of America* (1839). One wonders what Cooper might have accomplished had he had a computer.

In *Homeward Bound*, the protagonists are in continual motion. After twelve years of living in Europe, the featured characters—Eve Effingham, her father, and her older cousin—embark on a return voyage to the United States from London. They are buffeted by storms, chased by a British cruiser, and shipwrecked on the coast of Africa. There is a budding but not-quite-fulfilled romance, and a daring and successful rescue. They finally approach Sandy Hook, New Jersey, with New York City visible in the distance, only to be halted by the British cruiser before being permitted to land on American soil. In the second volume, *Home as Found*, Cooper began by placing the characters a few months later in New York City, where they engage in fashionable society and visit Wall Street, and then he brings them and others from *Homeward Bound* together again in Templeton, in central New York state, on the southern tip of Lake Otsego, where village life serves as a commentary on and counterpoint to the urban life of New York City. Although the journey from New York City to Templeton in chapter VIII is an important transition in this second novel, Cooper's focus is less on the characters' journey in space than on the nation's journey in time. From his point of view, the nation had changed tremendously in the preceding decade, and he wanted his readers to ponder the causes and consequences of that transformation.

The 1830s were a time of great social and cultural change in the United States. The election of Andrew Jackson as president in 1828 marked not just the emergence of a new democratic sensibility but the reconfiguration of economic, social, and cultural life in the new nation.[3] Writing in the same year the steamship was first put into commercial use for transatlantic journeys, Cooper has his characters cross the Atlantic in a wind-driven commercial packet. But in chapter VIII of *Home as Found*, those characters take a steamboat up the Hudson River, and the narrator remarks on their perception that the "great velocity of the boat" made objects on the shore appear and disappear in quick succession. The world was rapidly changing, and the pace of change is a persistent theme of *Home as Found*, manifested in new forms of communication and travel, new ways of quickly developing and marketing property on Wall Street, new ambitions of quickly climbing the social ladder, and new desires for more information quickly gathered and disseminated.

Two of the main characters are returning to the United States after twelve years abroad.[4] The heroine, Eve Effingham, spent her childhood and youth in Europe; she has relatively few preconceptions about the United States, and people and events appear new and often puzzling to her. She is a bit like Shakespeare's Miranda in *The Tempest*, curious about what at least some characters see as the "brave new world" of the young United States. Her father, Edward Effingham, contrasts the nation he left in his late thirties to the nation he sees before him at the age of fifty;[5] people and things seem shockingly different to him. The third main character, John Effingham, is technically Eve's cousin, but he plays the role of her uncle, being the same age as her father. John lived in Europe during those twelve years, but he also made several business trips back to the United States, and thus he is less surprised than Eve and Edward by what he sees in the world around them. He serves as a kind of jaded tour guide to his relatives. It is ironic at the end of the novel that John Effingham is humbled by his discovery that Paul Powis is his son. Rejected as a suitor by the woman who married his cousin, John had thoughtlessly and hurriedly married for the wrong reasons, then he abandoned his wife who, unbeknownst to him at the time, was pregnant. She died in childbirth, and the orphaned child was left to make his own way in the world. Careful readers will note how each character perceives the United States in the 1830s in light of her or his experiences.

Of course, Cooper wrote from his own personal experience about the shock of return. He, too, left the United States to live in Europe; and he, too, was surprised to learn upon his return seven years later that the United States had changed for what he thought was the worse. In these two fictions, however, Cooper creates leading characters who are less famous than he was but who are much wealthier; they move in lofty social circles because of their wealth. (In Europe, Cooper moved in some of those same social circles because of his *fame*.) Also, they remained in Europe for twelve years, not seven, and thus their shock is all the greater when they return. Home as they find it is not what they expected; one hundred years before Thomas Wolfe, Cooper has his characters discover that you can't go home again. And unlike Cooper, who knew that he was unlikely ever to return to Europe, they plan at the end of *Home as Found* to leave the United States and to return to Europe, perhaps forever. Those differences between the author and his characters seemed obvious to Cooper. He did not think he had written autobiographical novels. The reviewers disagreed.

It is useful to step back in time here. In the 1820s, Cooper's first great successes in novels like *The Spy* and *The Last of the Mohicans* had been read through the lens of Walter Scott's novels. In Cooper's early novels, readers discovered historical romances centered (like Scott's) on intrigue, suspense, and love. But from the beginning, Cooper understood himself as a kind of cultural critic, a gentleman who wrote in the service of his country and of broader enlightened ideas. He was surprised, baffled, and then angered by the reviews and sales of several works dating from the late 1820s and early 1830s, including the nonfictional *Notions of the Americans* (1828); the Swiftian political satire *The Monikins* (1835); and the trio of European political novels, *The Bravo* (1831), *The Heidenmauer* (1832), and *The Headsman* (1833). In 1834, Cooper threatened to stop writing novels altogether, and indeed spent much of the middle years of the 1830s completing the five volumes of his travel narratives, writing newspaper journalism for the *Evening Post*, planning his history of the US Navy, and purchasing and renovating the family house in Cooperstown.

He made his threat to give up novel writing in a long pamphlet, *A Letter to his Countrymen* (1834). In it, he paired personal and political issues. As James Beard put it, Cooper tried "to show how the unfriendly reception of his recent books in the *New-York American*, the *Morning Courier and New-York Enquirer*, and the *New-York Commercial Advertiser* was inspired directly or indirectly by foreign hostility to him as a representative of republican institutions and ideas" (*L&J* 3:7). However, his larger purpose in the pamphlet was to argue that the United States was too much under the influence of English thought, that the foreign press had been meddling in US affairs, and that some American representatives abroad were not holding fast to American principles. But his decision to conflate his personal complaints about the reception of his books with his political critique of the United States would have ramifications for the rest of his career. Most immediately, it led a number of Whig editors to attack Cooper for his egotism in thinking so highly of himself. Eventually, it would shape the reception of *Home as Found* and provoke Cooper into filing lawsuits to protect his reputation.

Cooper's decision to begin writing fiction again in the summer of 1837 was driven at least in part by practical realities. The panic of 1837 initiated a major recession in the United States that would last into the 1840s. Indeed, Cooper's portrait of wild Wall Street speculation in chapter VII of *Home as Found* was intended to demonstrate one cause of the panic and recession. Cooper's own investment income was greatly reduced because of the economic downturn, and he had no other obvious sources of income. He began to write fiction again because he needed to make money. However, even as the economy struggled in the 1830s and 1840s, the publishing industry was undergoing rapid change. Steam printing technology, cheaper paper, and the expansion of markets because of the speed and reach of new transportation networks allowed publishers to lower the prices on books. Cheap editions became widely available, and authors struggled to make profits. As always, American and British authors were readily pirated by foreign publishers, further siphoning off other potential sources of revenue. Relatively few authors directly benefited from these changes to the profession, although Cooper tried to be one of them. From the beginning of his career, he had aggressively managed his business practices, and into the 1840s he would experiment with new ways of managing the business end of his writing profession. For example, in the 1830s, he began to negotiate contracts that would make his publisher pay for the stereotyping of the work but allow him to own the stereotype plates. As copyright reverted to him after (typically) two years, he could then make a profit on future editions.[6] In the 1840s, in *The Autobiography of a Pocket Handkerchief* and *Jack Tier*, he followed Dickens's lead by using magazine publication as one source of income, followed by book publication.[7] Most of all, Cooper simply wrote at a very brisk pace after 1837. Of his thirty-two novels, fourteen were published between 1820 and 1835. The other eighteen were published between 1838 and 1850.

As Cooper planned the Effinghams' story in summer and fall 1837, he soon recognized that one novel could not contain all of the action and that the second novel would be quite different from the first. The first kept the characters at sea; it was driven by plot. Will the characters make it home to the United States? The second puts the characters in society; it is driven by social tensions. Will the characters be or feel at home in the United States after they return? When Cooper wrote to his British publisher in January 1838 to explain that there would need to be a continuation or sequel, he tried to persuade him "that the continuation will be better liked in England than America, as I do not spare the follies and peculiarities of this country [i.e., the United States]" (*L&J* 3:306). He understood that the sales of the second novel might be reduced in England because it was a continuation (or sequel), and that the second novel might be seen as provocative in the United States. He did not know just how provocative it would turn out to be.

The British edition has a different title from the US edition; it is titled *Eve Effingham; or, Home*. This may have been done to protect the British copyright, since the American edition was published first, and thus the novel would have been unprotected in England. (This was highly unusual. To protect copyright in the United States and in Great Britain, it was safest to print a novel first in the United States and then publish it first in Great Britain.) It is also possible that his British publisher wanted to emphasize that *Eve Effingham* was a stand-alone romance, not simply a sequel to *Homeward Bound*.

We do not know for sure why the novel has two different titles. The British edition also lacked the preface, which explicitly declared the second novel to be a sequel.

In that preface to the first American edition, Cooper argued that "It would be indeed a desperate undertaking, to think of making anything interesting in the way of a *Roman de Société* in this country" (iv). If the "novel of society" was a realistic fiction that grappled with the effects of social problems on specific groups of people, then Cooper was saying that in the United States the "frame" was too "homely" (iv), or too plain and uninteresting, to sustain critical investigation. The "field" in the United States, he wrote, is too "barren" for a writer of fiction (iv). He meant that social and cultural life in the United States took its cue from Europe; there was no native social or cultural center. The political capital of Washington DC bore little resemblance to European capitals like Paris or London. He seemed to mean that society in the United States was more homogeneous than in Europe, with no aristocracy on one end of the spectrum and little or no poverty on the other. Finally, he meant also that the American "character" was provincial and respectably average, lacking identifiable, prominent, or distinctive features. He complained that novels where the author wished to "illustrate a principle" were doomed to failure when featured in such a "homely" setting. Still, despite his sense that such an undertaking was doomed to failure, that was the frame he chose to work with in *Home as Found*! All of this contributed to the sense that the novel was fundamentally different from *Homeward Bound*. The first offered action and plot and thrilling changes of scenery; the second offered "principles" and ideas and a relatively "barren" field of action.[8]

In the preface to the American edition, Cooper says that the vital principle of *Home as Found* is the provincialism of the United States. The novel bears this out. He created characters who represent several kinds of provincialism, such as Howel with his unquestioning and naïve love of England and Wenham with his go-ahead boosterism of Young America. Other characters demonstrate the shallowness of an imitative culture, the duplicity of a new type of journalism, and the small-minded vanity of women. To careful readers, even the Effinghams come in for criticism. Eve and her father have never had to work for their money, so they find it difficult to understand or appreciate the successes of a man like Aristabulus Bragg; John Effingham turns out to have been a cad as a younger man, his sarcastic cynicism more self-directed than he is willing to admit; and the Effinghams are curiously self-involved, with Edward and John having tried to marry the same woman, Eve in the end marrying her own cousin, and the entire family retreating to Europe at the end of the novel. If the American characters are provincial, the Effinghams can be seen as snobs, equating social status with human worth and seldom crediting the young country for its success.

Most of the early readers of *Home as Found* came to the novel with preconceptions about the author and his criticisms of the young nation. Many believed that Cooper should stick to tales of the sea and forest. Many believed that fiction should strive to entertain, not teach or lecture. Many believed that English travelers to the United States like Mrs. Trollope and Basil Hall had unfairly criticized and even belittled the young nation in print.[9] They did not wish to be lectured at in a similar way by an American writer. Some had read, and many certainly knew about, the very early and very combative review of *Home as Found* published by James Watson Webb on 22 November 1838, one week after the book's publication. Webb had spent part of his teen years in Cooperstown before joining the US Army and rising to the rank of colonel. In 1827, he left the army and purchased a pro-Jackson newspaper, the *Morning Courier*. Two years later, he purchased a second newspaper, Mordecai Noah's *New York Courier*, forming the *Morning Courier and New York Enquirer*, a newspaper that by 1834 had become staunchly Whig. (Indeed, some sources credit Webb with supplying the name "Whig" for Henry Clay's National Republican Party, which coalesced in 1834.) It was one of the newspapers Cooper singled out for criticism in his 1834 pamphlet.

Webb's review of *Home as Found* ran to 3,500 words, not including a generous selection from the novel (extracts from chapters V and VI) to which he referred several times.[10] As a journalist in the *Daily Picayune* (New Orleans) reported a few weeks later, the review was "as caustic a stricture as we . . . have [ever] read. The way it poked Mr. Cooper about, and made him feel unhappy, was singular."[11] Webb "poked" at Cooper and his double novel in three different ways. He claimed that Cooper denigrated the United States in the novels to increase sales in England, that Cooper was angry that his countrymen did not welcome him as enthusiastically on his return to the United States in 1833 as they had welcomed Washington Irving in 1832, and that Cooper tried to paint himself as a noble aristocrat (70–71). Webb spent relatively little time in his review discussing *Homeward*

Bound, which had been published in the United States in August 1838 to fairly positive reviews and steady sales. He reserved most of his venom for *Home as Found*, repeatedly insisting that Cooper "is" the haughty aristocrat Edward Effingham, that he paints nearly all Americans in the novel as fools and knaves, and that Cooper's "insane vanity" is evident on every page (75). "As a novel," Webb concluded, "'Home as Found' is absolutely beneath criticism. It is void of plot, and was written for the vile purposes we have named, and to enable Mr. Cooper to pamper his insatiable vanity" (76). He and his novel deserved only "silent contempt" (77). Like Cooper in his 1834 pamphlet, Webb conflated the personal and the critical. He attacked the novel (not unfairly at times), but he also attacked the author ad hominem. To Webb, Cooper's novel was not fiction; it was an example of elitist, autobiographical, anti-American snobbery. Its author deserved to be punished.

Webb's review had three effects relevant to this historical introduction. First, Cooper responded on the same day with a letter to the New York *Evening Post*. He refuted several specific claims Webb made, including the notion that Cooper (like the Effinghams) called his house in Cooperstown "Temple Hall" and the idea that he tailored the plot to increase sales in England. Most significantly, he promised legal action over Webb's libels. This initiated a back-and-forth between Cooper and Webb. Webb returned fire by attacking Cooper again in May 1839, insisting that any attempt to silence him and other critics was an attack on the free press. Of course, Cooper's portrait of Steadfast Dodge did not help him throughout this controversy; his scorn for newspaper editors no doubt rankled Webb and other editors.

Second, Cooper did pursue legal action against Webb, securing two indictments for libel in spring 1839, one for Webb's initial review and the other for the attack in May 1839. (Cooper repeatedly tried and failed to secure a third indictment for libel against Webb for an article published in September 1839.) One of those indictments was brought to an end in 1841 when Webb agreed to retract the article published in May 1839. The other indictment (based on the 22 November 1838 review of *Home as Found*) resulted in three trials, in the first two of which the jury could not agree on a verdict and in the third Webb was found not guilty. That verdict was announced on 23 November 1843, almost exactly five years after Webb had published his offending review.

This lawsuit was merely one in a series of legal actions that Cooper initiated beginning in 1837, many of which were related in some way to *Home as Found*. A second set of actions grew out of the Three Mile Point controversy that Cooper fictionalizes in chapters XIV–XVI of the novel. In July 1837, just as he began writing *Homeward Bound*, Cooper issued a warning to local citizens to stop trespassing on the family land known as Three Mile Point. Like in *Home as Found*, the villagers held a meeting and drew up resolutions against the owner of the property. A local newspaper editor in a neighboring county, Elias Pellet, wrote about the controversy in August 1837, mocking Cooper in the process. Cooper defended himself in another local paper and even published the villagers' resolutions to demonstrate their silliness. Still another local newspaper editor, Andrew Barber, reprinted Pellet's article. Cooper sued them both for libel in September 1837. However, he did not push the suits until November 1838, when Webb's review provoked him into action. Cooper won a judgment of $400 against Barber in 1839. Pellet died before the other case could go to trial. Another set of legal actions grew out of Cooper's success against Barber, which no doubt emboldened him and, at the same time, rankled Whig newspaper editors. In 1839–41 Cooper brought suit for libel against four other newspaper editors (William Leete Stone, Park Benjamin, Thurlow Weed, and Horace Greeley) who had offended him in a variety of ways: reprinting articles against which judgment for libel had been made, attacking his *History of the United States Navy*, repeatedly needling him about his similarity to Edward Effingham (and more broadly about his "aristocratic" pretensions).[12] Some of those cases dragged on until 1845. Taken together, these cases are a tangled web involving politics (local and national), personality, the press, changing notions of authorship, and Cooper's pride.[13]

Third, Webb's early review of *Home as Found*, along with the resulting lawsuits over the next several years, inescapably shaped the reception of the novel. Cooper's legal actions kept him in court, constantly reminding readers of Webb's review and other criticisms, thus giving ammunition to Webb's claim that the aristocratic Effingham men were stand-ins for Cooper himself. Oscar Wilde's dictum "There is only one thing in life worse than being talked about, and that is not being talked about" was not true in the 1830s. To many readers, Cooper *was* the Effinghams.[14] This was the third effect of Webb's review: it colored the reception of the novel almost before anyone had a chance to read it. Other reviewers knew about Webb's review and about the lawsuits. Sales were affected. The novel did not sell as briskly as *Homeward Bound*, which had almost immediately gone into a second printing in September 1838, and it certainly did not sell as well as *The Pathfinder* would in 1840, which sold out its initial run and was reprinted twice in the 1840s. *Home as Found* was not reprinted or reissued in Cooper's lifetime, except as part of the complete set of his novels that the publishing firm of Stringer & Townsend began to issue in 1849 (using the stereotype plates of *Home as Found* that were made by Lea & Blanchard in November 1838).[15] What became known as the "Effingham Libels" framed all of the substantial reviews of the novel in the literary magazines. Although the reviewers in the literary magazines were slightly less vituperative than the newspaper editors, their critiques did not help the novel.

The longest and most substantial magazine review of *Home as Found* appeared in the *Southern Literary Messenger* in March 1839. The reviewer was well aware of Webb's review and Cooper's response to it:

> Soon after this novel made its appearance, both the author and his book were very severely handled by the editor of a New York paper—'The Morning Courier and Enquirer.' The attack upon Mr. Cooper's private character we must consider unjustifiable, and unworthy of a respectable journal. And the strictures upon the book itself, though by no means entirely devoid of legitimate force and truth, were, at least, not remarkable for their fairness. Certainly, Mr. Cooper should not have noticed this critique.[16]

This reviewer was not the last person to suggest that Cooper should simply have ignored his critics. But the reviewer goes on to critique the novel as a work of art. He thought the writing was poor at times and that the plot was "not only meagre, but also as badly conceived as that of any tale with which we have lately met, put forth by the most infantile magazine or newspaper contributor that the public forbearance has emboldened" (170). He maintained that the purpose of fiction was entertainment, and thus Cooper's opinions got in the way of the story: "Instead of endeavoring to throw the fascination of romance around his opinions, he has attempted to make the latter supply the interest which his story lacks" (169). He defended the right of an author to describe "scenes of his own life" in a novel, but he also considered "it imprudent [of Cooper] to have given such occasion for sarcastic criticism" by hewing so closely to places and events that are so clearly drawn from his life (172–73). There was too much "I"—too much of the author—in the novel. The reviewer emphasized Cooper's "principle" that the United States in 1838 was too provincial, and he largely agreed with it, while nonetheless suggesting that Cooper need not have written about it (174). *Home as Found*, the reviewer concluded, "is immeasurably inferior to any of the same author's former novels which we have read" (170). The novel was "written in a spirit soured by disappointment and rebuke . . . into spite and malignancy" (173); Cooper's motto on the title page ("Thou art perfect," from *Henry IV, Part 1*) was simply a bit of smug self-complacency if applied to the novel, because it was terribly flawed by "inconsistencies and absurdities" (175).

That was the best contemporaneous review of the novel!

The reviewer in the *New York Review* (January 1839) took on both *Homeward Bound* and *Home as Found*. He indicated his awareness of Webb's review and Cooper's hypersensitive personality with his observation that in drawing the character of Steadfast Dodge, Cooper was responding to the newspapers: "We are not aware that the newspaper press, upon which, in the person of Steadfast Dodge, its caricatured representative, [Cooper] has endeavored to throw so much obloquy, was ever made the subject of his ridicule, until it presumed to suggest, that it was possible even for him to nod."[17] The reviewer offered a lengthy defense of newspapers (though not, he says, those "penny sheets professedly devoted to slanders"; 212). Turning to *Home as Found*, he asserted that the novel is a "malicious work. It is evidently the bursting out of superabundant bile, and that after the manner of a general deluge. . . . We should respect a manly and fearless exposure of the vices and follies of our social system—for vices and follies it unquestionably has;—but there is a wide difference between faithful rebuke, proceeding from the spirit of true patriotism, and scornful sneers arising from morbid feeling, disaffection, disappointment, and assumed superiority" (214). Like many reviewers of Cooper's works in these years, he maintained that Americans were willing to be criticized—just not by Cooper. Cooper, he said, has "a strong determination to tarnish with the breath of calumny, every mirror which does not reflect his own admiration, as comely as it appears to himself" (212). In recent years, his "self love and vanity have corroded his heart and bedimmed his understanding" (221).

Other, shorter reviews appeared in the months after the novel's publication. For example, a reviewer in the *New-York Mirror* asserted that

> Mr. Cooper has been very generally and, we think, very justly
> rebuked for the publication of [*Home as Found*]. It is, in truth,
> an imposition upon the publick, put forth, as it is, in the form of
> a novel . . . it has about as much claim to be ranked under that
> head as a fourth of July oration, or a book of travels. . . . There is
> neither plot nor interest in the narrative, and neither fidelity nor
> effectiveness in the characters.[18]

The reviewer in the *Gentleman's Magazine and American Monthly
Review* called the novel Cooper's most "inane production." "Considered
as a novel, it is flat, stale, and miserably dull; as a literary composition, it is puerile and common place; as a national disquisition, it is
marked with undeniable strains of prejudice and ill-temper. It has been
severely, and generally, most justly handled by every portion of the
American press, for the anti-national sentiments and arrogant tone
observable in every page." The reviewer insinuated that Cooper was
insane: "From some physical defect, or some deeply seated disease
which has produced mental obscuration of the most dense description,
Mr. Cooper has, within these few years, found fault with all creation,
excepting alone his own immaculate self." The reviewer spent most
of the review attacking Cooper's European travel narratives as "TEN
VOLUMES of twaddle and ill-tempered gossip."[19] He did not engage
the plot or style or themes of *Home as Found*. The reviewer in the
Journal of Belles Lettres was no kinder: Cooper's "late works have
betrayed a mind ill at ease, a morbid sensibility to censure, and a
weakness of intellect, that is painful to his countrymen. . . . He chafes
under newspaper critiques at home in a manner so weak, and yet so
sensitively, as to make us fear for his mind." Pretending at least to
glance at the novel, the reviewer asserts that "We have looked in vain
for a single redeeming feature in the whole production. . . . [finding
instead] a succession of low caricatures, improbable events, and a
silly development, little calculated to excite sympathy for the author,
or interest in the characters."[20]
    These contemporary reviews circle around the same set of issues:
Home as Found is stronger on opinions than on plot, the novel is
too autobiographical, the novel is antidemocratic, the novel is unlike
Cooper's best work, Cooper's response to Webb's review and other
provocations in the press was too ill-tempered. Even the fairest reviewer,
in the *Southern Literary Messenger*, was unable to accept Cooper's
criticisms of the United States or consider the idea that Cooper was

not equating himself with the Effinghams. Added to the reviews in newspapers, they ensured that the novel would sell relatively few copies.

The British reviews of *Eve Effingham; or, Home* were just as negative but less personal. The unsigned reviewer in the *Literary Gazette* prefaced two columns of excerpts from the novel with the observation that although Cooper was more at home on the sea or in the forest, his sketches of American manners might interest some readers.[21] A week later, the reviewer in *The Atheneum* provided a few excerpts, all of them focused on the women of the novel, and concluded that the "tediousness of the incidents, the careful premeditated slowness of the arguments, [and] the solidity of the national vanity . . . compel us to express our opinion, that this is one of Mr. Cooper's poorest publications." The reviewer likens Cooper to a "he-Scheherazade" who had repeated his stories endlessly but over time has become less imaginative and less entertaining.[22]

The longest review in England appeared in the *Dublin Review* in May 1839. The reviewer began by accurately noting that *Homeward Bound* "was most cordially hailed," while *Home as Found* "has raised a loud and angry outcry against [Cooper]."[23] The reviewer noted that Cooper must have hit home with some of his observations, for his countrymen "denounce him with a vehemence and a fury which go far to prove that he must have spoken much truth" (491). Ironically, he said, Cooper spared the United States its worst sins: its "conduct toward the people of colour—the red man and the black" (491). Still, the reviewer went on to say, Cooper's satire is overly virulent; passing by America's worst sins, he focuses "on foibles and faults of a minor degree" (492). He noted that British commentators seem put out by Cooper's criticisms of the United States because he was intruding "upon their especial province" of unsparingly criticizing the new nation (492). He turned to a summary of *Homeward Bound*, including short excerpts to praise Cooper's "invention and ingenuity" (502). Before he turned to *Home as Found*, the reviewer explained that Cooper had mistaken "the bent of his own genius" in turning away from "the grave, calm, and dignified [voice of the] moralist and philosopher," as in *The Bravo* (1831), to adopt the voice of "the keen-witted, brilliant satirist, whose sharp-pointed weapon dazzles while it wounds" (509). This second novel, he said, was reminiscent "of that most puerile and unhappy of all [of Cooper's] productions, *The Monikins*" (509). To be clear, he insisted, the problem was not the accuracy of Cooper's portrait of the United States. The problem was twofold: Cooper had been personally offended by the nation and was intent on satisfying his pique, and his portrait was "rudely and inartistically limned" (510). In his summary of the novel, he emphasizes the role of class, arguing (as did the American reviewers) that the Effinghams' anxieties of social leveling and social pretentions were really Cooper's. We "do not relish . . . the constant and nervous anxiety Mr. Cooper displays, to impress upon the minds of all whom it may concern, that he considers himself no whit inferior, in position, to any person in any country" (522). He returned to the fact that Cooper, had he wished to reform his countrymen, could have chosen a different vehicle and to the glaring absence of the issue of race in a novel that wished to critique the United States (528).

An exhaustive review of *Homeward Bound* and *Home as Found* appeared two years after the novel was published in *The New World: A Weekly Family Journal of Popular Literature, Science, Art and News*. By Park Benjamin, one of the editors then under indictment for libeling Cooper, "Fenimore Cooper's Libels on America and Americans" covered nineteen newspaper columns over two successive weekly issues. In the first part, Benjamin used the double novel to demonstrate "by extracts from the publications themselves, that J. FENNIMORE [sic] COOPER and Mr. EDWARD EFFINGHAM are designed by the author to be one and the same individual."[24] In the second part, Benjamin broadens his case to argue that Cooper "has libeled America, Americans and every thing American, in a manner which should call forth the contempt and scorn of every man, woman and child in the country possessed of the smallest portion of patriotic feeling."[25] In the face of such relentlessly negative commentary, the more nuanced and thoughtful reviews in the *Dublin Review* and the *Southern Literary Messenger* could hardly be heard.

Even before the early reviews were in and even as he initiated several lawsuits, Cooper moved on other work. He had to. Soon after Webb's review appeared on 22 November 1838, he and his family moved to Philadelphia for the winter. There, he completed and read proofs for his *History of the Navy of the United States of America* (1839). It, too, would create controversy and generate lawsuits. By February he was thinking about writing a novel "in which *ships* should be the only actors" (*L&J* 3:369; it eventually became *The Two Admirals* [1842]). By June he was writing *The Pathfinder* (1840), a novel that would bring him great critical and commercial success. But there would be no time to slow down, ever again.

At this distance, we can see more clearly the significance of *Home as Found*. Its troubled reception reminds us that Cooper was often misunderstood. From the beginning of his career, he was invariably read as a mere romancer instead of as a serious political and social thinker. Ahead of contemporaries like Charles Dickens, Benjamin Disraeli, Harriet Beecher Stowe, and Victor Hugo, Cooper wished to use fiction to highlight social problems and articulate a political and historical vision. But because he wrote to make a living, he always had to try to shape his political and social ideas into a sellable commodity that could appeal to male and female readers. Try as he might to succeed in genres like biography, history, and political philosophy, he always had to return to a certain kind of sellable fiction. It was where the money was.

Home as Found demonstrates Cooper's inventiveness. When he floated an idea like writing a novel in which ships would be the only actors, his publisher replied that he was "at a loss to know how you can treat it." Few readers would be interested in such a story, he said. Constrained to making money as a novelist, Cooper was repeatedly urged by publishers and readers to be a certain kind of novelist. Experimentation was not encouraged. "I wish I could persuade you to undertake a naval story on your own inland Seas" (*L&J* 3:370, note 3), his publisher went on in response to Cooper's idea to write a novel with ships as the only actors. Presto, *The Pathfinder*. But in adopting an autobiographical frame for *Home as Found*, even more than in, say, *The Pioneers* (1823), Cooper anticipated the direction of the mainstream novel. In Hawthorne's "The Custom House" (1850), Melville's *Typee* (1846), Dana's *Two Years before the Mast* (1840), and Dickens's *David Copperfield* (1850), readers would soon grow accustomed to reading narratives grounded in the author's autobiographical experiences that blurred the line between fiction and memoir.

In continuing to interconnect his novels, Cooper anticipated the work of Balzac in the 1830s, Trollope in the 1850s, and dozens of later writers like Zola, Faulkner, and Proust. Beginning with *The Pioneers*, he interconnected five novels through the Leather-Stocking and three novels (*The Pioneers, Homeward Bound,* and *Home as Found*) through the Effinghams. In the 1840s, he would connect the Littlepage family through three interconnected novels. In a culture dominated by TV and film sequels, prequels, remakes, and reboots, this seems unremarkable to us. It was remarkable in the 1820s and 1830s.

After his death in 1851, Cooper's novels began to seem old-fashioned to critics grappling with innovative work by Melville, Rebecca Harding Davis, Henry James, and others. They remained very popular in numerous inexpensive collected editions, but they increasingly slipped into the category of adventure novels for boys. His Leather-Stocking Tales were notoriously mocked by Mark Twain in 1895. Relatively quickly, Cooper's novels came to seem less literary than Hawthorne's, less ambitious than Melville's, and less modern than James's. Cooper himself seemed somehow to be an aristocratic relic of an earlier age, almost Federalist (like his father!) in his politics. It was a strange turn of events for a supporter of Andrew Jackson and a lifelong Democrat.[26] In the twentieth century, some of Cooper's novels continued to be popularly successful. His plots served as the basis for a number of films, proved adaptable to comic books and television, and influenced a wide range of writers, from Owen Wister to Patrick O'Brian. However, literary critics often kept their distance. The New Criticism did his work no favors, biographical criticism was hindered until recently by the lack of source materials and by the Whig myth, and poststructuralist theorists gravitated to the work of Melville and Poe. Cooper seemed to some to be an apologist for the oppression of Native Americans, not a nuanced commentator on it.

Since the late nineteenth century, *Home as Found* seens to have been republished only once as a standalone print novel, in an inexpensive edition with an introduction by Lewis Leary.[27] That edition is still found in used bookstores. Copies are available online for $3. The novel has deserved a better fate, especially in a culture that has been more willing since the 1960s to critique itself, its history, and its place in the world. We can see more clearly than his contemporaries that Cooper loved his country, despite his criticisms of its political, social, and cultural life. We can see more clearly that he was committed to large-scale democracy, even as he remained suspicious about how that kind of democracy would affect public policy, religion, the press, and other institutions. *Home as Found* asks readers to engage critically with the problem of democratic change. It asks readers to be critical not just of the United States and not just of Cooper's specific objects of satire but of the narrator and his affinity for snobbish elites who pretend to be above the fray. As Cooper knew from personal experience, democracy is *in* the fray. It is always in the process of becoming, through arguments and disagreements and strife. The Effinghams retreat to Europe. Cooper remained, to continue to take part in that process. He asked the reader to do the same, offering not fixed formulas or pat answers but provocations. That's exactly how democracy is found.

NOTES

1. James Franklin Beard, ed., *The Letters and Journals of James Fenimore Cooper*, 6 vols. (Cambridge, MA: Belknap Press of Harvard University Press, 1960–68), 3:305. Cited parenthetically hereafter as *L&J*.

2. Cooper's letters demonstrate that he imagined the novel in three volumes as was expected by Bentley, his British publisher. He even agreed on payments in three installments, one per volume. Meanwhile his American publisher packaged the novel in two volumes, dividing the story as evenly as possible. Perhaps because there were an uneven number of chapters, however, the first volume proved to be slightly shorter than the second.

3. For example, see Daniel Walker Howe, *What Hath God Wrought: The Transformation of America, 1815–1848* (Oxford: Oxford University Press, 2007); David S. Reynolds, *Waking Giant: America in the Age of Jackson* (New York: Harper, 2008); Charles Sellers, *The Market Revolution: Jacksonian America, 1818–1846* (Oxford: Oxford University Press, 1991); and Sean Wilentz, *The Rise of American Democracy: Jefferson to Lincoln* (New York: Norton, 2005).

4. Several references in *Home as Found* suggest that the action of the novel takes place in the mid-1830s. For example, the great fire in New York described in chapter VII actually began on 16 December 1835. The "French quarrel" referenced in chapter VI alludes to Jackson's State of the Union addresses in December 1834 and December 1835. Eve and her father seem to have left the United States when James Monroe was president and returned near the end of Jackson's second term. Cooper himself spent the years 1826 through 1833 in Europe.

5. We learn in chapter V that John Effingham is "fifty."

6. On 25 August 1838, Cooper rejected Carey & Lea's offer to stereotype the second (revised) edition of *Homeward Bound* because the publisher wanted Cooper to pay for the stereotyping. See *L&J* 3:335, note 1. Cooper compromised in a letter dated 1 September, agreeing to reduce his compensation for the new contract by $200 (probably to contribute to the cost of stereotyping). In that second letter, he empowered Carey & Lea to stereotype *Home as Found*; J. Fagan of Philadelphia certainly stereotyped *Home as Found* and probably stereotyped *Homeward Bound*. In volume 2 of his biography of Cooper, Wayne Franklin explains that "The Careys paid Cooper $1800 for the right to stereotype the new book [*Home as Found*] at

their own expense and issue the first four thousand copies; they also agreed to pay him for additional copies over the two-year life of the agreement at the same rate and method as *Homeward Bound* (i.e., $500 per one thousand copies), after which the plates would be Cooper's" (Wayne Franklin, *James Fenimore Cooper: The Later Years* [New Haven, CT: Yale University Press, 2017], 630, note 20).

7. For a nuanced discussion of Cooper's innovative responses to the changing market in the 1830s and 1840s, see Franklin, *James Fenimore Cooper: The Later Years*, passim.

8. One might note here that the "field" was also limited by the fact that the narrator aligned himself with the Effinghams, which, as noted below, led many readers to identify the narrator (and thus Cooper) with Edward Effingham in particular. The "barren" social field was in part caused by that narrative choice, since the Effinghams are only willing to operate in their own social circle. This point was emphasized in many ways, such as when Mr. Jarvis (in chapter IV) informed his wife that he did not expect to be invited to entertainments at the Effinghams. They "think themselves too good to visit us," his wife complains. They are better than us, her husband replies. From the Effinghams' perspective, entire sections of American cultural and social life were simply beneath notice. For example, they watch the local Fourth of July custom referred to as "the fun of fire" (chapter XXI) from a distance, with condescending snobbery. It was "charming." Eve comments: "There is something refreshing, as the magazine writers term it, to find one of these miniature towns of ours condescending to be gay and happy in a village fashion." This was exactly the kind of comment that angered some of Cooper's contemporaries; they assumed it came from Cooper, not a character. Indeed, the Effinghams' response to the "fun of fire" is almost as dispassionate as their response to the great fire in New York City in chapter VII. Before the great fire is extinguished, John Effingham had already turned it into a moral lesson that others will learn soon enough; he already knew it. One might contrast the point of view in *Home as Found* with the point of view in some of Cooper's novels in the 1840s. In *Satanstoe* (1845), for example, Corny Littlepage observed and described in great detail the working-class and African American festival Pinkster.

9. Basil Hall, *Travels in North America in the years 1827 and 1828* (1829); Mrs. Trollope, *Domestic Manners of the* Americans (1832).

10. James Watson Webb, review of *Home as Found*, *Morning Courier and New York Enquirer*, 22 November 1838. Rpt. in Ethel Outland, *The "Effingham Libels" on Cooper: A Documentary History of the Libel Suits of James Fenimore Cooper Centering Around the Three Mile Point Controversy and the Novel HOME AS FOUND 1837–1845* (Madison: University of Wisconsin Press, 1929), 69–77. Further references are cited parenthetically.

11. "Cooper, the Novelist and Col. Webb," *Daily Picayune* (New Orleans), 13 December 1838, n.p.

12. Benjamin published what purported to be a review of *Home as Found* on 1 December 1838 in the *New-Yorker* (a weekly newspaper), reiterating many of Webb's claims, referring to Cooper as a "superlative dolt," and implying that he was insane. Cooper did not file a lawsuit in response to that review. In 1839, Benjamin became editor of the *New World* (a weekly newspaper), where he continued to attack Cooper.

13. See Outland, *The "Effingham" Libels on Cooper*; Dorothy Waples, *The Whig Myth of James Fenimore Cooper* (New Haven, CT: Yale University Press, 1938); and chapter 8, "Libels upon Libels," in Franklin, *James Fenimore Cooper: The Later Years*.

14. As Franklin points out, "In *Home as Found*, Cooper carried his autobiographical impulse to its logical—or rather illogical—conclusion. It is a curious book in its bearing on the author. Not only does it revisit, as he and his family had been doing, the literary territory of his (and its) past. It moreover so interlaces that territory with its fictional proxy from *The Pioneers* that it is at times hard to untangle the two" (2:199). Cooper made it easy for his detractors to see him as Edward Effingham.

15. Stringer and Townsend published *Home as Found* in their "New and Uniform Edition" of his "Standard Novels" in 1852, after Cooper's death, but as Wayne Franklin notes "the edition was neither new nor uniform" (*James Fenimore Cooper: The Later Years*, 476). Stringer and Townsend owned the stereotype plates for *Home as Found* and sight collation revealed that the 1852 edition was printed from them.

16. "'Home as Found': By the Author of 'Homeward Bound,'" *Southern Literary Messenger* 5.3 (March 1839): 175. Further references are noted parenthetically.

17. "Art[icle] 7.—*Homeward Bound* . . . [and] *Home as Found*," *New York Review* 4.7 (January 1839): 211. Further references are noted parenthetically.

18. "Literary Notices: *Home as Found*," *New-York Mirror: A Weekly Gazette of Literature and the Fine Arts* 16.24 (8 December 1838): 192.

19. "Review of New Books. The New American Novels," *Gentleman's Magazine and American Monthly Review* 4.1 (January 1839): 66.

20. *Journal of Belles Lettres* no. 22 (27 November 1838): n.p.

21. "'*Eve Effingham; or, Home*' by James Fenimore Cooper," *Literary Gazette, and Journal of Belles Letters*, no. 1142 (8 December 1838): 774–75.

22. "'*Eve Effingham; or, Home*' by James Fenimore Cooper," *Atheneum*, no. 581 (15 December 1838): 894.

23. "Art. X. '*Homeward Bound:*' A Tale of the Sea . . . [and] *Eve Effingham, or Home*," *Dublin Review* 6.12 (May 1839): 491. Further references are noted parenthetically.

24. [Park Benjamin,] "Fenimore Cooper's Libels on America and Americans," *New World; a Weekly Family Journal of Popular Literature, Science, Art and News* 1.13 (29 August 1840): 194.

25. [Park Benjamin,] "Fenimore Cooper's Libels on America and Americans [Concluded]," *New World; a Weekly Family Journal of Popular Literature, Science, Art and News* 1.14 (5 September 1840): 210.

26. Jerome McGann has argued that it is a "scandal" of Cooper studies that his work has been dismissed by so many readers as mere romance. "Cooper's pervading greatness as an artist," McGann writes, "is a function of how he engages with the violence that suffuses 'the American Dream.'" See Jerome McGann, "Fenimore Cooper's Anti-Aesthetic and the Representation of Conflicted History," *Modern Language Quarterly* 73 (2012): 123–55; quotations from 125 and 130.

27. James Fenimore Cooper, *Home as Found*, intro. Lewis Leary (New York: Capricorn, 1961). The novel was also republished in the many collected editions of Cooper's works, such as those by Hurd & Houghton (1871–72), Houghton, Mifflin (1876–1884), Appleton (1892), and Putnam's (1896–97).

Illustrations

Plate 1. F. O. C. Darley. Frontispiece engraving: "Aristabulus Bragg Proposing to Eve Effingham." *Home as Found*. New York: W. A. Townsend, 1860. Courtesy of HathiTrust.

> *"You are bashfully silent, Miss Eve! I make all due allowance for natural timidity, and shall say no more at present—though, as silence universally 'gives consent—' "* (262.28–30)

Felix Octavius Carr Darley (1822–1888) was a self-taught American illustrator. He created illustrations for the works of many mid-century authors including Washington Irving, Nathaniel Hawthorne, and Francis Parkman. The W. A. Townsend Co. commissioned him in 1856 to produce illustrations for their edition of Cooper's novels. He created approximately 350 images for the edition.

Plate 2. F. O. C. Darley. Title page engraving: "Ordeal Bumgrum Delivers Gossip to Mrs. Abbott." *Home as Found*. New York: W. A. Townsend, 1860. Courtesy of HathiTrust.

> *But Ordeal was out of breath, and although Jenny shook him, as if to shake the news out of him and Mrs. Abbott actually shook her fist, in her impatience to be enlightened, nothing could induce the child to speak until he had recovered his wind.* (203.32–35)

Plate 3. "Otsego Hall, Cooperstown, N.Y." Engraving by H. B. Hall after a daguerreotype, 1852. In *Homes of American Authors; Comprising Anecdotal, Personal, and Descriptive Sketches, by Various Writers*. New York: D. Appleton and Company, 1857; facing page 203. Courtesy of HathiTrust.

This engraving was produced from a daguerreotype commissioned by Cooper's children shortly after his death. He almost certainly had the house in mind when the narrator in chapter IX talks about the

Effingham house, the "Wigwam," "that model of the composite order, which owed its existance to the combined knowledge and taste of Mr Richard Jones and Mr Hiram Doolittle" (114).

Plate 4. One page from the author's manuscript, numbered 72 and corresponding to 113.12–114.20 of this edition. Cooper wrote on loose-leaf pages which were bound at some point after his death. Because the height of his manuscript pages varies, this image of a page in the bound volume also captures at the bottom lines that correspond in this edition to 147.3–6 and 148.14–18.

Plate 1. F. O. C. Darley. Frontispiece engraving: "Aristabulus Bragg
Proposing to Eve Effingham."

Plate 2. F. O. C. Darley. Title page engraving: "Ordeal Bumgrum Delivers Gossip to Mrs. Abbott."

Plate 3. "Otsego Hall, Cooperstown, N.Y." Engraving by H. B. Hall after a daguerreotype, 1852.

Plate 4. One page from the author's manuscript, numbered 72 and corresponding to 113.12–114.20 of this edition.

Home as Found

Preface.

THOSE who have done us the favour to read "Homeward Bound" will at once perceive that the incidents of this book commence at the point where those of the work just mentioned ceased. We are fully aware of the disadvantage of dividing the interest of a tale in this manner; but in the present instance, the separation has been produced by circumstances over which the writer had very little control. As any one who may happen to take up this volume will very soon discover that there is other matter which it is necessary to know, it may be as well to tell all such persons, in the commencement, therefore, that their reading will be bootless, unless they have leisure to turn to the pages of Homeward Bound for their cue.

We remember the despair with which that admirable observer of men, Mr. Mathews the comedian, confessed the hopelessness of success, in his endeavours to obtain a sufficiency of prominent and distinctive features to compose an entertainment founded on American character. The whole nation struck him as being destitute of salient points, and as characterized by a respectable mediocrity, that, however useful it might be in its way, was utterly without poetry, humour, or interest to the observer. For one who dealt principally with the more conspicuous absurdities of his fellow-creatures, Mr. Mathews was certainly right; we also believe him to have been right in the main, in the general tenor of his opinion; for this country, in its ordinary aspects, probably presents as barren a field to the writer of fiction, and to the dramatist, as any other on earth; we are not certain that we might not say the most barren. We believe that no attempt to delineate ordinary American life, either on the stage, or in the pages of a novel, has been rewarded with success. Even those works in which the desire to illustrate a principle has been the aim, when the picture has been brought within this homely frame, have had to contend with disadvantages that have been commonly found insurmountable. The latter being the intention of this book, the task has been undertaken with a perfect consciousness of all its difficulties, and with scarcely a hope of success. It would be indeed a desperate undertaking, to think of making anything interesting in the way of a *Roman de Société* in this country; still useful glances may possibly be made even in that direction, and we trust that the fidelity of one or two of our portraits will be recognized by the looker-on, although they will very likely be denied by the sitters themselves.

There seems to be a pervading principle in things, which gives an accumulating energy to any active property that may happen to be in the ascendant, at the time being.—Money produces money; knowledge is the parent of knowledge; and ignorance fortifies ignorance.—In a word, like begets like. The governing social evil of America is provincialism; a misfortune that is perhaps inseparable from her situation. Without a social capital, with twenty or more communities divided by distance and political barriers, her people, who are really more homogenous than any other of the same numbers in the world perhaps, possess no standard for opinion, manners, social maxims, or even language. Every man, as a matter of course, refers to his own particular experience, and praises or condemns agreeably to notions contracted in the circle of his own habits, however narrow, provincial, or erroneous they may happen to be. As a consequence, no useful stage can exist; for the dramatist who should endeavour to delineate the faults of society, would find a formidable party arrayed against him, in a moment, with no party to defend. As another consequence, we see individuals constantly assailed with a wolf-like ferocity, while society is everywhere permitted to pass unscathed.

That the American nation is a great nation, in some particulars the greatest the world ever saw, we hold to be true, and are as ready to maintain as any one can be; but we are also equally ready to concede, that it is very far behind most polished nations in various essentials, and chiefly, that it is lamentably in arrears to its own avowed principles. Perhaps this truth will be found to be the predominant thought, throughout the pages of "Home As Found."

CHAPTER I.

"Good morrow, coz."
"Good morrow, sweet Hero."

Much Ado About Nothing 3.4.39–40.

WHEN Mr. Effingham determined to return home, he sent orders to his agent to prepare his town-house in New-York for his reception, intending to pass a month or two in it, then to repair to Washington for a few weeks, at the close of its season, and to visit his country residence when the spring should fairly open. Accordingly, Eve now found herself at the head of one of the largest establishments, in the largest American town, within an hour after she had landed from the ship. Fortunately for her, however, her father was too just to consider a wife, or a daughter, a mere upper servant, and he rightly judged that a liberal portion of his income should be assigned to the procuring of that higher quality of domestic service, which can alone relieve the mistress of a household from a burthen so heavy to be borne. Unlike so many of those around him, who would spend on a single pretending and comfortless entertainment, in which the ostentatious folly of one contended with the ostentatious folly of another, a sum that, properly directed, would introduce order and system into a family for a twelvemonth, by commanding the time and knowledge of those whose study they had been, and who would be willing to devote themselves to such objects, and then permit their wives and daughters to return to the drudgery to which the sex seems doomed in this country, he first bethought him of the wants of social life before he aspired to its parade. A man of the world, Mr. Effingham possessed the requisite knowledge, and a man of justice, the requisite fairness, to permit those who depended on him so much for their happiness, to share equitably in the good things that Providence had so liberally bestowed on himself. In other words, he made two people comfortable, by paying a generous price for a housekeeper; his daughter, in the first place, by releasing her from cares that, necessarily, formed no more a part of her duties than it would be a part of her duty to sweep the pavement before the door; and, in the next place, a very respectable woman who was glad to obtain so good a home on so easy terms. To this simple and just expedient, Eve was indebted for being at the head of one of the quietest, most truly elegant, and best ordered establishments in America, with no other demands on her time than that which was necessary to issue a few orders in the morning, and to examine a few accounts once a week.

One of the first and the most acceptable of the visits that Eve received, was from her cousin, Grace Van Cortlandt, who was in the country at the moment of her arrival, but who hurried back to town to meet her old school-fellow and kinswoman, the instant she heard of her having landed. Eve Effingham and Grace Van Cortlandt were sisters' children, and had been born within a month of each other. As the latter was without father or mother, most of their time had been passed together, until the former was taken abroad, when a separation unavoidably ensued. Mr. Effingham ardently desired, and had actually designed, to take his niece with him to Europe, but her paternal grandfather, who was still living, objected his years and affection, and the scheme was reluctantly abandoned. This grandfather was now dead, and Grace had been left, with a very ample fortune, almost entirely the mistress of her own movements.

The moment of the meeting between these two warm-hearted and sincerely attached young women, was one of great interest and anxiety to both. They retained for each other the tenderest love, though the years that had separated them had given rise to so many new impressions and habits that they did not prepare themselves for the interview without apprehension. This interview took place about a week after Eve was established in Hudson Square, and at an hour earlier than was usual for the reception of visits. Hearing a carriage stop before the door, and the bell ring, our heroine stole a glance from behind a curtain and recognized her cousin as she alighted.

"*Qu'avez-vous, ma chère?*" demanded Mademoiselle Viefville, observing that her *élève* trembled and grew pale.

"It is my cousin, Miss Van Cortlandt—she whom I loved as a sister—we now meet for the first time in so many years!"

"*Bien—c'est une très jolie jeune personne!*" returned the governess, taking a glance from the spot Eve had just quitted. "*Sur le rapport de la personne, ma chère, vous devriez être contente, au moins.*"

"If you will excuse me, Mademoiselle, I will go down alone—I think I should prefer to meet Grace without witnesses in the first interview."

"*Très volontiers. Elle est parente, et c'est bien naturel.*"

Eve, on this expressed approbation, met her maid at the door, as she came to announce that *Mademoiselle de Cortlandt* was in the library, and descended slowly to meet her. The library was lighted from above by means of a small dome, and Grace had unconsciously placed herself in the very position that a painter would have chosen, had she been about to sit for her portrait. A strong, full, rich light fell obliquely on her as Eve entered, displaying her fine person and beautiful features to the very best advantage, and they were features and a person that are not seen every day, even in a country where female beauty is so common. She was in a carriage dress, and her toilette was rather more elaborate than Eve had been accustomed to see, at that hour, but still Eve thought she had seldom seen a more lovely young creature. Some such thoughts, also, passed through the mind of Grace herself, who, though struck, with a woman's readiness in such matters, with the severe simplicity of Eve's attire, as well as with its entire elegance, was more struck with the charms of her countenance and figure. There was, in truth, a strong resemblance between them, though each was distinguished by an expression suited to her character, and to the habits of her mind.

"Miss Effingham!" said Grace, advancing a step to meet the lady who entered, while her voice was scarcely audible and her limbs trembled.

"Miss Van Cortlandt!" said Eve, in the same low, smothered tone.

This formality caused a chill in both, and each unconsciously stopped and curtsied. Eve had been so much struck with the coldness of the American manner, during the week she had been at home, and Grace was so sensitive on the subject of the opinion of one who had seen so much of Europe, that there was great danger, at that critical moment, the meeting would terminate unpropitiously.

Thus far, however, all had been rigidly decorous, though the strong feelings that were glowing in the bosoms of both, had been so completely suppressed. But the smile, cold and embarrassed as it was, that each gave as she curtsied, had the sweet character of her childhood in it, and recalled to both the girlish and affectionate intercourse of their younger days.

"Grace!" said Eve, eagerly, advancing a step or two impetuously, and blushing like the dawn.

"Eve!"

Each opened her arms, and in a moment they were locked in a long and fervent embrace. This was the revival of their former intimacy, and before night Grace was domesticated in her uncle's house. It is true that Miss Effingham perceived certain peculiarities about Miss Van Cortlandt, that she had rather were absent; and Miss Van Cortlandt would have felt more at her ease, had Miss Effingham a little less reserve of manner, on certain subjects that the latter had been taught to think interdicted. Notwithstanding these slight separating shades in character, however, the natural affection was warm and sincere; and if Eve, according to Grace's notions, was a little stately and formal, she was polished and courteous, and if Grace, according to Eve's notions, was a little too easy and unreserved, she was feminine and delicate.

We pass over the three or four days that succeeded, during which Eve had got to understand something of her new position, and we will come at once to a conversation between the cousins, that will serve to let the reader more intimately into the opinions, habits and feelings of both, as well as to open the real subject of our narrative. This conversation took place in that very library which had witnessed their first interview, soon after breakfast, and while the young ladies were still alone.

"I suppose, Eve, you will have to visit the Green's.—They are Hajjis, and were much in society last winter."

"Hajjis!—You surely do not mean, Grace, that they have been to Mecca?"

"Not at all: only to Paris, my dear; that makes a Hajji in New-York."

"And does it entitle the pilgrim to wear the green turban?" asked Eve, laughing.

"To wear any thing, Miss Effingham; green, blue, or yellow, and to cause it to pass for elegance."

"And which is the favourite colour with the family you have mentioned?"

"It ought to be the first, in compliment to the name, but, if truth must be said, I think they betray an affection for all, with not a few of the half-tints in addition."

"I am afraid they are too *prononcées* for us, by this description. I am no great admirer, Grace, of walking rainbows."

"*Too* Green, you would have said, had you dared; but you are a Hajji too, and even the Greens know that a Hajji never puns, unless, indeed, it might be one from Philadelphia. But you will visit these people?"

"Certainly, if they are in society and render it necessary by their own civilities."

"They *are* in society, in virtue of their rights as Hajjis; but, as they passed three months at Paris, you probably know something of them."

"They may not have been there at the same time with ourselves," returned Eve, quietly, "and Paris is a very large town. Hundreds of people come and go, that one never hears of. I do not remember those you have mentioned."

"I wish you may escape them, for, in my untravelled judgment, they are anything but agreeable, notwithstanding all they have seen, or pretend to have seen."

"It is very possible to have been all over christendom, and to remain exceedingly disagreeable; besides one may see a great deal, and yet see very little of a good quality."

A pause of two or three minutes followed, during which Eve read a note, and her cousin played with the leaves of a book.

"I wish I knew your real opinion of us, Eve," the last suddenly exclaimed. "Why not be frank with so near a relative; tell me honestly, now—are you reconciled to your country?"

"You are the eleventh person who has asked me this question, which I find very extraordinary, as I have never quarrelled with my country."

"Nay, I do not mean exactly that. I wish to hear how our society has struck one who has been educated abroad."

"You wish, then, for opinions that can have no great value, since my experience at home, extends only to a fortnight. But you have many books on the country, and some written by very clever persons; why not consult them?"

"Oh! you mean the travellers. None of them are worth a second thought, and we hold them, one and all, in great contempt."

"Of that I can have no manner of doubt, as one and all, you are constantly protesting it, in the highways and by-ways. There is no more certain sign of contempt, than to be incessantly dwelling on its intensity!"

Grace had great quickness, as well as her cousin, and though provoked at Eve's quiet hit, she had the good sense and the good nature to laugh.

"Perhaps we do protest our disdain a little too strenuously for good taste, if not to gain believers; but surely, Eve, you do not support these travellers in all that they have written of us?"

"Not in half, I can assure you. My father and cousin Jack have discussed them too often in my presence to leave me in ignorance of the very many political blunders they have made in particular."

"Political blunders!—I know nothing of them, and had rather thought the travellers right, in most of what they said about our politics. But, surely, neither your father nor Mr. John Effingham corroborates what they say of our society!"

"I cannot answer for either, on that point."

"Speak then for yourself. Do *you* think them right?"

"You should remember, Grace, that I have not yet seen any society in New-York."

"No society, dear!—Why you were at the Henderson's, and the Morgan's, and the Drewett's; three of the greatest *réunions* that we have had in two winters!'"

"I did not know that by society you meant those unpleasant crowds."

"Unpleasant crowds! Why, child, that *is* society, is it not?'

"Not what I have been taught to consider such; I rather think it would be better to call it company."

"And is not this what is called society in Paris?"

"As far from it as possible; it may be an excrescence of society; one of its forms; but, by no means, society itself. It would be as true to call cards, which are sometimes introduced in the world, society, as to call a ball given in two small and crowded rooms, society. They are merely two of the modes in which idlers endeavour to vary their amusements."

"But we have little else than these balls, the morning visits, and an occasional evening, in which there is no dancing."

"I am sorry to hear it; for, in that case, you can have no society."

"And is it different at Paris—or Florence, or Rome?"

"Very. In Paris there are many houses open every evening to which one can go, with little ceremony. Our sex appears in them, dressed according to what a gentleman I overheard conversing at Mrs. Henderson's would call their 'ulterior intentions,' for the night; some attired in the simplest manner, others dressed for concerts, for the opera, for court even; some on the way from a dinner, and others going to a late ball. All this matter of course variety, adds to the ease and grace of the company, and coupled with perfect good manners, a certain knowledge of passing events, pretty modes of expression, an accurate and even utterance, the women usually find the means of making themselves agreeable. Their sentiment is sometimes a little heroic, but this one must overlook, and it is a taste, moreover, that is falling into disuse, as people read better books."

"And you prefer this heartlessness, Eve, to the nature of your own country!"

"I do not know that quiet, *retenue* and a good tone, are a whit more heartless than flirting, giggling and childishness. There may be more nature in the latter, certainly, but it is scarcely as agreeable, after one has fairly got rid of the nursery."

Grace looked vexed, but she loved her cousin too sincerely to be angry. A secret suspicion that Eve was right, too, came in aid of her affection, and while her little foot moved, she maintained her good-nature, a task not always attainable for those who believe that their own "superlatives" scarcely reach to other people's "positives." At this critical moment, when there was so much danger of a jar in the feelings of these two young females, the library door opened and Pierre, Mr. Effingham's own man, announced—

"Monsieur Bragg."

"Monsieur who?" asked Eve, in surprise.

"Monsieur Bragg," returned Pierre, in French, "desires to see Mademoiselle."

"You mean my father,—I know no such person."

"He inquired first for Monsieur, but understanding Monsieur was out, he next asked to have the honour of seeing Mademoiselle."

"Is it what they call a *person* in England, Pierre?"

Old Pierre smiled, as he answered—

"He has the air, Mademoiselle, though he esteems himself a *personnage*, if I might take the liberty of judging."

"Ask him for his card,—there must be a mistake, I think."

While this short conversation took place, Grace Van Cortlandt was sketching a cottage with a pen, without attending to a word that was said. But, when Eve received the card from Pierre and read aloud, with the tone of surprise that the name would be apt to excite in a novice in the art of American nomenclature, the words "Aristabulus Bragg," her cousin began to laugh.

"Who can this possibly be, Grace?—Did you ever hear of such a person, and what right can he have to wish to see me?"

"Admit him, by all means; it is your father's land agent, and he may wish to leave some message for my uncle. You will be obliged to make his acquaintance, sooner or later, and it may as well be done now as at another time."

"You have shown this gentleman into the front drawing-room, Pierre?"

"*Oui, Mademoiselle.*"

"I will ring when you are wanted."

Pierre withdrew, and Eve opened her secretary, out of which she took a small manuscript book, over the leaves of which she passed her fingers rapidly.

"Here it is," she said, smiling, "'Mr. Aristabulus Bragg, Attorney and Counsellor at Law, and the agent of the Templeton estate.' This precious little work, you must understand, Grace, contains sketches of the characters of such persons as I shall be the most likely to see, by John Effingham, A.M. It is a sealed volume, of course, but there can be no harm in reading the part that treats of our present visiter, and, with your permission, we will have it in common.—'Mr. Aristabulus Bragg was born in one of the western counties of Massachusetts, and emigrated to New-York, after receiving his education, at the mature age of nineteen; at twenty-one he was admitted to the bar, and for the last seven years he has been a successful practitioner in all the courts of Otsego, from the justice's to the circuit. His talents are undeniable, as he commenced his education at fourteen and terminated it at twenty-one, the law-course included. This man is an epitome of all that is good and all that is bad, in a very large class of his fellow citizens. He is quick-witted, prompt in action, enterprising in all things in which he has nothing to lose, but wary and cautious in all things in which he has a real stake, and ready to turn not only his hand, but his heart and his principles to any thing that offers an advantage. With him, literally, "nothing is too high to be aspired to, nothing too low to be done." He will run for Governor, or for town-clerk, just as opportunities occur, is expert in all the *practices* of his profession, has had a quarter's dancing, with three years in the classics, and turned his attention towards medicine and divinity, before he finally settled down into the law. Such a compound of shrewdness, impudence, common-sense, pretension, humility, cleverness, vulgarity, kind-heartedness, duplicity, selfishness, law-honesty, moral fraud and mother wit, mixed up with a smattering of learning and much penetration in practical things, can hardly be described, as any one of his prominent qualities is certain to be met by another quite as obvious that is almost its converse. Mr. Bragg, in short, is purely a creature of circumstances, his qualities pointing him out for either a member of congress or a deputy sheriff, offices that he is equally ready to fill. I have employed him to watch over the estate of your father, in the absence of the latter, on the principle that one practised in tricks is the best qualified to detect and expose them, and with the certainty that no man will trespass with impunity, so long as the courts continue to tax bills of costs with their present liberality? You appear to know the gentleman, Grace; is this character of him faithful?"

"I know nothing of bills of costs and deputy sheriffs, but I do know that Mr. Aristabulus Bragg is an amusing mixture of strut, humility, roguery and cleverness. He is waiting all this time in the drawing-room, and you had better see him, as he may, now, be almost considered part of the family. You know he has been living in the house at Templeton, ever since he was installed by Mr. John Effingham. It was there I had the honour first to meet him."

"First!—Surely you have never seen him any where else!"

"Your pardon, my dear. He never comes to town without honouring me with a call. This is the price I pay for having had the honour of being an inmate of the same house with him for a week."

Eve rang the bell, and Pierre made his appearance.

"Desire Mr. Bragg to walk into the library."

Grace looked demure while Pierre was gone to usher in their visiter, and Eve was thinking of the medley of qualities John Effingham had assembled in his description, as the door opened, and the subject of her contemplation entered.

"*Monsieur Aristabule*," said Pierre, eyeing the card, but sticking at the first name.

Mr. Aristabulus Bragg was advancing with an easy assurance to make his bow to the ladies, when the more finished air and quiet dignity of Miss Effingham, who was standing, so far disconcerted him, as completely to upset his self-possession. As Grace had expressed it, in consequence of having lived three years in the old residence at

Templeton, he had begun to consider himself a part of the family, and at home he never spoke of the young lady without calling her "Eve," or "Eve Effingham." But he found it a very different thing to affect familiarity among his associates, and to practise it in the very face of its subject; and, although seldom at a loss for words of some sort or another, he was now actually dumb-founded. Eve relieved his awkwardness by directing Pierre, with her eye, to hand a chair, and speaking first.

"I regret that my father is not in," she said, by way of turning the visit from herself; "but he is to be expected every moment. Are you lately from Templeton?"

Aristabulus drew his breath, and recovered enough of his ordinary tone of manner to reply with a decent regard to his character for self-command. The intimacy that he had intended to establish on the spot, was temporarily defeated, it is true, and without his exactly knowing how it had been effected; for it was merely the steadiness of the young lady, blended as it was with a polished reserve, that had thrown him to a distance he could not explain. He felt immediately, and with a tact that did his sagacity credit, that his footing in this quarter was only to be obtained by unusually slow and cautious means. Still, Mr. Bragg was a man of great decision, and, in his way, of very far-sighted views; and, singular as it may seem, at that unpropitious moment, he mentally determined that, at no very distant day, he would make Miss Eve Effingham his wife.

"I hope Mr. Effingham enjoys good health," he said, with some such caution as that with which a rebuked school-girl enters on the recitation of her task—"he enjoyed bad health I hear, (Mr. Aristabulus Bragg, though so shrewd, was far from critical in his modes of speech) when he went to Europe, and after travelling so far in such bad company, it would be no more than fair that he should have a little respite as he approaches home and old age."

Had Eve been told that the man who uttered this nice sentiment, and that too in accents as uncouth and provincial as the thought was finished and lucid, actually presumed to think of her as his bosom companion, it is not easy to say which would have predominated in her mind, mirth or resentment. But Mr. Bragg was not in the habit of letting his secrets escape him prematurely, and certainly this was one that none but a wizard could have discovered without the aid of a direct oral or written communication.

"Are you lately from Templeton?" repeated Eve, a little surprised that the gentleman did not see fit to answer the question, which was the only one that, as it seemed to her, could have a common interest with them both.

"I left home the day before yesterday," Aristabulus now deigned to reply.

"It is so long since I saw our beautiful mountains, and I was then so young, that I feel a great impatience to revisit them, though the pleasure must be deferred until spring."

"I conclude they are the handsomest mountains in the known world, Miss Effingham!"

"That is much more than I shall venture to claim for them; but, according to my imperfect recollection, and, what I esteem of far more importance, according to the united testimony of Mr. John Effingham and my father, I think they must be very beautiful."

Aristabulus looked up, as if he had a facetious thing to say, and he even ventured on a smile, while he made his answer.

"I hope Mr. John Effingham has prepared you for a great change in the house?"

"We know that it has been repaired and altered under his directions. That was done at my father's request."

"We consider it denationalized, Miss Effingham, there being nothing like it, west of Albany at least."

"I should be sorry to find that my cousin has subjected us to this imputation," said Eve smiling—perhaps a little equivocally; "the architecture of America being generally so simple and pure. Mr. Effingham laughs at his own improvements, however, in which, he says, he has only carried out the plans of the original *artiste*, who worked very much in what was called the composite order."

"You allude to Mr. Hiram Doolittle, a gentleman I never saw; though I hear he has left behind him many traces of his progress in the newer states. *Ex pede, Herculem*, as we say, in the classics, Miss Effingham. I believe it is the general sentiment that Mr. Doolittle's designs have been improved on, though most people think that the Grecian or Roman architecture, which is so much in use in America, would be more republican. But every body knows that Mr. John Effingham is not much of a republican."

Eve did not choose to discuss her kinsman's opinions with Mr. Aristabulus Bragg, and she quietly remarked that she "did not know that the imitations of the ancient architecture, of which there are so many in the country, were owing to attachment to republicanism."

"To what else can they be owing, Miss Eve?"

"Sure enough," said Grace Van Cortlandt; "these imitations are unsuited to the materials, the climate, and the uses; and some very powerful motive, like that mentioned by Mr. Bragg, could alone overcome these obstacles."

Aristabulus started from his seat, and making sundry apologies, declared his previous unconsciousness that Miss Van Cortlandt was present; all of which was true enough, as he had been so much occupied mentally, with her cousin, as not to have observed her, seated as she was partly behind a screen. Grace received the excuses favourably, and the conversation was resumed.

"I am sorry that my cousin should offend the taste of the country," said Eve, "but as we are to live in the house, the punishment will fall heaviest on the offenders."

"Do not mistake me, Miss Eve," returned Aristabulus, in a little alarm, for he too well understood the influence and wealth of John Effingham, not to wish to be on good terms with him; "do not mistake me. *I* admire the house, and know it to be a perfect specimen of a pure architecture in its way, but then public opinion is not yet quite up to it. *I* see all its beauties, I would wish you to know, but then there are many, a majority perhaps, who do not, and these persons think they ought to be consulted about such matters."

"I believe Mr. John Effingham thinks less of his own work than you seem to think of it yourself, sir, for I have frequently heard him laugh at it, as a mere enlargement of the merits of the composite order. He calls it a caprice, rather than a taste; nor do I see what concern a majority, as you term them, can have with a house that does not belong to them."

Aristabulus was surprised that any one could disregard a majority; for, in this respect, he a good deal resembled Mr. Dodge, though running a different career; and the look of surprise he gave was natural and open.

"I do not mean that the public has a legal right to control the tastes of the citizen," he said, "but in a *republican* government, you undoubtedly understand, Miss Eve, it *will* rule in all things."

"I can understand that one would wish to see his neighbour use good taste, as it helps to embellish a country; but the man who should consult the whole neighbourhood before he built, would be likely to erect a complicated house, if he paid much respect to the different opinions he received; or, what is quite as probable, have no house at all."

"I think you are mistaken, Miss Effingham, for the public sentiment, just now, runs almost exclusively and popularly into the Grecian school. We build little besides temples for our churches, our banks, our taverns, our court-houses, and our dwellings. A friend of mine has just built a brewery on the model of the Temple of the Winds."

"Had it been a mill, one might understand the conceit," said Eve, who now began to perceive that her visiter had some latent humour, though he produced it in a manner to induce one to think him any thing but a droll. "The mountains must be doubly beautiful, if they are decorated in the way you mention. I sincerely hope, Grace, that I shall find the hills as pleasant as they now exist in my recollection!"

"Should they not prove to be quite as lovely as you imagine, Miss Effingham," returned Aristabulus, who saw no impropriety in answering a remark made to Miss Van Cortlandt, or any one else, "I hope you will have the kindness to conceal the fact from the world."

"I am afraid that would exceed my power, the disappointment would be so strong. May I ask why you desire that I should keep so cruel a mortification to myself?"

"Why, Miss Eve," said Aristabulus, looking grave, "I am afraid that *our* people would hardly bear the expression of such an opinion from *you*."

"From *me!*—and why not from *me*, in particular?"

"Perhaps it is because they think you have travelled, and have seen other countries."

"And is it only those who have *not* travelled, and who have no means of knowing the value of what they see, that are privileged to criticise?"

"I cannot exactly explain my own meaning, perhaps, but I think Miss Grace will understand me. Do you not agree with me, Miss Van Cortlandt, in thinking it would be safer for one who never saw any other mountains to complain of the tameness and monotony of our own, than for one who had passed a whole life among the Andes and the Alps?"

Eve smiled, for she saw that Mr. Bragg was capable of detecting and laughing at provincial pride, even while he was so much under its influence; and Grace coloured, for she had the consciousness of having already betrayed some of this very silly sensitiveness, in her intercourse with her cousin, in connexion with other subjects. A reply was unnecessary, however, as the door just then opened, and John Effingham made his appearance. The meeting between the two gentlemen, for we suppose Aristabulus must be included in the category by courtesy, if not of right, was more cordial than Eve had expected to witness, for each really entertained a respect for the other, in reference to a merit of a particular sort; Mr. Bragg esteeming Mr. John Effingham as a wealthy and caustic cynic, and Mr. John Effingham regarding Mr. Bragg much as the owner of a dwelling regards a valuable house-dog. After a few moments of conversation, the two withdrew together, and just as the ladies were about to descend to the drawing-room, previously to dinner, Pierre announced that a plate had been ordered for the land agent.

CHAPTER II.

"I know that Deformed; 'a has been a vile thief this seven year; 'a goes up and down like a gentleman."

Much Ado About Nothing 3.3.125–127.

Eve, and her cousin, found Sir George Templemore and Captain Truck in the drawing-room, the former having lingered in New-York, with a desire to be near his friends, and the latter being on the point of sailing for Europe, in his regular turn. To these must be added Mr. Bragg and the ordinary inmates of the house, when the reader will get a view of the whole party.

Aristabulus had never before sat down to as brilliant a table, and for the first time in his life, he saw candles lighted at a dinner; but he was not a man to be disconcerted at a novelty. Had he been a European of the same origin and habits, awkwardness would have betrayed him fifty times, before the dessert made its appearance; but, being the man he was, one who overlooked a certain prurient politeness that rather illustrated his deportment, might very well have permitted him to pass among the *oi polloi* of the world, were it not for a peculiar management in the way of providing for himself. It is true, that he invited those near him to eat of everything he could reach, but he used his knife as a coal-heaver uses a shovel; the company he was in, however, though fastidious in its own deportment, was altogether above the silver-forkisms, and this portion of his demeanour, if it did not escape undetected, passed away unnoticed. Not so, however, with the peculiarity already mentioned as an exception. This touch of deportment, (or management, perhaps, is the better word,) being characteristic of the man, it deserves to be mentioned a little in detail.

The service at Mr. Effingham's table was made in the quiet, but thorough manner that distinguishes a French dinner. Every dish was removed, carved by the domestics, and handed in turn to each guest. But the delay and dignity of this arrangement suited neither Aristabulus's go-a-head-ism, nor his organ of acquisitiveness.

Instead of waiting, therefore, for the more graduated movements of the domestics, he began to take care of himself, an office that he performed with a certain dexterity that he had acquired by frequenting ordinaries—a school, by the way, in which he had obtained most of his notions of the proprieties of the table. One or two slices were obtained in the usual manner, or by means of the regular service; and, then, like one who had laid the foundation of a fortune, by some lucky windfall in the commencement of his career, he began to make accessions, right and left, as opportunity offered. Sundry *entremets*, or light dishes that had a peculiarly tempting appearance, came first under his grasp. Of these he soon accumulated all within his reach, by taxing his neighbours, when he ventured to send his plate, here and there, or wherever he saw a dish that promised to reward his trouble. By such means, which were resorted to, however, with a quiet and unobtrusive assiduity that escaped much observation, Mr. Bragg contrived to make his own plate an epitome of the first course. It contained in the centre, fish, beef, and ham; and around these staple articles, he had arranged *croquettes, rognons, râgouts*, vegetables, and other light things, until not only was the plate completely covered, but it was actually covered in double and triple layers; mustard, cold butter, salt, and even pepper, garnishing its edges. These different accumulations were the work of time and address, and most of the company had repeatedly changed their plates before Aristabulus had eaten a mouthful, the soup excepted. The happy moment when his ingenuity was to be rewarded, had now arrived, and the land agent was about to commence the process of mastication, or of deglutition rather, for he troubled himself very little with the first operation, when the report of a cork drew his attention towards the champaigne. To Aristabulus this wine never came amiss, for, relishing its piquancy, he had never gone far enough into the science of the table to learn which were the proper moments for using it. As respected all the others at table, this moment had in truth arrived, though, as respected himself, he was no nearer to it, according to a regulated taste, than when he first took his seat. Perceiving that Pierre was serving it, however, he offered his own glass, and enjoyed a delicious instant, as he swallowed a beverage that much surpassed any thing he had ever known to issue out of the waxed and leaded nozles that, pointed like so many enemies' batteries, loaded with headaches and disordered stomachs, garnished sundry village bars of his acquaintance.

Aristabulus finished his glass at a draught, and when he took breath, he fairly smacked his lips. That was an unlucky instant, his plate, burthened with all its treasures, being removed, at this unguarded moment; the man who performed the unkind office, fancying that a dislike to the dishes could alone have given rise to such an omnium-gatherum.

It was necessary to commence *de novo*, but this could no longer be done with the first course, which was removed, and Aristabulus set-to, with zeal, forthwith, on the game. Necessity compelled him to eat, as the different dishes were offered; and, such was his ordinary assiduity with the knife and fork, that, at the end of the second remove, he had actually disposed of more food than any other person at table. He now began to converse, and we shall open the conversation at the precise point in the dinner, when it was in the power of Aristabulus to make one of the interlocutors.

Unlike Mr. Dodge, he had betrayed no peculiar interest in the baronet, being a man too shrewd and worldly to set his heart on trifles of any sort; and Mr. Bragg no more hesitated about replying to Sir George Templemore, or Mr. Effingham, than he would have hesitated about answering one of his own nearest associates. With him age and experience formed no particular claims to be heard, and, as to rank, it is true he had some vague ideas about there being such a thing in the militia, but as it was unsalaried rank, he attached no great importance to it. Sir George Templemore was inquiring concerning the recording of deeds, a regulation that had recently attracted attention in England; and one of Mr. Effingham's replies contained some immaterial inaccuracy, which Aristabulus took occasion to correct, as his first appearance in the general discourse.

"I ask pardon, sir," he concluded his explanations by saying, "but I ought to know these little niceties, having served a short part of a term as a county clerk, to fill a vacancy occasioned by a death."

"You mean, Mr. Bragg, that you were employed to *write* in a county clerk's office," observed John Effingham, who so much disliked untruth, that he did not hesitate much about refuting it; or what he now fancied to be an untruth.

"As county clerk, sir. Major Pippin died a year before his time was out, and I got the appointment. As regular a county clerk, sir, as there is in the fifty-six counties of New-York."

"When I had the honour to engage you as Mr. Effingham's agent, sir," returned the other, a little sternly, for he felt his own character for veracity involved in that of the subject of his selection, "I believe, indeed, that you were writing in the office, but I did not understand it was as *the* clerk."

"Very true, Mr. John," returned Aristabulus, without discovering the least concern, "I was *then* engaged by my successor as *a* clerk; but a few months earlier, I filled the office myself."

"Had you gone on, in the regular line of promotion, my dear sir," pithily inquired Captain Truck, "to what preferment would you have risen by this time?"

"I believe I understand you, gentlemen," returned the unmoved Aristabulus, who perceived a general smile. "I know that some people are particular about keeping pretty much on the same level, as to office: but I hold to no such doctrine. If one good thing cannot be had, I do not see that it is a reason for rejecting another. I ran that year for sheriff, and finding I was not strong enough to carry the county, I accepted my successor's offer to write in the office, until something better might turn up."

"You practised all this time, I believe, Mr. Bragg," observed John Effingham.

"I did a little in that way, too, sir; or as much as I could. Law is flat with us, of late, and many of the attorneys are turning their attention to other callings."

"And pray, sir," asked Sir George, "what is the favourite pursuit with most of them, just now?"

"Some our way have gone into the horse-line; but much the greater portion are, just now, dealing in western cities."

"In western cities!" exclaimed the baronet, looking as if he distrusted a mystification.

"In such articles, and in mill-seats, and rail-road lines, and other expectations."

"Mr. Bragg means that they are buying and selling lands on which it is hoped all these conveniences may exist, a century hence," explained John Effingham.

"The *hope* is for next year, or next week, even, Mr. John," returned Aristabulus, with a sly look, "though you may be very right as to the *reality*. Great fortunes have been made on a capital of hopes, lately, in this country."

"And have you been able, yourself, to resist these temptations?" asked Mr. Effingham. "I feel doubly indebted to you, sir, that you should have continued to devote your time to my interests, while so many better things were offering."

"It was my duty, sir," said Aristabulus, bowing so much the lower, from the consciousness that he had actually deserted his post for some months, to embark in the western speculations that were then so active in the country, "not to say my pleasure. There are many profitable occupations in this country, Sir George, that have been overlooked in the eagerness to embark in the town-trade—"

"Mr. Bragg does not mean trade in town, but trade in towns," explained John Effingham.

"Yes, sir, the traffic in cities. I never come this way, without casting an eye about me, in order to see if there is any thing to be done that is useful; and I confess that several available opportunities have offered, if one had capital. Milk is a good business."

"*Le lait!*" exclaimed Mademoiselle Viefville, involuntarily.

"Yes, ma'am, for ladies as well as gentlemen. Sweet potatoes I have heard well spoken of, and peaches are really making some rich men's fortunes."

"All of which are honester and better occupations than the traffic in cities, that you have mentioned," quietly observed Mr. Effingham.

Aristabulus looked up in a little surprise, for with him every thing was eligible that returned a good profit, and all things honest that the laws did not actually prohibit. Perceiving, however, that the company was disposed to listen, and having, by this time, recovered the lost ground, in the way of food, he cheerfully resumed his theme.

"Many families have left Otsego, this and the last summer, Mr. Effingham, as emigrants for the west. The fever has spread far and wide."

"The fever! Is *old* Otsego," for so its inhabitants loved to call a county of half a century's existence, it being venerable by comparison, "is *old* Otsego losing its well established character for salubrity?"

"I do not allude to an animal fever, but to the western fever."

"*Ce pays de l'ouest, est-il bien malsain?*" whispered Mademoiselle Viefville.

"*Apparemment, Mademoiselle, sur plusieurs rapports.*"

"The western fever has seized old and young, and it has carried off many entire families from our part of the world," continued

Aristabulus, who did not understand the little aside just mentioned, and who, of course, did not heed it; "most of the counties adjoining our own have lost a considerable portion of their population."

"And they who have gone, do they belong to the permanent families, or are they merely the floating inhabitants?" inquired Mr. Effingham.

"Most of them belong to the regular movers."

"Movers!" again exclaimed Sir George—"is there any material part of your population who actually deserve this name?"

"As much so as the man who shoes a horse ought to be called a smith, or the man who frames a house a carpenter," answered John Effingham.

"To be sure," continued Mr. Bragg, "we have a pretty considerable leaven of them in our political dough, as well as in our active business. I believe, Sir George, that in England, men are tolerably stationary."

"We love to continue for generations on the same spot. We love the tree that our forefathers planted, the roof that they built, the fireside by which they sat, the sods that cover their remains."

"Very poetical, and I dare say there are situations in life, in which such feelings come in without much effort. It must be a great check to business operations, however, in your part of the world, sir!"

"Business operations!—what is business, as you term it, sir, to the affections, to the recollections of ancestry, and to the solemn feelings connected with history and tradition?"

"Why, sir, in the way of history, one meets with but few incumbrances in this country, but he may do very much as interest dictates, so far as that is concerned, at least. A nation is much to be pitied that is weighed down by the past, in this manner, since its industry and enterprize are constantly impeded by obstacles that grow out of its recollections. America may, indeed, be termed a happy and a free country, Mr. John Effingham, in this, as well as in all other things!"

Sir George Templemore was too well-bred to utter all he felt at that moment, as it would unavoidably wound the feelings of his hosts, but he was rewarded for his forbearance by intelligent smiles from Eve and Grace, the latter of whom the young baronet fancied, just at that moment, was quite as beautiful as her cousin, and if less finished in manners, she had the most interesting *naïveté*.

"I have been told that most old nations have to struggle with difficulties that we escape," returned John Effingham, "though I confess this is a superiority on our part, that never before presented itself to my mind."

"The political economists, and even the geographers have overlooked it, but practical men see and feel its advantages, every hour in the day. I have been told, Sir George Templemore, that in England, there are difficulties in running high-ways and streets through homesteads and dwellings; and that even a rail-road, or a canal, is obliged to make a curve to avoid a church-yard or a tomb-stone?"

"I confess to the sin, sir."

"Our friend Mr. Bragg," put in John Effingham, "considers life as all *means* and no *end*."

"An end cannot be got at without the means, Mr. John Effingham, as I trust you will, yourself, admit. I am for the end of the road, at least, and must say that I rejoice in being a native of a country in which as few impediments as possible exist to onward impulses. The man who should resist an improvement, in our part of the country, on account of his forefathers, would fare badly among his contemporaries."

"Will you permit me to ask, Mr. Bragg, if you feel no local attachments yourself," enquired the baronet, throwing as much delicacy into the tones of his voice, as a question that he felt ought to be an insult to a man's heart, would allow—"if one tree is not more pleasant than another; the house you were born in more beautiful than a house into which you never entered; or the altar at which you have long worshipped, more sacred than another at which you never knelt?"

"Nothing gives me greater satisfaction than to answer the questions of gentlemen that travel through our country," returned Aristabulus, "for I think, in making nations acquainted with each other, we encourage trade and render business more secure. To reply to your inquiry, a human being is not a cat, to love a locality rather than its own interests. I have found some trees much pleasanter than others, and the pleasantest tree I can remember was one of my own, out of which the sawyers made a thousand feet of clear stuff, to say nothing of middlings. The house I was born in was pulled down, shortly after my birth, as indeed has been its successor, so I can tell you nothing on that head; and as for altars, there are none in my persuasion."

"The church of Mr. Bragg has stripped itself as naked as he would strip every thing else, if he could," said John Effingham. "I much question if he ever knelt even; much less before an altar."

"We are of the standing order, certainly," returned Aristabulus, glancing towards the ladies to discover how they took his wit, "and Mr. John Effingham is as near right as a man need be, in a matter of faith. In the way of houses, Mr. Effingham, I believe it is the general opinion you might have done better with your own, than to have repaired it. Had the materials been disposed of, they would have sold well, and by running a street through the property, a pretty sum might have been realized."

"In which case I should have been without a home, Mr. Bragg."

"It would have been no great matter to get another on cheaper land. The old residence would have made a good factory, or an inn."

"Sir, I *am* a cat, and like the places I have long frequented."

Aristabulus, though not easily daunted, was awed by Mr. Effingham's manner, and Eve saw that her father's fine face had flushed. This interruption, therefore, suddenly changed the discourse, which has been related at some length, as likely to give the reader a better insight into a character that will fill some space in our narrative, than a more laboured description.

"I trust your owners, Captain Truck," said John Effingham, by way of turning the conversation into another channel, "are fully satisfied with the manner in which you saved their property from the hands of the Arabs?"

"Men, when money is concerned, are more disposed to remember how it was lost than how it was recovered, religion and trade being the two poles, on such a point," returned the old seaman, with a serious face. "On the whole, my dear sir, I have reason to be satisfied, however; and so long as you, my passengers and my friends, are not inclined to blame me, I shall feel as if I had done at least a part of my duty."

Eve rose from table, went to a side-board and returned, when she gracefully placed before the master of the Montauk a rich and beautifully chased punch-bowl, in silver. Almost at the same moment, Pierre offered a salver that contained a capital watch, a pair of small silver tongs to hold a coal, and a deck trumpet, in solid silver.

"These are so many faint testimonials of our feelings," said Eve— "and you will do us the favour to retain them, as evidences of the esteem created by skill, kindness, and courage."

"My dear young lady!" cried the old tar, touched to the soul by the feeling with which Eve acquitted herself of this little duty, "my dear young lady—well, God bless you—God bless you all—you too,

Mr. John Effingham, for that matter—and Sir George—that I should ever have taken that runaway for a gentleman and a baronet—though I suppose there are some silly baronets, as well as silly lords—retain them?"—glancing furiously at Mr. Aristabulus Bragg, "may the Lord forget me, in the heaviest hurricane, if I ever forget whence these things came, and why they were given."

Here the worthy captain was obliged to swallow some wine, by way of relieving his emotions, and Aristabulus, profiting by the opportunity, coolly took the bowl, which, to use a word of his own, he *hefted* in his hand, with a view to form some tolerably accurate notion of its intrinsic value. Captain Truck's eye caught the action, and he reclaimed his property quite as unceremoniously as it had been taken away, nothing but the presence of the ladies preventing an outbreaking that would have amounted to a declaration of war.

"With your permission, sir," said the captain, drily, after he had recovered the bowl, not only without the other's consent, but, in some degree, against his will; "this bowl is as precious in my eyes as if it were made of my father's bones."

"You may indeed think so," returned the land-agent, "for its cost could not be less than a hundred dollars."

"Cost, sir!—But, my dear young lady, let us talk of the real value. For what part of these things am I indebted to you?"

"The bowl is my offering," Eve answered, smilingly, though a tear glistened in her eye, as she witnessed the strong unsophisticated feeling of the old tar. "I thought it might serve sometimes to bring me to your recollection, when it was well filled in honour of 'sweethearts and wives.'"

"It shall—it shall, by the Lord; and Mr. Saunders needs look to it, if he do not keep this work as bright as a cruising frigate's bottom. To whom do I owe the coal-tongs?"

"Those are from Mr. John Effingham, who insists that he will come nearer to your heart than any of us, though the gift be of so little cost."

"He does not know me, my dear young lady—nobody ever got as near my heart as you; no, not even my own dear pious old mother. But I thank Mr. John Effingham from my inmost spirit, and shall seldom smoke without thinking of him. The watch I know is Mr. Effingham's, and I ascribe the trumpet to Sir George."

The bows of the several gentlemen assured the captain he was right, and he shook each of them cordially by the hand, protesting, in the fulness of his heart, that nothing would give him greater pleasure than to be able to go through the same perilous scenes as those from which they had so lately escaped, in their good company again.

While this was going on, Aristabulus, notwithstanding the rebuke he had received, contrived to get each article, in succession, into his hands, and by dint of poising it on a finger, or by examining it, to form some approximative notion of its inherent value. The watch he actually opened, taking as good a survey of its works as the circumstances of the case would very well allow.

"I respect these things, sir, more than you respect your father's grave," said Captain Truck sternly, as he rescued the last article from what he thought the impious grasp of Aristabulus again, "and cat or no cat, they sink or swim with me for the remainder of the cruise. If there is any virtue in a will, which I am sorry to say I hear there is not any longer, they shall share my last bed with me, be it ashore or be it afloat. My dear young lady, fancy all the rest, but depend on it, punch will be sweeter than ever taken from this bowl, and 'sweethearts and wives' will never be so honoured again."

"We are going to a ball this evening, at the house of one with whom I am sufficiently intimate to take the liberty of introducing a stranger, and I wish, gentlemen," said Mr. Effingham, bowing to Aristabulus and the captain, by way of changing the conversation, "you would do me the favour to be of our party."

Mr. Bragg acquiesced very cheerfully, and quite as a matter of course; while Captain Truck, after protesting his unfitness for such scenes, was finally prevailed on by John Effingham, to comply with the request also. The ladies remained at table but a few minutes longer, when they retired, Mr. Effingham having dropped into the old custom of sitting at the bottle, until summoned to the drawing-room, a usage that continues to exist in America, for a reason no better than the fact that it continues to exist in England;—it being almost certain that it will cease in New-York, the season after it is known to have ceased in London.

CHAPTER III.

"Thou art as wise as thou art beautiful."

A Midsummer Night's Dream 3.1.148.

AS Captain Truck asked permission to initiate the new coal-tongs by lighting a cigar, Sir George Templemore contrived to ask Pierre, in an aside, if the ladies would allow him to join them. The desired consent having been obtained, the baronet quietly stole from table, and was soon beyond the odours of the dining-room.

"You miss the censer and the frankincense," said Eve, laughing, as Sir George entered the drawing-room; "but you will remember we have no church establishment, and dare not take such liberties with the ceremonials of the altar."

"That is a short-lived custom with us, I fancy, though far from an unpleasant one. But you do me injustice in supposing I am merely running away from the fumes of the dinner."

"No, no; we understand perfectly well that you have something to do with the fumes of flattery, and we will at once fancy all has been said that the occasion requires. Is not our honest old captain a jewel in his way?"

"Upon my word, since you allow me to speak of your father's guests, I do not think it possible to have brought together two men who are so completely the opposites of each other, as Captain Truck and this Mr. Aristabulus Bragg. The latter is quite the most extraordinary person in his way, it was ever my good fortune to meet with."

"You call him a *person*, while Pierre calls him a *personnage*; I fancy he considers it very much as a matter of accident, whether he is to pass his days in the one character or in the other. Cousin Jack assures me, that, while this man accepts almost any duty that he chooses to assign him, he would not deem it at all a violation of the *convenances* to aim at the throne in the White House."

"Certainly with no hopes of ever attaining it!"

"One cannot answer for that. The man must undergo many essential changes, and much radical improvement, before such a climax to his fortunes can ever occur; but the instant you do away with the claims of hereditary power, the door is opened to a new chapter of accidents. Alexander of Russia styled himself *un heureux accident*; and should it ever be our fortune to receive Mr. Bragg as President, we shall only have to term him *un malheureux accident*. I believe that will contain all the difference."

"Your republicanism is indomitable, Miss Effingham, and I shall abandon the attempt to convert you to safer principles, more especially as I find you supported by both the Mr. Effinghams, who, while they condemn so much at home, seem singularly attached to their own system at the bottom."

"They condemn, Sir George Templemore, because they know that perfection is hopeless, and because they feel it to be unsafe and unwise to eulogize defects, and they are attached, because near views of other countries have convinced them that, comparatively at least, bad as we are, we are still better than most of our neighbours."

"I can assure you," said Grace, "that many of the opinions of Mr John Effingham, in particular, are not at all the opinions that are most in vogue here; he rather censures what we like, and likes what we censure. Even my dear uncle is thought to be a little heterodox on such subjects."

"I can readily believe it," returned Eve, steadily. "These gentlemen, having become familiar with better things, in the way of the tastes, and of the purely agreeable, cannot discredit their own knowledge so much as to extol that which their own experience tells them is faulty, or condemn that which their own experience tells them is relatively good. Now, Grace, if you will reflect a moment, you will perceive that people necessarily like the best of their own tastes, until they come to a knowledge of better; and that they as necessarily quarrel with the unpleasant facts that surround them; although these facts, as consequences of a political system, may be much less painful than those of other systems of which they have no knowledge. In the one case, they like their own best, simply because it is their own best; and they dislike their own worst, because it is their own worst. We cherish a taste, in the nature of things, without entering into any comparisons, for when the means of comparison offer, and we find improvements, it ceases to be a taste at all; while to complain of any positive grievance, is the nature of man, I fear!"

"I think a republic odious!"

"*La république est une horreur!*"

Grace thought a republic odious, without knowing any thing of any other state of society, and because it contained odious things; and Mademoiselle Viefville called a republic *une horreur*, because heads fell and anarchy prevailed in her own country, during its early struggles for liberty. Though Eve seldom spoke more sensibly, and never more temperately, than while delivering the foregoing opinions, Sir George Templemore doubted whether she had all that exquisite *finesse* and delicacy of features, that he had so much admired; and when Grace burst out in the sudden and senseless exclamation we have recorded, he turned towards her sweet and animated countenance, which, for the moment, he fancied the loveliest of the two.

Eve Effingham had yet to learn that she had just entered into the most intolerant society, meaning purely as society, and in connexion with what are usually called liberal sentiments, in christendom. We do not mean by this, that it would be less safe to utter a generous opinion in favour of human rights in America than in any other country, for the laws and the institutions become active in this respect, but simply, that the resistance of the more refined to the encroachments of the unrefined, has brought about a state of feeling—a feeling that is seldom just and never philosophical—which has created a silent but almost unanimous bias against the effects of the institutions, in what is called the world. In Europe, one rarely utters a sentiment of this nature, under circumstances in which it is safe to do so at all, without finding a very general sympathy in the auditors; but in the circle into which Eve had now fallen, it was almost considered a violation of the proprieties. We do not wish to be understood as saying more than we mean, however, for we have no manner of doubt that a large portion of the dissentients even, are so idly, and without reflection; or for the very natural reasons already given by our heroine; but we do wish to be understood as meaning that such is the outward appearance which American society presents to every stranger, and to every native of the country too, on his return from a residence among other people. Of its taste, wisdom and safety we shall not now speak, but content ourselves with merely saying that the effect of Grace's exclamation on Eve was unpleasant, and that, unlike the baronet, she thought her cousin was never less handsome than while her pretty face was covered with the pettish frown it had assumed for the occasion.

Sir George Templemore had tact enough to perceive there had
been a slight jar in the feelings of these two young women, and he
adroitly changed the conversation. With Eve he had entire confidence
on the score of provincialisms, and, without exactly anticipating the
part Grace would be likely to take in such a discussion, he introduced
the subject of general society in New-York.

"I am desirous to know," he said, "if you have your sets, as we
have them in London and Paris. Whether you have your *Faubourg
St. Germain* and your *Chaussée d'Antin*; your Piccadilly, Grosvenor
and Russell Squares."

"I must refer you to Miss Van Cortlandt for an answer to that
question," said Eve.

Grace looked up blushing, for there were both novelty and
excitement in having an intelligent foreigner question her on such
a subject.

"I do not know that I rightly understand the allusion," she said,
"although I am afraid Sir George Templemore means to ask if we
have distinctions in society?"

"And why *afraid*, Miss Van Cortlandt?"

"Because it strikes me such a question would imply a doubt of
our civilization."

"There are frequently distinctions made, when the differences are
not obvious," observed Eve. "Even London and Paris are not above
the imputation of this folly. Sir George Templemore, if I understand
him, wishes to know if we estimate gentility by streets, and quality
by squares."

"Not exactly that either, Miss Effingham—but, whether among
those, who may very well pass for gentlemen and ladies, you enter
into the minute distinctions that are elsewhere found. Whether you
have your exclusives, and your *élégants* and *élégantes*; or whether you
deem all within the pale as on an equality."

"*Les femmes américaines sont bien jolies!*" exclaimed Mademoiselle
Viefville.

"It is quite impossible that *coteries* should not form in a town of
three hundred thousand souls."

"I do not mean exactly even that. Is there no distinction between
coteries; is not one placed by opinion, by a silent consent, if not by
positive ordinances, above another?"

"Certainly, that to which Sir George Templemore alludes, is to
be found," said Grace, who gained courage to speak, as she found

the subject getting to be more clearly within her comprehension. "All the old families, for instance, keep more together than the others; though it is the subject of regret that they are not more particular than they are."

"Old families!" exclaimed Sir George Templemore, with quite as much stress as a well-bred man could very well lay on the words, in such circumstances.

"Old families," repeated Eve, with all that emphasis which the baronet himself had hesitated about giving. "As old, at least, as two centuries can make them; and this, too, with origins beyond that period, like those of the rest of the world. Indeed, the American has a better gentility than common, as, besides his own, he may take root in that of Europe."

"Do not misconceive me, Miss Effingham; I am fully aware that the people of this country are exactly like the people of all other civilized countries, in this respect; but my surprise is that, in a republic, you should have such a term even as that of 'old families.'"

"The surprise has arisen, I must be permitted to say, from not having sufficiently reflected on the real state of the country. There are two great causes of distinction every where, wealth and merit. Now, if a race of Americans continue conspicuous in their own society, through either or both of these causes, for a succession of generations, why have they not the same claims to be considered members of old families, as Europeans under the same circumstances? A republican history is as much a history as a monarchical history; and a historical name in one, is quite as much entitled to consideration, as a historical name in another. Nay, you admit this in your European republics, while you wish to deny it in ours."

"I must insist on having proofs; if we permit these charges to be brought against us without evidence, Mademoiselle Viefville, we shall finally be defeated through our own neglect."

"*C'est une belle illustration, celle de l'antiquité*" observed the governess, in a matter of course tone.

"If you insist on proof, what answer can you urge to the *Capponi?* '*Sonnez vos trompettes, et je vais faire sonner mes cloches*,'—or to the *Von Erlachs*, a family that has headed so many resistances to oppression and invasion, for five centuries?"

"All this is very true," returned Sir George, "and yet I confess it is not the way in which it is usual with us to consider American society."

"A descent from Washington, with a character and a social position to correspond, would not be absolutely vulgar, notwithstanding!"

"Nay, if you press me so hard, I must appeal to Miss Van Cortlandt for succour."

"On this point you will find no support in that quarter. Miss Van Cortlandt has an historical name herself, and will not forego an honest pride, in order to relieve one of the hostile powers from a dilemma."

"While I admit that time and merit must, in a certain sense, place families in America in the same situation with families in Europe, I cannot see that it is in conformity with your institutions to lay the same stress on the circumstance."

"In that we are perfectly of a mind, as I think the American has much the best reason to be proud of his family," said Eve, quietly.

"You delight in paradoxes, apparently, this evening, Miss Effingham, for I now feel very certain you can hardly make out a plausible defence of this new position."

"If I had my old ally, Mr. Powis, here," said Eve, touching the fender unconsciously with her little foot, and perceptibly losing the animation and pleasantry of her voice, in tones that were gentler, if not melancholy, "I should ask him to explain this matter to you, for he was singularly ready in such replies. As he is absent, however, I will attempt the duty myself. In Europe, office, power, and consequently, consideration, are all hereditary; whereas, in this country, they are not, but they depend on selection. Now, surely, one has more reason to be proud of ancestors who have been chosen to fill responsible stations, than of ancestors who have filled them through the accidents, *heureux ou malheureux*, of birth. The only difference between England and America, as respects family, is that you add positive rank to that to which we only give consideration. Sentiment is at the bottom of our nobility, and the great seal at the bottom of yours. And now, having established the fact that there are families in America, let us return whence we started, and enquire how far they have an influence in every-day society."

"To ascertain which, we must apply to Miss Van Cortlandt."

"Much less than they ought, if my opinion is to be taken," said Grace, laughing, "for the great inroad of strangers has completely deranged all the suitablenesses, in that respect."

"And yet, I dare say, these very strangers do good," rejoined Eve. "Many of them must have been respectable in their native places, and ought to be an acquisition to a society that, in its nature, must be, Grace, *tant soit peu*, provincial."

"Oh!" cried Grace, "I can tolerate any thing but the Hajjis!"

"The what?" asked Sir George, eagerly—"will you suffer me to ask an explanation, Miss Van Cortlandt."

"The Hajjis," repeated Grace laughing, though she blushed to the eyes.

The baronet looked from one cousin to the other, and then turned an inquiring glance on Mademoiselle Viefville. The latter gave a slight shrug, and seemed to ask an explanation of the young lady's meaning herself.

"A Hajji is one of a class, Sir George Templemore," Eve at length said, "to which you and I have both the honour of belonging."

"No, not Sir George Templemore," interrupted Grace, with a precipitation that she instantly regretted; "he is not an American."

"Then I, alone, of all present, have that honour. It means the pilgrimage to Paris, instead of Mecca; and the Pilgrim must be an American, instead of a Mahommedan."

"Nay, Eve, *you* are not a Hajji, neither."

"Then there is some qualification with which I am not yet acquainted. Will you relieve our doubts, Grace, and let us know the precise character of the animal."

"*You* stayed too long to be a Hajji—one must get innoculated merely; not take the disease and become cured, to be a true Hajji."

"I thank you, Miss Van Cortlandt, for this description," returned Eve in her quiet way. "I hope, as I have gone through the malady, it has not left me pitted."

"I should like to see one of these Hajjis," cried Sir George.—"Are they of both sexes?"

Grace laughed and nodded her head.

"Will you point it out to me, should we be so fortunate as to encounter one this evening?"

Again Grace laughed and nodded her head.

"I have been thinking, Grace," said Eve, after a short pause, "that we may give Sir George Templemore a better idea of the sets about which he is so curious, by doing what is no more than a duty of our own, and by letting him profit by the opportunity. Mrs. Hawker receives this evening without ceremony; we have not yet sent our answer to Mrs. Jarvis, and might very well look in upon her for half an hour, after which we shall be in very good season for Mrs. Houston's ball."

"Surely, Eve, you would not wish to take Sir George Templemore to such a house as that of Mrs. Jarvis!"

"*I* do not wish to take Sir George Templemore any where, for your Hajjis have opinions of their own on such subjects. But, as cousin Jack will accompany us, *he* may very well confer that important favour. I dare say, Mrs. Jarvis will not look upon it as too great a liberty."

"I will answer for it, that nothing Mr. John Effingham can do will be thought *mal à propos* by Mrs. Jared Jarvis. His position in society is too well established, and hers is too equivocal, to leave any doubt on that head."

"This, you perceive, settles the point of *coteries*," said Eve to the baronet. "Volumes might be written to establish principles; but when one can do any thing he or she pleases, any where that he or she likes, it is pretty safe to say that he or she is privileged."

"All very true, as to the fact, Miss Effingham; but I should like exceedingly to know the reason."

"Half the time, such things are decided without a reason at all. You are a little exacting in requiring a reason in New-York for that which is done in London without even the pretence of such a thing. It is sufficient that Mrs. Jarvis will be delighted to see you without an invitation, and that Mrs. Houston would, at least, think it odd, were you to take the same liberty with her."

"It follows," said Sir George, smiling, "that Mrs. Jarvis is much the most hospitable person of the two."

"But, Eve, what shall be done with Captain Truck and Mr. Bragg?" asked Grace. "We cannot take *them* to Mrs. Hawker's!"

"Aristabulus would, indeed, be a little out of place in such a house, but as for our excellent, brave, straight-forward, old captain, he is worthy to go any where. I shall be delighted to present *him* to Mrs. Hawker, myself."

After a little consultation between the ladies, it was settled that nothing should be said of the first two visits to Mr. Bragg, but that Mr. Effingham should be requested to bring him to the ball, at the proper hour, and that the rest of the party should go quietly off to the other places, without mentioning their projects. As soon as this was arranged the ladies retired to dress, Sir George Templemore passing into the library to amuse himself with a book the while; where, however, he was soon joined by John Effingham. Here the former revived the conversation on distinctions in society, with the confusion of thought that usually marks a European's notions of such matters.

CHAPTER IV.

"Ready."

"And I."

"And I."

"And I."

"Where shall we go?"

A Midsummer Night's Dream 3.1.163.

GRACE Van Cortlandt was the first to make her appearance after the retreat from the drawing-room. It has often been said that, pretty as the American females incontestably are, as a whole they appear better in *demi-toilette,* than when attired for a ball. With what would be termed high dress in other parts of the world, they are little acquainted; but reversing the rule of Europe, where the married bestow the most care on their personal appearance, and the single are taught to observe a rigid simplicity, Grace now seemed sufficiently ornamented in the eyes of the fastidious baronet, while, at the same time, he thought her less obnoxious to the criticism just mentioned, than most of her young countrywomen, in general.

An *embonpoint* that was just sufficient to distinguish her from most of her companions, a fine colour, brilliant eyes, a sweet smile, rich hair, and such feet and hands as Sir George Templemore had, somehow—he scarcely knew how, himself—fancied could only belong to the daughters of peers and princes, rendered Grace so strikingly attractive this evening, that the young baronet began to think her even handsomer than her cousin. There was also a charm in the unsophisticated simplicity of Grace, that was particularly alluring to a man educated amidst the coldness and mannerism of the higher classes of England. In Grace, too, this simplicity was chastened by perfect decorum and *retenue* of deportment; the exuberance of the new school of manners not having helped to impair the dignity of her character, or to weaken the charm of diffidence. She was less finished in her manners than Eve, certainly; a circumstance, perhaps, that induced Sir George Templemore to fancy her a shade more simple, but she was never unfeminine or unladylike; and the term vulgar, in despite of all the capricious and arbitrary rules of fashion, under no circumstances, could ever be applied to Grace Van Cortlandt. In this respect, nature seemed to have aided her; for had not her associations raised her above such an imputation, no one could believe that she would be obnoxious to the charge, had her lot in life been cast even many degrees lower than it actually was.

It is well known that, after a sufficient similarity has been created by education to prevent any violent shocks to our habits or principles, we most affect those whose characters and dispositions the least resemble our own. This was probably one of the reasons why Sir George Templemore, who, for some time, had been well assured of the hopelessness of his suit with Eve, began to regard her scarcely less lovely cousin, with an interest of a novel and lively nature. Quick-sighted and deeply interested in Grace's happiness, Miss Effingham had already detected this change in the young baronet's inclinations, and though sincerely rejoiced on her own account, she did not observe it without concern; for she understood better than most of her countrywomen how greatly the peace of mind of an American woman is endangered by transplanting her into the more artificial circles of the old world.

"I shall rely on your kind offices, in particular, Miss Van Cortlandt, to reconcile Mrs. Jarvis and Mrs. Hawker to the liberty I am about to take," cried Sir George, as Grace burst upon them in the library, in a blaze of beauty that, in her case, was aided by her attire; "and cold-hearted and unchristian-like women they must be, indeed, to resist such a mediator!"

Grace was unaccustomed to adulation of this sort; for though the baronet spoke gaily, and like one half trifling, his look of admiration was too honest to escape the intuitive perception of woman. She blushed deeply, and then recovering herself instantly, said with a *naïveté* that had a thousand charms with her listener—

"I do not see why Miss Effingham and myself should hesitate about introducing you at either place. Mrs. Hawker is a relative and an intimate—an intimate of mine, at least—and as for poor Mrs. Jarvis, she is the daughter of an old neighbour, and will be too glad to see us, to raise objections. I fancy any one of a certain—" Grace hesitated and laughed.

"Any one of a certain—?" said Sir George, inquiringly.

"Any one from this house," resumed the young lady, correcting the intended expression, "will be welcome in Spring street."

"Pure, native aristocracy!" exclaimed the baronet, with an air of affected triumph. "This you see, Mr. John Effingham, is in aid of my argument."

"I am quite of your opinion," returned the gentleman addressed— "as much native aristocracy as you please, but no hereditary."

The entrance of Eve and Mademoiselle Viefville interrupted this pleasantry, and the carriages being just then announced, John Effingham went in quest of Captain Truck, who was in the drawing-room with Mr. Effingham and Aristabulus.

"I have left Ned to discuss trespass suits and leases with his land-agent," said John Effingham, as he followed Eve to the street-door. "By ten o'clock, they will have taxed a pretty bill of costs between them!"

Mademoiselle Viefville followed John Effingham; Grace came next, and Sir George Templemore and the Captain brought up the rear. Grace wondered the young baronet did not offer her his arm, for she had been accustomed to receive this attention from the other sex, in a hundred situations in which it was rather an incumbrance than a service; while on the other hand, Sir George himself would have hesitated about offering such assistance, as an act of uncalled-for familiarity.

Miss Van Cortlandt, being much in society, kept a chariot for her own use, and the three ladies took their seats in it, while the gentlemen took possession of Mr. Effingham's coach. The order was given to drive to Spring street, and the whole party proceeded.

The acquaintance between the Effinghams and Mr. Jarvis had arisen from the fact of their having been near, and, in a certain sense, sociable neighbours in the country. Their town associations, however, were as distinct as if they dwelt in different hemispheres, with the exception of an occasional morning call, and, now and then, a family dinner given by Mr. Effingham. Such had been the nature of the intercourse previously to the family of the latter having gone abroad, and there were symptoms of its being renewed on the same quiet and friendly footing as formerly. But no two beings could be less alike, in certain essentials, than Mr. Jarvis and his wife. The former was a plain painstaking, sensible man of business, while the latter had an itching desire to figure in the world of fashion. The first was perfectly aware that Mr. Effingham, in education, habits, associations and manners, was, at least, of a class entirely distinct from his own; and without troubling himself to analyze causes, and without a feeling of envy, or unkindness of any sort, while totally exempt from any undue deference or unmanly cringing, he quietly submitted to let things take their course. His wife, on the other hand, not unfrequently expressed her surprise that any one in New-York should presume to be *better* than themselves; and the remark gave rise to the following short conversation, on the very morning of the day she gave the party, to which we are now conducting the reader.

"How do you know, my dear, that any one does think himself our *better*?" demanded the husband.

"Why do they not all visit us then!"

"Why do you not visit everybody yourself? A pretty household we should have, if you did nothing but visit every one who lives even in this street!"

"You surely would not have *me* visiting the grocers' wives at the corners, and all the other rubbish of the neighbourhood. What I mean is that all the people of a certain sort ought to visit all the other people of a certain sort, in the same town."

"You surely will make an exception, at least on account of numbers. I saw number three thousand six hundred and fifty this very day on a cart, and if the wives of all these carmen should visit one another, each would have to make ten visits daily in order to get through with the list in a twelvemonth."

"I have always bad luck in making you comprehend these things, Mr. Jarvis."

"I am afraid, my dear, it is because you do not very clearly comprehend them yourself. You first say that everybody ought to visit everybody, and then you insist on it, *you* will visit none but those you think good enough to be visited by Mrs. Jared Jarvis."

"What I mean is, that no one in New-York has a right to think himself, or herself, better than ourselves."

"Better?—In what sense better?"

"In such a sense as to induce them to think themselves too good to visit us."

"That may be your opinion, my dear, but others may judge differently. You clearly think yourself too good to visit Mrs. Onion, the grocer's wife, who is a capital woman in her way; and how do we know that certain people may not fancy we are not quite refined enough for them? Refinement is a positive thing, Mrs. Jarvis, and one that has much more influence on the pleasures of association than money. We may want a hundred little perfections that escape our ignorance, and which those who are trained to such matters deem essentials."

"I never met with a man of so little social spirit, Mr. Jarvis! Really, you are quite unsuited to be a citizen of a republican country."

"Republican!—I do not really see what republican has to do with the question. In the first place, it is a droll word for *you* to use in this sense at least; for, taking your own meaning of the term, you are as anti-republican as any woman I know. But a republic does not necessarily infer equality of condition, or even equality of rights,—it meaning merely the substitution of the right of the commonwealth for the right of a prince. Had you said a democracy there would have been some plausibility in using the word, though even then its application would have been illogical. If I am a freeman and a democrat, I hope I have the justice to allow others to be just as free and democratic as I am myself."

"And who wishes the contrary?—all I ask is a claim to be considered a fit associate for anybody in this country—in these United States of America."

"I would quit these United States of America next week, if I thought there existed any necessity for such an intolerable state of things."

"Mr. Jarvis!—and you, too, one of the Committee of Tammany Hall!"

"Yes, Mrs. Jarvis, and I one of the Committee of Tammany Hall! What, do you think I want the three thousand six hundred and fifty carmen running in and out of my house, with their tobacco saliva and pipes, all day long?"

"Who is thinking of your carmen and grocers!—I speak now only of genteel people."

"In other words, my dear, you are thinking only of those whom you fancy to have the advantage of you, and keep those who think of you in the same way, quite out of sight. This is not my democracy and freedom. I believe that it requires two people to make a bargain; and although I may consent to dine with A—, if A— will not consent to dine with me, there is an end of the matter."

"Now, you have come to a case in point. You often dined with Mr. Effingham before he went abroad, and yet you would never allow me to ask Mr. Effingham to dine with us. That is what I call meanness."

"It might be so, indeed, if it were done to save my money. I dined with Mr. Effingham because I like him; because he was an old neighbour; because he asked me, and because I found a pleasure in the quiet elegance of his table and society; and I did not ask him to dine with me, because I was satisfied he would be better pleased with such a tacit acknowledgement of his superiority in this respect, than by any bustling and ungraceful efforts to pay him in kind. Edward Effingham has dinners enough, without keeping a debtor and credit account with his guests, which is rather too New-Yorkish, even for me."

"Bustling and ungraceful!" repeated Mrs. Jarvis, bitterly; "I do not know that you are at all more bustling and ungraceful than Mr. Effingham himself."

"No, my dear, I am a quiet, unpretending man, like the great majority of my countrymen, thank God."

"Then why talk of these sorts of differences in a country in which the law establishes none?"

"For precisely the reason that I talk of the river at the foot of this street, or because there is a river. A thing may exist without there being a law for it. There is no law for building this house, and yet it is built. There is no law for making Dr. Verse a better preacher than Dr. Prolix, and yet he is a much better preacher; neither is there any law for making Mr. Effingham a more finished gentleman than I happen to be, and yet I am not fool enough to deny the fact. In the way of making out a bill of parcels, I will not turn my back to him, I can promise you."

"All this strikes me as being very spiritless, and as particularly anti-republican," said Mrs. Jarvis, rising to quit the room; "and if the Effinghams do not come this evening, I shall not enter their house this winter. I am sure they have no right to pretend to be our betters, and I feel no disposition to admit the impudent claim."

"Before you go, Jane, let me say a parting word," rejoined the husband, looking for his hat, "which is just this. If you wish the world to believe you the equal of any one, no matter whom, do not be always talking about it, lest they see you distrust the fact yourself. A positive thing will surely be seen, and they who have the highest claims are the least disposed to be always pressing them on the attention of the world. An outrage may certainly be done those social rights which have been established by common consent, and then it may be proper to resent it; but beware betraying a consciousness of your own inferiority, by letting every one see you are jealous of your station. Now, kiss me; here is the money to pay for your finery this evening, and let me see you as happy to receive Mrs. Jewett from Albion Place, as you would be to receive Mrs. Hawker herself."

"Mrs. Hawker!" cried the wife, with a toss of her head, "I would not cross the street to invite Mrs. Hawker and all her clan." Which was very true, as Mrs. Jarvis was thoroughly convinced the trouble would be unavailing, the lady in question being as near the head of fashion in New-York, as it was possible to be in a town that, in a moral sense, resembles an encampment, quite as much as it resembles a permanent and a long-existing capital.

Notwithstanding a great deal of management on the part of Mrs. Jarvis to get showy personages to attend her entertainment, the simple elegance of the two carriages that bore the Effingham party, threw all the other equipages into the shade. The arrival, indeed, was deemed a matter of so much moment, that intelligence was conveyed to the lady, who was still at her post in the inner drawing-room, of the arrival of a party altogether superior to any thing that had yet appeared in her rooms. It is true, this was not expressed in words, but it was made sufficiently obvious by the breathless haste and the air of importance of Mrs. Jarvis' sister, who had received the news from a servant, and who communicated it *propriâ personâ* to the mistress of the house.

The simple, useful, graceful, almost indispensable usage of announcing at the door, indispensable to those who receive much, and where there is the risk of meeting people known to us by name and not in person, is but little practised in America. Mrs. Jarvis would have shrunk from such an innovation, had she known that elsewhere the custom prevailed, but she was in happy ignorance on this point, as on many others that were more essential to the much-coveted social *éclat* at which she aimed. When Mademoiselle Viefville appeared, therefore, walking unsupported, as if she were out of leading-strings, followed by Eve and Grace and the gentlemen of their party, she at first supposed there was some mistake, and that her visiters had got into the wrong house; there being an opposition party in the neighbourhood.

"What brazen people!" whispered Mrs. Abijah Gross, who having removed from an interior New-England village, fully two years previously, fancied herself *au fait* of all the niceties of breeding and social tact. "There are positively two young ladies actually walking about without gentlemen!"

But it was not in the power of Mrs. Abijah Gross, with her audible whisper and obvious sneer and laugh, to put down two such lovely creatures as Eve and her cousin. The simple elegance of their attire, the indescribable air of polish, particularly in the former, and the surpassing beauty and modesty of mien of both, effectually silenced criticism, after this solitary outbreaking of vulgarity. Mrs. Jarvis recognized Eve and John Effingham, and her hurried compliments and obvious delight proclaimed to all near her, the importance she attached to their visit. Mademoiselle Viefville she had not recollected in her present dress, but as soon as she did she overwhelmed her with expressions of delight and satisfaction.

"I wish particularly to present to you a friend that we all prize exceedingly," said Eve, as soon as there was an opportunity of speaking. "This is Captain Truck, the gentleman who commands the Montauk, the ship of which you have heard so much. Ah! Mr. Jarvis," offering a hand to him with sincere cordiality, for Eve had known him from childhood, and always sincerely respected him—"*you* will receive my friend with a cordial welcome, I am certain."

She then explained to Mr. Jarvis who the honest captain was, when the former, first paying the proper respect to his other guests, led the old sailor aside, and began an earnest conversation on the subject of the recent passage.

John Effingham presented the baronet, whom Mrs. Jarvis, out of pure ignorance of his rank in his own country, received with perfect propriety and self-respect.

"We have very few people of note in town at present, I believe," said Mrs. Jarvis to John Effingham. "A great traveller, a most interesting man, is the only person of that sort I could obtain for this evening, and I shall have great pleasure in introducing you. He is there in that crowd, for he is in the greatest possible demand; he has seen so much.—Mrs. Snow, with your permission—really the ladies are thronging about him as if he were a Pawnee,—have the goodness to step a little this way, Mr. Effingham—Miss Effingham—Mrs. Snow, just touch his arm and let him know I wish to introduce a couple of friends.—Mr. Dodge, Mr. John Effingham, Miss Effingham, Miss Van Cortlandt. I hope you may succeed in getting him a little to yourselves, ladies, for he can tell you all about Europe—saw the king of France riding out to Nully, and has a prodigious knowledge of things on the other side of the water."

It required a good deal of Eve's habitual self-command to prevent a smile, but she had the tact and discretion to receive Steadfast as an utter stranger. John Effingham bowed as haughtily as man can bow, and then it was whispered that he and Mr. Dodge were rival travellers. The distance of the former, coupled with an expression of countenance that did not invite familiarity, drove nearly all the company over to the side of Steadfast, who, it was soon settled, had seen much the most of the world, understood society the best, and had moreover travelled as far as Timbuctoo in Africa. The *clientèle* of Mr. Dodge increased rapidly, as these reports spread in the rooms, and those who had not read the "delightful letters published in the Active Inquirer," furiously envied those who had enjoyed that high advantage.

"It is Mr. Dodge, the great traveller," said one young lady, who had extricated herself from the crowd around the "lion," and taken a station near Eve and Grace, and who, moreover, was a "blue" in her own set; "his beautiful and accurate descriptions have attracted great attention in England, and it is said they have actually been republished!"

"Have you read them, Miss Brackett?"

"Not the letters themselves, absolutely; but all the remarks on them in the last week's Hebdomad. Most delightful letters, judging from those remarks; full of nature and point, and singularly accurate in all their facts. In this respect they are invaluable, travellers do fall into such extraordinary errors!"

"I hope, ma'am," said John Effingham, gravely, "that the gentleman has avoided the capital mistake of commenting on things that actually exist. Comments on its facts are generally esteemed by the people of a country, impertinent and unjust; and your true way to succeed, is to treat as freely as possible its imaginary peculiarities."

Miss Brackett had nothing to answer to this observation, the Hebdomad having, among its other profundities, never seen proper to touch on the subject. She went on praising the "Letters," however, not one of which had she read, or would she read; for this young lady had contrived to gain a high reputation in her own *coterie* for taste and knowledge in books, by merely skimming the strictures of those who do not even skim the works they pretend to analyze.

Eve had never before been in so close contact with so much flippant ignorance, and she could not but wonder at seeing a man like her kinsman overlooked, in order that a man like Mr. Dodge should be preferred. All this gave John Effingham himself no concern, but retiring a little from the crowd, he entered into a short conversation with the young baronet.

"I should like to know your real opinions of this set," he said; "not that I plead guilty to the childish sensibility that is so common in all provincial circles to the judgments of strangers, but with a view to aid you in forming a just estimate of the real state of the country."

"As I know the precise connexion between you and our host, there can be no objection to giving a perfectly frank reply. The women strike me as being singularly delicate and pretty; well dressed, too, I might add; but, while there is a great air of decency, there is very little high finish; and what strikes me as being quite odd, under such circumstances, scarcely any downright vulgarity, or coarseness."

"A Daniel come to judgment! One who had passed a life here, would not have come so near the truth, simply because he would not have observed peculiarities, that require the means of comparison to be detected. You are a little too indulgent in saying there is no downright vulgarity; for some there is; though surprisingly little for the circumstances. But of the coarseness that would be so prominent elsewhere, there is hardly any. True, so great is the equality in all things, in this country, so direct the tendency to this respectable mediocrity, that what you now see here, to-night, may be seen in almost every village in the land, with a few immaterial exceptions in the way of furniture and other city appliances, and not much even in these."

"Certainly, as a mediocrity, this is respectable, though a fastidious taste might see a multitude of faults."

"I shall not say that the taste would be merely fastidious, for much is wanting that would add to the grace and beauty of society, while much that is wanting would be missed only by the over-sophisticated. Those young men, who are sniggering over some bad joke in the corner, for instance, are positively vulgar, as is that young lady who is indulging in practical coquetry; but, on the whole, there is little of this; and, even our hostess, a silly woman, devoured with the desire of being what neither her social position, education, habits nor notions fit her to be, is less obtrusive, bustling, and offensive, than a similar person, elsewhere."

"I am quite of your way of thinking, and intended to ask you to account for it."

"The Americans are an imitative people of necessity, and they are apt at this part of imitation, in particular. Then they are less artificial in all their practices, than older and more sophisticated nations; and this company has got that essential part of good breeding, simplicity, as it were *par force*. A step higher in the social scale, you will see less of it; for greater daring and bad models lead to blunders in matters that require to be exceedingly well done, if done at all. The faults here would be more apparent, by an approach near enough to get into the tone of mind, the forms of speech, and the attempts at wit."

"Which I think we shall escape to-night, as I see the ladies are already making their apologies and taking leave. We must defer this investigation to another time."

"It may be indefinitely postponed, as it would scarcely reward the trouble of an inquiry."

The gentlemen now approached Mrs. Jarvis, paid their parting compliments, hunted up Captain Truck, whom they tore by violence from the good-natured hospitality of the master of the house, and then saw the ladies into their carriage. As they drove off, the worthy mariner protested that Mr. Jarvis was one of the honestest men he had ever met, and announced that he intended giving him a dinner on board the Montauk, the very next day.

The dwelling of Mrs. Hawker was in Hudson Square; or in a portion of the city that the lovers of the grandiose are endeavouring to call St. John's Park; for it is rather an amusing peculiarity among a certain portion of the emigrants who have flocked into the Middle States, within the last thirty years, that they are not satisfied with permitting any family, or thing, to possess the name it originally enjoyed, if there exists the least opportunity to change it. There was but a carriage or two before the door, though the strong lights in the house showed that company had collected.

"Mrs. Hawker is the widow and the daughter of men of long established New-York families; she is childless, affluent, and universally respected where known, for her breeding, benevolence, good sense, and heart," said John Effingham, while the party was driving from one house to the other. "Were you to go into most of the sets of this town, and mention Mrs. Hawker's name, not one person in ten would know there is such a being in their vicinity; the *pêle mêle* of a migratory population keeping persons of her character and condition in life, quite out of view. The very persons who will prattle by the hour, of the establishments of Mrs. Peleg Pond, and Mrs. Jonah Twist, and Mrs. Abiram Wattles, people who first appeared on this island five or six years since, and, who having accumulated what to them are relatively large fortunes, have launched out into vulgar and uninstructed finery, would look with surprise at hearing Mrs. Hawker mentioned as one having any claims to social distinction. Her historical names are overshadowed in their minds by the parochial glories of certain local prodigies in the townships whence they emigrated; her manners would puzzle the comprehension of people whose imitation has not gone beyond the surface, and her polished and simple mind would find little sympathy among a class who seldom rise above a commonplace sentiment without getting upon stilts."

"Mrs. Hawker, then, is a lady," observed Sir George Templemore.

"Mrs. Hawker is a lady, in every sense of the word; by position, education, manners, association, mind, fortune and birth. I do not know that we ever had more of her class than exist to-day, but certainly we once had them more prominent in society."

"I suppose, sir," said Captain Truck, "that this Mrs. Hawker is of what is called the old school?"

"Of a very ancient school, and one that is likely to continue, though it may not be generally attended."

"I am afraid, Mr. John Effingham, that I shall be like a fish out of water in such a house. I can get along very well with your Mrs. Jarvis, and with the dear young lady in the other carriage; but the sort of woman you have described, will be apt to jam a plain mariner like myself. What in nature should I do, now, if she should ask me to dance a minuet?"

"Dance it agreeably to the laws of nature," returned John Effingham, as the carriages stopped.

A respectable, quiet, and aged black servant admitted the party, though even he did not announce the visiters, while he held the door of the drawing-room open for them, with respectful attention. Mrs. Hawker arose, and advanced to meet Eve and her companions, and, though she kissed the cousins affectionately, her reception of Mademoiselle Viefville was so simply polite as to convince the latter she was valued on account of her services. John Effingham, who was ten or fifteen years the junior of the old lady, gallantly kissed her hand, when he presented his two male companions. After paying the proper attention to the greatest stranger, Mrs. Hawker turned to Captain Truck and said—

"This, then, is the gentleman to whose skill and courage you all owe so much—*we* all owe so much, I might better have said—the commander of the Montauk?"

"I have the honour of commanding that vessel, ma'am," returned Captain Truck, who was singularly awed by the dignified simplicity of his hostess, although her quiet, natural, and yet finished manner, which extended even to the intonation of the voice, and the smallest movement, were as unlike what he had expected as possible; "and with such passengers as she had last voyage I can only say, it is a pity that she is not better off for one to take care of her."

"Your passengers give a different account of the matter, but, in order that I may judge impartially, do me the favour to take this chair, and let me learn a few of the particulars from yourself."

Observing that Sir George Templemore had followed Eve to the other side of the room, Mrs. Hawker now resumed her seat, and, without neglecting any to attend to one in particular, or attending to one in a way to make him feel oppressed, she contrived, in a few minutes, to make the captain forget all about the minuet, and to feel much more at his ease than would have been the case with Mrs. Jarvis, in a month's intercourse.

In the mean time, Eve had crossed the room to join a lady whose smile invited her to her side. This was a young, slightly framed female, of a pleasing countenance, but who would not have been particularly distinguished, in such a place, for personal charms. Still, her smile was sweet, her eyes were soft, and the expression of her face was what might almost be called illuminated. As Sir George Templemore followed her, Eve mentioned his name to her acquaintance, whom she addressed as Mrs. Bloomfield.

"You are bent on perpetrating further gaiety to-night," said the latter, glancing at the ball-dresses of the two cousins; "are you in the colours of the Houston faction, or in those of the Peabody."

"Not in pea-green, certainly," returned Eve, laughing—"as you may see; but in simple white."

"You intend then to be 'led a measure' at Mrs. Houston's. It were more suitable than among the other faction."

"Is fashion, then, factious, in New-York?" inquired Sir George.

"Fractious would be a better word, perhaps. But we have parties in almost every thing, in America; in politics, religion, temperance, speculations, and taste; why not in fashion?"

"I fear we are not quite independent enough to form parties on such a subject," said Eve.

"Perfectly well said, Miss Effingham; one must think a little originally, let it be ever so falsely, in order to get up a fashion. I fear we shall have to admit our insignificance on this point. You are a late arrival, Sir George Templemore?"

"As lately as the commencement of this month; I had the honour of being a fellow-passenger with Mr. Effingham and his family."

"In which voyage you suffered shipwreck, captivity, and famine, if half we hear be true."

"Report has a little magnified our risks; we encountered some serious dangers, but nothing amounting to the sufferings you have mentioned."

"Being a married woman, and having passed the crisis in which deception is not practised, I expect to hear truth again," said Mrs. Bloomfield, smiling. "I trust, however, you underwent enough to qualify you all for heroes and heroines, and shall content myself with knowing that you are here, safe and happy—if," she added, looking inquiringly at Eve, "one who has been educated abroad *can* be happy at home."

"One educated abroad *may* be happy at home, though possibly not in the modes most practised by the world," said Eve, firmly.

"Without an opera, without a court, almost without society!"

"An opera would be desirable, I confess; of courts I know nothing, unmarried females being cyphers in Europe; and I hope better things than to think I shall be without society."

"Unmarried females are considered cyphers too, here, provided there be enough of them with a good respectable digit at their head. I assure you no one quarrels with the cyphers under such circumstances. I think, Sir George Templemore, a town like this must be something of a paradox to you."

"Might I venture to inquire the reason for this opinion!"

"Merely because it is neither one thing nor another. Not a capital, nor yet merely a provincial place; with something more than commerce in its bosom, and yet with that something hidden under a bushel. A good deal more than Liverpool, and a good deal less than London. Better even than Edinburgh, in many respects, and worse than Wapping, in others."

"You have been abroad, Mrs. Bloomfield?"

"Not a foot out of my own country; scarcely a foot out of my own state. I have been at Lake George, the Falls, and the Mountain House; and, as one does not travel in a balloon, I saw some of the intermediate places. As for all else, I am obliged to go by report."

"It is a pity Mrs. Bloomfield was not with us, this evening, at Mrs. Jarvis's," said Eve, laughing. "She might then have increased her knowledge, by listening to a few cantos from the epic of Mr. Dodge."

"I have glanced at some of that author's wisdom," returned Mrs. Bloomfield, "but I soon found it was learning backwards. There is a never-failing rule, by which it is easy to arrive at a traveller's worth, in a negative sense, at least."

"That is a rule which may be worth knowing," said the baronet, "as it would save much useless wear of the eyes."

"When one betrays a profound ignorance of his own country, it is a fair presumption that he cannot be very acute in his observation of strangers. Mr. Dodge is one of these writers, and a single letter fully satisfied my curiosity. I fear, Miss Effingham, very inferior wares, in the way of manners, have been lately imported, in large quantities, into this country, as having the Tower mark on them."

Eve laughed, but declared that Sir George Templemore was better qualified than herself to answer such a question.

"We are said to be a people of facts, rather than a people of theories," continued Mrs. Bloomfield, without attending to the reference of the young lady, "and any coin that offers passes, until another that is better, arrives. It is a singular, but a very general mistake, I believe, of the people of this country, in supposing that they can exist under the present régime, when others would fail, because their opinions keep even pace with, or precede the actual condition of society; whereas, those who have thought and observed most on such subjects, agree in thinking the very reverse to be the case."

"This would be a curious condition for a government so purely conventional," observed Sir George, with interest, "and it certainly is entirely opposed to the state of things all over Europe."

"It is so, and yet there is no great mystery in it, after all. Accident has liberated us from trammels that still fetter you. We are like a vehicle on the top of a hill, which, the moment it is pushed beyond the point of resistance, rolls down of itself, without the aid of horses. One may follow with the team, and hook on when it gets to the bottom, but there is no such thing as keeping company with it until it arrives there."

"You will allow, then, that there is a bottom?'

"There is a bottom to every thing—to good and bad; happiness and misery; hope, fear, faith and charity; even to a woman's mind, which I have sometimes fancied the most bottomless thing in nature. There may, therefore, well be a bottom even to the institutions of America."

Sir George listened with the interest with which an Englishman of his class always endeavours to catch a concession that he fancies is about to favour his own political predilections, and he felt encouraged to push the subject further.

"And you think the political machine is rolling downwards towards this bottom?" he said, with an interest in the answer that, living in the quiet and forgetfulness of his own home, he would have laughed at himself for entertaining. But our sensibilities become quickened by collision, and opposition is known even to create love.

Mrs. Bloomfield was quick-witted, intelligent, cultivated and shrewd. She saw the motive at a glance, and, notwithstanding she saw and felt all its abuses, strongly attached to the governing principle of her country's social organization, as is almost universally the case with the strongest minds and most generous hearts of the nation, she was not disposed to let a stranger carry away a false impression of her sentiments on such a point.

"Did you ever study logic, Sir George Templemore?" she asked, archly.

"A little, though not enough I fear to influence my mode of reasoning, or even to leave me familiar with the terms."

"Oh! I am not about to assail you with *sequiturs* and *non sequiturs*, dialectics and all the mysteries of *Denk-Lehre*, but simply to remind you there is such a thing as the bottom of a subject. When I tell you we are flying towards the bottom of our institutions, it is in the intellectual sense, and not, as you have erroneously imagined, in an unintellectual sense. I mean that we are getting to understand them, which, I fear, we did not absolutely do at the commencement of the 'experiment.'"

"But I think you will admit, that as the civilization of the country advances, some material changes must occur; your people cannot always remain stationary; they must either go backwards or forward."

"Up or down, if you will allow me to correct your phraseology. The civilization of the country, in one sense at least, is retrogressive, and the people, as they cannot go 'up,' betray a disposition to go 'down.'"

"You deal in enigmas, and I am afraid to think I understand you."

"I mean, merely, that gallowses are fast disappearing, and that the people—*le peuple* you will understand—begin to accept money. In both particulars, I think there is a sensible change for the worse, within my own recollection."

Mrs. Bloomfield then changed her manner, and from using that light-hearted gaiety with which she often rendered her conversation *piquante*, and even occasionally brilliant, she became more grave and explicit. The subject soon turned to that of punishments, and few men could have reasoned more sensibly, justly or forcibly, on such a subject, than this slight and fragile-looking young woman. Without the least pedantry, with a beauty of language that the other sex seldom attains, and with a delicacy of discrimination, and a sentiment that were strictly feminine, she rendered a theme interesting, that, however important in itself, is forbidding, veiling all its odious and revolting features in the refinement and finesse of her own polished mind.

Eve could have listened all night, and, at every syllable that fell from the lips of her friend, she felt a glow of triumph; for she was proud of letting an intelligent foreigner see that America did contain women worthy to be ranked with the best of other countries, a circumstance that they who merely frequented what is called the world, she thought might be reasonably justified in distrusting. In one respect, she fancied Mrs. Bloomfield superior to those of her own sex whom she had so often admired abroad: for her knowledge and cleverness were untrammeled either by the prejudices incident to a factitious condition of society, or by their reaction; two circumstances that often obscured the sense and candour of those to whom she had so often listened with pleasure in other countries. The singularly feminine tone, too, of all that Mrs. Bloomfield said or thought, while it lacked nothing in strength, added to the charm of her conversation, and increased the pleasure of those that listened.

"Is the circle large to which Mrs. Hawker and her friends belong?" asked Sir George, as he assisted Eve and Grace to cloak, when they had taken leave. "A town which can boast of half-a-dozen such houses need not accuse itself of wanting society."

"Ah! there is but one Mrs. Hawker in New-York," answered Grace, "and not many Mrs. Bloomfields in the world. It would be too much to say, we have even half-a-dozen such houses."

"Have you not been struck with the admirable tone of this drawing-room," half whispered Eve. "It may want a little of that lofty ease that one sees among the better portion of the old *Princesses et Duchesses*, which is a relic of a school that, it is to be feared, is going out; but in its place there is a winning nature, with as much dignity as is necessary, and a truth that gives us confidence in the sincerity of those around us."

"Upon my word, I think Mrs. Hawker quite fit for a Duchess."

"You mean a *Duchesse*" said Eve, "and yet she is without the manner that we understand by such a word. Mrs. Hawker is a lady, and there can be no higher term."

"She is a delightful old woman," cried John Effingham, "and if twenty years younger and disposed to change her condition, I should really be afraid to enter the house."

"My dear sir," put in the captain, "I will make her Mrs. Truck to-morrow, and say nothing of years, if she could be content to take up with such an offer. Why, sir, she is no woman, but a saint in petticoats! I felt the whole time as if talking to my own mother, and as for ships, she knows more about them than I do!"

The whole party laughed at the strength of the captain's admiration, and getting into the carriages proceeded to the last of the houses they intended visiting that night.

CHAPTER V.

"So turns she every man the wrong side out,
And never gives to truth and virtue that
Which simpleness and merit purchaseth."

Much Ado About Nothing 3.1.68–70.

MRS. Houston was what is termed a fashionable woman in New-York. She, too, was of a family of local note, though of one much less elevated in the olden time than that of Mrs. Hawker. Still her claims were admitted by the most fastidious on such points, for a few do remain who think descent indisputable to gentility; and as her means were ample, and her tastes perhaps superior to those of most around her, she kept what was thought a house of better tone than common, even in the highest circle. Eve had but a slight acquaintance with her; but in Grace's eyes, Mrs. Houston's was the place of all others that she thought might make a favourable impression on her cousin. Her wish that this should prove to be the case was so strong, that, as they drove towards the door, she could not forbear from making an attempt to prepare Eve for what she was to meet.

"Although Mrs. Houston has a very large house for New-York, and lives in a uniform style, you are not to expect ante-chambers, and vast suites of rooms, Eve," said Grace; "such as you have been accustomed to see abroad."

"It is not necessary, my dear cousin, to enter a house of four or five windows in front, to see it is not a house of twenty or thirty. I should be very unreasonable to expect an Italian palazzo, or a Parisian hotel, in this good town."

"We are not old enough for that yet, Eve; a hundred years hence, Mademoiselle Viefville, such things may exist here."

"*Bien sûr. C'est naturel.*"

"A hundred years hence, as the world tends, Grace, they are not likely to exist any where, except as taverns, or hospitals, or manufactories. But what have we to do, coz, with a century ahead of us? young as we both are, we cannot hope to live that time."

Grace would have been puzzled to account satisfactorily to herself, for the strong desire she felt that neither of her companions should expect to see such a house as their senses so plainly told them did not exist in the place; but her foot moved in the bottom of the carriage, for she was not half satisfied with her cousin's answer.

"All I mean, Eve," she said, after a pause, "is, that one ought not to expect in a town as new as this, the improvements that one sees in an older state of society."

"And have Mademoiselle Viefville, or I, ever been so weak as to suppose, that New-York is Paris, or Rome, or Vienna?"

Grace was still less satisfied, for, unknown to herself, she *had* hoped that Mrs. Houston's ball might be quite equal to a ball in either of those ancient capitals; and she was now vexed that her cousin considered it so much a matter of course that it should not be. But there was no time for explanations, as the carriage now stopped.

The noise, confusion, calling out, swearing, and rude clamour before the house of Mrs. Houston, said little for the out-door part of the arrangements. Coachmen are nowhere a particularly silent and civil class; but the uncouth European peasants, who have been preferred to the honours of the whip in New-York, to the usual feelings of competition and contention, added that particular feature of humility which is known to distinguish "the beggar on horseback." The imposing equipages of our party, however, had that effect on most of these rude brawlers, which a display of wealth is known to produce on the vulgar-minded; and the ladies got into the house, through a lane of coachmen, by yielding a little to a *chevaux de frise* of whips, without any serious calamity.

"One hardly knows which is the most terrific," said Eve, involuntarily, as soon as the door closed on them—"the noise within, or the noise without!"

This was spoken rapidly, and in French, to Mademoiselle Viefville, but Grace heard and understood it, and for the first time in her life, she perceived that Mrs. Houston's company was not composed of nightingales. The surprise is that the discovery should have come so late.

"I am delighted at having got into this house," said Sir George, who, having thrown his cloak to his own servant, stood with the two other gentlemen waiting the descent of the ladies from the upper room, where the bad arrangements of the house compelled them to uncloak and to put aside their shawls, "as I am told it is the best house in town to see the other sex."

"To *hear them*, would be nearer the truth, perhaps," returned John Effingham. "As for pretty women, one can hardly go amiss in New-York; and your ears now tell you, that they do not come into the world to be seen only."

The baronet smiled, but he was too well bred to contradict or to assent. Mademoiselle Viefville, unconscious that she was violating the proprieties, walked into the rooms by herself, as soon as she descended, followed by Eve; but Grace shrank to the side of John Effingham, whose arm she took as a step necessary even to decorum.

Mrs. Houston received her guests with ease and dignity. She was one of those females that the American world calls gay; in other words, she opened her own house to a very promiscuous society, ten or a dozen times in a winter, and accepted the greater part of the invitations she got to other people's. Still, in most other countries, as a fashionable woman, she would have been esteemed a model of devotion to the duties of a wife and a mother, for she paid a personal attention to her household, and had actually taught all her children the Lord's prayer, the creed, and the ten commandments. She attended church twice every Sunday, and only staid at home from the evening lectures, that the domestics might have the opportunity of going (which, by the way, they never did) in her stead. Feminine, well-mannered, rich, pretty, of a very positive social condition, and naturally kind-hearted and disposed to sociability, Mrs. Houston, supported by an indulgent husband, who so much loved to see people with the appearance of happiness, that he was not particular as to the means, had found no difficulty in rising to the pinnacle of fashion, and of having her name in the mouths of all those who find it necessary to talk of somebodies, in order that they may seem to be somebodies themselves. All this contributed to Mrs. Houston's happiness, or she fancied it did; and as every passion is known to increase by indulgence, she had insensibly gone on in her much-envied career, until, as has just been said, she reached the summit.

"These rooms are very crowded," said Sir George, glancing his eyes around two very pretty little narrow drawing-rooms, that were beautifully, not to say richly, furnished; "one wonders that the same contracted style of building should be so very general, in a town that increases as rapidly as this, and where fashion has no fixed abode, and land is so abundant."

"Mrs. Bloomfield would tell you," said Eve, "that these houses are types of the social state of the country, in which no one is permitted to occupy more than his share of ground."

"But there are reasonably large dwellings in the place. Mrs. Hawker has a good house, and your father's for instance, would be thought so, too, in London even; and yet I fancy you will agree with me in thinking that a good room is almost unknown in New-York."

"I do agree with you, in this particular, certainly, for to meet with a good room, one must go into the houses built thirty years ago. We have inherited these snuggeries, however, England not having much to boast of in the way of houses."

"In the way of town residences, I agree with you entirely, as a whole, though we have some capital exceptions. Still, I do not think we are quite as compact as this—do you not fancy the noise increased in consequence of its being so confined?"

Eve laughed and shook her head quite positively.

"What would it be if fairly let out!" she said. "We must not lose the precious moments, however, but turn our eyes about us in quest of the *belles*. Grace, you who are so much at home, must be our cicerone, and tell us which are the idols we are to worship."

"*Dites-moi premièrement; que veut dire une belle à New-York?*" demanded Mademoiselle Viefville. "*Apparemment, tout le monde est joli.*"

"A *belle*, Mademoiselle," returned John Effingham, "is not necessarily beautiful, the qualifications for the character, being various and a little contradictory. One may be a *belle* by means of money, a tongue, an eye, a foot, teeth, a laugh, or any other separate feature, or grace; though no woman was ever yet a *belle*, I believe, by means of the head, considered collectively. But why deal in description, when the thing itself confronts us? The young lady standing directly before us, is a *belle* of the most approved stamp and silvery tone. Is it not Miss Ring, Grace?"

The answer was in the affirmative, and the eyes of the whole party turned towards the subject of this remark. The young lady in question was about twenty, rather tall for an American woman, not conspicuously handsome, but like most around her of delicate features and frame, and with such a *physique*, as, under proper training, would have rendered her the *beau idéal* of feminine delicacy and gentleness.

She had natural spirit, likewise, as appeared in her clear blue eye, and moreover she had the spirit to be a *belle.*

Around this young creature were clustered no less than five young men, dressed in the height of the fashion, all of whom seemed to be entranced with the words that fell from her lips, and each of whom appeared anxious to say something clever in return. They all laughed, the lady most, and sometimes all spoke at once. Notwithstanding these outbreakings, Miss Ring did most of the talking, and once or twice, as a young man would gape after a most exhilarating show of merriment, and discover an inclination to retreat, she managed to recall him to his allegiance, by some remark particularly pertinent to himself, or his feelings.

"*Qui est cette dame?*" asked Mademoiselle Viefville, very much as one would put a similar question, on seeing a man enter a church during service with his hat on.

"*Elle est demoiselle,*" returned Eve.

"*Quelle horreur!*"

"Nay, nay, Mademoiselle, I shall not allow you to set up France as immaculate on this point, neither—" said John Effingham, looking at the last speaker with an affected frown—"A young lady may have a tongue, and she may even speak to a young gentleman, and not be guilty of felony; although I will admit that five tongues are unnecessary, and that five listeners are more than sufficient, for the wisdom of twenty in petticoats."

"*C'est une horreur!*"

"I dare say Miss Ring would think it a greater horror to be obliged to pass an evening in a row of girls, unspoken to, except to be asked to dance, and admired only in the distance. But let us take seats on that sofa, and then we may go beyond the pantomime, and become partakers in the sentiment of the scene."

Grace and Eve were now led off to dance, and the others did as John Effingham had suggested. In the eyes of the *belle* and her admirers, they who had passed thirty were of no account, and our listeners succeeded in establishing themselves quietly within ear-shot—this was almost at duelling distance, too,—without at all interrupting the regular action of the piece. We extract a little of the dialogue, by way of giving a more dramatic representation of the scene.

"Do you think the youngest Miss Danvers beautiful?" asked the *belle,* while her eye wandered in quest of a sixth gentleman to "entertain," as the phrase is. "In my opinion, she is absolutely the prettiest female in Mrs. Houston's rooms this night."

The young men, one and all, protested against this judgment, and with perfect truth, for Miss Ring was too original to point out charms that every one could see.

"They say it will not be a match between her and Mr. Egbert, after every body has supposed it settled so long. What is your opinion, Mr. Edson?"

This timely question prevented Mr. Edson's retreat, for he had actually got so far in this important evolution, as to have gaped and turned his back. Recalled, as it were by the sound of the bugle, Mr. Edson was compelled to say something, a sore affliction to him always.

"Oh! I'm quite of your way of thinking; they have certainly courted too long to think of marrying."

"I detest long courtships; they must be perfect antidotes to love; are they not, Mr. Moreland?"

A truant glance of Mr. Moreland's eye was rebuked by this appeal, and instead of looking for a place of refuge, he now merely looked sheepish. He, however, entirely agreed with the young lady, as the surer way of getting out of the difficulty.

"Pray, Mr. Summerfield, how do you like the last Hajji—Miss Eve Effingham? To my notion, she is prettyish, though by no means as well as her cousin, Miss Van Cortlandt, who is really rather good-looking."

As Eve and Grace were the two most truly lovely young women in the rooms, this opinion, as well as the loud tone in which it was given, startled Mademoiselle Viefville quite as much as the subjects that the belle had selected for discussion. She would have moved, as listening to a conversation that was not meant for their ears; but John Effingham quietly assured her that Miss Ring seldom spoke in company without intending as many persons as possible to hear her.

"Miss Effingham is very plainly dressed for an only daughter," continued the young lady, "though that lace of her cousin's is real point! I'll engage it cost every cent of ten dollars a yard! They are both engaged to be married, I hear."

"*Ciel!*" exclaimed Mademoiselle Viefville.

"Oh! That is nothing," observed John Effingham, coolly. "Wait a moment, and you'll hear that they have been privately married these six months, if, indeed, you hear no more."

"Of course this is but an idle tale?" said Sir George Templemore with a concern, which, in despite of his good breeding, compelled him to put a question that, under other circumstances, would scarcely have been permissible.

"As true as the gospel. But listen to the *bell*, it is *ringing* for the good of the whole parish."

"The affair between Miss Effingham and Mr. Morpeth, who knew her abroad, I understand is entirely broken off; some say the father objected to Mr. Morpeth's want of fortune; others that the lady was fickle, while some accuse the gentleman of the same vice. Don't you think it shocking to jilt, in either sex, Mr. Mosely?"

The *retiring* Mr. Mosely was drawn again within the circle, and was obliged to confess that he thought it was very shocking, in either sex, to jilt.

"If I were a man," continued the *belle*, "I would never think of a young woman who had once jilted a lover. To my mind, it bespeaks a bad heart, and a woman with a bad heart cannot make a very amiable wife."

"What an exceedingly clever creature she is," whispered Mr. Mosely to Mr. Moreland, and he now made up his mind to remain and be "entertained" some time longer.

"I think poor Mr. Morpeth greatly to be pitied; for no man would be so silly as to be attentive seriously to a lady without encouragement. Encouragement is the *ne plus ultra* of courtship; are you not of my opinion, Mr. Walworth?"

Mr. Walworth was number five of the entertainees, and he did understand Latin, of which the young lady, though fond of using scraps, knew literally nothing. He smiled an assent, therefore, and the *belle* felicitated herself in having "entertained" *him* effectually; nor was she mistaken.

"Indeed, they say Miss Effingham had several affairs of the heart, while in Europe, but it seems she was unfortunate in them all."

"*Mais, ceci est trop fort! Je ne peux plus écouter.*"

"My dear Mademoiselle, compose yourself. The crisis is not yet arrived, by any means."

"I understand she still corresponds with a German Baron, and an Italian Marquis, though both engagements are absolutely broken off. Some people say she walks into company alone, unsupported by any gentleman, by way of announcing a firm determination to remain single for life."

A common exclamation from the young men proclaimed their disapprobation; and that night three of them actually repeated the thing, as a well established truth, and two of the three, failing of something better to talk about, also announced that Eve was actually engaged to be married.

"There is something excessively indelicate in a young lady's moving about a room without having a gentleman's arm to lean on! I always feel as if such a person was out of her place, and ought to be in the kitchen."

"But, Miss Ring, what well-bred person does it?" sputtered Mr. Moreland. "No one ever heard of such a thing in good society. 'Tis quite shocking! Altogether unprecedented."

"It strikes me as being excessively coarse!"

"Oh! manifestly; quite rustic!" exclaimed Mr. Edson.

"What can possibly be more vulgar?" added Mr. Walworth.

"I never heard of such a thing among the right sort!" said Mr. Mosely.

"A young lady who can be so brazen as to come into a room without a gentleman's arm to lean on, is, in my judgment at least, but indifferently educated, Hajji or no Hajji. Mr. Edson, have you ever felt the tender passion? I know you have been desperately in love, once, at least; do describe to me some of the symptoms, in order that I may know when I am seriously attacked myself by the disease."

"*Mais, ceci est ridicule! L'enfant s'est sauvée du Charenton de New-York.*"

"From the nursery rather, Mademoiselle; you perceive she does not yet know how to walk alone."

Mr. Edson now protested that he was too stupid to feel a passion as intellectual as love, and that he was afraid he was destined by nature to remain as insensible as a block.

"One never knows, Mr. Edson," said the young lady, encouragingly. "Several of my acquaintances, who thought themselves quite safe, have been seized suddenly, and, though none have actually died, more than one has been roughly treated, I assure you."

Here the young men, one and all, protested that she was excessively clever. Then succeeded a pause, for Miss Ring was inviting, with her eyes, a number six to join the circle, her ambition being dissatisfied with five entertainees, as she saw that Miss Trumpet, a rival belle, had managed to get exactly that number, also, in the other room. All the gentlemen availed themselves of the cessation in wit to gape, and Mr. Edson took the occasion to remark to Mr. Summerfield that he understood "lots had been sold in seven hundredth street that morning, as high as two hundred dollars a lot."

The *quadrille* now ended, and Eve returned towards her friends. As she approached, the whole party compared her quiet, simple, feminine, and yet dignified air, with the restless, beau-catching, and worldly look of the belle, and wondered by what law of nature, or of fashion, the one could possibly become the subject of the other's comments. Eve never appeared better than on that evening. Her dress had all the accuracy and finish of a Parisian toilette, being equally removed from exaggeration and neglect; and it was worn with the ease of one accustomed to be elegantly attired, and yet never decked with finery. Her step even was that of a lady, having neither the mincing tread of a Paris grisette, a manner that sometimes ascends even to the *bourgeoise*, the march of a cockneyess, nor the tiptoe swing of a *belle*; but it was the natural though regulated step, of a trained and delicate woman. Walk alone she could certainly, and always did, except on those occasions of ceremony that demanded a partner. Her countenance, across which an unworthy thought had never left a trace, was an index, too, to the purity, high principles and womanly self-respect that controlled all her acts, and, in these particulars, was the very reverse of the feverish, half-hoydenish half-affected expression of that of Miss Ring.

"They may say what they please," muttered Captain Truck, who had been a silent but wondering listener of all that passed; "she is worth as many of them as could be stowed in the Montauk's lower hold."

Miss Ring perceiving Eve approach, was desirous of saying something to her, for there was an *éclat* about a Hajji, after all, that rendered an acquaintance, or even an intimacy desirable, and she smiled and curtsied. Eve returned the salutation, but as she did not care to approach a group of six, of which no less than five were men, she continued to move towards her own party. This reserve compelled Miss Ring to advance a step or two, when Eve was obliged to stop. Curtsying to her partner, she thanked him for his attention, relinquished his arm, and turned to meet the lady. At the same instant the five "entertainees" escaped in a body, equally rejoiced at their release, and proud of their captivity.

"I have been dying to come and speak to you, Miss Effingham," commenced Miss Ring, "but these *five* giants (she emphasized the word we have put in italics) so beset me, that escape was quite impossible. There ought to be a law that but one gentleman should speak to a lady at a time."

"I thought there was such a law already," said Eve, quietly.

"You mean in good breeding; but no one thinks of those antiquated laws now-a-days. Are you beginning to be reconciled, a little, to your own country?"

"It is not easy to effect a reconciliation where there has been no misunderstanding. I hope I have never quarrelled with my country, or my country with me."

"Oh! it is not exactly that I mean. Cannot one need a reconciliation without a quarrel? What do you say to this, Mr. Edson?"

Miss Ring having detected some symptoms of desertion in the gentleman addressed, had thrown in this question by way of recall; when turning to note its effect, she perceived that all of her *clientelle* had escaped. A look of surprise and mortification and vexation it was not in her power to suppress, and then came one of horror.

"How conspicuous we have made ourselves, and it is all my fault!" she said, for the first time that evening permitting her voice to fall to a becoming tone. 'Why, here we actually are, two ladies conversing together, and no gentleman near us!"

"Is that being conspicuous?" asked Eve, with a simplicity that was entirely natural.

"I am sure, Miss Effingham, one who has seen as much of society as you, can scarcely ask that question seriously. I do not think I have done so improper a thing, since I was fifteen; and, dear me! dear me! how to escape is the question. You have permitted your partner to go, and I do not see a gentleman of my acquaintance near us, to give me his arm!"

"As your distress is occasioned by my company," said Eve, "it is fortunately in my power to relieve it." Thus saying, she quietly walked across the room, and took her seat next to Mademoiselle Viefville.

Miss Ring held up her hands in amazement, and then fortunately perceiving one of the truants gaping at no great distance, she beckoned him to her side.

"Have the goodness to give me your arm, Mr. Summerfield," she said, "I am dying to get out of this unpleasantly conspicuous situation; but you are the first gentleman that has approached me this twelvemonth. I would not for the world do so brazen a thing as Miss Effingham has just achieved; would you believe it, she positively went from this spot to her seat, quite alone!"

"The Hajjis are privileged."

"They make themselves so. But every body knows how bold and unwomanly the French females are. One could wish, notwithstanding, that our own people would not import their audacious usages into this country."

"It is a thousand pities that Mr. Clay, in his compromise, neglected to make an exception against that article. A tariff on impudence would not be at all sectional."

"It might interfere with the manufacture at home, notwithstanding," said John Effingham; for the lungs were strong, and the rooms of Mrs. Houston so small, that little was said that evening, which was not heard by any who chose to listen. But Miss Ring never listened, it being no part of the vocation of a *belle* to perform that inferior office, and sustained by the protecting arm of Mr. Summerfield, she advanced more boldly into the crowd, where she soon contrived to catch another group of even six "entertainees." As for Mr. Summerfield, he lived a twelvemonth on the reputation of the exceedingly clever thing he had just uttered.

"There come Ned and Aristabulus," said John Effingham, as soon as the tones of Miss Ring's voice were lost in the din of fifty others, pitched to the same key. "*A présent, Mademoiselle, je vais nous venger.*"

As John Effingham uttered this, he took Captain Truck by the arm, and went to meet his cousin and the land agent. The latter he soon separated from Mr. Effingham, and with this new recruit, he managed to get so near to Miss Ring as to attract her attention. Although fifty, John Effingham was known to be a bachelor, well connected, and to have twenty thousand a year. In addition, he was well preserved and singularly handsome, besides having an air that set all pretending gentility at defiance. These were qualities that no *belle* despised, and ill-assorted matches were, moreover, just coming into fashion in New-York. Miss Ring had an intuitive knowledge that he wished to speak to her, and she was not slow in offering the opportunity. The superior tone of John Effingham, his caustic wit and knowledge of the world, dispersed the five *beaux*, incontinently; these persons having a natural antipathy to every one of the qualities named.

"I hope you will permit me to presume on an acquaintance that extends back as far as your grandfather, Miss Ring," he said, "to present two very intimate friends; Mr. Bragg and Mr. Truck; gentlemen who will well reward the acquaintance."

The lady bowed graciously, for it was a matter of conscience with her to receive every man with a smile. She was still too much in awe of the master of ceremonies to open her batteries of attack, but John Effingham soon relieved her, by affecting a desire to speak to another lady. The *belle* had now the two strangers to herself, and having heard that the Effinghams had an Englishman of condition as a companion, who was travelling under a false name, she fancied herself very clever in detecting him at once in the person of Aristabulus; while by the aid of a lively imagination, she thought Mr. Truck was his travelling Mentor, and a divine of the church of England. The incognito she was too well bred to hint at, though she wished both the gentlemen to perceive that a *belle* was not to be mystified in this easy manner. Indeed, she was rather sensitive on the subject of her readiness in recognizing a man of fashion under any circumstances, and to let this be known was her very first object, as soon as she was relieved from the presence of John Effingham.

"You must be struck with the unsophisticated nature and the extreme simplicity of our society, Mr. Bragg," she said, looking at him significantly; "we are very conscious it is not what it might be, but do you not think it pretty well for beginners?"

Now, Mr. Bragg had an entire consciousness that he had never seen any society that deserved the name before this very night, but he was supported in giving his opinions by that secret sense of his qualifications to fill any station, which formed so conspicuous a trait in his character, and his answer was given with an *àplomb* that would have added weight to the opinion of the veriest *élégant* of the *Chaussée d'Antin*.

"It is indeed a good deal unsophisticated," he said, "and so simple that any body can understand it. I find but a single fault with this entertainment, which is, in all else, the perfection of elegance in my eyes, and that is, that there is too little room to swing the legs in dancing."

"Indeed!—I did not expect that—is it not the best usage of Europe, now, to bring a quadrille into the very minimum of space?"

"Quite the contrary, Miss. All good dancing requires evolutions. The dancing Dervishes, for instance would occupy quite as much space as both of these sets that are walking before us, and I believe it is now generally admitted that all good dancing needs room for the legs."

"We necessarily get a little behind the fashions, in this distant country. Pray, sir, is it usual for ladies to walk alone in society?"

"Woman was not made to move through life alone, Miss," returned Aristabulus with a sentimental glance of the eye, for he never let a good opportunity for preferment slip through his fingers, and, failing of Miss Effingham, or Miss Van Cortlandt, of whose estates and connections he had some pretty accurate notions, it struck him Miss Ring might, possibly, be a very eligible connection, as all was grist that came to his mill; "this I believe, is an admitted truth."

"By life you mean matrimony, I suppose."

"Yes, Miss, a man always means matrimony, when he speaks to a young lady."

This rather disconcerted Miss Ring, who picked her nosegay, for she was not accustomed to hear gentlemen talk to ladies of matrimony, but ladies to talk to gentlemen. Recovering her self-possession, however, she said with a promptitude that did the school to which she belonged infinite credit—

"You speak, sir, like one having experience."

"Certainly, Miss; I have been in love ever since I was ten years old; I may say I was born in love, and hope to die in love."

This a little out-Heroded Herod, but the *belle* was not a person to be easily daunted on such a subject. She smiled graciously, therefore, and continued the conversation with renewed spirit.

"You travelled gentleman get odd notions," she said, "and more particularly on such subjects. I always feel afraid to discuss them with foreigners, though with my own countrymen I have few reserves. Pray, Mr. Truck, are you satisfied with America?—Do you find it the country you expected to see?"

"Certainly, marm;" for so they pronounced this word in the river, and the captain cherished his first impressions; "when we sailed from Portsmouth, I expected that the first land we should make would be the Highlands of Navesink; and, although a little disappointed, I have had the satisfaction of laying eyes on it at last."

"Disappointment, I fear, is the usual fate of those who come from the other side. Is this dwelling of Mrs. Houston's equal to the residence of an English nobleman, Mr. Bragg?"

"Considerably better, Miss, especially in the way of republican comfort."

Miss Ring, like all *belles*, detested the word republican, their vocation being clearly to exclusion, and she pouted a little affectedly.

"I should distrust the quality of such comfort, sir," she said, with point; "but, are the rooms at all comparable with the rooms in Apsley House, for instance?"

"My dear Miss, Apsley House is a toll-gate lodge, compared to this mansion! I doubt if there be a dwelling in all England half as magnificent—indeed, I cannot imagine any thing more brilliant and rich."

Aristabulus was not a man to do things by halves, and it was a point of honour with him to know something of every thing. It is true he no more could tell where Apsley House is, or whether it was a tavern or a gaol, than he knew half the other things on which he delivered oracular opinions; but when it became necessary to speak, he was not apt to balk conversation from any ignorance, real or affected. The opinion he had just given, it is true, had a little surpassed Miss Ring's hopes; for the next thing, in her ambition to being a *belle*, and of "entertaining" gentlemen, was to fancy she was running her brilliant career in an orbit of fashion that lay parallel to that of the "nobility and gentry" of Great Britain.

"Well, this surpasses my hopes," she said, "although I was aware we are nearly on a level with the more improved tastes of Europe: still, I thought we were a little inferior to that part of the world, yet."

"Inferior, Miss! That is a word that should never pass your lips; you are inferior to nothing, whether in Europe or America, Asia or Africa."

As Miss Ring had been accustomed to do most of the flattering herself, as behoveth a *belle*, she began to be disconcerted with the directness of the compliments of Aristabulus, who was disposed to "make hay while the sun shines;" and she turned, in a little confusion, to the captain, by way of relief; we say confusion, for the young lady, although so liable to be misunderstood, was not actually impudent, but merely deceived in the relations of things; or, in other words, by some confusion in usages, she had hitherto permitted herself to do that in society, which female performers sometimes do on the stage; enact the part of a man.

"You should tell Mr. Bragg, sir," she said, with an appealing look at the captain, "that flattery is a dangerous vice, and one altogether unsuited to a Christian."

"It is, indeed, marm, and one that I never indulge in. No one under my orders, can accuse me of flattery."

By "under orders," Miss Ring understood curates and deacons; for she was aware the church of England had clerical distinctions of this sort, that are unknown in America.

"I hope, sir, you do not intend to quit this country without favouring us with a discourse."

"Not I, marm—I am discoursing pretty much from morning till night, when among my own people, though I own that this conversing rather puts me out of my reckoning. Let me get my foot on the planks I love, with an attentive audience, and a good cigar in my mouth, and I'll hold forth with any bishop in the universe."

"A cigar!" exclaimed Miss Ring, in surprise. "Do gentlemen of your profession use cigars when on duty!"

"Does a parson take his fees? Why, Miss, there is not a man among us, who does not smoke from morning till night."

"Surely not on Sundays!"

"Two for one, on those days, more than on any other."

"And your people, sir, what do they do, all this time?'

"Why, marm, most of them chew; and those that don't, if they cannot find a pipe, have a dull time of it. For my part, I shall hardly relish the good place itself, if cigars are prohibited."

Miss Ring was surprised; but she had heard that the English clergy were more free than our own, and then she had been accustomed to think every thing English of the purest water. A little reflection reconciled her to the innovation; and the next day, at a dinner party, she was heard defending the usage as a practice that had a precedent in the ancient incense of the altar. At the moment, however, she was dying to impart her discoveries to others; and she kindly proposed to the captain and Aristabulus to introduce them to some of her acquaintances, as they must find it dull, being strangers, to know no one. Introductions and cigars were the captain's hobbies, and he accepted the offer with joy, Aristabulus uniting cordially in the proposition, as he fancied he had a right, under the Constitution of the United States of America, to be introduced to every human being with whom he came in contact.

It is scarcely necessary to say how much the party with whom the two neophytes in fashion had come, enjoyed all this, though they concealed their amusement under the calm exterior of people of the world. From Mr. Effingham the mystification was carefully concealed by his cousin, as the former would have felt it due to Mrs. Houston, a well-meaning, but silly woman, to put an end to it. Eve and Grace laughed, as merry girls would be apt to laugh, at such an occurrence, and they danced the remainder of the evening with lighter hearts than ever. At one, the company retired in the same informal manner, as respects announcements and the calling of carriages, as that in which they had entered; most to lay their drowsy heads on their pillows, and Miss Ring to ponder over the superior manners of a polished young Englishman, and to dream of the fragrance of a sermon that was preserved in tobacco.

CHAPTER VI.

"Marry, our play is *The most lamentable comedy and most cruel death of Pyramus and Thisby.*"

A Midsummer Night's Dream 1.2.11–12.

OUR task in the way of describing town society will soon be ended. The gentlemen of the Effingham family had been invited to meet Sir George Templemore at one or two dinners, to which the latter had been invited in consequence of his letters, most of which were connected with his pecuniary arrangements. As one of these entertainments was like all the rest of the same character, a very brief account of it will suffice to let the reader into the secret of the excellence of the genus.

A well-spread board, excellent viands, highly respectable cookery, and delicious wines, were everywhere met. Two rows of men clad in dark dresses, a solitary female at the head of the table, or, if fortunate, with a supporter of the same sex near her, invariably composed the *convives*. The exaggerations of a province were seen ludicrously in one particular custom. The host, or perhaps it might have been the hostess, had been told there should be a contrast between the duller light of the reception-room, and the brilliancy of the table, and John Effingham actually hit his legs against a stool, in floundering through the obscurity of the first drawing-room he entered on one of the occasions in question.

When seated at table, the first great duty of restauration performed, the conversation turned on the prices of lots, speculations in towns, or the currency. After this came the regular assay of wines, during which it was easy to fancy the master of the house a dealer, for he usually sat either sucking a syphon or flourishing a cork-screw. The discourse would now have done credit to the annual meeting and dinner of the German exporters, assembled at Rudesheim to bid for the article.

Sir George was certainly on the point of forming a very erroneous judgment concerning the country, when Mr. Effingham extricated him from this set, and introduced him properly into his own. Here, indeed, while there was much to strike a European as peculiar, and even provincial, the young baronet fared much better. He met with the same quality of table, relieved by an intelligence that was always respectable, and a manliness of tone which, if not unmixed, had the great merit of a simplicity and nature that are not always found in more sophisticated circles. The occasional incongruities struck them all, more than the positive general faults; and Sir George Templemore did justice to the truth, by admitting frankly, the danger he had been in of forming a too hasty opinion.

All this time, which occupied a month, the young baronet got to be more and more intimate in Hudson Square, Eve gradually becoming more frank and unreserved with him, as she grew sensible that he had abandoned his hopes of success with herself, and Grace gradually more cautious and timid, as she became conscious of his power to please, and the interest he took in herself.

It might have been three days after the ball at Mrs. Houston's that most of the family was engaged to look in on a Mrs. Legend, a lady of what was called a literary turn, Sir George having been asked to make one of their party. Aristabulus was already returned to his duty in the country, where we shall shortly have occasion to join him, but an invitation had been sent to Mr. Truck, under the general, erroneous impression of his real character.

Taste, whether in the arts, literature, or any thing else, is a natural impulse, like love. It is true both may be cultivated and heightened by circumstances, but the impulses must be voluntary, and the flow of feeling, or of soul, as it has become a law to style it, is not to be forced, or commanded to come and go at will. This is the reason that all premeditated enjoyments connected with the intellect, are apt to baffle expectations, and why academies, literary clubs, coteries and dinners are commonly dull. It is true that a body of clever people may be brought together, and, if left to their own impulses, the characters of their mind will show themselves; wit will flash, and thought will answer thought spontaneously; but every effort to make the stupid agreeable, by giving a direction of a pretending intellectual nature to their efforts, is only rendering dullness more conspicuous by exhibiting it in contrast with what it ought to be to be clever, as a bad picture is rendered the more conspicuous by an elaborate and gorgeous frame.

The latter was the fate of most of Mrs. Legend's literary evenings, at which it was thought a distinction to understand even one foreign language. But, it was known that Eve was skilled in most of the European tongues, and, the good lady, not feeling that such accomplishments are chiefly useful as a means, looked about her in order to collect a set, among whom our heroine might find some one to converse with in each of the dialects with which she was familiar. Little was said about it, it is true, but great efforts were made to cause this evening to be memorable in the annals of *conversazioni.*

In carrying out this scheme, nearly all the wits, writers, artists and *literati,* as the most incorrigible members of the book clubs were styled, in New-York, were pressingly invited to be present. Aristabulus had contrived to earn such a reputation for the captain, on the night of the ball, that he was universally called a man of letters, and an article had actually appeared in one of the papers, speaking of the literary merits of the "Hon. and Rev. Mr. Truck, a gentleman travelling in our country, from whose liberality and just views, an account of our society was to be expected, that should, at last, do justice to our national character." With such expectations, then, every true American and Americaness, was expected to be at his or her post, for the solemn occasion. It was a rally of literature, in defence of the institutions—no, not of the institutions, for they were left to take care of themselves—but of the social character of the community.

Alas! it is easier to feel high aspirations on such subjects, in a provincial town, than to succeed; for merely calling a place an Emporium, is very far from giving it the independence, high tone, condensed intelligence and tastes of a capital. Poor Mrs. Legend, desirous of having all the tongues duly represented, was obliged to invite certain dealers in gin from Holland, a German linen merchant from Saxony, an Italian *Cavaliero,* who amused himself in selling beads, and a Spanish master, who was born in Portugal, all of whom had just one requisite for conversation in their respective languages, and no more. But such assemblies were convened in Paris, and why not in New-York?

We shall not stop to dwell on the awful sensations with which Mrs. Legend heard the first ring at her door, on the eventful night in question. It was the precursor of the entrance of Miss Annual, as regular a devotee of letters as ever conned a primer. The meeting was sentimental and affectionate. Before either had time, however, to disburthen her mind of one half of its prepared phrases, ring upon ring proclaimed more company, and the rooms were soon as much sprinkled with talent, as a modern novel with jests. Among those who came first, appeared all the foreign corps, for the refreshments entered as something into the account with them; and every blue of the place, whose social position in the least entitled her to be seen in such a house, Mrs. Legend belonging quite positively to good society.

The scene that succeeded was very characteristic. A professed genius does nothing like other people, except in cases that require a display of talents. In all minor matters he, or she, is *sui generis*; for sentiment is in constant ebullition in their souls; this being what is meant by the flow of that part of the human system.

We might here very well adopt the Homeric method, and call the roll of heroes and heroines, in what the French would term a *catalogue raisonnée*; but our limits compel us to be less ambitious, and to adopt a simpler mode of communicating facts. Among the ladies who now figured in the drawing-room of Mrs. Legend, besides Miss Annual, were Miss Monthly, Mrs. Economy, S.R.P., Marion, Longinus, Julietta, Herodotus, D.O.V.E., and Mrs. Demonstration; besides many others of less note; together with at least a dozen female Hajjis, whose claims to appear in such society were pretty much dependent on the fact, that having seen pictures and statues abroad, they necessarily must have the means of talking of them at home. The list of men was still more formidable in numbers, if not in talents. At its head stood Steadfast Dodge, Esquire, whose fame as a male Hajji had so far swollen since Mrs Jarvis's *réunion*, that, for the first time in his life, he now entered one of the better houses of his own country. Then there were the authors of "Lapis Lazuli," "The Aunts," "The Reformed," "The Conformed," "The Transformed," and "The Deformed;" with the editors of "The Hebdomad," "The Night Cap," "The Chrysalis," "The Real Maggot," and "The Seek no Further;" as also, "Junius," "Junius Brutus," "Lucius Junius Brutus," "Captain Kant," "Florio," the "Author of the History of Billy Linkum Tweedle," the celebrated Pottawattamie Prophet, "Single Rhyme," a genius who had prudently rested his fame in verse, on a couplet composed of one line; besides divers *amateurs* and *connoisseurs*, Hajjis, who *must* be men of talents, as they had acquired all they knew, very much as American Eclipse gained his laurels on the turf; that is to say, by a free use of the whip and spur.

As Mrs. Legend sailed about her rooms amid such a circle, her mind expanded, her thoughts diffused themselves among her guests on the principle of Animal Magnetism, and her heart was melting with the tender sympathies of congenial tastes. She felt herself to be at the head of American talents, and, in the secret recesses of her reason, she determined that, did even the fate of Sodom and Gomorrah menace her native town, as some evil disposed persons had dared to insinuate might one day be the case, here was enough to save it from destruction.

It was just as the mistress of the mansion had come to this consoling conclusion, that the party from Hudson Square rang. As few of her guests came in carriages, Mrs. Legend, who heard the rolling of wheels, felt persuaded that the lion of the night was now indeed at hand; and with a view to a proper reception, she requested the company to divide itself into two lines, in order that he might enter, as it were, between lanes of genius.

It may be necessary to explain, at this point of our narrative, that John Effingham was perfectly aware of the error which existed in relation to the real character of Captain Truck, wherein he thought great injustice had been done the honest seaman; and, the old man intending to sail for London next morning, had persuaded him to accept this invitation, in order that the public mind might be disabused in a matter of so much importance. With a view that this might be done naturally and without fuss, however, he did not explain the mistake to his nautical friend, believing it most probable that this could be better done incidentally, as it were, in the course of the evening; and feeling certain of the force of that wholesome apothegm, which says that "truth is powerful and must prevail." "If this be so," added John Effingham, in his explanations to Eve, "there can be no place where the sacred quality will be so likely to assert itself, as in a galaxy of geniuses, whose distinctive characteristic is 'an intuitive perception of things in their real colours.'"

When the door of Mrs. Legend's drawing-room opened, in the usual noiseless manner, Mademoiselle Viefville, who led the way, was startled at finding herself in the precise situation of one who is condemned to run the gauntlet. Fortunately, she caught a glimpse of Mrs. Legend, posted at the other end of the proud array, inviting her, with smiles, to approach. The invitation had been to a "*literary fête*," and Mademoiselle Viefville was too much of a Frenchwoman to be totally disconcerted at a little scenic effect on the occasion of a *fête* of any sort. Supposing she was now a witness of an American ceremony for the first time, for the want of *representation* in the country had been rather a subject of animadversion with her, she advanced steadily towards the mistress of the house, bestowing smile for smile, this being a part of the *programme* at which a *Parisienne* was not easily outdone. Eve followed, as usual, *sola*; Grace came next; then Sir George; then John Effingham; the captain bringing up the rear. There had been a friendly contest, for the precedency, between the two last, each desiring to yield it to the other on the score of merit; but the captain prevailed, by declaring "that he was navigating an unknown sea, and that he could do nothing wiser than to sail in the wake of so good a pilot as Mr. John Effingham."

As Hajjis of approved experience, the persons who led the advance in this little procession, were subjects of a proper attention and respect; but as the admiration of mere vulgar travelling would in itself be vulgar, care was taken to reserve the condensed feeling of the company for the celebrated English writer and wit, who was known to bring up the rear. This was not a common house, in which dollars had place, or *belles* rioted, but the temple of genius; and every one felt an ardent desire to manifest a proper homage to the abilities of the established foreign writer, that should be in exact proportion to their indifference to the twenty thousand a year of John Effingham, and to the nearly equal amount of Eve's expectations.

The personal appearance of the honest tar was well adapted to the character he was thus called on so unexpectedly to support. His hair had long been getting grey, but the intense anxiety of the chase, of the wreck, and of his other recent adventures, had rapidly, but effectually, increased this mark of time; and his head was now nearly as white as snow. The hale, fresh, red of his features, which was in truth the result of exposure, might very well pass for the tint of port, and his tread, which had always a little of the quarter-deck swing about it, might quite easily be mistaken by a tyro, for the human frame staggering under a load of learning. Unfortunately for those who dislike mystifications, the captain had consulted John Effingham on the subject of the toilette, and that kind and indulgent friend had suggested the propriety of appearing in black small-clothes for the occasion, a costume that he often wore himself of an evening. Reality, in this instance, then, did not disappoint expectation, and the burst of applause with which the captain was received, was accompanied by a general murmur in commendation of the admirable manner in which he "looked the character."

"What a Byronic head," whispered the author of "The Transformed" to D.O.V.E.; "and was there ever such a curl of the lip, before, to mortal man!"

The truth is, the captain had thrust his tobacco into "an aside," as a monkey is known to *empocher* a spare nut, or a lump of sugar.

"Do you think him Byronic?—To my eye, the cast of his head is Shaksperian, rather; though I confess there is a little of Milton about the forehead!"

"Pray," said Miss Annual, to Lucius Junius Brutus, "which is commonly thought to be the best of his works; that on a—a—a,—or that on e—e—e?"

Now, so it happened, that not a soul in the room, but the lion himself, had any idea what books he had written, and he knew only of some fifteen or twenty log-books. It was generally understood, that he was a great English writer, and this was more than sufficient.

"I believe the world generally prefers the a—a—a," said Lucius Junius Brutus; "but the few give a decided preference to the e—e—e—"

"Oh! out of all question preferable!" exclaimed half a dozen, in hearing.

"With what a classical modesty he pays his compliments to Mrs. Legend," observed "S. R. P."—"One can always tell a man of real genius, by his *tenue!*"

"He is so English!" cried Florio. "Ah! *they* are the only people, after all!"

This Florio was one of those geniuses who sigh most for the things that they least possess.

By this time Captain Truck had got through with listening to the compliments of Mrs. Legend, when he was seized upon by a circle of rabid literati, who badgered him with questions concerning his opinions, notions, inferences, experiences, associations, sensations, sentiments and intentions, in a way that soon threw the old man into a profuse perspiration. Fifty times did he wish, from the bottom of his soul, that soul which the crowd around him fancied dwelt so high in the clouds, that he was seated quietly by the side of Mrs. Hawker, who, he mentally swore, was worth all the *literati* in Christendom. But fate had decreed otherwise, and we shall leave him to his fortune, for a time, and return to our heroine and her party.

As soon as Mrs. Legend had got through with her introductory compliments to the captain, she sought Eve and Grace, with a consciousness that a few civilities were now their due.

"I fear, Miss Effingham, after the elaborate *soirées* of the literary circles in Paris, you will find our *réunions* of the same sort, a little dull; and yet I flatter myself with having assembled most of the talents of New-York on this memorable occasion, to do honour to your friend. Are you acquainted with many of the company?"

Now, Eve had never seen nor ever heard of a single being in the room, with the exception of Mr. Dodge and her own party, before this night, although most of them had been so laboriously employed in puffing each other into celebrity, for many weary years; and, as for elaborate *soirées*, she thought she had never seen one half as elaborate as this of Mrs. Legend's. As it would not very well do, however, to express all this in words, she civilly desired the lady to point out to her some of the most distinguished of the company, in order that she might know their persons at least.

"With the greatest pleasure, Miss Effingham," Mrs. Legend taking pride in dwelling on the merits of her guests.—"This heavy, grand-looking personage, in whose air one sees intellectual refinement and unequalled modesty at a glance, is Captain Kant, the editor of one of our most decidedly pious newspapers. His mind is distinguished for its intuitive perception of all that is delicate, reserved and finished in the intellectual world, while, in opposition to this quality, which is almost feminine, his character is just as remarkable for its unflinching love of truth. He was never known to publish a falsehood, and of his foreign correspondence, in particular, he is so exceedingly careful, that he assures me he has every word of it written under his own eye."

"On the subject of his religious scruples," added John Effingham, "he is so fastidiously exact, that I hear he 'says grace' over every thing that goes *from* his press, and 'returns thanks' for every thing that comes *to* it."

"You know him, Mr. Effingham, by this remark? Is he not, truly, a man of a vocation?"

"That, indeed, he is, ma'am. He may be succinctly said to have a newspaper mind, as he reduces every thing in nature or art to news, and commonly imparts to it so much of his own peculiar character, that it loses all identity with the subjects to which it originally belonged. One scarcely knows which to admire most about this man, the atmospheric transparency of his motives, for he is so disinterested as seldom even to think of paying for a dinner when travelling, and yet so conscientious as always to say something obliging of the tavern as soon as he gets home—his rigid regard to facts, or the exquisite refinement and delicacy that he imparts to every thing he touches.

Over all this, too, he throws a beautiful halo of morality and religion, never even prevaricating in the hottest discussion, unless with the unction of a saint!"

"Do you happen to know Florio?" asked Mrs. Legend, a little distrusting John Effingham's account of Captain Kant.

"If I do, it must indeed be by accident. What are his chief characteristics, ma'am?"

"Sentiment, pathos, delicacy, and all in rhyme, too. You, no doubt, have heard of his triumph over Lord Byron, Miss Effingham?"

Eve was obliged to confess that it was new to her.

"Why, Byron wrote an ode to Greece, commencing with 'The Isles of Greece! the Isles of Greece!' a very feeble line, as any one will see, for it contained a useless and an unmeaning repetition."

"And you might add vulgar, too, Mrs. Legend," said John Effingham, "since it made a palpable allusion to all those vulgar incidents that associate themselves in the mind, with these said common-place isles. The arts, philosophy, poetry, eloquence, and even old Homer, are brought unpleasantly to one's recollection, by such an indiscreet invocation."

"So Florio thought, and, by way of letting the world perceive the essential difference between the base and the pure coin, *he* wrote an ode on England, which commenced as such an ode *should!*"

"Do you happen to recollect any of it, ma'am?"

"Only the first line, which I greatly regret, as the rhyme is Florio's chief merit. But this line is, of itself, sufficient to immortalize a man."

"Do not keep us in torment, dear Mrs. Legend, but let us have it, of heaven's sake!"

"It began in this sublime strain, sir—'Beyond the wave!—Beyond the wave!' Now, Miss Effingham, that is what *I* call poetry!"

"And well you may, ma'am," returned the gentleman, who perceived Eve could scarce refrain from breaking out in a very unsentimental manner—"So much pathos."

"And so sententious and flowing!"

"Condensing a journey of three thousand miles, as it might be, into three words, and a note of admiration. I trust it was printed with a note of admiration, Mrs. Legend?"

"Yes, sir, with two—one behind each wave—and such waves, Mr. Effingham!"

"Indeed, ma'am, you may say so. One really gets a grand idea of them, England lying beyond each."

"So much expressed in so few syllables!"

"I think I see every shoal, current, ripple, rock, island, and whale, between Sandy Hook and the Land's End."

"He hints at an epic."

"Pray God he may execute one. Let him make haste, too, or he may get 'behind the age,' 'behind the age.'"

Here the lady was called away to receive a guest.

"Cousin Jack!"

"Eve Effingham?"

"Do you not sometimes fear offending?"

"Not a woman who begins with expressing her admiration of such a sublime thing as this. You are safe with such a person, any where short of a tweak of the nose."

"*Mais, tout ceci est bien drôle!*"

"You never were more mistaken in your life, Mademoiselle; every body here, but yourself, looks upon it as a matter of life and death."

The new guest was Mr. Pindar, one of those careless, unsentimental fellows, that occasionally throw off an ode that passes through Christendom, as dollars are known to pass from China to Norway, and yet, who never fancied spectacles necessary to his appearance, solemnity to his face, nor *soirées* to his renown. After quitting Mrs. Legend, he approached Eve, to whom he was slightly known, and accosted her.

"This is the region of taste, Miss Effingham," he said, with a shrug of the jaw, if such a member can shrug; "and I do not wonder at finding you here."

He then chatted pleasantly a moment, with the party, and passed on, giving an ominous gape, as he drew nearer to the *oi polloi* of literature. A moment after appeared Mr. Gray, a man who needed nothing but taste in the public, and the encouragement that would follow such a taste, to stand at, or certainly near, the head of the poets of our own time. He, too, looked shily at the galaxy, and took refuge in a corner. Mr. Pith followed; a man whose caustic wit needs only a sphere for its exercise, manners to portray, and a society with strong points about it to illustrate, in order to enrol his name high on the catalogue of satirists. Another ring announced Mr. Fun, a writer of exquisite humour, and of finished periods, but who, having perpetrated a little too much sentiment, in his time, was instantly seized upon by all the ultra ladies who were addicted to the same taste in that way, in the room.

These persons came late, like those who had already been too often dosed in the same way, to be impatient of repetitions. The three first soon got together in a corner, and Eve fancied they were laughing at the rest of the company; whereas, in fact, they were merely laughing at a bad joke of their own; their quick perception of the ludicrous having pointed out a hundred odd combinations and absurdities, that would have escaped duller minds.

"Who, in the name of the twelve Cæsars, has Mrs. Legend got to lionize, yonder, with the white summit and the dark base?" asked the writer of odes.

"Some English pamphleteer, by what I can learn," answered he of satire; "some fellow who has achieved a pert review, or written a Minerva Pressism, and who now flourishes among us like a green bay tree. A modern Horace, or a Juvenal on his travels."

"Fun is well badgered," observed Mr. Gray.—"Do you not see that Miss Annual, Miss Monthly, and that young alphabet D.O.V.E., have got him within the circle of their petticoats, where he will be martyred on a sigh?"

"He casts very longing looks this way; he wishes you to go to his rescue, Pith."

"I!—Let him take his fill of sentiment! I am no homœpathist in such matters. Large doses in quick succession, will soonest work a cure. Here comes the lion, and he breaks loose from his cage, like a beast that has been poked up with sticks."

"Good evening, gentlemen," said Captain Truck, wiping his face intensely, and who, having made his escape from a throng of admirers, took refuge in the first port that offered. "You seem to be enjoying yourselves here in a rational and agreeable way. Quite cool and refreshing in this corner, as I hope to be saved."

"And yet we have no doubt that both our reason and our amusement will receive a large increase from the addition of your society, sir," returned Mr. Pith.—"Do us the favour to take a seat, I beg of you, and rest yourself."

"With all my heart, gentlemen; for, to own the truth, these ladies make warm work about a stranger. I have just got out of what I call a category."

"You appear to have escaped with life, sir," observed Pindar, taking a cool survey of the other's person—"which is more than happens to every lion that is caged."

"Yes, thank God, I have done that, and it is pretty much all I have done," answered the captain, wiping his face. "I served in the French war—Truxtun's war, as we call it—and I had a touch with the English in the privateer trade, between twelve and fifteen; and here, quite lately, I was in an encounter with the savage Arabs down on the coast of Africa; and I account them all as so much snow-balling, compared with the yard-arm and yard-arm work of this very night. I wonder if it is permitted to try a cigar at these conversation-onies, gentlemen?"

"I believe it is, sir," returned Pindar, coolly. "Shall I help you to a light?"

"Oh! Mr. Truck!" cried Mrs. Legend, following the chafed animal to his corner, as one would pursue any other runaway, "instinct has brought you into this good company. You are, now, in the very focus of American talents."

"Having just escaped from the focus of American talons," whispered Pith.

"I must be permitted to introduce you myself. Mr. Truck, Mr. Pindar—Mr. Pith—Mr. Gray—gentlemen, you must be so happy to be acquainted, being, as it were, engaged in the same pursuits!"

The captain rose and shook each of the gentlemen cordially by the hand, for he had, at least, the consolation of a great many introductions that night. Mrs. Legend disappeared to say something equally clever to some other prodigy.

"Happy to meet you, gentlemen," said the captain. "In what trade do you sail?"

"By whatever name we may call it," answered Mr. Pindar—"we can scarcely be said to go before the wind."

"Not in the *Injee* business, then, or the monsoons would keep the stun'-sails set, at least."

"No, sir.—But yonder is Mr. Moccasin, who has lately set up, *secundum artem*, in the Indian business, having written two novels in that way already, and begun a third."

"Are you all regularly employed, gentlemen?"

"As regularly as inspiration permits," said Mr. Pith. "Men of our occupation must make fair weather of it, or we had better be doing nothing."

"So I often tell my owners, but 'go ahead' is the order of the day. When I was a youngster, a ship remained in port for a fair wind;

but, now, she goes to work and makes one. The world seems to get young, as I get old."

"This is a *rum litterateur*," Gray whispered to Pindar.

"It is an obvious mystification," was the answer; "poor Mrs. Legend has picked up some straggling porpoise, and converted him, by a touch of her magical wand, into a Boanerges of literature. The thing is as clear as day, for the worthy fellow smells of tar and cigar smoke. I perceive that Mr. Effingham is laughing out of the corner of his eyes, and will step across the room, and get the truth, in a minute."

The rogue was as good as his word, and was soon back again, when he contrived to let his friends understand the real state of the case. A knowledge of the captain's true character encouraged this trio in the benevolent purpose of aiding the honest old seaman in his desire to smoke, and Pith managed to give him a lighted paper, without becoming an open accessary to the plot.

"Will you take a cigar yourself, sir," said the captain, offering his box to Mr. Pindar.

"I thank you, Mr. Truck, I never smoke, but am a profound admirer of the flavour. Let me entreat you to begin as soon as possible."

Thus encouraged, Captain Truck drew two or three whiffs, when the rooms were immediately filled with the fragrance of a real Havana. At the first discovery, the whole literary pack went off on the scent. As for Mr. Fun, he managed to profit by the agitation that followed, in order to escape to the three wags in the corner, who were enjoying the scene, with the gravity of so many dervishes.

"As I live," cried Lucius Junius Brutus, "there is the author of a—a—a— actually smoking a cigar!—How excessively *piquant!*"

"Do my eyes deceive me, or is not that the writer of e—e—e— fumigating us all!" whispered Miss Annual.

"Nay, this cannot certainly be right," put in Florio, with a dogmatical manner. "All the periodicals agree that smoking is ungenteel in old England."

"You never were more mistaken, dear Florio," replied D.O.V.E. in a cooing tone. "The very last novel of society has a chapter in which the hero and heroine smoke in the declaration scene."

"Do they, indeed!—That alters the case. Really, one would not wish to get behind so great a nation, nor yet go much before it. Pray, Captain Kant, what do your friends in Canada say; is, or is not smoking permitted in good society there? the Canadians must, at least, be ahead of *us.*"

"Not at all, sir," returned the editor in his softest tones; "it is revolutionary and jacobinical."

But the ladies prevailed, and, by a process that is rather peculiar to what may be called a "credulous" state of society, they carried the day. This process was simply to make one fiction authority for another. The fact that smoking was now carried so far in England, that the clergy actually used cigars in the pulpits, was affirmed on the authority of Mr. Truck himself, and, coupled with his present occupation, the point was deemed to be settled. Even Florio yielded, and his plastic mind soon saw a thousand beauties in the usage, that had hitherto escaped it. All the literati drew round the captain in a circle, to enjoy the spectacle, though the honest old mariner contrived to throw out such volumes of vapour as to keep them at a safe distance. His four demure-looking neighbours got behind the barrier of smoke, where they deemed themselves entrenched against the assaults of sentimental petticoats, for a time, at least.

"Pray, Mr. Truck," inquired S.R.P., "is it commonly thought in the English literary circles, that Byron was a developement of Shakspeare, or Shakspeare a shadowing forth of Byron?"

"Both, marm," said the captain, with a coolness that would have done credit to Aristabulus, for he had been fairly badgered into impudence, and profiting by the occasion to knock the ashes off his cigar; "all incline to the first opinion, and some to the last."

"What finesse!" murmured one. "How delicate!" whispered a second. "A dignified reserve!" ejaculated a third. "So English!" exclaimed Florio.

"Do you think, Mr. Truck," asked D.O.V.E., "that the profane songs of Little have more pathos than the sacred songs of Moore; or that the sacred songs of Moore have more sentiment than the profane songs of Little?"

"A good deal of both, marm, and something to spare. I think there is little in one, and more in the other."

"Pray, sir," said S.R.P., "do you pronounce the name of Byron's lady-love, Guy-kee-oh-*ly*, or, Gwy-ky-o-*lee*?"

"That depends on how the wind is. If on shore, I am apt to say 'oh-lee;' and if off shore, 'oh-lie.'"

"That's capital!" cried Florio, in an extasy of admiration. "What man in this country could have said as crack a thing as that?"

"Indeed it is very witty," added Miss Monthly—"what does it mean?"

"Mean! More than is seen or felt by common minds. Ah! the English are truly a great nation!—How delightfully he smokes!"

"I think he is much the most interesting man we have had out here," observed Miss Annual, "since the last bust of Scott!"

"Ask him, dear D.O.V.E.," whispered Julietta, who was timid, from the circumstance of never having published, "which he thinks the most ecstatic feeling, hope or despair?"

The question was put by the more experienced lady, according to request, though she first said, in a hurried tone, to her youthful sister—"you can have felt but little, child, or you would know that it is despair, as a matter of course."

The honest captain, however, did not treat the matter so lightly, for he improved the opportunity to light a fresh cigar, throwing the still smoking stump into Mrs. Legend's grate, through a lane of literati, as he afterwards boasted, as coolly as he could have thrown it overboard, under other circumstances. Luckily for his reputation for sentiment, he mistook "ecstatic," a word he had never heard before, for "erratic;" and recollecting sundry roving maniacs that he had seen, he answered promptly—

"Despair, out and out."

"I knew it," said one.

"It's in nature," added a second.

"All can feel its truth," rejoined a third.

"This point may now be set down as established," cried Florio, "and I hope no more will be said about it."

"This is encouragement to the searchers after truth," put in Captain Kant.

"Pray, Hon. and Rev. Mr. Truck," asked Lucius Junius Brutus, at the joint suggestion of Junius Brutus and Brutus, "does the Princess Victoria smoke?"

"If she did not, sir, where would be the use in being a princess. I suppose you know that all the tobacco seized in England, after a deduction to informers, goes to the crown."

"I object to this usage," remarked Captain Kant, "as irreligious, French, and tending to *sans-culotteism*. I am willing to admit of this distinguished instance as an exception; but on all other grounds, I shall maintain that it savours of infidelity to smoke. The Prussian government, much the best of our times, never smokes."

"This man thinks he has a monopoly of the puffing, himself," Pindar whispered into the captain's ear; "whiff away, my dear sir, and you'll soon throw him into the shade."

The captain winked, drew out his box, lighted another cigar, and, by way of reply to the envious remark, he put one in each corner of his mouth, and soon had both in full blast, a state in which he kept them for near a minute.

"This is the very picturesque of social enjoyment," exclaimed Florio, holding up both hands in a glow of rapture. "It is absolutely Homeric, in the way of usages! Ah! the English are a very great nation!"

"I should like to know excessively if there was really such a person as Baron Mun-chaw-sen?" said Julietta, gathering courage from the success of her last question.

"There was, Miss," returned the captain, through his teeth, and nodding his head in the affirmative. "A regular traveller, that; and one who knew him well, swore to me that he hadn't related one half of what befel him."

"How very delightful to learn this from the highest quarter!" exclaimed Miss Monthly.

"Is Gatty (Goethe) really dead?" inquired Longinus, "or, is the account we have had to that effect, merely a metaphysical apotheosis of his mighty soul?"

"Dead, marm—stone dead—dead as a door-nail," returned the captain, who saw a present relief in killing as many as possible, even if they came to life, again, hereafter.

"You have been in France, Mr. Truck, beyond question?" observed Lucius Junius Brutus, in the way one puts a question.

"France!—I was in France before I was ten years old. I know every foot of the coast, from Havre de Grace to Marseilles."

"Will you then have the goodness to explain to us whether the soul of Chat-*to*-bri-*ong* is more expanded than his reason, or his reason more expanded than his soul?"

Captain Truck had a very tolerable notion of Baron Munchausen and of his particular merits; but Chateaubriand was a writer of whom he knew nothing. After pondering a moment, and feeling persuaded that a confession of ignorance might undo him; for the old man had got to be influenced by the atmosphere of the place; he answered coolly—

"Oh! Chat-*to*-bri-*ong*, is it you mean?—As whole-souled a fellow as I know. All soul, sir, and lots of reason, besides."

"How simple and unaffected!"

"Crack!" exclaimed Florio.

"A thorough Jacobin!" growled Captain Kant, who was always offended when any one but himself took liberties with the truth.

Here the four wags in the corner observed that head went to head in the crowd, and that the rear rank of the company began to disappear, while Mrs. Legend was in evident distress. In a few minutes, all the Romans were off; Florio soon after vanished, grating his teeth in a poetical frenzy; and even Captain Kant, albeit so used to look truth in the face, beat a retreat. The alphabet followed, and even the Annual and the Monthly retired, with leave-takings so solemn and precise, that poor Mrs. Legend was in total despair.

Eve, foreseeing something unpleasant, had gone away first, and, in a few minutes, Mr. Dodge, who had been very active in the crowd, whispering and gesticulating, made his bow also. The envy of this man had, in fact, become so intolerable, that he had let the cat out of the bag. No one now remained but the party entrenched behind the smoke, and the mistress of the house. Pindar solemnly proposed to the captain that they should go and enjoy an oyster-supper, in company; and, the proposal being cordially accepted, they rose in a body, to take leave.

"A most delightful evening, Mrs. Legend," said Pindar, with perfect truth, "much the pleasantest I ever passed in a house, where one passes so many that are agreeable."

"I cannot properly express my thanks for the obligation you have conferred by making me acquainted with Mr. Truck," added Gray. "I shall cultivate his society as far as in my power, for a more capital fellow never breathed."

"Really, Mrs. Legend, this has been a Byronic night!" observed Pith, as he made his bow. "I shall long remember it, and I think it deserves to be commemorated in verse."

Fun endeavoured to look sympathetic and sentimental, though the spirit within could scarcely refrain from grinning in Mrs. Legend's face. He stammered out a few compliments, however, and disappeared.

"Well, good night, marm," said Captain Truck, offering his hand cordially. "This has been a pleasant evening, altogether, though it was warm work at first. If you like ships, I should be glad to show you the Montauk's cabins when we get back; and if you ever think of Europe, let me recommend the London line as none of the worst. We'll try to make you comfortable, and trust to me to choose a state-room, a thing I am experienced in."

Not one of the wags laughed until they were fairly confronted with the oysters. Then, indeed, they burst out into a general and long fit of exuberant merriment, returning to it, between the courses from the kitchen, like the *refrain* of a song. Captain Truck, who was uncommonly well satisfied with himself, did not understand the meaning of all this boyishness, but he has often declared since, that a heartier or a funnier set of fellows he never fell in with, than his four last companions proved to be that night.

As for the literary *soirée*, the most profound silence has been maintained concerning it, neither of the wits there assembled having seen fit to celebrate it in rhyme, and Florio having actually torn up an impromptu for the occasion, that he had been all the previous day writing.

CHAPTER VII.

"There is a history in all men's lives,
Figuring the natures of the times deceas'd,
The which observ'd, a man may prophesy,
With a near aim, of the main chance of things
As yet not come to life. . . ."

2 Henry IV 3.1.80–84.

THE following morning the baronet breakfasted in Hudson Square. While at table, little was said concerning the events of the past night, though sundry smiles were exchanged, as eye met eye, and the recollection of the mystification returned. Grace alone looked grave, for she had been accustomed to consider Mrs. Legend a very discriminating person, and she had even hoped that most of those who usually figured in her rooms, were really the clever persons they laid claim to be.

The morning was devoted to looking at the quarter of the town which is devoted to business, a party having been made for that express purpose under the auspices of John Effingham. As the weather was very cold, although the distances were not great, the carriages were ordered, and they all set off about noon.

Grace had given up expecting a look of admiration from Eve in favor of any of the lions of New-York, her cousin having found it necessary to tell her, that, in a comparative sense at least, little was to be said in behalf of these provincial wonders. Even Mademoiselle Viefville, now that the freshness of her feelings were abated, had dropped quietly down into a natural way of speaking of things; and Grace, who was quick-witted, soon discovered that when she did make any allusions to similar objects in Europe, it was always to those that existed in some country town. A silent convention existed, therefore, to speak no more on such subjects; or if any thing was said, it arose incidentally and as inseparable from the regular thread of the discourse.

When in Wall street, the carriages stopped and the gentlemen
alighted. The severity of the weather kept the ladies in the chariot,
where Grace endeavoured to explain things as well as she could to
her companions.

"What are all these people running after, so intently?" inquired
Mademoiselle Viefville, the conversation being in French, but which
we shall render freely into English, for the sake of the general reader.

"Dollars, I believe, Mademoiselle; am I right, Grace?"

"I believe you are," returned Grace, laughing, "though I know
little more of this part of the town than yourself."

"*Quelle foule!* Is that building filled with dollars, into which the
gentlemen are now entering? Its steps are crowded."

"That is the *Bourse*, Mademoiselle, and it ought to be well lined,
by the manner in which some who frequent it live. Cousin Jack and
Sir George are going into the crowd, I see."

We will leave the ladies in their seats, a few minutes, and
accompany the gentlemen on their way into the Exchange.

"I shall now show you, Sir George Templemore," said John
Effingham,"what is peculiar to this country, and what, if properly
improved, it is truly worth a journey across the ocean to see. You
have been at the Royal Exchange in London, and at the *Bourse* of
Paris, but you have never witnessed a scene like that to which I am
about to introduce you. In Paris, you have beheld the unpleasant
spectacle of women gambling publicly in the funds; but it was in
driblets, compared to what you will see here."

While speaking, John Effingham led the way up stairs into the
office of one of the most considerable auctioneers. The walls were
lined with maps, some representing houses, some lots, some streets,
some entire towns.

"This is the focus of what Aristabulus Bragg calls the town trade,"
said John Effingham, when fairly confronted with all these wonders.
"Here, then, you may suit yourself with any species of real estate that
heart can desire. If a villa is wanted, there are a dozen. Of farms, a
hundred are in market; that is merely half-a-dozen streets; and here
are towns, of dimensions and value to suit purchasers."

"Explain this; it exceeds comprehension."

"It is simply what it professes to be. Mr. Hammer, do us the
favour to step this way. Are you selling to-day?"

"Not much, sir. Only a hundred or two lots on this island, and
some six or eight farms, with one smallish western village."

"Can you tell us the history of this particular piece of property, Mr. Hammer?"

"With great pleasure, Mr. Effingham; we know you to have means, and hope you may be induced to purchase. This was the farm of old Volkert Van Brunt, five years since, off of which he and his family had made a livelihood for more than a century, by selling milk. Two years since, the sons sold it to Peter Feeler for a hundred an acre; or for the total sum of five thousand dollars. The next spring Mr. Feeler sold it to John Search, as keen a one as we have, for twenty-five thousand. Search sold it, at private sale, to Nathan Rise for fifty thousand, the next week, and Rise had parted with it, to a company, before the purchase, for a hundred and twelve thousand cash. The map ought to be taken down, for it is now eight months since we sold it out in lots, at auction, for the gross sum of three hundred thousand dollars. As we have received our commission, we look at that land as out of the market, for a time."

"Have you other property, sir, that affords the same wonderful history of a rapid advance in value?" asked the baronet.

"These walls are covered with maps of estates in the same predicament. Some have risen two or three thousand per cent. within five years, and some only a few hundred. There is no calculating in the matter, for it is all fancy."

"And on what is this enormous increase in value founded?—Does the town extend to these fields?"

"It goes much farther, sir—that is to say, on paper. In the way of houses, it is still some miles short of them. A good deal depends on what you *call* a thing, in this market. Now, if old Volkert Van Brunt's property had been still called a farm, it would have brought a farm price; but, as soon as it was surveyed into lots, and mapped—"

"Mapped!"

"Yes, sir; brought into visible lines, with feet and inches, instead of acres. As soon as it was properly mapped, it rose to its just value. We have a good deal of the bottom of the sea that brings fair prices in consequence of being well mapped."

Here the gentlemen expressed their sense of the auctioneer's politeness, and retired.

"We will now go into the sales-room," said John Effingham, "where you shall judge of the spirit, or *energy*, as it is termed, which, at this moment, actuates this great nation."

Descending, they entered a crowd, where scores were eagerly bidding against each other, in the fearful delusion of growing rich by pushing a fancied value to a still higher point. One was purchasing ragged rocks, another the bottom of rivers, a third a bog, and all on the credit of maps. Our two observers remained some time silent spectators of the scene.

"When I first entered that room," said John Effingham, as they left the place, "it appeared to me to be filled with maniacs. Now, that I have been in it several times, the impression is not much altered."

"And all those persons are hazarding their means of subsistence on the imaginary estimate mentioned by the auctioneer?"

"They are gambling as recklessly as he who places his substance on the cast of the die. So completely has the mania seized every one, that the obvious truth, a truth which is as apparent as any other law of nature, that nothing can be sustained without a foundation, is completely overlooked, and he who should now proclaim, in this building, principles that bitter experience will cause every man to feel, within the next few years, would be happy if he escaped being stoned. I have witnessed many similar excesses in the way of speculations; but never an instance as gross, as wide-spread, and as alarming as this."

"You apprehend serious consequences, then, from the reaction?"

"In that particular, we are better off than older nations, the youth and real stamina of the country averting much of the danger; but I anticipate a terrible blow, and that the day is not remote when this town will awake to a sense of its illusion. What you see here is but a small part of the extravagance that exists, for it pervades the whole community, in one shape or another. Extravagant issues of paper-money, inconsiderate credits that commence in Europe, and extend throughout the land, and false notions as to the value of their possessions, in men who five years since had nothing, has completely destroyed the usual balance of things, and money has got to be so completely the end of life, that few think of it as a means. The history of the world, probably, cannot furnish a parallel instance, of an extensive country that is so absolutely under this malign influence, as is the fact with our own at this present instant. All principles are swallowed up in the absorbing desire for gain; national honour, permanent security, the ordinary rules of society, law, the constitution, and every thing that is usually so dear to men, are forgotten, or are perverted, in order to sustain this unnatural condition of things."

"This is not only extraordinary, but it is fearful!"

"It is both. The entire community is in the situation of a man who is in the incipient stages of an exhilarating intoxication, and who keeps pouring down glass after glass, in the idle notion that he is merely sustaining nature in her ordinary functions. This wide-spread infatuation extends from the coast to the extremest frontiers of the west; for, while there is a justifiable foundation for a good deal of this fancied prosperity, the true is so interwoven with the false, that none but the most observant can draw the distinction; and, as usual, the false predominates."

"By your account, sir, the tulip mania of Holland was trifling compared to this?"

"That was the same in principle as our own, but insignificant in extent. Could I lead you through these streets, and let you into the secret of the interests, hopes, infatuations and follies that prevail in the human breast, you, as a calm spectator, would be astonished at the manner in which your own species can be deluded. But let us move, and something may still occur to offer an example."

"Mr. Effingham—I beg pardon—Mr. Effingham," said a very gentlemanly-looking merchant, who was walking about the hall of the exchange, "what do you think now of our French quarrel?"

"I have told you, Mr. Bale, all I have to say on that subject. When in France, I wrote you that it was not the intention of the French government to comply with the treaty; you have since seen this opinion justified in the result; you have the declaration of the French minister of state, that, without an apology from this government, the money will not be paid; and I have given it as my opinion, that the vane on yonder steeple will not turn more readily than all this policy will be abandoned, should any thing occur in Europe to render it necessary, or could the French ministry believe it possible for this country to fight for a principle. These are my opinions, in all their phases, and you may compare them with facts and judge for yourself."

"It is all General Jackson, sir—all that monster's doings. But for his message, Mr. Effingham, we should have had the money long ago."

"But for his message, or some equally decided step, Mr. Bale, you would never have it, at all."

"Ah, my dear sir, I know your intentions are good, but I fear you are prejudiced against that excellent man, the King of France! Prejudice, Mr. Effingham, is a sad innovator on justice."

Here Mr. Bale shook his head, laughed, and disappeared in the crowd, perfectly satisfied that John Effingham was a prejudiced man, and that he, himself, was only liberal and just.

"Now, that is a man who wants for neither abilities nor honesty, and yet he permits his interests, and the influence of this very speculating mania, to overshadow all his sense of right, facts plain as noon-day, and the only principles that can rule a country in safety."

"He apprehends war, and has no desire to believe even facts, so long as they serve to increase the danger."

"Precisely so; for even prudence gets to be a perverted quality, when men are living under an infatuation like that which now exists. These men live like the fool who says 'there is no death.'"

Here the gentlemen rejoined the ladies, and the carriages drove through a succession of narrow and crooked streets, that were lined with warehouses filled with the products of the civilized world.

"Very much of all this is a part of the same lamentable delusion," said John Effingham, as the carriages made their way slowly through the encumbered streets. "The man who sells his inland lots at a profit, secured by credit, fancies himself enriched, and he extends his manner of living in proportion; the boy from the country becomes a merchant, or what is here called a merchant, and obtains a credit in Europe a hundred times exceeding his means, and caters to these fancied wants; and thus is every avenue of society thronged with adventurers, the ephemera of the same wide-spread spirit of reckless folly. Millions in value pass out of these streets, that go to feed the vanity of those who fancy themselves wealthy, because they hold some ideal pledges for the payment of advances in price like those mentioned by the auctioneer, and which have some such security for the eventual payment, as one can find in *calling* a thing, that is really worth a dollar, worth a hundred."

"Are the effects of this state of things apparent in your ordinary associations?"

"In every thing. The desire to grow suddenly rich has seized on all classes. Even women and clergymen are infected, and we exist under the active control of the most corrupting of all influences—'the love of money.' I should despair of the country altogether, did I not feel certain that the disease is too violent to last, and entertain a hope that the season of calm reflection and of repentance, that is to follow, will be in proportion to its causes."

After taking this view of the town, the party returned to Hudson Square, where the baronet dined, it being his intention to go to Washington on the following day. The leave-taking in the evening was kind and friendly; Mr. Effingham, who had a sincere regard for his late fellow-traveller, cordially inviting him to visit him in the mountains in June.

As Sir George took his leave, the bells began to ring for a fire. In New-York one gets so accustomed to these alarms, that near an hour had passed before any of the Effingham family began to reflect on the long continuance of the cries. A servant was then sent out to ascertain the reason, and his report made the matter more serious than usual.

We believe that in the frequency of these calamities, the question lies between Constantinople and New-York. It is a common occurrence for twenty or thirty buildings to be burnt down, in the latter place, and for the residents of the same ward to remain in ignorance of the circumstance, until enlightened on the fact by the daily prints; the constant repetition of the alarms hardening the ear and the feelings against the appeal. A fire of greater extent than common, had occurred only a night or two previously to this; and a rumour now prevailed, that the severity of the weather, and the condition of the hoses and engines, rendered the present danger double. On hearing this intelligence, the Messrs. Effinghams wrapped themselves up in their over-coats, and went together into the streets.

"This seems something more than usual, Ned," said John Effingham, glancing his eye upward at the lurid vault, athwart which gleams of fiery light began to shine; "the danger is not distant, and it seems serious."

Following the direction of the current, they soon found the scene of the conflagration, which was in the very heart of those masses of warehouses, or stores, that John Effingham had commented on, so lately. A short, narrow street of high buildings was already completely in flames, and the danger of approaching the furnace, added to the frozen condition of the apparatus, the exhaustion of the firemen from their previous efforts, and the intense coldness of the night, conspired to make the aspect of things in the highest degree alarming.

The firemen of New-York have that superiority over those of other places, that the veteran soldier obtains over the recruit. But the best troops can be appalled, and, on this memorable occasion, these celebrated firemen, from a variety of causes, became for a time, little more than passive spectators of the terrible scene.

There was an hour or two when all attempts at checking the conflagration seemed really hopeless, and even the boldest and the most persevering scarcely knew which way to turn, to be useful. A failure of water, the numerous points that required resistance, the conflagration extending in all directions from a common centre, by means of numberless irregular and narrow streets, and the impossibility of withstanding the intense heat, in the choked passages, soon added despair to the other horrors of the scene.

They who stood near the fiery masses, were freezing on one side with the Greenland cold of the night, while their bodies were almost blistered with the fierce flames on the other. There was something frightful in this contest of the elements, nature appearing to condense the heat within its narrowest possible limits, as if purposely to increase its fierceness. The effects were awful; for entire buildings would seem to dissolve at their touch, as the forked flames enveloped them in sheets of fire.

Every one being afoot, within sound of the alarm, though all the more vulgar cries had ceased, as men would deem it mockery to cry murder in a battle, Sir George Templemore met his friends, on the margin of this sea of fire. It was now drawing towards morning, and the conflagration was at its height, having already laid waste a nucleus of *blocks*, and it was extending by many lines, in every possible direction.

"Here is a fearful admonition for those who set their hearts on riches," observed Sir George Templemore, recalling the conversation of the previous day. "What, indeed, are the designs of man, as compared with the will of Providence!"

"I foresee that this is *le commencement de la fin*," returned John Effingham. "The destruction is already so great, as to threaten to bring down with it the usual safe-guards against such losses, insurance, and one pin knocked out of so frail and delicate a fabric, the whole will become loose, and fall to pieces."

"Will nothing be done to arrest the flames?"

"As men recover from the panic, their plans will improve and their energies will revive. The wider streets are already reducing the fire within more certain limits, and they speak of a favourable change of wind. It is thought five hundred buildings have already been consumed, in scarcely half a dozen hours."

That Exchange, which had so lately resembled a bustling temple of mammon, was already a dark and sheeted ruin, its marble walls being cracked, defaced, tottering, or fallen. It lay on the confines of the ruin, and our party was enabled to take their position near it, to observe the scene. All in their immediate vicinity was assuming the stillness of desolation, while the flushes of fierce light in the distance still marked the progress of the conflagration. Those who knew the localities, now began to speak of the natural or accidental barriers, such as the water, the slips, and the broader streets, as the only probable means of arresting the destruction. The crackling of the flames grew distant fast, and the cries of the firemen were soon scarcely audible.

At this period in the frightful scene, a party of seamen arrived, bearing powder, in readiness to blow up various buildings, in the streets that possessed of themselves, no sufficient barriers to the advance of the flame. Led by their officers, these gallant fellows, carrying in their arms the means of fire, and planted their kegs; laying their trains with the hardy indifference that practice can alone create, and with an intelligence that did infinite credit to their coolness. This deliberate courage was rewarded with complete success, and house crumbled to pieces after house, under the dull explosions, happily without an accident.

From this time the flames became less ungovernable, though the day dawned and advanced, and another night succeeded, before they could be said to have been got fairly under. Weeks, and even months passed, however, ere the smouldering ruins ceased to send up smoke, the fierce element continuing to burn, like a slumbering volcano, as it might be in the bowels of the earth.

The day that succeeded this disaster, was memorable for the rebuke it gave the rapacious longing for wealth. Men who had set their hearts on gold, and who prided themselves on its possession, and on that only, were made to feel its insecurity; and they who had walked abroad as gods, so lately, began to experience how utterly insignificant are the merely rich, when stripped of their possessions. Eight hundred buildings, containing fabrics of every kind, and the raw material in various forms, had been destroyed, as it were in the twinkling of an eye.

A faint voice was heard from the pulpit, and there was a moment when those who remembered a better state of things, began to fancy that principles would once more assert their ascendency, and that the community would, in a measure, be purified. But this expectation ended in disappointment, the infatuation being too wide-spread and corrupting, to be stopped by even this check, and the rebuke was reserved for a form that seems to depend on a law of nature, that of causing a vice to bring with it its own infallible punishment.

CHAPTER VIII.

"First, tell me, have you ever been at Pisa?"

The Taming of the Shrew 4.2.93.

THE conflagration alluded to, rather than described, in the preceding chapter, threw a gloom over the gaieties of New-York, if that ever could be properly called gay, which was little more than a strife in prodigality and parade, and leaves us little more to say of the events of the winter. Eve regretted very little the interruption to scenes in which she had found no pleasure, however much she lamented the cause; and she and Grace passed the remainder of the season quietly, cultivating the friendship of such women as Mrs. Hawker and Mrs. Bloomfield, and devoting hours to the improvement of their minds and tastes, without ever again venturing however, within the hallowed precincts of such rooms as those of Mrs. Legend.

One consequence of a state of rapacious infatuation, like that which we have just related, is the intensity of selfishness which smothers all recollection of the past, and all just anticipations of the future, by condensing life, with its motives and enjoyments, into the present moment. Captain Truck, therefore, was soon forgotten, and the literati, as that worthy seaman had termed the associates of Mrs. Legend, remained just as vapid, as conceited, as ignorant, as imitative, as dependent, and as provincial as ever.

As the season advanced, our heroine began to look with longings towards the country. The town life of an American offers little to one accustomed to a town life in older and more permanently regulated communities; and Eve was already heartily weary of crowded and noisy balls, (for a few were still given,) *belles*, the struggles of an uninstructed taste, and a representation in which extravagance was so seldom relieved by the elegance and convenience of a condition of society, in which more attention is paid to the fitness of things.

The American spring is the least pleasant of its four seasons, its character being truly that of "winter lingering in the lap of May." Mr. Effingham, who the reader will probably suspect, by this time, to be a descendant of a family of the same name, that we have had occasion to introduce in another work, had sent orders to have his country residence prepared for the reception of our party; and it was with a feeling of delight that Eve stepped on board a steam-boat to escape from a town that, while it contains so much that is worthy of any capital, contains so much more that is unfit for any place, in order to breathe the pure air, and to enjoy the tranquil pleasure of the country. Sir George Templemore had returned from his southern journey, and made one of the party, by express arrangement.

"Now, Eve," said Grace Van Cortlandt, as the boat glided along the wharves, "if it were any person but you, I should feel confident of having something to show that *would* extort admiration."

"You are safe enough, in that respect, for a more imposing object in its way, than this very vessel, eye of mine, never beheld. It is positively the only thing that deserves the name of magnificent I have yet seen, since our return,—unless, indeed, it may be magnificent projects."

"I am glad, dear coz, there is this one magnificent object, then, to satisfy a taste so fastidious."

As Grace's little foot moved, and her voice betrayed vexation, the whole party smiled; for the whole party, while it felt the justice of Eve's observation, saw the real feeling that was at the bottom of her cousin's remark. Sir George, however, though he could not conceal from himself the truth of what had been said by the one party, and the weakness betrayed by the other, had too much sympathy for the provincial patriotism of one so young and beautiful, not to come to the rescue.

"You should remember, Miss Van Cortlandt," he said, "that Miss Effingham has not had the advantage yet of seeing the Delaware, Philadelphia, the noble bays of the south, nor so much that is to be found out of the single town of New-York."

"Very true, and I hope yet to see her a sincere penitent for her unpatriotic admissions against her own country. *You* have seen the Capitol, Sir George Templemore; is it not, truly, one of the finest edifices of the world?"

"You will except St. Peter's, surely, my child," observed Mr. Effingham, smiling, for he saw that the baronet was embarrassed to give a ready answer.

"And the Cathedral at Milan," said Eve, laughing.

"*Et le Louvre!*" cried Mademoiselle Viefville, who had some such admiration for every thing Parisian, as Grace had for every thing American.

"And, most especially, the north-east corner of the south-west end of the north-west wing of Versailles," said John Effingham, in his usual dry manner.

"I see you are all against me," Grace rejoined, "but I hope, one day, to be able to ascertain for myself the comparative merits of things. As nature makes rivers, I hope the Hudson, at least, will not be found unworthy of your admiration, gentlemen and ladies."

"You are safe enough, there, Grace," observed Mr Effingham; "for few rivers, perhaps no river, offers so great and so pleasing a variety, in so short a distance, as this."

It was a lovely, bland morning, in the last week of May; and the atmosphere was already getting the soft hues of summer, or assuming that hazy and solemn calm that renders the season so quiet and soothing, after the fiercer strife of the elements in winter. Under such a sky, the Palisadoes, in particular, appeared well; for, though wanting in the terrific grandeur of an Alpine nature, and perhaps disproportioned to the scenery they adorned, they were bold and peculiar.

The great velocity of the boat added to the charm of the passage, the scene scarce finding time to pall on the eye; for, no sooner was one object examined in its outlines, than it was succeeded by another.

"An extraordinary taste is afflicting this country, in the way of architecture," said Mr. Effingham, as they stood gazing at the eastern shore; "nothing but a Grecian temple being deemed a suitable residence for a man, in these classical times. Yonder is a structure, for instance, of beautiful proportions, and, at this distance, apparently of a precious material, and yet it seems better suited to heathen worship than to domestic comfort."

"The malady has infected the whole nation," returned his cousin, "like the spirit of speculation. We are passing from one extreme to the other, in this, as in other things. One such temple, well placed in a wood, might be a pleasant object enough, but to see a river lined with them, with children trundling hoops before their doors, beef carried into their kitchens, and smoke issuing, moreover, from those unclassical objects chimnies, is too much even of a high class of tastes; one might as well live in a fever. Mr. Aristabulus Bragg, who is a wag in his way, informs me that there is one town in the interior that has actually a market-house on the plan of the Parthenon!"

"*Il Capo di Bove* would be a more suitable model for such a structure," said Eve, smiling. "But I think I have heard that the classical taste of our architects is any thing but rigid."

"This *was* the case, rather than *is*" returned John Effingham, "as witness all these temples. The country has made a quick and a great *pas, en avant*, in the way of the fine arts, and the fact shows what might be done with so ready a people, under a suitable direction. The stranger who comes among us is apt to hold the art of the nation cheap, but, as all things are comparative, let him inquire into its state ten years since, and look at it to-day. The fault just now, is perhaps to consult the books too rigidly, and to trust too little to invention; for no architecture, and especially no domestic architecture, can ever be above serious reproach, until climate, the uses of the edifice, and the situation, are respected as leading considerations. Nothing can be uglier, *per se*, than a Swiss cottage, or any thing more beautiful under its precise circumstances. As regards these mushroom temples, which are the offspring of mammon, let them be dedicated to whom they may, I should exactly reverse the opinion, and say, that while nothing can be much more beautiful, *per se*, nothing can be in worse taste, than to put them where they are."

"We shall have an opportunity of seeing what Mr. John Effingham can do in the way of architecture," said Grace, who loved to revenge some of her fancied wrongs, by turning the tables on her assailant, "for I understand he has been improving on the original labours of that notorious Palladio, Master Hiram Doolittle!"

The whole party laughed, and every eye was turned on the gentleman alluded to, expecting his answer.

"You will remember, good people," answered the accused by implication, "that my plans were handed over to me from my great predecessor, and that, moreover, they were originally of the composite order. If, therefore, the house should turn out to be a little complex and mixed, you will do me the justice to remember the last important fact. At all events, I have consulted comfort; and that I would maintain, in the face of Vitruvius himself, is a *sine quâ non* in domestic architecture."

"I took a run into Connecticut the other day," said Sir George Templemore, "and, at a place called New-Haven, I saw the commencement of a taste that bids fair to make a most remarkable town. It is true, you cannot expect structures of much pretension in the way of cost and magnitude in this country, but, so far as fitness and forms are concerned, if what I hear be true, and the next fifty years do as much in proportion for that little city, as I understand has been done in the last five, it will be altogether a wonder in its way. There are some abortions, it is true, but there are also some little jewels."

The baronet was rewarded for this opinion, by a smile from Grace, and the conversation changed. As the boat approached the mountains, Eve became excited, a very American state of the system by the way, and Grace still more anxious.

"The view of that bluff is Italian," said our heroine, pointing down the river at a noble headland of rock, that loomed grandly in the soft haze of the tranquil atmosphere. "One seldom sees a finer or a softer outline on the shores of the Mediterranean itself."

"But the Highlands, Eve!" whispered the uneasy Grace. "We are entering the mountains."

The river narrowed suddenly, and the scenery became bolder, but neither Eve nor her father expressed the rapture that Grace expected.

"I must confess, Jack," said the mild, thoughtful Mr. Effingham, "that these rocks strike my eyes as much less imposing than formerly. The passage is fine, beyond question, but it is hardly grand scenery."

"You never uttered a juster opinion, Ned, though after your eye loses some of the forms of the Swiss and Italian lakes, and of the shores of Italy, you will think better of these. The Highlands are remarkable for their surprises, rather than for their grandeur, as we shall presently see. As to the latter, it is an affair of feet and inches, and is capable of arithmetical demonstration. We have often been on lakes, beneath beetling cliffs of from three to six thousand feet in height; whereas, here, the greatest elevation is materially less than two. But, Sir George Templemore, and you, Miss Effingham, do me the favour to combine your cunning, and tell me whence this stream cometh, and whither we are to go?"

The boat had now approached a point where the river was narrowed to a width not much exceeding a quarter of a mile, and in the direction in which it was steering, the water seemed to become still more contracted until they were lost in a sort of bay, that appeared to be closed by high hills, through which, however, there were traces of something like a passage.

"The land in that direction looks as if it had a ravine-like entrance," said the baronet; "and yet it is scarcely possible that a stream like this can flow there!"

"If the Hudson truly passes through those mountains," said Eve, "I will concede all in its favour that you can ask, Grace."

"Where else can it pass?" demanded Grace, exultingly.

"Sure enough—I see no other place, and that seems insufficient."

The two strangers to the river now looked curiously around them, in every direction. Behind them was a broad and lake-like basin, through which they had just passed; on the left, a barrier of precipitous hills, the elevation of which was scarcely less than a thousand feet; on their right, a high but broken country, studded with villas, farm-houses, and hamlets; and in their front the deep but equivocal bay mentioned.

"I see no escape!" cried the baronet, gaily, "unless indeed, it be by returning."

A sudden and broad sheer of the boat caused him to turn to the left, and then they whirled round an angle of the precipice, and found themselves in a reach of the river, between steep declivities, running at right angles to their former course.

"This is one of the surprises of which I spoke," said John Effingham, "and which render the highlands so *unique*; for, while the Rhine is very sinuous, it has nothing like this."

The other travellers agreed in extolling this and many similar features of the scenery, and Grace was delighted; for, warm-hearted, affectionate, and true, Grace loved her country like a relative or a friend, and took an honest pride in hearing its praises. The patriotism of Eve, if a word of a meaning so lofty can be applied to feelings of this nature, was more discriminating, her tastes having been formed in a higher school, and her means of comparison being so much more ample. At West Point they stopped for the night, and here every body was in honest raptures; Grace, who had often visited the place before, being actually the least so of the whole party.

"Now, Eve, I know that you *do* love your country," she said, as she slipped an arm affectionately through that of her cousin. "This is feeling and speaking like an American girl, and as Eve Effingham should!"

Eve laughed, but she had discovered that the provincial feeling was so strong in Grace, a discussion would probably do no good. She dwelt, therefore, with sincere eloquence on the beauties of the place, and for the first time since they had met, her cousin felt as if there was no longer any point of dissension between them.

The following morning was the first of June, and it was another of those drowsy, dreamy days, that so much aid a landscape. The party embarked in the first boat that came up, and as they entered Newburgh bay, the triumph of the river was established. This is a spot, in sooth, that has few equals in any region, though Eve still insisted that the excellence of the view was in its softness rather than in its grandeur. The country houses, or boxes, for few could claim to be much more, were neat, well placed, and exceedingly numerous. The heights around the town of Newburgh, in particular, were fairly dotted with them, though Mr Effingham shook his head in disapprobation as he saw one Grecian temple appear after another.

"As we recede from the influence of the regular architects," he said, "we find imitation taking the place of instruction. Many of these buildings are obviously disproportioned, and then, like vulgar pretension of any sort, Grecian architecture produces less pleasure than even Dutch."

"I am surprised at discovering how little of a Dutch character, remains in this state," said the baronet; "I can scarcely trace that people in any thing, and yet, I believe, they had the moulding of your society, having carried the colony through its infancy."

"When you know us better, you will be surprised at discovering how little of any thing remains a dozen years," returned John Effingham. "Our towns pass away in generations like their people, and even the names of a place undergo periodical mutations, as well as every thing else. It is getting to be a predominant feeling in the American nature, I fear, to love change."

"But, cousin Jack, do you not overlook causes, in your censure. That a nation advancing as fast as this in wealth and numbers, should desire better structures than its fathers had either the means or the taste to build, and that names should change with persons, are both things quite in rule."

"All very true, Miss Effingham, though it does not account for the peculiarity I mean. Take Templeton, for instance. This little place has not essentially increased in numbers, within my memory, and yet fully one half its names are new. When he reaches his own home, your father will not know even the names of one half his neighbors. Not only will he meet with new faces, but he will find new feelings, new opinions in the place of traditions that he may love, an indifference to every thing but the present moment, and even those who may have better feelings, and a wish to cherish all that belongs to the holier sentiments of man, afraid to utter them, lest they meet with no sympathy."

"No cats, as Mr Bragg would say."

"Jack is one who never paints *en beau*," said Mr Effingham. "I should be very sorry to believe that a dozen short years can have made all these essential changes in my neighborhood."

"A dozen years, Ned! You name an age. Speak of three or four, if you wish to find any thing in America where you left it! The whole country is in such a constant state of mutation, that I can only liken it to that game of children, in which as one quits his corner, another runs in to it, and he that finds no corner to get into, is the laughing stock of the others. Fancy that dwelling the residence of one man from childhood to old age; let him then quit it for a year or two; on his return, he would find another in possession, who would treat him as an impertinent intruder, because he had been absent two years, and the other in possession for an eternity of the same period. An American 'always,' in the way of usages, extends no further back than eighteen months. In short, every thing is condensed into the present moment, and services, character, for evil as well as good unhappily, and all other things, cease to have weight, except as they influence the interests of the day."

"This is the coloring of a professed cynic—" observed Mr Effingham, smiling.

"But the law, Mr John Effingham," eagerly inquired the baronet— "surely the law would not permit a stranger to intrude in this manner on the rights of an owner?"

"The law *books* would do him that friendly office, perhaps, but what is a precept in the face of practices so ruthless. '*Les absents ont toujours tort*' is a maxim of peculiar application in America."

"Property is as secure in this country, as in any other, Sir George, and you will make allowances for the humours of the present annotator."

"Well, well, Ned; I hope you will find every thing *couleur de rose*, as you appear to expect. You will get quiet possession of your house, it is true, for I have put a Cerberus in it, that is quite equal to his task, difficult as it may be, and who has just as much relish for a bill of costs, as any squatter can have for a trespass; but, without some such guardian of your rights, I would not answer for it, that you would not be compelled to sleep in the highway."

"I trust Sir George Templemore knows how to make allowances for Mr John Effingham's pictures," cried Grace, unable to refrain from expressing her discontent any longer.

A laugh succeeded, and the beauties of the river, again attracted their attention. As the boat continued to ascend, Mr Effingham triumphantly affirmed that the appearance of things more than equalled his expectations, while both Eve and the baronet declared that a succession of lovelier landscapes could hardly be presented to the eye.

"Whited sepulchres!" muttered John Effingham—"all outside. Wait until you get a view of the deformity within."

As the boat approached Albany, Eve expressed her satisfaction in still stronger terms, and Grace was made perfectly happy, by hearing her and Sir George declare that the place entirely exceeded their expectations.

"I am glad to find, Eve, that you are so fast recovering your American feelings," said her beautiful cousin, after one of those expressions of agreeable disappointment, as they were seated at a late dinner, in an inn. "You have, at last, found words to praise the exterior of Albany, and I hope, by the time we return, you will be disposed to see New York with different eyes."

"I expected to see a capital in New York, Grace, and, in this, I have been grievously disappointed. Instead of finding the tastes, tone, conveniences, architecture, streets, churches, shops, and society of a capital, I found a huge expansion of common-place things, a commercial town, and the most mixed and the least regulated society that I had ever met with. Expecting so much, where so little was found, disappointment was natural. But in Albany, although a political capital, I knew the nature of the government too well, to expect more than a provincial town, and in this respect, I have found one much above the level of similar places in other parts of the world. I acknowledge that Albany has as much exceeded my expectations in one sense, as New York has fallen short of them, in another."

"In this simple fact, Sir George Templemore," said Mr Effingham, "you may read the real condition of the country. In all that requires something more than usual, a deficiency; in all that is deemed an average, better than common. The tendency is to raise every thing that is elsewhere degraded to a respectable height, when there commences an attraction of gravitation that draws all towards the centre, a little closer too, than could be wished perhaps."

"Ay, ay, Ned; this is very pretty, with your attractions and gravitations, but wait and judge for yourself of this average of which you now speak, so complacently."

"Nay, John, I borrowed the image from you; if it be not accurate, I shall hold you responsible for its defects."

"They tell me," said Eve, "that all American villages are the towns in miniature; children dressed in hoops and wigs. Is this so, Grace?"

"A little; there is too much desire to imitate the towns perhaps, and possibly too little feeling for country life."

"This is a very natural consequence, after all, of people's living entirely in such places," observed Sir George Templemore. "One sees much of this on the continent of Europe, because the country population is purely a country population, and less of it in England, perhaps, because those who are at the head of society, consider town and country, as very distinct things."

"*La campagne est vraiment délicieuse en Amérique!*" exclaimed Mademoiselle Viefville, in whose eyes, however, the whole country was little more than *campagne*.

The next morning, our travellers proceeded by the way of Schenectady, whence they ascended the beautiful valley of the Mohawk, by means of a canal boat, the cars that now rattle along its length not having commenced their active flights, at that time. With the scenery, every one was delighted, for while it differed essentially from that the party had passed through the previous day, it was scarcely less beautiful.

At a point where the necessary route diverged from the direction of the canal, carriages of Mr Effingham's were in readiness to receive the travellers, and here they were also favored with the presence of Mr Bragg, who fancied such an attention might be agreeable to the young ladies, as well as to his employer.

CHAPTER IX.

"Tell me where is fancy bred,
Or in the heart or in the head?
How begot, how nourished?"

The Merchant of Venice 3.2.63–65.

THE travellers were several hours ascending into the mountains, by a country road that could scarcely be surpassed by a French wheel-track of the same sort. Mademoiselle Viefville protested, twenty times in the course of the morning, that it was a thousand pities Mr Effingham had not the privilege of the *corvée*, that he might cause the approach to his *terres* to be kept in better condition. At length they reached the summit, a point where the waters began to flow south, when the road became tolerably level. From this time their progress became more rapid, and they continued to advance two or three hours longer at a steady pace.

Aristabulus now informed his companions that, in obedience to instructions from John Effingham, he had ordered the coachmen to take a road that led a little from the direct line of their journey, and that they had been travelling for some time, on one of the more ancient routes to Templeton.

"I was aware of this," said Mr Effingham, "though ignorant of the reason. We are on the Great Western Turnpike."

"Certainly, sir, and all according to Mr John's request. There would have been a great saving in distance, and agreeably to my notion, in horse flesh, had we quietly gone down the banks of the lake."

"Jack will explain his own meaning, in his own good time," returned Mr Effingham—"and he has stopped the other carriage, and alighted with Sir George, a hint, I fancy, that we are to follow their example."

Sure enough, the second carriage was now stopped, and Sir George hastened to open its door.

"Mr John Effingham, who acts as cicerone," cried the baronet, "insists that every one shall put *pied à terre*, at this precise spot, keeping the important reason a secret, however, in the recesses of his own bosom."

The ladies complied, and the carriages were ordered to proceed with the domestics, leaving the rest of the travellers by themselves, apparently in the heart of a forest.

"It is to be hoped, Mademoiselle, there are no banditti in America," said Eve, as they looked around them, at the novel situation, in which they were placed, apparently by a pure caprice of her cousin.

"*Ou des sauvages*," returned the governess, who, in spite of her ordinary intelligence and great good sense, had several times, that day, cast uneasy and stolen glances into the bits of dark wood they had occasionally passed.

"I will ensure your purses and your scalps, *mesdames*," cried John Effingham, gaily, "on condition that you will follow me implicitly; and by way of pledge for my faith, I solicit the honor of supporting Mademoiselle Viefville on this unworthy arm."

The governess laughingly accepted the conditions, Eve took the arm of her father, and Sir George offered his to Grace, Aristabulus, to his surprise, being left to walk entirely alone. It struck him, however, as so singularly improper that a young lady should be supported on such an occasion by her own father, that he frankly and gallantly proposed to Mr Effingham to relieve him of his burthen, an offer that was declined with quite as much distinctness as it was made.

"I suppose, cousin Jack, has a meaning to his melo-drama," said Eve, as they entered the forest, "and I dare say, dearest father, that you are behind the scenes, though I perceive determined secrecy in your face."

"John may have a cave to show us, or some tree of extraordinary height; such things existing in the country."

"We are very confiding, Mademoiselle, for I detect treachery in every face around us. Even Miss Van Cortlandt has the air of a conspirator, and seems to be in league with something, or somebody. Pray Heaven, it be not with wolves."

"*Des loups!*" exclaimed Mademoiselle Viefville, stopping short, with a mien so alarmed as to excite a general laugh—"*Est ce qu'il y a des loups et des sangliers dans cette forêt?*"

"No, Mademoiselle," returned her companion—"This is only barbarous America, and not civilized France. Were we in *le departement de la Seine* we might apprehend some such dangers, but being merely in the mountains of Otsego, we are reasonably safe."

"*Je l'espère*," murmured the governess, as she reluctantly and distrustfully proceeded, glancing her eyes incessantly to the right and to the left. The path now became steep and rather difficult; so much so, indeed, as to indispose them all to conversation. It led beneath the branches of lofty pines, though there existed, on every side of them, proofs of the ravages man had committed in that noble forest. At length they were compelled to stop for breath, after having ascended considerably above the road they had left.

"I ought to have said that the spot where we entered on this path, is memorable in the family history," observed John Effingham, to Eve—"for it was the precise place where one of our predecessors lodged a shot in the shoulder of another."

"Then I know precisely where we are!" cried our heroine, "though, I cannot yet imagine why we are led into this forest, unless it be to visit some spot hallowed by a deed of Natty Bumppo's!"

"Time will solve this mystery, as well as all others. Let us proceed."

Again they ascended, and, after a few more minutes of toil, they reached a sort of table land, and drew near an opening in the trees, where a small circle had evidently been cleared of its wood; though it was quite small, and untilled. Eve looked curiously about her, as did all the others to whom the place was novel, and she was lost in doubt.

"There seems to be a void beyond us," said the baronet— "I rather think Mr John Effingham has led us to the verge of a view."

At this suggestion, the party moved on in a body, and were well rewarded for the toil of the ascent, by a *coup d'œil* that was almost Swiss in character and beauty.

"Now, indeed, do I know where we are," exclaimed Eve, clasping her hands in rapture—"This is the 'Vision' and yonder is our blessed home!"

The whole artifice of the surprise was exposed, and after the first bursts of pleasure had subsided all to whom the scene was new, felt that they would not have missed this *piquante* introduction to the valley of the Susquehannah, on any account.

That the reader may understand the causes of so much delight, and why John Effingham had prepared this scene for his friends, we shall stop to give a short description of the objects that first met the eyes of the travellers.

It is known that they were in a small open spot in a forest, and on the verge of a precipitous mountain. The trees encircled them on every side but one, and on that lay the panorama, although the tops of tall pines, that grew in lines almost parallel to the declivity, rose nearly to a level with the eye. Hundreds of feet beneath them, directly in front, and stretching leagues to the right, was a lake embedded in woods and hills. On the side next the travellers, a fringe of forest broke the line of water, tree tops that intercepted the view of the shores, and on the other, high broken hills, or low mountains rather, that were covered with farms, beautifully relieved by patches of wood, in a way to resemble the scenery of a vast park, or a royal pleasure ground, limited the landscape. High valleys lay among these uplands, and in every direction, comfortable dwellings dotted the fields. The contrast between the dark hues of the evergreens, with which all the heights near the water were shaded, was in soft contrast to the livelier green of the other foliage, while the meadows and pastures were luxuriant with a verdure unsurpassed by that of England or Switzerland. Bays and points added to the exquisite outline of the glassy lake on this shore, while one of the former withdrew towards the northwest, in a way to leave the eye doubtful whether it saw the termination of the transparent sheet or not. Towards the south, bold, varied, but cultivated hills, also bounded the view, all teeming with the fruits of human labor, and yet all relieved by pieces of wood, in the way already mentioned, so as to give the entire region the character of park scenery. A wide, deep, even valley, commenced at the southern end of the lake, or nearly opposite to the stand of our travellers, and stretched away south, until concealed by a curvature in the ranges of the mountains. Like all the hill-tops, this valley was verdant, peopled, wooded in places, though less abundantly than the mountains, and teeming with the signs of life. Roads wound through its peaceful retreats, and might be traced working their way along the glens, and up the weary ascents, for miles, in every direction.

At the northern termination of this lovely valley, and immediately on the margin of the lake, lay the village of Templeton, immediately under the eyes of the party. The distance, in an air line, from their stand to the centre of the dwellings, could not be much less than a mile, but the atmosphere was so pure, and the day so calm, that it did not seem so far. The children and even the dogs were seen running about the streets, while the shrill cries of boys at their gambols, ascended distinctly to the ear.

As this was the Templeton of the Pioneers, and the progress of society during half a century is connected with the circumstance, we shall give the reader a more accurate notion of its present state, than can be obtained from incidental allusions. We undertake the office more readily because this is not one of those places that shoots up in a day, under the unnatural efforts of speculation, or which, favored by peculiar advantages in the way of trade, becomes a precocious city while the stumps still stand in its streets, but a sober county town that has advanced steadily, *pari passu*, with the surrounding region, and offers a fair specimen of the more regular advancement of the whole nation, in its progress towards civilization.

The appearance of Templeton, as seen from the height where it is now exhibited to the reader, was generally beautiful and map-like. There might be a dozen streets principally crossing each other at right angles, though sufficiently relieved from this precise delineation, to prevent a starched formality. Perhaps the greater part of the buildings were painted white, as is usual in the smaller American towns, tho a better taste was growing in the place, and many of the dwellings had the graver and chaster hues of the gray stones of which they were built. A general air of neatness and comfort pervaded the place, it being, in this respect, as unlike a continental European town, south of the Rhine, as possible, if indeed we except the picturesque bourgs of Switzerland. In England, Templeton would be termed a small market town, so far as size was concerned; in France, a large *bourg*; while, in America it was in common parlance, and by legal appellation, styled a village.

Of the dwellings of the place, fully twenty were of a quality that denoted ease in the condition of their occupants, and bespoke the habits of those accustomed to live in a manner superior to the great mass of their fellow creatures. Of these some six, or eight, had small lawns, carriage sweeps, and the other similar appliances of houses that were not deemed unworthy of the honour of bearing names of their own. No less than five little steeples, towers, or belfries, for neither word is exactly suitable to the architectural prodigies we wish to describe, rose above the roofs, denoting the sites of the same number of places of worship, an American village usually exhibiting as many of these proofs of liberty of conscience—*caprices of conscience* would perhaps be a better term,—as the dollars and cents of the neighborhood, will, by any practicable means, render attainable. Several light carriages, such as were suitable to a mountainous country, were passing to and fro in the streets, and, here and there, a single-horse vehicle was fastened before the door of a shop, or of a lawyer's office, denoting the presence of some customer, or client, from among the adjacent hills.

Templeton was not sufficiently a thoroughfare, to possess one of those monstrosities, a modern American tavern; or a structure whose roof should overtop that of all its neighbors, including even the churches. Still its inns were of respectable size, well *piazza'd*, to use a word of our own invention, and quite enough frequented.

Near the centre of the place, in grounds of rather limited extent, still stood that model of the composite order, which owed its existance to the combined knowledge and taste of Mr Richard Jones and Mr Hiram Doolittle. We will not say that it had been modernised, for the very reverse was the effect, in appearance at least; but, it had, since last presented to the reader, undergone material changes, that were directed by the more instructed intelligence of John Effingham.

This building was so conspicuous by position and size, that as soon as they had taken in glimpses of the entire landscape, which was not done without constant murmurs of pleasure, every eye became fastened on it, as the focus of interest. A long and common silence denoted how general was this feeling, and after the building had attracted their gaze, the whole party took seats on stumps and fallen trees, before a syllable was uttered. Aristabulus alone, permitted his look to wander, and he was curiously examining the countenance of Mr Effingham, near whom he sate, with a longing to discover whether the expression was that of approbation, or of disapprobation of the fruits of his cousin's genius.

"Mr John Effingham has considerably regenerated and re-vivified, not to say transmogrified the old dwelling," he said, cautiously using terms that might leave his own opinion of the changes doubtful. "The work of his hand has excited some speculation, a good deal of inquiry, and a little conversation, throughout the county. It has almost produced an excitement!"

"As my house came to me from my father," said Mr Effingham, across whose mild and handsome face, a smile was gradually stealing, "I knew its history; and when called on for an explanation of its singularities, could refer them confidently to the composite order. But, you, Jack, have supplanted all this, by a style of your own, for explanations of which I shall be compelled to consult the higher authorities."

"Do you dislike my taste, Ned?—To my eye, now, the structure has no bad appearance from this spot!"

"Fitness and comfort, are indispensable requisites for domestic architecture, to use your own argument. Are you quite sure that yonder castellated roof, for instance, is quite suited to the deep snows of these mountains?"

John Effingham whistled, as a gentleman will sometimes whistle, and endeavored to look unconcerned, for he well knew that the very first winter had demonstrated the unsuitableness of his plans, for such a climate. He had actually felt disposed to cause the whole to be altered privately, at his own expense, but, besides feeling certain his cousin would resent a liberty that inferred his indisposition to pay for his own buildings, he had a reluctance to admit, in the face of the whole country, that he had made so capital a mistake, in a branch of art, in which he prided himself rather more than common; almost as much, indeed, as his great predecessor, Mr Richard Jones.

"If you are not pleased with the appearance of your dwelling, Ned," he answered, "you can have, at least, the consolation of looking at some of your neighbors' houses, and of perceiving that they are a great deal uglier. Of all abortions of this sort, to my taste, a Grecian abortion is the worst—mine is only gothic, and that too, in a style so modest, that I should think it might pass, unmolested by any very furious criticism."

It was so unusual to see John Effingham on the defensive, that the whole party smiled, while Aristabulus, who stood in salutary fear of his caustic tongue, both smiled and wondered.

"Nay, do not mistake me, John," returned the proprietor of the edifice under discussion—"it is not your *taste* that I call in question, but your provision against the seasons. In the way of mere outward show, I really think you deserve high praise, for you have transformed a very ugly dwelling, into one that is almost handsome, in despite of proportions and of the necessity of regulating the alterations by prescribed limits. Still, I think, there is a little too much of the composite left about even the exterior."

"I hope, cousin Jack, you have not rashly innovated on the interior," cried Eve; "I think I shall remember that, and nothing is more pleasant than the *catism*, of seeing objects that you remember in childhood—pleasant, I mean, to those whom the mania of mutation has not afflicted."

"Do not be unnecessarily alarmed, Miss Effingham," replied her kinsman, with a pettishness of manner, that was altogether extraordinary in a man, whose mien, in common, was so singularly composed and masculine, "you will find all that you knew, when a kitten, in its proper place. I could not rake together, again, the ashes of Queen Dido, which were scattered to the four winds of Heaven, I fear; nor could I discover a reasonably good bust of Homer, but respectable substitutes are provided, and some of them have the great merit of puzzling all beholders, to tell to whom or what they belong; which I believe was the great characteristic of most of Mr Jones's inventions."

"I am glad to see, Cousin Jack, that you have, at least, managed to give a very respectable 'cloud-colour' to the whole house."

"Ay, it lay between that and an invisible green," the gentleman answered, losing his momentary spleen, in his natural love of the ludicrous—"but finding that the latter would be only too conspicuous in the droughts that sometimes prevail in this climate, I settled down into the yellowish drab, that, is, indeed, not unlike some of the richer volumes of the clouds."

"On the whole, I think you are fairly entitled, as Steadfast Dodge, Esquire, would say, to 'the meed of our thanks.'"

"What a lovely spot!" exclaimed Mr Effingham, who had already ceased to think of his own dwelling, and whose eye was roaming over the soft landscape, athwart which the lustre of a June noontide was throwing its richest glories; "this is truly a place, where one might fancy repose and content were to be found for the evening of a troubled life."

"Indeed, I have seldom looked upon a more bewitching scene," answered the baronet. "The lakes of Cumberland will scarce compete with this!"

"Or that of Brienz, or Lungeren, or Nemi," said Eve, smiling in a way that the other understood to be a hit at his nationality.

"*C'est charmant!*" murmured Mademoiselle Viefville. "*Un si beau calme fait penser à l'éternité.*"

"The farm you can see lying near yonder wood, Mr Effingham," coolly observed Aristabulus, "sold last spring for thirty dollars the acre, and was bought the summer before for twenty."

"*Chacun à son gout!* " said Eve.

"And yet, I fear, this glorious scene is marr'd by the envy, rapacity, uncharitableness, and all the other evil passions of man!" continued the more philosophical Mr Effingham—"Perhaps it were better, as it was so lately, when it lay in the solitude and peace of the wilderness, the resort of birds and beasts."

"Who prey on each other, dearest father, just as the worst of our own species prey on their fellows."

"True, child—true. And, yet, I never gaze on one of these scenes of holy calm, without wishing that the great tabernacle of nature might be tenanted only by those who have a feeling for its perfection."

"Do you see the lady," said Aristabulus, "that is just coming out on the lawn in front of the 'Wigwam,'" for that was the name John Effingham had seen fit to give the altered and amended abode. "Here, Miss Effingham, more in a line with the top of the pine beneath us."

"I see the person you mean; she seems to be looking in this direction."

"You are quite right, miss; she knows that we are to stop on the Vision, and no doubt sees us. That lady is your father's cook, Miss Effingham, and is thinking of the late breakfast that has been ordered to be in readiness against our arrival."

Eve concealed her amusement, for, by this time, she had discovered that Mr Bragg had a way peculiar to himself, or at least to his class, of using many of the commoner words of the English language. It would perhaps be expecting too much of Sir George Templemore, not to look for a smile, on such an occasion.

"Ah!" exclaimed Aristabulus, pointing towards the lake, across which several skiffs were stealing, some in one direction, and some in another. "There is a boat, that I think must contain the poet."

"Poet!" repeated John Effingham. "Have we reached that pass of luxury at Templeton?"

"Lord, Mr John Effingham, you must have very contracted notions of the place, if you think a poet a great novelty in it; the lake and mountains have been poetized, a dozen times, in the last ten years. Why, sir, we have caravans of wild beasts, nearly every summer!"

"This is, indeed, a step in advance, of which I was ignorant. Here then, in a region, that so lately was tenanted by beasts of prey, beasts are already brought as curiosities. You perceive the onward state of the country in this fact, Sir George Templemore."

"I do indeed; but I should like to hear from Mr Bragg, what sort of animals are in these caravans?"

"All sorts, sir, from monkeys to elephants. The last had a rhinoceros."

"Rhinoceros!—Why there was but one, lately, in all Europe. Neither the Zoological Gardens, nor the *Jardin des Plantes* had a rhinoceros! I never saw but one, and that was in a caravan at Rome, that travelled between St. Petersburgh and Naples."

"Well, sir, we have rhinocerosies here; and monkeys, and zebras, and poets, and painters, and congress-men, and bishops, and governors, and all other sorts of creatures."

"And who may the particular poet be, Mr Bragg," asked Eve, "that honors Templeton, with his presence, just at this moment?"

"That is more than I can tell you, Miss, for, though some eight or ten of us have done little else than try to discover his name for the last week, we have not got even as far as that one fact. He and the gentleman who travels with him, are both uncommonly close, on such matters, though I think we have some as good catechisers in Templeton, as can be found any where within fifty miles of us!"

"There is another gentleman with him—do you suspect them both of being poets?"

"Oh, no, Miss, the other is the waiter of the poet; that we know, as he serves him at dinner, and otherwise superintends his concerns; such as brushing his clothes, and keeping his room in order."

"This is being in luck for a poet, for they are of a class that are a little apt to neglect the decencies. May I ask why you suspect the master of being a poet, if the man be so assiduous?"

"Why, what else can he be? In the first place, Miss Effingham, he has no name."

"That is a reason in print," said John Effingham; "very few poets having names, now-a-days."

"Then he is out on the lake half his time, gazing up at the 'Silent Pine,' or conversing with the 'Speaking Rocks,' or drinking at the 'Fairy Spring.'"

"All suspicious circumstances, certainly; especially the dialogue with the rocks; though not absolutely conclusive."

"But, Mr John Effingham, the man does not take his food like other people. He rises early, and is out on the water, or up in the forest all the morning, and then returns to eat his breakfast in the middle of the forenoon. He goes into the woods, again, or on the lake, and comes back to dinner, just as I take my tea."

"This settles the matter. Any man who presumes to do all this, Mr Bragg, deserves to be called by some harder name, even, than that of a poet. Pray, sir, how long has this eccentric person, been a resident of Templeton."

"Hist—there he is, as I am a sinner!—and it was not he and the other gentlemen, that were in the boat."

The rebuked manner of Aristabulus, and the dropping of his voice, induced the whole party to look in the direction of his eye, and, sure enough, a gentleman approached them, in the half-rustic dress a man of the world is apt to assume in the country, an attire of itself that was sufficient to attract comment in a place where the prevailing wish was to be as much like town as possible. He came from the forest, along the table-land that crowned the mountain for some distance, following one of the foot-paths that the admirers of the beautiful landscape had made all over that pleasant wood. As he came out into the cleared spot, seeing it already in possession of a party, he bowed and was passing on, with a delicacy that Mr Bragg would be apt to deem eccentric, when suddenly hesitating, he gave a look of intense and eager interest at the whole party, smiled, advanced rapidly nearer, and discovered his entire person.

"I ought not to be surprised," he said, as he advanced so near as to render doubt any longer impossible, "for I knew you were hourly looked for, and indeed I waited for your arrival; and yet this meeting has been so unexpected, as to leave me scarcely in possession of my faculties."

It is needless to dwell upon the warmth and number of the greetings. To the surprise of Mr Bragg, his poet was not only known, but evidently much esteemed by all the party, with the exception of Miss Van Cortlandt, to whom he was soon cordially presented by the name of Powis. Eve managed, by an effort of womanly pride, to suppress the violence of her feelings, and the meeting passed off, as one of mutual surprise and pleasure, without any exhibition of emotion to attract unusual comment.

"We ought to express our wonder, at finding you here before us, my dear young friend," said Mr Effingham, still holding Paul's hand, affectionately between both his own; "and, even now, that my own eyes assure me of the fact, I can hardly believe you would arrive at New-York, and quit it, without giving us the satisfaction of seeing you."

"In that, sir, you are not wrong; certainly nothing could have deprived me of that pleasure, but the knowledge that it would not have been agreeable to yourselves. My sudden appearance, here, however, will be without mystery, when I tell you that I returned from England, by the way of Quebec, the Great Lakes, and the 'Falls,' having been induced by my friend Ducie, to take that route, in consequence of his ship's being sent to the St. Lawrence. A desire for novelty, and particularly a desire to see the celebrated cataract, which is almost *the* lion of America, did the rest."

"We are glad to have you with us, on any terms, and I take it as particularly kind, that you did not pass my door. You have been here some days."

"Quite a week. On reaching Utica, I diverged from the great route to see this place, not anticipating the pleasure of meeting you here so early, but hearing you were expected I determined to remain, with a hope, I rejoice to find was not vain, that you would not be sorry to see an old fellow traveller, once more."

Mr Effingham pressed his hands warmly, again, before he relinquished them, an assurance of welcome that Paul received with thrilling satisfaction.

"I have been in Templeton almost long enough," the young man resumed, laughing, "to set up as a candidate for the public favor, if I rightly understand the claims of a denizen. By what I can gather, from casual remarks, the old proverb that 'the new broom sweeps clean' applies with singular fidelity throughout all this region."

"Have you a copy of your last ode, or a spare epigram, in your pocket?" inquired John Effingham.

Paul looked surprised, and Aristabulus, for a novelty, was a little dashed. Paul looked surprised, as a matter of course, for, although he had been annoyed by the curiosity that is apt to haunt a village imagination, since his arrival in Templeton, he did not in the least suspect that his love of a beautiful nature had been imputed to devotion to the muses. Perceiving, however, by the smiles of those around him, that there was more meant than was expressed, he had the tact to permit the explanation to come from the person who had put the question, if it were proper it should come at all.

"We will defer the great pleasure that is in reserve," continued John Effingham, "to another time. At present, it strikes me that the lady of the lawn is getting to be impatient, and the *déjeuner à la fourchette*, that I have had the precaution to order is probably waiting our appearance. It must be eaten, though under the penalty of being thought moon-struck rhymers by the whole state. Come, Ned; if you are sufficiently satisfied with looking at the Wigwam in a bird's eye view, we will descend and put its beauties to the severer test of a close examination."

This proposal was readily accepted, though all tore themselves from that lovely spot with reluctance, and not until they had paused, again and again, to take another look.

"Fancy the shores of this lake lined with villas," said Eve—"church towers raising their dark heads among these hills; each mountain crowned with a castle, or a crumbling ruin, and all the other accessories of an old state of society, and what would then be the charms of the view."

"Less than they are to day, Miss Effingham," said Paul Powis, "for though poetry requires—you all smile, is it forbidden to touch on such subjects?"

"Not at all, so it be done in legitimate verse," returned the Baronet. "You ought to know that you are, now, expected even to speak in doggerel."

Paul ceased, not knowing what excuse to make, and the whole party walked away from the place, light-hearted and laughing; Aristabulus being quite as merry as any of them, though he scarce knew why. But it was a ruling trait in the character of this person, never to suffer himself to get behind the ages.

CHAPTER X.

"It is the spot I came to seek, –
My father's ancient burial-place . . .
It is the spot,—I know it well—
Of which our old traditions tell."

William Cullen Bryant, "An Indian At the Burial
Place of his Fathers," ll. 1–2, 5–6.

FROM the day after their arrival in New-York, or that on which the account of the arrests by the English cruiser had appeared in the journals, little had been said by any of our party concerning Paul Powis, or of the extraordinary manner in which he had left the packet, at the very moment she was about to enter her haven. It is true, that Mr Dodge, arrived at Dodgeopolis, had dilated on the subject in his hebdomadal, with divers additions and conjectures of his own, and this, too, in a way to attract a good deal of attention in the interior, but, it being a rule with those who are supposed to dwell at the fountain of foreign intelligence, not to receive any thing, from those, who ought not to be better informed than themselves, the Effinghams and their friends had never heard of his account of the matter.

While all thought the incident of the sudden return extraordinary, no one felt disposed to judge the young man harshly. The gentlemen knew that military censure, however unpleasant, did not always imply moral turpitude, and as for the ladies, they retained too lively a sense of his skill and gallantry, to wish to imagine evil on grounds so slight and vague. Still it had been impossible altogether to prevent the obtrusion of disagreeable surmises, and all now sincerely rejoiced at seeing their late companion, once more among them, seemingly in a state of mind that announced neither guilt nor degradation.

On quitting the mountain, Mr Effingham, who had a tender regard for Grace, offered her his arm as he would have given it to a second daughter, leaving Eve to the care of John Effingham. Sir George attended to Mademoiselle Viefville, and Paul walked by the side of our heroine and her cousin, leaving Aristabulus to be what he himself called a "miscellaneous companion;" or, in other words to thrust himself into either set, as inclination or accident might induce. Of course the parties conversed, as they walked, though those in advance would occasionally pause to say a word to those in the rear, and, as they descended, one or two changes occurred to which we may have occasion to allude.

"I trust you have had pleasant passages," said John Effingham to Paul, as soon as they were separated in the manner just mentioned. "Three trips across the Atlantic in so short a time would be hard duty to a landsman, though you, as a sailor, will probably think less of it."

"In this respect I have been fortunate, the Foam, as we know from experience, being a good traveller, and Ducie is altogether a fine fellow and an agreeable mess mate. You know I had him for a companion, both going and coming."

This was said naturally, and, while it explained so little directly, it removed all unpleasant uncertainty, by assuring his listeners that he had been on good terms, at last, with the person who had seemed to be his pursuer. John Effingham, too, well understood that no one messed with the commander of a vessel of war, in his own ship, who was, in any way, thought to be an unfit associate.

"You have made a material circuit to reach us, the distance by Quebec being nearly a fourth more than the direct road."

"Ducie desired it so strongly, that I did not like to deny him. Indeed, he made it a point, at first, to obtain permission to land me at New-York, where he had found me, as he said, but to this I would not listen, as I feared it might interfere with his promotion, of which he stood so good a chance, in consequence of his success in the affair of the money. By keeping constantly before the eyes of his superiors, on duty of interest, I thought his preferment would be more certain."

"And has his government thought his perseverance in the chase worthy of such a reward?"

"Indeed it has. He is now a post, and all owing to his good luck and judgment in that affair; though, in his country, rank in private life does no harm to rank in public life."

Eve liked the emphasis that Paul laid on "his country," and she thought the whole remark was made in a spirit that an Englishman would not be apt to betray.

"Has it ever occurred to you," continued John Effingham, "that our sudden and unexpected separation, has caused a grave neglect of duty in me, if not in both of us?"

Paul looked surprised, and, by his manner, he demanded an explanation.

"You may remember the sealed package of poor Mr Monday, that we were to open together, on our arrival in New-York, and on the contents of which, we were taught to believe depended the settling of some important private rights. I gave that package to you, at the moment it was received, and, in the hurry of leaving us, you overlooked the circumstance."

"All very true, and to my shame I confess that, until this instant, the affair has been quite forgotten by me. I had so much to occupy my mind while in England, that it was not likely to be remembered, and then the packet itself, has scarce been in my possession, since the day I left you."

"It is not lost, I trust!" said John Effingham, quickly.

"Surely not—It is safe, beyond a question, in the writing-desk in which I deposited it. But, the moment we reached Portsmouth, Ducie and myself proceeded to London, together, and, as soon as he had got through at the Admiralty, we went into Yorkshire, where we remained, much occupied with private matters of great importance to us both, while his ship was docked; and then it became necessary to make sundry visits to our relations—"

"Relations!" repeated Eve involuntarily, though she did not cease to reproach herself for the indiscretion, during the rest of the walk.

"Relations—" returned Paul, smiling. "Capt Ducie and myself are cousins-german, and we made pilgrimages together, to sundry family shrines. This duty occupied us, until a few days before we sailed for Quebec. On reaching our haven, I left the ship to visit the Great Lakes and Niagara, leaving most of my effects with Ducie, who has promised to bring them on with himself, when he follows on my track, as he expected soon to do, on his way to the West Indies, where he is to find a frigate. He owed me this attention, as he insisted, on account of having induced me to go so far out of my way, with so much luggage, to oblige him. The packet is, unluckily, left behind, with the other things."

"And do you expect Capt. Ducie to arrive in this country soon?— The affair of the packet ought not to be neglected much longer, for a promise to a dying man is doubly binding, as it appeals to all our generosity. Rather than neglect the matter, I would prefer sending a special messenger to Quebec."

"That will be quite unnecessary, as, indeed, it would be useless. Ducie left Quebec yesterday, and has sent his and my effects direct to New-York, under the care of his own steward. The writing case, containing other papers that are of interest to us both, he has promised not to lose sight of, but it will accompany him on the same tour, as that I have just made; for, he wishes to see Niagara and the lakes, also. He is now on my track, and will notify me, by letter, of the day he will be in Utica, in order that we may meet on the line of the canal, near this place, and proceed to New York, in company."

His companions listened to this brief statement, with an intense interest, with which the packet of poor Mr Monday, however, had very little connection. John Effingham called to his cousin, and, in a few words, stated the circumstances as they had just been related by the young man, without adverting to the papers of Mr Monday, which was an affair that he had hitherto kept to himself.

"It will be no more than a return of civility, if we invite Capt. Ducie to diverge from his road, and pass a few days with us, in the mountains," he added. "At what precise time do you expect him on the canal, Powis?"

"Within the fortnight. I feel certain he would be glad to pay his respects to this party, for he often expressed his sincere regrets at having been employed on a service that exposed the ladies to so much peril and delay."

"Capt. Ducie is a near kinsman of Mr Powis, dear father," added Eve, in a way to show her parent, that the invitation would be agreeable to herself, for Mr Effingham was so attentive to the wishes of his daughter, as never to ask a guest to his house, that he thought would prove disagreeable to its mistress.

"I shall do myself the pleasure to write to Capt. Ducie, this evening, urging him to honor us with his company," returned Mr Effingham. "We expect other friends in a few days, and I hope he will not find his time heavy on his hands, while in exile among us. Mr Powis will enclose my note in one of his letters, and will, I trust, second the request by his own solicitations."

Paul made his acknowledgments, and the whole party proceeded, though the interruption caused such a change in the *figure* of the promenade, as to leave the young man the immediate escort of Eve. By this time, they had not only reached the highway, but had again diverged from it, to follow the line of an old and abandoned wheel

track, that descended the mountain, along the side of the declivity, by a
wilder and more perilous direction than suited "modern enterprise;" it
having been one of those little calculated and rude roads, that the first
settlers of a country are apt to make, before there are time and means
to investigate and finish to advantage. Although much more difficult
and dangerous than its successor, as a highway, this relic of the infant
condition of the country, was by far the most retired and beautiful, and
pedestrians continued to use it, as a common foot-path to the Vision.
The seasons had narrowed its surface, and the second growth had
nearly covered it with their branches, shading it like an arbor, and Eve
expressed her delight with its wildness and boldness, mingled as both
were, with so pleasant a seclusion. Glimpses were constantly obtained
of the lake and the village, while they proceeded, and altogether, they
who were strangers to the scenery, were loud in its praises.

"Most persons who see this valley, for the first time," observed
Aristabulus, "find something to say in its favour; for my part, I
consider it as rather curious myself."

"Curious!" exclaimed Paul, "that gentleman is, at least, singular
in the choice of his expressions."

"You have met him, before to day," said Eve, laughing, for Eve
was now in a humour to laugh at trifles—. "This we know, since he
had prepared us to meet a poet, where we only find an old friend."

"Only, Miss Effingham!—Do you estimate poets so high, and old
friends, so low?"

"This extraordinary person, Mr Aristabulus Bragg, really deranges
all one's notions and opinions, in such a manner, as to destroy even the
usual signification of words, I believe. He seems so much in, and yet
so much out of his place; is both so *rusé* and so unpractised; so unfit
for what he is, and so ready at every thing, that I scarcely know how to
apply terms in any matter with which he has the smallest connection.
I fear he has persecuted you since your arrival, in Templeton?"

"Not at all; I am so much acquainted with men of his cast, that
I have acquired a tact in managing them. Perceiving that he was
disposed to suspect me of a disposition to 'poetize the lake,' to use his
own term, I took care to drop a couple of lines, roughly written off,
like a hasty and imperfect effusion, where I felt sure he would find
them, and have been living for a whole week on the fame, thereof."

"You do indulge in such tastes, then?" said Eve, smiling a little
saucily.

"I am as innocent of such an ambition, as of wishing to marry the heiress of the British throne, which, I believe, just now, is the goal of all the Icaruses of our own time. I am merely a rank plagiarist, for the rhyme on the fame of which I have rioted for a glorious week was two lines of Pope's, an author so effectually forgotten, in these palmy days of literature, in which all knowledge seems condensed into the productions of the last few years, that a man might almost pass off an entire classic for his own, without the fear of detection. It was merely the first couplet of the Essay on Man, which, fortunately, having an allusion to the 'pride of Kings,' would pass for original, as well as excellent, in nineteen villages in twenty, in America, in these piping times of ultra republicanism! No doubt, Mr Bragg thought a eulogy on the 'people' was to come next, to be succeeded by a glowing picture of Templeton and its environs."

"I do not know that I ought to admit these hits at liberty, from a foreigner," said Eve pretending to look graver, than she felt, for never before, in her life, had our heroine so strong a consciousness of happiness, as she had experienced that very morning.

"Foreigner! Miss Effingham!—And why a foreigner?"

"Nay, you know your own pretended cosmopolitism; and ought not the cousin of Capt Ducie to be an English man?"

"I shall not answer for the *ought*, the simple fact being a sufficient reply to the question. The cousin of Capt. Ducie is *not* an English man; nor, as I see you suspect, has he ever served a day in the British navy, or in any other navy than that of his native land."

"This is indeed taking us by surprise, and that most agreeably!" returned Eve, looking up at him with undisguised pleasure, while a bright glow, crimsoned her face. "We could not but feel an interest in one who had so effectually served us, and both my father and Mr John Effingham—"

"Cousin Jack—" interrupted the smiling Paul.

"Cousin Jack, then, if you dislike the formality I used; both my father and *cousin Jack*, examined the American navy register for your name, without success, as I understood, and the inference that followed was fair enough, I believe you will admit, yourself."

"Had they looked at a register of a few years date, they would have met with better luck. I have quitted the service, and am a sailor only in recollections. For the last few years, like yourselves, I have been a traveller by land, as well as by water."

Eve said no more, though every syllable that the young man uttered was received by attentive ears, and retained with a scrupulous fidelity of memory. They walked some distance in silence, until they reached the grounds of a house that was beautifully placed on the side of the mountain, near a lovely wood of pines. Crossing these grounds, until they reached a terrace in front of the dwelling, the village of Templeton lay directly in their front, perhaps a hundred feet beneath them, and yet so near, as to render the minutest object distinct. Here they all stopped to take a more distinct view of a place that had so much interest with most of the party.

"I hope you are sufficiently acquainted with the localities, to act as cicerone," said Mr. Effingham, to Paul. "In a visit of a week to this village, you have scarcely overlooked the Wigwam."

"Perhaps I ought to hesitate, or rather ought to blush to avow it," answered the young man, discharging the latter obligation by coloring to his temples, "but curiosity has proved so much stronger than manners, that I have been induced to trespass so far on the politeness of this gentleman, as to gain an admission to your dwelling, in and about which, more of my time has been passed, than has probably proved agreeable to its inmates."

"I hope the gentleman will not speak of it," said Aristabulus; "in this country, we live pretty much in common, and with me, it is a rule when a gentleman drops in, whether stranger or neighbor, to show him the civility to ask him to take off his hat."

"It appears to me," said Eve, willing to change the conversation, "that Templeton has an unusual number of steeples; for what purpose can so small a place possibly require so many buildings of that nature?"

"All in behalf of orthodoxy, Miss Eve," returned Aristabulus, who conceived himself to be the proper person to answer such interrogatories. "There is a shade of opinion, beneath every one of those steeples."

"Do you mean, sir, that there are as many shades of faith, in Templeton, as I now see buildings that have the appearance of being devoted to religious purposes?"

"Double the number, miss, and some to spare, in the bargain. You see but five meeting houses, and the county buildings, and we reckon seven regularly hostile denominations in the village, besides the diversities of sentiment on trifles. This edifice that you perceive here, in a line with the chimnies of the first house is New St. Paul's,

Mr Grant's old church; as orthodox a house, in its way, as there is in the diocese, as you may see by the windows. This is a gaining concern, though there has been some falling off of late, in consequence of the clergyman's having caught a bad cold, which has made him a little hoarse. I dare say he will get over it, however, and the church ought not to be abandoned on that account, serious as the matter undoubtedly is, for the moment. A few of us are determined to back up New St. Paul's in this crisis, and I make it a point to go there myself, quite half the time."

"I am glad we have so much of your company," said Mr Effingham, "for that is our own church, and in it my daughter was baptized. But, do you divide your religious opinions, in halves, Mr Bragg?"

"In as many parts, Mr Effingham, as there are denominations in the neighborhood, giving a decided preference to New St. Paul's notwithstanding, under the peculiar circumstances, particularly to the windows. The dark, gloomy-looking building, miss, off in the distance, yonder, is the methodist affair, of which not much need be said, methodism flourishing but little among us since the introduction of the New Lights, who have fairly managed to out-excite them. I believe, however, they stick pretty much to the old doctrine, which, no doubt, is one great reason of their present apathetick state, for the people *do* love novelties."

"Pray, sir, what building is this nearly in a line with New St. Paul's, and which resembles it a little, in colour and form?"

"Windows excepted; it has two rows of regular square topped windows, miss, as you may observe. That is the first Presbyterian, or the old standard; a very good house, and a pretty good faith, too, as times go. I make it a point to attend there, at least once every fortnight; change being so agreeable to the nature of man. I will say, miss, that my preference, so far as I have any, however, is for New St. Paul's, and I have experienced considerable regrets, that these presbyterians have gained a material advantage over us, in a very essential point, lately."

"I am sorry to hear that, Mr Bragg, for being an Episcopalian myself, and having great reliance on the antiquity and purity of my church, I should be sorry to find it put in the wrong, by any other."

"I fear we must give the point up notwithstanding, for these presbyterians have entirely outwitted the church people in that matter."

"And what is the point in which we have been so signally worsted?"

"Why, miss, their new bell weighs quite a hundred more than that of New St. Paul's, and has altogether the best sound. I know very well, that this advantage will not avail them anything to boast of, in the last great account, but it makes a surprising difference in the state of probation. You see the yellowish-looking building across the valley, with a heavy wall around it, and a belfry? That, in its regular character, is the county court house, and gaol, but, in the way of religion, it is used pretty much miscellaneously."

"Do you mean, really, sir, that divine service is ever actually performed in it, or that persons of all denominations are occasionally tried there?"

"It would be truer to say that all denominations occasionally try the court-house," said Aristabulus, simpering, "for, I believe, first and last, it has been used, in this way, by every shade of religion, short of the Jews. The ancient gothic tower in green wood, is the building of the Universalists, and the Grecian edifice that is not yet painted, the Baptists. The Quakers, I believe, worship chiefly at home, and the different shades of the Presbyterians meet, in different rooms, in private houses, about the place."

"Are there then shades of difference in the denominations, as well as all these denominations," asked Eve, in unfeigned surprise; "and this, too, in a population so small?"

"This is a free county, Miss Eve, and freedom loves variety. 'Many men, many minds.'"

"Quite true, sir," said Paul; "but here are many minds, among few men. Nor is this all; agreeably to your own account, some of these men do not exactly know their own minds. But, can you explain to us, what essential points are involved in all these shades of opinion?"

"It would require a life, sir, to understand the half of them. Some say that excitement is religion, and others that it is contentment. One set cries up practice, and another cries out against it. This man maintains that he will be saved if he does good, and that man affirms that if he only does good, he will be damned; a little evil is necessary to salvation, with one shade of opinion, while another thinks a man is never so near conversion as when he is deepest in sin."

"Subdivision is the order of the day," added John Effingham; "every county is to be subdivided that there may be more county towns, and county officers; every religion decimated, that there may be a greater variety and a better quality of saints."

Aristabulus nodded his head, and he would have winked could he have presumed to take such a liberty, with a man he held as much in habitual awe, as John Effingham.

"*Monsieur,*" inquired Mademoiselle Viefville, "is there no *église,* no *véritable église,* in Templeton?"

"Oh, yes Madame, several," returned Aristabulus, who would as soon think of admitting that he did not understand the meaning of *véritable église,* as one of the sects he had been describing would think of admitting that it was not infallible in its interpretation of christianity—"Several, but they are not be seen from this particular spot."

"How much more picturesque would it be, and even more christian-like in appearance, at least," said Paul, "could these good people consent to unite in worshipping God!—And how much does it bring into strong relief, the feebleness and ignorance of man, when you see him splitting hairs about doctrines, under which he has been told, in terms as plain as language can make it, that he is simply required to believe in the goodness and power of a Being whose nature and agencies exceed his comprehension!"

"All very true," cried John Effingham, "but what would become of liberty of conscience, in such a case? Most men, now-a-days, understand by faith, a firm reliance on their own opinions."

"In that case, too," put in Aristabulus, "we should want this handsome display of churches, to adorn our village. There is good comes of it, for any man would be more likely to invest in a place that has five churches, than in a place with but one. As it is, Templeton has as beautiful a set of churches as any village I know."

"Say rather, sir, a set of castors, for a stronger resemblance to vinegar cruets and mustard pots, than is borne by these architectural prodigies, eye never beheld."

"It is, nevertheless, a beautiful thing, to see the high pointed roof of the House of God, crowning an assemblage of houses, as one finds it in other countries," said Eve, "instead of a pile of taverns, as is too much the case in this dear home of ours."

When this remark was uttered, they descended the steps that led from the terrace, and proceeded towards the village. On reaching the gate of the Wigwam, the whole party stood confronted with that offspring of John Effingham's taste, for so great had been his improvements on the original production of Hiram Doolittle, that, externally at least, that distinguished architect could no longer have recognized the fruits of his own talents, in the house in question.

"This is certainly carrying out to the full, John, the conceits of the composite order," observed Mr Effingham, drily.

"I shall be sorry, Ned, if you dislike your house, as it is amended and corrected."

"Dear cousin Jack," cried Eve, "it is an odd jumble of the Grecian and gothic. One would like to know your authorities, for such a liberty."

"What do you think of the *façade* of the Cathedral of Milan, miss," laying emphasis on the last word, in imitation of the manner of Mr Bragg. "Is it such a novelty to see the two styles blended, or is architecture so pure in America, that you think I have committed the unpardonable sin."

"Nay, nothing, that is out of rule, ought to strike one, in a country, where imitation governs in all things immaterial, and originality unsettles all things sacred and dear."

"By way of punishment for that bold speech, I wish I had left the old rookery in the state I found it, that its beauties might have greeted your eyes, instead of this uncouth pile which seems so much to offend them. Mademoiselle Viefville, permit me to ask how you like that house?"

"*Mais, c'est un petit château.*"

"*Un château, Effinghamisé,*" said Eve, laughing.

"*Effinghamisé si vous voulez, ma chère; pourtant, c'est un petit château.*"

"The general opinion, in this part of the country is," said Aristabulus, "that Mr John Effingham has altered the building, on the plan of some edifice of Europe, though I forget the name of the particular temple; it is not, however, the Parthenon, nor the temple of Minerva."

"I hope, at least," said Mr Effingham, leading the way up a little lawn, "it will not turn out to be the Temple of the Winds."

CHAPTER XI.

"Nay, I'll come. If I lose a scruple of this sport, let me be boil'd
to death with melancholy."

Twelfth Night 2.5.2–3.

THE progress of society in America, has been distinguished by
several peculiarities that do not so properly belong to the more
regular and methodical advances of civilization, in other parts of the
world. On the one hand, the arts of life, like Minerva, who was struck
out of the intellectual being of her father at a blow, have started full
grown into existence, as the legitimate inheritance of the colonists,
while, on the other, every thing tends towards settling down into
a medium, as regards quality, a consequence of the community-
character of the institutions. Every thing she had seen that day,
had struck Eve as partaking of this mixed nature, in which, while
nothing was vulgar, little even approached to that high standard, that
her European education had taught her to esteem perfect. In the
Wigwam, however, as her father's cousin had seen fit to name the
family dwelling, there was more of keeping, and a closer attention to
the many little things she had been accustomed to consider essential
to comfort and elegance, and she was better satisfied with her future
home, than with most she had seen, since her return to America.

As we have described the interior of this house, in another work,
little remains to be said on the subject, at present, for, while John
Effingham had completely altered its external appearance, its internal
was not much changed. It is true, the cloud coloured covering had
disappeared, as had that stoop also, the columns of which were so
nobly upheld by their superstructure; the former having given place
to a less obtrusive roof, that was regularly embattled, and the latter
having been swallowed up by a small entrance tower, that the new
architect had contrived to attach to the building with quite as much
advantage to it, in the way of comfort, as in the way of appearance.

In truth, the Wigwam had none of the more familiar features of a modern American dwelling of its class. There was not a column about it, whether Grecian, Roman, or Egyptian; no Venetian blinds; no verandah, or piazza; no outside paint, nor any blending of colours. On the contrary it was a plain old structure, built with great solidity, of excellent materials, and in that style of respectable dignity and propriety, that was perhaps a little more peculiar to our fathers, than it is peculiar to their successors, our worthy selves. In addition to the entrance tower, or porch, on its northern front, John Effingham had also placed a prettily devised conceit on the southern, by means of which the abrupt transition from an inner room to the open air was adroitly avoided. He had moreover, removed the "firstly" of the edifice, and supplied its place with a more suitable addition that contained some of the offices, while it did not disfigure the building, a rare circumstance in an architectural after-thought.

Internally, the Wigwam had gradually been undergoing improvements, ever since that period, which, in the way of the arts, if not in the way of chronology, might be termed the dark ages of Otsego. The great hall had long before lost its characteristic decoration of the severed arm of Wolf, a gothic paper that was better adapted to the really respectable architecture of the room being its substitute, and even the urn that was thought to contain the ashes of Queen Dido, like the pitcher that goes too often to the well, had been broken in a war of extermination, that had been carried on against the cob-webs by a particularly notable housekeeper. Old Homer, too, had gone the way of all baked clay; Shakspeare, himself, had dissolved into dust, "leaving not a wreck behind;" and of Washington and Franklin, even, indigenous as they were, there remained no vestiges. Instead of these venerable memorials of the past, John Effingham, who retained a pleasing recollection of their beauties as they had presented themselves to his boyish eyes, had bought a few substitutes in a New-York shop, and *a* Shakspeare, and *a* Milton, and *a* Cæsar, and *a* Dryden, and *a* Locke, as the writers of heroick so beautifully express it, were now seated in tranquil dignity, on the old medallions, that had held their illustrious predecessors. Although time had, as yet, done little for this new collection in the way of colour, dust and neglect were already throwing around them the tint of antiquity.

"The lady," to use the language of Mr Bragg, who did the cooking of the Wigwam, having every thing, in readiness, our party took their seats at the breakfast table, which was spread in the great hall, as soon as each had paid a little attention to the *toilette*. As the service was neither very scientifick, nor sufficiently peculiar, either in the way of elegance, or of its opposite quality, to be worthy of notice, we shall pass it over in silence.

"One will not quite so much miss European architecture, in this house," said Eve, as she took her seat at the table, glancing an eye at the spacious and lofty room, in which they were assembled; "here is, at least, size and its comforts, if not elegance."

"Had you lost all recollection of this building, my child?" inquired her father, kindly. "I was in hopes you would feel some of the happiness of returning home, when you again found yourself beneath its roof!"

"I should greatly dislike to have all the anticks I have been playing in my own dressing room, exposed," returned Eve, rewarding the parental solicitude of her father, by a look of love—, "though Grace, between her laughing and her tears, has threatened me with such a disgrace. Anne Sidley has also been weeping, and, as even Annette, always courteous and considerate, has shed a few tears in the way of sympathy, you ought not to imagine that I have been altogether so stoical as not to betray some feeling, dear father. But the paroxysm is past, and I am beginning to philosophize. I hope, cousin Jack, you have not forgotten that the drawing room is a lady's empire!"

"I have respected your rights, Miss Effingham, though, with a wish to prevent any violence to your taste, I have caused sundry antediluvian paintings and engravings to be consigned to the—"

"Garret?" inquired Eve, so quickly as to interrupt the speaker.

"Fire—" coolly returned her cousin. "The garret is now much too good for them; that part of the house being converted into sleeping rooms for the maids. Mademoiselle Annette would go into the hystericks, were she to see the works of art, that satisfied the past generation of masters in this country, in too close familiarity with her Louvreized eyes."

"*Point du tout, monsieur*," said Mademoiselle Viefville, innocently; "*Annette a du goût dans son métier, sans doute*, but she is too well bred to expect *impossibilités*. No doubt, she would have conducted herself with decorum."

Every body laughed, for much light-heartedness prevailed at that board, and the conversation continued.

"I shall be satisfied if Annette escape convulsions," Eve added, "a refined taste being her weakness; and, to be frank, what I recollect of the works you mention, is not of the most flattering nature."

"And yet," observed Sir George, "nothing has surprised me more, than the respectable state of the arts of engraving and painting, in this country. It was unlooked for, and the pleasure has probably been in proportion to the surprise."

"In that you are very right, Sir George Templemore," John Effingham answered; "but the improvement is of very recent date. He who remembers an American town half a century ago, will see a very different thing in an American town of to-day, and this is equally true of the arts you mention, with the essential difference that the latter are taking a right direction, under a proper instruction, while the former are taking a wrong direction, under the influence of money that has no instruction. Had I left much of the old furniture, or any of the old pictures in the Wigwam we should have had the bland features of Miss Effingham in frowns, instead of bewitching smiles, at this very moment."

"And yet I have seen fine old furniture, in this country, cousin Jack."

"Very true, though not in this part of it. The means of conveyance were wanting, half a century since, and few people risk finery of any sort on corderoys. This very house had some respectable old things, that were brought here by dint of money, and they still remain; but the eighteenth century, in general, may be set down as a very dark antiquity, in all this region."

When the repast was over, Mr Effingham led his guests and daughter through the principal apartments, sometimes commending, and sometimes laughing at the conceits of his kinsman. The library was a good sized room, good sized at least for a country in which domestic architecture, as well as public architecture, is still in the chrysalis state. Its walls were hung, with an exceedingly pretty gothic paper, in green, but over each window was a chasm in the upper border, and as this border supplied the arches, the unity of the entire design was broken in no less than four places, that being the precise number of the windows. The defect soon attracted the eye of Eve, and she was not slow in demanding an explanation.

"The deficiency is owing to an American accident," returned her cousin; "one of those calamities of which you are fated to experience many, as the mistress of an American household. No more of the border was to be bought in the country, and this is a land of shops, and not of *fabricants*. At Paris, Mademoiselle, one would send to the paper-maker for a supply, but, alas! he that has not enough of a thing with us, is as badly off as if he had none. We are consumers, and not producers of works of art. It is a long way to send to France for ten or fifteen feet of paper hangings, and yet this must be done, or my beautiful gothic arches will remain forever without their key-stones!"

"One sees the inconvenience of this," observed Sir George—"We feel it, even in England, in all that relates to imported things."

"And we, in nearly all things, but food."

"And does not this show that America can never become a manufacturing country?" asked the baronet, with the interest an intelligent Englishman ever feels in that all absorbing question. "If you cannot manufacture an article as simple as that of paper-hangings, would it not be well to turn your attention, altogether, to agriculture?"

As the feeling of this interrogatory was much more apparent than its logic, smiles passed from one to the other, though John Effingham, who really had a regard for Sir George, was content to make an evasive reply, a singular proof of amity, in a man of his caustic temperament.

The survey of the house, on the whole, proved satisfactory to its future mistress, who complained, however, that it was furnished too much like a town residence.

"For," she added, "you will remember, cousin Jack, that our visits here will be something like a *villegiatura.*"

"Yes, yes, my fair lady; it will not be long before your Parisian and Roman tastes, will be ready to pronounce the whole country a *villegiatura!*"

"This is the penalty, Eve, one pays for being a Hajji,—" observed Grace, who had been closely watching the expression of the other's countenance; for, agreeably to her view of things, the Wigwam wanted nothing to render it a perfect abode. "The things that *we* enjoy, *you* despise."

"That is an argument, my dear coz, that would apply equally well, as a reason for preferring brown sugar to white."

"In coffee, certainly, Miss Eve," put in the attentive Aristabulus, who having acquired this taste, in virtue of an economical mother, really fancied it a pure one; "every body, in these regions, prefers the brown in coffee."

"*Oh, mon père et ma mère, comme je vous en veux,*" said Eve, without attending to the nice distinctions of Mr Bragg, which savored a little too much of the neophyte in cookery to find favor in the present company, "*comme je vous en veux* for having neglected so many beautiful sites, to place this building in the very spot it occupies."

"In that respect, my child, we may rather be grateful at finding so comfortable a house, at all. Compared with the civilization that then surrounded it, this dwelling was a palace at the time of its erection, bearing some such relation to the humbler structures around it, as the *chateau* bears to the cottage. Remember that brick had never before been piled on brick, in the walls of a house, in all this region, when the Wigwam was constructed. It is the Temple of Neptune of Otsego, if not of all the surrounding counties."

Eve pressed to her lips, the hand she was holding in both her own, and they all passed out of the library into another room. As they came in front of the hall windows, a party of apprentice boys were seen coolly making their arrangements to amuse themselves with a game of ball, on the lawn directly in front of the house.

"Surely, Mr Bragg," said the owner of the Wigwam, with more displeasure in his voice than was usual for one of his regulated mind, "you do not countenance this liberty?"

"Liberty, sir!—I am an advocate for liberty, wherever I can find it. Do you refer to the young men on the lawn, Mr Effingham?"

"Certainly to them, sir; and permit me to say, I think they might have chosen a more suitable spot for their sports. They are mistaking *liberties,* for liberty, I fear."

"Why, sir, I believe they have *always* played ball in that precise locality."

"*Always!*—I can assure you this is a great mistake. What private family, placed as we are in the center of a village, could allow of an invasion of its privacy in this rude manner? Well may the house be termed a wigwam, if this whooping is to be tolerated before its door."

"You forget, Ned," said John Effingham, with a sneer, "that an American *always* means just eighteen months. *Antiquity* is reached in five lustres, and the dark ages at the end of a human life. I dare say these amiable young gentlemen, who enliven their sports with so many agreeable oaths, would think you very unreasonable and encroaching to presume to tell them they are unwelcome."

"To own the truth, Mr John, it *would* be downright unpopular."

"As I cannot permit the ears of the ladies to be offended with these rude brawls, and shall never consent to have grounds that are so limited, and which so properly belong to the very privacy of my dwelling, invaded in this coarse manner, I beg, Mr Bragg, that you will, at once, desire these young men to pursue their sports some where else."

Aristabulus received this commission with a very ill grace, for, while his native sagacity told him that Mr Effingham was right, he too well knew the loose habits that had been rapidly increasing in the country, during the last ten years, not to foresee, that the order would do violence to all the apprentices' preconceived notions of their immunities; for, as he had truly stated, things move at so quick a pace in America, and popular feeling is so arbitrary, that a custom of a twelve month's existence, is deemed sacred, until the public, itself, sees fit to alter it. He was reluctantly quitting the party, on his unpleasant duty, when Mr Effingham turned to a servant who belonged to the place, and bade him go to the village barber, and desire him to come to the Wigwam, to cut his hair; Pierre, who usually performed that office for him, being busied in unpacking trunks.

"Never mind, Tom," said Aristabulus obligingly, as he took up his hat, "I am going into the street, and will give the message to Mr Lather."

"I cannot think, sir, of employing you on such a duty," hastily interposed Mr Effingham, who felt a gentleman's reluctance to impose an unsuitable office on any of his dependants—"Tom, I am sure will do me the favor."

"Do not name it, my dear sir; nothing makes me happier than to do these little errands, and, another time, you can do as much for me."

Aristabulus now went his way, more cheerfully, for he determined to go first to the barber, hoping that some expedient might suggest itself, by means of which he could coax the apprentices from the lawn, and thus escape the injury to his popularity, that he so much dreaded. It is true, these apprentices were not voters, but then some of them speedily would be, and all of them, moreover, had *tongues*, an instrument Mr Bragg held in quite as much awe, as some men dread salt-petre. In passing the ball-players, he called out, in a wheedling tone, to their ring-leader, a notorious street brawler—

"A fine time for sport, Dickey; dont you think there would be more room in the broad street, than on this crowded lawn, where you lose your ball so often in the shrubbery."

"This place will do, on a pinch," bawled Dickey—"though it might be better. If it warn't for that plagued house, we could'n't ask for a better ball ground."

"I dont see," put in another, "what folks built a house, just in that spot for; it has spoilt the very best play ground in the village."

"Some people have their notions, as well as others," returned Aristabulus; "but, gentlemen, if I were in your place, I would try the street. I feel satisfied you would find it much the most agreeable and convenient."

The apprentices thought differently, however, or they were indisposed to the change, and so they recommenced their yells, their oaths, and their game. In the mean while, the party in the house continued their examination of John Effingham's improvements, and when this was completed, they separated, each to his or her own room.

Aristabulus soon reappeared on the lawn, and approaching the ball-players, he began to execute his commission, as he conceived, in good earnest. Instead of simply saying, however, that it was disagreeable to the owner of the property to have such an invasion on his privacy, and thus putting a stop to the intrusion, for the future as well as at the present moment, he believed some address necessary to attain the desired end.

"Well, Dickey," he said, "there is no accounting for tastes, but, in my opinion, the street would be a much better place to play ball in, than this lawn. I wonder gentlemen of your observation should be satisfied with so cramped a play ground!"

"I tell you, Squire Bragg, this will do," roared Dickey; "we are in a hurry, and no way particular; for the Bosses will be after us, in half an hour. Heave away, Sam."

"There are so many fences hereabouts," continued Aristabulus, with an air of indifference; "it's true the village trustees say there *shall be no ball playing in the street*, but I conclude you dont much mind what *they* think or threaten."

"Let them sue for that, if they like," bawled a particularly amiable blackguard, called Peter, who struck his ball as he spoke, quite into the principal street of the village. "Who's a trustee, that he should tell gentlemen, where they are to play ball!"

"Sure enough," said Aristabulus, "and, now, by following up that blow, you can bring matters to an issue. I think the law very oppressive, and you can never have so good an opportunity to bring things to a crisis. Besides, it is very aristocratick to play ball among roses and dahlias."

The bait took, for what apprentice—American apprentice in particular—can resist an opportunity of showing how much he considers himself superior to the law. Then it had never struck any of the party before, that it was vulgar and aristocratick to pursue the sport among roses, and one or two of them actually complained that they had pricked their fingers, in searching for the ball.

"I know Mr Effingham will be very sorry to have you go," continued Aristabulus following up his advantage, "but gentlemen cannot always forego their pleasures for other folks."

"Who's Mr Effingham, I would like to know," cried Joe Wart; "if he warnts people to play ball on his premises, let him cut down his roses. Come, gentlemen, I conform to Squire Bragg, and invite you all to follow me into the street."

As the lawn was now evacuated *en masse*, Aristabulus proceeded with alacrity, to the house, and went into the library, where Mr Effingham was patiently waiting his return.

"I am happy to inform you, sir," commenced the ambassador, "that the ball players have adjourned, and as for Mr Lather, he declines your proposition."

"Declines my proposition!"

"Yes, sir; he dislikes to come, for he thinks it will be altogether a poor operation. His notion is, that if it be worth his while to come up to the Wigwam to cut your hair, it may be worth your while to go down to the shop, to have it cut. Considering the matter in all its bearings, therefore, he concludes he would rather not engage in the transaction at all."

"I regret, sir, to have consented to your taking so disagreeable a commission, and regret it the more, now I find that the barber is disposed to be troublesome."

"Not at all, sir. Mr Lather is a good man, in his way, and particularly neighborly. By the way, Mr Effingham, he asked me to propose to let him take down your garden fence, in order that he may haul some manure on his potatoe patch, which wants it dreadfully, he says."

"Certainly, sir. I cannot possibly object to his hauling his manure, even through this house, should he wish it. He is so very valuable a citizen, and one who knows his own business so well, that I am only surprised at the moderation of his request."

Here Mr Effingham rose, rang the bell for Pierre, and went to his own room, doubting, in his own mind, from all that he had seen, whether this was really the Templeton he had known in his youth, and whether he was in his own house or not.

As for Aristabulus, who saw nothing out of rule, or contrary to his own notions of propriety in what had passed, he hurried off to tell the barber, who was so ignorant of the first duty of his trade, that he was at liberty to pull down Mr Effingham's fence, in order to manure his own potatoe patch.

Lest the reader should suppose we are drawing caricatures, instead of representing an actual condition of society, it may be necessary to explain that Mr Bragg was a standing candidate for popular favor, that, like Mr Dodge, he considered every thing that presented itself in the name of the public, as sacred and paramount, and that so general and positive was his deference for majorities, that it was the bias of his mind to think half a dozen always in the right, as opposed to one, although that one, agreeably to the great decision of the real majority of the entire community, had not only the law on his side, but all the abstract merits of the disputed question. In short, to such a pass of freedom had Mr Bragg, in common with a large class of his countrymen, carried his notions, that he had really begun to imagine liberty was all means and no end.

CHAPTER XII.

"In sooth, thou wast in very gracious fooling last night, when thou spok'st of Pigrogromitus, of the Vapians passing the equinoctial of Queubus. 'Twas very good, i' faith."

Twelfth Night 2.3.22–25.

IT has just been said, that the progress of society in what is termed a "new country," is a little anomalous. At the commencement of a settlement, there is much of that sort of kind feeling and mutual interest, which men are apt to manifest towards each other, when they are embarked in an enterprise of common hazards. The distance that is unavoidably inseparable from education, habits and manners, is lessened by mutual wants and mutual efforts, and the gentleman, even while he may maintain his character and station, maintains them with that species of good-fellowship and familiarity, that mark the intercourse between the officer and the soldier, in an arduous campaign. Men, and even women, break bread together, and otherwise commingle, that, in different circumstances, would be strangers, the hardy adventures and rough living of the forest, apparently lowering the pretensions of the man of cultivation and mere mental resources, to something very near the level of those of the man of physical energy, and manual skill. In this rude intercourse, the parties meet, as it might be, on a sort of neutral ground, one yielding some of his superiority, and the other laying claim to an outward show of equality, that he secretly knows, however, is the result of the peculiar circumstances in which he is placed. In short, the state of society is favorable to the claims of mere animal force, and unfavorable to those of the higher mental qualities.

This period may be termed, perhaps, the happiest of the first century of a settlement. The great cares of life are so engrossing and serious, that small vexations are overlooked, and the petty grievances that would make us seriously uncomfortable, in a more regular state of society, are taken as matters of course, or laughed at, as the regular and expected incidents of the day. Good will abounds; neighbor comes cheerfully to the aid of neighbor; and life has much of the reckless gaiety, careless association, and buoyant merriment of childhood. It is found that they who have passed through this probation, usually look back to it with regret, and are fond of dwelling on the rude scenes, and ridiculous events that distinguish the history of a new settlement, as the hunter is known to pine for the forest.

To this period of fun, toil, neighborly feeling and adventure, succeeds another in which society begins to marshall itself, and the ordinary passions have sway. Now it is, that we see the struggles for place, the heart-burnings and jealousies of contending families, and the influence of mere money. Circumstances have probably established the local superiority of a few beyond all question, and the condition of these serves as a goal for the rest to aim at. The learned professions, the ministry included, or, what, by courtesy are so called, take precedence, as a matter of course, next to wealth, however, when wealth is at all supported by appearances. Then commence those gradations of social station, that set institutions at defiance, and which as necessarily follow civilization, as tastes and habits are a consequence of indulgence.

This is, perhaps, the least inviting condition of society that belongs to any country that can claim to be free and removed from barbarism. The tastes are too uncultivated to exercise any essential influence, and when they do exist, it is usually with the pretension and effort that so commonly accompany infant knowledge. The struggle is only so much the more severe, in consequence of the late *pêle mêle* while men lay claim to a consideration that would seem beyond their reach, in an older and more regulated community. It is during this period that manners suffer the most, since they want the nature and feeling of the first condition, while they are exposed to the rudest assaults of the coarse-minded and vulgar, for as men usually defer to a superiority that is long established, there being a charm about antiquity that is sometimes able to repress even the passions, in older communities the marshalling of time quietly regulates what is here the subject of strife. What has just been said, depends on a general and natural principle, perhaps, but the state of society we are describing has some features peculiar to itself. The civilization of America, even in those older districts, that supply the emigrants to the newer regions, is unequal; one state possessing a higher level than another. Coming, as it does, from different parts of this vast country, the population of a new settlement, while it is singularly homogenous for the circumstances, necessarily brings with it these local peculiarities. If to such elements there be added a sprinkling of Europeans of various nations and conditions, the effects of the commingling, and the temporary social struggles that follow, will occasion no surprise.

The third and last condition of society in a "new country," is that in which the influence of the particular causes enumerated ceases, and men and things come within the control of more general and regular laws. The effect, of course, is to leave the community in possession of a civilization that conforms to that of the whole region, be it higher or be it lower, and with a division into castes, that is more or less rigidly maintained, according to circumstances.

The periods, as the astronomers call the time taken in a celestial revolution, of the two first of these epochs in the history of a settlement, depend very much on its advancement in wealth and in numbers. In some places, the pastoral age, or that of good fellowship, continues for a whole life, to the obvious retrogression of the people, in most of the higher qualities, but to their manifest advantage, however, in the pleasures of the time being; while, in others, it passes away rapidly, like the buoyant animal joys, that live their time between fourteen and twenty.

The second period is usually of longer duration, the migratory habits of the American people, keeping society more unsettled than might otherwise prove to be the case. It may be said never to cease entirely, until the great majority of the living generation are natives of the region, knowing no other means of comparison than those under which they have passed their days. Even, when this is the case, there is commonly so large an infusion of the birds of passage, men who are adventurers in quest of advancement, and who live without the charities of a neighborhood, as they may be said almost to live without a home, that there is to be found, for a long time, a middle state of society, during which it may well be questioned whether a community belongs to the second, or to the third of the periods named.

Templeton was properly in this equivocal condition, for while the third generation of the old settlers were in active life, so many passers by, came and went, that their influence nearly neutralized that of time and the natural order of things. Its population was pretty equally divided between the descendants of the earlier inhabitants, and those who flitted like swallows and other migratory birds. All of those who had originally entered the region in the pride of manhood, and had been active in converting the wilderness into the abodes of civilized men, if they had not, in a physical sense, been literally gathered to their fathers, had been laid, the first of their several races, beneath those sods that were to cover the heads of so many of their descendants. A few still remained, among those who entered the wilderness in young manhood, but the events of the first period we have designated, and which we have imperfectly recorded in another work, were already passing into tradition. Among these original settlers, some portion of the feeling that had distinguished their earliest communion with their neighbors yet continued, and one of their greatest delights was to talk of the hardships and privations of their younger days, as the veteran loves to discourse of his marches, battles, sieges, and scars. It would be too much to say that these persons viewed the more ephemeral part of the population with distrust, for familiarity with changes accustomed them to new faces, but they had a secret inclination for each other, preferred those who could enter sincerely into their own feelings, and naturally loved that communion best, where they found the most sympathy. To this fragment of the community belonged nearly all there was to be found of that sort of sentiment which is connected with locality; adventure, with them, supplying the place of time; while, the natives of the spot, wanting in the recollections that had so many charms for their fathers, were not yet brought sufficiently within the influence of traditionary interest, to feel that hallowed sentiment in its proper force. As opposed in feeling, to these relics of the olden time, were the birds of passage, so often named, a numerous and restless class that, of themselves, are almost sufficient to destroy whatever there is of poetry or of local attachment, in any region where they resort.

In Templeton, and its adjacent district, however, the two hostile influences might be said to be nearly equal, the descendants of the fathers of the country, beginning to make a manly stand against the looser sentiments, or the want of sentiment, that so singularly distinguishes the migratory bands. The first did begin to consider the temple in which their fathers had worshipped more hallowed than strange altars, the sods that covered their fathers' heads, more sacred than the clods that were upturned by the plough, and the places of their childhood and childish sports, dearer than the highway trodden by a nameless multitude.

Such, then, were the elements of the society into which we have now ushered the reader, and with which it will be our duty to make him better acquainted, as we proceed in the regular narration of the incidents of our tale.

The return of the Effinghams after so long an absence, naturally produced a sensation in so small a place, and visiters began to appear in the Wigwam, as soon as propriety would allow. Many false rumours prevailed, quite as a matter of course, and Eve, it was reported, was on the point of being married to no less than three of the inmates of her father's house, within the first ten days, viz, Sir George Templemore, Mr Powis, and Mr Bragg; the latter story taking its rise, in some precocious hopes that had escaped the gentleman himself, in the "excitement" of helping to empty a bottle of bad Breton wine that was dignified with the name of champaigne. But these tales revived and died so often, in a state of society in which matrimony is so general a topic with the young of the gentler sex, that they brought with them their own refutation.

The third day, in particular, after the arrival of our party, was a reception day, at the Wigwam, the gentlemen and ladies making it a point to be at home and disengaged, after twelve o'clock, in order to do honor to their guests. One of the first who made his appearance was a Mr Howel, a bachelor of about the same age as Mr Effingham, and a man of easy fortune and quiet habits. Nature had done more towards making Mr Howel a gentleman, than either cultivation, or association, for he had passed his entire life, with very immaterial exceptions, in the valley of Templeton, where, without being what could be called a student, or a scholar, he had dreamed away his existence in an indolent communication with the current literature of the day. He was fond of reading, and being indisposed to contention, or activity of any sort, his mind had admitted the impressions of what he perused, as the stone receives a new form by the constant fall of drops of water. Unfortunately for Mr. Howel, he understood no language but his mother tongue, and, as all his reading was necessarily confined to English books, he had gradually, and unknown to himself, in his moral nature at least, got to be a mere reflection of those opinions, prejudices and principles, if such a word can properly be used for such a state of the mind, that it had suited the interests or passions of England to promulgate by means of the press. A perfect *bonne foi* prevailed in all his notions, and, though a modest man by nature, so very certain was he his authority was always right, that he was a little apt to be dogmatical on such points as he thought his authors appeared to treat as settled. Between John Effingham and Mr Howel, there were constant amicable skirmishes in the way of discussion, for, while the latter was so dependant, limited in knowledge by unavoidable circumstances, and disposed to an innocent credulity, the first was original in his views, accustomed to see and think for himself, and, moreover, a little apt to estimate his own advantages, at their full value.

"Here comes our good neighbor, and my old school fellow, Tom Howel," said Mr Effingham, looking out at a window, and perceiving the person mentioned crossing the little lawn in front of the house, by following a winding foot-path—, "as kind hearted a man, Sir George Templemore, as exists; one who is really American, for he has scarcely quitted the county half a dozen times in his life, and one of the honestest fellows of my acquaintance."

"Ay," put in John Effingham, "as real an American as any man can be, who uses English spectacles for all he looks at, English opinions for all he says, English prejudices for all he condemns, and an English palate for all he tastes. American, quotha!—The man is no more American than the Times' news paper, or Charing Cross! He actually made a journey to New York, last war, to satisfy himself with his own eyes, that a Yankee frigate had really brought an Englishman into port."

"His English predilections will be no fault in my eyes," said the baronet, smiling—"and I dare say we shall be excellent friends."

"I am sure Mr Howel is a very agreeable man," added Grace—"of all in your Templeton *côterie*, he is my greatest favorite."

"Oh! I foresee a tender intimacy between Templemore and Howel—" rejoined John Effingham, "and sundry wordy wars between the latter and Miss Effingham."

"In this you do me injustice, cousin Jack. I remember Mr Howel well, and kindly; for he was ever wont to indulge my childish whims, when a girl."

"The man is a second Burchell, and, I dare say, never came to the Wigwam when you were a child, without having his pockets stuffed with cakes, or *bon bons*."

The meeting was cordial, Mr Howel greeting the gentlemen like a warm friend, and expressing great delight at the personal improvements that had been made in Eve, between the ages of eight and twenty. John Effingham was no more backward than the others, for he, too, liked their simple minded, kind-hearted, but credulous neighbor.

"You are welcome back—you are welcome back—" added Mr Howel, blowing his nose, in order to conceal the tears that were gathering in his eyes. "I did think of going to New-York to meet you, but the distance at my time of life is very serious. Age, gentlemen, seems to be a stranger to you."

"And yet we, who are both a few months older than yourself, Howel," returned Mr Effingham, kindly, "have managed to overcome the distance you have just mentioned, in order to come and see *you!*"

"Ay, you are great travellers, gentlemen, very great travellers, and are accustomed to motion. Been quite as far as Jerusalem, I hear!"

"Into its very gates, my good friend, and I wish, with all my heart, we had had you in our company. Such a journey might cure you of the home-malady."

"I am a fixture, and never expect to look upon the ocean, now. I did, at one period of my life, fancy such an event might happen, but I have finally abandoned all hope on that subject. Well, Miss Eve, of all the countries in which you have dwelt, to which do you give the preference?"

"I think Italy is the general favorite," Eve answered, with a friendly smile; "although there are some agreeable things peculiar to almost every country."

"Italy!—Well that astonishes me, a good deal! I never knew there was any thing particularly interesting about Italy! I should have expected *you* to say, England."

"England is a fine country too, certainly, but it wants many things that Italy enjoys."

"Well, now, what?" said Mr Howel, shifting his legs from one knee to the other, in order to be more convenient to listen, or, if necessary, to object. "What *can* Italy possess, that England does not enjoy in a still greater degree?"

"Its recollections, for one thing, and all that interest which time and great events throw around a region."

"And is England wanting in recollections and great events? Are there not the Conqueror; or, if you will, King Alfred; and Queen Elizabeth, and Shakspeare—think of Shakspeare, my dear young lady—and Sir Walter Scott, and the Gun Powder Plot; and Cromwell—Oliver Cromwell, my dear Miss Eve—and Westminster Abbey, and London Bridge, and George IVth the descendant of a line of real kings,—what in the name of Heaven, can Italy possess, to equal the interest one feels in such things as these!"

"They are very interesting no doubt," said Eve, endeavoring not to smile, "but Italy has its relics of former ages, too; you forget the Cæsars."

"Very good sort of persons for barbarous times, I dare say, but what can they be to the English monarchs? I would rather look upon a *bonâ fide* English King, than see all the Cæsars that ever set fire to Rome. I never can think any man a real king, but the King of England."

"Not King Solomon!" cried John Effingham.

"Oh! he was a bible king, and one never thinks of them. Italy! Well, this I did not expect from your father's daughter! Your great-great-great-grandfather, must have been an Englishman born, Mr Effingham?"

"I have reason to think he was, sir."

"And Milton, and Dryden, and Newton, and Locke! These are prodigious names, and worth all the Cæsars put together. And Pope, too; what have they got in Italy, to compare to Pope?"

"They have at least *the* Pope," said Eve, laughing.

"And, then, there are the Boar's Head in East-Cheap; and the Tower; and Queen Anne and all the wits of her reign, and—and—and Titus Oates; and Bosworth Field, and Smithfield, where the martyrs were burned, and a thousand more spots and persons of intense interest in Old England!"

"Quite true," said John Effingham, with an air of sympathy— "but, Howel, you have forgotten Peeping Tom of Coventry, and the climate!"

"And Holyrood-house, and York Minster, and St Paul's," continued the worthy Mr Howel, too much bent on a catalogue of excellencies, that to him was sacred, to heed the interruption, "and, above all, Windsor Castle. What is there, in the world, to equal Windsor Castle, as a royal residence!"

Want of breath now gave Eve an opportunity to reply, and she seized it, with an eagerness that she was the first to laugh at herself, afterwards.

"Caserta is no mean house, Mr Howel, and, in my poor judgment, there is more real magnificence in its great stair case, than in all Windsor Castle united, if you except the chapel."

"But, St. Paul's!"

"Why, St. Peter's may be set down, quite fairly, I think, for its *pendant*, at least."

"True, the catholics *do* say so—" returned Mr Howel, with the deliberation one uses, when he greatly distrusts his own concession; "but I have always considered it one of their frauds. I don't think there *can* be any thing finer than St. Paul's. Then there are the noble ruins of England! *They* you must admit, are unrivalled."

"The Temple of Neptune, at Pæstum, is commonly thought an interesting ruin, Mr Howel."

"Yes, yes, for a *temple*, I dare say, though I do not remember to have ever heard of it before. But no temple can ever compare to a ruined *abbey*!"

"Taste is an arbitrary thing, Tom Howel, as you and I know when as boys we quarrelled about the beauty of our ponies," said Mr Effingham, willing to put an end to a discussion that he thought a little premature, after so long an absence. "Here are two young friends who shared the hazards of our late passage with us, and to whom, in a great degree, we owe our present happy security, and I am anxious to make you acquainted with them. This is our countryman Mr Powis, and this is an English friend, who, I am certain, will be happy to know so warm an admirer of his own country,—Sir George Templemore."

Mr Howel had never before seen a titled Englishman, and he was taken so much by surprise that he made his salutations rather awkwardly. As both the young men, however, met him with the respectful ease that denotes familiarity with the world, he soon recovered his self-possession.

"I hope you have brought back with you a sound American heart, Miss Eve," resumed the guest, as soon as this little interruption had ceased. "We have had sundry rumours of French Marquisses, and German Barons, but I have, all along, trusted too much to your patriotism to believe you would marry a foreigner."

"I hope you except Englishmen," cried Sir George, gaily: "we are almost the same people."

"I am proud to hear you say so, sir. Nothing flatters me more than to be thought English, and I certainly should not have accused Miss Effingham of a want of love of country had—"

"She married half a dozen English men," interrupted John Effingham, who saw that the old theme was in danger of being revived. "But, Howel, you have paid me no compliments on the changes in the house. I hope they are to your taste."

"A little too French, Mr John."

"French!—There is not a French feature in the whole animal. What has put such a notion into your head?"

"It is the common opinion, and I confess I should like the building better were it less continental."

"Why, my old friend, it is a non-descript-original—Effingham upon Doolittle, if you will; and, as for models, it is rather more *English* than any thing else."

"Well, Mr John; I am glad to hear this, for I do confess to a disposition rather to like the house. I am dying to know, Miss Eve, if you saw all our distinguished contemporaries when in Europe?—*that* to me, would be one of the greatest delights of travelling!"

"To say that we saw them *all*, might be too much; though we certainly did meet with many."

"Scott, of course."

"Sir Walter we had the pleasure of meeting, a few times, in London."

"And Southey, and Coleridge, and Wordsworth, and Moore, and Bulwer, and D'Israeli, and Rogers and Campbell, and the grave of Byron, and Horace Smith, and Miss Landon, and Barry Cornwall, and—"

"*Cum multis aliis,*" put in John Effingham, again, by way of arresting the torrent of names. "Eve saw many of these, and, as Tubal told Shylock, 'we often came where we did hear' of the rest. But you say nothing, friend Tom, of Goethe, and Tieck, and Schlegel, and la Martine, Chateaubriant, Hugo, Delavigne, Mickiewicz, Nota, Manzoni, Niccolini, &c. &c. &c. &c. &c. &c."

Honest, well-meaning Mr Howel listened to the catalogue that the other ran volubly over, in silent wonder, for, with the exception of one or two of these distinguished men, he had never even heard of them, and, in the simplicity of his heart, unconsciously to himself, he had got to believe that there was no great personage still living of whom he did not know something, or who did not pass most of his time in England.

"Ah, here comes young Wenham, by way of preserving the equilibrium," resumed John Effingham, looking out of a window— "I rather think you must have forgotten him, Ned, though you remember his father, beyond question."

Mr. Effingham and his cousin went out into the hall to receive the new guest, with whom the latter had become acquainted while superintending the repairs of the Wigwam.

Mr Wenham was the son of a successful lawyer in the county, and, being an only child, he had also succeeded to an easy independence. His age, however, brought him rather into the generation to which Eve belonged, than into that of the father, and, if Mr Howel was a reflection, or rather a continuation, of all the provincial notions that America entertained of England, forty years ago, Mr Wenham might almost be said to belong to the opposite school, and to be as ultra American, as his neighbor was ultra British. If there is *la Jeune France*, there is also *la Jeune Amérique*, although the votaries of the latter march with less hardy steps, than the votaries of the first. Mr Wenham fancied himself a paragon of national independence, and was constantly talking of American excellencies, though the ancient impressions still lingered in his moral system, as men, in after life, look askance for the ghosts which frightened their childhood, on crossing a church yard in the dark. John Effingham knew the *penchant* of the young man, and when he said that he came happily to preserve the equilibrium, he alluded to this striking difference in the characters of their two friends.

The introductions and salutations over, we shall resume the conversation, that succeeded in the drawing-room.

"You must be much gratified, Miss Effingham," observed Mr Wenham, who, like a true American, being a young man himself, supposed it *de rigueur* to address a young lady, in preference to any other person present, "with the great progress made by our country, since you went abroad."

Eve simply answered that her extreme youth when she left home, had prevented her from retaining any precise notions on such subjects.

"I dare say, it is all very true," she added, "but one, like myself, who remembers only older countries, is, I think, a little more apt to be struck with the deficiencies, than with what may, in truth, be improvements, though they still fall short of excellence."

Mr Wenham looked vexed, or indignant would be a better word, perhaps; but he succeeded in preserving his coolness, a thing that is not always easy to one of provincial habits and provincial education when he finds his own *beau idéal* lightly estimated by others.

"Miss Effingham must discover a thousand imperfections in this country," said Mr Howel, "coming, as she does, directly from England—That music, now—" alluding to the sounds of a flute that were heard through the open windows, issuing from a room in the adjacent village—"must be rude enough to her ear, after the music of London."

"The *street* music of London is certainly among the best, if not the very best, in Europe," returned Eve, with a glance of the eye at the Baronet, that caused him to smile, "and I think this fairly belongs to the class, being so freely given to the neighborhood."

"Have you read the articles signed Minerva, in the Hebdomad, Miss Effingham," inquired Mr Wenham, who was determined to try the young lady on a point of sentiment, having succeeded so ill in his first attempt to interest her—"they are generally thought to be a great acquisition to American Literature."

"Well, Wenham, you are a fortunate man," interposed Mr Howel, "if you can find any literature in America, to add to, or to substract from. Beyond almanacks, reports of cases badly got up, and newspaper verses, I know nothing that deserves such a name."

"We may not print on as fine paper, Mr Howel, or do up the books in as handsome binding as other people," said Mr Wenham, bridling and looking grave, "but so far as sentiments are concerned, or sound sense, American literature need turn its back, on no literature of the day."

"By the way, Mr Effingham, you were in Russia; did you happen to see the Emperor?"

"I had that pleasure, Mr Howel."

"And is he really the monster we have been taught to believe him?"

"Monster!" exclaimed the upright Mr Effingham, fairly recoiling a step in surprise. "In what sense a monster, my worthy friend; surely not in a physical!"

"I do not know that. I have somehow got the notion he is any thing but handsome. A mean, butchering, bloody minded looking little chap, I'll engage."

"You are libelling one of the finest men of the age."

"I think I would submit it to a jury. I cannot believe, after what I have read of him in the English publications, that he is so very handsome."

"But, my good neighbor, these English publications must be wrong; prejudiced perhaps, or even malignant."

"Oh! I am not the man to be imposed on, in that way. Besides, what motive could an English writer have for belying an Emperor of Russia?"

"Sure enough, what motive!" exclaimed John Effingham.—"You have your answer, Ned!"

"But you will remember, Mr Howel," Eve interposed, "that we have *seen* the Emperor Nicholas."

"I dare say, Miss Eve, that your gentle nature was disposed to judge him as kindly as possible; and, then, I think most Americans, ever since the treaty of Ghent, have been disposed to view all Russians too favorably. No, no; I am satisfied with the account of the English; they live much nearer to St. Petersburg than we do, and they are more accustomed, too, to give accounts of such matters."

"But living nearer, Tom Howel," cried Mr Effingham, with unusual animation, "in such a case, is of no avail, unless one lives near enough to see with his own eyes."

"Well—well—my good friend, we will talk of this another time. I know your disposition to look at every body with lenient eyes. I will now wish you all a good morning, and hope soon to see you again. Miss Eve, I have one word to say, if you dare trust yourself with a youth of fifty, for a minute in the library."

Eve rose cheerfully, and led the way to the room her father's visiter had named. When within it, Mr. Howel shut the door carefully, and then with a sort of eager delight, he exclaimed—

"For heaven's sake, my dear young lady, tell me who are these two strange gentlemen in the other room."

"Precisely the persons my father mentioned, Mr Howel; Mr Paul Powis, and Sir George Templemore."

"Englishmen, of course!"

"Sir George Templemore is, of course, as you say; but we may boast of Mr Powis as a countryman."

"Sir George Templemore!—What a superb looking young fellow!"

"Why, yes," returned Eve, laughing, "he, at least, you will admit is a handsome man."

"He is wonderful!—The other, Mr—a—a—a—I forget what you called him—he is pretty well too; but this Sir George is a princely youth."

"I rather think a majority of observers, would give the preference to the appearance of Mr Powis," said Eve, struggling to be steady, but permitting a blush to heighten her colour, in despite of the effort.

"What could have induced him to come up among these mountains—an English baronet!" resumed Mr. Howel, without thinking of Eve's confusion. "Is he a real lord?"

"Only a little one, Mr Howel. You heard what my father said of our having been fellow travellers."

"But what *does* he think of us. I am dying to know what such a man *really* thinks of us?"

"It is not always easy to discover what such men *really* think; although I am inclined to believe that he is disposed to think rather favorably of some of us."

"Ay, of you, and your father, and Mr John. You have travelled, and are more than half European; but what *can* he think of those who have never left America?"

"Even of some of those," returned Eve smiling, "I suspect he thinks partially."

"Well, I am glad of that. Do you happen to know his opinion of the Emperor Nicholas?"

"Indeed I do not remember to have heard him mention the Emperor's name; nor do I think he has ever seen him."

"That is extraordinary! Such a man should have seen every thing, and know every thing; but I'll engage, at the bottom, he does know all about him. If you happen to have any old English newspapers, as wrappers, or by any other accident, let me beg them of you. I care not how old they are. An English journal fifty years old, is more interesting than one of ours wet from the press."

Eve promised to send him a package, when they shook hands, and parted. As she was crossing the hall, to rejoin the party, John Effingham stopped her.

"Has Howel made proposals?" the gentleman inquired in an affected whisper.

"None, cousin Jack, beyond an offer to read the old English newspapers, I can send him."

"Yes, yes, Tom Howel will swallow all the nonsense that is *timbré à Londres.*"

"I confess a good deal of surprise at finding a respectable and intelligent man so weak minded as to give credit to such authorities, or to form his serious opinions on information derived from such sources."

"You may be surprised, Eve, at hearing so frank avowals of the weakness, but, as for the weakness itself, you are now in a country for which England does all the thinking, except on subjects that touch the current interests of the day."

"Nay, I will not believe this! If it were true, how came we independent of her—where did we get spirit to war against her."

"The man who has attained his majority is independent of his father's legal control, without being independent of the lessons he was taught when a child. The soldier sometimes mutinies, and after the contest is over, he is usually the most submissive man of the regiment."

"All this to me is very astonishing! I confess that a great deal has struck me unpleasantly, in this way, since our return; especially in ordinary society; but I never could have supposed it had reached the pass to which I see it existing, in our good neighbor Howel."

"You have witnessed one of the effects, in a matter of no great moment to ourselves; but, as time and years afford the means of observation and comparison, you will perceive the effects in matters of the last importance, in a national point of view. It is in human nature to undervalue the things with which we are familiar, and to form false estimates of those which are remote, either by time, or by distance. But go into the drawing room, and, in young Wenham, you will find one who fancies himself a votary of a new school, although his prejudices and mental dependance are scarcely less obvious than those of poor Tom Howel."

The arrival of more company, among whom were several ladies, compelled Eve to defer an examination of Mr Wenham's peculiarities to another opportunity. She found many of her own sex, whom she had left children, grown into womanhood, and not a few of them, at a period of life when they should be cultivating their physical and moral powers, already oppressed with the cares and feebleness that weigh so heavily on the young American wife.

CHAPTER XIII.

"Nay, we must longer kneel; I am a suitor."

Henry VIII 1.2.9.

THE Effinghams were soon regularly domesticated, and the usual civilities had been exchanged. Many of their old friends resumed their ancient intercourse, and some new acquaintances were made. The few first visits were, as usual, rather labored and formal, but things soon took their natural course, and, as the ease of country life, was the aim of the family, the temporary little bustle was quickly forgotten.

The dressing room of Eve, overlooked the lake, and, about a week after her arrival, she was seated in it, enjoying that peculiarly lady like luxury, which is to be found in the process of having another gently disposing of the hair. Annette wielded the comb, as usual, while Anne Sidley, who was unconsciously jealous that any one should be employed about her darling, even in this necessary manner, though so long accustomed to it, busied herself, in preparing the different articles of attire, that she fancied her young mistress might be disposed to wear that morning. Grace was also in the room, having escaped from the hands of her own maid, in order to look into one of those books which profess to give an account of the extraction and families of the higher classes of Great Britain; a copy of which Eve happened to possess, among a large collection of road books, *Almanacks de Gotha*, Court Guides, and other similar works that she had found it convenient to possess, as a traveller.

"Ah! here it is," said Grace, in the eagerness of one who is suddenly successful, after a long and vexatious search.

"Here is what, coz?"

Grace coloured, and she could have bitten her tongue for its indiscretion, but, too ingenuous to deceive, she reluctantly told the truth.

"I was merely looking for the account of Sir George Templemore's family; it is awkward to be domesticated with one, of whose family we are utterly ignorant."

"Have you found the name?"

"Yes; I see he has two sisters, both of whom are married, and a brother who is in the Guards. But—"

"But what, dear?"

"His title is not so *very* old."

"The title of no Baronet *can* be very old, the order, itself, having been instituted in the reign of James Ist."

"I did not know that. His ancestor was created a baronet in 1701, I see. Now, Eve—"

"Now, what, Grace?"

"We are both—" Grace would not confine the remark to herself— "we are both of older families than this! You have even a much higher English extraction, and I think I can claim for the Van Cortlandts more antiquity than one that dates from 1701!"

"No one doubts it, Grace, but what do you wish me to understand by this? Are we to insist on preceding Sir George, in going through a door?"

Grace blushed to the eyes, and yet she laughed, involuntarily.

"What nonsense! No one thinks of such things in America."

"Except at Washington, where, I am told 'Senators' ladies' do give themselves airs. But you are quite right, Grace; women have no rank in America, beyond their general social rank, as ladies or no ladies, and we will not be the first to set an example of breaking the rule. I am afraid our blood will pass for nothing, and that we must give place to the Baronet, unless, indeed, he recognizes the rights of the sex."

"You know I mean nothing so silly. Sir George Templemore does not seem to think of rank at all; even Mr Powis treats him, in all respects, as an equal, and Sir George seems to admit it to be right."

Eve's maid, at the moment, was twisting her hair, with the intention to put it up, but the sudden manner in which her young mistress turned to look at Grace, caused Annette to relinquish her grasp, and the shoulders of the beautiful and blooming girl were instantly covered with the luxuriant tresses.

"And why should *not* Mr Powis treat Sir George Templemore, as one every way his equal, Grace?" she asked, with an impetuosity unusual in one so trained in the forms of the world.

"Why, Eve, one is a baronet, and the other is but a simple gentleman."

Eve Effingham sat silent for quite a minute. Her little foot moved, and she had been carefully taught, too, that a lady-like manner, required that even this beautiful portion of the female frame should be quiet and unobtrusive. But America did not contain two of the same sex, years, and social condition, less alike in their opinions, or it might be said their prejudices, than the two cousins. Grace Van Cortlandt, of the best blood of her native land, had unconsciously imbibed, in childhood, the notions connected with hereditary rank, through the traditions of colonial manners, by means of novels, by hearing the vulgar reproached or condemned, for their obtrusion and ignorance, and too often justly reproached and condemned, and by the aid of her imagination, which contributed to throw a gloss and brilliancy over a state of things that singularly gains by distance. On the other hand, with Eve, every thing connected with such subjects was a matter of fact. She had been thrown early into the highest associations of Europe, she had not only seen royalty on its days of gala and representation, a mere raree show that is addressed to the senses, or purely an observance of forms that may possibly have their meaning, but which can scarcely be said to have their reasons, but she had lived long and intimately among the high born and great, and this, too, in so many different countries as to have destroyed the influence of the particular nation that has transmitted so many of its notions to America, as heir looms. By close observation, she knew that arbitrary and political distinctions made but little difference between men of themselves, and so far from having become the dupe of the glitter of life, by living so long within its immediate influence, she had learned to discriminate between the false and the real, and to perceive that which was truly respectable, and useful, and to know it from that which was merely arbitrary and selfish. Eve actually fancied that the position of an American gentleman might readily be—nay that it *ought* to be—the highest of all human stations, short of that of sovereigns. Such a man had no social superior in her eyes, with the exception of those who actually ruled, and this fact, she conceived, rendered him more than noble, as nobility is usually graduated. She had been accustomed to see her father and John Effingham moving in the best circles of Europe, respected for their information and independence, undistinguished by their manners, admired for their personal appearance, manly, courteous, and of noble bearing and principles, if not set apart from the rest of mankind by an arbitrary rule connected with rank. Rich, and possessing all the habits that properly mark refinement, of gentle extraction, of liberal attainments, walking abroad in the dignity of manhood, and with none between them and the Deity, Eve had learned to regard the gentlemen of her race as the equals in station of any of their European associates, and as the superiors of most, in every thing that is essential to true distinction. With her, even titular princes and dukes had no estimation, merely as princes and dukes, and, as her quick mind glanced over the long catalogue of artificial social gradations, and she found Grace actually attaching an importance to the equivocal and purely conventional station of an English baronet, a strong sense of the ludicrous connected itself with the idea.

"A simple gentleman, Grace!" she repeated slowly after her cousin; "and is not a simple gentleman; a simple *American* gentleman, the equal of any gentleman on earth—of a poor baronet, in particular?"

"Poor baronet, Eve!"

"Yes, dear, *poor* baronet; I know fully the extent and meaning of what I say. It is true, we do not know as much of Mr Powis' family," and here Eve's colour heightened, though she made a mighty effort to be steady and unmoved—"as we might; but, we know he is an *American*; that, at least, is something; and we see he is a gentleman; and what American gentleman, a real American gentleman, *can* be the inferior of an English baronet? Would your uncle, think you; would cousin Jack; proud, lofty-minded cousin Jack, think you, Grace, consent to receive so paltry a distinction as a baronetcy, were our institutions to be so far altered as to admit of such social classifications?"

"Why, what would they be, Eve, if not baronets?"

"Earls, Counts, Dukes, nay Princes! These are the designations of the higher classes of Europe and such titles, or those that are equivalent, would belong to the higher classes here."

"I fancy that Sir George Templemore would not be persuaded to admit all this!"

"If you had seen Miss Eve, surrounded and admired by Princes, as I have seen her, Miss Grace," said Anne Sidley, earnestly, "you would not think any simple Sir George, half good enough for her."

"Our good Nanny means, *a* Sir George," interrupted Eve, laughing, "and not *the* Sir George in question. But, seriously, dearest coz, it depends more on ourselves, and less on others, in what light they are to regard us, than is commonly supposed. Do you not know that there are families in America who, if disposed to raise any objections beyond those that are purely personal, would object to baronets, and the wearers of red ribbands as unfit matches for their daughters, on the ground of rank? What an absurdity would it be for *a* Sir George, or *the* Sir George either, to object to a daughter of a President of the United States for instance, on account of station, and yet I'll answer for it, *you* would think it no personal honour, if Mr Jackson had a son that he should propose to my dear father for you. Let us respect ourselves properly, take care to be truly ladies and gentlemen, and so far from titular rank's being necessary to us, before a hundred lustres are past, we shall bring all such distinctions into discredit; by showing that they are not necessary to any one important interest, or to true happiness and respectability any where."

"And do you not believe, Eve, that Sir George Templemore thinks of the difference in station, between us?"

"I cannot answer for that," said Eve, calmly. "The man is naturally modest; and, it is possible, when he sees that we belong to the highest social condition of a great country, he may regret that such has not been his own good fortune, in his native land; especially, Grace, since he has known *you*."

Grace blushed, looked pleased, delighted even, and yet surprised. It is unnecessary to explain the causes of the three first expressions of her emotions, but the last may require a short examination. Nothing but time and a change of circumstances, can ever raise a province, or a provincial town, to the independant state of feeling that so strikingly distinguishes a metropolitan country, or a capital. It would be as rational to expect that the tenants of the nursery should disregard the opinions of the drawing room, as to believe that the provincial should do all his own thinking. Political dependency, moreover, is much more easily thrown aside, than mental dependency. It is not surprising, therefore, that Grace Van Cortlandt, with her narrow associations, general notions of life, origin, and provincial habits, should be the very opposite of Eve in all that relates to independence of thought, on subjects like those that they were now discussing. Had Grace been a native of New England, even, she would have been less influenced by the mere social rank of the Baronet, than was actually the case, for, while the population of that part of the Union feels more of the general subserviency to Great Britain, than the population of any other portion of the republick, it probably feels less of it in this particular form, from the circumstance that its colonial habits were less connected with the aristocratical usages of the mother country. Grace was allied by blood, too, with the higher classes of England, as indeed was the fact with most of the old families among the New York gentry, and the traditions of her race came in aid of the traditions of her colony, to continue the profound deference she felt for an English title. Eve might have been equally subjected to the same feelings, had she not been removed into another sphere, at so early a period of life, where she imbibed the notions already mentioned; notions that were quite as effectually rooted in her moral system, as those of Grace herself could be in her own.

"This is a strange way of viewing the rank of a Baronet, Eve!" Grace exclaimed, as soon as she had a little recovered from the confusion caused by the personal allusion. "I greatly question, if you can induce Sir George Templemore to see his own position with your eyes."

"No, my dear, I think he will be much more likely to regard, not only that, but most other things, with the eyes of another person. We will now talk of more agreeable things, however, for I confess, when I do dwell on titles, I have a taste for the more princely appellations, and that a simple *chevalier*, can scarce excite a feeling—"

"Nay, Eve," interrupted Grace with spirit, "an *English* Baronet is noble; Sir George Templemore assured me that, as lately as last evening. The heralds, I believe, have quite recently established that fact to their own satisfaction."

"I am glad of it, dear," returned Eve, with difficulty refraining from gaping, "as it will be of great importance to them in their own eyes. At all events, I concede that Sir George Templemore, Knight or Baronet, big baron, or little baron, or rag baron, as they call it in this country, is a noble fellow, and what more can any reasonable person desire. Do you know, sweet coz, that the Wigwam will be full to overflowing next week?—That it will be necessary to light our Council Fire, and to smoke the pipe of many welcomes?"

"I have understood Mr Powis, that his kinsman Capt. Ducie will arrive on Monday."

"And Mrs Hawker will come on Tuesday, Mr and Mrs Bloomfield on Wednesday, and honest, brave, straight forward, literati-hating, segar-smoking Capt. Truck, on Thursday at the latest. We shall be a large country circle, and I hear the gentlemen talking of the boats, and other amusements. But, I believe my father has a consultation in the library, at which he wishes us to be present; we will now join him, if you please."

As Eve's toilette was completed, the two ladies rose, and descended together to join the party below. Mr Effingham was standing at a table that was covered with maps, while two or three respectable-looking men, master mechanics, were at his side. The manners of these men were quiet, civil, and respectful, having a mixture of manly simplicity with a proper deference for the years and station of the master of the house; and, yet, all but one, wore their hats! The one who formed the exception had become refined by a long intercourse with this particular family, and his acquired taste had taught him that respect for himself, as well as for decency, rendered it necessary to observe the long established rules of decorum, in his intercourse with others. His companions, though without a particle of coarseness, or any rudeness of intention, were less decorous, simply from a loose habit that is insensibly taking the place of the ancient laws of propriety in such matters, and which habit, it is to be feared, has a part of its origin in false and impracticable political notions, that have been stimulated by the arts of demagogues. Still, not one of these three hard-working, really civil, and even humane men, who now stood covered in the library of Mr Effingham, was probably conscious of the impropriety of which he was guilty, or was doing more than insensibly yielding to a vicious and vulgar practice.

"I am glad you have come, my love," said Mr Effingham, as his daughter entered the room, "for I find I need support in maintaining my own opinions, here. John is obstinately silent, and, as for all these other gentlemen, I fear they have decidedly taken sides against me."

"You can usually count on my support, dearest father, feeble as it may be; but, what is the disputed point, to-day?"

"There is a proposition to alter the interior of the church, and our neighbor Gouge has brought the plans on which, as he says, he has lately altered several churches in the county. The idea is to remove the pews entirely, converting them into what are called 'slips,' to lower the pulpit, and to raise the floor, amphitheatre fashion."

"Can there be a sufficient reason for this change?" demanded Eve, with surprise. "Slips! The word has a vulgar sound even, and savors of a useless innovation. I doubt its orthodoxy."

"It is very popular, Miss Eve," answered Aristabulus, advancing from a window, where he had been whispering apart. "This fashion takes universally, and is getting to prevail in all denominations."

Eve turned involuntarily, and to her surprise she perceived that the Editor of the Active Inquirer was added to their party. The salutations, on the part of the young lady, were distant and stately, while Mr Dodge, who had not been able to resist public opinion and had actually parted with his moustachies, simpered and wished to have it understood by the spectators, that he was on familiar terms with all the family.

"It may be popular, Mr Bragg," returned Eve, as soon as she rose from her profound curtsey to Mr Dodge, "but it can scarcely be said to be seemly. This is, indeed, changing the order of things, by elevating the sinner and depressing the saint."

"You forget, Miss Eve, that under the old plan, the people could not see; they were kept unnaturally down, if one can so express it, while nobody had a good look out, but the parson, and the singers in the front row of the gallery. This was unjust."

"I do not conceive, sir, that a 'good look-out,' as you term it, is at all essential to devotion, or that one cannot as well listen to instruction when beneath the teacher, as when above him."

"Pardon me, miss—" Eve recoiled, as she always did when Mr Bragg used this vulgar and contemptuous mode of address—"we put no-body up, or down; all we aim at is a just equality. We place all, as near as possible, on a level."

Eve gazed about her in wonder; and then she hesitated a moment, as if distrusting her ears.

"Equality! Equality with what? Surely not with the ordained ministers of the church, in the performance of their sacred duties! Surely not with the Deity!"

"We do not look at it exactly in this light, ma'am. The people build the church, *that* you will allow, Miss Effingham—even *you* will allow *this*, Mr Effingham."

Both the parties appealed to, bowed a simple assent to so plain a proposition, but neither spoke.

"Well, the people building the church, very naturally ask themselves for what purpose it was built?"

"For the worship of God—" returned Eve, with a steady solemnity that a little abashed even the ordinarily indomitable and self satisfied Aristabulus.

"Yes, miss, for the worship of God, and the accommodation of the public."

"Certainly," added Mr Dodge, "for the public accommodation, and for public worship," laying due emphasis on the adjectives.

"Father, you, at least, will never consent to this!"

"Not readily, my love. I confess it shocks all my notions of propriety, to see the sinner, even when he professes to be the most humble and penitent, thrust himself up ostentatiously, as if filled with his own self love, and self importance."

"You will allow, Mr Effingham," rejoined Aristabulus, "that churches are built to accommodate the public, as Mr Dodge has so well remarked."

"No, sir, they are built for the worship of God, as my daughter has so well remarked."

"Yes, sir, that, too, I grant you,—"

"As secondary to the main object, the public convenience, Mr Bragg unquestionably means," put in John Effingham, speaking for the first time that morning, on the subject, and with his usual point.

Eve turned quickly, and looked towards her kinsman. He was standing near the table, with folded arms, and his fine face expressed all the sarcasm and contempt that a countenance so singularly calm and gentleman like, could betray.

"Cousin Jack," she said earnestly, "this ought not to be."

"Cousin Eve, nevertheless, this will be."

"Surely not—surely not! Men can never so far forget appearances as to convert the temple of God, into a theatre, in which the convenience of the spectators is the one great object to be kept in view!"

"*You* have travelled, sir," said John Effingham, indicating by his eye that he addressed Mr Dodge in particular, "and must have entered places of worship in other parts of the world. Did not the simple beauty of the manner in which all classes, the great and the humble, the rich and the poor, kneel in a common humility before the altar, strike you agreeably, on such occasions, in Catholic countries in particular?"

"Bless me no, Mr John Effingham. I was disgusted at the meanness of their rites, and really shocked at the abject manner in which the people knelt on the cold damp stones, as if they were no better than beggars."

"And were they not beggars?" asked Eve, with almost a severity of tone—"Ought they not so to consider themselves, when petitioning for mercy of the one great and omnipotent God?"

"Why, Miss Effingham, the people *will* rule, and it is useless to pretend to tell *them* that they shall not have the highest seats in the church, as well as in the state. Really, I can see no ground why a parson should be raised above his parishioners. The new-order churches consult the public convenience, and place every body on a level, as it might be. Now, in old times a family was buried in its pew; it could neither see, nor be seen, and I can remember when I could just get a look of our clergyman's wig, for he was an old-school man, and, as for his fellow creatures, one might as well be praying in his own closet. I must say I am a supporter of liberty, if it be only in pews."

"I am sorry, Mr Dodge," answered Eve, mildly, "you did not extend your travels into the countries of the Musselmauns, where, most christian sects might get some useful notions concerning that part of worship, at least, that is connected with 'appearances.' There you would have seen no seats, but sinners bowing down, in a mass, on the cold stones, and all thoughts of cushioned pews, and drawing room conveniences, unknown. We protestants have not improved on our Catholic forefathers, in this respect, and the innovation of which you now speak, in my eyes, is an irreverent, almost a sinful invasion of the proprieties of the temple."

"Ah, Miss Eve, this comes from substituting forms for the substance of things!" exclaimed the editor. "For my part, I can say I was truly shocked with the extravagances I witnessed, in the way of worship, in most of the countries I visited. Would you think it, Mr Bragg; rational beings, real *bonâ fide*, living men and women, kneeling on the stone pavement, like so many camels in the Desert, ready to receive the burthens of their masters;"—Mr. Dodge loved to draw his images from the different parts of the world he had seen—"not a pew, not a cushion, not a single comfort that is suitable to a free and intelligent being, but every thing conducted in the most abject manner, as if accountable human souls were no better than so many mutes in a Turkish palace."

"You ought to mention this in the Active Inquirer," said Aristabulus.

"All in good time, sir; I have many things in reserve, among which I propose to give a few remarks (I dare say they will be very worthless ones) on the impropriety of a rational being's ever kneeling. To my notion, gentlemen and ladies, God never intended an American to kneel."

The respectable mechanics who stood around the table did not absolutely assent to this proposition, for one of them actually remarked that "he saw no great harm in a man's kneeling to the Deity," but they evidently inclined to the opinion that the new-school of pews was far better than the old.

"It always appears to me, Miss Effingham," said one, "that I hear and understand the sermon better, in one of the low pews, than in one of the old high-backed things, that look so much like pounds."

"But can you withdraw into yourself better, sir?—Can you more truly devote all your thoughts, with a suitable singleness of heart, to the worship of God?"

"You mean in the prayers, now, I rather conclude?"

"Certainly, sir, I mean in the prayers and the thanksgivings."

"Why we leave them pretty much to the parson, though I will own it is not quite as easy leaning on the edge of one of the new-school pews, as on one of the old. They are better for sitting, but not so good for leaning, but then the sitting posture at prayers, is quite coming into favour among our people, Miss Effingham, as well as among yours. The sermon is the main chance, after all."

"Yes," observed Mr Gouge, "give me good stirring preaching, any day, in preference to good praying. A man may get along with second rate prayers, but he stands in need of first-rate preaching."

"These gentlemen consider religion a little like a cordial on a cold day," observed John Effingham, "which is to be taken in sufficient doses to make the blood circulate. They are not the men to be *pounded* in pews, like lost sheep, not they."

"Mr John will always have his say," one remarked, and then Mr Effingham dismissed the party by telling them he would think of the matter.

When the mechanics were gone, the subject was discussed at some length between those that remained, all the Effinghams agreeing that they would oppose the innovation, as irreverent in appearance, unsuited to the retirement and self abasement that best comported with prayer, and opposed to the delicacy of their own habits; while Messrs Bragg and Dodge contended to the last, that such changes were loudly called for by the popular sentiment, that it was unsuited to the dignity of a man to be 'pounded' even in a church, and, virtually, that a good 'stirring' sermon, as they called it, was of far more account in public worship, than all the prayers and praises that could issue from the heart or throat.

CHAPTER XIV.

"We'll follow Cade, we'll follow Cade!"

2 Henry VI 4.8.33.

"THE views of this Mr Bragg, and of our old fellow traveller, Mr Dodge, on the subject of religious forms, appear to be peculiar," observed Sir George Templemore, as he descended the little lawn before the Wigwam, in company with the three ladies, Paul Powis, and John Effingham, on their way to the lake. "I should think it would be difficult to find another christian, who objects to kneeling at prayer."

"Therein you are mistaken, Templemore," answered Paul, "for this country, to say nothing of one particular sect which holds it in pious horror, is filled with them. Our worthy ancestors, like neophytes, ran into extremes on the subject of forms, as well as in other matters. When you go to Philadelphia, Miss Effingham, you will see an instance, of a most ludicrous nature—ludicrous, if there were not something painfully revolting mingled with it—of the manner in which men can strain at a gnat and swallow a camel, and which, I am sorry to say, is immediately connected with our own church."

It was music to Eve's ears, to hear Paul Powis speak of his "worthy ancestors" as having been Americans, and to find him so thoroughly identifying himself with her own native land; for, while condemning so many of its practices, and so much alive to its absurdities and contradictions, our heroine had seen too much of other countries, not to take an honest pride in the real excellencies of her own. There was, also, a soothing pleasure, in hearing him openly own that he belonged to that church which she herself so deeply reverenced.

"And what is there ridiculous, in Philadelphia in particular, and in connection with our own church?" she asked; "I am not so easily disposed to find fault when the venerable church is concerned."

"You know that the protestants, in their horror of idolatry, discontinued, in a great degree, the use of the cross, as an outward religious symbol, and that there was probably a time, when there was not a single cross to be seen in the whole of a country, that was settled by those who made the profession of love for Christ, and a dependence on his expiation, the great business of their lives?"

"Certainly, we all know our predecessors were a little over rigid and scrupulous on all the points connected with outward appearances."

"They certainly contrived to render the religious rites as little pleasing to the senses as possible, by aiming at a sublimation that peculiarly favors spiritual pride, and a pious conceit. I do not know whether travelling has had the same effect on you, as it has produced on me, but I find all my inherited antipathies to the mere visible representation of the cross, superseded by a sort of solemn affection for it, as a symbol, more particularly when it is plain, and unaccompanied by any of those bloody and minute accessories that are so often seen around it in catholic countries. The German protestants, who usually ornament the altar with a cross, first cured me of the disrelish I had imbibed for such things, in childhood."

"We also, I think, Cousin John, were agreeably struck with the same usage in Germany. From feeling a species of nervousness at the sight of a cross, I came to love to see it, and I think you must have undergone a similar change, for I have discovered no less than two among the ornaments of the great window of the entrance tower, at the Wigwam."

"You might have discovered one also, in every door of the building, whether great or small, young lady. Our worthy ancestors, as Powis calls them, much of whose piety, by the way, was any thing but meliorated with spiritual humility, or christian charity, were such ignoramuses as to set up crosses in every door they built, even while they veiled their eyes in holy horror, whenever the sacred symbol was seen in a church."

"Every door!" exclaimed the protestants of the party.

"Yea, literally, in every door, I might almost say; certainly in every pannelled door, that was constructed twenty years since. I first discovered the secret of our blunder, when visiting a castle in France, that dated back from the time of the crusades. It was a *château* of the Montmorencies, that had passed into the hands of the Condé family, by marriage; and the courtly old domestic who showed me the curiosities pointed out to me the stone *croix* in the windows, which has caused the latter to be called *croisées*, as a pious usage of the crusaders. Turning to a door, I saw the same crosses in the wooden stiles, and if you cast an eye on the first humble door that you may pass in this village, you will detect the same symbol staring you boldly in the face, in the very heart of a population that would almost expire, at the thought of placing such a sign of the beast, on their thresholds."

The whole party expressed their surprise, but the first door they passed corroborated this account, and proved the accuracy of John Effingham's statements. Catholic zeal and ingenuity could not have wrought more accurate symbols of this peculiar sign of the sect, and yet here they stood staring every passenger in the face, as if mocking the ignorant and exaggerated pretention which would lay undue stress on the minor points of a religion, the essence of which was faith and humility.

"And the Philadelphia church," said Eve, quickly, so soon as her curiosity was satisfied on the subject of the doors, "I am now more impatient than ever, to learn what silly blunder we have also committed there."

"Impious would almost be a better term," Paul answered. "The only church spire that existed for half a century in that town, was surmounted by a *mitre*, while the *cross* was studiously rejected!"

A silence followed, for there is often more true argument in simply presenting the facts of a case, than in all the rhetoric and logic that could be urged, in the way of auxiliaries. Every one saw the egregious folly, not to say presumption, of the mistake, and, at the moment, every one wondered how a common sense community could have committed it. We are mistaken; there was one exception to the general feeling in the person of Sir George Templemore. To his church and state notions, and anti-catholic prejudices, which were quite as much political as religious, there was every thing that was proper, and nothing that was wrong, in rejecting a cross for a mitre.

"The church, no doubt, was Episcopal, Powis," he remarked, "and it was not Roman. What better symbol than the mitre could be chosen?"

"Now, I reflect it is not so very strange," said Grace hastily, "for, you will remember, Mr Effingham, that protestants attach the idea of idolatry to the cross, as it is used by catholics."

"And of bishops, peers in parliament, church and state, to a mitre!"

"Yes, but the church in question I have seen, and it was erected before the war of the revolution. It was an English rather than an American church."

"It was, indeed, an English church, rather than an American, and Templemore is very right to defend it, mitre and all."

"I dare say a bishop officiated at its altar?"

"I dare say—nay, I know he did, and, I will add, he would rather that the mitre were two hundred feet in the air, than down on his own simple, white-haired, apostolical looking head. But enough of divinity for the morning; yonder is Tom with the boat, let us to our oars."

The party were now on the little wharf, that served as a village landing, and the boatman mentioned, lay off in waiting for the arrival of his fare. Instead of using him, however, the man was dismissed, the gentlemen preferring to handle the oars themselves. Aquatick excursions were of constant occurrence, in the warm months, on that beautifully limpid sheet of water, and it was the practice to dispense with the regular boatmen, whenever good oarsmen were to be found among the company.

As soon as the light buoyant skiff was brought to the side of the wharf, the whole party embarked; and Paul and the Baronet taking the oars, they soon urged the boat from the shore.

"The world is getting to be too confined for the adventurous spirit of the age," said Sir George, as he and his companion pulled leisurely along, taking the direction of the eastern shore, beneath the forest-clad cliffs, towards which the ladies had expressed a wish to be rowed; "here are Powis and myself actually rowing together on a mountain lake of America, after having boated as companions, on the coast of Africa, and on the margin of the Great Desert. Polynesia and Terra Australis may yet see us in company, as hardy cruisers."

"The spirit of the age, is, indeed, working wonders, in the way you mean," said John Effingham. "Countries of which our fathers merely read, are getting to be as familiar as our own houses, to their sons, and, with you, one can hardly foresee to what a pass of adventure the generation or two that will follow us, may not reach."

"*Vraiment, c'est fort extraordinaire de se trouver sur un lac américain!*" exclaimed Mademoiselle Viefville.

"More extraordinary than to find one's self on a Swiss lake, think you, my dear Mademoiselle Viefville?"

"*Non—non, mais tout aussi extraordinaire pour une Parisienne.*"

"I am now about to introduce you, Mr John Effingham and Miss Van Cortlandt excepted," Eve continued, "to the wonders and curiosities of this lake and region. There, near the small house, that is erected over a spring of delicious water, stood the hut of Natty Bumppo, once known throughout all these mountains as a renowned hunter, a man who had the simplicity of a woodsman, the heroism of a savage, the faith of a christian, and the feelings of a poet. A better than he, after his fashion, seldom lived."

"We have all heard of him," said the Baronet looking round curiously, "and must feel an interest in what concerns so brave and just a man. I would, I could see his counterpart."

"Alas!" said John Effingham, "the days of the 'Leatherstockings' have passed away. He preceded me in life, and I see few remains of his character, in a region where speculation is more rife than morality, and emigrants are plentier than hunters. Natty probably chose that spot for his hut, on account of the vicinity of the spring; is it not so, Miss Effingham?"

"He did; and yonder little fountain that you see gushing from the thicket, and which comes glancing like diamonds into the lake, is called the 'Fairy Spring,' by some flight of poetry, that, like so many of our feelings, must have been imported, for I see no connection between the name and the character of the country, fairies having never been known even by tradition, in Otsego."

The boat now came under a shore, where the trees fringed the very water, frequently overhanging the element that mirrored their fantastick forms. At this point a light skiff was moving leisurely along in their own direction, a short distance in advance. On a hint from John Effingham, a few vigorous strokes of the oars brought the two boats near each other.

"This is the flag ship," half whispered John Effingham, as they came near the other skiff, "containing no less a man than the 'commodore.' Formerly the chief of the Lake was an Admiral, but that was in times when, living nearer to the monarchy, we retained some of the European terms; now, no man rises higher than a Commodore in America, whether it be on the ocean or on the Otsego, whatever may be his merits or his services. A charming day, commodore; I rejoice to see you still afloat, in your glory."

The commodore, a tall, thin, athletic man of seventy, with a white head, and movements that were quick as those of a boy, had not glanced aside at the approaching boat, until he was thus saluted in the well known voice of John Effingham. He then turned his head, however, and scanning the whole party through his spectacles, he smiled good naturedly, made a flourish with one hand, while he continued paddling with the other, for he stood erect and straight in the stern of his skiff, and answered heartily—

"A fine morning, Mr John, and the right time of the moon for boating. This is not a real scientifick day for the fish, perhaps, but I have just come out to see that all the points and bays are in their right places."

"How is it, commodore, that the water near the village is less limpid than common, and that even up here, we see so many specks floating on its surface?"

"What a question for Mr John Effingham to ask on his native water! So much for travelling in far countries, where a man forgets quite as much as he learns, I fear." Here the commodore turned entirely round, and raising an open hand in an oratorical manner, he added—"You must know, ladies and gentlemen, that the lake is in blow."

"In blow, commodore; I did not know that the lake bore its blossoms!"

"It does, sir, nevertheless; ay, Mr John, and its fruits too; but the last must be dug for by those who have the knack. There have been no miraculous draughts of the fishes of late years, in the Otsego, ladies and gentlemen, but it needs the scientifick touch, and the knowledge of baits to get a fin of any of your true game above the water, now a days. Well, I have had the head of the sogdollager thrice in the open air, in my time, though I am told the admiral actually got hold of him once with his hand."

"The socdollager," said Eve, much amused with the singularities of the man, whom she perfectly remembered to have been commander of the lake, even in her own infancy; "we must be indebted to you for an explanation of that term, as well as for the meaning of your allusion to the head and to the open air."

"A sogdollager, young lady, is the perfection of a thing; I know Mr Grant, when he was alive, used to say there was no such word in the dictionary, but then there are many words that ought to be in the dictionaries, that have been forgotten by the printers. In the way of salmon trout, the sogdollager is their commodore. Now, ladies and gentlemen, I should not like to tell you all I know about the patriarch of this lake, for you would scarcely believe me, but if he would not weigh a hundred when cleaned, there is not an ox in the county that will weigh a pound on its legs!"

"You say you had his head above water?" said John Effingham.

"Thrice, Mr. John. The first time was thirty years ago, and I confess I lost him on that occasion, by want of science, for the art is not learned in a day, and I had then followed the business but ten years. The second time was five years later, and I had then been fishing expressly for the old gentleman, about a month. For near a minute it was a matter of dispute between us, whether he should come out of the lake, or I go into it, but I actually got his gills in plain sight. That was a glorious haul! Washington did not feel better the night Cornwallis surrendered, than I felt on that great occasion!"

"One never knows the feelings of another, it seems. I should have thought disappointment at the loss would have been the prevailing sentiment on that great occasion, as you so justly term it."

"So it would have been, Mr John, with an unscientifick fisherman, but we experienced hands know better. Glory is to be measured by quality, and not by quantity, ladies and gentlemen, and I look on it as a greater feather in a man's cap, to see the sogdollager's head above water, for half a minute, than to bring home a skiff filled with pickerel. The last time I had a look at the old gentleman, I did not try to get him into the boat, but we sat and conversed, for near two minutes, he in the water and I in the skiff."

"Conversed!" exclaimed Eve. "With a fish, too! What could the animal have to say!"

"Why, young lady, a fish can talk as well as one of ourselves; the only difficulty is to understand what he says. I have heard the old settlers affirm, that the Leatherstocking used to talk for hours at a time, with the animals of the forest, and even with the trees."

"You knew the Leatherstocking, commodore?"

"No, young lady, I am sorry to say I never had the pleasure of looking at him even. He *was* a great man! They may talk of their Jeffersons and Jacksons, but I set down Washington and Natty Bumppo as the two only really great men of my time."

"What do you think of Bonaparte, commodore?" inquired Paul.

"Well, sir, Bonaparte had some strong points about him, I do really believe. But he would have been nothing to the Leatherstocking in the woods! It's no great matter, young gentleman, to be a great man among your inhabitants of cities—what I call umbrella people. Why, Natty was almost as great with the spear, as with the rifle, though, I own, I never heard that he got a sight of the sogdollager."

"We shall meet again this summer, commodore," said John Effingham, "the ladies wish to hear the echoes, and we must leave you."

"All very natural, Mr John," returned the commodore laughing, and again flourishing his hand in his own peculiar manner. "The women all love to hear these echoes, for they are not often satisfied with what they have once said, but like to have it over again. I never knew a lady come on the Otsego water, but one of the first things she did was to get paddled to the Speaking Rocks, to have a chat with herself. They come out in such numbers, sometimes, and then all talk at once, in a way to confuse the echo. I suppose you have heard, young lady, the opinion people have now got, concerning these voices?"

"I cannot say I have ever heard more than that they are some of the most perfect echoes known," answered Eve, turning her body, so as to face the old man, as the skiff of the party passed that of the veteran fisherman.

"Some people maintain that there is no echo at all, and that the sounds we hear come from the spirit of the Leatherstocking, which keeps about its old haunts, and repeats every thing we say, in mockery of our ignorance, and as a taunt for our invasion of the woods. I do not say this notion is true, or that it is my own, but we all know that Natty *did* dislike to see a new settler arrive in the mountains, and that he loved a tree as much as a muskrat loves water. They show a pine up, here, on the side of the Vision, which he notched at every new comer, until reaching seventeen his honest old heart could go no farther, and he gave the matter up, in despair."

"This is so poetical, commodore, it is a pity it cannot be true. I like this explanation of the 'Speaking Rocks,' much better than that implied by the name of 'Fairy Spring.'"

"You are quite right, young lady," called out the fisherman, as the boats separated still farther; "there never was any fairy known in Otsego, but the time has been when we could boast of a Natty Bumppo."

Here the commodore flourished his hand, again, and Eve nodded her adieus. The skiff of the party continued to pull slowly along the fringed shore, occasionally sheering more into the lake to avoid some overhanging and nearly horizontal tree, and then returning so closely to the land as barely to clear the pebbles of the narrow strand with the oar. Eve thought she had never beheld a more wild, or beautifully variegated foliage, than that which the whole leafy mountain-side presented. More than half the forest of tall, solemn pines, that had veiled the earth when the country was first settled, had already disappeared, but, agreeably to one of the mysterious laws by which nature is governed, a vigorous second growth, that included nearly every variety of American wood, had shot up in their places. The rich Rembrandt-like hemlocks, in particular, were perfectly beautiful, contrasting admirably with the livelier tints of the various deciduous trees. Here and there, some flowering shrub, rendered the picture gay, while masses of the rich chestnut, in blossom, lay in clouds of natural glory, among the dark tops of the pines.

The gentlemen pulled the light skiff fully a mile under this overhanging foliage, occasionally frightening some migratory bird from a branch, or a water-fowl from the narrow strand. At length John Effingham desired them to cease rowing, and managing the skiff, for a minute or two, with the paddle which he had used in steering, he desired the whole party to look up, announcing to them, that they were beneath the "Silent Pine."

A common exclamation of pleasure succeeded the upward glance, for it is seldom that a tree is seen to more advantage, than that which immediately attracted every eye. The pine stood on the bank, with its roots embedded in the earth a few feet higher than the level of the lake, but in such a situation as to bring the distance above the water into the apparent height of the tree. Like all of its kind, that grow in the dense forests of America, its increase, for a thousand years, had been upward, and it now stood in solitary glory, a memorial of what the mountains which were yet so rich in vegetation, had really been in their days of pride. For near a hundred feet above the eye, the even round trunk was branchless, and then commenced the dark green masses of foliage, which clung around the stem, like smoke ascending in wreaths. The tall, column-like tree, had inclined towards the light, when struggling among its fellows, and it now so far overhung the lake, that its summit may have been some ten or fifteen feet without the base. A gentle, graceful curve added to the effect of this variation from the perpendicular, and infused enough of the fearful with the grand, to render the picture sublime. Although there was not a breath of wind on the lake, the currents were strong enough above the forest to move this lofty object, and it was just possible to detect a slight, graceful yielding of the very uppermost bows to the passing air.

"This pine is ill named," cried Sir George Templemore, "for it is the most eloquent tree eye of mine has ever looked on!"

"It is indeed eloquent," answered Eve; "one hears it speak, even now, of the fierce storms that have whistled round its top, of the seasons that have passed, since it extricated that verdant cap from the throng of sisters that grew beneath it, and of all that has passed on the Otsego water, when this limpid lake lay, like a gem embedded in the forest. When the Conqueror first landed in England, this tree stood on the spot where it now stands! Here, then, is at last, an American antiquity!"

"A true and regulated taste, Miss Effingham," said Paul, "has pointed out to you, one of the real charms of the country. Were we to think less of the artificial, and more of our natural excellencies, we should render ourselves less liable to criticism."

Eve was never inattentive when Paul spoke, and her colour heightened as he paid this compliment to her taste, but still her soft blue eye was rivetted on the pine.

"Silent it may be, in one respect, but it is indeed all eloquence in another," she resumed, with a fervour that was not lessened by Paul's remark. "That crest of verdure, which resembles a plume of feathers, speaks of a thousand things to the imagination."

"I have never known a person of any poetry, who came under this tree," said John Effingham, "that did not fall into this very train of thought. I once brought a man celebrated for his genius, here, and after gazing for a minute or two at the high, green, tuft, that tops the tree, he exclaimed, 'that mass of green waved in the fierce light, when Columbus first ventured in to the unknown sea!' It is indeed eloquent, for it tells the same glowing tale to all who approach it; a tale fraught with feeling and recollections."

"And yet its silence is, after all, its eloquence," added Paul, "and the name is not so misapplied as one might at first think."

"It probably obtained its name from some fancied contrast to the garrulous rocks that lie up yonder, half concealed by the forest. If you will ply the oars, gentlemen, we will now hold a little communion with the spirit of the Leatherstocking."

The young men complied, and in about five minutes, the skiff was pulled off in the lake, at the distance of fifty rods from the shore, where the whole mountain side came at one glance into the view. Here they lay on their oars, and John Effingham called out to the rocks a "good morning," in a clear distinct voice. The mocking sounds were thrown back again, with a closeness of resemblance that actually startled the novice. Then followed other calls, and other repetitions of the echoes, in which the latter did not lose the minutest intonation of the voice.

"This actually surpasses the celebrated echoes of the Rhine," cried the delighted Eve, "for though those do give the strains of the bugle so clearly, I do not think they answer to the voice with so much fidelity."

"You are very right, Eve," replied her kinsman; "I can recall no place where so perfect and accurate an echo is to be heard, as at these Speaking Rocks. By increasing our distance to half a mile, and using a bugle, as I well know from actual experiment, we should get back entire passages of an air. The interval between the sound and the echo, too, would be distinct, and would give time for an undivided attention. Whatever may be said of the Pine, these rocks are most aptly named, and if the spirit of Leatherstocking has any concern with the matter, he is a mocking spirit."

John Effingham now looked at his watch, and then he explained to the party a pleasure he had in store for them. On a sort of small public promenade, that lay at the point where the river flowed out of the lake, stood a rude shell of a building, that was called the "gun house." Here, a speaking picture of the entire security of the country from foes within, as well as from foes without, were kept two or three pieces of field artillery with doors, so open, that any one might enter the building, and even use the guns at will, although they properly belonged to an organized corps of the state. One of these guns had been sent a short distance down the valley, and John Effingham informed his companions that they might look, momentarily, for its reports to arouse the slumbering echoes of the mountains. He was still speaking, when the gun was fired, its muzzle being turned eastward. The sound first reached the side of the Vision abreast of the village, whence the reverberations reissued, and rolled along the range, from cave to cave, cliff to cliff, and wood to wood, until they were lost, like distant thunder, two or three leagues to the northward. The experiment was thrice repeated, and always with the same magnificent effect, the western hills, actually echoing the echoes of the eastern mountains, like the dying strains of some fearful music.

"Such a locality would be a treasure in the vicinity of a melo-dramatick theatre," said Paul smiling, "for, certainly, no artificial thunder, I have ever heard, has equalled this! A sheet of water like this, might even receive a gondola."

"And yet I fear one accustomed to the boundless horizon of the ocean might, in time, weary of it," answered John Effingham, significantly.

Paul protested earnestly to the contrary, and the party rowed away in silence.

"Yonder is the spot where we have so long been accustomed to resort for Pic-Nics," said Eve pointing out a lovely place, that was beautifully shaded by old oaks, and on which stood a rude house, that was much dilapidated and indeed injured by the hands of man. John Effingham smiled, as his cousin showed the place to her companions, promising them an early and a nearer view of its beauties.

"By the way, Miss Effingham," he said, "I suppose you flatter yourself with being the heiress of that desirable retreat?"

"It is very natural that, at some day, though I trust a very distant one, I should succeed to that which belongs to my dear father."

"Both natural and legal, my fair cousin, but you are yet to learn that there is a power that threatens to rise up and dispute your claim."

"What power—human power, at least,—can dispute the lawful claim of an owner to his property? That point has been ours, ever since civilized man has dwelt among these hills; who will presume to rob us of it!"

"You will be much surprised to discover that there is such a power, and that there is actually a disposition to exercise it. The public, the all-powerful, omnipotent, over-ruling, law-making, law-breaking public, has a passing caprice to possess itself of your beloved Point, and Ned Effingham must show unusual energy, or it will get it."

"This can hardly be serious, Cousin Jack?"

"As serious as the magnitude of the subject can render a responsible being, as Mr Dodge would say."

Eve said no more, but she looked vexed, and remained silent until they landed, when she hastened to seek her father, with a view to communicate what she had just heard. Mr Effingham listened to his daughter, as he always did, with tender interest, and when she had done, he kissed her glowing cheek, bidding her not to believe, that which she seemed so seriously to dread, possible.

"But, cousin John would not trifle with me, on such a subject, father," Eve continued, "he knows how much I prize all those little heir-looms that are connected with the affections."

"We can inquire further into the affair, my child, if it be your desire; ring for Pierre, if you please."

Pierre answered, and a message was sent to Mr Bragg, requiring his presence in the library.

Aristabulus appeared, by no means in the best humour, for he greatly disliked having been omitted in the late excursion on the lake, fancying that he had a community-right to share in all his neighbor's amusements, though he had sufficient self-command to conceal his feelings.

"I wish to know, sir," Mr Effingham commenced, without introduction, "whether there can be any mistake concerning the ownership of the Fishing Point, on the west side of the Lake."

"Certainly not sir; it belongs to the public."

Mr Effingham's cheek glowed, and he looked astonished; but he remained calm.

"The public! Do you gravely affirm, Mr Bragg, that the public pretends to claim that point."

"Claim, Mr Effingham; as long as I have resided in this county, I have never heard its right disputed."

"Your residence in this county, sir, is not of very ancient date, and nothing is easier than that *you* may be mistaken. I confess some curiosity to know in what manner the public has acquired its title to this spot. You are a lawyer, Mr Bragg, and may give an intelligible account of it."

"Why, sir, your father gave it to them in his life time. Every body, in all this region, will tell you as much as this."

"Do you suppose, Mr Bragg, there is any body in all this region, who will swear to that fact. Proof, you well know, is very requisite even to obtain justice."

"I much question, sir, if there be any body in all this region, that will not swear to the fact. It is the common tradition of the whole country, and to be frank with you, sir, there is a little displeasure because Mr John Effingham has talked of giving private entertainments on the Point."

"This, then, only shows how idly and inconsiderately the traditions of the country take their rise. But, as I wish to understand all the points of the case, do me the favor to walk into the village, and inquire of those whom you think the best informed in the matter, what they know of the Point, in order that I may regulate my course accordingly. Be particular, if you please, on the subject of title, as one would not wish to move in the dark."

Aristabulus quitted the house immediately, and, Eve, perceiving that things were in the right train, left her father alone to meditate on what had just passed. Mr Effingham walked up and down his library for some time, much disturbed, for the spot in question was identified with all his early feelings and recollections, and if there were a foot of land on earth, to which he was more attached than to all others, next to his immediate residence, it was this. He could not conceal from himself, moreover, in despite of his opposition to John Effingham's sarcasms, that his native country had undergone many changes since he last resided in it, and that some of these changes were quite sensibly for the worse. The spirit of misrule was abroad, and the lawless and unprincipled held bold language, when it suited their purpose to intimidate. As he ran over in his mind, however, the facts of the case, and the nature of his right, he smiled to think that any one should contest it, and sat down to his writing, almost forgetting that there had been any question at all, on the unpleasant subject.

Aristabulus was absent for several hours, nor did he return until Mr Effingham was dressed for dinner, and alone in the library, again, having absolutely lost all recollection of the commission he had given his agent.

"It is as I told you, sir, the public insists that it owns the Point, and, I feel it my duty to say, Mr Effingham, that the public is determined to maintain its claim."

"Then, Mr Bragg, it is proper I should tell the public that it is *not* the owner of the Point, but that *I* am its owner, and that I am determined to maintain *my* claim."

"It is hard to kick against the pricks, Mr Effingham."

"It is so, sir, as the public may discover, if it persevere in invading a private right."

"Why, sir, some of those with whom I have conversed have gone so far, as to desire me to tell you,—I trust my motive will not be mistaken—"

"If you have any communication to make, Mr Bragg, do it without reserve. It is proper I should know the truth, exactly."

"Well, then, sir, I am the bearer of something like a defiance; the people wish you to know that they hold your right cheaply, and that they laugh at it. Not to mince matters, they defy you."

"I thank you for this frankness, Mr Bragg, and it increases my respect for your character. Affairs are now at such a pass, that it is necessary to act. If you will amuse yourself with a book, for a moment, I shall have further occasion for your kindness."

Aristabulus did not read, for he was too much filled with wonder at seeing a man so coolly set about contending with that awful public, which he himself as habitually deferred to, as any asiatick slave defers to his monarch. Indeed, nothing but his being sustained by that omnipotent power, as he viewed the power of the public to be, had emboldened him to speak so openly to his employer, for Aristabulus felt a secret confidence that, right or wrong, it was always safe in America to make the most fearless professions in favor of the great body of the community. In the mean time, Mr Effingham wrote a simple advertisement against trespassing on the property in question, and handed it to the other, with a request that he would have it inserted in the number of the village paper that was to appear next morning. Mr Bragg took the advertisement, and went to execute the duty, without comment.

The evening arrived before Mr Effingham was again alone, when, being by himself in the library once more, Mr Bragg entered, full of his subject. He was followed by John Effingham, who had gained an inkling of what had passed.

"I regret to say, Mr Effingham," Aristabulus commenced, "that your advertisement has created one of the greatest excitements it has ever been my ill fortune to witness in Templeton."

"All of which ought to be very encouraging to us, Mr Bragg; as men under excitement are usually wrong."

"Very true, sir, as regards individual excitements, but this is a public excitement."

"I am not at all aware that this fact, in the least, alters the case. If one excited man is apt to do silly things, half a dozen backers will be very likely to increase his folly."

Aristabulus listened with increasing wonder, for excitement was one of the means for effecting public objects, so much practised by men of his habits, that it had never crossed his mind any single individual could be indifferent to its existence. To own the truth, he had anticipated so much unpopularity, from his unavoidable connection with the affair, as to have contributed himself in producing this very excitement, with the hope of "choking Mr Effingham off," as he had elegantly expressed it to one of his intimates, in the vernacular of the country.

"A public excitement is a powerful engine, Mr Effingham!" he exclaimed in a sort of politico-pious horror.

"I am fully aware, sir, that it may be even a fearfully powerful engine. Excited men, acting in masses, compose what are called mobs, and have committed a thousand excesses and crimes."

"Your advertisement is to the last degree disrellished; to be very sincere, it is awfully unpopular!"

"I suppose it is always what you term an unpopular act, so far as the individuals opposed are concerned, to resist aggression."

"But they call your advertisement aggression, sir."

"In that simple fact, exists all the merits of the question. If I own this property, the public, or that portion of it, which is connected with this affair are aggressors; and so much more in the wrong that they are many against one; if *they* own the property, I am not only wrong, but very indiscreet."

The calmness with which Mr Effingham spoke had an effect on Aristabulus, and, for a moment, he was staggered. It was only for a moment, however, as the pains and penalties of unpopularity presented themselves afresh to an imagination that had been so long accustomed to study the popular caprices, that it had got to deem the public favor the one great good of life.

"But *they* say, *they* own the Point, Mr Effingham."

"And *I* say, they do *not* own the Point, Mr Bragg; never *did* own it; and, with my consent, never *shall* own it."

"This is purely a matter of fact," observed John Effingham, "and I confess I am curious to know how, or whence this potent public derives its title. You are lawyer enough, Mr Bragg, to know that the public can hold property only by use, or by especial statute. Now, under which title does this claim present itself?"

"First, by use, sir, and then by especial gift."

"The use, you are aware, must be adverse, or as opposed to the title of the other claimants. Now, I am a living witness that my late uncle *permitted* the public to use this Point, and that the publick accepted the conditions. Its use, therefore, has not been adverse, or, at least, not for a time sufficient to make title. Every hour that my cousin has *permitted* the public to enjoy his property, adds to *his* right, as well as to the obligation conferred on that publick, and increases the duty of the latter to cease intruding, whenever he may desire it. If there is an especial gift, as I understand you to say, from my late uncle, there must also be a law to enable the public to hold the property, or a trustee; which is the fact?"

"I admit, Mr John Effingham, that I have seen neither deed, nor law, and I doubt if the latter exist. Still the public *must* have some claim, for it is impossible that every body should be mistaken."

"Nothing is easier, nor any thing more common, than for whole communities to be mistaken and more particularly, when they commence with 'excitement.'"

While his cousin was speaking, Mr Effingham went to a secretary, and taking out a large bundle of papers, he laid it down on the table, unfolding several parchment deeds, to which massive seals bearing the arms of the late Colony, as well as those of England, were pendant.

"Here are my titles, sir," he said, addressing Aristabulus pointedly; "if the public has a better, let it be produced, and I shall at once submit to its claim."

"No one doubts that the King, through his authorized agent, the Governor of the Colony of New York, granted this estate to your predecessor, Mr Effingham; or that it descended legally to your immediate parent; but all contend that your parent gave this spot to the publick, as a place of publick resort."

"I am glad that the question is narrowed down within limits that are so easily examined. What evidence is there of this intention, on the part of my late father?"

"Common report; I have talked with twenty people in the village, and they all agree that the 'Point' has been used by the publick, as publick property, from time immemorial."

"Will you be so good, Mr Bragg, as to name some of those, who affirm this."

Mr Bragg complied, naming quite the number of persons he had mentioned, with a readiness that proved he thought he was advancing testimony that could not easily be rebutted.

"Of all the names you have mentioned," returned Mr Effingham, "I never heard but three, and these are the names of mere boys. The first dozen are certainly the names of persons who can know no more of this village, than they have gleaned in the last few years, and several of them, I understand, have dwelt among us but a few weeks; nay, days."

"Have I not told you, Ned," interrupted John Effingham, "that to an American 'always' means eighteen months, and that 'time immemorial' is only since the last general crisis in the money market!"

"The persons I have mentioned, compose a part of the population, sir," added Mr Bragg, "and, one and all, they are ready to swear that your father, by some means or other, they are not very particular as to minutiæ, gave them the right to use this property."

"They are mistaken, and I should be sorry that any one among them, should swear to such a falsehood. But here are my titles, let them show better, or, if they can, any."

"Perhaps your father abandoned the place to the publick; this might make a good claim."

"That he did not, I am a living proof to the contrary; he left it to his heirs at his death, and I myself, exercised full right of ownership over it, until I went abroad. I did not travel with it in my pocket, sir, it is true, but I left it to the protection of the laws, which I trust are as available to the rich, as to the poor, although this is a free country."

"Well, sir, I suppose a jury must determine the point, as you seem firm; though I warn you, Mr Effingham, as one who knows his country, that a verdict, in the face of a popular feeling, is rather a hopeless matter. If they prove that your late father intended to abandon or to give this to the publick, your case will be lost."

Mr Effingham looked among the papers a moment, and selecting one, he handed it to Mr Bragg, first pointing out to his notice a particular paragraph.

"This, sir, is my late father's will," Mr Effingham said mildly; "and in that particular clause, you will find that he makes a special devise of this very Point, leaving it to his heirs, in such terms, as to put any intention to give it to the public quite out of the question. This, at least, is the latest evidence, I, his only son, executor, and heir possess of his final wishes; if that wandering and time-immemorial publick of which you speak, has a better, I wait with patience that it may be produced."

The composed manner of Mr Effingham had deceived Aristabulus, who did not anticipate any proof so completely annihilating to the pretentions of the public, as that he now held in his hand. It was a simple, brief devise, disposing of the piece of property in question, and left it without dispute, that Mr Effingham had succeeded to all the rights of his father, with no reservation, or condition, of any sort.

"This is very extraordinary!" exclaimed Mr Bragg, when he had read the clause seven times, each perusal contributing to make the case still clearer in favor of his employer, the individual, and still stronger against the hoped for future employers, the people. "The public ought to have known of this bequest of the late Mr Effingham."

"I think it ought, sir, before it pretended to deprive his child of his property; or, rather, it ought to be certain, at least, that there was no such devise."

"You will excuse me, Mr Effingham, but I think it is incumbent on a private citizen, in a case of this sort, when the publick has taken up a wrong notion, as I now admit is clearly the fact as regards the Point, to enlighten it, and to inform it that it does not own the spot."

"This has been done already, Mr Bragg, in the advertisement you had the goodness to carry to the printers, although I deny that there exists any such obligation."

"But, sir, they object to the mode you have chosen to set them right."

"The mode is usual, I believe, in the case of trespasses."

"They expect something different, sir, in an affair in which the publick is—is—is—all—"

"Wrong," put in John Effingham pointedly. "I have heard something of this out of doors, Ned, and blame you for your moderation. Is it true that you had told several of your neighbors that you have no wish to prevent them from using the Point, but that your sole object is merely to settle the question of right, and to prevent intrusions on your family, when it is enjoying its own place of retirement?"

"Certainly, John, my only wish is to preserve the property for those to whom it is especially devised, to allow those who have the best, nay the only right to it, its undisturbed possession, occasionally, and to prevent any more of that injury to the trees that has been committed by some of those rude men, who always fancy themselves so completely all the publick, as to be masters, in their own particular persons, whenever the publick has any claim. I can have no wish to deprive my neighbors of the innocent pleasure of visiting the Point, though I am fully determined they shall not deprive me of my property."

"You are far more indulgent than I should be, or perhaps than you will be yourself when you read this."

As John Effingham spoke, he handed his kinsman a small handbill, which purported to call a meeting, for that night, of the inhabitants of Templeton to resist his arrogant claim to the disputed property. This handbill had the usual marks of a feeble and vulgar malignancy about it, affecting to call Mr Effingham, "*one* Mr Effingham," and it was anonymous.

"This is scarcely worth our attention, John," said Mr Effingham, mildly. "Meetings of this sort cannot decide a legal title, and no man who respects himself will be the tool of so pitiful an attempt to frighten a citizen from maintaining his rights."

"I agree with you as respects the meeting, which has been conceived in ignorance and low malice, and will probably end, as all such efforts end, in ridicule. But—"

"Excuse me, Mr John," interrupted Aristabulus, "there is an awful excitement! Some have even spoken of Lynching!"

"Then," said Mr Effingham, "it does, indeed, require that we should be more firm. Do *you*, sir, know of any person who has dared to use such a menace?"

Aristabulus quailed before the stern eye of Mr Effingham, and he regretted having communicated so much, though he had communicated nothing but the truth. He stammered out an obscure and half intelligible explanation, and proposed to attend the meeting, in person, in order that he might be in the way of understanding the subject, without falling into the danger of mistake. To this Mr Effingham assented, as he felt too indignant at this outrage on all his rights, whether as a citizen, or as a man, to wish to pursue the subject with his agent, that night. Aristabulus departed, and John Effingham remained closetted with his kinsman, until the family had retired. During this long interview the former communicated many things to the latter, in relation to this very affair, of which the owner of the property, until then, had been profoundly ignorant.

CHAPTER XV.

"There shall be in England seven halfpenny loaves sold for a penny; the three-hoop'd pot shall have ten hoops, and I will make it felony to drink small beer. All the realm shall be in common, and in Cheapside shall my palfrey go to grass."

2 Henry VI 4.2.65–69.

THOUGH the affair of the Point continued to agitate the village of Templeton next day, and for many days, it was little remembered in the Wigwam. Confident of his right, Mr Effingham, though naturally indignant at the abuse of his long liberality, through which alone the public had been permitted to frequent the place, and this too, quite often, to his own discomfort and disappointment, had dismissed the subject temporarily from his mind, and was already engaged in his ordinary pursuits. Not so, however, with Mr Bragg. Agreeably to promise, he had attended the meeting, and now he seemed to regulate all his movements, by a sort of mysterious self-importance, as if the repository of some secret of unusual consequence. No one regarded his manner, however, for Aristabulus, and his secrets, and opinions, were all of too little value, in the eyes of most of the party, to attract peculiar attention. He found a sympathetic listener in Mr Dodge, happily, that person having been invited, through the courtesy of Mr Effingham, to pass a few days with those, in whose company, though very unwillingly on the editor's part certainly, he had gone through so many dangerous trials. These two, then, soon became intimate, and to have seen their shrugs, significant whisperings, and frequent conferences in corners, one who did not know them, might have fancied their shoulders burthened with the weight of the state.

But all this pantomime, which was intended to awaken curiosity, was lost on the company in general. The ladies, attended by Paul and the Baronet, proceeded into the forest on foot, for a morning's walk, while the two Messrs Effingham continued to read the daily journals, that were received from town each morning, with a most provoking indifference. Neither Aristabulus, nor Mr Dodge, could resist any longer, and, after exhausting their ingenuity, in the vain effort to induce one of the two gentlemen to question them in relation to the meeting of the previous night, the desire to be doing fairly overcame their affected mysteriousness, and a formal request was made to Mr Effingham to give them an audience in the library. As the latter, who suspected the nature of the interview, requested his kinsman to make one in it, the four were soon alone, in the apartment so often named.

Even now, that his own request for the interview was granted, Aristabulus hesitated about proceeding, until a mild intimation from Mr Effingham that he was ready to hear his communication, told the agent that it was too late to change his determination.

"I attended the meeting, last night, agreeably to our arrangement, Mr Effingham," Aristabulus commenced, "and I feel the utmost regret at being compelled to lay the result before a gentleman for whom I entertain so profound a respect."

"There was then a meeting?" said Mr Effingham, inclining his body slightly, by way of acknowledgment for the other's compliment.

"There was, sir, and I think, Mr Dodge, we may say an overflowing one."

"The public was fairly represented," returned the editor, "as many as fifty or sixty having been present."

"The public has a perfect right to meet, and to take counsel on its claims to anything it may conceive itself entitled to enjoy," observed Mr. Effingham; "I can have no possible objection to such a course, though I think it would have consulted its own dignity more, had it insisted on being convoked by more respectable persons than those who, I understand, were foremost in this affair, and in terms better suited to its own sense of propriety."

Aristabulus glanced at Mr. Dodge, and Mr. Dodge glanced back at Mr. Bragg, for neither of these political mushrooms could conceive of the dignity and fair-mindedness with which a gentleman could view an affair of this nature.

"They passed a set of resolutions, Mr. Effingham," Aristabulus resumed, with the gravity with which he ever spoke of things of this nature. "A set of resolutions, sir!"

"That was to be expected," returned his employer, smiling; "the Americans are a set-of-resolutions-passing people. Three cannot get together, without naming a chairman and secretary, and a resolution is as much a consequence of such an 'organization,'—I believe that is the approved word,—as an egg is the accompaniment of the cackling of a hen."

"But, sir, you do not yet know the nature of those resolutions!"

"Very true, Mr. Bragg; that is a piece of knowledge I am to have the pleasure of obtaining from you."

Again Aristabulus glanced at Steadfast, and Steadfast threw back the look of surprise, for, to both it was matter of real astonishment that any man should be so indifferent to the resolutions of a meeting that had been regularly organized, with a chairman and secretary at its head, and which so unequivocally professed to be the public.

"I am reluctant to discharge this duty, Mr. Effingham, but as you insist on its performance it must be done. In the first place, they resolved that your father meant to give them the Point."

"A decision that must clearly settle the matter, and which will destroy all my father's own resolutions on the same subject. Did they stop at the Point, Mr. Bragg, or did they resolve that my father also gave them his wife and children?"

"No, sir, nothing was said concerning the latter."

"I cannot properly express my gratitude for the forbearance, as they had just as good a right to pass this resolution, as to pass the other."

"The public's is an awful power, Mr. Effingham!"

"Indeed it is, sir, but fortunately, that of the re-public is still more awful, and I shall look to the latter for support, in this 'crisis'—that is the word, too, is it not, Mr. John Effingham?"

"If you mean a change of administration, the upsetting of a stage, or the death of a cart-horse; they are all equally crises, in the American vocabulary."

"Well, Mr. Bragg, having resolved that it knew my late father's intentions better than he knew them himself, as is apparent from the mistake he made in his will, what next did the public dispose of, in the plenitude of its power?"

"It resolved, sir, that it was your duty to carry out the intentions of your father."

"In that, then, we are perfectly of a mind; as the public will most probably discover, before we get through with this matter. This is one of the most pious resolutions I ever knew the public to pass. Did it proceed any farther?"

Mr. Bragg, notwithstanding the long-encouraged truckling to the sets of men, whom he was accustomed to dignify with the name of the public, had so profound a deference for the principles, character, and station of Mr. Effingham, that no sophistry, or self-encouragement in the practices of social confusion, could overcome; and he paused before he communicated the next resolution to his employer. But perceiving that both the latter and his cousin were quietly waiting to hear it, he was fain to overcome his scruples.

"They have openly libelled you, by passing resolutions declaring you to be odious."

"That, indeed, is a strong measure, and, in the interest of good manners and of good morals, it may call for a rebuke. No one can care less than myself, Mr. Bragg, for the opinions of those who have sufficiently demonstrated that their opinions are of no value, by the heedless manner in which they have permitted themselves to fall into this error; but it is proceeding too far, when a few members of the community presume to take these liberties with a private individual, and that, moreover, in a case affecting a pretended claim of their own; and I desire you to tell those concerned, that if they dare to publish their resolution declaring me to be odious, I will teach them what they now do not appear to know, that we live in a country of laws. I shall not prosecute them, but I shall indict them for the offence, and I hope this is plainly expressed."

Aristabulus stood aghast! To indict the public was a step he had never heard of before, and he began to perceive that the question actually had two sides. Still, his awe of public meetings, and his habitual regard for popularity, induced him not to give up the matter, without another struggle.

"They have already ordered their proceedings to be published, Mr. Effingham!" he said, as if such an order were not to be countermanded.

"I fancy, sir, that when it comes to the issue, and the penalties of a prosecution present themselves, their leaders will begin to recollect their individuality, and to think less of their public character. They who hunt in droves, like wolves, are seldom very valiant when singled out from their pack. The end will show."

"I heartily wish this unpleasant affair might be amicably settled," added Aristabulus.

"One might, indeed, fancy so," observed John Effingham, "since no one likes to be persecuted."

"But, Mr. John, the public thinks *itself* persecuted, in this affair."

"The term, as applied to a body that not only makes, but which executes, the law, is so palpably absurd, that I am surprised any man can presume to use it. But, Mr. Bragg, you have seen documents that cannot err, and know that the public has not the smallest right to this bit of land."

"All very true, sir; but you will please to remember, that the people do not know what I now know."

"And you will please to remember, sir, that when people choose to act affirmatively, in as high-handed a manner as this, they are *bound* to know what they are about. Ignorance in such a matter, is like the drunkard's plea of intoxication; it merely makes the offence worse."

"Do you not think, Mr. John, that Mr. Effingham might have acquainted these citizens with the real state of the case? Are the people so very wrong that they have fallen into a mistake?"

"Since you ask this question plainly, Mr. Bragg, it shall be answered with equal sincerity. Mr. Effingham is a man of mature years; the known child, executor, and heir of one who, it is admitted all round, was the master of the controverted property. Knowing his own business, this Mr. Effingham, in sight of the grave of his fathers, beneath the paternal roof, has the intolerable impudence—"

"Arrogance is the word, Jack," said Mr. Effingham, smiling.

"Aye, the intolerable arrogance to suppose that his own is his own; and this he dares to affirm, without having had the politeness to send his title-deeds, and private papers, round to those who have been so short a time in the place, that they might well know nothing of that which has occurred in it for the last half century. Oh thou naughty, arrogant fellow, Ned!"

"Mr. John, you appear to forget that the public has more claims to be treated with attention, than a single individual. If it has fallen into error, it ought to be undeceived."

"No doubt, sir; and I advise Mr. Effingham to send you, his agent, to every man, woman and child in the county, with the Patent of the King, all the mesne conveyances and wills, in your pocket, in order that you may read them at length to each individual, with a view that every man, woman and child, may be satisfied that he or she is not the owner of Edward Effingham's lands!"

"Nay, sir, a shorter process might be adopted."

"It might, indeed, sir, and such a process has been adopted by my cousin, in giving the usual notice, in the news-paper, against trespassing. But, Mr. Bragg, you must know that I took great pains, three years since, when repairing this house, to correct the mistake on this very point, into which I found that your immaculate public had fallen, through its disposition to know more of other people's affairs, than those concerned knew of themselves."

Aristabulus said no more, but gave the matter up in despair. On quitting the house, he proceeded forthwith, to inform those most interested of the determination of Mr. Effingham, not to be trampled on by any pretended meeting of the public. Common sense, not to say common honesty, began to resume its sway, and prudence put in its plea, by way of applying the corrective. Both he and Mr. Dodge, however, agreed that there was an unheard-of temerity in thus resisting the people, and this too without a commensurate object, as the pecuniary value of the disputed point was of no material consequence to either party.

The reader is not, by any means, to suppose that Aristabulus Bragg and Steadfast Dodge belonged to the same variety of the human species, in consequence of their unity of sentiment in this affair, and certain other general points of resemblance in their manner and modes of thinking. As a matter of necessity, each partook of those features of caste, condition, origin, and association that characterize their particular set; but when it came to the nicer distinctions that mark true individuality, it would not have been easy to find two men more essentially different. The first was bold, morally and physically, aspiring, self-possessed, shrewd, singularly adapted to succeed in his schemes where he knew the parties, intelligent, after his tastes, and apt. Had it been his fortune to be thrown earlier into a better sphere, the same natural qualities that rendered him so expert in his present situation, would have conduced to his improvement, and most probably would have formed a gentleman, a scholar, and one who could have contributed largely to the welfare, principles and tastes of his fellow-creatures. That such was not his fate, was more his misfortune than his fault, for his plastic character had readily taken the impression of those things that from propinquity alone, pressed hardest on it. On the other hand Steadfast was a hypocrite by nature, cowardly, envious, and malignant; and circumstances had only lent their aid to the natural tendencies of his disposition. That two men so differently constituted at their births, should meet, as it might be in a common centre, in so many of their habits and opinions, was merely the result of accident and education.

Among the other points of resemblance between these two persons, was that fault of confounding the cause with the effects of the peculiar institutions under which they had been educated and lived. Because the law gave to the public, that authority which, under other systems, is entrusted either to one, or to the few, they believed the public was invested with far more power than a right understanding of their own principles would have shown. In a word, both these persons made a mistake which is getting to be too common in America, that of supposing the institutions of the country were all means and no end. Under this erroneous impression they saw only the machinery of the government, becoming entirely forgetful that the power which was given to the people collectively, was only so given to secure to them as perfect a liberty as possible, in their characters of individuals. Neither had risen sufficiently above vulgar notions, to understand that public opinion, in order to be omnipotent, or even formidable beyond the inflictions of the moment, must be right; and that, if a solitary man renders himself contemptible by taking up false notions inconsiderately and unjustly, bodies of men, falling into the same error, incur the same penalties, with the additional stigma of having acted as cowards.

There was also another common mistake into which Messrs. Bragg and Dodge had permitted themselves to fall, through the want of a proper distinction between principles. Resisting the popular will, on the part of an individual, they considered arrogance and aristocracy, *per se*, without at all entering into the question of the right, or the wrong. The people, rightly enough in the general signification of the term, they deemed to be sovereign; and they belonged to a numerous class, who view disobedience to the sovereign in a democracy, although it be in his illegal caprices, very much as the subject of a despot views disobedience to his prince.

It is scarcely necessary to say, that Mr. Effingham and his cousin viewed these matters differently. Clear-headed, just-minded, and liberal in all his practices, the former, in particular, was greatly pained by the recent occurrence; and he paced his library in silence, for several minutes after Mr. Bragg and his companion had withdrawn, really too much grieved to speak.

"This is, altogether, a most extraordinary procedure, John," he at length observed, "and, it strikes me, that it is but an indifferent reward for the liberality with which I have permitted others to use my property, these thirty years; often, very often, as you well know, to my own discomfort, and to that of my friends."

"I have told you, Ned, that you were not to expect the America on your return, that you left behind you on your departure for Europe.

I insist that no country has so much altered for the worse, in so short a time."

"That unequalled pecuniary prosperity should sensibly impair the manners of what is termed the world, by introducing suddenly large bodies of uninstructed and untrained men and women into society, is a natural consequence of obvious causes; that it should corrupt morals, even, we have a right to expect, for we are taught to believe it the most corrupting influence under which men can live; but, I confess, I did not expect to see the day, when a body of strangers, birds of passage, creatures of an hour, should assume a right to call on the old and long-established inhabitants of a country, to prove their claims to their possessions, and this, too, in an unusual and unheard-of manner, under the penalty of being violently deprived of them!"

"Long established!" repeated John Effingham, laughing; "what do you term long established? Have you not been absent a dozen years, and do not these people reduce everything to the level of their own habits. I suppose, now, you fancy you can go to Rome, or Jerusalem, or Constantinople, and remain four or five lustres, and then come coolly back to Templeton, and, on taking possession of this house again, call yourself an old resident."

"I certainly do suppose I have that right. How many English, Russians, and Germans, did we meet in Italy, the residents of years, who still retained all their natural and local rights and feelings!"

"Ay, that is in countries where society is permanent, and men get accustomed to look on the same objects, hear the same names, and see the same faces, for their entire lives. I have had the curiosity to inquire, and have ascertained that none of the old, permanent families have been active in this affair of the Point, but that all the clamour has been made by those you call the birds of passage. But what of that? These people fancy everything reduced to the legal six months required to vote; and that rotation in persons is as necessary to republicanism as rotation in office."

"Is is not extraordinary that persons who can know so little on the subject, should be thus indiscreet and positive?"

"It is not extraordinary in America. Look about you, Ned, and you will see adventurers uppermost everywhere; in the government, in your towns, in your villages, in the country, even. We are a nation of changes. Much of this, I admit, is the fair consequence of legitimate causes, as an immense region, in forest, cannot be peopled on any other conditions. But this necessity has infected the entire national character, and men get to be impatient of any sameness, even though it be useful. Everything goes to confirm this feeling, instead of opposing it. The constant recurrences of the elections accustom men to changes in their public functionaries; the great increase in the population brings new faces; and the sudden accumulations of property place new men in conspicuous stations. The architecture of the country is barely becoming sufficiently respectable to render it desirable to preserve the buildings, without which we shall have no monuments to revere. In short, everything contributes to produce such a state of things, painful as it may be to all of any feeling, and little to oppose it."

"You colour highly, Jack; and no picture loses in tints, in being retouched by you."

"Look into the first paper that offers, and you will see the *young men* of the country hardily invited to meet by themselves, to consult concerning public affairs, as if they were impatient of the counsels and experience of their fathers. No country can prosper, where the ordinary mode of transacting the business connected with the root of the government, commences with this gross impiety."

"This is a disagreeable feature in the national character, certainly; but we must remember the arts employed by the designing to practise on the inexperienced."

"Had I a son, who presumed to denounce the wisdom and experience of his father, in this disrespectful manner, I would disinherit the rascal!"

"Ah, Jack, bachelor's children are notoriously well educated, and well mannered. We will hope, however, that time will bring its changes also, and that one of them will be a greater constancy in persons, things, and the affections."

"Time *will* bring its changes, Ned; but all of them that are connected with individual rights, as opposed to popular caprice, or popular interests, are likely to be in the wrong direction."

"The tendency is certainly to substitute popularity for the right, but we must take the good with the bad. Even you, Jack, would not exchange this popular oppression for any other system under which you have lived."

"I don't know that—I don't know that. Of all tyranny, a vulgar tyranny is to me the most odious."

"You used to admire the English system, but I think observation has lessened your particular admiration in that quarter," said Mr. Effingham, smiling in a way that his cousin perfectly understood.

"Harkee, Ned; we all take up false notions in youth, and this was one of mine; but, of the two, I should prefer the cold, dogged domination of English law, with its fruits, the heartlessness of a sophistication without parallel, to being trampled on by every arrant blackguard that may happen to traverse this valley, in his wanderings after dollars. There is one thing you yourself must admit; the public is a little too apt to neglect the duties it ought to discharge, and to assume duties it has no right to fulfil."

This remark, which was teeming with truth, ended the discourse.

CHAPTER XVI.

Her breast was a brave palace, a Broad-street,
Where all heroic ample thoughts did meet.
Where nature such a tenement had ta'en,
That other's souls, to hers, dwelt in a lane.

John Norton, "Dirge for the Tenth Muse," ll. 77–80.

THE village of Templeton, it has been already intimated, was a miniature town. Although it contained within the circle of its houses, half-a-dozen residences with grounds, and which were dignified with names, as has been also said, it did not cover a surface of more than a mile square; that disposition to concentration, which is as peculiar to an American town, as the disposition to diffusion is peculiar to the country population, and which seems almost to prescribe that a private dwelling shall have but three windows in front, and a *façade* of twenty-five feet, having presided at the birth of this spot, as well as at the birth of so many of its predecessors and contemporaries. In one of its more retired streets (for Templeton had its publicity and retirement, the latter after a very village-fashion, however,) dwelt a widow-bewitched of small worldly means, five children, and of great capacity for circulating intelligence. Mrs. Abbott, for so was this demi-relict called, was just on the verge of what is termed the "good society" of the village, the most uneasy of all positions for an ambitious and *ci-devant* pretty woman to be placed in. She had not yet abandoned the hope of obtaining a divorce and its *suites*; was singularly, nay, rabidly devout, if we may coin the adverb; in her own eyes she was perfection, in those of her neighbours slightly objectionable; and she was altogether a droll, and by no means an unusual compound of piety, censoriousness, charity, proscription, gossip, kindness, meddling, ill-nature, and decency.

The establishment of Mrs. Abbott, like her house, was necessarily very small, and she kept no servant but a girl she called her help, a very suitable appellation, by the way, as they did most of the work of the *mènage* in common. This girl, in addition to doing the cooking and the washing, was the confidant of all her employer's wandering notions of mankind in general, and of her neighbours in particular; as often helping her mistress in circulating her comments on the latter, as in anything else.

Mrs. Abbott knew nothing of the Effinghams, except by a hearsay that got its intelligence from her own school, being herself a late arrival in the place. She had selected Templeton as a residence on account of its cheapness, and, having neglected to comply with the forms of the world, by hesitating about making the customary visit to the Wigwam, she began to resent, in her spirit at least, Eve's delicate forbearance from obtruding herself, where, agreeably to all usage, she had a perfect right to suppose she was not desired. It was in this spirit, then, that she sat, conversing with Jenny, as the maid of all work was called, the morning after the conversation related in the last chapter, in her snug little parlour, sometimes plying her needle, and oftener thrusting her head out of a window which commanded a view of the principal street of the place, in order to see what her neighbours might be about.

"This is a most extraordinary course Mr. Effingham has taken concerning the Point," said Mrs. Abbott, "and I *do* hope the people will bring him to his senses. Why, Jenny, the public has used that place ever since I can remember, and I have now lived in Templeton quite fifteen months.—What *can* induce Mr. Howel to go so often to that barber's shop, which stands directly opposite the parlour windows of Mrs. Bennett—one would think the man was all beard."

"I suppose Mr. Howel gets shaved sometimes," said the logical Jenny.

"Not he; or if he does, no decent man would think of posting himself before a lady's window to do such a thing.—Orlando Furioso Samuel," calling to her eldest son, a boy of eleven, "run over to Mr. Jones's store, and listen to what the people are talking about, and bring me back the news, as soon as any thing worth hearing drops from any body; and stop as you come back, my son, and borrow neighbour Brown's gridiron. Jenny, it is most time to think of putting over the potatoes."

"Ma' "—cried Orlando Furioso Samuel, from the front door, Mrs. Abbott being very rigid in requiring that all her children should call her "ma'," being so much behind the age as actually not to know that 'mother' had got to be much the genteeler term of the two; "Ma'," roared Orlando Furioso Samuel, "suppose there is no news at Mr. Jones's store?"

"Then go to the nearest tavern; something must be stirring this fine morning, and I'm dying to know what it can possibly be. Mind you bring something besides the gridiron back with you. Hurry, or never come home again as long as you live! As I was saying, Jenny, the right of the public, which is our right, for we are a part of the public, to this Point, is as clear as day, and I am only astonished at the impudence of Mr. Effingham in pretending to deny it. I dare say his French daughter has put him up to it. They say she is monstrous arrogant!"

"Is Eve Effingham, French," said Jenny, studiously avoiding any of the usual terms of civility and propriety, by way of showing her breeding—"well, I had always thought her nothing but Templeton born!"

"What signifies where a person was born? where they *live*, is the essential thing; and Eve Effingham has lived so long in France, that she speaks nothing but broken English; and Miss Debby told me last week, that in drawing up a subscription paper for a new cushion to the reading-desk of her people, she actually spelt 'charity' 'carrotty.'"

"Is that French, Miss Abbott?"

"I rather think it is, Jenny; the French are very niggardly, and give their poor carrots to live on, and so they have adopted the word, I suppose. You, Byansy-Alzumy-Ann, (Bianca-Alzuma-Ann!")

"Marm!"

"Byansy-Alzumy-Ann! who taught you to call me marm! Is this the way you have learned your catechism? Say, ma', this instant."

"Ma."

"Take your bonnet, (this word by the way of brevity, Mrs Abbott chose to call bunnet)—Take your bonnet, my child, and run down to Mrs. Wheaton's, and ask her if any thing new has turned up about the Point, this morning; and, do you hear, Byansy-Alzumy-Ann Abbott—how the child starts away, as if she were sent on a matter of life and death!"

"Why, ma', I want to hear the news, too."

"Very likely, my dear, but, by stopping to get your errand, you may learn more than by being in such a hurry. Stop in at Mrs. Green's, and ask how the people liked the lecture of the strange parson, last evening—and beg her if she can lend me a watering pot, too. Now, run, and be back as soon as possible. Never loiter when you carry news, child."

"No one has a right to stop the mail, I believe, Miss Abbott," put in Jenny, very appositely.

"That, indeed, have they not, or else we could not calculate the consequences. You may remember, Jenny, the pious, even, had to give up that point, public convenience being too strong for religion, even. Roger-Demetrius-Benjamin!"—calling to a second boy, two years younger than his brother—"your eyes are better than mine—who are all those people collected together in the street. Is not Mr. Howel among them?"

"I do not know, ma'!" answered Roger-Demetrius-Benjamin, gaping.

"Then run, this minute, and see, and don't stop to look for your hat. As you come back, step into the tailor's shop and ask if your new jacket is most done, and what the news is? I rather think, Jenny, we shall find out something worth hearing, in the course of the day. By the way, they do say that Grace Van Cortlandt, Eve Effingham's cousin, is under concern."

"Well, she is the last person I should think would be troubled about any thing, for every body says she is so desperate rich she might eat off of silver, if she liked; and she is sure of being married, some time or other."

"That ought to lighten her concern, you think. Oh! it does my heart good when I see any of those flaunty people right well exercised! Nothing would make me happier than to see Eve Effingham herself, groaning fairly in the spirit! That would teach her to take away the people's Points."

"But, Miss Abbott, then she would become almost as good a woman as you are yourself."

"Not she, indeed! Though I am a miserable, graceless, awfully wicked sinner! Twenty times a day do I doubt whether I am actually converted or not. Sin has got such a hold of my very heart-strings, that I sometimes think they will crack before it lets go. Rinaldo-Rinaldini-Timothy, my child, do you toddle across the way, and give my compliments to Mrs. Hulbert, and inquire if it be true that young Dickson, the lawyer, is really engaged to Aspasia Tubbs or not? and borrow a skimmer, or a tin pot, or any thing you can carry, for we may want something of the sort in the course of the day. I do believe, Jenny, that a worse creature than myself is hardly to be found in Templeton."

"Why, Miss Abbott," returned Jenny, who had heard too much of this self-abasement to be much alarmed about it, "this is giving almost as bad an account of yourself, as I heard somebody, that I won't name, give of you last week."

"And who is your somebody, I should like to know? I dare say, one no better than a formalist, who thinks that reading prayers out of a book, kneeling, bowing, and changing gowns, is religion! Thank Heaven, I'm pretty indifferent to the opinions of such people. Harkee, Jenny; if I thought I was no better than some persons I could name, I'd give the point of salvation up, in despair!"

"Miss Abbott," roared a ragged, dirty-faced, bare-footed boy, who bolted in without knocking, and stood in the middle of the room, with his hat on, with a suddenness that denoted great readiness in entering other people's possessions; "Miss Abbott, ma' wants to know if you are likely to go from home this week?"

"Why, what in nature can she want to know that for, Ordeal Bumgrum?" Mrs. Abbott pronounced this singular name, however, "Ordeel."

"Oh! she *warnts* to know."

"So do I *warnt* to know; and know I will. Run home this instant, and ask your mother why she has sent you here with this message. Jenny, I am much exercised to find out the reason Mrs. Bumgrum should have sent Ordeal over with such a question."

"I did hear that Miss Bumgrum intended to make a journey herself, and she may want your company."

"Here comes Ordeal back, and we shall soon be out of the clouds. What a boy that is for errands! He is worth all my sons put together. You never see him losing time by going round by the streets, but away he goes over the garden fences like a cat, or he will whip through a house, if standing in his way, as if he were its owner, should the door happen to be open. Well, Ordeal?"

But Ordeal was out of breath, and although Jenny shook him, as if to shake the news out of him, and Mrs. Abbott actually shook her fist, in her impatience to be enlightened, nothing could induce the child to speak, until he had recovered his wind.

"I believe he does it on purpose," said the provoked maid.

"It's just like him!" cried the mistress; "the very best news-carrier in the village is actually spoilt, because he is thick-winded."

"I wish folks wouldn't make their fences so high," Ordeal exclaimed, the instant he found breath. "I can't see of what use it is to make a fence people can't climb!"

"What does your mother say?" cried Jenny repeating her shake, *con amore*.

"Ma' wants to know, Miss Abbott, if you don't intend to use it yourself, if you will lend her your name for a few days, to go to Utica with? She says folks don't treat her half as well when she is called Bumgrum, as when she has another name, and she thinks she'd like to try yours, this time."

"Is that all!—You need n't have been so hurried about such a trifle, Ordeal. Give my compliments to your mother, and tell her she is quite welcome to my name, and I hope it will be serviceable to her."

"She says she is willing to pay for the use of it, if you will tell her what the damage will be."

"Oh! it's not worth while to speak of such a trifle; I dare say she will bring it back quite as good as when she took it away. I am no such unneighbourly or aristocratical person as to wish to keep my name all to myself. Tell your mother she is welcome to mine, and to keep it as long as she likes, and not to say any thing about pay; I may want to borrow hers, or something else, one of these days, though, to say the truth, my neighbours *are* apt to complain of me as unfriendly and proud for not borrowing as much as a good neighbour ought."

Ordeal departed, leaving Mrs. Abbott in some such condition as that of the man who had no shadow. A rap at the door interrupted the further discussion of the old subject, and Mr. Steadfast Dodge appeared in answer to the permission to enter. Mr. Dodge and Mrs. Abbott were congenial spirits, in the way of news, he living by it, and she living on it.

"You are very welcome, Mr. Dodge," the mistress of the house commenced; "I hear you passed the day, yesterday, up at the Effinghamses."

"Why, yes, Mrs. Abbott, the Effinghamses insisted on it, and I could not well get over the sacrifice, after having been their shipmate so long. Besides it is a little relief to talk French, when one has been months in the daily practice of it."

"I hear there is company at the house?"

"Two of our fellow-travellers, merely. An English baronet, and a young man of whom less is known than one could wish. He is a mysterious person, and I hate mystery, Mrs. Abbott."

"In that, then, Mr. Dodge, you and I are alike. I think every thing should be known. Indeed, that is not a free country in which there are any secrets. I keep nothing from my neighbours, and, to own the truth, I do not like my neighbours to keep any thing from me."

"Then you'll hardly like the Effinghams, for I never yet met with a more close-mouthed family. Although I was so long in the ship with Miss Eve, I never heard her once speak of her want of appetite, of sea-sickness, or of any thing relating to her ailings even; nor can you imagine how close she is on the subject of the beaux; I do not think I ever heard her use the word, or so much as allude to any walk or ride she ever took with a man in her life. I set her down, Mrs. Abbott, as unqualifiedly artful!"

"That you may with certainty, sir, for there is no more sure sign that a young woman is all the while thinking of the beaux, than her never mentioning them."

"That I believe to be human nature; no ingenuous person ever thinks much of the particular subject of conversation. What is your opinion, Mrs. Abbott, of the contemplated match at the Wigwam?"

"Match!" exclaimed Mrs. Abbott, much as a dog would snap at a bone.—"What, already! It is the most indecent thing I ever heard of! Why, Mr. Dodge, the family has not been home a fortnight, and to think so soon of getting married! It is quite as bad as a widower's marrying within the month."

Mrs. Abbott made a distinction, habitually, between the cases of widowers and widows, as the first, she maintained, might get married whenever they pleased, and the latter only when they got offers; and she felt just that sort of horror of a man's thinking of marrying too soon after the death of his wife, as might be expected in one who actually contemplated a second husband before the first was dead.

"Why, yes," returned Steadfast, "it is a little premature, perhaps, though they have been long acquainted. Still, as you say, it would be more decent to wait and see what may turn up in a country, that, to them, may be said to be a foreign land."

"But, who are the parties, Mr. Dodge."

"Miss Eve Effingham, and Mr. John Effingham"

"Mr. John Effingham!" exclaimed the lady, who had lent her name to a neighbour, aghast, for this was knocking one of her own day-dreams in the head, "well this is too much! But he shall not marry her, sir; the law will prevent it, and we live in a country of laws. A man cannot marry his own niece."

"It is excessively improper, and ought to be put a stop to. And yet these Effinghams do very much as they please."

"I am very sorry to hear that; they are extremely disagreeable," said Mrs. Abbott, with a look of eager inquiry, as if afraid the answer might be in the negative.

"As much so as possible; they have hardly a way that you would like, my dear marm; and are as close-mouthed as if they were always afraid of committing themselves."

"Desperate bad news-carriers, I am told, Mr. Dodge. There is Dorindy (Dorinda) Mudge, who was employed there by Eve and Grace one day; she tells me she tried all sorts of ways to get them to talk, by speaking of the most common things; things that one of my children knew all about; such as the affairs of the neighbourhood, and how people are getting on; and, though they would listen a little, and that is something, I admit, not a syllable could she get in the way of answer, or remark. She tells me that, several times, she had a mind to quit, for it is monstrous unpleasant to associate with your tongue-tied folks."

"I dare say Miss Effingham could throw out a hint now and then, concerning the voyage and her late fellow-travellers," said Steadfast, casting an uneasy glance at his companion.

"Not she. Dorindy maintains that it is impossible to get a sentiment out of her concerning a single fellow-creature. When she talked of the late unpleasant affair of poor neighbour Bronson's family—a melancholy transaction that, Mr. Dodge, and I shouldn't wonder if it went to nigh break Mrs. Bronson's heart—but when Dorindy mentioned this, which is bad enough to stir the sensibility of a frog, neither of my young ladies replied, or put a single question. In this respect Grace is as bad as Eve, and Eve is as bad as Grace, they say. Instead of so much as seeming to wish to know any more, what does my Miss Eve do, but turn to some daubs of paintings, and point out to her cousin what she was pleased to term peculiarities in Swiss scenery. Then the two hussies would talk of nature, 'our beautiful nature' Dorindy says Eve had the impudence to call it, and, as if human nature and its failings and backsliding were not a fitter subject for a young woman's discourse, than a silly conversation about lakes, and rocks, and trees, and as if she *owned* the nature about Templeton. It is my opinion, Mr. Dodge, that downright ignorance is at the bottom of it all, for Dorindy says that they actually know no more of the intricacies of the neighbourhood than if they lived in Japan."

"All pride, Mrs. Abbott; rank pride. They feel themselves too great to enter into the minutiæ of common folks' concerns. I often tried Miss Effingham, coming from England; and things touching private interests, that I know she did and must understand, she always disdainfully refused to enter into. Oh! she is a real Tartar, in her way; and what she does not wish to do, you never can make her do!"

"Have you heard that Grace is under concern?"

"Not a breath of it; under whose preaching was she sitting, Mrs. Abbott?"

"That is more than I can tell you; not under the church parson's, I'll engage; no one ever heard of a real, active, regenerating, soul-reviving, spirit-groaning and fruit-yielding conversion under *his* ministry."

"No, there is very little unction in that persuasion generally. How cold and apathetic they are, in these soul-stirring times! Not a sinner has been writhing on *their* floor, I'll engage, nor a wretch transferred into a saint, in the twinkling of an eye, by *that* parson. Well, *we* have every reason to be grateful, Mrs. Abbott."

"That we have, for most glorious have been our privileges! To be sure that is a sinful pride that can puff up a wretched, sinful being like Eve Effingham to such a pass of conceit, as to induce her to think she is raised above thinking of, and taking an interest in the affairs of her neighbours. Now, for my part, conversion has so far opened *my* heart, that I do actually feel as if I wanted to know all about the meanest creature in Templeton."

"That's the true spirit, Mrs. Abbott; stick to that, and your redemption is secure. I only edit a newspaper, by way of showing an interest in mankind."

"I hope, Mr. Dodge, the press does not mean to let this matter of the Point sleep; the press is the true guardian of the public rights, and I can tell you the whole community looks to it for support, in this crisis."

"We shall not fail to do our duty," said Mr. Dodge, looking over his shoulder, and speaking lower. "What! shall one insignificant individual, who has not a single right above that of the meanest citizen in the county, oppress this great and powerful community! What if Mr. Effingham does own this point of land—"

"But he does *not* own it," interrupted Mrs. Abbott. "Ever since I have known Templeton, the public has owned it. The public, moreover, says it owns it, and what the public says, in this happy country, is law."

"But, allowing that the public does not own—"

"It *does* own it, Mr. Dodge," the nameless repeated, more positively.

"Well, marm, own or no own, this is not a country in which the press ought to be silent, when a solitary, insignificant individual undertakes to trample on the public. Leave that matter to us, Mrs. Abbott; it is in good hands, and shall be well taken care of."

"I'm piously glad of it!"

"I mention this to you, as to a friend," continued Mr. Dodge, cautiously drawing from his pocket a manuscript, which he prepared to read to his companion, who sat with a devouring a curiosity, ready to listen.

The manuscript of Mr. Dodge contained a professed account of the affair of the Point. It was written obscurely, and was not without its contradictions, but the imagination of Mrs. Abbott supplied all the vacuums, and reconciled all the inconsistencies. The article was so liberal of its professions of contempt for Mr. Effingham, that every rational man was compelled to wonder, why a quality, that is usually so passive, should, in this particular instance, be aroused to so sudden and violent activity. In the way of facts, not one was faithfully stated; and there were several deliberate, unmitigated falsehoods, which went essentially to colour the whole account.

"I think this will answer the purpose," said Steadfast, "and we have taken means to see that it shall be well circulated."

"This will do them good," cried Mrs. Abbott; almost breathless with delight. "I hope folks will believe it."

"No fear of that. If it were a party thing, now, one half would believe it, as a matter of course, and the other half would not believe it, as a matter of course; but, in a private matter, lord bless you, marm, people are always ready to believe any thing that will give them something to talk about."

Here the *tête à tête* was interrupted by the return of Mrs. Abbott's different messengers, all of whom, unlike the dove sent forth from the ark, brought back something in the way of hopes. The Point was a common theme, and, though the several accounts flatly contradicted each other, Mrs. Abbott, in the general benevolence of her pious heart, found the means to extract corroboration of her wishes from each.

Mr. Dodge was as good as his word, and the account appeared. The press throughout the country seized with avidity on any thing that helped to fill its columns. No one appeared disposed to inquire into the truth of the account, or after the character of the original authority. It was in print, and that struck the great majority of the editors and their readers, as a sufficient sanction. Few, indeed, were they, who lived so much under a proper self-control, as to hesitate; and this rank injustice was done a private citizen, as much without moral restraint, as without remorse, by those, who, to take their own accounts of the matter, were the regular and habitual champions of human rights!

John Effingham pointed out this extraordinary scene of reckless wrong, to his wondering cousin, with the cool sarcasm, with which he was apt to assail the weaknesses and crimes of the country. His firmness, united to that of his cousin, however, put a stop to the publication of the resolutions of Aristabulus's meeting, and when a sufficient time had elapsed to prove that these prurient denouncers of their fellow-citizens had taken wit in their anger, he procured them, and had them published himself, as the most effectual means of exposing the real character of the senseless mob, that had thus disgraced liberty, by assuming its professions and its usages, while it so unequivocally betrayed that it knew nothing of its spirit.

To an observer of men, the end of this affair presented several strong points for comment. As soon as the truth became generally known, in reference to the real ownership of the spot in dispute, and the public came to ascertain that instead of hitherto possessing a right, it had, in fact been merely enjoying a favour, those who had committed themselves by their arrogant assumptions of facts, and their indecent outrages, fell back on their self-love, and began to seek excuses for their own conduct in that of the other party. Mr. Effingham was loudly condemned for not having done the very thing, he, in truth, had done, viz: telling the public it did not own his property; and when this was shown to be an absurdity, the complaint followed that what he had done, had been done in the mode he had adopted, although it was precisely the mode constantly used by every one else. From these vague and indefinite accusations, those most implicated in the wrong, began to deny all their own original assertions, by insisting that they had known all along, that Mr. Effingham owned the property, but that they did not choose he, or any other man, should presume to tell them what they knew so well already. In short, the end of this affair exhibited human nature in its usual aspects of prevarication, untruth, contradiction, and inconsistency, and notwithstanding the high profession of liberty made by those implicated, they who had been the most guilty of wrong, were loudest in their complaints, as if they alone had suffered.

"This is not exhibiting the country to us, certainly, after so long an absence, in its best appearance," said Mr. Effingham, "I must admit, John; but error belongs to all regions, and to all classes of institutions."

"Ay, Ned, make the best of it, as usual; but, if you do not come round to my way of thinking, before you are a twelvemonth older, I shall renounce prophesying. I wish we could get at the bottom of Miss Effingham's thoughts, on this occasion."

"Miss Effingham has been grieved, disappointed, nay, shocked," said Eve, "but, still she will not despair of the republic. None of our respectable neighbours, in the first place, have shared in this transaction, and that is something; though I confess I feel some surprise that any considerable portion of a community, that respects itself, should quietly allow an ignorant fragment of its own numbers, to misrepresent it so grossly, in an affair that so nearly touches its own character for common sense and justice."

"You have yet to learn, Miss Effingham, that men can get to be so saturated with liberty, that they become insensible to the nicer feelings. The grossest enormities are constantly committed in this good republic of ours, under the pretence of being done by the public, and for the public. The public have got to bow to that bugbear, quite as submissively as Gesler could have wished the Swiss to bow to his own cap, as that of Rodolph's substitute. Men will have idols, and the Americans have merely set up themselves."

"And yet, cousin Jack, you would be wretched were you doomed to live under a system less free. I fear you have the affectation of sometimes saying that which you do not exactly feel."

CHAPTER XVII.

"Come, these are no times to talk of dreams . . .
We'll talk of dreams hereafter."

William Lisle Bowles, "The Sanctuary: A Dramatic
Sketch," ll. 51, 53.

THE day succeeding that in which the conversation just mentioned occurred, was one of great expectation and delight in the Wigwam. Mrs. Hawker and the Bloomfields were expected, and the morning passed away rapidly, under the gay buoyancy of the feelings that usually accompany such anticipations in a country-house. The travellers were to leave town the previous evening, and, though the distance was near two hundred and thirty miles, they were engaged to arrive by the usual dinner hour. In speed, the Americans, so long as they follow the great routes, are unsurpassed; and even Sir George Templemore, coming, as he did, from a country of MacAdamized roads and excellent posting, expressed his surprise, when given to understand that a journey of this length, near a hundred miles of which were by land, moreover, was to be performed in twenty-four hours, the stops included.

"One particularly likes this rapid travelling," he remarked, "when it is to bring us such friends as Mrs. Hawker."

"And Mrs. Bloomfield," added Eve, quickly. "I rest the credit of the American females on Mrs. Bloomfield."

"More so, than on Mrs. Hawker, Miss Effingham?"

"Not in all that is amiable, respectable, feminine, and lady-like; but certainly more so, in the way of mind. I know, Sir George Templemore, as a European, what your opinion is of our sex in this country."

"Good heaven, my dear Miss Effingham!—My opinion of your sex, in America! It is impossible for any one to entertain a higher opinion of your countrywomen—as I hope to show—as, I trust, my respect and admiration have always proved—nay, Powis, you, as an

American, will exonerate me from this want of taste—judgment—feeling—"

Paul laughed, but told the embarrassed and really distressed baronet, that he should leave him in the very excellent hands into which he had fallen.

"You see yonder bird, that is sailing so prettily above the roofs of the village," said Eve, pointing with her parasol in the direction she meant; for the three were walking together on the little lawn, in waiting for the appearance of the expected guests; "and I dare say you are ornithologist enough to tell its vulgar name."

"You are in the humour to be severe this morning—the bird is but a common swallow."

"One of which will not make a summer, as every one knows. Our cosmopolitism is already forgotten, and with it, I fear, our frankness."

"Since Powis has hoisted his national colours, I do not feel as free on such subjects as formerly," returned Sir George, smiling. "When I thought I had a secret ally in him, I was not afraid to concede a little in such things, but his avowal of his country has put me on my guard. In no case, however, shall I admit my insensibility to the qualities of your countrywomen. Powis, as a native, may take that liberty; but, as for myself, I shall insist they are, at least, the equals of any females I know."

"In *naiveté*, prettiness, delicacy of appearance, simplicity, and sincerity—"

"In sincerity, think you, dear Miss Effingham?"

"In sincerity, above all things, dear Sir George Templemore. Sincerity—nay, frankness is the last quality I should think of denying them."

"But to return to Mrs. Bloomfield—she is clever, exceedingly clever, I allow; in what is her cleverness to be distinguished from that of one of her sex, on the other side of the ocean?"

"In nothing, perhaps, did there exist no differences in national characteristics. Naples and New-York are in the same latitude, and yet, I think you will agree with me, that there is little resemblance in their populations."

"I confess I do not understand the allusion—are you quicker witted, Powis?"

"I will not say that," answered Paul; "but I think I do comprehend Miss Effingham's meaning. You have travelled enough to know, that, as a rule, there is more aptitude in a southern, than in a northern people. They receive impressions more readily, and are quicker in all their perceptions."

"I believe this to be true; but, then, you will allow that they are less constant, and have less perseverance?"

"In that we are agreed, Sir George Templemore," resumed Eve, "though we might differ as to the cause. The inconstancy of which you speak, is more connected with moral than physical causes, perhaps, and we, of this region, might claim an exemption from some of them. But, Mrs. Bloomfield is to be distinguished from her European rivals, by a frame so singularly feminine as to appear fragile, a delicacy of exterior, that, were it not for that illumined face of hers, might indicate a general feebleness, a sensitiveness and quickness of intellect that amount almost to inspiration; and, yet all is balanced by a practical common sense, that renders her as safe a counsellor as she is a warm friend. This latter quality causes you sometimes to doubt her genius, it is so very homely and available. Now it is in this, that I think the American woman, when she does rise above mediocrity, is particularly to be distinguished from the European. The latter, as a genius, is almost always in the clouds, whereas, Mrs. Bloomfield, in her highest flights, is either all heart, or all good sense. The nation is practical, and the practical qualities get to be imparted even to its highest order of talents."

"The English women are thought to be less excitable, and not so much under the influence of sentimentalism, as some of their continental neighbours."

"And very justly—but—"

"But, what, Miss Effingham—there is, in all this, a slight return to the cosmopolitism, that reminds me of our days of peril and adventure. Do not conceal a thought, if you wish to preserve that character."

"Well, to be sincere, I shall say that your women live under a system too sophisticated and factitious to give fair play to common sense, at all times. What, for instance, can be the habitual notions of one, who, professing the doctrines of Christianity, is accustomed to find money placed so very much in the ascendant, as to see it daily exacted in payment for the very first of the sacred offices of the church? It would be as rational to contend that a mirror which had been cracked into radii, by a bullet, like those we have so often seen in Paris, would reflect faithfully, as to suppose a mind familiarized to such abuses would be sensitive on practical and common sense things."

"But, my dear Miss Effingham, this is all habit."

"I know it is all habit, Sir George Templemore, and a very bad habit it is. Even your devoutest clergymen get so accustomed to it, as not to see the capital mistake they make. I do not say it is absolutely sinful, where there is no compulsion; but, I hope you agree with me, Mr. Powis, when I say I think a clergyman ought to be so sensitive on such a subject, as to refuse even the little offerings for baptisms, that it is the practice of the wealthy of this country to make."

"I agree with you entirely, for it would denote a more just perception of the nature of the office they are performing; and they who wish to give can always make occasions."

"A hint might be taken from Franklin, who is said to have desired his father to ask a blessing on the pork-barrel, by way of condensation," put in John Effingham, who joined them as he spoke, and who had heard a part of the conversation. "In this instance, an average might be struck in the marriage fee, that should embrace all future baptisms. But here comes neighbour Howel to favour us with his opinion. Do you like the usages of the English church, as respects baptisms, Howel?"

"Excellent, the best in the world, John Effingham."

"Mr. Howel is so true an Englishman," said Eve, shaking hands cordially with their well-meaning neighbour, "that he would give a certificate in favour of polygamy, if it had a British origin."

"And is not this a more natural sentiment for an American than that which distrusts so much, merely because it comes from the little island?" asked Sir George, reproachfully.

"That is a question I shall leave Mr. Howel himself to answer."

"Why, Sir George," observed the gentleman alluded to, "I do not attribute my respect for your country, in the least, to origin. I endeavour to keep myself free from all sorts of prejudices. My admiration of England arises from conviction, and I watch all her movements with the utmost jealousy, in order to see if I cannot find her tripping, though I feel bound to say I have never yet detected her in a single error. What a very different picture, France—I hope your governess is not within hearing, Miss Eve; it is not her fault; she was born a French woman, and we would not wish to hurt her feelings—but what a different picture France presents! I have watched her narrowly too, these forty years, I may say, and I have never yet found her right; and this, you must allow, is a great deal to be said by one who is thoroughly impartial."

"This is a terrible picture, indeed, Howel, to come from an unprejudiced man," said John Effingham; "and I make no doubt Sir George Templemore will have a better opinion of himself for ever after—he for a valiant lion, and you for a true prince. But yonder is the 'exclusive extra,' which contains our party."

The elevated bit of lawn on which they were walking commanded a view of the road that led into the village, and the travelling vehicle engaged by Mrs. Hawker and her friends, was now seen moving along it at a rapid pace. Eve expressed her satisfaction, and then all resumed their walk, as some minutes must still elapse previously to the arrival.

"Exclusive extra!" repeated Sir George; "that is a peculiar phrase, and one that denotes any thing but democracy."

"In any other part of the world a thing would be sufficiently marked, by being 'extra,' but here it requires the addition of 'exclusive,' in order to give it the 'tower stamp,'" said John Effingham, with a curl of his handsome lip. "Any thing may be as exclusive as it please, provided it bear the public impress. A stagecoach being intended for every body, why, the more exclusive it is, the better. The next thing we shall hear of will be exclusive steamboats, exclusive rail-roads, and both for the uses of the exclusive people."

Sir George now seriously asked an explanation of the meaning of the term, when Mr. Howel informed him that an 'extra' in America meant a supernumerary coach, to carry any excess of the ordinary number of passengers; whereas an 'exclusive extra' meant a coach expressly engaged by a particular individual.

"The latter, then, is American posting," observed Sir George.

"You have got the best idea of it that can be given," said Paul. "It is virtually posting with a coachman, instead of postillions, few persons in this country, where so much of the greater distances is done by steam, using their own travelling carriages. The American 'exclusive extra' is not only posting, but, in many of the older parts of the country, it is posting of a very good quality."

"I dare say, now, this is all wrong, if we only knew it," said the simple-minded Mr. Howel. "There is nothing exclusive in England, ha, Sir George?"

Every body laughed except the person who put this question, but the rattling of wheels and the tramping of horses on the village bridge, announced the near approach of the travellers. By the time the party had reached the great door in front of the house, the carriage was already in the grounds, and at the next moment, Eve was in the arms of Mrs. Bloomfield. It was apparent, at a glance, that more than the expected number of guests was in the vehicle; and as its contents were slowly discharged, the spectators stood around it, with curiosity, to observe who would appear.

The first person that descended, after the exit of Mrs. Bloomfield, was Captain Truck, who, however, instead of saluting his friends, turned assiduously to the door he had just passed through, to assist Mrs. Hawker to alight. Not until this office had been done, did he even look for Eve; for, so profound was the worthy captain's admiration and respect for this venerable lady, that she actually had got to supplant our heroine, in some measure, in his heart. Mr. Bloomfield appeared next, and an exclamation of surprise and pleasure proceeded from both Paul and the baronet, as they caught a glimpse of the face of the last of the travellers that got out.

"Ducie!" cried Sir George. "This is even better than we expected."

"Ducie!" added Paul, "you are several days before the expected time, and in excellent company."

The explanation, however, was very simple. Captain Ducie had found the facilities for rapid motion much greater than he had expected, and he reached Fort Plain, in the eastward cars, as the remainder of the party arrived in the westward. Captain Truck, who had met Mrs. Hawker's party in the river boat, had been intrusted with the duty of making the arrangements, and recognizing Captain Ducie, to their mutual surprise, while engaged in this employment, and ascertaining his destination, the latter was very cordially received into the "exclusive extra."

Mr. Effingham welcomed all his guests with the hospitality and kindness for which he was distinguished. We are no great admirers of the pretension to peculiar national virtues, having ascertained, to our own satisfaction, by tolerably extensive observation, that the moral difference between men is of no great amount; but we are almost tempted to say, on this occasion, that Mr. Effingham received his guests with American hospitality; for if there be one quality that this people can claim to possess in a higher degree than that of most other christian nations, it is that of a simple, sincere, confiding hospitality. For Mrs. Hawker, in common with all who knew her, the owner of the Wigwam entertained a profound respect; and though his less active mind did not take as much pleasure as that of his daughter, in the almost intuitive intelligence of Mrs. Bloomfield, he also felt for this lady a very friendly regard. It gave him pleasure to see Eve surrounded by persons of her own sex, of so high a tone of thought and breeding; a tone of thought and breeding, moreover, that was as far removed as possible from anything strained or artificial: and his welcomes were cordial in proportion. Mr. Bloomfield was a quiet, sensible, gentleman-like man, whom his wife fervently loved, without making any parade of her attachment; and he was also one who had the good sense to make himself agreeable wherever he went. Captain Ducie, who, Englishman-like, had required some urging to be induced to present himself at the Wigwam before the precise hour named in his own letter, and who had seriously contemplated passing several days in a tavern, previously to showing himself there, was agreeably disappointed at a reception, that would have been just as frank and warm, had he come without any notice at all: for the Effinghams knew that the usages which sophistication and a crowded population perhaps render necessary in older countries, were not needed in their own; and then the circumstance that their quondam pursuer was so near a kinsman of Paul Powis', did not fail to act essentially in his favour.

"We can offer but little, in these retired mountains, to interest a traveller and a man of the world, Captain Ducie," said Mr. Effingham, when he went to pay his compliments more particularly, after the whole party was in the house; "but there is a common interest in our past adventures to talk about, after all other topics fail. When we met on the ocean, and you deprived us so unexpectedly of our friend Powis, we did not know that you had the better claim of affinity to his company."

Captain Ducie coloured slightly, but he made his answer with a proper degree of courtesy and gratitude.

"It is very true," he added, "Powis and myself are relatives, and I shall place all my claims to your hospitality to his account; for I feel that I have been the unwilling cause of too much suffering to your party, to bring with me any very pleasant recollections, notwithstanding your kindness in including me as a friend, in the adventures of which you speak."

"Dangers that are happily past, seldom bring very unpleasant recollections, more especially when they were connected with scenes of excitement. I understand, sir, that the unhappy young man, who was the principal cause of all that passed, anticipated the sentence of the law, by destroying himself."

"He was his own executioner, and the victim of a silly weakness that, I should think, your state of society was yet too young and simple to encourage. The idle vanity of making an appearance, a vanity, by the way, that seldom besets gentlemen, or the class to which it may be thought more properly to belong, ruins hundreds of young men in England, and this poor creature was of the number. I never was more rejoiced than when he quitted my ship, for the sight of so much weakness sickened one of human nature. Miserable as his fate proved to be, and pitiable as his condition really was, while in my charge, his case has the alleviating circumstance with me, of having made me acquainted with those whom it might not otherwise have been my good fortune to meet!"

This civil speech was properly acknowledged, and Mr. Effingham addressed himself to Captain Truck, to whom, in the hurry of the moment, he had not yet said half that his feelings dictated.

"I am rejoiced to see you under my roof, my worthy friend," taking the rough hand of the old seaman between his own whiter and more delicate fingers, and shaking it with cordiality, "for this *is* being under my roof, while those town residences have less the air of domestication and familiarity. You will spend many of your holidays here, I trust; and when we get to be a few years older, we will begin to prattle about the marvels we have seen in company."

The eye of Captain Truck glistened, and, as he returned the shake by another of twice the energy, and the gentle pressure of Mr. Effingham by a squeeze like that of a vice, he said in his honest off-hand manner—

"The happiest hour I ever knew was that in which I discharged the pilot, the first time out, as a ship-master; the next great event of my life, in the way of happiness, was the moment I found myself on the deck of the Montauk, after we had given those greasy Arabs a hint that their room was better than their company; and I really think this very instant must be set down as the third. I never knew, my dear sir, how much I truly loved you and your daughter, until both were out of sight."

"That is so kind and gallant a speech, that it ought not to be lost on the person most concerned. Eve, my love, our worthy friend has just made a declaration which will be a novelty to you, who have not been much in the way of listening to speeches of this nature."

Mr. Effingham then acquainted his daughter with what Captain Truck had just said.

"This is certainly the first declaration of the sort I ever heard, and with the simplicity of an unpractised young woman, I here avow that the attachment is reciprocal," said the smiling Eve. "If there is an indiscretion in this hasty acknowledgement, it must be ascribed to surprise, and to the suddenness with which I have learned my power, for your *parvenues* are not always perfectly regulated."

"I hope Mam'selle V.A.V. is well," returned the Captain, cordially shaking the hand the young lady had given him, "and that she enjoys herself to her liking in this outlandish country?"

"Mademoiselle Viefville will return you her thanks in person, at dinner; and I believe she does not yet regret *la belle France* unreasonably; as I regret it myself, in many particulars, it would be unjust not to permit a native of the country some liberty in that respect."

"I perceive a strange face in the room—one of the family, my dear young lady?"

"Not a relative, but a very old friend.—Shall I have the pleasure of introducing you, Captain?"

"I hardly dared to ask it, for I know you must have been overworked in this way, lately, but I confess I *should* like an introduction; I have neither introduced, nor been introduced since I left New-York, with the exception of the case of Captain Ducie, whom I made properly acquainted with Mrs. Hawker and her party as you may suppose. They know each other regularly now, and you are saved the trouble of going through the ceremony yourself."

"And how is it with you and the Bloomfields? Did Mrs. Hawker name you to them properly?"

"That is the most extraordinary thing of the sort I ever knew! Not a word was said in the way of introduction, and yet I slid into an acquaintance with Mrs. Bloomfield so easily, that I could not tell how it was done, if my life depended on it. But this very old friend of yours, my dear young lady—"

"Captain Truck, Mr. Howel; Mr. Howel, Captain Truck;" said Eve, imitating the most approved manner of the introductory spirit of the day with admirable self-possession and gravity. "I am fortunate in having it in my power to make two persons whom I so much esteem acquainted."

"Captain Truck is the gentleman who commands the Montauk?" said Mr. Howel, glancing at Eve, as much as to say, "am I right?"

"The very same, and the brave seaman to whom we are all indebted for the happiness of standing here at this moment."

"You are to be envied, Captain Truck; of all the men in your calling, you are exactly the one I should most wish to supplant. I understand you actually go to England twice every year!"

"Three times, sir, when the winds permit. I have even seen the old island four times, between January and January."

"What a pleasure! It must be the very acme of navigation to sail between America and England!"

"It is not unpleasant, sir, from April to November, but the long nights, thick weather, and heavy winds knock off a good deal of the satisfaction for the rest of the year."

"But I speak of the country; of old England itself; not of the passages."

"Well, England has what I call a pretty fair coast. It is high, and great attention is paid to the lights; but of what account is either coast or lights, if the weather is so thick, you cannot see the end of your flying-jib-boom!"

"Mr. Howel alludes more particularly to the country, inland," said Eve; "to the towns, the civilization, and to the other proofs of cultivation and refinement. To the government, especially."

"In my judgment, sir, the government is much too particular about tobacco, and some other trifling things I could name. Then it restricts pennants to King's ships, whereas, to my notion, my dear young lady, a New-York packet is as worthy of wearing a pennant as any vessel that floats. I mean, of course, ships of the regular European lines, and not the Southern traders."

"But these are merely spots on the sun, my good sir," returned Mr. Howel; "putting a few such trifles out of the question, I think you will allow that England is the most delightful country in the world?"

"To be frank with you, Mr. Howel, there is a good deal of hang-dog weather, along in October, November and December. I have known March any thing but agreeable, and then April is just like a young girl with one of your melancholy novels, now smiling, and now blubbering."

"But the morals of the country, my dear sir; the moral features of England must be a source of never-dying delight to a true philanthropist," resumed Mr. Howel, as Eve, who perceived that the discourse was likely to be long, went to join the ladies. "An Englishman has most reason to be proud of the moral excellencies of his country!"

"Why, to be frank with you, Mr. Howel, there are some of the moral features of London, that are any thing but very beautiful. If you could pass twenty-four hours in the neighbourhood of St. Catharine's, you would see sights that would throw Templeton into fits. The English are a handsome people, I allow; but their morality is none of the best-featured."

"Let us be seated, sir; I am afraid we are not exactly agreed on our terms, and, in order that we may continue this subject, I beg you will let me take a seat next you, at table."

To this Captain Truck very cheerfully assented, and then the two took chairs, continuing the discourse very much in the blind and ambiguous manner in which it had been commenced; the one party insisting on seeing every thing through the medium of an imagination that had got to be diseased on such subjects, or with a species of monomania; while the other seemed obstinately determined to consider the entire country as things had been presented to his limited and peculiar experience, in the vicinity of the docks.

"We have had a very unexpected, and a very agreeable attendant in Captain Truck," said Mrs Hawker, when Eve had placed herself by her side, and respectfully taken one of her hands. "I really think if I were to suffer shipwreck, or to run the hazard of captivity, I should choose to have both occur in his good company."

"Mrs. Hawker makes so many conquests," observed Mrs. Bloomfield, "that we are to think nothing of her success with this mer-man; but what will you say, Miss Effingham, when you learn that I am also in favour, in the same high quarter. I shall think the better of masters, and boatswains, and Trinculos and Stephanos, as long as I live, for this specimen of their craft."

"Not Trinculos and Stephanos, dear Mrs. Bloomfield; for, *à l' exception pres de* Saturday-nights, and sweet-hearts and wives, a more exemplary person in the way of libations does not exist than our excellent Captain Truck. He is much too religious and moral for so vulgar an excess as drinking."

"Religious!" exclaimed Mrs, Bloomfield, in surprise. "This is a merit to which I did not know he possessed the smallest claims. One might imagine a little superstition, and some short-lived repentances in gales of wind; but scarcely any thing as much like a trade wind, as religion!"

"Then you do not know him; for a more sincerely devout man, though I acknowledge it is after a fashion that is perhaps peculiar to the ocean, is not often met with. At any rate, you found him attentive to our sex?"

"The pink of politeness, and, not to embellish, there is a manly deference about him, that is singularly agreeable to our frail vanity. This comes of his packet-training, I suppose, and we may thank you for some portion of his merit. His tongue never tires in your praises, and did I not feel persuaded that your mind is made up never to be the wife of any republican American, I should fear this visit exceedingly. Notwithstanding the remark I made concerning my being in favour, the affair lies between Mrs. Hawker and yourself. I know it is not your habit to trifle even on that very popular subject with young ladies, matrimony; but this case forms so complete an exception to the vulgar passion, that I trust you will overlook the indiscretion. Our *golden* captain, for *copper* he is not, protests that Mrs. Hawker is the most delightful old lady he ever knew, and that Miss Eve Effingham is the most delightful young lady he ever knew. Here, then, each may see the ground she occupies, and play her cards accordingly. I hope to be forgiven for touching on a subject so delicate."

"In the first place," said Eve, smiling, "I should wish to hear Mrs. Hawker's reply."

"I have no more to say, than to express my perfect gratitude," answered that lady, "to announce a determination not to change my condition, yet, on account of extreme youth, and a disposition to abandon the field to my younger, if not fairer, rival."

"Well, then," resumed Eve, anxious to change the subject, for she saw that Paul was approaching their group, "I believe it will be wisest in me to suspend a decision, circumstances leaving so much at my disposal. Time must show what that decision will be."

"Nay," said Mrs. Bloomfield, who saw no feeling involved in the trifling, "this is unjustifiable coquetry, and I feel bound to ascertain how the land lies. You will remember I am the Captain's confidant, and you know the fearful responsibility of a friend in an affair of this sort; that of a friend in the duello being insignificant in comparison. That I may have testimony at need, Mr. Powis shall be made acquainted with the leading facts. Captain Truck is a devout admirer of this young lady, sir, and I am endeavouring to discover whether he ought to hang himself on her father's lawn, this evening, as soon as the moon rises, or live another miserable week. In order to do this, I shall pursue the categorical and inquisitorial method—and so defend yourself Miss Effingham. Do you object to the country of your admirer?"

Eve, though inwardly vexed at the turn this pleasantry had taken, maintained a perfectly composed manner, for she knew that Mrs. Bloomfield had too much feminine propriety to say any thing improper, or any thing that might seriously embarrass her.

"It would, indeed, be extraordinary, should I object to a country which is not only my own, but which has so long been that of my ancestors," she answered steadily. "On this score, my knight has nothing to fear."

"I rejoice to hear this," returned Mrs. Bloomfield, glancing her eyes, unconsciously to herself, however, towards Sir George Templemore, "and, Mr. Powis, you, who I believe are a European, will learn humility in the avowal. Do you object to your swain that he is a seaman?"

Eve blushed, notwithstanding a strong effort to appear composed, and, for the first time since their acquaintance, she felt provoked with Mrs. Bloomfield. She hesitated before she answered in the negative, and this too in a way to give more meaning to her reply, although nothing could be farther from her intentions.

"The happy man *may* then be an American and a seaman! Here is great encouragement. Do you object to sixty?"

"In any other man I should certainly consider it a blemish, as my own dear father is but fifty."

Mrs. Bloomfield was struck with the tremor in the voice, and with the air of embarrassment, in one who usually was so easy and collected; and with feminine sensitiveness she adroitly abandoned the subject, though she often recurred to this stifled emotion in the course of the day, and from that moment she became a silent observer of Eve's deportment with all her father's guests.

"This is hope enough for one day," she said, rising; "the profession and the flag must counterbalance the years as best they may, and the Truck lives another revolution of the sun! Mrs. Hawker, we shall be late at dinner, I see by that clock, unless we retire soon."

Both the ladies now went to their rooms; Eve, who was already dressed for dinner, remaining in the drawing-room. Paul still stood before her, and, like herself, he seemed embarrassed.

"There are men who would be delighted to hear even the little that has fallen from your lips in this trifling," he said, as soon as Mrs. Bloomfield was out of hearing. "To be an American and a seaman, then, are not serious defects in your eyes?"

"Am I to be made responsible for Mrs. Bloomfield's caprices and pleasantries?"

"By no means; but I do think you hold yourself responsible for Miss Effingham's truth and sincerity. I can conceive of your silence, when questioned too far, but scarcely of any direct declaration, that shall not possess both these high qualities."

Eve looked up gratefully, for she saw that profound respect for her character dictated the remark; but rising, she observed—

"This is making a little *badinage* about our honest, lion-hearted, old captain, a very serious affair. And now, to show you that I am conscious of, and thankful for, your own compliment, I shall place you on the footing of a friend to both the parties, and request you will take Captain Truck into your especial care, while he remains here. My father and cousin are both sincerely his friends, but their habits are not so much those of their guest, as yours will probably be; and to you, then, I commit him, with a request that he may miss his ship and the ocean as little as possible."

"I would I knew how to take this charge, Miss Effingham!— To be a seaman is not always a recommendation with the polished, intelligent, and refined."

"But when one is polished, intelligent, and refined, to be a seaman is to add one other particular and useful branch of knowledge to those which are more familiar. I feel certain Captain Truck will be in good hands, and now I will go and do my devoirs to my own especial charges, the ladies."

Eve bowed as she passed the young man, and she left the room with as much haste as at all became her. Paul stood motionless quite a minute after she had vanished, nor did he awaken from his reverie, until aroused by an appeal from Captain Truck, to sustain him, in some of his matter-of-fact opinions concerning England, against the visionary and bookish notions of Mr. Howel.

"Who is this Mr. Powis?" asked Mrs. Bloomfield of Eve, when the latter appeared in her dressing-room, with an unusual impatience of manner.

"You know, my dear Mrs. Bloomfield, that he was our fellow-passenger in the Montauk, and that he was of infinite service to us, in escaping from the Arabs."

"All this I know, certainly; but he is a European, is he not?"

Eve scarcely ever felt more embarrassed than in answering this simple question.

"I believe not; at least, I think not; we thought so when we met him in Europe, and even until quite lately; but he has avowed himself a countryman of our own, since his arrival at Templeton."

"Has he been here long?"

"We found him in the village on reaching home. He was from Canada, and has been waiting for his cousin, Captain Ducie, who came with you."

"His cousin!—He has English cousins, then! Mr. Ducie kept this to himself, with true English reserve. Captain Truck whispered something of the latter's having taken out one of his passengers, *the* Mr. Powis, the hero of the rocks, but I did not know of his having found his way back to our—to his country. Is he as agreeable as Sir George Templemore?"

"Nay, Mrs. Bloomfield, I must leave you to judge of that for yourself. I think them both agreeable men; but there is so much caprice in a woman's tastes, that I decline thinking for others."

"He is a seaman, I believe," observed Mrs. Bloomfield, with an abstracted manner—"he *must* have been, to have manoeuvred and managed as I have been told he did. Powis—Powis—that is not one of our names, neither—I should think he must be from the south."

Here Eve's habitual truth and dignity of mind did her good service, and prevented any further betrayal of embarrassment.

"We do not know his family," she steadily answered. "That he is a gentleman, we see; but of his origin and connections he never speaks."

"His profession would have given him the notions of a gentleman, for he was in the navy I have heard, although I had thought it the British navy. I do not know of any Powises in Philadelphia, or Baltimore, or Richmond, or Charleston; he must surely be from the interior."

Eve could scarcely condemn her friend for a curiosity that had not a little tormented herself, though she would gladly have changed the discourse.

"Mr. Powis would be much gratified, did he know what a subject of interest he has suddenly become with Mrs. Bloomfield," she said, smiling.

"I confess it all; to be very sincere, I think him the most distinguished young man, in air, appearance, and expression of countenance, I ever saw. When this is coupled with what I have heard of his gallantry and coolness, my dear, I should not be woman to feel no interest in him. I would give the world to know of what State he is a native, if native, in truth, he be."

"For that we have his own word. He was born in this country, and was educated in our own marine."

"And yet from the little that fell from him, in our first short conversation, he struck me as being educated above his profession."

"Mr. Powis has seen much as a traveller; when we met him in Europe, it was in a circle particularly qualified to improve both his mind and his manners."

"Europe! Your acquaintance did not then commence, like that with Sir George Templemore, in the packet?"

"Our acquaintance with neither, commenced in the packet. My father had often seen both these gentlemen, during our residences in different parts of Europe."

"And your father's daughter?"

"My father's daughter, too," said Eve, laughing. "With Mr. Powis, in particular, we were acquainted under circumstances that left a vivid recollection of his manliness and professional skill. He was of almost as much service to us on one of the Swiss lakes, as he has subsequently been on the ocean."

All this was news to Mrs. Bloomfield, and she looked as if she thought the intelligence interesting. At this moment the dinner-bell rang, and all the ladies descended to the drawing-room. The gentlemen were already assembled, and as Mr. Effingham led Mrs. Hawker to the table, Mrs. Bloomfield gaily took Eve by the arm, protesting that she felt herself privileged, the first day, to take a seat near the young mistress of the Wigwam.

"Mr. Powis and Sir George Templemore will not quarrel about the honour," she said, in a low voice, as they proceeded towards the table.

"Indeed you are in error, Mrs. Bloomfield; Sir George Templemore is much better pleased with being at liberty to sit next my cousin Grace."

"Can this be so!" returned the other, looking intently at her young friend.

"Indeed it is so, and I am very glad to be able to affirm it. How far Miss Van Cortlandt is pleased that it is so, time must show: but the baronet betrays every day, and all day, how much he is pleased with her."

"He is then a man of less taste, and judgment, and intelligence, than I had thought him."

"Nay, dearest Mrs. Bloomfield, this is not necessarily true; or, if true, need it be so openly said?"

"*Se non è vero, è ben trovato.*"

CHAPTER XVIII.

"Thine for a space are they—
Yet shalt thou yield thy treasures up at last;
Thy gates shall yet give way,
Thy bolts shall fall, inexorable Past."

William Cullen Bryant, "The Past," ll. 35–38.

CAPTAIN Ducie had retired for the night, and was sitting reading, when a low tap at the door roused him from a brown study. He gave the necessary permission, and the door opened.

"I hope, Ducie, you have not forgotten the secretary I left among your effects," said Paul entering the room, "and concerning which I wrote you when you were still at Quebec."

Captain Ducie pointed to the case, which was standing among his other luggage, on the floor of the room.

"Thank you for this care," said Paul, taking the secretary under his arm, and retiring towards the door; "it contains papers of much importance to myself, and some that I have reason to think are of importance to others."

"Stop, Powis—a word before you quit me. Is Templemore *de trop*?"

"Not at all; I have a sincere regard for Templemore, and should be sorry to see him leave us."

"And yet I think it singular a man of his habits should be rusticating among these hills, when I know that he is expected to look at the Canadas, with a view to report their actual condition at home."

"Is Sir George really entrusted with a commission of that sort?" inquired Paul, with interest.

"Not with any positive commission, perhaps, for none was necessary. Templemore is a rich fellow, and has no need of appointments; but, it is hoped and understood, that he will look at the provinces, and report their condition to the government. I dare say he will not be impeached for his negligence, though it may occasion surprise."

"Good night, Ducie; Templemore prefers a wigwam to your walled Quebec, and *natives* to colonists; *voilà tout!*"

In a minute, Paul was at the door of John Effingham's room, where he again tapped, and was again told to enter.

"Ducie has not forgotten my request, and this is the secretary that contains poor Mr. Monday's papers," he remarked, as he laid his load on a toilet-table, speaking in a way to show that the visit was expected. "We have, indeed, neglected this duty too long, and it is to be hoped no injustice, or wrong to any, will be the consequence."

"Is that the package?" demanded John Effingham, extending a hand to receive a bundle of papers that Paul had taken from the secretary. "We will break the seals this moment, and ascertain what ought to be done, before we sleep."

"These are papers of my own, and very precious are they," returned the young man, regarding them a moment, with interest, before he laid them on the toilet. "Here are the papers of Mr. Monday."

John Effingham received the package from his young friend, placed the lights conveniently on the table, put on his spectacles, and invited Paul to be seated. The gentlemen were placed opposite each other, the duty of breaking the seals, and first casting an eye at the contents of the different documents, devolving, as a matter of course, on the senior of the two, who, in truth, had alone been entrusted with them.

"Here is something signed by poor Monday himself, in the way of a general certificate," observed John Effingham, who first read the paper, and then handed it to Paul. It was, in form, an unsealed letter; and it was addressed "to all whom it may concern." The certificate itself was in the following words:

"I, John Monday, do declare and certify, that all the accompanying letters and documents are genuine and authentic. Jane Dowse, to whom and from whom, are so many letters, was my late mother, she having intermarried with Peter Dowse, the man so often named, and who led her into acts for which I know she has since been deeply repentant. In committing these papers to me, my poor mother left me the sole judge of the course I was to take, and I have put them in this form, in order that they may yet do good, should I be called suddenly away. All depends on discovering who the person called Bright actually is, for he was never known to my mother, by any other name. She knows him to have been an Englishman, however, and thinks he was, or had been, an upper servant in a gentleman's family. John Monday."

This paper was dated several years back, a sign that the disposition to do right had existed some time in Mr. Monday; and all the letters and other papers had been carefully preserved. The latter also appeared to be regularly numbered, a precaution that much aided the investigations of the two gentlemen. The original letters spoke for themselves, and the copies had been made in a clear, strong, mercantile hand, and with the method of one accustomed to business. In short, so far as the contents of the different papers would allow, nothing was wanting to render the whole distinct and intelligible.

John Effingham read the paper No. 1, with deliberation, though not aloud; and when he had done, he handed it to his young friend, coolly remarking—

"That is the production of a deliberate villain."

Paul glanced his eye over the document, which was an original letter signed, "David Bright," and addressed to "Mrs. Jane Dowse." It was written with exceeding art, made many professions of friendship, spoke of the writer's knowledge of the woman's friends in England, and of her first husband in particular, and freely professed the writer's desire to serve her, while it also contained several ambiguous allusions to certain means of doing so, which should be revealed whenever the person to whom the letter was addressed might discover a willingness to embark in the undertaking. This letter was dated Philadelphia, was addressed to one in New-York, and it was old.

"This is, indeed, a rare specimen of villany," said Paul, as he laid down the paper, "and has been written in some such spirit as that employed by the devil when he tempted our common mother. I think I never read a better specimen of low, wily, cunning."

"And, judging by all that we already know, it would seem to have succeeded. In this letter you will find the gentleman a little more explicit; and but a little; though he is evidently encouraged by the interest and curiosity betrayed by the woman in this copy of the answer to his first epistle."

Paul read the letter just named, and then he laid it aside to wait for the next, which was still in the hands of his companion.

"This is likely to prove a history of unlawful love, and of its miserable consequences," said John Effingham in his cool manner, as he handed the answer to letter No. 1, and letter No. 2, to Paul. "The world is full of such unfortunate adventures, and I should think the parties English, by a hint or two you will find in this very honest and conscientious communication. Strongly artificial, social and political distinctions render expedients of this nature more frequent, perhaps, in Great Britain, than in any other country. Youth is the season of the passions, and many a man in the thoughtlessness of that period lays the foundation of bitter regret in after life."

As John Effingham raised his eyes, in the act of extending his hand towards his companion, he perceived that the fresh ruddy hue of his embrowned cheek deepened, until the colour diffused itself over the whole of his fine brow. At first an unpleasant suspicion flashed on John Effingham, and he admitted it with regret, for Eve and her future happiness had got to be closely associated, in his mind, with the character and conduct of the young man; but when Paul took the papers, steadily, and by an effort seemed to subdue all unpleasant feelings, the calm dignity with which he read them completely effaced the disagreeable distrust. It was then John Effingham remembered that he had once believed Paul himself might be the fruits of the heartless indiscretion he condemned. Commiseration and sympathy instantly took the place of the first impression, and he was so much absorbed with these feelings that he had not taken up the letter which was to follow, when Paul laid down the paper he had last been required to read.

"This does, indeed, sir, seem to foretell one of those painful histories of unbridled passion, with the still more painful consequences," said the young man with the steadiness of one who was unconscious of having a personal connexion with any events of a nature so unpleasant. "Let us examine farther."

John Effingham felt emboldened by these encouraging signs of unconcern, and he read the succeeding letters aloud, so that they learned their contents simultaneously. The next six or eight communications betrayed nothing distinctly, beyond the fact that the child which formed the subject of the whole correspondence, was to be received by Peter Dowse and his wife, and to be retained as their own offspring, for the consideration of a considerable sum, with an additional engagement to pay an annuity. It appeared by these letters also, that the child, which was hypocritically alluded to under the name of the "pet," had been actually transferred to the keeping of Jane Dowse, and that several years passed, after this arrangement, before the correspondence terminated. Most of the later letters referred to the payment of the annuity, although they all contained cold inquiries after the 'pet,' and answers so vague and general, as sufficiently to prove that the term was singularly misapplied. In the whole, there were some thirty or forty letters, each of which had been punctually answered, and their dates covered a space of near twelve years. The perusal of all these papers consumed more than an hour, and when John Effingham laid his spectacles on the table, the village clock had struck the hour of midnight.

"As yet," he observed, "we have learned little more than the fact that a child was made to take a false character, without possessing any other clue to the circumstances than is given in the names of the parties, all of whom are evidently obscure, and one of the most material of whom, we are plainly told, must have borne a fictitious name. Even poor Monday, in possession of so much collateral testimony that we want, could not have known what was the precise injustice done, if any, or, certainly, with the intentions he manifests, he would not have left that important particular in the dark."

"This is likely to prove a complicated affair," returned Paul, "and it is not very clear that we can be of any immediate service. As you are probably fatigued, we may without impropriety defer the further examination to another time."

To this John Effingham assented, and Paul, during the short conversation that followed, brought the secretary from the toilet to the table, along with that bundle of important papers that belonged to himself, to which he had alluded, and busied himself in replacing the whole in the drawer from which they had been taken.

"All the formalities about the seals, that we observed when poor Monday gave us the packet, would seem to be unnecessary," he remarked, while thus occupied, "and it will probably be sufficient if I leave the secretary in your room, and keep the keys myself."

"One never knows," returned John Effingham, with the greater caution of experience and age. "We have not read all the papers, and there are wax and lights before you; each has his watch and seal, and it will be the work of a minute only, to replace every thing as we left the package, originally. When this is done, you may leave the secretary, or remove it, at your own pleasure."

"I will leave it; for, though it contains so much that I prize, and which is really of great importance to myself, it contains nothing for which I shall have immediate occasion."

"In that case, it were better that I place the package in which we have a common interest in an *armoire*, or in my secretary, and that you keep your precious effects more immediately under your own eye."

"It is immaterial, unless the case will inconvenience you, for I do not know that I am not happier when it is out of my sight, so long as I feel certain of its security, than when it is constantly before my eyes."

Paul said this with a forced smile, and there was a sadness in his countenance that excited the sympathy of his companion. The latter, however, merely bowed his assent, and the papers were replaced, and the secretary was locked and deposited in an *armoire*, in silence. Paul was then about to wish the other good night, when John Effingham seized his hand, and by a gentle effort induced him to resume his seat. An embarrassing, but short pause succeeded, when the latter spoke.

"We have suffered enough in company, and have seen each other in situations of sufficient trial to be friends," he said. "I should feel mortified, did I believe you could think me influenced by an improper curiosity, in wishing to share more of your confidence than you are perhaps willing to bestow; I trust you will attribute to its right motive the liberty I am now taking. Age makes some difference between us, and the sincere and strong interest I feel in your welfare, ought to give me a small claim not to be treated as a total stranger. So jealous and watchful has this interest been, I might with great truth call it affection, that I have discovered you are not situated exactly as other men in your condition of life are situated, and I feel persuaded that the sympathy, perhaps the advice, of one so many years older than yourself, might be useful. You have already said so much to me, on the subject of your personal situation, that I almost feel a right to ask for more."

John Effingham uttered this in his mildest and most winning manner; and few men could carry with them, on such an occasion, more of persuasion in their voices and looks. Paul's features worked, and it was evident to his companion that he was moved, while, at the same time, he was not displeased.

"I am grateful, deeply grateful, sir, for this interest in my happiness," Paul answered, "and if I knew the particular points on which you feel any curiosity, there is nothing that I can desire to conceal. Have the further kindness to question me, Mr. Effingham, that I need not touch on things you do not care to hear."

"All that really concerns your welfare, would have interest with me. You have been the agent of rescuing not only myself, but those whom I most love, from a fate worse than death; and, a childless bachelor myself, I have more than once thought of attempting to supply the places of those natural friends that I fear you have lost. Your parents—"

"Are both dead. I never knew either," said Paul, who spoke huskily, "and will most cheerfully accept your generous offer, if you will suffer me to attach to it a single condition."

"Beggars must not be choosers," returned John Effingham, "and if you will suffer me to feel this interest in you, and occasionally to share in the confidence of a father; I shall not insist on any unreasonable terms. What is your condition?"

"That the word money may be struck out of our vocabulary, and that you leave your will unaltered. Were the world to be examined, you could not find a worthier or a lovelier heiress, than the one you have already selected, and whom Providence itself has given you. Compared with yourself, I am not rich; but I have a gentleman's income, and as I shall probably never marry, it will suffice for all my wants."

John Effingham was more pleased than he cared to express with this frankness, and with the secret sympathy that had existed between them; but he smiled at the injunction; for, with Eve's knowledge, and with her father's entire approbation, he had actually made a codicil to his will, in which their young protector was left one half of his large fortune.

"The will may remain untouched, if you desire it," he answered, evasively, "and that condition is disposed of. I am glad to learn so directly from yourself, what your manner of living and the reports of others had prepared me to hear, that you are independent. This fact, alone, will place us solely on our mutual esteem, and render the friendship that I hope is now brought within a covenant, if not now first established, more equal and frank. You have seen much of the world, Powis, for one of your years and profession?"

"It is usual to think that men of my profession see much of the world, as a consequence of their pursuits; though I agree with you, sir, that this is seeing the world only in a very limited circle. It is now several years since circumstances, I might almost say the imperative order of one whom I was bound to obey, induced me to resign, and since that time I have done little else but travel. Owing to certain adventitious causes, I have enjoyed an access to European society that few of our countrymen possess, and I hope the advantage has not been entirely thrown away. It was as a traveller on the continent of Europe, that I had the pleasure of first meeting with Mr. and Miss Effingham. I was much abroad, even as a child, and owe some little skill in foreign languages to that circumstance."

"So my cousin has informed me. You have set the question of country at rest, by declaring that you are an American, and yet I find you have English relatives. Captain Ducie, I believe, is a kinsman?"

"He is; we are sisters' children, though our friendship has not always been such as the connexion would infer. When Ducie and myself met at sea, there was an awkwardness, if not a coolness, in the interview, that, coupled with my sudden return to England, I fear did not make the most favourable impression, on those who witnessed what passed."

"We had confidence in your principles," said John Effingham, with a frank simplicity, "and, though the first surmises were not pleasant, perhaps, a little reflection told us that there was no just ground for suspicion."

"Ducie is a fine, manly fellow, and has a seaman's generosity and sincerity. I had last parted from him on the field, where we appeared as enemies; and the circumstance rendered the unexpected meeting awkward. Our wounds no longer smarted, it is true; but, perhaps, we both felt shame and sorrow that they had ever been inflicted."

"It should be a very serious quarrel that could arm sisters' children against each other," said John Effingham, gravely.

"I admit as much. But, at that time, Captain Ducie was not disposed to admit the consanguinity, and the offence grew out of an intemperate resentment of some imputations on my birth; between two military men, the issue could scarcely be avoided. Ducie challenged, and I was not then in the humour to balk him. A couple of flesh-wounds happily terminated the affair. But an interval of three years had enabled my enemy to discover that he had not done me justice; that I had been causelessly provoked to the quarrel, and that we ought to be firm friends. The generous desire to make suitable expiation, urged him to seize the first occasion of coming to America that offered; and when ordered to chase the Montauk, in obedience to a telegraphic communication from London, he was hourly expecting to sail for our seas, where he wished to come, expressly that we might meet. You will judge, therefore, how happy he was to find me unexpectedly in the vessel that contained his principal object of pursuit, thus killing, as it might be, two birds with one stone."

"And did he carry you away with him, with any such murderous intention?" demanded John Effingham, smiling.

"By no means; nothing could be more amicable than Ducie and myself got to be, when we had been a few hours together in his cabin. As often happens, when there have been violent antipathies and unreasonable prejudices, a nearer view of each other's character and motives removed every obstacle; and long before we reached England, two warmer friends could not be found, or a more frank intercourse between relatives could not be desired. You are aware, sir, that our English cousins do not often view their cis-atlantic relatives with the most lenient eyes."

"This is but too true," said John Effingham proudly, though his lip quivered as he spoke, "and it is, in a great measure, the fault of that miserable mental bondage which has left this country, after sixty years of nominal independence, so much at the mercy of a hostile opinion. It is necessary that we respect ourselves in order that others respect us."

"I agree with you, sir, entirely. In my case, however, previous injustice disposed my relatives to receive me better, perhaps, than might otherwise have been the case. I had little to ask in the way of fortune, and feeling no disposition to raise a question that might disturb the peerage of the Ducies, I became a favourite."

"A peerage!—Both your parents, then, were English?"

"Neither, I believe; but the connection between the two countries was so close, that it can occasion no surprise a right of this nature should have passed into the colonies. My mother's mother became the heiress of one of those ancient baronies, that pass to the heirs-general, and, in consequence of the deaths of two brothers, these rights, which however were never actually possessed by any of the previous generation, centered in my mother and my aunt. The former being dead, as was contended, without issue—"

"You forget yourself!"

"Lawful issue," added Paul, reddening to the temples, "I should have added—Mrs. Ducie, who was married to the younger son of an English nobleman, claimed and obtained the rank. My pretension would have left the peerage in abeyance, and I probably owe some little of the opposition I found, to that circumstance. But, after Ducie's generous conduct, I could not hesitate about joining in the application to the crown, that, by its decision, the abeyance might be determined in favour of the person who was in possession; and Lady Dunluce is now quietly confirmed in her claim."

"There are many young men in this country, who would cling to the hopes of a British peerage with greater tenacity!"

"It is probable there are; but my self-denial is not of a very high order, for, it could scarcely be expected the English ministers would consent to give the rank to a foreigner who did not hesitate about avowing his principles and national feelings. I shall not say I did not covet this peerage, for it would be supererogatory; but I am born an American, and will die an American; and an American who swaggers about such a claim, is like the daw among the peacocks. The less that is said about it, the better."

"You are fortunate to have escaped the journals, which, most probably, would have *begraced* you, by elevating you at once to the rank of a duke."

"Instead of which, I had no other station than that of a dog in the manger. If it makes my aunt happy to be called Lady Dunluce, I am sure she is welcome to the privilege; and when Ducie succeeds her, as will one day be the case, an excellent fellow will be a peer of England. *Voila tout!* You are the only countryman, sir, to whom I have ever spoken of the circumstance, and with you I trust it will remain a secret"

"What! am I precluded from mentioning the facts in my own family? I am not the only sincere, the only warm friend, you have in this house, Powis."

"In that respect, I leave you to act your pleasure, my dear sir. If Mr. Effingham feel sufficient interest in my fortunes, to wish to hear what I have told you, let there be no silly mysteries,—or—or Mademoiselle Viefville—"

"Or Nanny Sidley, or Annette," interrupted John Effingham, with a kind smile. "Well, trust to me for that; but, before we separate for the night, I wish to ascertain beyond question one other fact, although the circumstances you have stated scarce leave a doubt of the reply."

"I understand you, sir, and did not intend to leave you in any uncertainty on that important particular. If there can be a feeling, more painful than all others, with a man of any pride, it is to distrust the purity of his mother. Mine was beyond reproach, thank God, and so it was most clearly established, or I could certainly have had no legal claim to the peerage."

"Or your fortune—" added John Effingham, drawing a long breath, like one suddenly relieved from an unpleasant suspicion.

"My fortune comes from neither parent, but from one of those generous dispositions, or caprices, if you will, that sometimes induce men to adopt those who are alien to their blood. My guardian adopted me, took me abroad with him, placed me, quite young, in the navy, and dying, he finally left me all he possessed. As he was a bachelor, with no near relative, and had been the artisan of his own fortune, I could have no hesitation about accepting the gift he so liberally bequeathed. It was coupled with the condition that I should retire from the service, travel for five years, return home, and marry. There is no silly forfeiture exacted in either case, but such is the general course solemnly advised by a man who showed himself my true friend for so many years."

"I envy him the opportunity he enjoyed of serving you. I hope he would have approved of your national pride, for I believe we must put that at the bottom of your disinterestedness, in the affair of the peerage."

"He would, indeed, although he never knew any thing of the claim which arose out of the death of the two lords who preceded my aunt, and who were the brothers of my grandmother. My guardian was in all respects a man, and, in nothing more, than in a manly national pride. While abroad a decoration was offered him, and he declined it with the character and dignity of one who felt that distinctions which his country repudiated, every gentleman belonging to that country ought to reject; and yet he did it with a respectful gratitude for the compliment, that was due to the government from which the offer came."

"I almost envy that man," said John Effingham, with warmth. "To have appreciated you, Powis, was a mark of a high judgment; but it seems he properly appreciated himself, his country, and human nature."

"And yet he was little appreciated in his turn. That man passed years in one of our largest towns, of no more apparent account among its population than any one of its commoner spirits, and of not half as much as one of its bustling brokers, or jobbers."

"In that there is nothing surprising. The class of the chosen few is too small every where, to be very numerous at any given point, and more especially so in a scattered population like that of America. The broker will as naturally appreciate the broker, as the dog appreciates the dog, or the wolf the wolf. Least of all is the manliness you have named, likely to be valued among a people who have been put into men's clothes before they are out of leading-strings. I am older than you, my dear Paul," it was the first time John Effingham ever used so familiar an appellation, and the young man thought it sounded kindly—"I am older than you, my dear Paul, and will venture to tell you an important fact that may hereafter lessen some of your own mortifications. In most nations there is a high standard to which man at least affects to look; and acts are extolled and seemingly appreciated, for their naked merits. Little of this exists in America, where no man is much praised for himself, but for the purposes of party, or to feed national vanity. In the country in which, of all others, political opinion ought to be the freest, it is the most persecuted, and the community-character of the nation induces every man to think he has a right of property in all its fame. England exhibits a great deal of this weakness and injustice, which, it is to be feared, is a vicious fruit of liberty; for it is certain that the sacred nature of opinion is most appreciated in those countries in which it has the least efficiency. We are constantly deriding those governments which fetter opinion, and yet I know of no nation in which the expression of opinion is so certain to attract persecution and hostility as our own, though it may be, and is so free, by law."

"This arises from its potency. Men quarrel about opinion here, because opinion rules. It is but one mode of struggling for power. But to return to my guardian; he was a man to think and act for himself, and as far from the magazine and newspaper existence that most Americans, in a moral sense, pass, as any man could be."

"It is indeed a newspaper and magazine existence," said John Effingham, smiling at Paul's terms, "to know life only through such mediums! It is as bad as the condition of those English who form their notions of society from novels written by men and women who have no access to it, and from the records of the court journal. I thank you sincerely, Mr. Powis, for this confidence, which has not been idly solicited on my part, and which shall not be abused. At no distant day we will break the seals again, and renew our investigations into this affair of the unfortunate Monday, which is not yet, certainly, very promising in the way of revelations."

The gentlemen shook hands cordially, and Paul, lighted by his companion, withdrew. When the young man was at the door of his own room, he turned, and saw John Effingham following him with his eye. The latter then renewed the good night, with one of those winning smiles that rendered his face so brilliantly handsome, and each retired.

CHAPTER XIX.

"Item, a capon . . . . . 2*s*. 2*d*.
Item, sauce . . . . . 4*d*.
Item, sack, two gallons . . . . . 5*s*. 8*d*. . . .
Item, bread . . . . . ob."

Henry IV, Part 1 2.4.535–537, 539.

THE next day John Effingham made no allusion to the conversation of the previous night, though the squeeze of the hand given to Paul, when they met, was an assurance that nothing was forgotten. As he had a secret pleasure in obeying any injunction of Eve's, the young man himself sought Captain Truck, even before they had breakfasted, and, as he had made an acquaintance with 'the commodore,' on the lake, previously to the arrival of the Effinghams, that worthy was summoned, and regularly introduced to the honest ship-master. The meeting between these two distinguished men was grave, ceremonious and dignified, each probably feeling that he was temporarily the guardian of a particular portion of an element that was equally dear to both. After a few minutes passed, as it might be, in the preliminary points of etiquette, a better feeling and more confidence were established, and it was soon settled that they should fish in company, the rest of the day; Paul promising to row the ladies out on the lake, and to join them in the course of the afternoon.

As the party quitted the breakfast-table, Eve took an occasion to thank the young man for his attention to their common friend, who, it had been reported, had taken his morning's repast at an early hour, and was already on the lake, the day by this time having advanced within two hours of noon.

"I have dared even to exceed your instructions, Miss Effingham," said Paul, "for I have promised the Captain to endeavour to persuade you, and as many of the ladies as possible, to trust yourselves to my seamanship, and to submit to be rowed to the spot where we shall find him and his friend the commodore riding at anchor, or to repair to the Point for a pic nic, as you may determine."

"An engagement that my influence shall be used to see fulfilled. Mrs. Bloomfield has already expressed a desire to go on the Otsego-Water, and I make no doubt I shall find other companions. Once more let me thank you for this little attention, for I too well know your tastes, not to understand that you might find a more agreeable ward."

"Upon my word, I feel a sincere regard for our old Captain, and could often wish for no better companion. Were he, however, as disagreeable as I find him, in truth, pleasant and frank, your wishes would conceal all his faults."

"You have learned, Mr. Powis, that small attentions are as much remembered as important services, and after having saved our lives, wish to prove that you can discharge *les petits devoirs socials*, as well as perform great deeds. I trust you will persuade Sir George Templemore to be of our party, and at four we shall be ready to accompany you; until then I am contracted to a gossip with Mrs. Bloomfield in her dressing-room."

We shall now leave the party on the land, and follow those who have already taken boat, or the fishermen. The beginning of the intercourse between the salt-water navigator and his fresh-water companion was again a little constrained and critical. Their professional terms agreed as ill as possible, for when the Captain used the expression 'ship the oars,' the commodore understood just the reverse of what it had been intended to express; and, once, when he told his companion to 'give way,' the latter took the hint so literally as actually to cease his efforts. All these professional niceties induced the worthy ship-master to undervalue his companion, who, in the main, was very skilful in his particular pursuit, though it was a skill that he exerted after the fashions of his own lake, and not after the fashions of the ocean. Owing to several contre-tems of this nature, by the time they reached the fishing-ground the Captain began to entertain a feeling for the commodore, that ill comported with the deference due to his titular rank.

"I have come out with you, commodore," said Captain Truck, when they had got to their station, and laying a peculiar emphasis on the appellation he used, "in order to *enjoy* myself, and you will confer an especial favour on me by not using such phrases as 'cable-rope,' 'casting anchor,' and 'titivating.' As for the two first, no seaman ever uses them; and I never heard such a word on board a ship, as the last. D—e, sir, if I believe it is to be found in the dictionary, even."

"You amaze me, sir! 'Casting anchor,' and 'cable-rope' are both Bible phrases, and they must be right."

"That follows by no means, commodore, as I have some reason to know; for my father having been a parson, and I being a seaman, we may be said to have the whole subject, in the family. St. Paul—you have heard of such a man as St. Paul, commodore?—"

"I know him almost as well as I know this lake, sir; but St. Peter and St. Andrew were the men most after my heart. Ours is an ancient calling, sir, and in those two instances you see to what a fisherman can rise. I do not remember to have ever heard of a sea-captain who was converted into a saint."

"Ay, ay, there is always too much to do on board ship to leave time to be much more than a beginner in religion. There was my mate, v'y'ge before last, Tom Leach, who is now master of a ship of his own, had he been brought up to it properly, he would have made as conscientious a parson as did his grandfather before him. Such a man would have been a seaman, as well as a parson. I have little to say against St. Peter or St. Andrew, but, in my judgment, they were none the better saints for having been fishermen; and, if the truth were known, I dare say they were at the bottom of introducing such lubberly phrases into the Bible, as 'casting-anchor,' and 'cable-rope.'"

"Pray, sir," asked the commodore, with dignity, "what are *you* in the practice of saying, when you speak of such matters; for, to be frank with you, *we* always use these terms on these lakes."

"That I can believe, for there is a strong fresh-water smell about them. We say 'anchor,' or 'let go the anchor,' or 'dropped the anchor,' or some such reasonable expression, and not 'cast anchor,' as if a bit of iron, weighing two or three tons, is to be jerked about like a stone big enough to kill a bird with. As for the 'cable-rope,' as you call it, we say the 'cable,' or 'the chain,' or 'the ground tackle,' according to reason and circumstances. You never hear a real 'salt' flourishing his 'cable-ropes,' and his 'casting-anchors,' which are altogether too sentimental and particular for his manner of speaking. As for 'ropes,' I suppose you have not got to be a commodore, and need being told how many there are in a ship."

"I do not pretend to have counted them, but I have seen a ship, sir, and one under full sail, too, and I know there were as many ropes about her as there are pines on the Vision."

"Are there more than seven of these trees on your mountain? for that is just the number of ropes in a merchant-man; though a man-of-war's-man counts one or two more."

"You astonish me, sir! But seven ropes in a ship?—I should have said there are seven hundred!"

"I dare say, I dare say; that is just the way in which a landsman pretends to criticise a vessel. As for the ropes, I will now give you their names, and then you can lay athwart hawse of these canoe gentry, by the hour, and teach them rigging and modesty, and both at the same time. In the first place," continued the captain, jerking uselessly at his line, and then beginning to count on his fingers— "There is the 'man-rope;' then come the 'bucket-rope,' the 'tiller-rope,' the 'bolt-rope,' the 'foot-rope,' the 'top-rope,' and the 'limber-rope.' I have followed the seas, now, more than half a century, and never yet heard of a 'cable-rope,' from any one who could hand, reef, and steer."

"Well, sir, every man to his trade," said the commodore, who just then pulled in a fine pickerel, which was the third he had taken, while his companion rejoiced in no more than a few fruitless bites. "You are more expert in ropes than in lines, it would seem. I shall not deny your experience and knowledge; but in the way of fishing, you will at least allow that the sea is no great school. I dare say, now, if you were to hook the 'sogdollager,' we should have you jumping into the lake to get rid of him. Quite probably, sir, you never before heard of that celebrated fish?"

Notwithstanding the many excellent qualities of Captain Truck, he had a weakness that is rather peculiar to a class of men, who, having seen so much of this earth, are unwilling to admit they have not seen it all. The little brush in which he was now engaged with the commodore, he conceived due to his own dignity, and his motive was duly to impress his companion with his superiority, which being fairly admitted, he would have been ready enough to acknowledge that the other understood pike-fishing much better than himself. But it was quite too early in the discussion to make any such avowal, and the supercilious remark of the commodore's putting him on his mettle, he was ready to affirm that he had eaten 'sogdollagers' for breakfast, a month at a time, had it been necessary.

"Pooh! pooh! man," returned the captain, with an air of cool indifference, "you do not surely fancy that you have any thing in a lake like this, that is not to be found in the ocean! If you were to see a whale's flukes thrashing your puddle, every cruiser among you would run for a port; and as for 'sogdollagers,' we think little of them in salt-water; the flying-fish, or even the dry dolphin, being much the best eating."

"Sir," said the commodore, with some heat, and a great deal of emphasis, "there is but *one* 'sogdollager' in the world, and he is in this lake. No man has ever seen him, but my predecessor, the 'Admiral,' and myself."

"Bah!" ejaculated the captain, "they are as plenty as soft clams, in the Mediterranean, and the Egyptians use them as a pan-fish. In the East, they catch them to bait with, for hallibut, and other middling sized creatures, that are particular about their diet. It is a good fish, I own, as is seen in this very circumstance."

"Sir," repeated the commodore, flourishing his hand, and waxing warm with earnestness, "there is but one 'sogdollager' in the universe, and that is in Lake Otsego. A 'sogdollager' is a salmon trout, and not a species; a sort of father to all the salmon trout in this part of the world; a scaly patriarch."

"I make no doubt *your* 'sogdollager' is scaly enough; but what is the use in wasting words about such a trifle? A whale is the only fish fit to occupy a gentleman's thoughts. As long as I have been at sea, I have never witnessed the taking of more than three whales."

This allusion happily preserved the peace; for, if there were any thing in the world for which the commodore entertained a profound, but obscure reverence, it was for a whale. He even thought better of a man for having actually seen one, gambolling in the freedom of the ocean; and his mind became suddenly oppressed by the glory of a mariner, who had passed his life among such gigantic animals. Shoving back his cap, the old man gazed steadily at the captain a minute, and his displeasure about the 'sogdollagers' vanished, though, in his inmost mind, he set down all that the other had told him on that particular subject, as so many parts of a regular 'fish story.'

"Captain Truck," he said, with solemnity, "I acknowledge myself to be but an ignorant and inexperienced man, one who has passed his life on this lake, which, broad and beautiful as it is, must seem a pond in the eyes of a seaman like yourself, who have passed your days on the Atlantic—"

"Atlantic!" interrupted the captain contemptuously, "I should have but a poor opinion of myself, had I seen nothing but the Atlantic! Indeed, I never can believe I am at sea at all, on the Atlantic, the passages between New-York and Portsmouth being little more than so much canalling along a tow-path. If you wish to say any thing about oceans, talk of the Pacific, or of the Great South Sea, where a man may run a month with a fair wind, and hardly go from island to island. Indeed, that is an ocean in which there is a manufactory of islands, for they turn them off in lots to supply the market, and of a size to suit customers."

"A manufactory of islands!" repeated the commodore, who began to entertain an awe of his companion, that he never expected to feel for any human being on Lake Otsego; "are you certain, sir, there is no mistake in this?"

"None in the least; not only islands, but whole Archipelagos are made annually, by the sea insects in that quarter of the world; but, then, you are not to form your notions of an insect in such an ocean, by the insects you may find in a bit of water as this."

"As big as our pickerel, or salmon trout, I dare say?" returned the commodore, in the simplicity of his heart, for by this time his local and exclusive conceit was thoroughly humbled, and he was almost ready to believe any thing.

"I say nothing of their size, for it is to their numbers and industry that I principally allude now. A solitary shark, I dare say, would set your whole Lake in commotion?"

"I think we might manage a shark, sir. I once saw one of those animals, and I do really believe the sogdollager would outweigh him. I do think we might manage a shark, sir."

"Ay, you mean an in-shore, high-latitude fellow. But what would you say to a shark as long as one of those pines on the mountain?"

"Such a monster would take in a man, whole?"

"A man! He would take in a platoon, Indian file. I dare say one of those pines, now, may be thirty or forty feet high!"

A gleam of intelligence and of exultation shot across the weather-beaten face of the old fisherman, for he detected a weak spot in the other's knowledge. The worthy Captain, with that species of exclusiveness which accompanies excellence in any one thing, was quite ignorant of most matters that pertain to the land. That there should be a tree, so far inland, that was larger than his main-yard, he did not think probable, although that yard itself was made of part of a tree; and, in the laudable intention of duly impressing his companion with the superiority of a real seaman over a mere fresh-water navigator, he had inadvertently laid bare a weak spot in his estimate of heights and distances, that the Commodore seized upon, with some such avidity as the pike seizes the hook. This accidental mistake alone saved the latter from an abject submission, for the cool superiority of the Captain had so far deprived him of his conceit, that he was almost ready to acknowledge himself no better than a dog, when he caught a glimpse of light through this opening.

"There is not a pine, that can be called of age, on all the mountain, which is not more than a hundred feet high, and many are nearer two," he cried in exultation, flourishing his hand, furiously. "The sea may have its big monsters, Captain, but our hills have their big trees. Did you ever see a shark of half that length?"

Now, Captain Truck was a man of truth, although so much given to occasional humorous violations of its laws, and, withal, a little disposed to dwell upon the marvels of the great deep, in the spirit of exaggeration, and he could not, in conscience, affirm any thing so extravagant as this. He was accordingly obliged to admit his mistake, and from this moment, the conversation was carried on with a greater regard to equality. They talked, as they fished, of politics, religion, philosophy, human nature, the useful arts, abolition, and most other subjects that would be likely to interest a couple of Americans who had nothing to do but to twitch, from time to time, at two lines dangling in the water. Although few people possess less of the art of conversation than our own countrymen, no other nation takes as wide a range in its discussions. He is but a very indifferent American that does not know, or thinks he knows, a little of every thing, and neither of our worthies was in the least backward in supporting the claims of the national character in this respect. This general discussion completely restored amity between the parties; for, to confess the truth, our old friend the Captain was a little rebuked about the affair of the tree. The only peculiarity worthy of notice, that occurred in the course of their various digressions, was the fact, that the commodore insensibly began to style his companion "General;" the courtesy of the country in his eyes, appearing to require that a man who had seen so much more than himself, should, at least, enjoy a title equal to his own in rank, and that of Admiral being proscribed by the sensitiveness of republican principles. After fishing a few hours, the old laker pulled the skiff up to the Point so often mentioned, where he lighted a fire on the grass, and prepared a dinner. When every thing was ready, the two seated themselves, and began to enjoy the fruits of their labours in a way that will be understood by all sportsmen.

"I have never thought of asking you, general," said the commodore, as he began to masticate a perch, "whether you are an aristocrat or a democrat. We have had the government pretty much upside-down, too, this morning, but this question has escaped me."

"As we are here by ourselves under these venerable oaks, and talking like two old messmates," returned the general, "I shall just own the truth, and make no bones of it. I have been captain of my own ship so long, that I have a most thorough contempt for all equality. It is a vice that I deprecate, and, whatever may be the laws of this country, I am of opinion, that equality is no where borne out by the Law of Nations; which, after all, commodore, is the only true law for a gentleman to live under."

"That is the law of the strongest, if I understand the matter, general."

"But, reduced to rules. The Law of Nations, to own the truth to you, is full of categories, and this will give an enterprising man an opportunity to make his fortune. Would you believe, commodore, that there are countries, in which they lay taxes on tobacco?"

"Taxes on tobacco! Sir, I never heard of such an act of oppression under the forms of law! What has tobacco done, that any one should think of taxing it?"

"I believe, commodore, that its greatest offence is being so general a favourite. Taxation, I have found, differs from most other things, generally attacking that which men most prize."

"This is quite new to me, general. A tax on tobacco! The law-makers in those countries cannot chew. I drink to your good health, sir, and to many happy returns of such banquets as this."

Here the commodore raised to his lips a large silver punch-bowl, which Pierre had furnished, and fastening his eyes on the boughs of a knarled oak, he looked like a man who was taking an observation, for near a minute. All this time, the captain regarded him, with a sympathetic pleasure, and when the bowl was free, he imitated the example, levelling his own eye at a cloud, that seemed floating at an angle of forty-five degrees above him, expressly for that purpose.

"There is a lazy cloud!" exclaimed the general, as he let go his hold to catch breath; "I have been watching it near a minute, and it has not moved so much as an inch."

"Tobacco!" repeated the commodore, drawing a long breath, as if he was just recovering the play of his lungs, "I should as soon think of laying a tax on punch. The country that pursues such a policy must, sooner or later, meet with a downfall. I never knew good come of persecution."

"I find you are a sensible man, commodore, and regret I did not make your acquaintance earlier in life. Have you yet made up your mind on the subject of religious faith?"

"Why, my dear general, not to be nibbling like a sucker with a sore mouth, with a person of your liberality, I shall give you a plain history of my adventures, in the way of experiences, that you may judge for yourself. I was born an Episcopalian, if one can say so, but was converted to Presbyterianism at twenty. I stuck to this denomination about five years, when I thought I would try the Baptists, having got to be fond of the water, by this time. At thirty-two I fished a while with the Methodists; since which conversion, I have chosen to worship God pretty much by myself, out here on the lake."

"Do you consider it any harm, to hook a fish of a Sunday?"

"No more than it is to eat a fish of a Sunday. I go altogether by faith, in my religion, general, for they talked so much to me of the uselessness of works, that I've got to be very unparticular as to what I do. Your people who have been converted four or five times, are like so many pickerel, which strike at every hook."

"This is very much my case. Now, on the river—of course you know where the river is?"

"Certain," said the commodore; "it is at the foot of the lake."

"My dear commodore, when we say 'the river,' we always mean the Connecticut; and I am surprised a man of your sagacity should require to be told this. There are people on the river who contend that a ship should heave-to of a Sunday. They did talk of getting up an Anti-Sunday-Sailing-Society, but the ship-masters were too many for them, since they threatened to start a society to put down the growing of inyens, (the captain would sometimes use this pronunciation) except of week-days. Well, I started in life, on the platform tack, in the way of religion, and I believe I shall stand on the same course till orders come to 'cast anchor,' as you call it. With you, I hold out for faith, as the one thing needful. Pray, my good friend, what are your real sentiments concerning 'Old Hickory.'"

"Tough, sir;—Tough as a day in February on this lake. All fins, and gills, and bones."

"That is the justest character I have yet heard of the old gentleman; and it says a great deal in a few words; no category about it. I hope the punch is to your liking?"

On this hint the old fisherman raised the bowl to his lips a second time, and renewed the agreeable duty of letting its contents flow down his throat, in a pleasant stream. This time, he took aim at a gull that was sailing over his head, only relinquishing the draught as the bird settled into the water. The 'general' was more particular; for selecting a stationary object, in the top of an oak, that grew on the mountain near him, he studied it with an admirable abstruseness of attention, until the last drop was drained. As soon as this startling fact was mentioned, however, both the *convives* set about repairing the accident, by squeezing lemons, sweetening water, and mixing liquors, *secundem artem*. At the same instant, each lighted a cigar, and the conversation, for some time, was carried on between their teeth.

"We have been so frank with each other to-day, my excellent commodore," said Captain Truck, "that did I know your true sentiments concerning Temperance Societies, I should look on your inmost soul as a part of myself. By these free communications men get really to know each other."

"If liquor is not made to be drunk, for what is it made? Any one may see that this lake was made for skiffs and fishing; it has a length, breadth, and depth, suited to such purposes. Now, here is liquor distilled, bottled, and corked, and I ask if all does not show that it was made to be drunk. I dare say your temperance men are ingenious, but let them answer that if they can."

"I wish, from my heart, my dear sir, we had known each other fifty years since. That would have brought you acquainted with salt-water, and left nothing to be desired in your character. We think alike, I believe, in every thing but on the virtues of fresh-water. If these temperance people had their way, we should all be turned into so many Turks, who never taste wine, and yet marry a dozen wives."

"One of the great merits of fresh-water, general, is what I call its mixable quality."

"There would be an end to Saturday nights, too, which are the seamen's tea-parties."

"I question if many of them fish in the rain, from sunrise to sunset."

"Or, stand their watches in wet pee-jackets, from sunset to sunrise. Splicing the main brace at such times, is the very quintessence of human enjoyments."

"If liquors were not made to be drunk," put in the commodore, logically, "I would again ask for what are they made? Let the temperance men get over that difficulty if they can."

"Commodore, I wish you twenty more good hearty years of fishing in this lake, which grows, each instant, more beautiful in my eyes, as I confess does the whole earth; and to show you that I say no more than I think, I will clench it with a draught."

Captain Truck now brought his right eye to bear on the new moon, which happened to be at a convenient height, closed the left one, and continued in that attitude until the commodore began seriously to think he was to get nothing besides the lemon-seeds for his share. This apprehension, however, could only arise from ignorance of his companion's character, than whom a juster man, according to the notions of ship-masters, did not live; and had one measured the punch that was left in the bowl when this draught was ended, he would have found that precisely one half of it was still untouched, to a thimblefull. The commodore now had his turn; and before he got through, the bottom of the vessel was as much uppermost as the butt of a clubbed firelock. When the honest fisherman took breath after this exploit, and lowered his cup from the vault of heaven to the surface of the earth, he caught a view of a boat crossing the lake, coming from the Silent Pine, to that Point on which they were enjoying so many agreeable hallucinations on the subject of temperance.

"Yonder is the party from the Wigwam," he said, "and they will be just in time to become converts to our opinions, if they have any doubts on the subjects we have discussed. Shall we give up the ground to them, by taking to the skiff, or do you feel disposed to face the women?"

"Under ordinary circumstances, commodore, I should prefer your society to all the petticoats in the State, but there are two ladies in that party, either of whom I would marry, any day, at a minute's warning."

"Sir," said the commodore with a tone of warning, "we, who have lived bachelors so long, and are wedded to the water, ought never to speak lightly on so grave a subject."

"Nor do I. Two women, one of whom is twenty, and the other seventy—and hang me if I know which I prefer."

"You would soonest be rid of the last, my dear general, and my advice is to take her."

"Old as she is, sir, a king would have to plead hard to get her consent. We will, now, make them some punch, that they may see we were mindful of them in their absence."

To work these worthies went in earnest, in order to anticipate the arrival of the party, and as the different compounds were in the course of mingling, the conversation did not flag. By this time both the salt-water and the fresh-water sailor were in that condition when men are apt to think aloud, and the commodore had lost all his awe of his companion.

"And so you have become a laker in your religion, my dear commodore," continued the general, between his teeth, while he smoked and squeezed a lemon at the same time, "and do your worshipping on the water?"

"Altogether of late, and more especially since my dream."

"Dream! My dear sir, I should think you altogether too innocent a man to dream."

"The best of us have our failings, general. I do sometimes dream, I own, as well as the greatest sinner of them all."

"And of what did you dream—the sogdollager?"

"I dreamt of death."

"Of slipping the cable!" cried the general, looking up suddenly. "Well, what was the drift?"

"Why, sir, having no wings, I went down below, and soon found myself in the presence of the old gentleman himself."

"That was pleasant—had he a tail? I have always been curious to know whether he really has a tail or not."

"I saw none, sir, but then we stood face to face, like gentlemen, and I cannot describe what I did not see."

"Was he glad to see you, commodore?"

"Why, sir, he was civilly spoken, but his occupation prevented many compliments."

"Occupation!"

"Certainly, sir; he was cutting out shoes, for his imps to travel about in, in order to stir up mischief."

"And did he set you to work?—This is a sort of State-Prison affair, after all!"

"No sir, he was too much of a gentleman to set me at making shoes as soon as I arrived. He first inquired what part of the country I was from, and when I told him, he was curious to know what most of the people were about in our neighbourhood."

"You told him, of course, commodore?"

"Certainly, sir, I told him their chief occupation was quarrelling about religion; making saints of themselves, and sinners of their neighbours. 'Hollo!' says the Devil, calling out to one of his imps, 'boy, run and catch my horse—I must be off, and have a finger in that pie. What denominations have you in that quarter, commodore?' So I told him, general, that we had Baptists, and Quakers, and Universalists, and Episcopalians, and Presbyterians, old-lights, new-lights, and blue-lights; and Methodists—. 'Stop,' said the Devil, 'that's enough; you imp, be nimble with that horse.—Let me see, commodore, what part of the country did you say you came from?' I told him the name more distinctly this time—"

"The very spot?"

"Town and county."

"And what did the Devil say to that?"

"He called out to the imp, again—'Hollo, you boy, never mind that horse; *these* people will all be here before I can get there.'"

Here the commodore and the general began to laugh, until the arches of the forest rang with their merriment. Three times they stopped, and as often did they return to their glee, until, the punch being ready, each took a fresh draught, in order to ascertain if it were fit to be offered to the ladies.

"My dear sir," said the commodore, as soon as he had recovered breath, "I am a thousand times sorry you came from that river, for, to tell you my mind without any concealment, my only objection to you is that you are not of the middle states. I admit the good qualities of the Yankees, in a general way, and yet they are the very worst neighbours that a man can have."

"This is a new character of them, commodore, as they generally pass for the best, in their own eyes. I should like to hear you explain your meaning."

"I call him a bad neighbour who never remains long enough in a place to love any thing but himself. Now, sir, I have a feeling for every pebble on the shore of this lake, a sympathy with every wave,"— here the commodore began to twirl his hand about, with the fingers standing apart, like so many spikes in a *chevaux-de-frise*—"and each hour, as I row across it, I find I like it better; and yet, sir, would you believe me, I often go away of a morning to pass the day on the water, and, on returning home at night, find half the houses filled with new faces."

"What becomes of the old ones?" demanded Captain Truck; for this, it struck him, was getting the better of him with his own weapons. "Do you mean that the people come and go like the tides?"

"Exactly so, sir; just as it used to be with the herrings in the Otsego, before the Susquehannah was dammed, and is still, with the swallows."

"Well, well, my good friend, take consolation. You'll meet all the faces you ever saw here, one day, in heaven."

"Never; not a man of them will stay there, if there be such a thing as moving. Depend on it, sir," added the commodore gravely, in the simplicity of his heart, "heaven is no place for a Yankee, if, by hook or crook, he can get farther west. They are all too uneasy for any steady occupation. You, who are a navigator, must know something concerning the stars; is there such a thing as another world, that lies west of this?"

"That can hardly be, commodore, since the points of the compass only refer to objects on this earth. You know, I suppose, that a man starting from this spot, and travelling due west, would arrive, in time, at this very point, coming in from the east; so that what is west to us, in the heavens, on this side of the world, is east to those on the other."

"This I confess I did not know, general. I have understood that what is good in one man's eyes, will be bad in another's; but never before have I heard that what is west to one man, lies east to another. I am afraid, general, that there is a little of the sogdollager bait in this?"

"Not enough, sir, to catch the merest fresh-water gudgeon that swims. No, no; there is neither east nor west off the earth, nor any up and down; and so we Yankees must try and content ourselves with heaven. Now, commodore, hand me the bowl, and we will get it ready down to the shore, and offer the ladies our homage, and some punch."

CHAPTER XX.

"O Romeo, Romeo, wherefore art thou Romeo?"

Romeo and Juliet 2.2.33.

THE usual effect of punch is to cause people to see double; but, on this occasion, the mistake was the other way, for two boats had touched the strand, instead of the one announced by the commodore, and they brought with them the whole party from the Wigwam, Steadfast and Aristabulus included. A domestic or two had also been brought to prepare the customary repast.

Captain Truck was as good as his word, as respects the punch, and the beverage was offered to each of the ladies in form, as soon as her feet had touched the green sward which covers that beautiful spot. Mrs. Hawker declined drinking, in a way to delight the gallant seaman; for so completely had she got the better of all his habits and prejudices, that every thing she did seemed right and gracious in his eyes.

The party soon separated into groups, or pairs, some being seated on the margin of the limpid water, enjoying the light cool airs, by which it was fanned, others lay off in the boats fishing, while the remainder plunged into the woods, that, in their native wildness, bounded the little spot of verdure, which, canopied by old oaks, formed the arena so lately in controversy. In this manner, an hour or two soon slipped away, when a summons was given for all to assemble around the viands.

The repast was laid on the grass, notwithstanding Aristabulus more than hinted that the public, his beloved public, usually saw fit to introduce rude tables for that purpose. The Messrs. Effinghams, however, were not to be taught by a mere bird of passage, how a rustic fête so peculiarly their own, ought to be conducted, and the attendants were directed to spread the dishes on the turf. Around this spot, rustic seats were *improvisés*, and the business of *restauration* proceeded. Of all there assembled, the Parisian feelings of Mademoiselle Viefville were the most excited; for to her, the scene was one of pure delights, with the noble panorama of forest-clad mountains, the mirror-like lake, the overshadowing oaks, and the tangled brakes of the adjoining woods.

"*Mais, vraiment ceci surpasse les Tuileries, même dans leur propre genre!*" she exclaimed, with energy. "*On passerait volontiers par les dangers du désert pour y parvenir.*"

Those who understood her, smiled at this characteristic remark, and most felt disposed to join in the enthusiasm. Still, the manner in which their companions expressed the happiness they felt, appeared tame and unsatisfactory to Mr. Bragg and Mr. Dodge, these two persons being accustomed to see the young of the two sexes indulge in broader exhibitions of merry-making than those in which it comported with the tastes and habits of the present party to indulge. In vain Mrs. Hawker, in her quiet dignified way, enjoyed the ready wit and masculine thoughts of Mrs. Bloomfield, appearing to renew her youth; or, Eve, with her sweet simplicity, cultivated mind and improved tastes, seemed like a highly-polished mirror, to throw back the flashes of thought and memory, that so constantly gleamed before both; all was lost on these thoroughly matter-of-fact utilitarians. Mr. Effingham, all courtesy and mild refinement, was seldom happier; and John Effingham was never more pleasant, for he had laid aside the severity of his character, to appear, what he ought always to have been, a man in whom intelligence and quickness of thought could be made to seem secondary to the gentler qualities. The young men were not behind their companions, either, each, in his particular way, appearing to advantage, gay, regulated, and full of a humour that was rendered so much the more agreeable, by drawing its images from a knowledge of the world, that was tempered by observation and practice.

Poor Grace, alone, was the only one of the whole party, always excepting Aristabulus and Steadfast, who, for those fleeting but gay hours, was not thoroughly happy. For the first time in her life, she felt her own deficiencies, that ready and available knowledge, so exquisitely feminine in its nature and exhibition, which escaped Mrs. Bloomfield and Eve, as it might be from its own excess; which the former possessed almost intuitively, a gift of Heaven, and which the latter enjoyed, not only from the same source, but as a just consequence of her long and steady self-denial, application, and a proper appreciation of her duty to herself, was denied one who, in ill-judged compliance with the customs of a society that has no other apparent aim than the love of display, had precluded herself from enjoyments that none but the intellectual can feel. Still Grace was beautiful and attractive; and though she wondered where her cousin, in general so simple and unpretending, had acquired all those stores of thought, that, in the *abandon* and freedom of such a fête, escaped her in rich profusion, embellished with ready allusions and a brilliant though chastened wit, her generous and affectionate heart could permit her to wonder without envying. She perceived, for the first time, on this occasion, that if Eve were indeed a Hajji, it was not a Hajji of a common school; and, while her modesty and self-abasement led her bitterly to regret the hours irretrievably wasted in the frivolous levities so common to those of her sex with whom she had been most accustomed to mingle, her sincere regret did not lessen her admiration for one she began tenderly to love.

As for Messrs. Dodge and Bragg, they both determined, in their own minds, that this was much the most stupid entertainment they had ever seen on that spot, for it was entirely destitute of loud laughing, noisy merriment, coarse witticisms, and practical jokes. To them, indeed, it appeared the height of arrogance, for any particular set of persons to presume to come to a spot, rendered sacred by the public suffrage in its favour, in order to indulge in these outlandish dog-in-the-mangerisms.

Towards the close of this gay repast, and when the party were about to yield their places to the attendants, who were ready to re-ship the utensils, John Effingham observed—

"I trust, Mrs. Hawker, you have been duly warned of the fatal-character of this point, on which woman is said never to have been wooed in vain. Here are Captain Truck and myself, ready at any moment to use these carving knives, *faute des Bowies*, in order to show our desperate devotion; and I deem it no more than prudent in you, not to smile again this day, lest the cross readings of jealousy should impute a wrong motive."

"Had the injunction been against laughing, sir, I might have resisted, but smiles are far too feeble to express one's approbation, on such a day as this; you may, therefore, trust to my discretion. Is it then true, however, that Hymen haunts these shades?"

"A bachelor's history of the progress of love, may be, like the education of his children, distrusted; but so sayeth tradition; and I never put my foot in the place, without making fresh vows of constancy to myself. After this announcement of the danger, dare you accept an arm, for I perceive signs that life cannot be entirely wasted in these pleasures, great as they may prove."

The whole party arose, and separating naturally, they strolled in groups or pairs again, along the pebbly strand, or beneath the trees, while the attendants made the preparations to depart. Accident, as much as design, left Sir George and Grace alone, though neither observed the circumstance until they had passed a little rise in the formation of the ground, and were beyond the view of their companions. The baronet was the first to perceive how much he had been favoured by fortune, and his feelings were touched by the air of gentle melancholy, that shaded the usually bright and brilliant countenance of the beautiful girl.

"I should have thrice enjoyed this pleasant day," he said, with an interest in his manner, that caused the heart of Grace to beat quicker, "had I not seen that to you it has been less productive of satisfaction, than to most of those around you. I fear you may not be as well, as usual?"

"In health, never better, though not in spirits, perhaps."

"I could wish I had a right to inquire why you, who have so few causes in general to be out of spirits, should have chosen a moment so little in accordance with the common feeling."

"I have chosen no moment; the moment has chosen me, I fear. Not until this day, Sir George Templemore, have I ever been truly sensible of my great inferiority to my cousin, Eve."

"An inferiority that no one but yourself would observe or mention."

"No, I am neither vain enough, nor ignorant enough, to be the dupe of this flattery," returned Grace, shaking her handsome head, while she forced a smile; for even the delusion those we love pour into our ears, is not without its charms. "When I first met my cousin, after her return, my own imperfections rendered me blind to her superiority; but she herself has gradually taught me to respect her mind, her womanly character, her tact, her delicacy, principles, breeding, every thing that can make a woman estimable, or worthy to be loved! Oh! how have I wasted in childish amusements, and frivolous vanities, the precious moments of that girlhood which can never be recalled, and left myself scarcely worthy to be an associate of Eve Effingham!"

The pent feelings of Grace had so far gotten the control, that she scarce knew what she said, or to whom she was speaking; she even wrung her hands, in the momentary bitterness of her regrets, and in a way to arouse all the sympathy of a lover.

"No one but yourself would say this, Miss Van Cortlandt, and least of all your admirable cousin."

"She is, indeed, my admirable cousin! But what are *we*, in comparison with such a woman. Simple and unaffected as a child, with the intelligence of a scholar; with all the graces of a woman, she has the learning and mind of a man. Mistress of so many languages—"

"But you, too, speak several, my dear Miss Van Cortlandt."

"Yes," said Grace, bitterly, "I *speak* them, as the parrot repeats words that he does not understand. But Eve Effingham has used these languages as means, and she does not tell you merely what such a phrase or idiom signifies, but what the greatest writers have thought and written."

"No one has a more profound respect for your cousin than myself, Miss Van Cortlandt, but justice to you requires that I should say her great superiority over yourself has escaped me."

"This may be true, Sir George Templemore, and for a long time it escaped me too. I have only learned to prize her as she ought to be prized by an intimate acquaintance; hour by hour, as it might be. But even you must have observed how quick and intuitively my cousin and Mrs. Bloomfield have understood each other to-day; how much extensive reading, and what polished tastes they have both shown, and all so truly feminine! Mrs. Bloomfield is a remarkable woman, but she loves these exhibitions, for she knows she excels in them. Not so with Eve Effingham, who, while she so thoroughly enjoys every thing intellectual, is content, always, to seem so simple. Now, it happens, that the conversation turned once to-day on a subject that my cousin, no later than yesterday, fully explained to me, at my own earnest request; and I observed that, while she joined so naturally with Mrs. Bloomfield in adding to our pleasure, she kept back half what she knew, lest she might seem to surpass her friend. No—no—no—there is not such another woman as Eve Effingham in this world!"

"So keen a perception of excellence in others, denotes an equal excellence in yourself."

"I know my own great inferiority now, and no kindness of yours, Sir George Templemore, can ever persuade me into a better opinion of myself. Eve has travelled, seen much in Europe that does not exist here, and, instead of passing her youth in girlish trifling, has treated the minutes as if they were all precious, as she well knew them to be."

"If Europe, then, does indeed possess these advantages, why not yourself visit it, dearest Miss Van Cortlandt?"

"I—I a Hajji!" cried Grace with childish delight, though her colour heightened, and, for a moment, Eve and her superiority was forgotten.

Certainly Sir George Templemore did not come out on the lake that day with any expectation of offering his baronetcy, his fair estate, with his hand, to this artless, half-educated, provincial, but beautiful girl. For a long time he had been debating with himself the propriety of such a step, and it is probable that, at some later period, he would have sought an occasion, had not one now so opportunely offered, notwithstanding all his doubts and reasonings with himself. If the "woman who hesitates is lost," it is equally true that the man who pretends to set up his reason alone against beauty, is certain to find that sense is less powerful than the senses. Had Grace Van Cortlandt been more sophisticated, less natural, her beauty might have failed to make this conquest; but the baronet found a charm in her *naiveté*, that was singularly winning to the feelings of a man of the world. Eve had first attracted him by the same quality: the early education of American females being less constrained and artificial than that of the English; but in Eve he found a mental training and acquisitions that left the quality less conspicuous, perhaps, than in her scarcely less beautiful cousin; though, had Eve met his admiration with any thing like sympathy, her power over him would not have been easily weakened. As it was, Grace had been gradually winding herself around his affections, and he now poured out his love, in a language that her unpractised and already favourably disposed feelings had no means of withstanding. A very few minutes were allowed to them, before the summons to the boat; but when this summons came, Grace rejoined the party, elevated in her own good opinion, as happy as a cloudless future could make her, and without another thought of the immeasurable superiority of her cousin.

By a singular coincidence, while the baronet and Grace were thus engaged on one part of the shore, Eve was the subject of a similar proffer on another. She had left the circle, attended by Paul, her father, and Aristabulus; but no sooner had they reached the margin of the water, than the two former were called away by Captain Truck, to settle some controverted point between the latter and the commodore. By this unlooked-for desertion, Eve found herself alone with Mr. Bragg.

"That was a funny and comprehensive remark Mr. John made about the 'Point,' Miss Eve," Aristabulus commenced, as soon as he found himself in possession of the ground. "I should like to know if it be really true that no woman was ever unsuccessfully wooed beneath these oaks? If such be the case, we gentlemen ought to be cautious how we come here."

Here Aristabulus simpered, and looked, if possible, more amiable than ever; though the quiet composure and womanly dignity of Eve, who respected herself too much, and too well knew what was due to her sex, ever to enter into, or, so far as it depended on her will, to permit any of that common-place and vulgar trifling about love and matrimony, which formed a never-failing theme between the youthful of the two sexes in Mr. Bragg's particular circle, sensibly curbed his ambitious hopes. Still he thought he had made too good an opening, not to pursue the subject.

"Mr. John Effingham sometimes indulges in pleasantries," Eve quietly answered, "that would lead one astray who might attempt to follow."

"Love *is* a jack-o'-lantern," rejoined Aristabulus, sentimentally. "That I admit; and it is no wonder so many get swamped in following his lights. Have you ever felt the tender passion, Miss Eve?"

Now, Aristabulus had heard this precise question put at the *soirée* of Mrs. Houston, more than once, and he believed himself to be in the most polite road for a regular declaration. An ordinary woman, who felt herself offended by this question, would, most probably, have stepped back, and, raising her form to its utmost elevation, answered by an emphatic "sir!" Not so with Eve. She felt the distance between Mr. Bragg and herself to be so great, that by no probable means could he even offend her by any assumption of equality. This distance was the result of opinions, habits, and education, rather than of condition, however; for, though Eve Effingham could become the wife of a gentleman only, she was entirely superior to those prejudices of the world that depend on purely factitious causes. Instead of discovering surprise, indignation, or dramatic dignity, therefore, at this extraordinary question, she barely permitted a smile to curl her handsome mouth; and this so slightly, as to escape her companion's eye.

"I believe we are to be favoured with as smooth water, in returning to the village, as we had in the morning, while coming to this place," she simply said. "You row sometimes, I think, Mr. Bragg?"

"Ah! Miss Eve, such another opportunity may never occur again, for you foreign ladies are so difficult of access! Let me, then, seize this happy moment, here, beneath the hymeneal oaks, to offer you this faithful hand and this willing heart. Of fortune you will have enough for both, and I say nothing about the miserable dross. Reflect, Miss Eve, how happy we might be, protecting and soothing the old age of your father, and in going down the hill of life in company; or, as the song says, 'and hand in hand we'll go, and sleep the'gither at the foot, John Anderson, my Joe.'"

"You draw very agreeable pictures, Mr Bragg, and with the touches of a master!"

"However agreeable you find them, Miss Eve, they fall infinitely short of the truth. The tie of wedlock, besides being the most sacred, is also the dearest; and happy, indeed, are they who enter into the solemn engagement with such cheerful prospects as ourselves. Our ages are perfectly suitable, our disposition entirely consonant, our habits so similar as to obviate all unpleasant changes, and our fortunes precisely what they ought to be to render a marriage happy, with confidence on one side, and gratitude on the other. As to the day, Miss Eve, I could wish to leave you altogether the mistress of that, and shall not be urgent. It is the privilege of your sex."

Eve had often heard John Effingham comment on the cool impudence of a particular portion of the American population, with great amusement to herself; but never did she expect to be the subject of an attack like this in her own person. By way of rendering the scene perfect, Aristabulus had taken out his penknife, cut a twig from a bush, and he now rendered himself doubly interesting by commencing the favourite occupation of whittling. A better picture of a rational passion could not well have been drawn.

"You are bashfully silent, Miss Eve! I make all due allowances for natural timidity, and shall say no more at present—though, as silence universally 'gives consent—'"

"If you please, sir," interrupted Eve, hastily, with a slight motion of her parasol, that implied a check. "I presume our habits and opinions, notwithstanding you seem to think them so consonant with each other, are sufficiently different to cause you not to see the impropriety of one, who is situated like yourself, abusing the confidence of a parent, by making such a proposal to a daughter without her father's knowledge; and, on that point, I shall say nothing. But as you have done me the honour of making me a very unequivocal offer of your hand, I wish that the answer may be as distinct as the proposal. I decline the advantage and happiness of becoming your wife, sir—"

"Time flies, Miss Eve!"

"Time does fly, Mr. Bragg; and, if you remain much longer in the employment of Mr. Effingham, you may lose an opportunity of advancing your fortunes at the west, whither I understand it has long been your intention to emigrate—"

"I will readily relinquish all my hopes at the west, for your sake."

"No, sir, I cannot be a party to such a sacrifice. I will not say forget *me*, but forget your hopes here, and renew those you have so unreflectingly abandoned beyond the Mississippi. I shall not represent this conversation to Mr. Effingham in a manner to create any unnecessary prejudices against you; and while I thank you, as every woman should, for an offer that must infer some portion, at least, of your good opinion, you will permit me again to wish you all lawful success in your western enterprises."

Eve gave Mr. Bragg no farther opportunity to renew his suit; for, she curtsied and left him, as she ceased speaking. Mr. Dodge, who had been a distant observer of the interview, now hastened to join his friend, curious to know the result, for it had been privately arranged between these modest youths, that each should try his fortune in turn, with the heiress, did she not accept the first proposal, as, however, it was rather supposed she might. To the chagrin of Steadfast, and probably to the reader's surprise, Aristabulus informed his friend that Eve's manner and language had been full of encouragement.

"She thanked me for the offer, Mr. Dodge," he said, "and her wishes for my future prosperity at the west, were warm and repeated. Eve Effingham is, indeed, a charming creature!"

"At the west! Perhaps she meant differently from what you imagine. I know her well; the girl is full of art."

"Art, sir! she spoke as plainly as woman could speak, and I repeat that I feel considerably encouraged. It is something, to have had so plain a conversation with Eve Effingham."

Mr. Dodge swallowed his discontent, and the whole party soon embarked, to return to the village; the commodore and general taking a boat by themselves, in order to bring their discussions on human affairs in general, to a suitable close.

That night, Sir George Templemore, asked an interview with Mr. Effingham, when the latter was alone in his library.

"I sincerely hope this request is not the forerunner of a departure," said the host kindly, as the young man entered, "in which case I shall regard you as one unmindful of the hopes he has raised. You stand pledged by implication, if not in words, to pass another month with us."

"So far from entertaining an intention so faithless, my dear sir, I am fearful that you may think I trespass too far on your hospitality."

He then communicated his wish to be allowed to make Grace Van Cortlandt his wife. Mr. Effingham heard him with a smile, that showed he was not altogether unprepared for such a demand, and his eye glistened as he squeezed the other's hand.

"Take her with all my heart, Sir George," he said, "but remember you are transferring a tender plant into a strange soil. There are not many of your countrymen to whom I would confide such a trust, for I know the risk they run who make ill-assorted unions—"

"Ill-assorted unions, Mr. Effingham!"

"Yours will not be one, in the ordinary acceptation of the term, I know; for in years, birth and fortune, you and my dear niece are as much on an equality as can be desired: but it is too often an ill-assorted union for an American woman to become an English wife. So much depends on the man, that with one in whom I have less confidence than I have in you, I might justly hesitate. I shall take a guardian's privilege, though Grace be now her own mistress, and give you one solemn piece of advice—always respect the country of the woman you have thought worthy to bear your name."

"I hope always to respect every thing that is hers; but, why this particular caution?—Miss Van Cortlandt is almost English in her heart."

"An affectionate wife will generally take her bias in such matters, from her husband. Your country will be her country, your God her God. Still, Sir George Templemore, a woman of spirit and sentiment can never wholly forget the land of her birth. You love us not in England, and one who settles there will often have occasion to hear gibes and sneers on the land from which she came—"

"Good God, Mr. Effingham, you do not think I shall take my wife into society where—"

"Bear with a proser's doubts, Templemore. You will do all that is well-intentioned and proper, I dare say, in the usual acceptation of the words; but I wish you to do more; that which is wise. Grace has now a sincere reverence and respect for England, feelings that in many particulars are sustained by the facts, and will be permanent; but, in some things, observation, as it usually happens with the young and sanguine, will expose the mistakes into which she has been led by enthusiasm and the imagination. As she knows other countries better, she will come to regard her own with more favourable and discriminating eyes, losing her sensitiveness on account of peculiarities she now esteems, and taking new views of things. Perhaps you will think me selfish, but I shall add, also, that if you wish to cure your wife of any homesickness, the surest mode will be to bring her back to her native land."

"Nay, my dear sir," said Sir George, laughing, "this is very much like acknowledging its blemishes."

"I am aware it has that appearance, and yet the fact is otherwise. The cure is as certain with the Englishman as with the American; and with the German as with either. It depends on a general law, which causes us all to over-estimate by-gone pleasures and distant scenes, and to undervalue those of the present moment. You know I have always maintained there is no real philosopher short of fifty, nor any taste worth possessing that is a dozen years old."

Here Mr. Effingham rang the bell, and desired Pierre to request Miss Van Cortlandt to join him in the library. Grace entered blushing and shy, but with a countenance beaming with inward peace. Her uncle regarded her a moment intently, and a tear glistened in his eye, again, as he tenderly kissed her burning cheek.

"God bless you, love," he said—"'tis a fearful change for your sex, and yet you all enter into it radiant with hope, and noble in your confidence. Take her, Templemore," giving her hand to the baronet, "and deal kindly by her. You will not desert us entirely. I trust I shall see you both once more in the Wigwam before I die."

"Uncle—uncle—" burst from Grace, as, drowned in tears, she threw herself into Mr. Effingham's arms; "I am an ungrateful, inconsiderate girl, thus to abandon all my natural friends. I have acted wrong—"

"Wrong, dearest Miss Van Cortlandt!"

"Selfishly, then, Sir George Templemore," the simple-hearted girl ingenuously added, scarcely knowing how much her words implied— "Perhaps this matter might be reconsidered."

"I am afraid little would be gained by that, my love," returned the smiling uncle, wiping his eyes at the same instant. "The second thoughts of ladies usually confirm the first, in such matters. God bless you, Grace;—Templemore, may Heaven have you, too, in its holy keeping. Remember what I have said, and to-morrow we will converse further on the subject. Does Eve know of this, my niece?"

The colour went and came rapidly in Grace's cheek, and she looked to the floor, abashed.

"We ought then to send for her," resumed Mr. Effingham, again reaching towards the bell.

"Uncle—" and Grace hurriedly interposed, in time to save the string from being pulled. "Could I keep such an important secret from my dearest cousin!"

"I find that I am the last in the secret, as is generally the case with old fellows, and I believe I am even now *de trop.*"

Mr. Effingham kissed Grace again affectionately, and, although she strenuously endeavoured to detain him, he left the room.

"We must follow," said Grace, hastily wiping her eyes, and rubbing the traces of tears from her cheeks—"Excuse me, Sir George Templemore; will you open—"

He did open,—not the door—but his arms. Grace seemed like one that was rendered giddy by standing on a precipice, but when she fell, the young baronet was at hand to receive her. Instead of quitting the library that instant, the bell had announced the appearance of the supper-tray, before she even remembered that she had so earnestly intended to do so.

CHAPTER XXI.

"This day, no man think
Has business at his house. . . ."

Henry VIII 5.4.74–75.

THE warm weather, which was always a little behind that of the lower counties, had now set in among the mountains, and the season had advanced into the first week in July. "Independence Day," as the fourth of that month is termed by the Americans, arrived; and the wits of Templeton were taxed, as usual, in order that the festival might be celebrated with the customary intellectual and moral treat. The morning commenced with a parade of the two or three uniformed companies of the vicinity, much gingerbread and spruce-beer were consumed in the streets, no light potations of whiskey were swallowed in the groceries, and a great variety of drinks, some of which bore very ambitious names, shared the same fate in the taverns.

Mademoiselle Viefville had been told that this was the great American *fête*; the festival of the nation; and she appeared that morning in gay ribands, and with her bright, animated face, covered with smiles for the occasion. To her surprise, however, no one seemed to respond to her feelings; and as the party rose from the breakfast-table, she took an opportunity to ask an explanation of Eve, in a little 'aside.'

"*Est-ce que je me suis trompée, ma chère?*" demanded the lively Frenchwoman. "Is not this *la célébration de votre indépendance?*"

"You are not mistaken, my dear Mademoiselle Viefville, and great preparations are made to do it honour. I understand there is to be a military parade, an oration, a dinner, and fire-works."

"*Monsieur votre père—?*"

"*Monsieur mon père* is not much given to rejoicings, and he takes this annual joy, much as a valetudinarian takes his morning draught."

"*Et Monsieur Jean Effingham—?*"

"Is always a philosopher; you are to expect no antics from him."

"*Mais ces jeunes gens, Monsieur Bragg, Monsieur Dodge, et Monsieur Powis, même!*"

"*Se réjouissent en Américains.* I presume you are aware that Mr. Powis has declared himself to be an American?"

Mademoiselle Viefville looked towards the streets, along which divers tall, sombre-looking countrymen, with faces more lugubrious than those of the mutes of a funeral, were sauntering, with a desperate air of enjoyment; and she shrugged her shoulders, as she muttered to herself, "*que ces Americains sont drôles!*"

At a later hour, however, Eve surprised her father, and indeed most of the Americans of the party, by proposing that the ladies should walk out into the street, and witness the fête.

"My child, this is a strange proposition to come from a young lady of twenty," said her father.

"Why strange, dear sir?—We always mingled in the village fêtes in Europe."

"*Certainement,*" cried the delighted Mademoiselle Viefville; "*c'est de rigueur, même.*"

"And it is *de rigueur,* here, Mademoiselle Viefville, for young ladies to keep out of them," put in John Effingham. "I should be very sorry to see either of you three ladies in the streets of Templeton to-day."

"Why so, cousin Jack? Have we any thing to fear from the rudeness of our countrymen? I have always understood, on the contrary, that in no other part of the world is woman so uniformly treated with respect and kindness, as in this very republic of ours; and yet, by all these ominous faces, I perceive that it will not do for her to trust herself in the streets of a village on a *festa.*"

"You are not altogether wrong, in what you now say, Miss Effingham, nor are you wholly right. Woman, as a whole, is well treated in America; and yet it will not do for a *lady* to mingle in scenes like these, as ladies may and do mingle with them in Europe."

"I have heard this difference accounted for," said Paul Powis, "by the fact that women have no legal rank in this country. In those nations where the station of a lady is protected by legal ordinances, it is said she may descend with impunity; but, in this, where all are equal before the law, so many misunderstand the real merits of their position, that she is obliged to keep aloof from any collisions with those who might be disposed to mistake their own claims."

"I wish for no collisions, no associations, Mr. Powis, but simply to pass through the streets, with my cousin and Mademoiselle Viefville, to enjoy the sight of the rustic sports, as one would do in France, or Italy, or even in republican Switzerland, if you insist on a republican example."

"Rustic sports!" repeated Aristabulus with a frightened look— "the people will not bear to hear their sports called rustic, Miss Effingham."

"Surely, sir,"—Eve never spoke to Mr. Bragg, now, without using a repelling politeness—"surely, sir, the people of these mountains will hardly pretend that their sports are those of a capital."

"I merely mean, ma'am, that the *term* would be monstrously unpopular; nor do I see why the sports in a city"—Aristabulus was much too peculiar in his notions, to call any place that had a mayor and aldermen a town,—"should not be just as rustic as those of a village. The contrary supposition violates the principle of equality."

"And do *you* decide against us, dear sir?" Eve added, looking at Mr. Effingham.

"Without stopping to examine causes, my child, I shall say that I think you had better all remain at home."

"*Voilà, Mademoiselle Viefville, une fête Americaine!*"

A shrug of the shoulders was the significant reply.

"Nay, my daughter, you are not entirely excluded from the festivities; all gallantry has not quite deserted the land."

"A young lady shall walk *alone* with a young gentleman—shall ride alone with him—shall drive out alone with him—shall not move *without* him, *dans le monde, mais,* she shall not walk in the crowd, to look at *une fête avec son père!*" exclaimed Mademoiselle Viefville, in her imperfect English. "*Je désespère, vraiment,* to understand some *habitudes Americaines!*"

"Well, Mademoiselle, that you may not think us altogether barbarians, you shall, at least, have the benefit of the oration."

"You may well call it *the* oration, Ned; for, I believe one, or, certainly one skeleton, has served some thousand orators annually, any time these sixty years."

"Of this skeleton, then, the ladies shall have the benefit. The procession is about to form, I hear; and by getting ready immediately, we shall be just in time to obtain good seats."

Mademoiselle Viefville was delighted; for, after trying the theatres, the churches, sundry balls, the opera, and all the admissable gaieties of New-York, she had reluctantly come to the conclusion that America was a very good country *pour s'ennuyer,* and for very little else; but here was the promise of a novelty. The ladies completed their preparations, and, accordingly, attended by all the gentlemen, they made their appearance in the assembly, at the appointed hour.

The orator, who, as usual, was a lawyer, was already in possession of the pulpit, one of the village churches having been selected as the scene of the ceremonies. He was a young man, who had recently been called to the bar, it being as much in rule for the legal tyro to take off the wire-edge of his wit in a Fourth of July oration, as it was formerly for a Mousquetaire to prove his spirit in a duel. The academy which, formerly, was a servant of all work to the public, having been equally used for education, balls, preaching, town-meetings, and caucuses, had shared the fate of most American edifices in wood; lived its hour and been burned; and the collection of people, whom we have formerly had occasion to describe, appeared to have also vanished from the earth, for nothing could be less alike in exterior, at least, than those who had assembled under the ministry of Mr. Grant, and their successors, who were now collected to listen to the wisdom of Mr. Writ. Such a thing as a coat of two generations was no longer to be seen; the latest fashion, or what was thought to be the latest fashion, being as rigidly respected by the young farmer, or the young mechanic, as by the more admitted bucks, the law student, and the village shop-boy. All the red cloaks, too, had long since been laid aside to give place to imitation merino shawls, or, in cases of unusual moderation and sobriety, to mantles of silk. As Eve glanced her eye around her, she perceived Tuscan hats, bonnets of gay colours and flowers, and dresses of French chintzes, where fifty years ago would have been seen even men's woollen hats, and homely English calicoes. It is true that the change among the men was not quite as striking, for their attire admits of less variety; but the black stock had superseded the check handkerchief and the bandanna; gloves had taken the places of mittens; and the coarse and clownish shoe of "cow-hide" was supplanted by the calf-skin boot.

"Where are your peasants, your rustics, your milk and dairy maids—*the people*, in short"—whispered Sir George Templemore to Mrs. Bloomfield, as they took their seats; "or is this occasion thought to be too intellectual for them, and the present assembly composed only of the *élite?*"

"These *are* the people, and a pretty fair sample, too, of their appearance and deportment. Most of these men are what you in

England would call operatives, and the women are their wives, daughters, and sisters."

The baronet said nothing at the moment, but he sat looking around him with a curious eye for some time, when he again addressed his companion.

"I see the truth of what you say, as regards the men, for a critical eye can discover the proofs of their occupations; but, surely, you must be mistaken as respects your own sex; there is too much delicacy of form and feature for the class you mean."

"Nevertheless, I have said naught but truth."

"But look at the hands and the feet, dear Mrs. Bloomfield. Those are French gloves, too, or I am mistaken."

"I will not positively affirm that the French gloves actually belong to the dairy-maids, though I have known even this prodigy; but, rely on it, you see here the proper female counterparts of the men, and singularly delicate and pretty females are they, for persons of their class. This is what you call democratic coarseness and vulgarity, Miss Effingham tells me, in England."

Sir George smiled, but, as what it is the fashion of the country to call 'the exercises,' just then began, he made no other answer.

These exercises commenced with instrumental music, certainly the weakest side of American civilization. That of the occasion of which we write, had three essential faults, all of which are sufficiently general to be termed characteristic, in a national point of view. In the first place, the instruments themselves were bad; in the next place, they were assorted without any regard to harmony; and, in the last place, their owners did not know how to use them. As in certain American *cities*—the word is well applied here—she is esteemed the greatest belle who can contrive to utter her nursery sentiments in the loudest voice, so in Templeton, was he considered the ablest musician who could give the greatest *éclat* to a false note. In a word, clamour was the one thing needful, and as regards time, that great regulator of all harmonies, Paul Powis whispered to the captain that the air they had just been listening to, resembled what the sailors call a 'round robin;' or a particular mode of signing complaints practised by seamen, in which the nicest observer cannot tell which is the beginning, or which the end.

It required all the Parisian breeding of Mademoiselle Viefville to preserve her gravity during this overture, though she kept her bright animated, French-looking eyes, roaming over the assembly, with an air of delight that, as Mr. Bragg would say, made her very popular. No one else in the party from the Wigwam, Captain Truck excepted, dared look up, but each kept his or her eyes riveted on the floor, as if in silent enjoyment of the harmonies. As for the honest old seaman, there was as much melody in the howling of a gale to his unsophisticated ears, as in any thing else. He saw no great difference, therefore, between this feat of the Templeton band and the sighings of old Boreas; and, to say the truth, our nautical critic was not very much out of the way.

Of the oration it is scarcely necessary to say much, for if human nature is the same in all ages, and under all circumstances, so is a fourth of July oration. There were the usual allusions to Greece and Rome, between the republics of which and that of this country there exists some such affinity as is to be found between a horse-chestnut and a chestnut-horse; or that of mere words; and a long catalogue of national glories that might very well have sufficed for all the republics, both of antiquity and of our own time. But when the orator came to speak of the American character, and particularly of the intelligence of the nation, he was most felicitous, and made the largest investments in popularity. According to his account of the matter, no other people possessed a tithe of the knowledge, or a hundredth part of the honesty and virtue of the very community he was addressing; and after labouring for ten minutes to convince his hearers that they already knew every thing, he wasted several more in trying to persuade them to undertake further acquisitions of the same nature.

"How much better all this might be made," said Paul Powis, as the party returned towards the Wigwam, when the "exercises" were ended, "by substituting a little plain instruction on the real nature and obligations of the institutions, for so much unmeaning rhapsody. Nothing has struck me with more surprise and pain, than to find how far, or it might be better to say, how high, ignorance reaches on such subjects, and how few men, in a country where all depends on the institutions, have clear notions concerning their own condition."

"Certainly this is not the opinion we usually entertain of ourselves," observed John Effingham. "And yet it ought to be. I am far from underrating the ordinary information of the country, which, as an average information, is superior to that of almost every other people; nor am I one of those who, according to the popular European notion, fancy the Americans less gifted than common in intellect; there can be but one truth in any thing, however, and it falls to the lot of very few, any where, to master it. The Americans, moreover, are a people of facts and practices, paying but little attention to principles, and giving themselves the very minimum of time for investigations that lie beyond the reach of the common mind; and it follows that they know little of that which does not present itself in their every-day transactions. As regards the practice of the institutions, it is regulated here, as elsewhere, by party, and party is never an honest or a disinterested expounder."

"Are you, then, more than in the common dilemma," asked Sir George, "or worse off than your neighbours?"

"We are worse off than our neighbours, for the simple reason that it is the intention of the American system, which has been deliberately framed, and which is moreover the result of a bargain, to carry out its theory in practice; whereas, in countries where the institutions are the results of time and accidents, *improvement* is only obtained by *innovations*. Party invariably assails and weakens power. When power is the possession of a few, the many gain by party; but when power is the legal right of the many, the few gain by party. Now, as party has no ally as strong as ignorance and prejudice, a right understanding of the principles of a government is of far more importance in a popular government, than in any other. In place of the eternal eulogies on facts, that one hears on all public occasions in this country, I would substitute some plain and clear expositions of principles; or, indeed, I might say, of facts as they are connected with principles."

"*Mais, la musique, Monsieur*," interrupted Mademoiselle Viefville, in a way so droll as to raise a general smile, "*qu'en pensez-vous?*"

"That it is music, my dear Mademoiselle, in neither fact nor principle."

"It only proves that a people can be free, Mademoiselle," observed Mrs. Bloomfield, "and enjoy fourth of July orations, without having very correct notions of harmony or time. But do our rejoicings end here, Miss Effingham?"

"Not at all—there is still something in reserve for the day, and all who honour it. I am told the evening, which promises to be sufficiently sombre, is to terminate with a fête that is peculiar to Templeton, and which is called 'The Fun of Fire.'"

"It is an ominous name, and ought to be a brilliant ceremony."

As this was uttered, the whole party entered the Wigwam.

"The Fun of Fire" took place, as a matter of course, at a later hour. When night had set in, every body appeared in the main street of the village, a part of which, from its width and form, was particularly adapted to the sports of the evening. The females were mostly at the windows, or on such elevated stands as favoured their view, and the party from the Wigwam occupied a large balcony that topped the piazza of one of the principal inns of the place.

The sports of the night commenced with rockets, of which a few, that did as much credit to the climate as to the state of the pyrotechnics of the village, were thrown up, as soon as the darkness had become sufficiently dense to lend them brilliancy. Then followed wheels, crackers and serpents, all of the most primitive kind, if, indeed, there be any thing primitive in such amusements. A balloon or two succeeded. The "Fun of Fire" was to close the rejoicings, and it was certainly worth all the other sports of that day, united, the gingerbread and spruce beer included.

A blazing ball cast from a shop-door, was the signal for the commencement of the Fun. It was merely a ball of common yarn, or of some other similar material, saturated with turpentine, and it burned with a bright, fierce flame until consumed. As the first of these fiery meteors sailed into the street, a common shout from the boys, apprentices, and young men, proclaimed that the fun was at hand. It was followed by several more, and in a few minutes the entire area was gleaming with glancing light. The whole of the amusement consisted in tossing the fire-balls with boldness, and in avoiding them with dexterity, something like competition soon entering into the business of the scene.

The effect was singularly beautiful. Groups of dark objects became suddenly illuminated, and here a portion of the throng might be seen beneath a brightness like that produced by a bonfire, while all the back-ground of persons and faces were gliding about in a darkness that almost swallowed up a human figure. Suddenly all this would be changed; the brightness would pass away, and a ball alighting in a spot that had seemed abandoned to gloom, it would be found peopled with merry countenances, and active forms. The constant changes from brightness to deep darkness, with all the varying gleams of light and shadow, made the beauty of the scene, which soon extorted admiration from all in the balcony.

"*Mais, c'est charmant!*" exclaimed Mademoiselle Vielville, who was enchanted at discovering something like gaiety and pleasure among the "*tristes Américains*," and who had never even suspected them of being capable of so much apparent enjoyment.

"These are the prettiest village sports I have ever witnessed," said Eve, "though a little dangerous, one would think. There is something refreshing, as the magazine writers term it, to find one of these miniature towns of ours condescending to be gay and happy in a village fashion. If I were to bring my strongest objection to American country life, it would be its ambitious desire to ape the towns, converting the ease and *abandon* of a village, into the formality and stiffness that render children in the clothes of grown people so absurdly ludicrous."

"What!" exclaimed John Effingham; "do you fancy it possible to reduce a free-man so low, as to deprive him of his stilts! No, no, young lady; you are now in a country where if you have two rows of flounces on your frock, your maid will make it a point to have three, by way of maintaining the equilibrium. This is the noble ambition of liberty."

"Annette's foible is a love of flounces, cousin Jack, and you have drawn that image from your eye, instead of your imagination. It is a French, as well as an American ambition, if ambition it be."

"Let it be drawn whence it may, it is true. Have you not remarked, Sir George Templemore, that the Americans will not even bear the ascendency of a capital? Formerly, Philadelphia, then the largest town in the country, was the political capital; but it was too much for any one community to enjoy the united consideration that belongs to extent and politics; and so the honest public went to work to make a capital, that should have nothing else in its favour, but the naked fact that it was the seat of government, and I think it will be generally allowed, that they have succeeded to admiration. I fancy Mr. Dodge will admit that it would be quite intolerable, that country should not be town, and town country."

"This is a land of equal rights, Mr. John Effingham, and I confess that I see no claims that New-York possesses, which do not equally belong to Templeton."

"Do you hold, sir," inquired Captain Truck, "that a ship is a brig, and a brig a ship."

"The case is different; Templeton *is* a town, is it not, Mr. John Effingham?"

"*A* town, Mr. Dodge, but not town. The difference is essential."

"I do not see it, sir. Now, New-York, to my notion is not a *town*, but a *city*."

"Ah! This is the critical acumen of the editor! But you should be indulgent, Mr. Dodge, to us laymen, who pick up our phrases by merely wandering about the world; or in the nursery perhaps, while you, of the favoured few, by living in the condensation of a province, obtain a precision and accuracy to which we can lay no claim."

The darkness prevented the editor of the Active Inquirer from detecting the general smile, and he remained in happy ignorance of the feeling that produced it. To say the truth, not the smallest of the besetting vices of Mr. Dodge had their foundation in a provincial education, and in provincial notions; the invariable tendency of both being to persuade their subject that he is always right, while all opposed to him in opinion are wrong. That well-known line of Pope, in which the poet asks, "what can we reason, but from what we know?" contains the principle of half our foibles and faults, and perhaps explains fully that proportion of those of Mr. Dodge, to say nothing of those of no small number of his countrymen. There are limits to the knowledge, and tastes, and habits of every man, and, as each is regulated by the opportunities of the individual, it follows of necessity, that no one can have a standard much above his own experience. That an isolated and remote people should be a provincial people, or, in other words, a people of narrow and peculiar practices and opinions, is as unavoidable as that study should make a scholar; though in the case of America, the great motive for surprise is to be found in the fact that causes so very obvious should produce so little effect. When compared with the bulk of other nations, the Americans, though so remote and insulated, are scarcely provincial, for it is only when the highest standard of this nation is compared with the highest standard of other nations, that we detect the great deficiency that actually exists. That a moral foundation so broad should uphold a moral superstructure so narrow, is owing to the circumstance that the popular sentiment rules, and as every thing is referred to a body of judges that, in the nature of things, must be of very limited and superficial attainments, it cannot be a matter of wonder to the reflecting, that the decision shares in the qualities of the tribunal. In America, the gross mistake has been made of supposing, that, because the mass rules in a political sense, it has a right to be listened to and obeyed in all other matters, a practical deduction that can only lead, under the most favourable exercise of power, to a very humble mediocrity. It is to be hoped, that time, and a greater concentration of taste, liberality, and knowledge than can well distinguish a young and scattered population, will repair this evil, and that our children will reap the harvest of the broad fields of intelligence that have been sowed by ourselves. In the mean time, the present generation must endure that which cannot easily be cured; and, among its other evils, it will have to submit to a great deal of very questionable information, not a few false principles, and an unpleasant degree of intolerant and narrow bigotry, that are propagated by such apostles of liberty and learning as Steadfast Dodge, Esquire.

We have written in vain, if it now be necessary to point out a multitude of things in which that professed instructor and Mentor of the public, the editor of the Active Inquirer, had made a false estimate of himself, as well as of his fellow-creatures. That such a man should be ignorant, is to be expected, as he had never been instructed; that he was self-sufficient was owing to his ignorance, which oftener induces vanity than anything else; that he was intolerant and bigoted, follows as a legitimate effect of his provincial and contracted habits; that he was a hypocrite, came from his homage of the people; and that one thus constituted, should be permitted, periodically, to pour out his vapidity, folly, malice, envy, and ignorance, on his fellow-creatures, in the columns of a newspaper, was owing to a state of society in which the truth of the wholesome adage "that what is every man's business is nobody's business," is exemplified not only daily, but hourly, in a hundred other interests of equal magnitude, as well as to a capital mistake, that leads the community to fancy that whatever is done in their name, is done for their good.

As the "Fun of Fire" had, by this time, exhibited most of its beauties, the party belonging to the Wigwam left the balcony, and, the evening proving mild, they walked into the grounds of the building, where they naturally broke into groups, conversing on the incidents of the day, or of such other matters as came uppermost. Occasionally, gleams of light were thrown across them from a fire-ball; or a rocket's starry train was still seen drawn in the air, resembling the wake of a ship at night, as it wades through the ocean.

CHAPTER XXII.

Gentle Octavia,
Let your best love draw to that point, which seeks
Best to preserve it.

Antony and Cleopatra 3.4.20–22.

WE shall not say it was an accident that brought Paul and Eve side by side, and a little separated from the others; for a secret sympathy had certainly exercised its influence over both, and probably contributed as much as any thing else towards bringing about the circumstance. Although the Wigwam stood in the centre of the village, its grounds covered several acres, and were intersected with winding walks, and ornamented with shrubbery, in the well-known English style, improvements also of John Effingham; for, while the climate and forests of America offer so many inducements to encourage landscape gardening, it is the branch of art that, of all the other ornamental arts, is perhaps the least known in this country. It is true, time had not yet brought the labours of the projector to perfection, in this instance; but enough had been done to afford very extensive, varied, and pleasing walks. The grounds were broken, and John Effingham had turned the irregularities to good account, by planting and leading paths among them, to the great amusement of the lookers-on, however, who, like true disciples of the Manhattanese economy, had already begun to calculate the cost of what they termed grading the lawns, it being with them as much a matter of course to bring pleasure grounds down to a mathematical surface, as to bring a rail-road route down to the proper level.

Through these paths, and among the irregularities, groves, and shrubberies, just mentioned, the party began to stroll; one group taking a direction eastward, another south, and a third westward, in a way soon to break them up into five or six different divisions. These several portions of the company ere long got to move in opposite directions, by taking the various paths, and while they frequently met, they did not often re-unite. As has been already intimated, Eve and Paul were alone, for the first time in their lives, under circumstances that admitted of an uninterrupted confidential conversation. Instead of profiting immediately, however, by this unusual occurrence, as many of our readers may anticipate, the young man continued the discourse, in which the whole party had been engaged when they entered the gate that communicated with the street.

"I know not whether you felt the same embarrassment as myself, to-day, Miss Effingham," he said, "when the orator was dilating on the glories of the republic, and on the high honours that accompany the American name. Certainly, though a pretty extensive traveller, I have never yet been able to discover that it is any signal advantage abroad to be one of the 'fourteen millions of freemen.'"

"Are we to attribute the mystery that so long hung over your birth-place, to this fact," Eve asked, a little pointedly.

"If I have made any seeming mystery, as to the place of my birth, it has been involuntary on my part, Miss Effingham, so far as you, at least, have been concerned. I may not have thought myself authorized to introduce my own history into our little discussions, but I am not conscious of aiming at any unusual concealments. At Vienna, and in Switzerland, we met as travellers; and now that you appear disposed to accuse me of concealment, I may retort, and say that, neither you nor your father ever expressly stated in my presence that you were Americans."

"Was that necessary, Mr. Powis?"

"Perhaps not; and I am wrong to draw a comparison between my own insignificance, and the éclat that attended you and your movements."

"Nay," interrupted Eve, hastily, "do not misconceive me. My father felt an interest in you, quite naturally, after what had occurred on the lake of Lucerne, and I believe he was desirous of making you out a countryman,—a pleasure that he has at length received."

"To own the truth, I was never quite certain, until my last visit to England, on which side of the Atlantic I was actually born, and to this uncertainty, perhaps, may be attributed some of that cosmopolitism to which I made so many high pretensions in our late passage."

"Not know where you were born!" exclaimed Eve, with an involuntary haste, that she immediately repented.

"This, no doubt, sounds odd to you, Miss Effingham, who have always been the pride and solace of a most affectionate father, but it has never been my good fortune to know either parent. My mother, who was the sister of Ducie's mother, died at my birth, and the loss of my father even preceded hers. I may be said to have been born an orphan."

Eve, for the first time in her life, had taken his arm, and the young man felt the gentle pressure of her little hand, as she permitted this expression of sympathy to escape her, at a moment she found so intensely interesting to herself.

"It was, indeed, an irreparable misfortune, Mr. Powis; I fear you were put into the navy through the want of those who would feel a natural concern in your welfare."

"The navy was my own choice; partly, I think, from a certain love of adventure, and quite as much, perhaps, with a wish to settle the question of my birth-place, practically at least, by enlisting in the service of the country that I first knew, and certainly best loved."

"But of that birth-place, I understand there is now no doubt?" said Eve, with more interest than she was herself conscious of betraying.

"None whatever; I am a native of Philadelphia; that point was conclusively settled in my late visit to my aunt, Lady Dunluce, who was present at my birth."

"Is Lady Dunluce also an American?"

"She is; never having quitted the country until after her marriage to Colonel Ducie. She was a younger sister of my mother's, and, notwithstanding some jealousies and a little coldness that I trust have now disappeared, I am of opinion she loved her; though one can hardly answer for the durability of the family ties in a country where the institutions and habits are as artificial as in England."

"Do you think there is less family affection, then, in England than in America?"

"I will not exactly say as much, though I am of opinion that neither country is remarkable in that way. In England, among the higher classes, it is impossible that the feelings should not be weakened by so many adverse interests. When a brother knows that nothing stands between himself and rank and wealth, but the claims of one who was born a twelvemonth earlier than himself, he gets to feel more like a rival than a kinsman, and the temptation to envy or dislike, or even hatred, sometimes becomes stronger than the duty to love."

"And yet the English, themselves, say that the services rendered by the elder to the younger brother, and the gratitude of the younger to the elder, are so many additional ties."

"It would be contrary to all the known laws of feeling, and all experience, if this were so. The younger applies to the elder for aid in preference to a stranger, because he thinks he has a claim; and what man who fancies he has a claim, is ever disposed to believe justice is fully done him; or who that is required to discharge a duty, imagines he has not done more than could be properly asked?"

"I fear your opinion of men is none of the best, Mr. Powis!"

"There may be exceptions, but such I believe to be the common fate of humanity. The moment a duty is created, a disposition to think it easily discharged follows; and of all sentiments, that of a continued and exacting gratitude is the most oppressive. I fear more brothers are aided, through family pride, than through natural affection."

"What, then, loosens the tie among ourselves, where no law of primogeniture exists?"

"That which loosens every thing. A love of change that has grown up with the migratory habits of the people; and which, perhaps, is, in some measure, fostered by the institutions. Here is Mr. Bragg to confirm what I say, and we may hear his sentiments on this subject."

As Aristabulus, with whom walked Mr. Dodge, just at that moment came out of the shrubbery, and took the same direction with themselves, Powis put the question, as one addresses an acquaintance in a room.

"Rotation in feelings, sir," returned Mr. Bragg, "is human nature, as rotation in office is natural justice. Some of our people are of opinion that it might be useful could the whole of society be made periodically to change places, in order that every one might know how his neighbour lives."

"You are, then, an Agrarian, Mr. Bragg?"

"As far from it as possible; nor do I believe you will find such an animal in this county. Where property is concerned, we are a people that never let go, as long as we can hold on, sir; but, beyond this we like lively changes. Now, Miss Effingham, every body thinks frequent changes of religious instructors in particular, necessary. There can be no vital piety without keeping the flame alive with excitement."

"I confess, sir, that my own reasoning would lead to a directly contrary conclusion, and that there can be no vital piety, as you term it, *with* excitement."

Mr. Bragg looked at Mr. Dodge, and Mr. Dodge looked at Mr. Bragg. Then each shrugged his shoulders, and the former continued the discourse.

"That may be the case in France, Miss Effingham," he said, pointedly, and as he thought with dignity, "but, in America, we look to excitement as the great purifier. We should as soon expect the air in the bottom of a well to be elastic, as that the moral atmosphere shall be clear and salutary, without the breezes of excitement. For my part, Mr. Dodge, I think no man should be a judge, in the same court, more than ten years at a time, and a priest gets to be rather common-place and flat after five. There are men that may hold out a little longer, I acknowledge; but to keep real, vital, soul-saving regeneration stirring, a change should take place as often as once in five years, in a parish; that is my opinion, at least."

"But, sir," rejoined Eve, "as the laws of religion are immutable, the modes by which it is known universal, and the promises, mediation, and obligations are every where the same, I do not see what you propose to gain by so many changes."

"Why, Miss Effingham, we change the dishes at table, and no family of my acquaintance, more than this of your honourable father's; and I am surprised to find you opposed to the system."

"Our religion, sir," answered Eve, gravely, "is a duty, and rests on revelation and obedience; while our diet may, very innocently, be a matter of mere taste, or even of caprice, if you will."

"Well, I confess I see no great difference, the main object in this life being to stir people up, and to go ahead. I presume you know, Miss Eve, that many people think that we ought to change our own parson, if we expect a blessing on the congregation."

"I should sooner expect a curse would follow an act of so much heartlessness, sir. Our clergyman has been with us since his entrance into the duties of his holy office, and it will be difficult to suppose that the Divine favour would follow the commission of so selfish and capricious a step, with a motive no better than the desire for novelty."

"You quite mistake the object, Miss Eve, which is to stir the people up; a hopeless thing, I fear, so long as they always sit under the same preaching."

"I have been taught to believe that piety is increased, Mr. Bragg, by the aid of the Holy Spirit's sustaining and supporting us in our good desires; and I cannot persuade myself that the Deity finds it necessary to save a soul, by the means of any of those human agencies by which men sack towns, turn an election, or incite a mob. I hear that extraordinary scenes are witnessed in this country, in some of the other sects; but I trust never to see the day, when the apostolic, reverend, and sober church, in which I have been nurtured, shall attempt to advance the workings of that Divine power, by a profane, human hurrah."

All this was Greek to Messrs. Dodge and Bragg, who, in furthering their objects, were so accustomed to "stirring people up," that they had quite forgotten that the more a man was in "an excitement," the less he had to do with reason. The exaggerated religious sects, which first peopled America, have had a strong influence in transmitting to their posterity false notions on such subjects; for while the old world is accustomed to see Christianity used as an ally of government, and perverted from its one great end to be the instrument of ambition, cupidity, and selfishness, the new world has been fated to witness the reaction of such abuses, and to run into nearly as many errors in the opposite extreme. The two persons just mentioned, had been educated in the provincial school of religious notions, that is so much in favour, in a portion of this country; and they were striking examples of the truth of the adage, that "what is bred in the bone will be seen in the flesh," for their common character, common in this particular at least, was a queer mixture of the most narrow superstitions and prejudices, that existed under the garb of religious training, and of unjustifiable frauds, meannesses, and even vices. Mr. Bragg was a better man than Mr. Dodge, for he had more self-reliance, and was more manly; but, on the score of religion, he had the same contradictory excesses, and there was a common point, in the way of vulgar vice, towards which each tended, simply for the want of breeding and tastes, as infallibly as the needle points to the pole. Cards were often introduced in Mr. Effingham's drawing-room, and there was one apartment expressly devoted to a billiard-table; and many was the secret fling, and biting gibe, that these pious devotees passed between themselves, on the subject of so flagrant an instance of immorality, in a family of so high moral pretensions; the two worthies not unfrequently concluding their comments by repairing to some secret room in a tavern, where, after carefully locking the door, and drawing the curtains, they would order brandy, and pass a refreshing hour in endeavouring to relieve each other of the labour of carrying their odd sixpences, by means of little shoemaker's loo.

On the present occasion, however, the earnestness of Eve produced a pacifying effect on their consciences, for, as our heroine never raised her sweet voice above the tones of a gentlewoman, its very mildness and softness gave force to her expressions. Had John

Effingham uttered the sentiments to which they had just listened, it is probable Mr. Bragg would have attempted an answer; but, under the circumstances, he preferred making his bow, and diverging into the first path that offered, followed by his companion. Eve and Paul continued their circuit of the grounds, as if no interruption had taken place.

"This disposition to change is getting to be universal in the country," remarked the latter, as soon as Aristabulus and his friend had left them, "and I consider it one of the worst signs of the times; more especially since it has become so common to connect it with what it is the fashion to call excitement."

"To return to the subject which these gentlemen interrupted," said Eve, "that of the family ties; I have always heard England quoted as one of the strongest instances of a nation in which this tie is slight, beyond its aristocratical influence; and I should be sorry to suppose that we are following in the footsteps of our good-mother, in this respect at least."

"Has Mademoiselle Viefville never made any remark on this subject?"

"Mademoiselle Viefville, though observant, is discreet. That she believes the standard of the affections as high in this as in her own country, I do not think; for, like most Europeans, she believes the Americans to be a passionless people, who are more bound up in the interests of gain, than in any other of the concerns of life."

"She does not know us!" said Paul so earnestly as to cause Eve to start at the deep energy with which he spoke. "The passions lie as deep, and run in currents as strong here, as in any other part of the world, though, there not being as many factitious causes to dam them, they less seldom break through the bounds of propriety."

For near a minute the two paced the walk in silence, and Eve began to wish that some one of the party would again join them, that a conversation which she felt was getting to be awkward, might be interrupted. But no one crossed their path again, and without rudeness, or affectation, she saw no means of effecting her object. Paul was too much occupied with his own feelings to observe his companion's embarrassment, and, after the short pause mentioned, he naturally pursued the subject, though in a less emphatic manner than before.

"It was an old, and a favourite theory, with the Europeans," he said, with a sort of bitter irony, "that all the animals of this hemisphere have less gifted natures than those of the other; nor is it a theory of which they are yet entirely rid. The Indian was supposed to be passionless, because he had self-command; and what in the European would be thought exhibiting the feelings of a noble nature, in him has been represented as ferocity and revenge. Miss Effingham, you and I have seen Europe, have stood in the presence of its wisest, its noblest and its best; and what have they to boast beyond the immediate results of their factitious and laboured political systems, that is denied to the American—or rather would be denied to the American, had the latter the manliness and mental independence, to be equal to his fortunes?"

"Which, you think he is not."

"How can a people be even independent that imports its thoughts, as it does its wares,—that has not the spirit to invent even its own prejudices?"

"Something should be allowed to habit, and to the influence of time. England, herself, probably has inherited some of her false notions, from the Saxons and Normans."

"That is not only possible, but probable; but England, in thinking of Russia, France, Turkey, or Egypt, when induced to think wrong, yields to an English, and not to an American interest. Her errors are at least requited, in a degree, by serving her own ends, whereas ours are made, too often, to oppose our most obvious interests. We are never independent unless when stimulated by some strong and pressing moneyed concern, and not often then beyond the plainest of its effects.—But, here is one, apparently, who does not belong to our party."

Paul interrupted himself, in consequence of their meeting a stranger in the walk, who moved with the indecision of one uncertain whether to advance or to recede. Rockets frequently fell into the grounds, and there had been one or two inroads of boys, which had been tolerated on account of the occasion; but this intruder was a man in the decline of life, of the condition of a warm tradesman seemingly, and he clearly had no connection with sky-rockets, as his eyes were turned inquiringly on the persons of those who passed him, from time to time, none of whom had he stopped, however, until he now placed himself before Paul and Eve, in a way to denote a desire to speak.

"The young people are making a merry night of it," he said, keeping a hand in each coat-pocket, while he unceremoniously occupied the centre of the narrow walk, as if determined to compel a parley.

Although sufficiently acquainted with the unceremonious habits of the people of the country to feel no surprise at this intrusion, Paul was vexed at having his tête à tête with Eve so rudely broken; and he answered with more of the hauteur of the quarter-deck, than he might otherwise have done, by saying coldly—

"Perhaps, sir, it is your wish to see Mr. Effingham—or—" hesitating an instant, as he scanned the stranger's appearance—"some of his people. The first will soon pass this spot, and you will find most of the latter on the lawn, watching the rockets."

The man regarded Paul a moment, and then he removed his hat respectfully.

"Please, sir, can you inform me if a gentleman called Captain Truck—one that sails the packets between New-York and England, is staying at the Wigwam at present."

Paul told him that the captain was walking with Mr. Effingham, and that the next pair that approached would be they. The stranger fell back, keeping his hat respectfully in his hand, and the two passed.

"That man has been an English servant, but he has been a little spoiled by the reaction of an excessive liberty to do as he pleases. The 'please, sir,' and the attitude can hardly be mistaken, while the *nonchalance* of his manner '*à nous aborder*' sufficiently betrays the second edition of his education."

"I am curious to know what this person can want with our excellent captain—it can scarcely be one of the Montauk's crew!"

"I will answer for it, that the fellow has not enough seamanship about him to whip a rope," said Paul, laughing; "for if there be two temporal pursuits that have less affinity than any two others, they are those of the pantry and the tar-bucket. I think it will be seen that this man has been an English servant, and he has probably been a passenger on board some ship commanded by our honest old friend."

Eve and Paul now turned, and they met Mr. Effingham and the captain just as the two latter reached the spot where the stranger stood waiting their arrival.

"This is Captain Truck, the gentleman for whom you inquired," said Paul.

The stranger looked hard at the captain, and the captain looked hard at the stranger, the obscurity rendering a pretty close scrutiny necessary, to enable either to distinguish features. The examination seemed to be mutually unsatisfactory, for each retired a little, like a man who had not found a face that he knew.

"There must be two Captain Trucks, then, in the trade," said the stranger; "this is not the gentleman I used to know."

"I think you are as right in the latter part of your remark, friend, as you are wrong in the first," returned the captain. "Know you, I do not, and yet there are no more two Captain Trucks in the English trade, than there are two Miss Eve Effinghams, or two Mrs. Hawkers in the universe. I am John Truck, and no other man of that name ever sailed a ship between New York and England, in my day, at least."

"Did you ever command the Dawn, sir?"

"The Dawn! That I did; and the Regulus, and the Manhattan, and the Wilful Girl, and the Deborah-Angelina, and the Sukey and Katy, which, my dear young lady, I may say, was my first love. She was only a fore-and-after, carrying no standing topsail, even, and we named her after two of the river girls, who were flyers, in their way; at least, I thought so then; though a man by sailing a packet comes to alter his notions about men and things, or, for that matter, about women and things, too. I got into a category, in that schooner, that I never expect to see equalled; for I was driven ashore to windward in her, which is gibberish to you, my dear young lady, but which Mr. Powis will very well understand, though he may not be able to explain it."

"I certainly know what you mean," said Paul, "though I confess I am in a category, as well as the schooner, so far as knowing how it could have happened."

"The Sukey and Katy ran away with me, that's the upshot of it. Since that time I have never consented to command a vessel that was called after *two* of our river young women, for I do believe that one of them is as much as a common mariner can manage. You see, Mr. Effingham, we were running along a weather-shore, as close in as we could get, to be in the eddy, when a squall struck her a-beam, and she luffed plump on to the beach. No helping it. Helm hard up, peak down, head sheets to windward, and main sheet flying, but it was all too late; away she went dead ashore to windward. But for that accident, I think I might have married."

"And what connexion could you find between matrimony and this accident, captain?" demanded the laughing Eve.

"There was an admonition in it, my dear young lady, that I thought was not to be disregarded. I tried the Wilful Girl next, and she was thrown on her beam-ends with me; after which I renounced all female names, and took to the Egyptian."

"The Egyptian!"

"Certainly, Regulus, who was a great snake-killer, they tell me, in that part of the world. But I never saw my way quite clear as bachelor, until I got the Dawn. Did you know that ship, friend?"

"I believe, sir, I made two passages in her while you commanded her."

"Nothing more likely; we carried lots of your countrymen, though mostly forward of the gangways. I commanded the Dawn more than twenty years ago."

"It is all of that time since I crossed with you, sir; you may remember that we fell in with a wreck, ten days after we sailed, and took off her crew and two passengers. Three or four of the latter had died with their sufferings, and several of the people."

"All this seems but as yesterday! The wreck was a Charleston ship, that had started a butt."

"Yes, sir—yes, sir—that is just it—she had started, *but* could not get in. That is just what they said at the time. I am David, sir—I should think you *cannot* have forgotten David."

The honest captain was very willing to gratify the other's harmless self-importance, though, to tell the truth, he retained no more personal knowledge of the David of the Dawn, than he had of David, King of the Jews.

"Oh, David!" he cried, cordially—"are *you* David? Well, I did not expect to see you again in this world, though I never doubted where we should be, hereafter. I hope you are very well, David; what sort of weather have you made of it since we parted? If I recollect aright, you worked your passage;—never at sea before."

"I beg your pardon, sir; I never was at sea before the *first* time, it is true; but I did not belong to the crew. I was a passenger."

"I remember, now, you were in the steerage," returned the captain, who saw daylight ahead.

"Not at all, sir, but in the cabin."

"Cabin!" echoed the captain, who perceived none of the requisites of a cabin-passenger in the other—"Oh! I understand, in the pantry?"

"Exactly so, sir. You may remember my master—he had the left-hand state-room to himself, and I slept next to the scuttle-butt. You recollect master, sir?"

"Out of doubt, and a very good fellow he was. I hope you live with him still?"

"Lord bless you, sir, he is dead!"

"Oh! I recollect hearing of it, at the time. Well, David, I hope if ever you cross again, we shall be ship-mates once more. We were beginners, then, but we have ships worth living in, now.—Good night."

"Do you remember Dowse, sir, that we got from the wreck?" continued the other, unwilling to give up his gossip so soon. "He was a dark man, that had had the small-pox badly. I think, sir, you will recollect *him*, for he was a hard man in other particulars, besides his countenance."

"Somewhat flinty about the soul; I remember the man well; and so, David, good night; you will come and see me, if you are ever in town. Good night, David."

David was now compelled to leave the place, for Captain Truck, who perceived that the whole party was getting together again, in consequence of the halt, felt the propriety of dismissing his visiter, of whom, his master, and Dowse, he retained just as much recollection as one retains of a common stage-coach companion after twenty years. The appearance of Mr. Howel, who just at that moment approached them, aided the manœuvre, and, in a few minutes the different groups were again in motion, though some slight changes had taken place in the distribution of the parties.

CHAPTER XXIII.

"How silver-sweet sound lovers' tongues by night,
Like softest music to attending ears!"

Romeo and Juliet 2.2.165–166.

"A poor matter, this of the fire-works," said Mr. Howel, who, with an old bachelor's want of tact, had joined Eve and Paul in their walk. "The English would laugh at them famously, I dare say. Have you heard Sir George allude to them at all, Miss Eve?"

"It would be great affectation for an Englishman to deride the fire-works of any *dry* climate," said Eve laughing; "and I dare say, if Sir George Templemore has been silent on the subject, it is because he is conscious he knows little about it."

"Well, that is odd! I should think England the very first country in the world for fire-works. I hear, Miss Eve, that, on the whole, the baronet is rather pleased with us; and I must say that he is getting to be very popular in Templeton."

"Nothing is easier than for an Englishman to become popular in America," observed Paul, "especially if his condition in life be above that of the vulgar. He has only to declare himself pleased with America; or, to be sincerely hated, to declare himself displeased."

"And in what does America differ from any other country, in this respect?" asked Eve, quickly.

"Not much, certainly; love induces love, and dislike, dislike. There is nothing new in all this; but the people of other countries, having more confidence in themselves, do not so sensitively inquire what others think of them. I believe this contains the whole difference."

"But Sir George does *rather* like us?" inquired Mr. Howel, with interest.

"He likes some of us particularly well," returned Eve. "Do you not know that my cousin Grace is to become Mrs.—I beg her pardon—Lady Templemore, very shortly?"

"Good God!—Is that possible—Lady Templemore!—Lady Grace Templemore!"

"Not Lady Grace Templemore, but Grace, Lady Templemore, and graceful Lady Templemore in the bargain."

"And this honour, my dear Miss Eve, they tell me you refused!"

"They tell you wrong then, sir," answered the young lady, a little startled with the suddenness and *brusquerie* of the remark, and yet prompt to do justice to all concerned. "Sir George Templemore never did me the honour to propose *to* me, or *for* me, and consequently he *could* not be refused."

"It is very extraordinary!—I hear you were actually acquainted in Europe?"

"We were, Mr. Howel, actually acquainted in Europe, but I knew hundreds of persons in Europe, who have never dreamed of asking me to marry them."

"This is very strange—quite unlooked for—to marry Miss Van Cortlandt! Is Mr. John Effingham in the grounds?"

Eve made no answer, but Paul hurriedly observed—

"You will find him in the next walk, I think, by returning a short distance, and taking the first path to the left."

Mr. Howel did as told, and was soon out of sight.

"That is a most earnest believer in English superiority, and, one may say, by his strong desire to give you an English husband, Miss Effingham, in English merit."

"It is the weak spot in the character of a very honest man. They tell me such instances were much more frequent in this country thirty years since, than they are to-day."

"I can easily believe it, for I think I remember some characters of the sort, myself. I have heard those who are older than I am, draw a distinction like this between the state of feeling that prevailed forty years ago, and that which prevails to-day; they say that, formerly, England absolutely and despotically thought for America, in all but those cases in which the interests of the two nations conflicted; and I have even heard competent judges affirm, that so powerful was the influence of habit, and so successful the schemes of the political managers of the mother country, that even many of those who fought for the independence of America, actually doubted of the propriety of their acts, as Luther is known to have had fits of despondency concerning the justness of the reformation he was producing; while, latterly, the leaning towards England is less the result of a simple mental dependence,—though of that there still remains a disgraceful amount—than of calculation, and a desire in a certain class to defeat the dominion of the mass, and to establish that of a few in its stead."

"It would, indeed, be a strange consummation of the history of this country, to find it becoming monarchical!"

"There are a few monarchists no doubt springing up in the country, though almost entirely in a class that only knows the world through the imagination and by means of books; but the disposition, in our time, is to aristocracy, and not to monarchy. Most men that get to be rich, discover that they are no happier for their possessions; perhaps every man who has not been trained and prepared to use his means properly, is in this category, as our friend the captain would call it, and then they begin to long for some other untried advantages. The example of the rest of the world is before our own wealthy, and, *faute d'imagination*, they imitate because they cannot invent. Exclusive political power is also a great ally in the accumulation of money, and a portion have the sagacity to see it; though I suspect more pine for the vanities of the exclusive classes, than for the substance. Your sex, Miss Effingham, as a whole, is not above this latter weakness, as I think you must have observed in your intercourse with those you met abroad."

"I met with some instances of weakness, in this way," said Eve, with reserve, and with the pride of a woman, "though not more, I think, than among the men; and seldom, in either case, among those whom we are accustomed to consider people of condition at home. The self-respect and the habits of the latter, generally preserved them from betraying this feebleness of character, if indeed they felt it."

"The Americans abroad may be divided into two great classes; those who go for improvement in the sciences or the arts, and those who go for mere amusement. As a whole, the former have struck me as being singularly respectable, equally removed from an apish servility and a swaggering pretension of superiority; while, I fear, a majority of the latter have a disagreeable direction towards the vanities."

"I will not affirm the contrary," said Eve, "for frivolity and pleasure are only too closely associated in ordinary minds. The number of those who prize the elegancies of life, for their intrinsic value, is every where small, I should think; and I question if Europe is much better off than ourselves, in this respect."

"This may be true, and yet one can only regret that, in a case where so much depends on example, the tone of our people was not more assimilated to their facts. I do not know whether you were struck with the same peculiarity, but, whenever I felt in the mood to hear high monarchical and aristocratical doctrines blindly promulgated, I used to go to the nearest American Legation."

"I have heard this fact commented on," Eve answered, "and even by foreigners, and I confess it has always struck me as singular. Why should the agent of a republic make a parade of his anti-republican sentiments?"

"That there are exceptions, I will allow; but, after the experience of many years, I honestly think that such is the rule. I might distrust my own opinion, or my own knowledge; but others, with opportunities equal to my own, have come to the same conclusion. I have just received a letter from Europe, complaining that an American Envoy Extraordinary, who would as soon think of denouncing himself, as utter the same sentiments openly at home, has given an opinion against the effects of one of the commonest and most popular features of the American state governments; and this, too, under circumstances that might naturally be thought to produce practical consequences, on his hearers."

"*Tant pis.* To me all this is inexplicable!"

"It has its solution, Miss Effingham, like any other problem. In ordinary times, extraordinary men seldom become prominent, power passing into the hands of clever managers. Now, the very vanity, and the petty desires, that betray themselves in glittering uniforms, puerile affectations, and feeble imitations of other systems, probably induce more than half of those who fill the foreign missions to apply for them, and it is no more than we ought to expect that the real disposition should betray itself, when there was no longer any necessity for hypocrisy."

"But I should think this necessity for hypocrisy would never cease! Can it be possible that a people, as much attached to their institutions as the great mass of the American nation is known to be, will tolerate such a base abandonment of all they cherish!"

"How are they to know any thing about it? It is a startling fact, that there is a man at this instant, who has not a single claim to such a confidence, either in the way of mind, principles, manners, or attainments, filling a public trust abroad, who, on all occasions, except those which he thinks will come directly before the American people, not only proclaims himself opposed to the great principles of the institutions, but who, in a recent controversy with a foreign nation, actually took sides against his own country, informing that of the opposing nation, that the administration at home would not be supported by the legislative part of the government!"

"And why is not this publicly exposed?"

"*Cui bono!* The presses that have no direct interest in the matter, would treat the affair with indifference or levity, while a few would mystify the truth. It is quite impossible for a man in a private station to make the truth available in any country, in a matter of public interest; and those in public stations seldom or never attempt it, unless they see a direct party end to be obtained. This is the reason that we see so much infidelity to the principles of the institutions, among the public agents abroad, for they very well know that no one will be able to expose them. In addition to this motive, there is so strong a desire in that portion of the community which is considered the highest, to effect a radical change in these very institutions, that infidelity to them, in their eyes, would be a merit, rather than an offence."

"Surely, surely, other nations are not treated in this cavalier manner!"

"Certainly not. The foreign agent of a prince, who should whisper a syllable against his master, would be recalled with disgrace; but the servant of the people is differently situated, since there are so many to be persuaded of his guilt. I could always get along with all the attacks that the Europeans are so fond of making on the American system, but those which they quoted from the mouths of our own diplomatic agents."

"Why do not our travellers expose this?"

"Most of them see too little to know any thing of it. They dine at a diplomatic table, see a star or two, fancy themselves obliged, and puff elegancies that have no existence, except in their own brains. Some think with the unfaithful, and see no harm in the infidelity. Others calculate the injury to themselves, and no small portion would fancy it a greater proof of patriotism to turn a sentence in favour of the comparative 'energies' and 'superior intelligence' of their own people, than to point out this or any other disgraceful fact, did they even possess the opportunities to discover it. Though no one thinks more highly of these qualities in the Americans, considered in connexion with practical things, than myself, no one probably gives them less credit for their ability to distinguish between appearances and reality, in matters of principle."

"It is probable that were we nearer to the rest of the world, these abuses would not exist, for it is certain they are not so openly practised at home. I am glad, however, to find that, even while you felt some uncertainty concerning your own birth-place, you took so much interest in us, as to identify yourself in feeling, at least, with the nation."

"There was one moment when I was really afraid that the truth would show I was actually born an Englishman—"

"Afraid!" interrupted Eve; "that is a strong word to apply to so great and glorious a people."

"We cannot always account for our prejudices, and perhaps this was one of mine; and, now that I know that to be an Englishman is not the greatest possible merit in your eyes, Miss Effingham, it is in no manner lessened."

"In my eyes, Mr. Powis! I do not remember to have expressed any partiality for, or any prejudice against the English: so far as I can speak of my own feelings, I regard the English the same as any other foreign people."

"In words you have not certainly; but acts speak louder than words."

"You are disposed to be mysterious to-night. What act of mine has declared *pro* or *con* in this important affair."

"You have at least done what, I fear, few of your countrywomen would have the moral courage and self-denial to do, and especially those who are accustomed to living abroad—refused to be the wife of an English baronet of a good estate and respectable family."

"Mr. Powis," said Eve, gravely, "this is an injustice to Sir George Templemore, that my sense of right will not permit to go uncontradicted, as well as an injustice to my sex and me. As I told Mr. Howel, in your presence, that gentleman has never proposed for me, and of course cannot have been refused. Nor can I suppose that any American gentlewoman can deem so paltry a thing as a baronetcy, an inducement to forget her self-respect."

"I fully appreciate your generous modesty, Miss Effingham; but you cannot expect that I, to whom Templemore's admiration gave so much uneasiness, not to say pain, am to understand you, as Mr. Howel has probably done, too broadly. Although Sir George may not have positively proposed, his readiness to do so, on the least encouragement, was too obvious to be overlooked by a near observer."

Eve was ready to gasp for breath, so completely by surprise was she taken, by the calm, earnest, and yet respectful manner, in which Paul confessed his jealousy. There was a tremor in his voice, too, usually so clear and even, that touched her heart, for, when there exists a real sympathy between the sexes, feeling responds to feeling, as echo answers sound. She felt the necessity of saying something, and yet they had walked some distance, ere it was in her power to utter a syllable.

"I fear my presumption has offended you, Miss Effingham," said Paul, speaking more like a corrected child, than the lion-hearted young man he had proved himself.

There was deep homage in the emotion he betrayed, and Eve, although she could barely distinguish his features, was not slow in discovering this proof of the extent of her power over his feelings.

"Do not call it presumption," she said; "for, one who has done so much for us all, can surely claim some right to take an interest in those he has so well served. As for Sir George Templemore, you have probably mistaken the feeling created by our common adventures for one of more importance. He is warmly and sincerely attached to my cousin, Grace Van Cortlandt."

"That he is so now, I fully believe; but that a very different magnet first kept him from the Canadas, I am sure.—We treated each other generously, Miss Effingham, and had no concealments, during that long and anxious night, when all expected that the day would dawn on our captivity. Templemore is too manly and honest to deny his former desire to obtain you for a wife, and I think even he would admit that it depended entirely on yourself to be so, or not."

"This is an act of self-humiliation that he is not called onto perform," Eve hurriedly replied; "such allusions, now, are worse than useless, and they might pain my cousin, were she to hear them."

"I am mistaken in my friend's character, if he leave his betrothed in any doubt, on this subject. Five minutes of perfect frankness now, might obviate years of distrust, hereafter."

"And would you, Mr. Powis, avow a former weakness of this sort, to the woman you had finally selected for your wife?"

"I ought not to quote myself for authority, for or against such a course, since I have never loved but one, and her with a passion too single and too ardent ever to admit of competition. Miss Effingham, there would be something worse than affectation—it would be trifling with one who is sacred in my eyes, were I now to refrain from speaking explicitly, although what I am about to say is forced from me by circumstances, rather than voluntary, and is almost uttered without a definite object. Have I your permission to proceed?'

"You can scarcely need a permission, being the master of your own secrets, Mr. Powis."

Paul, like all men agitated by strong passion, was inconsistent, and far from just; and Eve felt the truth of this, even while her mind was ingeniously framing excuses for his weaknesses. Still, the impression that she was about to listen to a declaration that possibly ought never to be made, weighed upon her, and caused her to speak with more coldness than she actually felt. As she continued silent, however, the young man saw that it had become indispensably necessary to be explicit.

"I shall not detain you, Miss Effingham, perhaps vex you," he said, "with the history of those early impressions, which have gradually grown upon me, until they have become interwoven with my very existence. We met, as you know, at Vienna, for the first time. An Austrian of rank, to whom I had become known through some fortunate circumstances, introduced me into the best society of that capital, in which I found you the admiration of all who knew you. My first feeling was that of exultation, at seeing a young countrywoman—you were then almost a child, Miss Effingham—the greatest attraction of a capital celebrated for the beauty and grace of its women—"

"Your national partialities have made you an unjust judge towards others, Mr. Powis," Eve interrupted him by saying, though the earnestness and passion with which the young man uttered his feelings, made music to her ears: "what had a young, frightened, half-educated American girl to boast of, when put in competition with the finished women of Austria?"

"Her surpassing beauty, her unconscious superiority, her attainments, her trembling simplicity and modesty, and her meek purity of mind. All these did you possess, not only in my eyes, but in those of others; for these are subjects on which I dwelt too fondly to be mistaken."

A rocket passed near them at the moment, and, while both were too much occupied by the discourse to heed the interruption, its transient light enabled Paul to see the flushed cheeks and tearful eyes of Eve, as the latter were turned on him, in a grateful pleasure, that his ardent praises extorted from her, in despite of all her struggles for self-command.

"We will leave to others this comparison, Mr. Powis," she said, "and confine ourselves to less doubtful subjects."

"If I am then to speak only of that which is beyond all question, I shall speak chiefly of my long cherished, devoted, unceasing attachment. I adored you at Vienna, Miss Effingham, though it was at a distance, as one might worship the sun; for, while your excellent father admitted me to his society, and I even think honoured me with some portion of his esteem, I had but little opportunity to ascertain the value of the jewel that was contained in so beautiful a casket; but when we met the following summer in Switzerland, I first began truly to love. Then I learned the justness of thought, the beautiful candour, the perfectly feminine delicacy of your mind; and, although I will not say that these qualities were not enhanced in the eyes of so young a man, by the extreme beauty of their possessor, I will say that, as weighed against each other, I could a thousand times prefer the former to the latter, unequalled as the latter almost is, even among your own beautiful sex."

"This is presenting flattery in its most seductive form, Powis."

"Perhaps my incoherent and abrupt manner of explaining myself deserves a rebuke; though nothing can be farther from my intentions than to seem to flatter, or in any manner to exaggerate. I intend merely to give a faithful history of the state of my feelings, and of the progress of my love."

Eve smiled faintly, but very sweetly, as Paul would have thought, had the obscurity permitted more than a dim view of her lovely countenance.

"Ought I to listen to such praises, Mr. Powis," she asked; "praises which only contribute to a self-esteem that is too great already?"

"No one but yourself would say this; but your question does, indeed, remind me of the indiscretion that I have fallen into, by losing that command of my feelings, in which I have so long exulted. No man should make a woman the confidant of his attachment, until he is fully prepared to accompany the declaration with an offer of his hand;—and such is not my condition."

Eve made no dramatic start, assumed no look of affected surprise, or of wounded dignity; but she turned on her lover, her serene eyes, with an expression of concern so eloquent, and of a wonder so natural, that, could he have seen it, it would probably have overcome every difficulty on the spot, and produced the usual offer, notwithstanding the difficulty that he seemed to think insurmountable.

"And yet," he continued, "I have now said so much, involuntarily as it has been, that I feel it not only due to you, but in some measure to myself, to add that the fondest wish of my heart, the end and aim of all my day-dreams, as well as of my most sober thoughts for the future, centre in the common wish to obtain you for a wife."

The eye of Eve fell, and the expression of her countenance changed, while a slight but uncontrollable tremor ran through her frame. After a short pause, she summoned all her resolution, and in a voice, the firmness of which surprised even herself, she asked—

"Powis, to what does all this tend?"

"Well may you ask that question, Miss Effingham! You have every right to put it, and the answer, at least, shall add no further cause of self-reproach. Give me, I entreat you, but a minute to collect my thoughts, and I will endeavour to acquit myself of an imperious duty, in a manner more manly and coherent, than I fear has been observed for the last ten minutes."

They walked a short distance in profound silence, Eve still under the influence of astonishment, in which an uncertain and indefinite dread of, she scarce knew what, began to mingle; and Paul, endeavouring to quiet the tumult that had been so suddenly aroused within him. The latter then spoke:

"Circumstances have always deprived me of the happiness of experiencing the tenderness and sympathy of your sex, Miss Effingham, and have thrown me more exclusively among the colder and ruder spirits of my own. My mother died at the time of my birth, thus cutting me off, at once, from one of the dearest of earthly ties. I am not certain that I do not exaggerate the loss in consequence of the privations I have suffered; but, from the hour when I first learned to feel, I have had a yearning for the tender, patient, endearing, disinterested love of a mother. You, too, suffered a similar loss, at an early period, if I have been correctly informed—"

A sob—a stifled, but painful sob, escaped Eve; and, inexpressibly shocked, Paul ceased dwelling on his own sources of sorrow, to attend to those he had so unintentionally disturbed.

"I have been selfish, dearest Miss Effingham," he exclaimed— "have overtaxed your patience—have annoyed you with griefs and losses that have no interest for you, which can have no interest, with one happy and blessed as yourself."

"No, no, no, Powis—you are unjust to both. I, too, lost my mother when a mere child, and never knew her love and tenderness. Proceed; I am calmer, and earnestly intreat you to forget my weakness, and to proceed."

Paul did proceed, but this brief interruption in which they had mingled their sorrows for a common misfortune, struck a new chord of feeling, and removed a mountain of reserve and distance, that might otherwise have obstructed their growing confidence.

"Cut off in this manner, from my nearest and dearest natural friend," Paul continued, "I was thrown, an infant, into the care of hirelings; and, in this at least, my fortune was still more cruel than your own; for the excellent woman who has been so happy as to have had the charge of your infancy, had nearly the love of a natural mother, however she may have been wanting in the attainments of one of your own condition in life."

"But we had both of us, our fathers, Mr. Powis. To me, my excellent, high principled, affectionate—nay tender father, has been every thing. Without him, I should have been truly miserable; and with him, notwithstanding these rebellious tears, tears that I must ascribe to the infection of your own grief, I have been truly blest."

"Mr. Effingham deserves this from you, but I never knew my father, you will remember."

"I am an unworthy confidant, to have forgotten this so soon. Poor Powis, you were, indeed, unhappy!"

"He had parted from my mother before my birth, and either died soon after, or has never deemed his child of sufficient worth to make him the subject of interest sufficient to excite a single inquiry into his fate."

"Then he never knew that child!" burst from Eve, with a fervour and frankness, that set all reserves, whether of womanly training, or of natural timidity, at defiance.

"Miss Effingham!—dearest Miss Effingham—Eve, my own Eve, what am I to infer from this generous warmth! Do not mislead me! I can bear my solitary misery, can brave the sufferings of an isolated existence; but I could not live under the disappointments of such a hope, a hope fairly quickened by a clear expression from your lips."

"You teach me the importance of caution, Powis, and we will now return to your history, and to that confidence of which I shall not again prove a faithless repository. For the present at least, I beg that you will forget all else."

"A command so kindly—so encouragingly given—do I offend, dearest Miss Effingham?"

Eve, for the second time in her life, placed her own light arm and beautiful hand, through the arm of Paul, discovering a bewitching but modest reliance on his worth and truth, by the very manner in which she did this simple and every-day act, while she said more cheerfully—

"You forget the substance of the command, at the very moment you would have me suppose you most disposed to obey it."

"Well, then, Miss Effingham, you shall be more implicitly minded. *Why* my father left my mother so soon after their union, I never knew. It would seem that they lived together but a few months, though I have the proud consolation of knowing that my mother was blameless. For years I suffered the misery of doubt on a point that is ever the most tender with man, a distrust of his own mother; but all this has been happily, blessedly, cleared up, during my late visit to England. It is true that Lady Dunluce was my mother's sister, and as such might have been lenient to her failings; but a letter from my father, that was written only a month before my mother's death, leaves no doubt not only of her blamelessness as a wife, but it bears ample testimony to the sweetness of her disposition. This letter is a precious document for a son to possess, Miss Effingham!"

Eve made no answer; but Paul fancied that he felt another gentle pressure of the hand, which, until then, had rested so lightly on his own arm, that he scarcely dared to move the latter, lest he might lose the precious consciousness of its presence.

"I have other letters from my father to my mother," the young man continued, "but none that are so cheering to my heart as this. From their general tone, I cannot persuade myself that he ever truly loved her. It is a cruel thing, Miss Effingham, for a man to deceive a woman on a point like that!"

"Cruel, indeed!" said Eve, firmly. "Death itself were preferable to such a delusion."

"I think my father deceived himself as well as my mother; for there is a strange incoherence and a want of distinctness in some of his letters, that caused feelings, keen as mine naturally were on such a subject, to distrust his affection from the first."

"Was your mother rich?" Eve asked innocently; for, an heiress herself, her vigilance had early been directed to that great motive of deception and dishonesty.

"Not in the least. She had little besides her high lineage, and her beauty. I have her picture, which sufficiently proves the latter; had, I ought rather to say, for it was her miniature, of which I was robbed by the Arabs, as you may remember, and I have not seen it since.

In the way of money, my mother had barely the competency of a gentlewoman; nothing more."

The pressure on Paul was more palpable, as spoke of the miniature; and he ventured to touch his companion's arm, in order to give it a surer hold of his own.

"Mr. Powis was not mercenary, then, and it is a great deal," said Eve, speaking as if she were scarcely conscious that she spoke at all.

"Mr. Powis!—He was every thing that was noble and disinterested. A more generous, or a less selfish man, never existed than Francis Powis!"

"I thought you never knew your father personally!" exclaimed Eve in surprise.

"Nor did I. But, you are in an error, in supposing that my father's name was Powis, when it was Assheton."

Paul then explained the manner in which he had been adopted while still a child, by a gentleman called Powis, whose name he had taken, on finding himself deserted by his own natural parent, and to whose fortune he had succeeded, on the death of his voluntary protector.

"I bore the name of Assheton until Mr. Powis took me to France, when he advised me to assume his own, which I did the more readily, as he thought he had ascertained that my father was dead, and that he had bequeathed the whole of a very considerable estate to his nephews and nieces, making no allusion to me in his will, and seemingly anxious even to deny his marriage; at least, that person passed among his acquaintances for a bachelor to his dying day."

"There is something so unusual and inexplicable in all this, Mr. Powis, that it strikes me you have been to blame, in not inquiring more closely into the circumstances than, by your own account, I should think had been done."

"For a long time, for many bitter years, I was afraid to inquire, lest I should learn something injurious to a mother's name. Then there was the arduous and confined service of my profession, which kept me in distant seas; and the last journey and painful indisposition of my excellent benefactor, prevented even the wish to inquire after my own family. The offended pride of Mr. Powis, who was justly hurt at the cavalier manner in which my father's family met his advances, aided in alienating me from that portion of my relatives, and put a stop to all additional proffers of intercourse from me. They even affected to doubt the fact that my father had ever married."

"But of that you had proof?" Eve earnestly asked.

"Unanswerable. My aunt Dunluce was present at the ceremony, and I possess the certificate given to my mother by the clergyman who officiated. Is it not strange, Miss Effingham, that with all these circumstances in favour of my legitimacy, even Lady Dunluce and her family, until lately, had doubts of the fact."

"That is indeed unaccountable, your aunt having witnessed the ceremony."

"Very true; but some circumstances, a little aided perhaps by the strong desire of her husband, General Ducie, to obtain the revival of a barony that was in abeyance, and of which she would be the only heir, assuming that my rights were invalid, inclined her to believe that my father was already married, when he entered into the solemn contract with my mother. But from that curse too, I have been happily relieved."

"Poor Powis!" said Eve, with a sympathy that her voice expressed more clearly even than her words; "you have, indeed, suffered cruelly, for one so young."

"I have learned to bear it, dearest Miss Effingham, and have stood so long a solitary and isolated being, one in whom none have taken any interest—"

"Nay, say not that—*we*, at least, have always felt an interest in you—have always esteemed you, and now have learned to—"

"Learned to—?"

"Love you," said Eve, with a steadiness that afterwards astonished herself; but she felt that a being so placed, was entitled to be treated with a frankness different from the reserve that it is usual for her sex to observe on similar occasions.

"Love!" cried Paul, dropping her arm. "Miss Effingham!—Eve—but that *we*!"

"I mean my dear father—cousin Jack—myself."

"Such a feeling will not heal a wound like mine. A love that is shared with even such men as your excellent father, and your worthy cousin, will not make me happy. But, why should I, unowned, bearing a name to which I have no legal title, and virtually without relatives, aspire to one like you!"

The windings of the path had brought them near a window of the house, whence a stream of strong light gleamed upon the sweet countenance of Eve, as raising her eyes to those of her companion, with a face bathed in tears, and flushed with natural feeling and modesty, the struggle between which even heightened her loveliness, she smiled an encouragement that it was impossible to misconstrue.

"Can I believe my senses! Will *you—do* you—*can* you listen to the suit of one like me?" the young man exclaimed, as he hurried his companion past the window, lest some interruption might destroy his hopes.

"Is there any sufficient reason why I should not, Powis?"

"Nothing but my unfortunate situation in respect to my family, my comparative poverty, and my general unworthiness."

"Your unfortunate situation in respect to your relatives would, if any thing, be a new and dearer tie with us; your comparative poverty is merely comparative, and can be of no account, where there is sufficient already; and as for your general unworthiness, I fear it will find more than an offset, in that of the girl you have so rashly chosen from the rest of the world."

"Eve—dearest Eve—" said Paul, seizing both her hands, and stopping her at the entrance of some shrubbery, that densely shaded the path, and where the little light that fell from the stars enabled him still to trace her features—"you will not leave me in doubt on a subject of this nature—am I really so blessed?"

"If accepting the faith and affection of a heart that is wholly yours, Powis, can make you happy, your sorrows will be at an end—"

"But your father?" said the young man, almost breathless in his eagerness to know all.

"Is here to confirm what his daughter has just declared," said Mr. Effingham, coming out of the shrubbery beyond them, and laying a hand kindly on Paul's shoulder. "To find that you so well understand each other, Powis, removes from my mind one of the greatest anxieties I have ever experienced. My cousin John, as he was bound to do, has made me acquainted with all you have told him of your past life, and there remains nothing further to be revealed. We have known you for years, and receive you into our family with as free a welcome as we could receive any precious boon from Providence."

"Mr. Effingham!—dear sir," said Paul, almost gasping between surprise and rapture—"this is indeed beyond all my hopes—and this generous frankness, too, in your lovely daughter—"

Paul's hands had been transferred to those of the father, he knew not how; but releasing them hurriedly, he now turned in quest of Eve again, and found she had fled. In the short interval between the address of her father and the words of Paul, she had found means to disappear, leaving the gentlemen together. The young man would have followed, but the cooler head of Mr. Effingham perceiving that the occasion was favourable to a private conversation with his accepted son-in-law, and quite as unfavourable to one, or at least to a very rational one, between the lovers, he quietly took the young man's arm, and led him towards a more private walk. Half an hour of confidential discourse calmed the feelings of both, and rendered Paul Powis one of the happiest of human beings.

CHAPTER XXIV.

"You shall do marvell's wisely, good Reynaldo,
Before you visit him, to make inquire
Of his behaviour."

Hamlet 2.1.3–5.

ANNE Sidley was engaged among the dresses of Eve, as she loved
to be, although Annette held her taste in too low estimation ever to
permit her to apply a needle, or even to fit a robe to the beautiful
form that was to wear it, when our heroine glided into the room and
sunk upon a sofa. Eve was too much absorbed with her own feelings
to observe the presence of her quiet unobtrusive old nurse, and too
much accustomed to her care and sympathy to heed it, had it been
seen. For a moment she remained, her face still suffused with blushes,
her hands lying before her folded, her eyes fixed on the ceiling, and
then the pent emotions found an outlet in a flood of tears.

Poor Anne could not have felt more shocked, had she heard of
any unexpected calamity, than she was at this sudden outbreaking
of feeling in her child. She went to her, and bent over her with the
solicitude of a mother, as she inquired into the causes of her apparent
sorrow.

"Tell me, Miss Eve, and it will relieve your mind," said the faithful
woman; "your dear mother had such feelings sometimes, and I never
dared to question her about them; but you are my own child, and
nothing can grieve you without grieving me."

The eyes of Eve were brilliant, her face continued to be suffused,
and the smile which she gave through her tears was so bright, as to
leave her poor attendant in deep perplexity as to the cause of a gush
of feeling that was very unusual in one of the other's regulated mind.

"It is not grief, dear Nanny,"—Eve at length murmured—"any
thing but that! I am not unhappy. Oh! no; as far from unhappiness
as possible."

"God be praised it is so, ma'am! I was afraid that this affair of the English gentleman and Miss Grace might not prove agreeable to you, for he has not behaved as handsomely as he might, in that transaction."

"And why not, my poor Nanny?—I have neither claim, nor the wish to possess a claim, on Sir George Templemore. His selection of my cousin has given me sincere satisfaction, rather than pain; were he a countryman of our own, I should say unalloyed satisfaction, for I firmly believe he will strive to make her happy."

Nanny now looked at her young mistress, then at the floor; at her young mistress again, and afterwards at a rocket that was sailing athwart the sky. Her eyes, however, returned to those of Eve, and encouraged by the bright beam of happiness that was glowing in the countenance she so much loved, she ventured to say—

"If Mr. Powis were a more presuming gentleman than he is, ma'am—"

"You mean a less modest, Nanny," said Eve, perceiving that her nurse paused.

"Yes, ma'am—one that thought more of himself, and less of other people, is what I wish to say."

"And were this the case?"

"I might think *he* would find the heart to say what I know he feels."

"And did he find the heart to say what you know he feels, what does Anne Sidley think should be my answer?"

"Oh, ma'am, I know it would be just as it ought to be. I cannot repeat what ladies say on such occasions, but I know that it is what makes the hearts of the gentlemen leap for joy."

There are occasions in which woman can hardly dispense with the sympathy of woman. Eve loved her father most tenderly, had more than the usual confidence in him, for she had never known a mother; but had the present conversation been with him, notwithstanding all her reliance on his affection, her nature would have shrunk from pouring out her feelings as freely as she might have done with her other parent, had not death deprived her of such a blessing. Between our heroine and Anne Sidley, on the other hand, there existed a confidence of a nature so peculiar, as to require a word of explanation before we exhibit its effects. In all that related to physical wants, Anne had been a mother, or even more than a mother to Eve, and this alone had induced great personal dependence in the one, and a sort of supervisory care in the other, that had brought her to fancy she was responsible for the bodily health and well-doing of her charge. But this was not all. Nanny had been the repository of Eve's childish griefs, the confidant of her girlish secrets; and though the years of the latter soon caused her to be placed under the management of those who were better qualified to store her mind, this communication never ceased; the high-toned and educated young woman reverting with unabated affection, and a reliance that nothing could shake, to the long-tried tenderness of the being who had watched over her infancy. The effect of such an intimacy was often amusing; the one party bringing to the conferences, a mind filled with the knowledge suited to her sex and station, habits that had been formed in the best circles of christendom, and tastes that had been acquired in schools of high reputation; and the other, little more than her single-hearted love, a fidelity that ennobled her nature, and a simplicity that betokened perfect purity of thought. Nor was this extraordinary confidence without its advantages to Eve; for, thrown so early among the artificial and calculating, it served to keep her own ingenuousness of character active, and prevented that cold, selfish, and unattractive sophistication, that mere women of fashion are apt to fall into, from their isolated and factitious mode of existence. When Eve, therefore, put the questions to her nurse, that have already been mentioned, it was more with a real wish to know how the latter would view a choice on which her own mind was so fully made up, than any silly trifling on a subject that engrossed so much of her best affections.

"But you have not told me, dear Nanny," she continued, "what *you* would have that answer be. Ought I, for instance, ever to quit my beloved father?"

"What necessity would there be for that, ma'am? Mr. Powis has no home of his own; and, for that matter, scarcely any country—"

"How can you know this, Nanny?" demanded Eve, with the jealous sensitiveness of a fervent love.

"Why, Miss Eve, his man says this much, and he has lived with him long enough to know it, if he had a home. Now, I seldom sleep without looking back at the day, and often have my thoughts turned to Sir George Templemore and Mr. Powis; and when I have remembered that the first had a house and a home, and that the last had neither, it has always seemed to me that *he* ought to be the one."

"And then, in all this matter, you have thought of convenience, and what might be agreeable to others, rather than of me."

"Miss Eve!"

"Nay, dearest Nanny, forgive me; I know your last thought, in every thing, is for yourself. But surely, the mere circumstance that he had no home, ought not to be a sufficient reason for selecting any man, for a husband. With most women it would be an objection."

"I pretend to know very little of these feelings, Miss Eve. I have been wooed, I acknowledge; and once I do think I might have been tempted to marry, had it not been for a particular circumstance."

"You! You marry, Anne Sidley!" exclaimed Eve, to whom the bare idea seemed as odd and unnatural, as that her own father should forget her mother, and take a second wife. "This is altogether new, and I should be glad to know what the lucky circumstance was, which prevented what, to me, might have proved so great a calamity."

"Why, ma'am, I said to myself, what does a woman do, who marries? She vows to quit all else to go with her husband, and to love him before father and mother, and all other living beings on earth—is it not so, Miss Eve?"

"I believe it is so, indeed, Nanny—nay, I am quite certain it is so," Eve answered, the colour deepening on her cheek, as she gave this opinion to her old nurse, with the inward consciousness that she had just experienced some of the happiest moments of her life, through the admission of a passion that thus overshadowed all the natural affections. "It is, truly, as you say."

"Well, ma'am, I investigated my feelings, I believe they call it, and after a proper trial, I found that I loved you so much better than any one else, that I could not, in conscience, make the vows."

"Dearest Nanny! my kind, good, faithful old nurse! let me hold you in my arms: and, I, selfish, thoughtless, heartless girl, would forget the circumstance that would be most likely to keep us together, for the remainder of our lives! Hist! there is a tap at the door. It is Mrs. Bloomfield; I know her light step. Admit her, my kind Anne, and leave us together."

The bright searching eye of Mrs. Bloomfield was riveted on her young friend, as she advanced into the room; and her smile, usually so gay and sometimes ironical, was now thoughtful and kind.

"Well, Miss Effingham," she cried, in a manner that her looks contradicted, "am I to condole with you, or to congratulate?—For a more sudden, or a more miraculous change did I never before witness in a young lady, though whether it be for the better or the worse—

These are ominous words, too—for 'better or worse, for richer or poorer'—"

"You are in fine spirits this evening, my dear Mrs. Bloomfield, and appear to have entered into the gaieties of the Fun of Fire, with all your—"

"Might, will be a homely, but an expressive word. Your Templeton Fun of Fire is fiery fun, for it has cost us something like a general conflagration. Mrs. Hawker has been near a downfall, like your great namesake, by a serpent's coming too near her dress; one barn, I hear, has actually been in a blaze, and Sir George Templemore's heart is in cinders. Mr. John Effingham has been telling me that he should not have been a bachelor, had there been two Mrs. Bloomfields in the world, and Mr. Powis looks like a rafter dugout of Herculaneum, nothing but coal."

"And what occasions this pleasantry?" asked Eve, so composed in manner that her friend was momentarily deceived.

Mrs. Bloomfield took a seat on the sofa, by the side of our heroine, and regarding her steadily for near a minute, she continued—

"Hypocrisy and Eve Effingham can have little in common, and my ears must have deceived me."

"Your ears, dear Mrs. Bloomfield!"

"My ears, dear Miss Effingham. I very well know the character of an eaves-dropper, but if gentlemen will make passionate declarations in the walks of a garden, with nothing but a little shrubbery between his ardent declarations and the curiosity of those who may happen to be passing, they must expect to be overheard."

Eve's colour had gradually increased as her friend proceeded; and when the other ceased speaking, as bright a bloom glowed on her countenance, as had shone there when she first entered the room.

"May I ask the meaning of all this?" she said, with an effort to appear calm.

"Certainly, my dear; and you shall also know the *feelings* that prompt it, as well as the meaning," returned Mrs. Bloomfield, kindly taking Eve's hand in a way to show that she did not mean to trifle further on a subject that was of so much moment to her young friend. "Mr. John Effingham and myself were star-gazing at a point where two walks approach each other, just as you and Mr. Powis were passing in the adjoining path. Without absolutely stopping our ears, it was quite impossible not to hear a portion of your conversation. We both tried to behave honourably; for I coughed, and your kinsman actually hemmed, but we were unheeded."

"Coughed and hemmed!" repeated Eve, in greater confusion than ever. "There must be some mistake, dear Mrs. Bloomfield, as I remember to have heard no such signals."

"Quite likely, my love, for there was a time when I too had ears for only one voice; but you can have affidavits to the fact, *à la mode de New England*, if you require them. Do not mistake my motive, nevertheless, Miss Effingham, which is any thing but vulgar curiosity"—here Mrs. Bloomfield looked so kind and friendly, that Eve took both her hands and pressed them to her heart—"you are motherless; without even a single female connexion of a suitable age to consult with on such an occasion, and fathers after all are but men—"

"Mine is as kind, and delicate, and tender, as any woman can be, Mrs. Bloomfield."

"I believe it all, though he may not be quite as quick-sighted, in an affair of this nature.—Am I at liberty to speak to you as if I were an elder sister?"

"Speak, Mrs. Bloomfield, as frankly as you please, but leave me the mistress of my answers."

"It is, then, as I suspected," said Mrs. Bloomfield, in a sort of musing manner; "the men have been won over, and this young creature has absolutely been left withhout a protector in the most important moment of her life!"

"Mrs. Bloomfield!—What does this mean?—What *can* it mean?"

"It means merely general principles, child; that your father and cousin have been parties concerned, instead of vigilant sentinels; and, with all their pretended care, that you have been left to grope your way in the darkness of female uncertainty, with one of the most pleasing young men in the country constantly before you, to help the obscurity."

It is a dreadful moment, when we are taught to doubt the worth of those we love; and Eve became pale as death, as she listened to the words of her friend. Once before, on the occasion of Paul's return to England, she had felt a pang of that sort, though reflection, and a calm revision of all his acts and words since they first met in Germany, had enabled her to get the better of indecision, and when she first saw him on the mountain, nearly every unpleasant apprehension and distrust had been dissipated by an effort of pure reason. His own explanations had cleared up the unpleasant affair, and, from that moment, she had regarded him altogether with the eyes of a confiding partiality. The speech of Mrs. Bloomfield now sounded like words of doom to her, and, for an instant, her friend was frightened with the effects of her own imperfect communication. Until that moment Mrs. Bloomfield had formed no just idea of the extent to which the feelings of Eve were interested in Paul, for she had but an imperfect knowledge of their early association in Europe, and she sincerely repented having introduced the subject at all. It was too late to retreat, however, and, first folding Eve in her arms, and kissing her cold forehead, she hastened to repair a part, at least, of the mischief she had done.

"My words have been too strong, I fear," she said, "but such is my general horror of the manner in which the young of our sex, in this country, are abandoned to the schemes of the designing and selfish of the other, that I am, perhaps, too sensitive when I see any one that I love thus exposed. You are known, my dear, to be one of the richest heiresses of the country; and, I blush to say that no accounts of European society that we have, make fortune-hunting a more regular occupation there, than it has got to be here."

The paleness left Eve's face, and a look of slight displeasure succeeded.

"Mr. Powis is no fortune-hunter, Mrs. Bloomfield," she said, steadily; "his whole conduct for three years has been opposed to such a character; and, then, though not absolutely rich, perhaps, he has a gentleman's income, and is removed from the necessity of being reduced to such an act of baseness."

"I perceive my error, but it is now too late to retreat. I do not say that Mr. Powis is a fortune-hunter, but there are circumstances connected with his history, that you ought at least to know, and that immediately. I have chosen to speak to you, rather than to speak to your father, because I thought you might like a female confidant on such occasion, in preference even to your excellent natural protector. The idea of Mrs. Hawker occurred to me, on account of her age; but I did not feel authorised to communicate to her a secret of which I had myself become so accidentally possessed."

"I appreciate your motive fully, dearest Mrs. Bloomfield," said Eve, smiling with all her native sweetness, and greatly relieved, for she now began to think that too keen a sensitiveness on the subject of Paul had unnecessarily alarmed her, "and beg there may be no reserves between us. If you know a reason why Mr. Powis should not be received as a suitor, I entreat you to mention it."

"Is he Mr. Powis at all?"

Again Eve smiled, to Mrs. Bloomfield's great surprise, for, as the latter had put the question with sincere reluctance, she was astonished at the coolness with which it was received.

"He is not Mr. Powis, legally perhaps, though he might be, but that he dislikes the publicity of an application to the legislature. His paternal name is Assheton."

"You know his history, then!"

"There has been no reserve on the part of Mr. Powis; least of all, any deception."

Mrs. Bloomfield appeared perplexed, even distressed; and there was a brief space, during which her mind was undecided as to the course she ought to take. That she had committed an error by attempting a consultation, in a matter of the heart, with one of her own sex, after the affections were engaged, she discovered when it was too late; but she prized Eve's friendship too much, and had too just a sense of what was due to herself, to leave the affair where it was, or without clearing up her own unasked agency in it.

"I rejoice to learn this," she said, as soon as her doubts had ended, "for frankness, while it is one of the safest, is one of the most beautiful traits in human character; but beautiful though it be, it is one that the other sex uses least to our own."

"Is our own too ready to use it to the other?"

"Perhaps not: it might be better for both parties, were there less deception practised during the period of courtship, generally: but as this is hopeless, and might destroy some of the most pleasing illusions of life, we will not enter into a treatise on the frauds of Cupid. Now to my own confessions, which I make all the more willingly, because I know they are uttered to the ear of one of a forgiving temperament, and who is disposed to view even my follies favourably."

The kind but painful smile of Eve, assured the speaker she was not mistaken, and she continued, after taking time to read the expression of the countenance of her young friend—

"In common with all of New-York, that town of babbling misses, who prattle as water flows, without consciousness or effort, and of whiskered masters, who fancy Broadway the world, and the flirtations of miniature drawing-rooms, human nature, I believed, on your return from Europe, that an accepted suitor followed in your train, in the person of Sir George Templemore."

"Nothing in my deportment, or in that of Sir George, or in that of any of my family, could justly have given rise to such a notion," said Eve, quickly.

"Justly! What has justice, or truth, or even probability, to do with a report, of which love and matrimony are the themes? Do you not know *society* better than to fancy this improbability, child?"

"I know that our own sex would better consult their own dignity and respectability, my dear Mrs. Bloomfield, if they talked less of such matters; and that they would be more apt to acquire the habits of good taste, not to say of good principles, if they confined their strictures more to things and sentiments than they do, and meddled less with persons."

"And pray, is there no tittle-tattle, no scandal, no commenting on one's neighbours, in other civilized nations besides this?"

"Unquestionably; though I believe, as a rule, it is every where thought to be inherently vulgar, and a proof of low associations."

"In that, we are perfectly of a mind; for, if there be any thing that betrays a consciousness of inferiority, it is our rendering others of so much obvious importance to ourselves, as to make them the subjects of our constant conversation. We may speak of virtues, for therein we pay an homage to that which is good; but when we come to dwell on personal faults, it is rather a proof that we have a silent conviction of the superiority of the subject of our comments to ourselves, either in character, talents, social position, or something else that is deemed essential, than of our distaste for his failings. Who, for instance, talks scandal of his grocer, or of his shoemaker, or his coachman? No, no, our pride forbids this; we always make our betters the subject of our strictures by preference, taking up with our equals only when we can get none of a higher class."

"This quite reconciles me to having been given to Sir George Templemore, by the world of New-York," said Eve, smiling.

"And well it may, for they who have prattled of your engagement, have done so principally because they are incapable of maintaining a conversation on any thing else. But, all this time, I fear I stand accused in your mind, of having given advice unasked, and of feeling an alarm in an affair that affected others, instead of myself, which is the very sin that we lay at the door of our worthy compeers. In common with all around me, then, I fancied Sir George Templemore an accepted lover, and, by habit, had gotten to associate you together in my pictures. On my arrival here, however, I will confess that Mr. Powis, whom, you will remember, I had never seen before, struck me as much the most dangerous man.—Shall I own all my absurdity?"

"Even to the smallest shade."

"Well, then, I confess to having supposed that, while the excellent father believed you were in a fair way to become Lady Templemore, the equally excellent daughter thought the other suitor, infinitely the most agreeable person."

"What! in contempt of a betrothal?"

"Of course I ascribed that part of the report, at once, to the usual embellishments. We do not like to be deceived in our calculations, or to discover that even our gossip has misled us. In pure resentment at my own previous delusion, I began to criticise this Mr. Powis—"

"Criticise, Mrs. Bloomfield!"

"To find fault with him, my dear; to try to think he was not just the handsomest and most engaging young man I had ever seen; to imagine what he ought to be, in place of what he was; and among other things, to inquire *who* he was?"

"You did not think proper to ask that question of any of *us*," said Eve, gravely.

"I did not; for I discovered by instinct, or intuition, or conjecture—they mean pretty much the same thing, I believe—that there was a mystery about him; something that even his Templeton friends did not quite understand, and a lucky thought occurred of making my inquiries of another person."

"They were answered satisfactorily," said Eve, looking up at her friend, with the artless confidence that marks her sex, when the affections have gotten the mastery of reason.

"*Cosi, cosi.* Bloomfield has a brother who is in the Navy, as you know, and I happened to remember that he had once spoken of an officer of the name of Powis, who had performed a clever thing in the West Indies, when they were employed together against the pirates. I wrote to him one of my usual letters, that are compounded of all things in nature and art, and took an occasion to allude to a certain Mr. Paul Powis, with a general remark that he had formerly served, together with a particular inquiry if he knew any thing about him. All this, no doubt, you think very officious; but believe me, dear Eve, where there was as much interest as I felt and feel in you, it was very natural."

"So far from entertaining resentment, I am grateful for your concern, especially as I know it was manifested cautiously, and without any unpleasant allusions to third persons."

"In that respect I believe I did pretty well. Tom Bloomfield—I beg his pardon, Captain Bloomfield, for so he calls himself, at present— knows Mr. Powis well; or, rather *did* know him, for they have not met for years, and he speaks of his personal qualities and professional merit highly, but takes occasion to remark that there was some mystery connected with his birth, as, before he joined the service he understood he was called Assheton, and at a later day, Powis, and this without any public law, or public avowal of a motive. Now, it struck me that Eve Effingham ought not to be permitted to form a connection with a man so unpleasantly situated, without being apprised of the fact. I was waiting for a proper occasion to do this ungrateful office myself, when accident made me acquainted with what has passed this evening, and perceiving that there was no time to lose, I came hither, more led by interest in you, my dear, perhaps, than by discretion."

"I thank you sincerely for this kind concern in my welfare, dear Mrs. Bloomfield, and give you full credit for the motive. Will you permit me to inquire how much you know of that which passed this evening?"

"Simply that Mr. Powis is desperately in love, a declaration that I take it is always dangerous to the peace of mind of a young woman, when it comes from a very engaging young man."

"And my part of the dialogue—" Eve blushed to the eyes as she asked this question, though she made a great effort to appear calm—"my answer?"

"There was too much of woman in me—of true, genuine, loyal, native woman, Miss Effingham, to listen to that, had there been an opportunity. We were but a moment near enough to hear any thing, though that moment sufficed to let us know the state of feelings of the gentleman. I ask no confidences, my dear Eve, and now that I have made my explanations, lame though they be, I will kiss you and repair to the drawing-room, where we shall both be soon missed. Forgive me, if I have seemed impertinent in my interference, and continue to ascribe it to its true motive."

"Stop, Mrs. Bloomfield, I entreat, for a single moment; I wish to say a word before we part. As you have been accidentally made acquainted with Mr. Powis's sentiments towards me, it is no more than just that you should know the nature of mine towards him—"

Eve paused involuntarily, for, though she had commenced her explanation, with a firm intention to do justice to Paul, the bashfulness of her sex held her tongue tied, at the very moment her desire to speak was the strongest. An effort conquered the weakness, and the warm-hearted, generous-minded girl succeeded in commanding her voice.

"I cannot allow you to go away with the impression, that there is a shade of any sort on the conduct of Mr. Powis," she said. "So far from desiring to profit by the accidents that have placed it in his power to render us such essential service, he has never spoken of his attachment until this evening, and then under circumstances in which feeling, naturally, perhaps I might say uncontrollably, got the ascendency."

"I believe it all, for I feel certain Eve Effingham would not bestow her heart heedlessly."

"Heart!—Mrs. Bloomfield!"

"Heart, my dear; and now I insist on the subject's being dropped, at least for the present. Your decision is probably not yet made—you are not yet an hour in possession of your suitor's secret, and prudence demands deliberation. I shall hope to see you in the drawing-room; until then, adieu."

Mrs. Bloomfield signed for silence, and quitted the room with the same light tread as that with which she had entered it.

CHAPTER XXV.

". . . to show virtue her feature, scorn her own image, and the very age and body of the time his form and pressure."

Hamlet 3.2.22–24.

WHEN Mrs. Bloomfield entered the drawing-room, she found nearly the whole party assembled. The Fun of Fire had ceased, and the rockets no longer gleamed athwart the sky; but the blaze of artificial light within, was more than a substitute for that which had so lately existed without.

Mr. Effingham and Paul were conversing by themselves, in a window-seat, while John Effingham, Mrs. Hawker, and Mr. Howel were in an animated discussion on a sofa; Mr. Wenham had also joined the party, and was occupied with Captain Ducie, though not so much so as to prevent occasional glances at the trio just mentioned. Sir George Templemore and Grace Van Cortlandt were walking together in the great hall, and were visible through the open door, as they passed and repassed.

"I am glad of your appearance among us, Mrs. Bloomfield," said John Effingham, "for, certainly more Anglo-mania never existed than that which my good friend Howel manifests this evening, and I have hopes that your eloquence may persuade him out of some of those notions, on which my logic has fallen like seed scattered by the way-side."

"I can have little hopes of success where Mr. John Effingham has failed."

"I am far from being certain of that; for, somehow, Howel has taken up the notion that I have gotten a grudge against England, and he listens to all I say with distrust and distaste."

"Mr. John uses strong language habitually, ma'am," cried Mr. Howel, "and you will make some allowances for a vocabulary that has no very mild terms in it; though, to be frank, I do confess that he seems prejudiced on the subject of that great nation."

"What is the point in immediate controversy, gentlemen?" asked Mrs. Bloomfield, taking a seat.

"Why here is a review of a late American work, ma'am, and I insist that the author is skinned alive, whereas, Mr. John insists that the reviewer exposes only his own rage, the work having a national character, and running counter to the reviewer's feelings and interests."

"Nay, I protest against this statement of the case, for I affirm that the reviewer exposes a great deal more than his rage, since his imbecility, ignorance, and dishonesty, are quite as apparent as any thing else."

"I have read the article," said Mrs. Bloomfield, after glancing her eye at the periodical, "and I must say that I take sides with Mr. John Effingham in his opinion of its character."

"But do you not perceive, ma'am, that this is the idol of the nobility and gentry; the work that is more in favour with people of consequence in England than any other. Bishops are said to write for it!"

"I know it is a work expressly established to sustain one of the most factitious political systems that ever existed, and that it sacrifices every high quality to attain its end."

"Mrs. Bloomfield, you amaze me! The first writers of Great Britain figure in its pages."

"That I much question, in the first place; but even if it were so, it would be but a shallow mystification. Although a man of character might write one article in a work of this nature, it does not follow that a man of no character does not write the next. The principles of the communications of a periodical are as different as their talents."

"But the editor is a pledge for all.—The editor of this review is an eminent writer himself."

"An eminent writer may be a very great knave, in the first place, and one fact is worth a thousand conjectures in such a matter. But we do not know that there is any responsible editor to works of this nature at all, for there is no name given in the title-page, and nothing is more common than vague declarations of a want of this very responsibility. But if I can prove to you that this article *cannot* have been written by a man of common honesty, Mr. Howel, what will you then say to the responsibility of your editor?"

"In that case I shall be compelled to admit that he had no connexion with it."

"Any thing in preference to giving up the beloved idol!" said John Effingham laughing. "Why not add at once, that he is as great a knave as the writer himself? I am glad, however, that Tom Howel has fallen into such good hands, Mrs. Bloomfield, and I devoutly pray you may not spare him."

We have said that Mrs. Bloomfield had a rapid perception of things and principles, that amounted almost to intuition. She had read the article in question, and, as she glanced her eyes through its pages, had detected its fallacies and falsehoods, in almost every sentence. Indeed, they had not been put together with ordinary skill, the writer having evidently presumed on the easiness of the class of readers who generally swallowed his round assertions, and were so clumsily done that any one who had not the faith to move mountains would have seen through most of them without difficulty. But Mr. Howel belonged to another school, and he was so much accustomed to shut his eyes to the palpable mystification mentioned by Mrs. Bloomfield, that a lie, which, advanced in most works, would have carried no weight with it, advanced in this particular periodical, with him became elevated to the dignity of truth.

Mrs. Bloomfield turned to an article on America, in the periodical in question, and read from it several disparaging expressions concerning Mr. Howel's native country, one of which was, "The American's first plaything is the rattle-snake's tail."

"Now, what do you think of this assertion in particular, Mr. Howel?" she asked, reading the words we have just quoted.

"Oh! that is said in mere pleasantry—it is only wit."

"Well, then, what do you think of it as wit?"

"Well, well, it may not be of a very pure water, but the best of men are unequal at all times, and more especially in their wit."

"Here," continued Mrs. Bloomfield, pointing to another paragraph, "is a positive statement, or a positive misstatement, which makes the cost of the 'civil department of the United States Government,' about six times more than it really is."

"Our government is so extremely mean, that I ascribe that error to generosity."

"Well," continued the lady, smiling, "here the reviewer asserts that Congress passed a law *limiting* the size of certain ships, in order to please the democracy; and that the Executive privately evaded this law, and built vessels of a much greater size; whereas the provision of the law is just the contrary, or it expressly commands that the ships should not be *less* than of seventy-four guns; a piece of information, by the way, that I obtained from Mr. Powis."

"Ignorance, ma'am; a stranger cannot be supposed to know all the laws of a foreign country."

"Then why make bold and false assertions about them, that are intended to discredit the country? Here is another assertion—'ten thousand of the men that fought at Waterloo would have marched through North America?' Do you believe that, Mr. Howel?"

"But that is merely an opinion, Mrs. Bloomfield; any man may be wrong in his opinion."

"Very true, but it is an opinion uttered in the year of our Lord one thousand eight hundred and twenty-eight; and after the battles of Bunker Hill, Cowpens, Plattsburg, Saratoga, and New-Orleans! And, moreover, after it had been proved that something very like ten thousand of the identical men who fought at Waterloo, could not march even ten miles into the country."

"Well, well, all this shows that the reviewer is sometimes mistaken."

"Your pardon Mr. Howel; I think it shows, according to your own admission, that his wit, or rather its wit, for there is no *his* about it—that its wit is of a very indifferent quality as witticisms even; that it is ignorant of what it pretends to know; and that its opinions are no better than its knowledge: all of which, when fairly established against one who, by his very pursuit, professes to know more than other people, is very much like making it appear contemptible."

"This is going back eight or ten years—let us look more particularly at the article about which the discussion commences."

"*Volontiers.*"

Mrs. Bloomfield now sent to the library for the work reviewed, and opening the review she read some of its strictures; and then turning to the corresponding passages in the work itself, she pointed out the unfairness of the quotations, the omissions of the context, and, in several flagrant instances, witticisms of the reviewer, that were purchased at the expense of the English language. She next showed several of those audacious assertions, for which the particular periodical was so remarkable, leaving no doubt with any candid person, that they were purchased at the expense of truth.

"But here is an instance that will scarce admit of cavilling or objection on your part, Mr. Howel," she continued; "do me the favour to read the passage in the review."

Mr. Howel complied, and when he had done, he looked expectingly at the lady.

"The effect of the reviewer's statement is to make it appear that the author has contradicted himself, is it not?"

"Certainly, nothing can be plainer."

"According to your favourite reviewer, who accuses him of it, in terms. Now let us look at the fact. Here is the passage in the work itself. In the first place you will remark that this sentence, which contains the alleged contradiction, is mutilated; the part which is omitted, giving a directly contrary meaning to it, from that it bears under the reviewer's scissors."

"It has some such appearance, I do confess."

"Here you perceive that the closing sentence of the same paragraph, and which refers directly to the point at issue, is displaced, made to appear as belonging to a separate paragraph, and as conveying a different meaning from what the author has actually expressed."

"Upon my word, I do not know but you are right!"

"Well, Mr. Howel, we have had wit of no very pure water, ignorance as relates to facts, and mistakes as regards very positive assertions. In what category, as Captain Truck would say, do you place this?"

"Why does not the author reviewed expose this?"

"Why does not a gentleman wrangle with a detected pickpocket?"

"It is literary swindling," said John Effingham, "and the man who did it, is inherently a knave."

"I think both these facts quite beyond dispute," observed Mrs. Bloomfield, laying down Mr. Howel's favourite review with an air of cool contempt; "and I must say I did not think it necessary to prove the general character of the work, at this late date, to any American of ordinary intelligence; much less to a sensible man, like Mr. Howel."

"But, ma'am, there may be much truth and justice in the rest of its remarks," returned the pertinacious Mr. Howel, "although it has fallen into these mistakes."

"Were you ever on a jury, Howel?" asked John Effingham, in his caustic manner.

"Often; and on grand juries, too."

"Well, did the judge never tell you, when a witness is detected in lying on one point, that his testimony is valueless on all others?"

"Very true; but this is a review, and not testimony."

"The distinction is certainly a very good one," resumed Mrs. Bloomfield, laughing, "as nothing, in general, can be less like honest testimony than a review!"

"But I think, my dear ma'am, you will allow that all this is excessively biting and severe—I can't say I ever read any thing sharper in my life."

"It strikes me, Mr. Howel, as being nothing but epithets, the cheapest and most contemptible of all abuse. Were two men, in your presence, to call each other such names, I think it would excite nothing but disgust in your mind. When the thought is clear and poignant, there is little need to have recourse to mere epithets; indeed, men never use the latter, except when there is a deficiency of the first."

"Well, well, my friends," cried Mr. Howel, as he walked away towards Grace and Sir George, "this is a different thing from what I at first thought it, but still I think you undervalue the periodical, in general."

"I hope this little lesson will cool some of Mr. Howel's faith in foreign morality," observed Mrs. Bloomfield, as soon as the gentleman named was out of hearing; "a more credulous and devout worshipper of the idol, I have never before met."

"The school is diminishing, but it is still large. Men like Tom Howel, who have thought in one direction all their lives, are not easily brought to change their notions, especially when the admiration which proceeds from distance, distance 'that lends enchantment to the view,' is at the bottom of their faith. Had this very article been written and printed round the corner of the street in which he lives, Howel would be the first to say that it was the production of a fellow without talents or principles, and was unworthy of a second thought."

"I still think he will be a wiser, if not a better man, by the exposure of its frauds."

"Not he. If you will excuse a homely and a coarse simile, 'he will return like a dog to his vomit, or the sow to its wallowing in the mire.' I never knew one of that school thoroughly cured, until he became himself the subject of attack, or, by a close personal communication, was made to feel the superciliousness of European superiority. It is only a week since I had a discussion with him on the subject of the humanity and the relish for liberty in his beloved model; and when I cited the instance of the employment of the tomahawk, in the wars between England and this country, he actually affirmed that the Indian savages killed no women and children, but the wives and offspring of their enemies; and when I told him that the English, like most other people, cared very little for any liberty but their own, he coolly affirmed that their own was the only liberty worth caring for!"

"Oh yes," put in young Mr. Wenham, who had overheard the latter portion of the conversation, "Mr. Howel is so thoroughly English, that he actually denies that America is the most civilized country in the world, or that we speak our language better than any nation was ever before known to speak its own language."

"This is so manifest an act of treason," said Mrs. Bloomfield, endeavouring to look grave, for Mr. Wenham was any thing but accurate in the use of words himself, commonly pronouncing "been," "ben," "does," "dooze," "nothing," "nawthing," "few," "foo," &c. &c. &c., "that, certainly, Mr. Howel should be arraigned at the bar of public opinion for the outrage."

"It is commonly admitted, even by our enemies, that our mode of speaking is the very best in the world, which, I suppose, is the real reason why our literature has so rapidly reached the top of the ladder."

"And is that the fact?" asked Mrs. Bloomfield, with a curiosity that was not in the least feigned.

"I believe no one denies *that*. *You* will sustain me in this, I fancy, Mr. Dodge?"

The editor of the Active Inquirer had approached, and was just in time to catch the subject in discussion. Now the modes of speech of these two persons, while they had a great deal in common, had also a great deal that was not in common. Mr. Wenham was a native of New-York, and his dialect was a mixture that is getting to be sufficiently general, partaking equally of the Doric of New England, the Dutch cross, and the old English root; whereas, Mr. Dodge spoke the pure, unalloyed Tuscan of his province, rigidly adhering to all its sounds and significations. "Dissipation," he contended, meant "drunkenness;" "ugly," "vicious;" "clever," "good-natured;" and "humbly," (homely) "ugly." In addition to this finesse in significations, he had a variety of pronunciations that often put strangers at fault, and to which he adhered with a pertinacity that obtained some of its force from the fact, that it exceeded his power to get rid of them. Notwithstanding all these little peculiarities, peculiarities as respects every one but those who dwelt in his own province, Mr. Dodge had also taken up the notion of his superiority on the subject of language, and always treated the matter as one that was placed quite beyond dispute, by its publicity and truth.

"The progress of American Literature," returned the editor, "is really astonishing the four quarters of the world. I believe it is very generally admitted, now, that our pulpit and bar are at the very summit of these two professions. Then we have much the best poets of the age, while eleven of our novelists surpass any of all other countries. The American Philosophical Society is, I believe, generally considered the most acute learned body now extant, unless, indeed, the New-York Historical Society may compete with it, for that honour. Some persons give the palm to one, and some to the other; though I myself think it would be difficult to decide between them. Then to what a pass has the drama risen of late years! Genius is getting to be quite a drug in America!"

"You have forgotten to speak of the press, in particular," put in the complacent Mr. Wenham. "I think we may more safely pride ourselves on the high character of the press, than any thing else."

"Why, to tell you the truth, sir," answered Steadfast, taking the other by the arm, and leading him so slowly away, that a part of what followed was heard by the two amused listeners, "modesty is so infallibly the companion of merit, that *we* who are engaged in that high pursuit do not like to say any thing in our own favour. You never detect a newspaper in the weakness of extolling itself; but, between ourselves, I may say, after a close examination of the condition of the press in other countries, I have come to the conclusion, that, for talents, taste, candour, philosophy, genius, honesty, and truth, the press of the United States stands at the very—"

Here Mr. Dodge passed so far from the listeners, that the rest of the speech became inaudible, though from the well-established modesty of the man and the editor, there can be little doubt of the manner in which he concluded the sentence.

"It is said in Europe," observed John Effingham, his fine face expressing the cool sarcasm in which he was so apt to indulge, "that there are *la vieille* and *la Jeune France*. I think we have now had pretty fair specimens of *old* and *young* America; the first distrusting every thing native, even to a potatoe; and the second distrusting nothing, even to itself."

"There appears to be a sort of pendulum-uneasiness in mankind," said Mrs. Bloomfield, "that keeps opinion always vibrating around the centre of truth, for I think it the rarest thing in the world to find man or woman who has not a disposition, as soon as an error is abandoned, to fly off into its opposite extreme. From believing we had nothing worthy of a thought, there is a set springing up who appear to have jumped to the conclusion that we have every thing."

"Ay, this is *one* of the reasons that all the rest of the world laugh at us."

"Laugh at us, Mr. Effingham! Even *I* had supposed the American name had, at last, got to be in good credit in other parts of the world."

"Then even *you*, my dear Mrs. Bloomfield, are notably mistaken. Europe, it is true, is beginning to give us credit for not being quite as bad as she once thought us; but we are far, very far, from being yet admitted to the ordinary level of nations, as respects goodness."

"Surely they give us credit for energy, enterprize, activity—"

"Qualities that they prettily term, rapacity, cunning, and swindling! I am far, very far, however, from giving credit to all that it suits the interests and prejudices of Europe, especially of our venerable kinswoman, Old England, to circulate and think to the prejudice of this country, which, in my poor judgment, has as much substantial merit to boast of as any nation on earth; though, in getting rid of a set of ancient vices and follies, it has not had the sagacity to discover that it is fast falling into pretty tolerable—or if you like it better—intolerable substitutes."

"What then do *you* deem our greatest error—our weakest point?"

"Provincialisms, with their train of narrow prejudices, and a disposition to set up mediocrity as perfection, under the double influence of an ignorance that unavoidably arises from a want of models, and of the irresistible tendency to mediocrity, in a nation where the common mind so imperiously rules."

"But does not the common mind rule every where? Is not public opinion always stronger than law?"

"In a certain sense, both these positions may be true. But in a nation like this, without a capital, one *that is all provinces*, in which intelligence and tastes are scattered, this common mind wants the usual direction, and derives its impulses from the force of numbers, rather than from the force of knowledge. Hence the fact, that the public opinion never or seldom rises to absolute truth. I grant you that *as* a mediocrity, it is well; much better than common even; but it is still a mediocrity."

"I see the justice of your remark, and I suppose we are to ascribe the general use of superlatives, which is so very obvious, to these causes."

"Unquestionably; men have gotten to be afraid to speak the truth, when that truth is a little beyond the common comprehension; and thus it is that you see the fulsome flattery that all the public servants, as they call themselves, resort to, in order to increase their popularity, instead of telling the wholesome facts that are needed."

"And what is to be the result?"

"Heaven knows. While America is so much in advance of other nations, in a freedom from prejudices of the old school, it is fast substituting a set of prejudices of its own, that are not without serious dangers. We may live through it, and the ills of society may correct themselves, though there is one fact that menaces more evil than any thing I could have feared."

"You mean the political struggle between money and numbers, that has so seriously manifested itself of late!" exclaimed the quick-minded and intelligent Mrs. Bloomfield.

"*That* has its dangers; but there is still another evil of greater magnitude. I allude to the very general disposition to confine political discussions to political men. Thus, the private citizen, who should presume to discuss a political question, would be deemed fair game for all who thought differently from himself. He would be injured in his pocket, reputation, domestic happiness, if possible; for, in this respect, America is much the most intolerant nation I have ever visited. In all other countries, in which discussion is permitted at all, there is at least the *appearance* of fair play, whatever may be done covertly; but here, it seems to be sufficient to justify falsehood, frauds, nay, barefaced rascality, to establish that the injured party has had the audacity to meddle with public questions, not being what the public chooses to call a public man. It is scarcely necessary to say that, when such an opinion gets to be effective, it must entirely defeat the real intentions of a popular government."

"Now you mention it," said Mrs. Bloomfield, "I think I have witnessed instances of what you mean."

"Witnessed, dear Mrs. Bloomfield! Instances are to be seen as often as a man is found freeman enough to have an opinion independent of party. It is not for connecting himself with party that a man is denounced in this country, but for daring to connect himself with truth. Party will bear with party, but party will not bear with truth. It is in politics as in war, regiments or individuals may desert, and they will be received by their late enemies with open arms, the honour of a soldier seldom reaching to the pass of refusing succour of any sort; but both sides will turn and fire on the countrymen who wish merely to defend their homes and firesides."

"You draw disagreeable pictures of human nature, Mr. Effingham."

"Merely because they are true, Mrs. Bloomfield. Man is worse than the beasts, merely because he has a code of right and wrong, which he never respects. They talk of the variation of the compass, and even pretend to calculate its changes, though no one can explain the principle that causes the attraction or its vagaries at all. So it is with men; they pretend to look always at the right, though their eyes are constantly directed obliquely; and it is a certain calculation to allow of a pretty wide variation—but here comes Miss Effingham, singularly well attired, and more beautiful than I have ever before seen her!"

The two exchanged quick glances, and then, as if fearful of betraying to each other their thoughts, they moved towards our heroine, to do the honours of the reception.

CHAPTER XXVI.

"Happily, when I shall wed,
That lord whose hand must take my plight shall carry
Half my love with him, half my care and duty."

King Lear 1.1.100–102.

AS no man could be more gracefully or delicately polite than John Effingham, when the humour seized him, Mrs. Bloomfield was struck with the kind and gentlemanlike manner with which he met his young kinswoman on this trying occasion, and the affectionate tones of his voice, and the winning expression of his eye, as he addressed her. Eve herself was not unobservant of these peculiarities, nor was she slow in comprehending the reason. She perceived at once that he was acquainted with the state of things between her and Paul. As she well knew the womanly fidelity of Mrs. Bloomfield, she rightly enough conjectured that the long observation of her cousin, coupled with the few words accidentally overheard that evening, had even made him better acquainted with the true condition of her feelings, than was the case with the friend with whom she had so lately been conversing on the subject.

Still Eve was not embarrassed by the conviction that her secret was betrayed to so many persons. Her attachment to Paul was not the impulse of girlish caprice, but the warm affection of a woman. It had grown with time, was sanctioned by her reason, and if it was tinctured with the more glowing imagination and ample faith of youth, it was also sustained by high principles and her sense of right. She knew that both her father and cousin esteemed the man of her own choice, nor did she believe the little cloud that hung over his birth could do more than leave a temporary influence on his own sensitive feelings. She met John Effingham, therefore, with a frank composure, returned the kind pressure of his hand, with a smile such as a daughter might bestow on an affectionate parent, and turned to salute the remainder of the party, with that lady-like ease which had got to be a part of her nature.

"There goes one of the most attractive pictures that humanity can offer," said John Effingham to Mrs. Bloomfield, as Eve walked away; "a young, timid, modest, sensitive girl, so strong in her principles, so conscious of rectitude, so pure of thought, and so warm in her affections, that she views her selection of a husband, as others view their acts of duty and religious faith. With her love has no shame, as it has no weakness."

"Eve Effingham is as faultless as comports with womanhood; and yet I confess ignorance of my own sex, if she receive Mr. Powis as calmly as she received her cousin."

"Perhaps not, for in that case, she could scarcely feel the passion. You perceive that he avoids oppressing her with his notice, and that the meeting passes off without embarrassment. I do believe there is an elevating principle in love, that, by causing us to wish to be worthy of the object most prized, produces the desired effects by stimulating exertion. There, now, are two as perfect beings as one ordinarily meets with, each oppressed by a sense of his or her unworthiness to be the choice of the other."

"Does love, then, teach humility; successful love, too?"

"Does it not? It would be hardly fair to press this matter on you, a married woman; for, by the pandects of American society, a man may philosophize on love, prattle about it, trifle on the subject, and even analyze the passion with a miss in her teens, and yet he shall not allude to it, in a discourse with a matron. Well, *chacun à son goût*; we are, indeed, a little peculiar in our usages, and have promoted a good deal of village coquetry, and the flirtations of the may-pole, to the drawing-room."

"Is it not better that such follies should be confined to youth, than that they should invade the sanctity of married life, as I understand is too much the case elsewhere?"

"Perhaps so; though I confess it is easier to dispose of a straight-forward proposition from a mother, a father, or a commissioned friend, than to get rid of a young lady, who, *propriâ personâ*, angles on her own account. While abroad, I had a dozen proposals—"

"Proposals!" exclaimed Mrs. Bloomfield, holding up both hands, and shaking her head incredulously.

"Proposals! Downright, *bonâ fide*, blushes-causing proposals! Why not, ma'am?—am I more than fifty? am I not reasonably youthful for that period of life, and have I not six or eight thousand a year—"

"Eighteen, or you are much scandalized."

"Well, eighteen, if you will," coolly returned the other, in whose eyes money was no merit, for he was born to a fortune, and always treated it as a means, and not as the end of life; "every dollar is a magnet, after one has turned forty. Do you suppose that a single man, of tolerable person, well-born, and with a hundred thousand francs of *rentes*, could entirely escape proposals from the ladies in Europe?"

"This is so revolting to all our American notions, that, though I have often heard of such things, I have always found it difficult to believe them!"

"And is it more revolting for the friends of young ladies to look out for them, on such occasions, than that the young ladies should take the affair into their own hands, as is so often practised quite as openly, here?"

"It is well you are a confirmed bachelor, or declarations like these would mar your fortunes. I will admit that the school is not as retiring and diffident as formerly; for we are all ready enough to say that no times are equal to our own times; but I shall strenuously protest against your interpretation of the nature and artlessness of an American girl."

"Artlessness!" repeated John Effingham, with a slight lifting of the eye-brows; "we live in an age when new dictionaries and vocabularies are necessary to understand each other's meaning. It is artlessness, with a vengeance, to beset an old fellow of fifty, as one would besiege a town. Hist!—Ned is retiring with his daughter, my dear Mrs. Bloomfield, and it will not be long before I shall be summoned to a family council. Well, we will keep the secret until it is publicly proclaimed."

John Effingham was right, for his two cousins left the room together, and retired to the library, but in a way to attract no particular attention, except in those who were enlightened on the subject of what had already passed that evening. When they were alone, Mr. Effingham turned the key, and then he gave a free vent to his paternal feelings.

Between Eve and her parent, there had always existed a confidence exceeding that which it is common to find between father and daughter. In one sense, they had been all in all to each other, and Eve had never hesitated about pouring those feelings into his breast, which, had she possessed another parent, would more naturally have been confided to the affection of a mother. When their eyes first met, therefore, they were mutually beaming with an expression of confidence and love, such as might, in a measure, have been expected between two of the gentler sex. Mr Effingham folded his child to his heart, pressed her there tenderly for near a minute in silence, and then kissing her burning cheek he permitted her to look up.

"This answers all my fondest hopes, Eve"—he exclaimed; "fulfils my most cherished wishes for thy sake."

"Dearest sir!"

"Yes, my love, I have long secretly prayed that such might be your good fortune; for, of all the youths we have met, at home or abroad, Paul Powis is the one to whom I can consign you with the greatest confidence that he will cherish and love you as you deserve to be cherished and loved!"

"Dearest father, nothing but this was wanting to complete my perfect happiness."

Mr. Effingham kissed his daughter again, and he was then enabled to pursue the conversation with greater composure.

"Powis and I have had a full explanation," he said, "though in order to obtain it, I have been obliged to give him strong encouragement—"

"Father!"

"Nay, my love, your delicacy and feelings have been sufficiently respected, but he has so much diffidence of himself, and permits the unpleasant circumstances connected with his birth to weigh so much on his mind, that I have been compelled to tell him, what I am sure you will approve, that we disregard family connections, and look only to the merit of the individual."

"I hope, father, nothing was said to give Mr. Powis reason to suppose we did not deem him every way our equal."

"Certainly not. He is a gentleman, and I can claim to be no more. There is but one thing in which connections ought to influence an American marriage, where the parties are suited to each other in the main requisites, and that is to ascertain that neither should be carried, necessarily, into associations for which their habits have given them too much and too good tastes to enter into. A *woman*, especially, ought never to be transplanted from a polished to an unpolished circle; for, when this is the case, if really a lady, there will be a dangerous clog on her affection for her husband. This one great point assured, I see no other about which a parent need feel concern."

"Powis, unhappily, has no connections in this country; or none with whom he has any communications; and those he has in England are of a class to do him credit."

"We have been conversing of this, and he has manifested so much proper feeling that it has even raised him in my esteem. I knew his father's family, and must have known his father, I think, though there were two or three Asshetons of the name of John. It is a highly respectable family of the middle states, and belonged formerly to the colonial aristocracy. Jack Effingham's mother was an Assheton."

"Of the same blood, do you think, sir? I remembered this when Mr. Powis mentioned his father's name, and intended to question cousin Jack on the subject."

"Now you speak of it, Eve, there *must* be a relationship between them. Do you suppose that our kinsman is acquainted with the fact that Paul is, in truth, an Assheton?"

Eve told her father that she had never spoken with their relative on the subject, at all.

Then ring the bell and we will ascertain at once how far my conjecture is true. You can have no false delicacy, my child, about letting your engagement be known to one as near and as dear to us, as John."

"Engagement, father!"

"Yes, engagement," returned the smiling parent, "for such I already deem it. I have ventured, in your behalf, to plight your troth to Paul Powis, or what is almost equal to it; and in return I can give you back as many protestations of unequalled fidelity, and eternal constancy, as any reasonable girl can ask."

Eve gazed at her father in a way to show that reproach was mingled with fondness, for she felt that, in this instance, too much of the precipitation of the other sex had been manifested in her affairs; still, superior to coquetry and affectation, and much too warm in her attachments to be seriously hurt, she kissed the hand she held, shook her head reproachfully, even while she smiled, and did as had been desired.

"You have, indeed, rendered it important to us to know more of Mr. Powis, my beloved father," she said, as she returned to her seat, "though I could wish matters had not proceeded quite so fast."

"Nay, all I promised was conditional, and dependent on yourself. You have nothing to do, if I have said too much, but to refuse to ratify the treaty made by your negotiator."

"You propose an impossibility," said Eve, taking the hand, again, that she had so lately relinquished, and pressing it warmly between her own; "the negotiator is too much revered, has too strong a right to command, and is too much confided in to be thus dishonoured. Father, I *will*, I *do*, ratify all you *have*, all you *can* promise in my behalf."

"Even, if I annul the treaty, darling?"

"Even, in that case, father. I will marry none without your consent, and have so absolute a confidence in your tender care of me, that I do not even hesitate to say, I will marry him to whom you contract me."

"Bless you, bless you, Eve; I do believe you, for such have I ever found you, since thought has had any control over your actions. Desire Mr. John Effingham to come hither"—then, as the servant closed the door, he continued,—"and such I believe you will continue to be until your dying day."

"Nay, reckless, careless father, you forget that you yourself have been instrumental in transferring my duty and obedience to another. What if this sea-monster should prove a tyrant, throw off the mask, and show himself in his real colours? Are you prepared, then, thoughtless, precipitate, parent"—Eve kissed Mr, Effingham's cheek with childish playfulness, as she spoke, her heart swelling with happiness the whole time, "to preach obedience where obedience would then be due?"

"Hush, precious—I hear the step of Jack; he must not catch us fooling in this manner."

Eve rose; and when her kinsman entered the room, she held out her hand kindly to him, though it was with an averted face and a tearful eye.

"It is time I was summoned," said John Effingham, after he had drawn the blushing girl to him and kissed her forehead, "for what between *tête à têtes* with young fellows, and *tête à têtes* with old fellows, this evening, I began to think myself neglected. I hope I am still in time, however, to render a very decided disapprobation available?"

"Cousin Jack!" exclaimed Eve, with a look of reproachful mockery, "*you* are the last person who ought to speak of disapprobation, for you have done little else but sing the praises of the applicant, since you first met him."

"Is it even so? then, like others, I must submit to the consequences of my own precipitation and false conclusions. Am I summoned to inquire how many thousands a year I shall add to the establishment of the new couple? As I hate business, say five at once; and when the papers are ready, I will sign them, without reading,"

"Most generous cynic," cried Eve, "I would I dared, now, to ask a single question!"

"Ask it without scruple, young lady, for this is the day of your independence and power. I am mistaken in the man, if Powis do not prove to be the captain of his own ship, in the end."

"Well, then, in whose behalf is this liberality really meant; mine, or that of the gentleman?"

"Fairly enough put," said John Effingham, laughing, and again drawing Eve towards him and saluting her cheek; "for if I were on the rack, I could scarcely say which I love best, although you have the consolation of knowing, pert one, that you get the most kisses."

"I am almost in the same state of feeling myself, John, for a son of my own could scarcely be dearer to me than Paul."

"I see, indeed, that I *must* marry," said Eve hastily, dashing the tears of delight from her eyes, for what could give more delight than to hear the praises of her beloved, "if I wish to retain my place in your affections. But, father, we forget the question you were to put to cousin Jack."

"True, love. John, your mother was an Assheton?"

"Assuredly, Ned; you are not to learn my pedigree at this time of day, I trust."

"We are anxious to make out a relationship between you and Paul; can it not be done?"

"I would give half my fortune, Eve consenting, were it so!—What reason is there for supposing it probable, or even possible?"

"You know that he bears the name of his friend, and adopted parent, while that of his family is really Assheton."

"Assheton!" exclaimed the other, in a way to show that this was the first he had ever heard of the fact.

"Certainly; and as there is but one family of this name, which is a little peculiar in the spelling—for here it is spelt by Paul himself, on this card—we have thought that he must be a relation of yours. I hope we are not to be disappointed."

"Assheton!—It is, as you say, an unusual name; nor is there more than one family that bears it in this country, to my knowledge. Can it be possible that Powis is truly an Assheton?"

"Out of all doubt," Eve eagerly exclaimed; "we have it from his own mouth. His father was an Assheton, and his mother was—"

"Who!" demanded John Effingham, with a vehemence that startled his companions.

"Nay, that is more than I can tell you, for he did not mention the family name of his mother; as she was a sister of Lady Dunluce, however, who is the wife of General Ducie, the father of our guest, it is probable her name was Dunluce."

"I remember no relative that has made such a marriage, or who *can* have made such a marriage; and yet do I personally and intimately know every Assheton in the country."

Mr. Effingham and his daughter looked at each other, for it at once struck them all painfully, that there must be Asshetons of another family.

"Were it not for the peculiar manner in which this name is spelled," said Mr. Effingham, "I could suppose that there are Asshetons of whom we know nothing, but it is difficult to believe that there can be such persons of a respectable family of whom we have never heard, for Powis said his relatives were of the Middle States—"

"And that his mother was called Dunluce?" demanded John Effingham earnestly, for he too appeared to wish to discover an affinity between himself and Paul.

"Nay, father, this I think he did not say; though it is quite probable; for the title of his aunt is an ancient barony, and those ancient baronies usually became the family name."

"In this you must be mistaken, Eve, since he mentioned that the right was derived through his mother's mother, who was an Englishwoman."

"Why not send for him at once, and put the question?" said the simple-minded Mr. Effingham; "next to having him for my own son, it would give me pleasure, John, to learn that he was lawfully entitled to that which I know you have done in his behalf."

"That is impossible," returned John Effingham. "I am an only child, and as for cousins through my mother, there are so many who stand in an equal degree of affinity to me, that no one in particular can be my heir-at-law. If there were, I am an Effingham; my estate came from Effinghams, and to an Effingham it should descend in despite of all the Asshetons in America."

"Paul Powis included!" exclaimed Eve, raising a finger reproachfully.

"True, to him I have left a legacy; but it was to a Powis, and not to an Assheton."

"And yet he declares himself legally an Assheton, and not a Powis."

"Say no more of this, Eve; it is unpleasant to me. I hate the name of Assheton, though it was my mother's, and could wish never to hear it again."

Eve and her father were mute, for their kinsman, usually so proud and self-restrained, spoke with suppressed emotion, and it was plain that, for some hidden cause, he felt even more than he expressed. The idea that there should be any thing about Paul that could render him an object of dislike to one as dear to her as her cousin, was inexpressibly painful to the former, and she regretted that the subject had ever been introduced. Not so with her father. Simple, direct, and full of truth, Mr. Effingham rightly enough believed that mysteries in a family could lead to no good, and he repeated his proposal of sending for Paul, and having the matter cleared up at once.

"You are too reasonable, Jack," he concluded, "to let an antipathy against a name that was your mother's, interfere with your sense of right. I know that some unpleasant questions arose concerning your succession to my aunt's fortune, but that was all settled in your favour twenty years ago, and I had thought to your entire satisfaction."

"Unhappily, family quarrels are ever the most bitter, and usually they are the least reconcileable," returned John Effingham, evasively.— "I would that this young man's name were any thing but Assheton! I do not wish to see Eve plighting her faith at the altar, to any one bearing that accursed name!"

"I shall plight my faith, if ever it be done, dear cousin John, to the man, and not to his name."

"No, no—he must keep the appellation of Powis, by which we have all learned to love him, and to which he has done so much credit."

"This is very strange, Jack, for a man who is usually as discreet and as well regulated as yourself. I again propose that we send for Paul, and ascertain precisely to what branch of this so-much-disliked family he really belongs."

"No, father, if you love me, not now!" cried Eve, arresting Mr. Effingham's hand as it touched the bell-cord; "it would appear distrustful, and even cruel, were we to enter into such an inquiry so soon. Powis might think we valued his family, more than we value himself."

"Eve is right, Ned; but I will not sleep without learning all. There is an unfinished examination of the papers left by poor Monday, and

I will take an occasion to summon Paul to its completion, when an opportunity will offer to renew the subject of his own history; for it was at the other investigation that he first spoke frankly to me, concerning himself."

"Do so, cousin Jack, and let it be at once," said Eve earnestly. "I can trust you with Powis alone, for I know how much you respect and esteem him in your heart. See, it is already ten."

"But, he will naturally wish to spend the close of an evening like this engaged in investigating something very different from Mr. Monday's tale," returned her cousin; the smile with which he spoke chasing away the look of chilled aversion that had so lately darkened his noble features.

"No, not to-night," answered the blushing Eve. "I have confessed weakness enough for one day. Tomorrow, if you will—if he will,—but not to-night. I shall retire with Mrs. Hawker, who already complains of fatigue; and you will send for Powis to meet you in your own room, without unnecessary delay."

Eve kissed John Effingham coaxingly, and as they walked together out of the library, she pointed towards the door that led to the chambers. Her cousin laughingly complied, and when in his own room, he sent a message to Paul to join him.

"Now, indeed, may I call you a kinsman," said John Effingham, rising to receive the young man, towards whom he advanced, with extended hands, in his most winning manner. "Eve's frankness and your own discernment have made us a happy family!"

"If any thing could add to the felicity of being acceptable to Miss Effingham," returned Paul, struggling to command his feelings, "it is the manner in which her father and yourself have received my poor offers."

"Well, we will now speak of it no more. I saw from the first which way things were tending, and it was my plain-dealing that opened the eyes of Templemore to the impossibility of his ever succeeding, by which means his heart has been kept from breaking."

"Oh! Mr. Effingham, Templemore never loved Eve Effingham! I thought so once, and he thought so, too; but it could not have been a love like mine."

"It certainly differed in the essential circumstance of reciprocity, which, in itself, singularly qualifies the passion, so far as duration is concerned. Templemore did not exactly know the reason why he preferred Eve; but, having seen so much of the society in which he lived, I was enabled to detect the cause. Accustomed to an elaborate sophistication, the singular union of refinement and nature caught his fancy; for the English seldom see the last separated from vulgarity; and when it is found, softened by a high intelligence and polished manners, it has usually great attractions for the *blasés.*"

"He is fortunate in having so readily found a substitute for Eve Effingham!"

"This change is not unnatural, neither. In the first place, I, with this truth-telling tongue, destroyed all hope, before he had committed himself by a declaration; and then Grace Van Cortlandt possesses the great attraction of nature, in a degree quite equal to that of her cousin. Besides, Templemore, though a gentleman, and a brave man, and a worthy one, is not remarkable for qualities of a very extraordinary kind. He will be as happy as is usual for an Englishman of his class to be, and he has no particular right to expect more. I sent for you, however, less to talk of love, than to trace its unhappy consequences in this affair, revealed by the papers of poor Monday. It is time we acquitted ourselves of that trust. Do me the favour to open the dressing-case that stands on the toilet-table; you will find in it the key that belongs to the bureau, where I have placed the secretary that contains the papers."

Paul did as desired. The dressing-case was complicated and large, having several compartments, none of which were fastened. In the first opened, he saw a miniature of a female so beautiful, that his eye rested on it, as it might be, by fascination. Notwithstanding some difference produced by the fashions of different periods, the resemblance to the object of his love, was obvious at a glance. Borne away by the pleasure of the discovery, and actually believing that he saw a picture of Eve, drawn in a dress that did not in a great degree vary from the present attire, fashion having undergone no very striking revolution in the last twenty years, he exclaimed—

"This is indeed a treasure, Mr. Effingham, and most sincerely do I envy you its possession. It is like, and yet, in some particulars, it is unlike—it scarcely does Miss Effingham justice about the nose and forehead!"

John Effingham started when he saw the miniature in Paul's hand, but recovering himself, he smiled at the eager delusion of his young friend, and said with perfect composure—

"It is not Eve, but her mother. The two features you have named in the former came from my family; but in all the others, the likeness is almost identical."

"This then is Mrs. Effingham!" murmured Paul, gazing on the face of the mother of his love, with a respectful melancholy, and an interest that was rather heightened than lessened by a knowledge of the truth. "She died young, sir?"

"Quite; she can scarcely be said to have become an angel too soon, for she was always one."

This was said with a feeling that did not escape Paul, though it surprised him. There were six or seven miniature-cases in the open compartment of the dressing-box, and supposing that the one which lay uppermost belonged to the miniature in his hand, he raised it, and opened the lid with a view to replace the picture of Eve's mother, with a species of pious reverence. Instead of finding an empty case, however, another miniature met his eye. The exclamation that now escaped the young man was one of delight and surprise.

"That must be my grandmother, with whom you are in such raptures, at present," said John Effingham, laughing—"I was comparing it yesterday with the picture of Eve, which is in the Russia-leather case, that you will find somewhere there. I do not wonder, however, at your admiration, for she was a beauty in her day, and no woman is fool enough to be painted after she grows ugly."

"Not so—not so—Mr. Effingham! This is the miniature I lost in the Montauk, and which I had given up as booty to the Arabs. It has, doubtless, found its way into your state-room, and has been put among your effects by your man, through mistake. It is very precious to me, for it is nearly every memorial I possess of my own mother!"

"Your mother!" exclaimed John Effingham rising involuntarily. "I think there must be some mistake, for I examined all those pictures this very morning, and it is the first time they have been opened since our arrival from Europe. It cannot be the missing picture."

"Mine it is certainly; in that I cannot be mistaken!"

"It would be odd indeed, if one of my grandmothers, for both the pious ladies are there, should prove to be your mother.—Powis, will you have the goodness to let me see the picture you mean."

Paul brought the miniature and a light, placing both before the eyes of his friend.

"That!" exclaimed John Effingham, his voice sounding harsh and unnatural to the listener,—"that picture like *your* mother!"

"It is her miniature—*the* miniature that was transmitted to me, from those who had charge of my childhood. I cannot be mistaken as to the countenance, or the dress."

"And your father's name was Assheton?"

"Certainly—John Assheton, of the Asshetons of Pennsylvania."

John Effingham groaned aloud; when Paul stepped back equally shocked and surprised, he saw that the face of his friend was almost livid, and that the hand which held the picture shook like the aspen.

"Are you unwell, dear Mr. Effingham?"

"No—no—'tis impossible! This lady never had a child. Powis, you have been deceived by some fancied, or some real resemblance. This picture is mine, and has not been out of my possession these five and twenty years."

"Pardon me, sir, it is the picture of my mother, and no other; the very picture lost in the Montauk."

The gaze that John Effingham cast upon the young man was ghastly; and Paul was about to ring the bell, but a gesture of denial prevented him.

"See," said John Effingham, hoarsely, as he touched a spring in the setting, and exposed to view the initials of two names interwoven with hair—"is this, too, yours?"

Paul looked surprised and disappointed.

"That certainly settles the question; my miniature had no such addition; and yet I believe that sweet and pensive countenance to be the face of my own beloved mother, and of no one else."

John Effingham struggled to appear calm; and, replacing the pictures, he raised the key from the dressing case, and, opening the bureau, he took out the secretary. This he signed for Powis, who had the key, to open; throwing himself into a chair, though every thing was done mechanically, as if his mind and body had little or no connection with each other.

"Some accidental resemblance has deceived you as to the miniature," he said, while Paul was looking for the proper number among the letters of Mr. Monday. "No—no—that *cannot* be the picture of your mother. She left no child. Assheton did you say, was the name of your father?"

"Assheton—John Assheton—about that, at least, there can have been no mistake. This is the number at which we left off—will you, sir, or shall I, read?"

The other made a sign for Paul to read; looking, at the same time, as if it were impossible for him to discharge that duty himself.

"This is a letter from the woman who appears to have been entrusted with the child, to the man Dowse," said Paul, first glancing his eyes over the page,—"it appears to be little else but gossip—ha!—what is this, I see?"

John Effingham raised himself suddenly in his chair, and he sat gazing at Paul, as one gazes who expects some extraordinary developement, though of what nature he knew not.

"This is a singular passage," Paul continued—"so much so as to need elucidation. 'I have taken the child with me to get the picture from the jeweller, who has mended the ring, and the little urchin knew it at a glance.'"

"What is there remarkable in that? Others beside ourselves have had pictures; and this child knows its own better than you."

"Mr. Effingham, such a thing occurred to myself! It is one of those early events of which I still retain, have ever retained, a vivid recollection. Though little more than an infant at the time, well do I recollect to have been taken in this manner to a jeweller's, and the delight I felt at recovering my mother's picture, that which is now lost, after it had not been seen for a month or two."

"Paul Blunt—Powis—Assheton"—said John Effingham, speaking so hoarsely as to be nearly unintelligible, "remain here a few minutes—I will rejoin you."

John Effingham arose, and, notwithstanding he rallied all his powers, it was with extreme difficulty he succeeded in reaching the door, steadily rejecting the offered assistance of Paul, who was at a loss what to think of so much agitation in a man usually so self-possessed and tranquil. When out of the room, John Effingham did better, and he proceeded to the library, followed by his own man, whom he had ordered to accompany him with a light.

"Desire Captain Ducie to give me the favour of his company for a moment," he then said, motioning to the servant to withdraw. "You will not be needed any longer."

It was but a minute before Captain Ducie stood before him. This gentleman was instantly struck with the pallid look, and general agitation of the person he had come to meet, and he expressed an apprehension that he was suddenly taken ill. But a motion of the hand forbade his touching the bell-cord, and he waited in silent wonder at the scene which he had been so unexpectedly called to witness.

"A glass of that water, if you please, Captain Ducie," said John Effingham, endeavouring to smile with gentlemanlike courtesy, as he made the request, though the effort caused his countenance to appear ghastly again. A little recovered by this beverage, he said more steadily—

"You are the cousin of Powis, Captain Ducie."

"We are sisters' children, sir."

"And your mother is—"

"Lady Dunluce—a peeress in her own right."

"But, what—her family name?"

"Her own family name has been sunk in that of my father, the Ducies claiming to be as old and as honourable a family, as that from which my mother inherits her rank. Indeed the Dunluce barony has gone through so many names, by means of females, that I believe there is no intention to revive the original appellation of the family which was first summoned."

"You mistake, me—your mother—when she married—was—"

"Miss Warrender."

"I thank you, sir, and will trouble you no longer," returned John Effingham, rising and struggling to make his manner second the courtesy of his words—"I have troubled you, abruptly—incoherently I fear—your arm—"

Captain Ducie stepped hastily forward, and was just in time to prevent the other from falling senseless on the floor, by receiving him in his own arms.

CHAPTER XXVII.

"What's Hecuba to him, or he to Hecuba,
That he should weep for her?"

Hamlet 2.2.559–560.

THE next morning, Paul and Eve were alone in that library which had long been the scene of the confidential communications of the Effingham family. Eve had been weeping, nor were Paul's eyes entirely free from the signs of his having given way to strong sensations. Still happiness beamed in the countenance of each, and the timid but affectionate glances with which our heroine returned the fond, admiring look of her lover, were any thing but distrustful of their future felicity. Her hand was in his, and it was often raised to his lips, as they pursued the conversation.

"This is so wonderful," exclaimed Eve, after one of the frequent musing pauses in which both indulged, "that I can scarcely believe myself awake. That you, Blunt, Powis, Assheton, should, after all, prove an Effingham!

"And that I, who have so long thought myself an orphan, should find a living father, and he a man like Mr. John Effingham!"

"I have long thought that something heavy lay at the honest heart of cousin Jack—you will excuse me, Powis, but I shall need time to learn to call him by a name of greater respect."

"Call him always so, love, for I am certain it would pain him to meet with any change in you. He *is* your cousin Jack"

"Nay, he may some day unexpectedly become *my* father too, as he has so wonderfully become yours," rejoined Eve, glancing archly at the glowing face of the delighted young man; "and then cousin Jack might prove too familiar and disrespectful a term."

"So much stronger does your claim to him appear than mine, that I think, when that blessed day shall arrive, Eve, it will convert him into *my* cousin Jack, instead of your father. But call *him* as you may, why do you still insist on calling *me* Powis?"

"That name will ever be precious in my eyes! You abridge me of my rights, in denying me a change of name. Half the young ladies of the country marry for the novelty of being called Mrs. Somebody else, instead of the Misses they were, while I am condemned to remain Eve Effingham for life."

"If you object to the appellation, I can continue to call myself Powis. This has been done so long now as almost to legalize the act."

"Indeed, no—you are an Effingham, and as an Effingham ought you to be known. What a happy lot is mine! Spared even the pain of parting with my old friends, at the great occurrence of my life, and finding my married home the same as the home of my childhood!"

"I owe every thing to you, Eve, name, happiness, and even a home."

"I know not that. Now that it is known that you are the great-grandson of Edward Effingham, I think your chance of possessing the Wigwam would be quite equal to my own, even were we to look different ways in quest of married happiness. An arrangement of that nature would not be difficult to make, as John Effingham might easily compensate a daughter for the loss of her house and lands by means of those money-yielding stocks and bonds, of which he possesses so many."

"I view it differently. *You* were Mr.—my father's heir—how strangely the word father sounds in unaccustomed ears!—But you were my father's chosen heir, and I shall owe to you, dearest, in addition to the treasures of your heart and faith, my fortune."

"Are you so very certain of this, ingrate?—Did not Mr. John Effingham—cousin Jack—adopt you as his son even before he knew of the natural tie that actually exists between you?"

"True, for I perceive that you have been made acquainted with most of that which has passed. But I hope, that in telling you his own offer, Mr.—that my father did not forget to tell you of the terms on which it was accepted?"

"He did you ample justice, for he informed me that you stipulated there should be no altering of wills, but that the unworthy heir already chosen, should still remain the heir."

"And to this Mr—"

"Cousin Jack," said Eve, laughing, for the laugh comes easy to the supremely happy.

"To this cousin Jack assented?"

"Most true, again. The will would not have been altered, for your interests were already cared for."

"At the expense of yours, dearest Eve!"

"It would have been at the expense of my better feelings, Paul, had it not been so. However, that will can never do either harm or good to any, now."

"I trust it will remain unchanged, beloved, that I may owe as much to you as possible."

Eve looked kindly at her betrothed, blushed even deeper than the bloom which happiness had left on her cheek, and smiled like one who knew more than she cared to express.

"What secret meaning is concealed behind that look of portentous signification?"

"It means, Powis, that I have done a deed that is almost criminal. I have destroyed a will."

"Not my father's!"

"Even so—but it was done in his presence, and if not absolutely with his consent, with his knowledge. When he informed me of your superior rights, I insisted on its being done, at once, so, should any accident occur, you will be heir at law, as a matter of course. Cousin Jack affected reluctance, but I believe he slept more sweetly, for the consciousness that this act of justice had been done."

"I fear he slept little, as it was; it was long past midnight before I left him, and the agitation of his spirits was such as to appear awful in the eyes of a son!"

"And the promised explanation is to come, to renew his distress! Why make it at all? is it not enough that we are certain that you are his child? and for that, have we not the solemn assurance, the declaration of almost a dying man!"

"There should be no shade left over my mother's fame. Faults there have been, somewhere, but it is painful, oh! how painful! for a child to think evil of a mother."

"On this head you are already assured. Your own previous knowledge, and John Effingham's distinct declarations, make your mother blameless."

"Beyond question; but this sacrifice must be made to my mother's spirit. It is now nine; the breakfast-bell will soon ring, and then we are promised the whole of the melancholy tale. Pray with me, Eve, that it may be such as will not wound the ear of a son!"

Eve took the hand of Paul within both of hers, and kissed it with a sort of holy hope, that in its exhibition caused neither blush nor shame. Indeed so bound together were these young hearts, so ample and confiding had been the confessions of both, and so pure was their love, that neither regarded such a manifestation of feeling, differently from what an acknowledgement of a dependence on any other sacred principle would have been esteemed. The bell now summoned them to the breakfast-table, and Eve, yielding to her sex's timidity, desired Paul to precede her a few minutes, that the sanctity of their confidence might not be weakened by the observation of profane eyes.

The meal was silent; the discovery of the previous night, which had been made known to all in the house, by the declarations of John Effingham as soon as he was restored to his senses, Captain Ducie having innocently collected those within hearing to his succour, causing a sort of moral suspense that weighed on the vivacity if not on the comforts of the whole party, the lovers alone excepted.

As profound happiness is seldom talkative, the meal was a silent one; and when it was ended, they who had no tie of blood with the parties most concerned with the revelations of the approaching interview, delicately separated, making employments and engagements that left the family at perfect liberty; while those who had been previously notified that their presence would be acceptable, silently repaired to the dressing-room of John Effingham. The latter party was composed of Mr. Effingham, Paul, and Eve, only. The first passed into his cousin's bed-room, where he had a private conference that lasted half an hour. At the end of that time, the two others were summoned to join him.

John Effingham was a strong-minded and a proud man, his governing fault being the self-reliance that indisposed him to throw himself on a greater power, for the support, guidance, and counsel, that all need. To humiliation before God, however, he was not unused, and of late years it had got to be frequent with him, and it was only in connexion with his fellow-creatures that his repugnance to admitting even of an equality existed. He felt how much more just, intuitive, conscientious even, were his own views than those of mankind, in general; and he seldom deigned to consult with any as to the opinions he ought to entertain, or as to the conduct he ought to pursue. It is scarcely necessary to say, that such a being was one of strong and engrossing passions, the impulses frequently proving too imperious for the affections, or even for principles. The scene that he was now compelled to go through, was consequently one of sore mortification and self-abasement; and yet, feeling its justice no less than its necessity, and having made up his mind to discharge what had now become a duty, his very pride of character led him to do it manfully, and with no uncalled-for reserves. It was a painful and humiliating task, notwithstanding; and it required all the self-command, all the sense of right, and all the clear perception of consequences, that one so quick to discriminate could not avoid perceiving, to enable him to go through it with the required steadiness and connexion.

John Effingham received Paul and Eve, seated in an easy chair; for, while he could not be said to be ill, it was evident that his very frame had been shaken by the events and emotions of the few preceding hours. He gave a hand to each, and, drawing Eve affectionately to him, he imprinted a kiss on a cheek that was burning, though it paled and reddened in quick succession, the heralds of the tumultuous thoughts within. The look he gave Paul was kind and welcome, while a hectic spot glowed on each cheek, betraying that his presence excited pain as well as pleasure. A long pause succeeded this meeting, when John Effingham broke the silence.

"There can now be no manner of question, my dear Paul," he said, smiling affectionately but sadly, as he looked at the young man, "about your being my son. The letter written by John Assheton to your mother, after the separation of your parents, would settle that important point, had not the names, and the other facts that have come to our knowledge, already convinced me of the precious truth; for precious and very dear to me is the knowledge that I am the father of so worthy a child. You must prepare yourself to hear things that it will not be pleasant for a son to listen—"

"No, no—cousin Jack—*dear* cousin Jack!" cried Eve, throwing herself precipitately into her kinsman's arms, "we will hear nothing of the sort. It is sufficient that you are Paul's father, and we wish to know no more—will hear no more."

"This is like yourself, Eve, but it will not answer what I conceive to be the dictates of duty. Paul had two parents; and not the slightest suspicion ought to rest on one of them, in order to spare the feelings of the other. In showing me this kindness you are treating Paul inconsiderately."

"I beg, dear sir, you will not think too much of me, but entirely consult your own judgment—your own sense of—in short, dear father, that you will consider yourself before your son."

"I thank you, my children—what a word, and what a novel sensation is this, for me, Ned!—I feel all your kindness, but if you would consult my peace of mind, and wish me to regain my self-respect, you will allow me to disburthen my soul of the weight that oppresses it. This is strong language; but, while I have no confessions of deliberate criminality, or of positive vice to make, I feel it to be hardly too strong for the facts. My tale will be very short, and I crave your patience, Ned, while I expose my former weakness to these young people." Here John Effingham paused, as if to recollect himself; then he proceeded with a seriousness of manner that caused every syllable he uttered to tell on the ears of his listeners. "It is well known to your father, Eve, though it will probably be new to you," he said, "that I felt a passion for your sainted mother, such as few men ever experience for any of your sex. Your father and myself were suitors for her favour at the same time, though I can scarcely say, Edward, that any feeling of rivalry entered into the competition."

"You do me no more than justice, John, for if the affection of my beloved Eve could cause me grief, it was because it brought you pain."

"I had the additional mortification of approving of the choice she made; for, certainly, as respected her own happiness, your mother did more wisely in confiding it to the regulated, mild, and manly virtues of your father, than in placing her hopes on one as eccentric and violent as myself."

"This is injustice, John. You may have been positive, and a little stern, at times, but never violent, and least of all with a woman."

"Call it what you will, it unfitted me to make one so meek, gentle, and yet high-souled, as entirely happy as she deserved to be, and as you did make her, while she remained on earth. I had the courage to stay and learn that your father was accepted, (though the marriage was deferred two years in consideration for my feelings,) and then with a heart, in which mortified pride, wounded love, a resentment that was aimed rather against myself than against your parents, I quitted home, with a desperate determination never to rejoin my family again. This resolution I did not own to myself, even, but it lurked in my intentions unowned, festering like a mortal disease; and it caused me, when I burst away from the scene of happiness of which I had been a compelled witness, to change my name, and to make several inconsistent and extravagant arrangements to abandon my native country even."

"Poor John!" exclaimed his cousin, involuntarily, "this would have been a sad blot on our felicity, had we known it!"

"I was certain of that, even when most writhing under the blow you had so unintentionally inflicted, Ned; but the passions are tyrannical and inconsistent masters. I took my mother's name, changed my servant, and avoided those parts of the country where I was known. At this time, I feared for my reason, and the thought crossed my mind, that by making a sudden marriage I might supplant the old passion, which was so near destroying me, by some of that gentler affection which seemed to render you so blest, Edward."

"Nay, John, this was, itself, a temporary tottering of the reasoning faculties,"

"It was simply the effect of passions, over which reason had never been taught to exercise a sufficient influence. Chance brought me acquainted with Miss Warrender, in one of the southern states, and she promised, as I fancied, to realize all my wild schemes of happiness and resentment."

"Resentment, John?"

"I fear I must confess it, Edward, though it were anger against myself. I first made Miss Warrender's acquaintance as John Assheton, and some months had passed before I determined to try the fearful experiment I have mentioned. She was young, beautiful, well-born, virtuous and good; if she had a fault, it was her high spirit—not high temper, but she was high-souled and proud."

"Thank God, for this!" burst from the inmost soul of Paul, with unrestrainable feeling.

"You have little to apprehend, my son, on the subject of your mother's character; if not perfect, she was wanting in no womanly virtue, and might, nay ought to have made any reasonable man happy. My offer was accepted, for I found her heart disengaged. Miss Warrender was not affluent, and, in addition to the other unjustifiable motives that influenced me, I thought there would be a satisfaction in believing that I had been chosen for myself, rather than for my wealth. Indeed, I had got to be distrustful and ungenerous, and then I disliked the confession of the weakness that had induced me to change my name. The simple, I might almost say, loose laws of this country, on the subject of marriage, removed all necessity for explanations, there being no bans nor license necessary, and the christian name only being used in the ceremony. We were married, therefore, but I was not so unmindful of the rights of others, as to neglect to procure a certificate, under a promise of secrecy, in my own name. By going to the place where the ceremony was performed, you will also find the marriage of John Effingham and Mildred Warrender duly registered in the books of the church to which the officiating clergyman belonged. So far, I did what justice required, though, with a motiveless infatuation for which I can now hardly account, which *cannot* be accounted for, except by ascribing it to the inconsistent cruelty of passion, I concealed my real name from her with whom there should have been no concealment. I fancied, I tried to fancy I was no impostor, as I was of the family I represented myself to be, by the mother's side; and I wished to believe that my peace would easily be made when I avowed myself to be the man I really was. I had found Miss Warrender and her sister living with a well-intentioned but weak aunt, and with no male relative to make those inquiries which would so naturally have suggested themselves to persons of ordinary worldly prudence. It is true, I had become known to them under favourable circumstances, and they had good reason to believe me an Assheton from some accidental evidence that I possessed, which unanswerably proved my affinity to that family, without betraying my true name. But there is so little distrust in this country, that, by keeping at a distance from the places in which I was personally known, a life might have passed without exposure."

"This was all wrong, dear cousin Jack," said Eve, taking his hand and affectionately kissing it, while her face kindled with a sense of her sex's rights, "and I should be unfaithful to my womanhood were I to say otherwise. You had entered into the most solemn of all human contracts, and evil is the omen when such an engagement is veiled by any untruth. But, still, one would think you might have been happy with a virtuous and affectionate wife!"

"Alas! it is but a hopeless experiment to marry one, while the heart is still yearning towards another. Confidence came too late; for, discovering my unhappiness, Mildred extorted a tardy confession from me; a confession of all but the concealment of the true name; and justly wounded at the deception of which she had been the dupe, and yielding to the impulses of a high and generous spirit, she announced to me that she was unwilling to continue the wife of any man on such terms. We parted, and I hastened into the south-western states, where I passed the next twelvemonth in travelling, hurrying from place to place, in the vain hope of obtaining peace of mind. I plunged into the prairies, and most of the time mentioned was lost to me as respects the world, in the company of hunters and trappers."

"This, then, explains your knowledge of that section of the country," exclaimed Mr. Effingham, "for which I have never been able to account! We thought you among your old friends in Carolina, all that time."

"No one knew where I had secreted myself, for I passed under another feigned name, and had no servant, even. I had, however, sent an address to Mildred, where a letter would find me; for, I had begun to feel a sincere affection for her, though it might not have amounted to passion, and looked forward to being reunited, when her wounded feelings had time to regain their tranquillity. The obligations of wedlock are too serious to be lightly thrown aside, and I felt persuaded that neither of us would be satisfied in the end, without discharging the duties of the state into which we had entered."

"And why did you not hasten to your poor wife, cousin Jack," Eve innocently demanded, "as soon as you returned to the settlements?"

"Alas! my dear girl, I found letters at St. Louis announcing her death. Nothing was said of any child, nor did I in the least suspect that I was about to become a father. When Mildred died, I thought all the ties, all the obligations, all the traces of my ill-judged marriage were extinct; and the course taken by her relations, of whom, in this country, there remained very few, left me no inclination to proclaim it. By observing silence, I continued to pass as a bachelor, of course; though had there been any apparent reason for avowing what had occurred, I think no one who knows me, can suppose I would have shrunk from doing so."

"May I inquire, my dear sir," Paul asked, with a timidity of manner that betrayed how tenderly he felt it necessary to touch on the subject at all—"may I inquire, my dear sir, what course was taken by my mother's relatives?"

"I never knew Mr. Warrender, my wife's brother, but he had the reputation of being a haughty and an exacting man. His letters were not friendly; scarcely tolerable; for he affected to believe I had given a false address at the west, when I was residing in the middle states, and he threw out hints that to me were then inexplicable, but which the letters left with me, by Paul, have sufficiently explained. I thought him cruel and unfeeling at the time, but he had an excuse for his conduct."

"Which was, sir—?" Paul eagerly inquired.

"I perceive by the letters you have given me, my son, that your mother's family had imbibed the opinion, that I was John Assheton, of Lancaster, a man of singular humours, who had made an unfortunate marriage in Spain, and whose wife, I believe, is still living in Paris, though lost to herself and her friends. My kinsman lived retired, and never recovered the blow. As he was one of the few persons of the name, who could have married your mother, her relatives appear to have taken up the idea that he had been guilty of bigamy, and of course that Paul was illegitimate. Mr. Warrender, by his letters, appears even to have had an interview with this person, and, on mentioning his wife, was rudely repulsed from the house. It was a proud family, and Mildred being dead, the concealment of the birth of her child was resorted to, as a means of averting a fancied disgrace. As for myself, I call the all-seeing eye of God to witness, that the thought of my being a parent never crossed my mind, until I learned that a John Assheton was the father of Paul, and that the miniature of Mildred Warrender, that I received at the period of our engagement, was the likeness of his mother. The simple declaration of Captain Ducie concerning the family name of his mother, removed all doubt."

"But, cousin Jack, did not the mention of Lady Dunluce, of the Ducies, and of Paul's connections, excite curiosity?"

"Concerning what, dear? I could have no curiosity about a child of whose existence I was ignorant. I did know that the Warrenders had pretensions to both rank and fortune in England, but never heard the title, and cared nothing about money that would not, probably, be Mildred's. Of General Ducie I never even heard, as he married after my separation, and subsequently to the receipt of my brother-in-law's letters, I wished to forget the existence of the family. I went to Europe, and remained abroad seven years, and as this was at a time when the continent was closed against the English, I was not in a way to hear any thing on the subject. On my return, my wife's aunt was dead; the last of my wife's brothers was dead; her sister must then have long been Mrs. Ducie; no one mentioned the Warrenders, all traces of whom were nearly lost in this country, and to me the subject was too painful to be either sought or dwelt on. It is a curious fact, that, in 1829, during our late visit to the old world, I ascended the Nile with General Ducie for a travelling companion. We met at Alexandria, and went to the cataracts and returned in company. He knew me as John Effingham, an American traveller of fortune, if of no particular merit, and I knew him as an agreeable English general officer. He had the reserve of an Englishman of rank, and seldom spoke of his family, and it was only on our return, that I found he had letters from his wife, Lady Dunluce; but little did I dream that Lady Dunluce was Mabel Warrender. How often are we on the very verge of important information, and yet live on in ignorance and obscurity! The Ducies appear finally to have arrived at the opinion that the marriage was legal, and that no reproach rests on the birth of Paul, by the inquiries made concerning the eccentric John Assheton."

"They fancied, in common with my uncle Warrender, for a long time, that the John Assheton whom you have mentioned, sir," said Paul, "was my father. But some accidental information, at a late day, convinced them of their error, and then they naturally enough supposed that it was the only other John Assheton that could be heard of, who passes, and probably with sufficient reason, for a bachelor. This latter gentleman I have myself always supposed to be my father, though he has treated two or three letters I have written to him, with the indifference with which one would be apt to treat the pretensions of an impostor. Pride has prevented me from attempting to renew the correspondence lately."

"It is John Assheton of Nescopeck, my mother's brother's son, as inveterate a bachelor as is to be found in the Union!" said John Effingham, smiling, in spite of the grave subject and deep emotions that had so lately been uppermost in his thoughts. "He must have supposed your letters were an attempt at mystification on the part of some of his jocular associates, and I am surprised that he thought it necessary to answer them at all."

"He did answer but one, and that reply certainly had something of the character you suggest, sir. I freely forgive him, now I understand the truth, though his apparent contempt gave me many a bitter pang at the time. I saw Mr. Assheton once in public, and observed him well, for, strange as it is, I have been thought to resemble him."

"Why strange? Jack Assheton and myself have, or rather had a strong family likeness to each other, and, though the thought is new to me, I can now easily trace this resemblance to myself. It is rather an Assheton than an Effingham look, though the latter is not wanting."

"These explanations are very clear and satisfactory," observed Mr. Effingham, "and leave little doubt that Paul is the child of John Effingham and Mildred Warrender; but they would be beyond all cavil, were the infancy of the boy placed in an equally plain point of view, and could the reasons be known why the Warrenders abandoned him to the care of those who yielded him up to Mr. Powis."

"I see but little obscurity in that," returned John Effingham. "Paul is unquestionably the child referred to in the papers left by poor Monday, to the care of whose mother he was intrusted, until, in his fourth year, she yielded him to Mr. Powis, to get rid of trouble and expense, while she kept the annuity granted by Lady Dunluce.

The names appear in the concluding letters; and had we read the latter through at first, we should earlier have arrived at the same conclusion. Could we find the man called Dowse, who appears to have instigated the fraud, and who married Mrs. Monday, the whole thing would be explained."

"Of this I am aware," said Paul, for he and John Effingham had perused the remainder of the Monday papers together, after the fainting fit of the latter, as soon as his strength would admit; "and Captain Truck is now searching for an old passenger of his, who I think will furnish the clue. Should we get this evidence, it would settle all legal questions."

"Such questions will never be raised," said John Effingham, holding out his hand affectionately to his son; "you possess the marriage certificate given to your mother, and I avow myself to have been the person therein styled John Assheton. This fact I have endorsed on the back of the certificate; while here is another given to me in my proper name, with the endorsement made by the clergyman that I passed by another name, at the ceremony."

"Such a man, cousin Jack, was unworthy of his cloth!" said Eve with energy.

"I do not think so, my child. He was innocent of the original deception. The certificate and entry in the church books were both made some time after the marriage, and might do good, whereas they could not do harm. The clergyman in question is now a bishop, and is still living. He may give evidence if necessary, to the legality of the marriage."

"And the clergyman by whom I was baptized is also alive," cried Paul, "and has never lost sight of me He was, in part, in the confidence of my mother's family, and even after I was adopted by Mr. Powis, he kept me in view as one of his little Christians as he termed me. It was no less a person than Dr.—."

"This alone would make out the connection and identity," said Mr. Effingham, "without the aid of the Monday witnesses. The whole obscurity has arisen from John's change of name, and his ignorance of the fact that his wife had a child. The Ducies appear to have had plausible reasons, too, for distrusting the legality of the marriage; but all is now clear, and as a large estate is concerned, we will take care that no further obscurity shall rest over the affair."

"The part connected with the estate is already secured," said John Effingham, looking at Eve with a smile. "An American can always make a will, and one that contains but a single bequest is soon written. Mine is executed, and Paul Effingham, my son by my marriage with Mildred Warrender, and lately known in the United States' Navy as Paul Powis, is duly declared my heir. This will suffice for all legal purposes, though we shall have large draughts of gossip to swallow."

"Cousin Jack!"

"Daughter Eve!"

"Who has given cause for it?"

"He who commenced one of the most sacred of his earthly duties, with an unjustifiable deception. The wisest way to meet it, will be to make our avowals of the relationship as open as possible."

"I see no necessity, John, of entering into details," said Mr. Effingham; "you were married young, and lost your wife within a year of your marriage. She was a Miss Warrender, and the sister of Lady Dunluce; Paul and Ducie are declared cousins, and the former proves to be your son, of whose existence you were ignorant. No one will presume to question any of us, and it really strikes me that all rational people ought to be satisfied with this simple account of the matter."

"Father!" exclaimed Eve, with her pretty little hands raised in the attitude of surprise, "in what capital even, in what part of the world, would such a naked account appease curiosity? Much less will it suffice here, where every human being, gentle or simple, learned or ignorant, refined or vulgar, fancies himself a constitutional judge of all the acts of all his fellow-creatures?"

"We have at least the consolation of knowing that no revelations will make the matter any worse, or any better," said Paul, "as the gossips would tell their own tale, in every case, though its falsehood were as apparent as the noon-day sun. A gossip is essentially a liar, and truth is the last ingredient that is deemed necessary to his or her qualifications; indeed, a well authenticated fact is a death-blow to a gossip. I hope, my dear sir, you will say no more than that I am your son, a circumstance much too precious to me to be omitted."

John Effingham looked affectionately at the noble young man, whom he had so long esteemed and admired; and the tears forced themselves to his eyes, as he felt the supreme happiness that can gladden a parent's heart, only.

CHAPTER XXVIII.

"For my part, I care not; I say little; but when time shall serve, there shall be smiles—"

Henry V 2.1.5–6.

ALTHOUGH Paul Effingham was right, and Eve Effingham was also right, in their opinions of the art of gossiping, they both forgot one qualifying circumstance, that, arising from different causes, produces the same effect, equally in a capital and in a province. In the first, marvels form a nine days' wonder from the hurry of events; in the latter, from the hurry of talking. When it was announced in Templeton that Mr. John Effingham had discovered a son in Mr. Powis, as that son had conjectured, every thing but the truth was rumoured and believed, in connection with the circumstance. Of course it excited a good deal of a natural and justifiable curiosity and surprise in the trained and intelligent, for John Effingham had passed for a confirmed bachelor; but they were generally content to suffer a family to have feelings and incidents that were not to be paraded before a neighbourhood. Having some notions themselves of the delicacy and sanctity of the domestic affections, they were willing to respect the same sentiments in others. But these few excepted, the village was in a tumult of surmises, reports, contradictions, confirmations, rebutters, and sur-rebutters, for a fortnight. Several village *élégants*, whose notions of life were obtained in the valley in which they were born, and who had turned up their noses at the quiet, reserved, gentlemanlike Paul, because he did not happen to suit their tastes, were disposed to resent his claim to be his father's son, as if it were an injustice done to their rights; such commentators on men and things uniformly bringing every thing down to the standard of self. Then the approaching marriages at the Wigwam had to run the gauntlet, not only of village and county criticisms, but that of the mighty Emporium itself, as it is the fashion to call the confused and tasteless collection of flaring red brick houses, marten-box churches, and colossal taverns, that stands on the island of Manhattan; the discussion of marriages being a topic of never-ending interest in that well regulated social organization, after the subjects of dollars, lots, and wines, have been duly exhausted. Sir George Templemore was transformed into the Honourable Lord George Templemore, and Paul's relationship to Lady Dunluce was converted, as usual, into his being the heir apparent of a Duchy of that name; Eve's preference for a nobleman, as a matter of course, to the *aristocratical* tastes imbibed during a residence in foreign countries; Eve, the intellectual, feminine, instructed Eve, whose European associations, while they had taught her to prize the refinement, grace, *retenue*, and tone of an advanced condition of society, had also taught her to despise its mere covering and glitter! But, as there is no protection against falsehood, so is there no reasoning with ignorance.

A sacred few, at the head of whom were Mr. Steadfast Dodge and Mrs. Widow-Bewitched Abbott, treated the matter as one of greater gravity, and as possessing an engrossing interest for the entire community.

"For my part, Mr. Dodge," said Mrs. Abbott, in one of their frequent conferences, about a fortnight after the *éclaircissement* of the last chapter, "I do not believe that Paul Powis is Paul Effingham at all. You say that you knew him by the name of Blunt when he was a younger man?"

"Certainly, ma'am. He passed universally by that name formerly, and it may be considered as at least extraordinary that he should have had so many aliases. The truth of the matter is, Mrs. Abbott, if truth could be come at, which I always contend is very difficult in the present state of the world—"

"You never said a juster thing, Mr. Dodge!" interrupted the lady, feelings impetuous as hers seldom waiting for the completion of a sentence, "I never can get hold of the truth of any thing now; you may remember you insinuated that Mr. John Effingham himself was to be married to Eve, and, lo and behold! it turns out to be to his son!"

"The lady may have changed her mind, Mrs. Abbott: she gets the same estate with a younger man."

"She's monstrous! And I'm sure it will be a relief to the whole village when she is married, let it be to the father, or to the son. Now, do you know, Mr. Dodge, I have been in a desperate taking about one thing, and that is to find that, bony fie-dy, the two old Effinghams are not actually brothers! I knew that they *called* each other cousin

Jack and cousin Ned, and that Eve affected to call her uncle *cousin* Jack, but then she has so many affectations, and the old people are so foreign, that I looked upon all that as mere pretence; I said to myself a neighbourhood *ought* to know better about a man's family than he *can* know himself, and the neighbourhood all declared they were brothers; and yet it turns out, after all, that they are only cousins!"

"Yes, I do believe that, for once, the family was right in that matter, and the public mistaken."

"Well, I should like to know who has a better right to be mistaken than the public, Mr. Dodge. This is a free country, and if the people can't sometimes be wrong, what is the mighty use of their freedom? We are all sinful wretches, at the best, and it is vain to look for any thing but vice from sinners."

"Nay, my dear Mrs. Abbott, you are too hard on yourself, for every body allows that *you* are as exemplary as you are devoted to your religious duties."

"Oh! I was not speaking particularly of myself, sir; I am no egotist in such things, and wish to leave my own imperfections to the charity of my friends and neighbours. But, do you think, Mr. Dodge, that a marriage between Paul Effingham, for so I suppose he must be called, and Eve Effingham, will be legal? Can't it be set aside, and if that should be the case, wouldn't the fortune go to the public?"

"It *ought* to be so, my dear ma'am, and I trust the day is not distant when it will be so. The people are beginning to understand their rights, and another century will not pass, before they will enforce them by the necessary penal statutes. We have got matters so now, that a man can no longer indulge in the aristocratic and selfish desire to make a will, and, take my word for it, we shall not stop until we bring every thing to the proper standard."

The reader is not to suppose from his language that Mr. Dodge was an agrarian, or that he looked forward to a division of property, at some future day; for, possessing in his own person already, more than what could possibly fall to an individual share, he had not the smallest desire to lessen its amount by a general division. In point of fact he did not know his own meaning, except as he felt envy of all above him, in which, in truth, was to be found the whole secret of his principles, his impulses, and his doctrines. Any thing that would pull down those whom education, habits, fortune, or tastes, had placed in positions more conspicuous than his own, was, in his eyes, reasonable and just—as any thing that would serve him, in person, the same ill turn, would have been tyranny and oppression. The institutions of America, like every thing human, have their bad as well as their good side; and while we firmly believe in the relative superiority of the latter, as compared with other systems, we should fail of accomplishing the end set before us in this work, did we not exhibit, in strong colours, one of the most prominent consequences that has attended the entire destruction of factitious personal distinctions in the country, which has certainly aided in bringing out in bolder relief than common, the prevalent disposition in man to covet that which is the possession of another, and to decry merits that are unattainable.

"I rejoice to hear this," returned Mrs. Abbott, whose principles were of the same loose school as those of her companion, "for I think no one should have rights but those who have experienced religion, if you would keep vital religion in a country. There goes that old sea-lion, Truck, and his fishing associate, the commodore, with their lines and poles, as usual, Mr. Dodge; I beg you will call to them, for I long to hear what the first can have to say about his beloved Effinghams, now?"

Mr. Dodge complied, and the navigator of the ocean and the navigator of the lake, were soon seated in Mrs. Abbott's little parlour, which might be styled the focus of gossip, near those who were so lately its sole occupants.

"This is wonderful news, gentlemen," commenced Mrs. Abbott, as soon as the bustle of the entrance had subsided. "Mr. Powis is Mr. Effingham, and it seems that Miss Effingham is to become Mrs. Effingham. Miracles will never cease, and I look upon this as one of the most surprising of my time."

"Just so, ma'am," said the commodore, winking his eye, and giving the usual flourish with a hand; "your time has not been that of a day neither, and Mr. Powis has reason to rejoice that he is the hero of such a history. For my part, I could not have been more astonished, were I to bring up the sogdollager with a trout-hook, having a cheese paring for the bait."

"I understand," continued the lady, "that there are doubts after all, whether this miracle be really a true miracle. It is hinted that Mr. Powis is neither Mr. Effingham nor Mr. Powis, but that he is actually a Mr. Blunt. Do you happen to know any thing of the matter, Captain Truck?"

"I have been introduced to him, ma'am, by all three names, and I consider him as an acquaintance in each character. I can assure you, moreover, that he is A. No. 1, on whichever tack you take him; a man who carries a weather helm in the midst of his enemies."

"Well, I do not consider it a very great recommendation for one to be A. No. 1, or even No. 2; or have enemies, at all. Now, I dare say, Mr. Dodge, *you* have not an enemy on earth!"

"I should be sorry to think that I had, Mrs. Abbott. I am every man's friend, particularly the poor man's friend, and I should suppose that every man *ought* to be my friend. I hold the whole human family to be brethren, and that they ought to live together as such."

"Very true, sir; quite true—we *are* all sinners, and ought to look favourably on each other's failings. It is no business of mine—I say it is no business of ours, Mr. Dodge, who Miss Eve Effingham marries; but were she *my* daughter, I do think I should not like her to have three family names, and to keep her own in the bargain!"

"The Effinghams hold their heads very much up, though it is not easy to see *why*; but so they do, and the more names the better, perhaps, for such people," returned the editor. "For my part, I treat them with condescension, just as I do every body else; for it is a rule with me, Captain Truck, to make use of the same deportment to a king on his throne, as I would to a beggar in the street."

"Merely to show that you do not feel yourself to be above your betters. We have many such philosophers in this country."

"Just so," said the commodore.

"I wish I knew," resumed Mrs. Abbott; for there existed in her head, as well as in that of Mr. Dodge, such a total confusion on the subject of deportment, that neither saw nor felt the cool sarcasm of the old sailor; "I wish I knew, now, whether Eve Effingham has really been regenerated! What is your opinion, commodore?"

"Re-what, ma'am?" said the commodore, who was not conscious of ever having heard the word before; for, in his Sabbaths on the water, where he often worshipped God devoutly in his heart, the language of the professedly pious was never heard; "I can only say she is as pretty a skiff as floats, but I can tell you nothing about resuscitation—indeed, I never heard of her having been drowned."

"Ah, Mrs. Abbott, the very best friends of the Effinghams will not maintain that they are pious. I do not wish to be invidious, or to say unneighbourly things; but were I upon oath, I could testify to a great many things, which would unqualifiedly show, that none of them have ever experienced, or even been exercised."

"Now, Mr. Dodge, you know how much I dislike scandal," the widow-bewitched cried affectedly, "and I cannot tolerate such a sweeping charge. I insist on the proofs of what you say, in which, no doubt, these gentlemen will cordially join me."

By proofs, Mrs. Abbott meant allegations.

"Well, ma'am, since you insist on my *proving* what I have said, you shall not be disappointed. In the first place, then, they *read* their family prayers out of a book."

"Ay, ay," put in the captain; "but that merely shows they have some education; it is done every where."

"Your pardon, sir; no people but the Catholics and the church people commit this impiety. The idea of *reading* to the Deity, Mrs. Abbott, is particularly shocking to a pious soul."

"As if the Lord stood in need of letters! *That* is very bad, I allow; for at *family* prayers, a form becomes mockery."

"Yes, ma'am; but what do you think of cards?"

"Cards!" exclaimed Mrs. Abbott, holding up her pious hands, in holy horror.

"Even so; foul paste-board, marked with kings and queens," said the captain. "Why this is worse than a common sin, being unqualifiedly anti-republican."

"I confess I did not expect this! I had heard that Eve Effingham was guilty of indiscretions, but I did not think she was so lost to virtue, as to touch a card. Oh! Eve Effingham; Eve Effingham, for what is your poor diseased soul destined!"

"She dances, too, I suppose you know that," continued Mr. Dodge, who finding his popularity a little on the wane, had joined the meeting himself, a few weeks before, and who did not fail to manifest the zeal of a new convert.

"Dances!" repeated Mrs. Abbott, in holy horror.

"Reels, jigs, and fiddle de di!" echoed Captain Truck.

"Just so," put in the commodore; "I have seen it with my own eyes. But, Mrs. Abbott, I feel bound to tell you that your own daughter—"

"Biansy-Alzumy-Anne!" exclaimed the mother in alarm.

"Just so; my-aunty-and-sue-me-anne, if that is her name. Do you know, ma'am, that I have seen your own blessed daughter, my-aunty-Anne, do a worse thing, even, than dancing!"

"Commodore, you are awful! What *could* a child of mine do that is worse than dancing?"

"Why, ma'am, if you *will* hear all, it is my duty to tell you. I saw aunty-Anne (the commodore was really ignorant of the girl's name) jump a skipping-rope, yesterday morning, between the hours of seven and eight. As I hope ever to see the sogdollager, again, ma'am, I did!"

"And do you call this as bad as dancing?"

"Much worse, ma'am, to my notion. It is jumping about without music, and without any grace, either, particularly as it was performed by my-aunty-Anne."

"You are given to light jokes. Jumping the skipping-rope is not forbidden in the bible."

"Just so; nor is dancing, if I know any thing about it; nor, for that matter, cards."

"But waste of time is; a sinful waste of time; and evil-passions, and all unrighteousness."

"Just so. My-aunty-Anne was going to the pump for water—I dare say you sent her—and she was misspending her time; and as for evil passions, she did not enjoy the hop, until she and your neighbour's daughter had pulled each other's hair for the rope, as if they had been two she-dragons. Take my word for it, ma'am, it wanted for nothing to make it sin of the purest water, but a cracked fiddle."

While the commodore was holding Mrs. Abbott at bay, in this manner, Captain Truck, who had given him a wink to that effect, was employed in playing off a practical joke at the expense of the widow. It was one of the standing amusements of these worthies, who had gotten to be sworn friends and constant associates, after they had caught as many fish as they wished, to retire to the favourite spring, light, the one his cigar, the other his pipe, mix their grog, and then relieve their ennui, when tired of discussing men and things, by playing cards on a particular stump. Now, it happens that the captain had the identical pack which had been used on all such occasions in his pocket, as was evident in the fact that the cards were nearly as distinctly marked on their backs, as on their faces. These cards he showed secretly to his companion, and when the attention of Mrs. Abbott was altogether engaged in expecting the terrible announcement of her daughter's errors, the captain slipped them, kings, queens and knaves, high, low, jack and the game, without regard to rank, into the lady's work-basket. As soon as this feat was successfully performed, a sign was given to the commodore that the conspiracy was effected, and that disputant in theology gradually began to give ground, while he continued to the last to maintain that jumping the rope was a sin, though it might be one of the venial class. There is little doubt, had he possessed a smattering of phrases, a greater command of biblical learning, and more zeal, that the fisherman might have established a new shade of the Christian faith; for, while mankind still persevere in disregarding the plainest mandates of God, as respects humility, the charities, and obedience, nothing seems to afford them more delight than to add to the catalogue of the offences against his divine supremacy. It was perhaps lucky for the commodore, who was capital at casting a pickerel line, but who usually settled his polemics with the fist, when hard pushed, that Captain Truck found leisure to come to the rescue.

"I'm amazed, ma'am," said the honest packet-master, "that a woman of your sanctity should deny that jumping the rope is a sin, for I hold that point to have been settled by all our people, these fifty years. You will admit that the rope cannot be well-jumped without levity."

"Levity, Captain Truck! I hope you do not insinuate that a daughter of mine discovers levity?"

"Certainly, ma'am; she is called the best rope-jumper in the village, I hear; and levity, or lightness of carriage, is the great requisite for skill in the art. Then there are 'vain repetitions' in doing the same thing over and over so often, and 'vain repetitions' are forbidden even in our prayers. I can call both father and mother to testify to that fact."

"Well, this is news to me! I must speak to the minister about it."

"Of the two, the skipping-rope is rather more sinful than dancing, for the music makes the latter easy; whereas, one has to force the spirit to enter into the other. Commodore, our hour has come, and we must make sail. May I ask the favour, Mrs. Abbott, of a bit of thread to fasten this hook afresh?"

The widow-bewitched turned to her basket, and raising a piece of calico, to look for the thread "high, low, jack and the game," stared her in the face. When she bent her eyes towards her guests, she perceived all three gazing at the cards, with as much apparent surprise and curiosity, as if two of them knew nothing of their history.

"Awful!" exclaimed Mrs. Abbott, shaking both hands,—"awful— awful—awful! The powers of darkness have been at work here!"

"They seem to have been pretty much occupied, too," observed the captain, "for a better thumbed pack I never yet found in the forecastle of a ship."

"Awful—awful—awful!—This is equal to the forty days in the wilderness, Mr. Dodge."

"It is a trying cross, ma'am."

"To my notion, now," said the captain, "those cards are not worse than the skipping-rope, though I allow that they might have been cleaner."

But Mrs. Abbott was not disposed to view the matter so lightly. She saw the hand of the devil in the affair, and fancied it was a new trial offered to her widowed condition.

"Are these actually cards!" she cried, like one who distrusted the evidence of her senses.

"Just so, ma'am," kindly answered the commodore; "This is the ace of spades, a famous fellow to hold when you have the lead; and this is the Jack, which counts one, you know, when spades are trumps. I never saw a more thorough-working pack in my life."

"Or a more thoroughly worked pack," added the captain, in a condoling manner.

"Well, we are not all perfect, and I hope Mrs. Abbott will cheer up and look at this matter in a gayer point of view. For myself I hold that a skipping-rope is worse than the Jack of spades, sundays or week days. Commodore, we shall see no pickerel to-day, unless we tear ourselves from this good company."

Here the two wags took their leave, and retreated to the skiff; the captain, who foresaw an occasion to use them, considerately offering to relieve Mrs. Abbott from the presence of the odious cards, intimating that he would conscientiously see them fairly sunk in the deepest part of the lake.

When the two worthies were at a reasonable distance from the shore, the commodore suddenly ceased rowing, made a flourish with his hand, and incontinently began to laugh, as if his mirth had suddenly broken through all restraint. Captain Truck, who had been lighting a cigar, commenced smoking, and, seldom indulging in boisterous merriment, he responded with his eyes, shaking his head from time to time, with great satisfaction, as thoughts more ludicrous than common came over his imagination.

"Harkee, commodore," he said, blowing the smoke upward, and watching it with his eye until it floated away in a little cloud, "neither of us is a chicken. You have studied life on the fresh water, and I have studied life on the salt. I do not say which produces the best scholars, but I know that both make better Christians than the jack-screw system."

"Just so. I tell them in the village that little is gained in the end by following the blind; that is my doctrine, sir."

"And a very good doctrine it would prove, I make no doubt, were you to enter into it a little more fully—"

"Well, sir, I can explain—"

"Not another syllable is necessary. I know what you mean as well as if I said it myself, and, moreover, short sermons are always the best. You mean that a pilot ought to know where he is steering, which is perfectly sound doctrine. My own experience tells me, that if you press a sturgeon's nose with your foot, it will spring up as soon as it is loosened. Now the jack-screw will heave a great strain, no doubt; but the moment it is let up, down comes all that rests on it, again. This Mr. Dodge, I suppose you know, has been a passenger with me once or twice?"

"I have heard as much—they say he was tigerish in the fight with the niggers—quite an out-and-outer."

"Ay, I hear he tells some such story himself; but harkee, commodore, I wish to do justice to all men, and I find there is very little of it inland, hereaway. The hero of that day is about to marry your beautiful Miss Effingham; other men did their duty too, as, for instance, was the case with Mr. John Effingham; but Paul Blunt-Powis-Effingham finished the job. As for Mr. Steadfast Dodge, sir, I say nothing, unless it be to add that he was nowhere near *me* in that transaction; and if any man felt like a hungry alligator, on that occasion, it was your humble servant."

"Which means that he was not nigh the enemy, I'll swear before a magistrate."

"And no fear of perjury. Any one who saw Mr. John Effingham and Mr. Powis on that day, might have sworn that they were father and son; and any one who *did not see* Mr. Dodge might have said at once, that he did not belong to their family. That is all, sir; I never disparage a passenger, and, therefore, shall say no more than merely to add, that Mr. Dodge is no warrior."

"They say he has experienced religion, lately, as they call it."

"It is high time, sir, for he had experienced sin quite long enough, according to my notion. I hear that the man goes up and down the country disparaging those whose shoe-ties he is unworthy to unloose, and that he has published some letters in his journal, that are as false as his heart; but let him beware, lest the world should see, some rainy day, an extract from a certain log-book belonging to a ship called the Montauk. I am rejoiced at this marriage after all, commodore, or marriages rather, for I understand that Mr. Paul Effingham and

Sir George Templemore intend to make a double bowline of it to-morrow morning. All is arranged, and as soon as my eyes have witnessed that blessed sight, I shall trip for New-York again."

"It is clearly made out then, that the young gentleman is Mr. John Effingham's son?"

"As clear as the north-star in a bright night. The fellow who spoke to me at the Fun of Fire has put us in a way to remove the last doubt, if there were any doubt. Mr. Effingham himself, who is so cool-headed and cautious, says there is now sufficient proof to make it good in any court in America, That point may be set down as settled, and, for my part, I rejoice it is so, since Mr. John Effingham has so long passed for an old bachelor, that it is a credit to the corps to find one of them the father of so noble a son."

Here the commodore dropped his anchor, and the two friends began to fish. For an hour neither talked much, but having obtained the necessary stock of perch, they landed at the favourite spring, and prepared a fry. While seated on the grass, alternating between the potations of punch, and the mastication of fish, these worthies again renewed the dialogue in their usual discursive, philosophical, and sentimental manner.

"We are citizens of a surprisingly great country, commodore," commenced Mr. Truck, after one of his heaviest draughts; "every body says it, from Maine to Florida, and what every body says must be true."

"Just so, sir. I sometimes wonder how so great a country ever came to produce so little a man as myself."

"A good cow may have a bad calf, and that explains the matter. Have you many as virtuous and pious women in this part of the world, as Mrs. Abbott?"

"The hills and valleys are filled with them. You mean persons who have got so much religion that they have no room for any thing else?"

"I shall mourn to my dying day, that you were not brought up to the sea! If you discover so much of the right material on fresh-water, what would you have been on salt? The people who suck in nutriment from a brain and a conscience like those of Mr. Dodge, too, commodore, must get, in time, to be surprisingly clear-sighted."

"Just so; his readers soon overreach themselves. But it's of no great consequence, sir; the people of this part of the world keep nothing long enough to do much good, or much harm with it."

"Fond of change, ha?"

"Like unlucky fishermen, always ready to shift the ground. I don't believe, sir, that in all this region you can find a dozen graves of sons, that lie near their fathers. Every body seems to have a mortal aversion to stability,"

"It is hard to love such a country, commodore!"

"Sir, I never try to love it. God has given me a pretty sheet of water, that suits my fancy and wants, a beautiful sky, fine green mountains, and I am satisfied. One may love God, in such a temple, though he love nothing else."

"Well, I suppose if you love nothing, nothing loves you, and no injustice is done."

"Just, so, sir. Self has got to be the idol, though in the general scramble a man is sometimes puzzled to know whether he is himself, or one of the neighbours."

"I wish I knew your political sentiments, commodore; you have been communicative on all subjects but that, and I have taken up the notion that you are a true philosopher."

"I hold myself to be but a babe in swaddling-clothes compared to yourself, sir; but such as my poor opinions are, you are welcome to them. In the first place, then, sir, I have lived long enough on this water to know that every man is a lover of liberty in his own person, and that he has a secret distaste for it in the persons of other people. Then, sir, I have got to understand that patriotism means bread and cheese, and that opposition is every man for himself."

"If the truth were known, I believe, commodore, you have buoyed out the channel!"

"Just so. After being pulled about by the salt of the land, and using my freeman's privileges at their command, until I got tired of so much liberty, sir, I have resigned, and retired to private life, doing most of my own thinking out here on the Otsego-Water, like a poor slave as I am."

"You ought to be chosen the next President!"

"I owe my present emancipation, sir, to the sogdollager. I first began to reason about such a man as this Mr. Dodge, who has thrust himself and his ignorance together into the village, lately, as an expounder of truth, and a ray of light to the blind. Well, sir, I said to myself, if this man be the man I know him to be as a man, can he be any thing better as an editor?"

"That was a home question put to yourself, commodore; how did you answer it?"

"The answer was satisfactory, sir, to myself, whatever it might be to other people. I stopped his paper, and set up for myself. Just about that time the sogdollager nibbled, and instead of trying to be a great man, over the shoulders of the patriots and sages of the land, I endeavoured to immortalize myself by hooking him. I go to the elections now, for that I feel to be a duty, but instead of allowing a man like this Mr. Dodge to tell me how to vote, I vote for the man in public that I would trust in private, and for no other."

"Excellent! I honour you more and more every minute I pass in your society. We will now drink to the future happiness of those who will become brides and bridegrooms to-morrow. If all men were as philosophical and as learned as you, commodore, the human race would be in a fairer way than they are to-day."

"Just so; I drink to them with all my heart. Is it not surprising, sir, that people like Mrs. Abbott and Mr. Dodge should have it in their power to injure such as those whose happiness we have just had the honour of commemorating in advance?"

"Why, commodore, a fly may bite an elephant, if he can find a weak spot in his hide. I do not altogether understand the history of the marriage of John Effingham, myself; but we see the issue of it has been a fine son. Now I hold that when a man fairly marries, he is bound to own it, the same as any other crime; for he owes it to those who have not been as guilty as himself, to show the world that he no longer belongs to them."

"Just so; but we have flies in this part of the world that will bite through the toughest hide."

"That comes from there being no quarter-deck in your social ship, commodore. Now aboard of a well-regulated packet, all the thinking is done aft; they who are desirous of knowing whereabouts the vessel is, being compelled to wait till the observations are taken, or to sit down in their ignorance. The whole difficulty comes from the fact that sensible people live so far apart in this quarter of the world, that fools have more room than should fall to their share. You understand me, commodore?"

"Just so," said the commodore, laughing, and winking. "Well, it is fortunate that there are some people who are not quite as weak-minded as some other people. I take it, Captain Truck, that you will be present at the wedding?"

The captain now winked in his turn, looked around him to make sure no one was listening, and laying a finger on his nose, he answered, in a much lower key than was usual for him—

"You can keep a secret, I know, commodore. Now what I have to say is not to be told to Mrs. Abbott, in order that it may be repeated and multiplied, but is to be kept as snug as your bait, in the bait-box."

"You know your man, sir."

"Well then, about ten minutes before the clock strikes nine, to-morrow morning, do you slip into the gallery of New St. Paul's, and you shall see beauty and modesty, when 'unadorned, adorned the most.' You comprehend?"

"Just so," and the hand was flourished even more than usual.

"It does not become us bachelors to be too lenient to matrimony, but I should be an unhappy man, were I not to witness the marriage of Paul Powis to Eve Effingham."

Here both the worthies, "freshened the nip," as Captain Truck called it, and then the conversation soon got to be too philosophical and contemplative for this unpretending record of events and ideas.

CHAPTER XXIX.

"Then plainly know my heart's dear love is set
On the fair daughter of rich Capulet.
As mine on hers, so hers is set on mine,
And all combin'd, save what thou must combine
By holy marriage."

Romeo and Juliet 2.3.57–61.

THE morning chosen for the nuptials of Eve and Grace arrived, and all the inmates of the Wigwam were early afoot, though the utmost care had been taken to prevent the intelligence of the approaching ceremony from getting into the village. They little knew, however, how closely they were watched; the mean artifices that were resorted to by some who called themselves their neighbours, to tamper with servants, to obtain food for conjecture, and to justify to themselves their exaggerations, falsehoods, and frauds. The news did leak out, as will presently be seen, and through a channel that may cause the reader, who is unacquainted with some of the peculiarities of American life, a little surprise.

We have frequently alluded to Annette, the *femme de chambre* that had followed Eve from Europe, although we have had no occasion to dwell on her character, which was that of a woman of her class, as that class is well known to exist in France. Annette was young, had bright, sparkling black eyes, was well made, and had the usual tournure and manner of a Parisian grisette. As it is the besetting weakness of provincial habits to mistake graces for grace, flourishes for elegance, and exaggeration for merit, Annette soon acquired a reputation in her circle, as a woman of more than usual claims to distinction. Her attire was in the height of the fashion, being of Eve's cast-off clothes, and of the best materials, and attire is also a point that is not without its influence on those who are unaccustomed to the world.

As the double ceremony was to take place before breakfast, Annette was early employed about the person of her young mistress, adorning it in the bridal robes. While she worked at her usual employment, the attendant appeared unusually agitated, and several times pins were badly pointed, and new arrangements had to supersede or to supply the deficiencies of her mistakes. Eve was always a model of patience, and she bore with these little oversights with a quiet that would have given Paul an additional pledge of her admirable self-command, as well as of a sweetness of temper that, in truth, raised her almost above the common failings of mortality.

"*Vous êtes un peu agitée, ce matin, ma bonne Annette,*" she merely observed, when her maid had committed a blunder more material than common.

"*J'espère que Mademoiselle a été contente de moi, jusqu' à present,*" returned Annette, vexed with her own awkwardness, and speaking in the manner in which it is usual to announce an intention to quit a service.

"Certainly, Annette, you have conducted yourself well, and are very expert in your *métier*. But why do you ask this question, just at this moment?"

"*Parceque*—because—with mademoiselle's permission, I intended to ask for my *congé*."

"*Congé!* Do you think of quitting me, Annette?"

"It would make me happier than anything else to die in the service of mademoiselle, but we are all subject to our destiny"—the conversation was in French—"and mine compels me to cease my services as a *femme de chambre*."

"This is a sudden, and for one in a strange country, an extraordinary resolution. May I ask, Annette, what you propose to do?"

Here, the woman gave herself certain airs, endeavoured to blush, did look at the carpet with a studied modesty that might have deceived one who did not know the genus, and announced her intention to get married, too, at the end of the present month.

"Married!" repeated Eve—"surely not to old Pierre, Annette!"

"Pierre, Mademoiselle! I shall not condescend to look at Pierre. *Je vais me marier avec un avocat*."

"*Un avocat!*"

"*Oui Mademoiselle*. I will marry myself with Monsieur Aristabule Bragg, if Mademoiselle shall permit."

Eve was perfectly mute with astonishment, notwithstanding the proofs she had often seen of the wide range that the ambition of an American of a certain class allows itself. Of course, she remembered the conversation on the Point, and it would not have been in nature, had not a mistress who had been so lately wooed, felt some surprise at finding her discarded suitor so soon seeking consolation in the smiles of her own maid. Still her surprise was less than that which the reader will probably experience at this announcement; for, as has just been said, she had seen too much of the active and pliant enterprise of the lover, to feel much wonder at any of his moral *tours de force*. Even Eve, however, was not perfectly acquainted with the views and policy that had led Aristabulus to seek this consummation to his matrimonial schemes, which must be explained explicitly, in order that they may be properly understood.

Mr. Bragg had no notion of any distinctions in the world, beyond those which came from money, and political success. For the first he had a practical deference that was as profound as his wishes for its enjoyments; and for the last he felt precisely the sort of reverence, that one educated under a feudal system, would feel for a feudal lord. The first, after several unsuccessful efforts, he had found unattainable by means of matrimony, and he turned his thoughts towards Annette, whom he had for some months held in reserve, in the event of his failing with Eve and Grace (for on both these heiresses had he entertained designs) as a *pis aller*. Annette was a dress-maker of approved taste, her person was sufficiently attractive, her broken English gave piquancy to thoughts of no great depth, she was of a suitable age, and he had made her proposals and had been accepted, as soon as it was ascertained that Eve and Grace were irretrievably lost to him. Of course, the Parisienne did not hesitate an instant about becoming the wife of *un avocat*; for, agreeably to her habits, matrimony was a legitimate means of bettering her condition in life. The plan was soon arranged. They were to be married as soon as Annette's month's notice had expired, and then they were to emigrate to the far west, where Mr. Bragg proposed to practise law, to keep school, or to go to Congress, or to turn trader, or to saw lumber, or, in short, to turn his hand to any thing that offered; while Annette was to help along with the *ménage*, by making dresses, and teaching French; the latter occupation promising to be somewhat peripatetic, the population being scattered, and few of the dwellers in the interior deeming it necessary to take more than a quarter's instruction in any of the higher branches of education; the object being to *study*, as it is called, and not to *learn*. Aristabulus, who was filled with *go-aheadism*, would have shortened the delay, but this Annette positively resisted; her *esprit de corps* as a servant, and all her notions of justice, repudiating the notion that the connexion which had existed so long between Eve and herself, was to be cut off at a moment's warning. So diametrically were the ideas of the *fiancés* opposed to each other, on this point, that at one time it threatened a rupture, Mr. Bragg asserting the natural independence of man to a degree that would have rendered him independent of all obligations that were not effectually enacted by the law, and Annette maintaining the dignity of a European *femme de chambre,* whose sense of propriety demanded that she should not quit her place without giving a month's warning. The affair was happily decided by Aristabulus's receiving a commission to tend a store, in the absence of its owner; Mr. Effingham, on a hint from his daughter, having profited by the annual expiration of the engagement, to bring their connexion to an end.

This termination to the passion of Mr. Bragg would have afforded Eve a good deal of amusement at any other moment; but a bride cannot be expected to give too much of her attention to the felicity and prospects of those who have no natural or acquired claims to her affection. The cousins met, attired for the ceremony, in Mr. Effingham's room, where he soon came in person, to lead them to the drawing-room. It is seldom that two more lovely young women are brought together on similar occasions. As Mr. Effingham stood between them, holding a hand of each, his moistened eyes turned from one to the other in honest pride, and in an admiration that even his tenderness could not restrain. The *toilettes* were as simple as the marriage ceremony will permit; for it was intended that there should be no unnecessary parade; and, perhaps, the delicate beauty of each of the brides was rendered the more attractive by this simplicity, as it has often been justly remarked, that the fair of this country are more winning in dress of a less conventional character, than when in the elaborate and regulated attire of ceremonies. As might have been expected, there was most of soul and feeling in Eve's countenance, though Grace wore an air of charming modesty and nature. Both were unaffected, simple and graceful, and we may add that both trembled as Mr. Effingham took their hands.

"This is a pleasing and yet a painful hour," said that kind and excellent man; "one in which I gain a son, and lose a daughter."

"And *I*, dearest uncle," exclaimed Grace, whose feelings trembled on her eye-lids, like the dew ready to drop from the leaf, "have *I* no connexion with your feelings?"

"You are the daughter that I lose, my child, for Eve will still remain with me. But Templemore has promised to be grateful, and I will trust his word."

Mr. Effingham then embraced with fervour both the charming young women, who stood apparelled for the most important event of their lives, lovely in their youth, beauty, innocence, and modesty; and taking an arm of each, he led them below. John Effingham, the two bridegrooms, Captain Ducie, Mr. and Mrs. Bloomfield, Mrs. Hawker, Captain Truck, Mademoiselle Viefville, Annette, and Anne Sidley, were all assembled in the drawing-room, ready to receive them; and as soon as shawls were thrown around Eve and Grace, in order to conceal the wedding dresses, the whole party proceeded to the church.

The distance between the Wigwam and New St. Paul's was very trifling, the solemn pines of the church-yard blending, from many points, with the gayer trees in the grounds of the former; and as the buildings in this part of the village were few, the whole of the bridal train entered the tower, unobserved by the eyes of the curious. The clergyman was waiting in the chancel, and as each of the young men led the object of his choice immediately to the altar, the double ceremony began without delay. At this instant Mr. Steadfast Dodge and Mrs. Abbott advanced from the rear of the gallery, and coolly took their seats in its front. Neither belonged to this particular church, though, having discovered that the marriages were to take place that morning by means of Annette, they had no scruples on the score of delicacy about thrusting themselves forward on the occasion; for, to the latest moment, that publicity-principle which appeared to be interwoven with their very natures, induced them to think that nothing was so sacred as to be placed beyond the reach of curiosity. They entered the church, because the church they held to be a public place, precisely on the principle that others of their class conceive if a gate be blown open by accident, it removes all the moral defences against trespassers, in removing the physical.

The solemn language of the prayers and vows proceeded none the less for the presence of these unwelcome intruders; for, at that grave moment, all other thoughts were hushed in those that more properly belonged to the scene. When the clergyman made the usual appeal to know if any man could give a reason why those who stood before him should not be united in holy wedlock, Mrs. Abbott nudged Mr. Dodge, and, in the fulness of her discontent, eagerly inquired in a whisper, if it were not possible to raise some valid objection. Could she have had her pious wish, the simple, unpretending, meek, and *church*-going Eve, should never be married at all. But the editor was not a man to act openly in any thing, his particular province lying in insinuations and innuendoes. As a hint would not now be available, he determined to postpone his revenge to a future day. We say revenge, for Steadfast was of the class that consider any happiness, or advantage, in which they are not ample participators, wrongs done to themselves.

That is a wise regulation of the church, which makes the marriage ceremony brief, for the intensity of the feelings it often creates would frequently become too powerful to be suppressed, were it unnecessarily prolonged. Mr. Effingham gave away both the brides, the one in the quality of parent, the other in that of guardian, and neither of the bridegrooms got the ring on the wrong finger. This is all we have to say of the immediate scene at the altar. As soon as the benediction was pronounced, and the brides were released from the first embraces of their husbands, Mr. Effingham, without even kissing Eve, threw the shawls over their shoulders, and, taking an arm of each, he led them rapidly from the church, for he felt reluctant to suffer the holy feelings that were uppermost in his heart to be the spectacle of rude and obtrusive observers. At the door, he relinquished Eve to Paul, and Grace to Sir George, with a silent pressure of the hand of each, and signed for them to proceed towards the Wigwam. He was obeyed, and in less than half an hour from the time they had left the drawing-room, the whole party was again assembled in it.

What a change had been produced in the situation of so many, in that brief interval!

"Father!" Eve whispered, while Mr. Effingham folded her to his heart, the unbidden tears falling from both their eyes—"I am still thine!"

"It would break my heart to think otherwise, darling. No, no—I have not lost a daughter, but have gained a son."

"And what place am I to occupy in this scene of fondness?" inquired John Effingham, who had considerately paid his compliments to Grace first, that she might not feel forgotten at such a moment, and who had so managed that she was now receiving the congratulations of the rest of the party; "am I to lose both son and daughter?"

Eve, smiling sweetly through her tears, raised herself from her own father's arms, and was received in those of her husband's parent. After he had fondly kissed her forehead several times, without withdrawing from his bosom, she parted the rich hair on his forehead, passing her hand down his face, like an infant, and said softly—

"Cousin Jack!"

"I believe this must be my rank and estimation still! Paul shall make no difference in our feeling; we will love each other as we have ever done."

"Paul can be nothing new between you and me. You have always been a second father in my eyes, and in my heart, too, dear—dear cousin Jack."

John Effingham pressed the beautiful, ardent, blushing girl to his bosom again; and as he did so, both felt, notwithstanding their language, that a new and dearer tie than ever bound them together. Eve now received the compliments of the rest of the party, when the two brides retired to change the dresses in which they had appeared at the altar, for their more ordinary attire.

In her own dressing-room, Eve found Anne Sidley, waiting with impatience to pour out her feelings, the honest and affectionate creature being much too sensitive to open the floodgates of her emotions in the presence of third parties.

"Ma'am—Miss Eve—Mrs. Effingham!" she exclaimed as soon as her young mistress entered, afraid of saying too much, now that her nursling had become a married woman.

"My kind and good Nanny!" said Eve, taking her old nurse in her arms, their tears mingling in silence for near a minute. "You have seen your child enter on the last of her great earthly engagements, Nanny, and I know you pray that they may prove happy."

"I do—I do—I do—ma'am—madam—Miss Eve—what am I to call you in future, ma'am?"

"Call me Miss Eve, as you have done since my childhood, dearest Nanny."

Nanny received this permission with delight, and twenty times that morning she availed herself of the permission. She continued to use the term until, two years later, she danced a miniature Eve on her knee, as she had done its mother before her, when matronly rank began silently to assert its rights, and our present bride became Mrs. Effingham.

"I shall not quit you, ma'am, now that you are married?" Anne Sidley timidly asked; for, although she could scarcely think such an event within the bounds of probability, and Eve had already more than once assured her to the contrary with her own tongue, still did she love to have assurance made doubly sure. "I hope nothing will ever happen to make me quit you, ma'am?"

"Nothing of that sort, with my consent, ever shall happen, my excellent Nanny. And now that Annette is about to get married, I shall have more than the usual necessity for your services."

"And Mamerzelle, ma'am?" inquired Nanny, with sparkling eyes; "I suppose she, too, will return to her own country, now you know every thing, and have no farther occasion for her?"

"Mademoiselle Viefville will return to France in the autumn, but it will be with us all; for my dear father, cousin Jack, my husband—" Eve blushed as she pronounced the novel word—"and myself, not forgetting you my old nurse, will all sail for England, with Sir George and Lady Templemore, on our way to Italy, the first week in October."

"I care not, ma'am, so that I go with you. I would rather we did not live in a country where I cannot understand all that the people say to you, but wherever you are will be my earthly paradise."

Eve once more kissed the true-hearted woman, and, Annette entering, she changed her dress.

The two brides met at the head of the great stairs, on their way back to the drawing-room. Eve was a little in advance, but, with a half-concealed smile, she gave way to Grace, curtsying gravely, and saying—

"It does not become *me* to precede Lady Templemore—I, who am only Mrs. Paul Effingham."

"Nay, dear Eve, I am not so weak as you imagine. Do you not think I should have married him had he not been a baronet?"

"Templemore, my dear coz, is a man any woman might love, and I believe, as firmly as I hope it sincerely, that he will make you happy."

"And yet there is one woman who would not love him, Eve!"

Eve looked steadily at her cousin for a moment, was startled, and then she felt gratified that Sir George had been so honest, for the frankness and manliness of his avowal was a pledge of the good faith and sincerity of his character. She took her cousin affectionately by the hand, and said—

"Grace, this confidence is the highest compliment you can pay me, and it merits a return. That Sir George Templemore may have had a passing inclination for one who so little deserved it, is possibly true—but my affections were another's before I knew him."

"You never would have married Templemore, Eve; he says himself, now, that you are quite too continental, as he calls it, to like an Englishman."

"Then I shall take the first good occasion to undeceive him; for I do *like* an Englishman, and he is the identical man."

As few women are jealous on their wedding-day, Grace took this in good part, and they descended the stairs together, side by side, reflecting each other's happiness, in their timid but conscious smiles. In the great hall, they were met by the bridegrooms, and each taking the arm of him who had now become of so vast importance to her, they paced the room to and fro, until summoned to the *déjeuner à la fourchette*, which had been prepared under the especial superintendence of Mademoiselle Viefville, after the manner of her country.

Wedding-days, like all formally prepared festivals, are apt to go off a little heavily. Such, however, was not the case with this, for every appearance of premeditation and preparation vanished with this meal. It is true the family did not quit the grounds, but, with this exception, ease and tranquil happiness reigned throughout. Captain Truck was alone disposed to be sentimental, and, more than once, as he looked about him, he expressed his doubts whether he had pursued the right course to attain happiness,

"I find myself in a solitary category," he said, at the dinner-table, in the evening. "Mrs. Hawker, and both the Messrs. Effinghams, *have been* married; every body else *is* married, and I believe I must take refuge in saying that I *will be* married, if I can now persuade any one to have me. Even Mr. Powis, my right-hand man, in all that African affair, has deserted me, and left me like a single dead pine in one of your clearings, or a jewel-block dangling at a yard-arm, without a sheave. Mrs. Bride—" the captain styled Eve thus, throughout the day, to the utter neglect of the claims of Lady Templemore—"Mrs. Bride, we will consider my forlorn condition more philosophically, when I shall have the honour to take you, and so many of this blessed party, back again to Europe, where I found you. Under your advice I think I might even yet venture."

"And I am overlooked entirely," cried Mr. Howel, who had been invited to make one at the wedding-feast; "what is to become of me, Captain Truck, if this marrying mania go any further?"

"I have long had a plan for your welfare, my dear sir, that I will take this opportunity to divulge; I propose, ladies and gentlemen, that we enlist Mr. Howel in our project for this autumn, and that we carry him with us to Europe. I shall be proud to have the honour of introducing him to his old friend, the island of Great Britain."

"Ah! that is a happiness, I fear, that is not in reserve for me!" said Mr. Howel, shaking his head. "I have thought of these things, in my time, I confess, but age will now defeat any such hopes."

"Age, Tom Howel!" said John Effingham; "you are but fifty, like Ned and myself. We were all boys together, forty years ago, and yet you find us, who have so lately returned, ready to take a fresh departure. Pluck up heart; there may be a steam-boat ready to bring you back, by the time you wish to return."

"Never," said Captain Truck, positively. "Ladies and gentlemen, it is morally impossible that the Atlantic should ever be navigated by steamers. That doctrine I shall maintain to my dying day; but what need of a steamer, when we have packets like palaces?"

"I did not know, captain, that you entertained so hearty a respect for Great Britain—it is encouraging, really, to find so generous a feeling toward the old island in one of her descendants. Sir George and Lady Templemore, permit me to drink to your lasting felicity."

"Ay—ay—I entertain no ill-will to England, though her tobacco laws are none of the genteelest. But my wish to export you, Mr. Howel, is less from a desire to show you England, than to let you perceive that there are other countries in Europe—"

"Other countries!—Surely you do not suppose I am so ignorant of geography, as to believe that there are no other countries in Europe—no such places as Hanover, Brunswick, and Brunswick Lunenberg, and Denmark; the sister of old George the Third married the king of that country; and Wurtemberg, the king of which married the Princess Royal—"

"And Mecklenburg-Strelitz," added John Effingham, gravely, "a princess of which actually married George the Third *propriâ personâ*, as well as by proxy. Nothing can be plainer than your geography, Howel; but, in addition to these particular regions, our worthy friend the captain wishes you to know also, that there are such places as France, and Austria, and Russia, and Italy; though the latter can scarcely repay a man for the trouble of visiting it."

"You have guessed my motive, Mr. John Effingham, and expressed it much more discreetly than I could possibly have done," cried the captain. "If Mr. Howel will do me the honour to take passage with me, going and coming, I shall consider the pleasure of his remarks on men and things, as one of the greatest advantages I ever possessed."

"I do not know but I might be induced to venture as far as England, but not a foot farther."

"*Pas à Paris!*" exclaimed Mademoiselle Viefville, who wondered why any rational being would take the trouble to cross the Atlantic, merely to see *Ce melancolique Londres;* "you will go to *Paris,* for my sake, Monsieur Howel?"

"For your sake, indeed, Mam'selle, I would do any thing, but hardly for my own. I confess I have thought of this, and I will think of it farther. I should like to see the King of England and the House of Lords, I confess, before I die."

"Ay, and the Tower, and the Boar's-Head at East-Cheap, and the statue of the Duke of Wellington, and London Bridge, and Richmond Hill, and Bow Street, and Somerset House, and Oxford Road, and Bartlemy Fair, and Hungerford Market, and Charing-Cross—*old* Charing-Cross, Tom Howel!"—added John Effingham, with a good-natured nod of the head.

"A wonderful nation!" cried Mr. Howel, whose eyes sparkled as the other proceeded in his enumeration of wonders. "I do not think, after all, that I can die in peace, without seeing *some* of these things—*all* would be too much for me. How far is the Isle of Dogs, now, from St. Catherine's Docks, captain?"

"Oh! but a few cables' lengths. If you will only stick to the ship until she is fairly docked, I will promise you a sight of the Isle of Dogs before you land, even. But then you must promise me to carry out no tobacco!"

"No fear of me; I neither smoke nor chew, and it does not surprise me that a nation as polished as the English should have this antipathy to tobacco. And one might really see the Isle of Dogs before landing? It *is* a wonderful country! Mrs. Bloomfield, will you ever be able to die tranquilly without seeing England?"

"I hope, sir, whenever that event shall arrive, that it may be met tranquilly, let what may happen previously. I do confess, in common with Mrs. Effingham, a longing desire to see Italy; a wish that I believe she entertains from her actual knowledge, and which I entertain from my bright anticipations."

"Now, this really surprises me. What *can* Italy possess to repay one for the trouble of travelling so far?"

"I trust, cousin Jack," said Eve, colouring at the sound of her own voice, for on that day of supreme happiness and intense emotions, she had got to be so sensitive as to be less self-possessed than common, "that our friend Mr. Wenham will not be forgotten, but that he may be invited to join the party."

This representative of *la jeune Amérique* was also present at the dinner, out of regard to his deceased father, who was a very old friend of Mr. Effingham's, and, being so favourably noticed by the bride, he did not fail to reply.

"I believe an American has little to learn from any nation but his own," observed Mr. Wenham, with the complacency of the school to which he belonged, "although one might wish that all of this country should travel, in order that the rest of the world might have the benefit of the intercourse."

"It is a thousand pities," said John Effingham, "that one of our universities, for instance, was not ambulant. Old Yale was so, in its infancy; but unlike most other creatures, it went about with greater ease to itself when a child, than it can move in manhood."

"Mr. John Effingham loves to be facetious," said Mr. Wenham with dignity; for, while he was as credulous as could be wished, on the subject of American superiority, he was not quite as blind as the votaries of the Anglo-American school, who usually yield the control of all their faculties and common sense to their masters, on the points connected with their besetting weaknesses. "Every body is agreed, I believe, that the American imparts more than he receives, in his intercourse with Europeans."

The smiles of the more experienced of this young man's listeners were well-bred and concealed, and the conversation turned to other subjects. It was easy to raise the laugh on such an occasion, and contrary to the usages of the Wigwam, where the men usually left the table with the other sex, Captain Truck, John Effingham, Mr. Bloomfield, and Mr. Howel, made what is called a night of it. Much delicious claret was consumed, and the honest captain was permitted to enjoy his cigar. About midnight he swore he had half a mind to write a letter to Mrs. Hawker, with an offer of his hand; as for his heart, that she well knew she had possessed for a long time.

The next day, about the hour when the house was tranquil, from the circumstance that most of its inmates were abroad on their several avocations of boating, riding, shopping, or walking, Eve was in the library, her father having left it, a few minutes before, to mount his horse. She was seated at a table, writing a letter to an aged relative of her own sex, to communicate the circumstance of her marriage. The door was half open, and Paul appeared at it unexpectedly, coming in search of his young bride. His step had been so light, and so intently was our heroine engaged with her letter, that his approach was unnoticed, though it had now been a long time since the ear of Eve had learned to know his tread, and her heart to beat at its welcome sound. Perhaps a beautiful woman is never so winningly lovely as when, in her neat morning attire, she seems fresh and sweet as the new-born day. Eve had paid a little more attention to her toilette than usual even, admitting just enough of a properly selected jewelry, a style of ornament that so singularly denotes the refinement of a gentlewoman, when used understandingly, and which so infallibly betrays vulgarity under other circumstances, while her attire had rather more than its customary finish, though it was impossible not to perceive, at a glance, that she was in an undress. The Parisian skill of Annette, on which Mr. Bragg based so many of his hopes of future fortune, had cut and fitted the robe to her faultlessly beautiful person, with a tact, or it might be truer to say a contact, so perfect, that it even left more charms to be imagined than it displayed, though the outline of the whole figure was that of the most lovely womanhood. But, notwithstanding the exquisite modelling of the whole form, the almost fairy lightness of the full, swelling, but small foot, about which nothing seemed lean and attenuated, the exquisite hand that appeared from among the ruffles of the dress, Paul stood lost in nearly breathless admiration of the countenance of his "bright and blooming bride." Perhaps there is no sentiment so touchingly endearing to a man, as that which comes over him as he contemplates the beauty, confiding faith, holy purity and truth that shine in the countenance of a young, unpractised, innocent woman, when she has so far overcome her natural timidity as to pour out her tenderness in his behalf, and to submit to the strongest impulses of her nature. Such was now the fact with Eve. She was writing of her husband, and, though her expressions were restrained by modesty, taste and education, they partook of her unutterable fondness and devotion. The tears stood in her eyes, the pen trembled in her hand, and she shaded her face as if to conceal the weakness from herself. Paul was alarmed, he knew not why, but Eve in tears was a sight painful to him. In a moment he was at her side, with an arm placed gently around her waist, and he drew her fondly towards his bosom.

"Eve—dearest Eve!" he said—"what mean these tears?"

The serene eye, the radiant blush, and the meek tenderness that rewarded his own burst of feeling, reassured the husband, and, deferring to the sensitive modesty of so young a bride, he released his hold, retaining only a hand.

"It is happiness, Powis—nothing but excess of happiness, which makes us women weaker, I fear, than even sorrow."

Paul kissed her hands, regarded her with an intensity of admiration, before which the eyes of Eve rose and fell, as if dazzled while meeting his looks, and yet unwilling to lose them; and then he reverted to the motive which had brought him to the library.

"My father—*your* father, that is now—"

"Cousin Jack!"

"Cousin Jack, if you will, has just made me a present, which is second only to the greater gift I received from your own excellent parent, yesterday, at the altar. See, dearest Eve, he has bestowed this lovely image of yourself on me; lovely, though still so far from the truth. And here is the miniature of my poor mother, also, to supply the place of the one carried away by the Arabs."

Eve gazed long and wistfully at the beautiful features of this image of her husband's mother. She traced in them that pensive thought, that winning kindness, that had first softened her heart towards Paul, and her lips trembled as she pressed the insensible glass against them.

"She must have been very handsome, Eve, and there is a look of melancholy tenderness in the face, that would seem almost to predict an unhappy blighting of the affections."

"And yet this young, ingenuous, faithful woman entered on the solemn engagement we have just made, Paul, with as many reasonable hopes of a bright future as we ourselves!"

"Not so, Eve—confidence and holy truth were wanting at the nuptials of my parents. When there is deception at the commencement of such a contract, it is not difficult to predict the end."

"I do not think, Paul, you ever deceived; that heart of yours is too generous!"

"If any thing can make a man worthy of such a love, dearest, it is the perfect and absorbing confidence with which your sex throw themselves on the justice and faith of ours. Did that spotless heart ever entertain a doubt of the worth of any living being on which it had set its affections?"

"Of itself, often, and they say self-love lies at the bottom of all our actions."

"You are the last person to hold this doctrine, beloved, for those who live most in your confidence, declare that all traces of self are lost in your very nature."

"Most in my confidence! My father—my dear, kind father, has then been betraying his besetting weakness, by extolling the gift he has made."

"Your kind, excellent father, knows too well the total want of necessity for any such thing. If the truth must be confessed, I have been passing a quarter of an hour with worthy Anne Sidley."

"Nanny—dear old Nanny!—and you have been weak enough, traitor, to listen to the eulogiums of a nurse on her child!"

"All praise of thee, my blessed Eve, is grateful to my ears, and who can speak more understandingly of those domestic qualities which lie at the root of domestic bliss, than those who have seen you in your most intimate life, from childhood down to the moment when you have assumed the duties of a wife?"

"Paul, Paul, thou art beside thyself; too much learning hath made thee mad!"

"I am not mad, most beloved and beautiful Eve, but blessed to a degree that might indeed upset a stronger reason."

"We will now talk of other things," said Eve, raising his hand to her lips in respectful affection, and looking gratefully up into his fond and eloquent eyes; "I hope the awkwardness of which you so lately spoke has subsided, and that you no longer feel yourself a stranger in the dwelling of your own family."

"Now that I can claim a right through you, I confess that my conscience is getting to be easier on this point. Have you been yet told of the arrangement that the older heads meditate in reference to our future means?"

"I would not listen to my dear father when he wished to introduce the subject, for I found that it was a project that made distinctions between Paul Effingham and Eve Effingham, two that I wish, henceforth, to consider as one in all things."

"In this, darling, you may do yourself injustice as well as me. But perhaps you may not wish *me* to speak on the subject, neither."

"What would my lord?"

"Then listen, and the tale is soon told. We are each other's natural heirs. Of the name and blood of Effingham, neither has a relative nearer than the other, for, though but cousins in the third degree, our family is so small as to render the husband, in this case, the natural heir of the wife, and the wife the natural heir of the husband. Now your father proposes that his estates be valued, and that my father settle on you a sum of equal amount, which his wealth, will fully enable him to do, and that I become the possessor in reversion, of the lands that would otherwise have been yours."

"You possess me, my heart, my affections, my duty; of what account is money after this!"

"I perceive that you are so much and so truly woman, Eve, that we must arrange all this without consulting you at all."

"Can I be in safer hands? A father that has always been too indulgent of my unreasonable wishes—a second parent that has only contributed too much to spoil me in the same thoughtless manner—and a—"

"Husband," added Paul, perceiving that Eve hesitated at pronouncing to his face a name so novel though so endearing, "who will strive to do more than either in the same way."

"Husband," she added, looking up into his face with a smile innocent as that of an infant, while the crimson tinge covered her forehead, "if the formidable word must be uttered, who is doing all he can to increase a self-esteem that is already so much greater than it ought to be."

A light tap at the door caused Eve to start and to look embarrassed, like one detected in a fault; Paul released the hand that he had continued to hold during the brief dialogue.

"Sir—ma'am"—said the timid, meek voice of Anne Sidley, as she held the door ajar, without presuming to look into the room; "Miss Eve—Mr. Powis."

"Enter, my good Nanny," said Eve, recovering her self-composure in a moment, the presence of her nurse always appearing to her as no more than a duplication of herself. "What is your wish?"

"I hope I am not unreasonable, but I knew that Mr. Effingham was alone with you, here, and I wished—that is, ma'am,—Miss Eve—Sir—"

"Speak your wishes, my good old nurse—am I not your own child, and is not this your own child's"—again Eve hesitated, blushed, and smiled, ere she pronounced the word—"husband."

"Yes, ma'am; and God be praised that it is so. I dreamt, it is now four years, Miss Eve; we were then travelling among the Denmarkers, and I dreamt that you were married to a great prince—"

"But your dream has not come true, my good Nanny, and you see by this fact that it is not always safe to trust in dreams."

"Ma'am, I do not esteem princes by the kingdoms and crowns, but by their qualities—and if Mr. Powis be not a prince, who is?"

"That, indeed, changes the matter," said the gratified young wife; "and I believe, after all, dear Nanny, that I must become a convert to your theory of dreams."

"While I must always deny it, good Mrs Sidley, if this is a specimen of its truth," said Paul, laughing. "But, perhaps this prince proved unworthy of Miss Eve, after all?"

"Not he, sir; he made her a most kind and affectionate husband; not humouring all her idle wishes, if Miss Eve could have had such wishes, but cherishing her, and counselling her, and protecting her, showing as much tenderness for her as her own father, and as much love for her as I had myself."

"In which case, my worthy nurse, he proved an invaluable husband," said Eve, with glistening eyes—"and I trust, too, that he was considerate and friendly to you?"

"He took me by the hand, the morning after the marriage, and said, Faithful Anne Sidley, you have nursed and attended my beloved when a child, and as a young lady; and I now entreat you will continue to wait on and serve her as a wife to your dying day. He did, indeed, ma'am; and I think I can now hear the very words he spoke so kindly. The dream, so far, has come good."

"My faithful Anne," said Paul, smiling, and taking the hand of the nurse, "you have been all that is good and true to my best beloved, as a child, and as a young lady; and now I earnestly entreat you to continue to wait on her, and to serve her as *my* wife, to your dying day."

Nanny clapped her hands with a scream of delight, and bursting into tears, she exclaimed, as she hurried from the room,

"It has all come true—it has all come true!"

A pause of several minutes succeeded this burst of superstitious but natural feeling.

"All who live near you appear to think you the common centre of their affections," Paul resumed, when his swelling heart permitted him to speak.

"We have hitherto been a family of love—God grant it may always continue so."

Another delicious silence, which lasted still longer than the other, followed. Eve then looked up into her husband's face with a gentle curiosity, and observed—

"You have told me a great deal, Powis—explained all but one little thing, that, at the time, caused me great pain. Why did Ducie, when you were about to quit the Montauk together, so unceremoniously stop you, as you were about to get into the boat first; is the etiquette of a man-of-war so rigid as to justify so much rudeness, I had almost called it—?"

"The etiquette of a vessel of war is rigid certainly, and wisely so. But what you fancied rudeness, was in truth a compliment. Among us sailors, it is the inferior who goes first *into* a boat, and who *quits* it last."

"So much, then, for forming a judgment, ignorantly! I believe it is always safer to have no opinion, than to form one without a perfect knowledge of all the accompanying circumstances."

"Let us adhere to this safe rule through life, dearest, and we may find its benefits. An absolute confidence, caution in drawing conclusions, and a just reliance on each other, may keep us as happy to the end of our married life, as we are at this blessed moment, when it is commencing under auspices so favourable as to seem almost providential."

Explanatory Notes

3.18   As any one who may happen to take up this volume: In a letter of 22 February 1838, Cooper's British publisher, Richard Bentley, warned Cooper about the difficulty of marketing "sequels": "My experience has always proved that sequels do not sell to the same extent as the earlier portion" (cited in *L&J* 3:306, n. 2). Bentley might have omitted this preface in his edition of the novel precisely because Cooper calls attention to *Home as Found* as a sequel.

3.25   Mr. Mathews, the comedian: The English actor Charles Mathews (1776–1835) was well known for his imitations and improvisations. He made two tours of the United States, the first in 1822–23 and the second in 1834–35. During the first tour, he performed a variety of "types" of American characters (including one as an African American, possibly in blackface).

4.6   *Roman de Société*: Known as the social novel in the Anglo-American tradition, a "novel of society" dramatized problems like poverty, child labor, and slavery. By 1838, Cooper had read "condition-of-England" novels by authors like Benjamin Disraeli, as well as Balzac's early social novels. He might well have been aware of Dickens's *Oliver Twist*, which began serial publication in *Bentley's Miscellany* in February 1837. Cooper seems to be discussing realism and, as a subset of it, the novel of society: no realistic novel (delineating "ordinary American life") has been successful in the United States, he says, much less a novel that desired "to illustrate a principle" (*Roman de Société*). His syntax is ambiguous: is his intention in the novel before us just to "delineate ordinary American life" (realism), or is it "to illustrate a principle . . . within [a] homely frame" (*Roman de Société*)?

6.29   Hudson Square: The Effinghams live in a fashionable neighborhood in what is today lower Manhattan. Also known as St. Johns Park, Hudson Square was bounded by Varick Street, Laight Street, Hudson Street, and Beach Street. The neighborhood featured townhouses arranged around a private park; it reached the peak of its fashionable popularity in the 1830s and 1840s. Mrs. Hawker (chapter IV) also lives in Hudson Square. In the Bentley edition, Cooper placed the Effingham townhouse on State Street, at the very south end of Manhattan. State Street was also a fashionable and desirable neighborhood in 1830s, but it was longer established than Hudson Square and perhaps more recognizable to British readers.

6.33   "*Qu'avez-vous, ma chère?*": "Is something the matter, my dear?" Mademoiselle Viefville refers here to Eve as her pupil ("*élève*"). Viefville's surname contains an unusual spelling in French; her name translated might mean "old town" ("vieille ville") or "old girl" ("vieille fille").

6.37   "*Bien – c'est . . . moins.*": "Very well, she is an attractive young lady. . . . From how she presents herself, my dear, you must be satisfied."

7.4   "*Très volontiers. . . . naturel.*": "Certainly. She's a relation and that is only natural."

9.1   *prononcès*: Pronounced.

10.21   *réunions*: Assemblies, gatherings.

11.14   *retenue*: Restraint, moderation.

11.33   *person* and *personnage*: A person (i.e., somebody important) versus a character.

12.21   John Effingham, A. M.: The Master of arts degree (M.A.) was at one time referred to by the initialism A. M. (*artium magister* in postclassical Latin). Eve is almost certainly being facetious.

15.30   Hiram Doolittle: A character in Cooper's *The Pioneers* (1823). Along with Richard Jones, a cousin of Judge Marmaduke Temple, he designed the family home in Templeton.

15.32   *Ex pede, Herculem*: From his foot, (we can measure) Hercules. This is a Latin proverb about the proportionality of part to whole, ascribed to Pythagoras.

17.8   Temple of the Winds: The Tower of the Winds in the public marketplace of ancient Athens. Also known as the Horologion or "timepiece" of Andonicus of Cyrrhus, it was a marble clock tower and weathervane.

17.12   a droll: A funny or waggish fellow; a humorist or jester. It is less often used today as a noun.

19.32   silver-forkisms: Beginning around 1830, "silver-fork" was used "to designate a school of novelists . . . distinguished by an affectation of gentility" (*OED*). In other words, the characters in this scene had good manners; they did not affect them. They choose not to call attention to Bragg's lack of good manners—though they did notice it.

19.41   organ of acquisitiveness: An allusion to phrenology, which theorized that the brain was composed of multiple, distinct, innate "organs" or tendencies, manifested on the skull by bumps, protrusions, and depressions.

23.7   The "western speculations" discussed here and the "western fever" discussed later on this page refer to the real estate speculation boom of the 1830s, fueled in part by the cession of land in Illinois, Wisconsin, and Iowa by Native American tribes after the Black Hawk War of 1832.

23.35   *"Ce pays. . . . rapports."*: "This country to the west, is it really unhealthy?" Viefville asks. "Apparently, according to some reports."

26.1   standing order: The Standing Order referred to the loose association of Congregational Churches in New England in the late eighteenth and early nineteenth centuries. Bragg puns on the idea that Protestants, unlike Catholics, typically do not kneel during church services.

29.40   *convenances*: Proprieties.

30.5   *un heureux accident*: A fortunate accident, contrasted a line later with an unfortunate accident.

31.2   *"La république est une horreur!"*: "A republic is a horror!"

32.8   "your *Faubourg St. Germain* and your *Chausée d'Antin"*: Aristocratic, fashionable neighborhoods in Paris.

30.5   Alexander of Russia: Alexander I (ruled 1801–1825) used liberal rhetoric to promise constitutional and social reforms, most of which were never carried out. It is a "happy accident" that a powerful autocrat would support democratic reforms. If Bragg were to become president, Eve says, it would be "an unhappy (or unfortunate) accident."

32.30   *élégants* and *élégantes*: Fashionable young men and women.

32.32   *"Les femmes américaines sont bien jolies!"*: "American women are very attractive!"

33.33   *"C'est une belle illustration, celle de l'antiquité"*: "Antiquity does indeed offer a striking example."

33.35   Capponi and von Erlachs: Piero Capponi was a fifteenth-century Florentine statesman who negotiated with the invading king, Charles VIII of France, after the last of the Medici had been expelled from Florence in 1494. Charles offered harsh terms of surrender to the city, which Capponi rejected. Charles then offered to "blow his trumpets," that is, send his men to battle. Capponi replied: "Blow your trumpets and we will ring our bells ('*Sonnez vos trompettes . . .*'), that is, they would resist. Charles moderated his claim and signed a treaty with the city. From the fourteenth century to the early nineteenth century, the Erlach family played an important role in the political, military, and social life of Bern (Switzerland).

35.2   *tant-soi peu*: A tiny bit.

38.22   *demi-toilette*: Dress that is slightly more relaxed and less elaborate than full evening dress.

38.30   *embonpoint*: Plumpness, curviness.

42.26   Committee of Tammany Hall: Tammany Hall, or the Society of St. Tammany, was a New York City political organization founded in the late eighteenth century. It supported Democratic-Republican candidates (and later Democratic candidates) for local and national offices. Originally founded as a club for "pure" Americans—the name refers somewhat ironically to Lenape chief Tamenend—Tammany Hall became increasingly associated with immigrants, particularly the Irish, in the nineteenth century. Though associated with strong-arm political patronage from the beginning, it was infamous for graft and corruption under William "Boss" Tweed in the 1860s and 1870s.

44.34   *éclat*: Brilliance.

45.3   *au fait*: Familiar with.

45.37   Pawnee: Cooper is alluding to the eastern tour in 1821 of a delegation of Native American chiefs from the lower Missouri and Platte River tribes, including Pawnee leader Petalesharo. In romanticized retellings, Petalesharo had been celebrated in the press in 1817 for preventing his tribe from sacrificing a Comanche girl captured as an enemy. More recently, Black Hawk and other defeated leaders of the Black Hawk War had been forced to tour eastern cities in defeat in 1833. The Sauk, Meskwaki, and Kickapoo leaders were treated as celebrities.

46.4   Nully: Neuilly is a French commune just west of Paris and adjacent to it.

46.21   "blue": A blue, or bluestocking, refers to an educated intellectual woman. The term originated in reference to the Blue Stockings Society in London in the mid-eighteenth century. Led by hostess and critic Elizabeth Montagu, the informal club promoted education for women.

48.9   *par force*: By force.

49.2   *pêle mêle*: Chaos, confused jumble.

52.6   Lake George, the Falls, and the Mountain House: As upstate and western New York became more accessible in the early nineteenth century, these became tourist destinations: Lake George (the lake and a village at its southern end, also named Lake George); Niagara Falls; and the Catskill Mountain House near Palenville, New York, in the

Catskill Mountains. All three were noted for their spectacular views of nature.

52.24   Tower mark: The tower stamp (or mark, or hallmark) on gold and silver articles guaranteed the quality or purity of the metal. See also 215.16.

53.33   *Denk-Lehre*: German, logic or dialectics.

54.9   *le peuple*: The people of the United States, understood as an ethnic or national group with a shared identity.

56.37   *"Bien sûr. C'est naturel."*: "Of course. That's clear."

57.22   beggar on horseback: The complete proverb is "set a beggar on horseback, and he'll ride to the devil." Someone unaccustomed to power or luxury will abuse it or be corrupted by it.

57.26   *chevaux de frise*: Literally, "Frisian horses," medieval defensive anticavalry obstacles composed of wooden frames and iron or wooden spikes.

59.22   *"Dites-moi premièrement. . . . tout le monde est joli."*: "First tell me what does it mean to be a beauty in New York? Everyone there is fashionable."

60.13   *"Qui est cette dame?"*: "Who is that lady?" "She is an unmarried lady," Eve replies. "How appalling!" Viefville comments with some disgust, and then adds a few lines later, "Absolutely appalling!"

61.37   *"Ciel!"*: "Good heavens!"

62.24   *ne plus ultra*: Literally, not further beyond; metaphorically, the best or most extreme example of something.

62.33   *"Mais, ceci . . ."*: "This is just too much. I cannot listen anymore."

63.24   "Mais, ceci . . .": "Why, this is ridiculous! The child ran away from New York's Charenton." Charenton was a famous lunatic asylum located on the outskirts of Paris. The Marquis de Sade spent the last years of his life there.

66.6   Mr. Clay, in his compromise: The so-called Compromise Tariff of 1833 was proposed by Henry Clay and John Calhoun as part of the resolution of the Nullification Crisis. It generally reduced tariffs that had been introduced in 1828, making most imports cheaper, and it included a specific reduction of the tariff to zero ("an exception") on some raw materials.

66.21   "*À présent, Mademoiselle . . .*": "Now, Miss, I shall now avenge us both."

67.27   Chaussée d'Antin: In the 1830s, a fashionable area in the ninth arrondissement in Paris.

68.40   Apsley House: A mansion near Hyde Park in London, made famous when it was purchased by the Duke of Wellington in 1817.

72.25   *convives*: Guests.

74.7   *conversazioni*: Plural, singular *conversazione*, borrowed from Italian, the word in English came to mean an assembly or soiree connected to the arts.

75.13   *catalogue raisonné*: A descriptive catalog of works of art.

75.35   American Eclipse (1814–1847): An undefeated American thoroughbred race horse.

75.39   Animal Magnetism: The name given by the German doctor Franz Mesmer in the late eighteenth century to what he believed to be an invisible natural force possessed by all living things.

78.2   *empocher*: Pocket, put in a bag.

78.20   *tenue*: Dress, attire.

81.14   "*Mais, tout ceci est bien drôle!*": "Why, all this is most amusing!"

82.13   Minerva Pressism: The Minerva Press was a publishing house founded by William Lane in London in the 1790s. Lane focused on the lucrative market of gothic romances, hence the term came to refer to writing typical of or resembling those romantic, sometimes sensational novels.

82.21   homœpathist: Homeopathy is a system of alternative medicine developed in the late eighteenth century by Samuel Hahnemann. He believed that a disease could be cured by a substance (administered in small doses) that produced similar symptoms in healthy people.

83.3   "Truxtun's War" and "twelve and fifteen": Captain Truck refers to the "Quasi-War," an undeclared war between the United States and France fought almost entirely at sea from 1798 to 1800. He then refers to the War of 1812, between the United States and Great Britain from 1812 to 1815.

83.32   *secundem artem*: According to the art or practice.

83.29   *Injee* business: India business, or trade with the East Indies.

84.3   *rum litterateur*: As an adjective, *rum* could colloquially mean "odd, strange, or suspect," but it could also serve a complementary adjective as in "rum-looking." Gray says here that Truck is suspect as a literary man, but ironically the three writers soon discover that he is a worthy interlocutor.

84.6   Boanerges of literature: *Boanerges* is a Greek word meaning "sons of thunder." Jesus gave the name to two of his disciples, James and John, on account of their fiery temper.

85.34   Guy-kee-oh-*ly*, or, Gwy-ky-o-*lee*: Teresa, Countess Guiccioli, was the married lover of Lord Byron while he was writing the early cantos of *Don Juan* in 1818–22. She later wrote an autobiographical account, *Lord Byron's Life in Italy*, which remained unpublished until 2005.

86.33   *sans-culotteism*: The sans-culottes ("without breeches") were lower- and working-class republicans during the French Revolution. Here, the term refers any extreme republican or revolutionary movement.

87.9   Baron Munchausen: A fictional German nobleman created by the writer Rudolph Erich Raspe in his 1785 novel *Baron Munchausen's Narrative of his Marvelous Travels and Campaigns in Russia*.

91.11   *"Quelle foule!"*: "What a crowd!" Grace then explains that they are observing the Stock Exchange (*"Bourse"*).

94.18   our French quarrel: Compensation claims by the United States for the capture by the French of US ships and sailors during the Napoleonic wars caused strained relations between the United States and France into the early 1830s. The French government signed a reparations treaty in 1831 only to become delinquent in its payments in 1832–33 because of internal political difficulties. President Andrew Jackson reprimanded the French government in his December 1834 State of the Union address and refused to soften his language a year later in his 1835 address. American reparations were finally paid in February 1836. This reference, and the Great Fire recounted later in the chapter, place the action of the novel in 1835–36.

95.9   the fool who says 'there is no death': An allusion to Psalms 14.1, "The fool has said in his heart, There is no God."

96.4   bells began to ring: Cooper describes in the next several pages the Great Fire of New York, which began on the evening of December 16, 1835. More than 500 buildings were destroyed over a large area in lower Manhattan.

97.26   *la commencement de la fin*: The beginning of the end.

99.41   winter lingering in the lap of May: Adapted from Oliver Goldsmith, *The Traveler; or, A Prospect of Society* (1764), "But winter, ling'ring chills the lap of May" (l. 173).

101.1   *"Et le Louvre!"*: "And the Louvre!" The Louvre in Paris is the world's largest art museum and a historic landmark.

102.3   *Il Capo di Bove*: Now an archaeological site on the Appian Way outside of Rome. Thermal baths were in use there as early as the second century; there was a working farm on the site in the nineteenth century. Tourists would have been familiar with the site while traveling the Appian Way. The Parthenon was a temple dedicated to the goddess Athena on the Acropolis in Athens, Greece.

102.8   *pas, en avant*: Step forward.

106.8   *en beau*: In beautiful (ways). Ned is saying that Jack always paints a gloomy picture.

106.29   '*Les absents ont toujours tort.*': 'The absent are always wrong.'

107.9   Whited sepulchers: See Mark 23.27.

108.16   "*La campagne est vraiment délicieuse en Amérique!*": "The countryside is truly delightful in America!"

109.18   *corvée*: Unpaid labor by a feudal vassal owed to a lord.

109.19   *terres*: Property, land.

110.2   *pied à terre*: Foot on the ground.

110.11   *ou des sauvages*: Or savages.

110.37   "*Des loups! . . .*": "Wolves! . . . Are there wolves and wild boars in this forest?"

111.4   "*Je l'espère*": I hope so.

111.28   *coup d'œil*: A look or view.

113.9   *pari passu*: Side by side, simultaneously.

114.8   Cooper struggled to spell the word "piazzaed," settling in his emendation on the amanuensis copy on *piazza'd*. He did not invent it; the word had been in use since the late seventeenth century according to the *OED*.

116.33   "*C'est charmant! . . . à l'éternité.*": "How charming! . . . Such a beautiful calm makes one think of eternity." Several lines later Eve adds in French, "Taste is a personal matter." Eve uses an American variation of the French aphorism "*À chacun son gout*," to each their own. She repeats the saying at 330.26.

120.6   James Kirke Paulding's play *The Lion of the West* was first performed in 1831, treating Davy Crockett as a larger-than-life figure on the American frontier.

120.36   *déjeuner à la fourchette*: A luncheon or light meal.

126.28   *rusé*: Cunning.

127.5   two lines of Pope's: Alexander Pope's *Essay on Man* (1733–34) begins with an address to philosopher Henry St. John, Viscount Bolingbroke, "Awake, my St. John! Leave all meaner things / To low ambition, and the pride of kings."

127.33   American navy register: *The Register of the Commissioned and Warrant Officers of the United States Navy and Marine Corps* was published yearly by the US government.

130.25   Many men, many minds: From the Latin proverb, "Quot homines, tot sententiae," there are as many opinions as there are men.

131.6   *église . . . veritable église*: Church . . . real church.

132.25   "*Mais, c'est . . . .*": "Why, it's a small château," Viefville says. "An Effinghamized château," Eve responds. "Effinghamized, if you like, my dear; nevertheless it's a small château."

132.32–35   Parthenon, Temple of Minerva, Temple of the Winds: The Pantheon (as AMAN and B have it) is a Roman temple honoring all (Roman) gods. The Parthenon is a Greek temple in Athens honoring Athena. There is more than one Temple of Minerva; they are all Roman, as Minerva is the Roman equivalent of Athena. See 17.8 for Temple of the Winds.

134.27   leaving not a wreck behind: From *The Tempest* 4.1.156. Prospero has just promised his daughter, Miranda, to Ferdinand but warned him not to "break the virgin knot" before the ceremony. He commands Ariel and other spirits to put on a short play for the couple, presaging their blessing by Ceres, goddess of fertility and motherhood. When the vision disappears, he remarks that his "insubstantial pageant" has faded as will life and the Earth itself, "leaving not a wrack behind."

135.33 *"Point du tout, monsieur . . . "*: "Not at all, sir . . . Annette's good taste doubtless reflects her trade, but she is too well bred to expect impossibilities."

136.20 corderoys, or corduroys: Corduroy roads are constructed by placing logs perpendicular to the direction traveled on swampy or wet areas.

136.39 *fabricants*: Manufacturers.

137.23 *villegiatura*: A rural or suburban retreat; a holiday in the country.

137.38 *"Oh, mon père et ma mère . . .* : "Oh, father and mother, how I blame you. . . . how I blame you . . . ." Eve is quoting from Molière's well-known comedy, *Le Bourgeois Gentilhomme* (1670), where Monsieur Jourdain, a draper having made a fortune, comically rails against his parents for not having taught him aristocratic refinements.

138.15 a game of ball: The apprentices were probably not playing baseball, as it is generally accepted by sports historians that the first team to play baseball under modern rules was the New York Knickerbockers in 1845. They were probably playing rounders, cricket, or another folk game that made use of a ball and a bat, such as stoolball or trap ball.

147.39 *bonne foi*: Good faith, sincerity.

148.33 a second Burchell: William John Burchell (1781–1863) was an English naturalist, explorer, artist, traveler, and author. From his travels to Africa and South America, he brought thousands of plant and insect specimens to England.

150.25 Peeping Tom of Coventry: A tailor in English legend who was struck blind as he watched Lady Godiva ride naked through the streets of Coventry. She was protesting against the heavy taxes imposed by her husband on his tenants and had asked the villagers to keep their windows shut as she passed by on horseback.

152.21 *Cum multis alias*: With many others.

152.22 as Tubal told Shylock: Asked by Shylock if he had found his daughter in Genoa, Tubal replies, "I often came where I did hear of her, but cannot find her" (*Merchant of Venice* III.i.85–86).

153.8 *la jeune France*: European reform movements in the 1830s gave rise to nationalist youth movements in many countries, including Germany (*Junges Deutschland*), Italy (*La Giovine Italia*), and France. The Young America movement began to coalesce in the 1830s.

156.28 *timbré à Londres*: Stamped in London.

158.32 *Almanachs de Gotha*: A directory of Europe's royalty and higher nobility, first published in 1763. It was published annually until 1944.

159.23 Possibly an allusion to Peggy Eaton, who married Senator John Henry Eaton in 1829. The marriage was scandalous, in part because she married him soon after the death of her first husband; rumors circulated that he committed suicide because of an affair between her and Eaton. In 1929, Andrew Jackson appointed Eaton Secretary of War, and Peggy was snubbed by a number of wives in Washington social circles. She was the daughter of a tavern owner in Washington DC; class resentment played a role in the scandal.

172.33 *"Vraiment, c'est fort . . .* : "Really, it's most extraordinary to be on an American lake," Viefville says. In response to Eve's question, she then says, "No, no, but every bit as extraordinary for a Parisienne."

182.28 kick against the pricks: To strike the foot against sharp or piercing weapons; more generally, to show defiance to figures of authority.

199.32 *ci-devant*: Formerly.

210.22 Albrecht or Hermann Gessler was a legendary bailiff at Altdort, whose brutal rule led to the William Tell rebellion and the independence of the Swiss confederacy. Rodolph probably refers to Rudolph I, Count of Hapsburg and King of the Romans in the late thirteenth century.

214.12 A hint might be taken from Franklin: The story of Benjamin Franklin urging his father to say grace over the whole pork barrel, rather than every day over servings of pork, circulated widely in the early nineteenth century. The anecdote does not appear in Franklin's *Autobiography* or letters.

221.27 Trinculos and Stephanos: Characters in Shakespeare's *The Tempest*. Trinculo is King Alonso's jester, Stephano is his boisterous and sometimes-drunk butler.

221.29 *à l'exception pres de*: With the exception.

224.9 *badinage*: Banter.

227.3 *Se non è vero, è ben trovato*: Even if it is not true, it is a good story.

229.4 *voilà tout!*: That's all!

242.15 *les petits devoirs socials*: The little social duties.

255.39 *improvisés*: Improvised.

256.5 "*Mais, vraiment ceci surpasse . . .*": "But truly, this surpasses even the Garden of the Tuileries! . . . One would pass willingly through the dangers of the desert to reach it." The Tuileries Garden, near the Louvre in Paris, was designed in the 16th century, and became a public park after the French Revolution.

257.30 *faute des Bowies*: As Bowies, or in place of Bowies. The Bowie knife emerged as a fixed-blade fighting knife in the 1820s.

262.6 and hand in hand we'll go: A reference to a well-known poem by Robert Burns, "John Anderson, my Jo," which was often set to music.

262.29 as silence universally 'gives consent—': The notion that silence gives consent is a proverb in English. There is also a legal concept that silence gives consent, although it is not valid in all contexts. With the quotation marks, Cooper has Aristabulus allude to one or both ideas.

267.31 *"Est-ce que . . . votre indépendance"*: "Am I wrong, my dear? . . . Is not this the celebration of your independence?"

267.36 *"Monsieur votre père?"*: "Your distinguished father?"

268.1 *"Mais ces jeunes . . . Américains."*: Viefville asks, "But the young men, Mr. Bragg, Mr. Dodge, and Mr. Powis, even!" Eve responds: "They rejoice as Americans."

268.17 *"Certainement . . . même!"*: "Certainly . . . it is strictly required (that is, by fashion or etiquette)."

269.19 *"Voilà . . . une fête Americaine!"*: "There you go, Mademoiselle Viefville, an American celebration!"

269.23 *"dans le monde, mais . . . "*: Viefville complains with exasperation that in the United States a young woman can be alone with a man "in the world," but she cannot be seen in a crowd of strangers, even with her father. "I really despair," she says, at understanding American habits.

273.28 *"Mais, le musique . . . "*: "But what do you think of the music?" she asks.

274.40 *"Mais, c'est charmant!"*: "Why, it's lovely!" She is pleased to find something pleasant among the "sad Americans."

276.13 well-known line of Pope: "Say first, of God above, or man below, / What can we reason, but from what we know?" (*The Essay on Man*, ll. 17–18).

279.13 fourteen millions of freemen: This phrase begins to appear in the 1830s, even though the US census of 1830 put the total population at only 13 million, of which 2 million were slaves. The census of 1840 counted 17 million, of which 2.5 million were slaves.

281.28 Agrarian: Radical political reformer Thomas Skidmore founded the short-lived Working Man's Party in 1829. The next year he founded another short-lived party, the Agrarian Party. Skidmore published an ambitious treatise arguing for property redistribution, *The Rights of Man to Property* (1829).

283.17 what is bred in the bone will be seen in the flesh: A proverb in circulation since the fifteenth century.

283.36 little shoemaker's loo: Loo is a trick-taking card game that originated in the seventeenth century. This is either a regional variation of the game or a local name for the game.

286.23 *à nous aborder*: To approach us.

292.15 *faute d'imagination*: Lack of imagination.

293.20 *Tant pis*: Never mind, or oh well.

294.5 *Cui bono*: To whom is it a benefit, a Latin phrase about identifying crime suspects.

315.28 *Cosi, cosi*: So-so.

321.29 *"Volontiers."*: Gladly.

323.25 distance 'that lends enchantment to the view': The idea that distance lends enchantment (to a view) is proverbial, but Thomas Campbell, a poet whose works Cooper knew, also used the phrase in "The Pleasures of Hope" (1799): "'Tis distance lends enchantment to the view / And robes the mountain in its azure hue" (ll. 7–8). Cooper's American publisher, Carey & Lea, republished Campbell's poem in an 1830 collection, *Poetical Works of Rogers, Campbell, J. Montgomery, Lamb, and Kirke White*.

323.32 he will return like a dog to his vomit: "Of them the proverbs are true: 'A dog returns to its vomit' and 'A sow that is washed returns to her wallowing in the mud'" (2 Peter 2:22). For the first proverb, Peter is citing Proverbs 26.11.

325.4   the four quarters of the world: In 1820, in a review of Adam Seybert's *Statistical Annals of the United States* in the *Edinburgh Review*, Sydney Smith had asked: "In the four quarters of the globe, who reads an American book? Or goes to an American play? or looks at an American picture or statue?" His comments were read with scorn by Americans with a nationalist agenda.

325.34 la Jeune France: See explanatory note at 153.8.

330.35 *propriâ personâ*: For herself, on her own account.

339.6   *blasés*: Jaded.

359.31 agrarian: See the explanatory note at 281.28.

370.7   unadorned, adorned the most: Commonly attributed to St. Jerome, but Cooper likely knew the quotation from James Thomson, *The Seasons* (Autumn): "For loveliness / Needs not the foreign aid of ornament, / But is when unadorned adorned the most."

372.11 "*Vous êtes un peu agitée . . .*": "You are a little agitated this morning, my good Annette." Annette responds: "I hope that Mademoiselle has been content with me until now."

372.23 *Congé*: Take leave, quit.

372.37 "*Je vais me marier avec un avocat.*": "I'm going to marry a lawyer."

373.24 *pis aller*: Last resort.

374.29 *toilettes*: Manner or style of dressing.

381.5   "*Pas à Paris!*": "Not to Paris!" Viefville then asks why anyone would cross the Atlantic merely to see "dreary London."

383.26 bright and blooming bride: A cliché in the early nineteenth century, used in many works of literature.

Textual Commentary

In July 1837, Cooper set out to write a novel portraying the fictional town of "Templeton in 1837."[1] Templeton was Cooper's version of Cooperstown, the village in central New York state at the southern tip of Lake Otsego. It was the setting of his third novel, *The Pioneers* (1823), in which he traced events in the lives of its villagers in the mid-1790s. In two novels since then, Cooper had returned to the life of one of the main characters of that novel, Natty Bumppo, but he had not used Templeton as a setting for a novel.[2]

His original plan for the new novel was to devote the first two volumes of a British "triple decker" to a handful of characters—descendants of several characters in *The Pioneers*—who would travel by ship, rail, and carriage from England to Templeton. He told his British publisher, Richard Bentley, that the characters would reach Templeton by the third volume (*L&J* 3:298). However, by December he realized that he could not get the characters home until the end of volume three. "I thought this book would be part sea and part shore," he wrote Bentley, but "I find it necessary to make it nearly all sea" (*L&J* 3:302). He decided he needed a second novel in which to write the "shore" part of the tale. After completing the manuscript of the first novel, *Homeward Bound*, in January 1838, Cooper immediately began to write the "shore" part of the story, the novel we now know as *Home as Found*. "You have had many caricatures of our society," he wrote Bentley, but "my aim [in this sequel] is to give a true picture, *coute qui coute* [i.e., cost what it may]" (*L&J* 3:306). That picture would include New York City and the village of Templeton, the two extremes of social life in the young United States. He could not have imagined just then what the "cost" of this "true picture" of American society would be.[3]

Cooper understood that from a publisher's point of view sequels typically did not sell as well as earlier work, and even before he began writing the new novel, tentatively titled *At Home*, he offered to sell it to Bentley for a lower price than he otherwise would have asked. But he composed the novel with enthusiasm even as he worked simultaneously on other projects like *The American Democrat* (1838) and the *History of the Navy of the United States of America* (1839), sending the first volume in February or March, the second in May, and the third and final volume in July.[4]

To secure copyright in the United States and England, Cooper technically needed to have his novel *printed* first in the United States but *published* first in England. Indeed, since 1833, he had adopted the "plan of printing [his works first] in Philadelphia or New York and sending the sheets to London,"[5] where his publisher would set type for the British edition from the printed and proofed sheets. Under that system, Cooper could read proof on the American sheets and make changes during the production process that would apply simultaneously to the American and the British editions.

However, with *Homeward Bound* and then with *Home as Found*, Cooper adopted a slightly different practice, one that has significant implications for the textual history of the novel. As he wrote in his own usual small, crabbed handwriting (author's holograph manuscript, first authorial witness; hereafter referred to as AMS), his daughters copied the novel in their more legible handwriting (amanuensis copy, first nonauthorial witness implicated in the transmission of the text, as determined by editorial examination; hereafter referred to as AMAN). AMS was used by his American publisher, Lea & Blanchard,[6] to set type for the American edition (co-second authorial witness implicated in the transmission of the text, as determined by editorial examination; hereafter referred to as A). This fact was proved by internal evidence on the still-extant portion of AMS. It revealed stint marks and gathering marks that correspond to the Lea & Blanchard edition; clearly, the compositor at Lea & Blanchard followed AMS (and not AMAN) quite faithfully. In addition, internal evidence in A revealed that Cooper must have edited proof sheets before the novel was printed, because substantive changes were made between AMS and A. Those proof sheets are not extant. Because A contained substantive differences from AMS, the editor treated it as a second authorial witness. Cooper clearly authorized changes to A, even though we must infer those changes without being able to demonstrate them through his written directive.

Meanwhile, even as he continued to compose AMS, Cooper edited AMAN with varying degrees of rigor (co-second authorial witness, Cooper's editorial work on the amanuensis copy; hereafter referred to as CAMAN). These changes to AMAN were marked noticeably on the page with the use of different ink, and they were made in what is clearly Cooper's handwriting. In one case, Cooper even wrote a note on AMAN directly to the compositor, reminding him to print a name "as it is in the former sheets": he could not remember how he had written it earlier. Even in cases when the evidence was slight that Cooper made changes to AMAN—as with punctuation marks made with a darker ink—the editor accepted many changes made to AMAN as Cooper's. There was certainly evidence that other hands wrote on AMAN, including stint marks and gathering marks, but the evidence suggested that only one hand, Cooper's, edited the amanuenses' words, phrasing, and punctuation.

AMAN/CAMAN was sent in three installments to his publisher in London and used by compositors there to set type for the British edition (second nonauthorial witness implicated in the transmission of the text, as determined by editorial examination; hereafter referred to as B). Internal evidence on AMAN/CAMAN indicated very clearly that Bentley's compositor used it to set type: stint marks and gathering marks were legible; wording and phrasing consistently followed AMAN, not AMS; and the compositor picked up unique changes made in Cooper's hand (as CAMAN). In theory, Cooper could have sent edited proof sheets to London in August or September, but of course the amanuensis copy was produced specifically to obviate that need. He sent AMAN/CAMAN in installments without having to wait for the proof sheets of the whole novel to be printed in Philadelphia sometime after he completed it in July.

CAMAN and A were treated as co-second authorial witnesses because the editor had no way of knowing when Cooper edited (the lost proof sheets for) A or when he made the editorial changes referred to here as CAMAN. Logic would suggest that Cooper edited AMAN before he edited proof sheets to A, because the entire manuscript of AMAN/CAMAN was mailed to Bentley by the end of July 1838, and in September he was still negotiating with Lea & Blanchard to stereotype the novel. Indeed, in advance of the November publication date, he could have been editing proof sheets for A well into October or even early November. The proof sheets, if they existed, would constitute another authorial witness; as it is, evidence that they existed survives only circumstantially, as emendations to the author's manuscript visible in A only when the author's manuscript is extant. Cooper sometimes made identical changes at presumably different times to AMS and AMAN. But the evidence also reveals that his changes to the proof sheets of A often differed from changes he made at identical points to AMAN. And as far as we can tell from that evidence, he was not overly concerned about making his editorial changes either to AMS or to the lost proof sheets accord with those he made to AMAN.

Sometimes, it is true, his changes to AMAN accord with changes made on AMS (and then printed in A). Such changes are triply authorized by Cooper: emended on AMS, emended on AMAN, and proofed (via the lost proof sheets) in A. For example, at 138.21–22 Cooper first wrote the sentence, "Certainly to them, sir; and permit me to say, I think they might have chosen a more suitable spot for their sports." The amanuensis copied it correctly. Cooper then interlined the following sentence into both AMS and AMAN: "They are mistaking *liberties*, for liberty, I fear." At 139.18, to take another example, he altered the name of the local barber from Soap to Lather, making the change on both AMS and AMAN. In these two cases, the printed texts—A and B—deriving from the authorial emendations are identical. These changes, however, were not noted on the lists of emendations or rejected readings, because in all cases the "emended" reading derived from the copy-text (either AMS when it was extant or A).

On some occasions, a change authorized by Cooper on AMS did not accord with a change authorized on AMAN. For example, at 120.34 Cooper in AMS had a character say: "But we will defer the pleasure that is in reserve." The amanuensis copied it correctly. Then, on AMAN, he changed the sentence to "We will defer the pleasure of an examination." In A the sentence was altered from AMS, but not in the same way it was in AMAN: "We will defer the great pleasure that is in reserve." In cases like these, Cooper authorized two variants, one as CAMAN (appearing in B) and one via the lost proof sheets (appearing in A). In most of these cases, the editor accepted the variant from A. This was done for two reasons: because A was almost certainly corrected in proof sheets in the fall of 1838, after the revised amanuensis copy had been mailed to England; and because A is a complete extant text (unlike AMAN/CAMAN; see the discussion of each witness below).

Thus, AMS was the first authorial witness, a now incomplete holograph in Cooper's hand. When it is extant, it served as the copy-text. The editor treated two authorial witnesses, A and CAMAN, as co-second authorial witnesses. Each was the product of Cooper's editorial changes to a transcription of the text, one a typeset transcription of the holograph (via edited proof sheets set from AMS) and the other a handwritten transcription of the holograph made by an amanuensis and edited by Cooper. AMAN itself was the first nonauthorial witness, and B was the second nonauthorial witness.

The transmission of the text is as follows:

- Cooper composed the holograph manuscript (AMS) between January and July 1838.

- Serving as amanuenses, his daughters copied the author's manuscript for use by compositors in London (AMAN), with volume two being sent on 15 May and volume three on 25 July. (Cooper's letters do not indicate exactly when the first volume was sent.)

- While still composing AMS, Cooper made changes to the amanuensis copy (CAMAN) and to AMS. Those changes were often, but not always, in agreement. They vary in frequency across the three volumes; they were generally less frequent in volume three, though at that point only AMAN/CAMAN was extant for the editor to examine.

- Using AMS as source text, the printing firm of I. Ashmead in Philadelphia printed the novel for Lea & Blanchard, and it was published as *Home as Found* on 15 November 1838 (A). J. Fagan of Philadelphia stereotyped the first edition. Cooper made changes to the text on lost proof sheets and those changes are revealed in A when AMS is extant; he could have been making changes to the sheets well into October and early November, long after he had mailed volume three of the amanuensis copy to Bentley on 25 July. Significantly, the first American edition was both printed and published prior to the British first edition.

- Using the amanuensis copy (AMAN) including Cooper's handwritten variants (CAMAN) as his copy-text, Richard Bentley published the novel in London on 28 November 1838 (B) under a different title, *Eve Effingham; Or, Home*. This may have obviated the necessity to publish first to obtain a quasi-copyright in Britain. As will be discussed below, B reveals hundreds of substantive and accidental differences from A, as well as two very substantial differences.

No other edition of the novel was called for in Cooper's lifetime. He did not edit the novel for either Putnam's *The Works of James Fenimore Cooper (Author's Revised Edition)* (1849–1851) or Bentley's *The Selected Novels of James Fenimore Cooper* (1831–1855). Thus, there are no authorial witnesses after 1838.

Copy-Texts

The transmission process of the text was made more complex for the editor because neither AMS nor AMAN/CAMAN came down to us intact. Approximately 22 percent of AMS has survived; approximately 81 percent of AMAN/CAMAN has survived. Fortunately, the entirety of the surviving portion of AMS coincided with a surviving portion of AMAN/CAMAN, meaning that for 22 percent of the novel we have a fairly complete picture of the textual transmission process. Examination of the witnesses revealed that we are certainly missing proof sheets edited by Cooper for the publication of A, because A contained substantive variants that must have been authorized by him at some stage after the completion of AMS.

Following the guidelines of the Cooper Edition, the editor made AMS the copy-text where it has survived. In that section of the novel, AMS was closest to the author's hand, and thus was closest to his original intentions. Keyed to the pagination of this volume, the author's manuscript is thus the copy-text for 104.32–190.22.

For the remainder of the novel, the editor could have chosen a copy-text or copy-texts from among the four remaining witnesses: AMAN, CAMAN, A, and B. B was nonauthorial and was farthest from Cooper's hand, since the compositors' work at Bentley was mediated by the transcription of the amanuensis and because there was no evidence that Cooper edited proof sheets from the American printer or from the British printer for it. (See the discussion below about Bentley's substantive and unauthorized editorial changes.)

However, AMAN/CAMAN (taken together) and A had an almost identical authority as a copy-text when AMS was not extant. Both were transcribed from AMS, and then proofed and edited by Cooper. AMAN/CAMAN had the virtue of showing us Cooper's handwritten changes to the amanuenses' transcription, whereas A revealed changes certainly made by Cooper, but the editor had to infer his agency on lost proof sheets. This was an argument for using AMAN/CAMAN as copy-text. Both AMAN/CAMAN and A made repeated changes to the text at the level of accidentals, the amanuensis for personal and sometimes idiosyncratic reasons, and the compositor at Lea & Blanchard for reasons of house style. The compositors of A were, however, more consistent than the amanuenses, no doubt because they were imposing a standard house style, while the several daughters brought individual attitudes and attention spans to the transcription of the text.[7] This was an argument for A. Cooper also presumably had access to AMS and the lost proof sheets at a later date than AMAN/CAMAN, since the final volume of AMAN/CAMAN was sent to London on 20 July. We know that Cooper was in Philadelphia several times in fall 1838 and that he consulted with his publisher on those visits. He could have been editing AMS and proof sheets well into October or early November. This was a second argument for using A as the copy-text where AMS is not extant. A third and clinching point in favor of A was the fact that AMAN/CAMAN is not extant in its entirety. For 19 percent of the text, the editor would necessarily have had to make use of A as the copy-text, because only it and B survive.

Thus, the Cooper edition of *Home as Found* uses two copy-texts. From 104.32 to 190.22, AMS served as the copy-text. From 3.1 to 104.32 and from 190.22 to 388.19, A served as copy-text. The editor's rationale for copy-text is explained in more detail for each section in which multiple witnesses are extant, beginning with the section where AMS is still extant.

- 104.32–190.22. AMS, a holograph in Cooper's hand, is the copy-text. It represents his first intentions and, through revisions made on the holograph itself, later reconsiderations. AMAN/CAMAN is extant here, and the copy-text can be emended on the authority of Cooper's changes in CAMAN. A exists, and the copy-text can be emended on the authority of substantive changes made to it which must have been authorized by Cooper at a late stage in the production process on the lost proof sheets. B exists, but variants that are only in B (and not in AMAN/CAMAN) can be accepted as emendations only on the authority of the editor, since we know from the witnesses that Cooper did not specifically authorize variants found only in B. In this section of the novel where AMS is extant, we can see Cooper emending the copy-text in three different ways: making simultaneous and identical or very similar emendations to AMS and to the amanuensis copy as CAMAN (thus putting A and B into general agreement); making changes as CAMAN only (and thus putting A and B into disagreement); and making changes at the proof stage that are visible in A only in their deviation from AMS and AMAN/CAMAN (and thus putting A and B into disagreement).

- 76.24–104.32, 190.22–388.19.[8] A is the copy-text for reasons discussed earlier. A and CAMAN have relatively equal authority because each is one step from Cooper's hand; the compositor and the amanuensis were both attempting to reproduce AMS accurately, and Cooper edited the work of both. A can be emended on the authority of CAMAN. In these two large sections of the novel, then, CAMAN, AMAN, and B are additional witnesses to A, the first being authorial and second two nonauthorial. Of course, many variants first printed in B are accepted as emendations of the copy-text because they have been authorized by Cooper via CAMAN. However, there is a bit of a trade-off in these sections, because we know that Cooper sometimes edited the same word or clause or sentence differently in CAMAN and in A. Without AMS in hand here, we cannot tell for sure if the variant in A was Cooper's initial thought (revised in CAMAN) or a revision (after CAMAN) that first appeared in A. By accepting a change from CAMAN that we know Cooper made, we might be rejecting a change in the Lea & Blanchard edition that he might have made at a later date (on AMS or on the lost proof sheets) or made more emphatically on the proof sheets. Still, the editor accepted many variants in CAMAN as emendations to the copy-text. Some cases are addressed in detail in the Textual Notes.

- 5.1–76.24. A serves as copy-text, and B is the only other extant witness. Here, there is little reason to emend A, based as it was on AMS and (presumably) on the lost proof sheets. B was set from AMAN/CAMAN, and although Cooper certainly made changes to AMAN here, we lack the textual evidence that he authorized any particular variant that appears in B. While we thus "lose" some variants that Cooper no doubt authorized via CAMAN, we reject variants in B caused by a variety of factors: the amanuensis mistranscribing AMS; the amanuensis or Cooper failing to transcribe an emendation Cooper made to AMS; the compositor or editor in B introducing a variant on his own initiative; and so on. B contains more substantive variants than can be accounted for by the typical method of production of Cooper's novels in the 1830s and 1840s; for whatever reason, the compositor or editor of B introduced many substantive variants. He was editing to bring the text into conformity with house style and with British spellings and locution, but some tinkering went beyond that. For example, at 77.16 (where AMS is no longer extant), Cooper authorized in A the clause "an ardent desire to manifest a proper homage to." The amanuensis had written "an ardent desire to manifest a homage to," indicating that Cooper had probably emended his first thought (recorded accurately by AMAN) on the lost proof sheets. In place of that clause, Bentley printed "a veneration for." This was a substantive change, which a compositor would not normally make, and there was absolutely no evidence that Cooper made or authorized it. It was a variant introduced by Bentley, perhaps acting with Cooper's tacit or explicit permission to edit the text, as when Bentley retitled the novel, but not specifically authorized by Cooper based on the evidence we have in hand. When AMS is no longer extant, the editor has accepted some variants from B as emendations, but did so sparingly: (1) to correct obvious errors by the compositor at Lea & Blanchard, (2) to assign attribution to the epigraphs, (3) to enforce standard modern publishing conventions, (4) to correct misspellings of foreign words, and (5) to sharpen or clarify a thought based on the editor's experience in understanding how Cooper tended to emend his initial thoughts. Approximately sixty-five emendations were made to A in this section of the novel, and more than 600 substantive changes printed in B were rejected.[9]

- 3.1–4.35. A serves as copy-text, and there are no other witnesses. The preface is found only in Lea & Blanchard.

Author's Manuscript (AMS)

The surviving section of the holograph manuscript that served as the copy-text for the Cooper Edition of *Home as Found* from 104.32 to 190.22 was composed between January 1838 and May 1838. We know that Cooper completed this extant section of AMS before June because he mailed volume two of the British edition on 15 May, and volume two (of the British edition) included all of the text that appears in this section of the novel. The partial manuscript is held at the Historical Society of Pennsylvania, which received the manuscript as a gift from Lea Brothers & Co on 2 April 1887. A typewritten note prefacing the manuscript states that it is the "Latter Part of Manuscript / 'Home as Found,'" and that "Mr. Cooper has the rest [of the manuscript]. He requested that it should be left with Messrs. Lea and Blanchard." That note was dated 25 October 1838. Because it was typewritten, the note was probably a transcription of a lost page prefacing the partial manuscript; it was perhaps typewritten in 1887 at the time of presentation. It is not clear why Cooper had "the rest" of the manuscript in the fall of 1838, nor why "it" (this part of the manuscript) should have needed to be left with Lea & Blanchard, since stint marks and page references keyed to the Lea & Blanchard edition indicate clearly that it had been used by the compositor. Given that Cooper mailed the third and final volume of the novel to Bentley on 25 July, and thus that he had completed the entirety of AMS by that date, it is possible that he was still reading proof sheets of the Lea & Blanchard edition against the author's manuscript in late October 1838, before the November publication date. He perhaps needed to keep the second half of novel in his possession after 25 October as he was proofing the second volume of the US edition.

Cooper always numbered his manuscript pages; the partial manuscript is numbered consecutively from 66 to 125, suggesting that the entire AMS must have been approximately 260 pages in length. The final extant page includes a few sentences from the end of chapter XIV and then the first few paragraphs of chapter XV. A line is drawn across the page at the end of chapter XIV and a hand other than Cooper's has written "End of Vol. I." Two stint marks in this section of the manuscript include a name, and several gatherings of twelve printed pages are marked with brackets. At nine different locations, someone has marked the beginning/end of a printed page (keyed to A) with a circled page number. These do not correspond to gatherings; they might be stint marks, or they might suggest that the compositor or even Cooper was calculating the length of volume 1.

Cooper wrote on ruled paper, always making use of all of the space on the page. His handwriting is crabbed but legible. There are remarkably few cross outs or interlineations. To offer one example, he made nineteen changes on a single manuscript page (see Plate 4). Only twice did he write a word or short phrase, cross it out, and then continue with a new word or new phrase on the same line. At those moments, we can see him thinking "in the moment" as he wrote. In five places, he interlined single words after writing his first thought. So to his initial thought, "Near the centre of the place, in grounds of rather limited extent, stood that model of the composite order" (114.10–11), he interlined the adverb "still" before "stood." In seven places, he crossed out a word or very short phrase and interlined the change above it: "Much" became "Perhaps" (113.16), and "as many different" became "the same number of" (113.35). In one place, he simply deleted a word he deemed unnecessary. In another place he looked at what he had written, interlined a word, and then deleted the interlined word (returning to his first thought). These changes on AMS were not recorded on the lists of Emendations and Rejected Readings; the editor did not try to construct a genetic text of AMS.

Cooper's handwriting presents some recurrent problems. For example, it can be difficult to make a distinction between lower-case and capital initial letters. Words like "Christian" and "Protestant" often appear to begin with a lower-case letter, even though most printers of the era capitalized them. Cooper was careful to punctuate, but his scribbled additions in the margins or above the line sometimes duplicated or deleted his apparent intentions regarding commas and dashes. And he typically wrote the titles "Mr." and "Mrs." without the initial; readers will note this fact when the copy-text shifts from A to AMS, and vice-versa. Unless Cooper made an obvious mistake, however—as when he misspelled the word "athwart" (116.24)—the editor faithfully transcribed Cooper's manuscript.

Changes to AMS as the copy-text were typically accepted as emendations only when authorized by CAMAN or by a substantive change in A that must have been authorized by Cooper in proof sheets. In a few cases, however, emendations for the purposes of clarity or correctness were drawn from AMAN or B. At 128.38, for example, Cooper wrote "regular" in AMS (and AMAN has the same word), revised it to "regularily" in CAMAN, and B printed it correctly as "regularly." At 190.23, Cooper wrote "consult" in A (and AMAN has the same word), changed it to "to take council" in CAMAN, and B printed it correctly as "to take counsel."

All emendations of AMS as copy-text were noted on the Emendations list.

Amanuensis Copy (AMAN) and Cooper's Corrections (CAMAN)

Cooper continued the practice he employed in writing *Homeward Bound* of having his daughters transcribe AMS. That amanuensis copy was then used to set type for B by his publisher in London, while the author's manuscript was used to set type for A by his publisher in Philadelphia. This was a deviation from Cooper's practice (since *The Prairie*) of having proof sheets of each text printed locally—since 1833 that would have been in Philadelphia or New York—and then distributing corrected proof sheets to printers in London, the United States, or elsewhere. While working on *Homeward Bound* in 1837, he had told Bentley that the daughters copied it "pretty plainly" and he himself had "corrected it with some care" (*L&J* 3:298). Bentley could simply set type from the corrected amanuensis copy.

Textual evidence in the amanuensis copy of *Home as Found* demonstrated that it was used by Bentley to set type for the first British edition. Gatherings were always marked in ink at intervals of twenty-four printed pages, and each page number and gathering indicator corresponded to the Bentley edition. Stint marks were regularly recorded in pencil, typically at intervals of four to six manuscript pages.

The manuscript of AMAN/CAMAN is held in the Barrett Collection in the Albert and Shirley Small Special Collections Library at the University of Virginia Library. It is now in a bound volume. The manuscript pages are numbered, beginning with 88 (76.24) and continuing consecutively to 158, the end of volume 1. Volume 2 is numbered consecutively from 1 to 148, volume 3 from 1 to 142. At the beginning of the second and third volumes, someone (probably Cooper) has written in ink the new volume number, and someone else (presumably at Bentley's publishing house) has written the British title "Eve Effingham."

Textual evidence in AMAN repeatedly confirmed that Cooper proofed and edited it. Corrections, alterations, and additions in his handwriting (CAMAN) are visible throughout the manuscript. Many of these variants were accepted by the editor as Cooper's emendations of his original intent, and others as emendations of the amanuenses' mistranscriptions. However, some of these authorial variants were rejected for reasons described elsewhere in this Textual Commentary. Cooper's hand was also seen in the epigraph (or "motto," as he called it) to each chapter. It was always in his hand.[10]

In general, several different types of variants were noted in AMAN/CAMAN, and the editor handled each type differently. One set of variants included mistranscriptions by the amanuensis, which were obvious when AMS was extant but had to be inferred when it was not. Many variants in the hand of the amanuensis were rejected and were typically not listed on the Rejected Readings lists. Mistranscriptions by the amanuensis hold no value for the scholar.

Some changes made by the amanuensis were, however, accepted as emendations, most often when A also changed the copy-text in the same manner. These included misspellings, missing punctuation, confusing punctuation, and misspellings of foreign words in the AMS copy-text. On these occasions, the editor treated AMAN and A as co-equals, noting in all cases on the Emendations list which text or texts (AMAN and/or A) was used to authorize the emendation. For example, at 126.35, in AMS Cooper had Paul say that he "took care to drop a few couple of lines" of poetry around Templeton; he had neglected to cross out either "few" or "couple of." Both the amanuensis and the compositor at Lea & Blanchard (or Cooper in proofs) corrected this by deleting "few."

When AMS served as copy-text, all changes via CAMAN that brought AMAN/CAMAN into alignment with the copy-text or were identical to a change in Cooper's hand made on the copy-text were unrecorded on the list of Emendations. Such changes demonstrated that Cooper was editing the amanuensis copy and trying to keep it in alignment with the copy-text, but the editor did not deem it useful to list the specific cases when Cooper did this. In more than 150 instances, Cooper simply emended a mistranscription in the amanuensis copy, bringing it into alignment with the copy-text. These range from single word mistranscriptions to more substantial ones. At 174.13, for example, Cooper had written "oratorical" and the amanuensis transcribed it as "aristocratical"; Cooper corrected it. They also included more substantial mistranscriptions, such as when the amanuensis left out an entire line of the author's manuscript. For example at 162.2–3, she left out a whole line: "those that are purely personal, would object to baronets, and the wearers of red ribbands as unfit matches." Instead, she wrote "those, fit matches." Cooper interlined the missing words as CAMAN. A few lines later, the amanuensis again dropped an entire line, but Cooper did not catch that mistake (162.29–30). B did not print that missing line, of course.

When AMS served as copy-text, changes made as CAMAN that differ from AMS/A were typically accepted by the editor as emendations of the copy-text. For example, at 115.19, Cooper had John Effingham say to his brother: "you can have, at least, the consolation of looking at some of your neighbors' houses, and of perceiving that they are a great deal worse off." In CAMAN, he crossed out "worse off" and wrote "uglier." Not noted in AMS or in A, this change was accepted as an emendation to the copy-text. More than 250 changes in Cooper's hand on the amanuensis copy were accepted as emendations in this section of the manuscript where AMS is extant. They were all recorded on the list of Emendations.

Cooper's subtlety and complexity were often hindered by the production process and his own (over)commitments. He did not always proofread carefully enough. For example, in chapter IX, the group traveling to Templeton stops at "The Vision" to enjoy the panoramic view looking out over the lake and toward the village. Aristabulus Bragg tells them that a poet has been frequenting the area; this is, it turns out, Paul Powis. "How do you know he is a poet?" someone asks Bragg. "Why, what else can he be," Bragg responds, since "he has no name?" To which John Effingham replies, "That is a reason in print . . . very few poets having names" (118.27). The compositor at A and the amanuensis both transcribed the word "point" here, instead of the word "print." Now the joke comes into focus: "That is a reason in *print* . . . very few poets having names." Those familiar with the conventions of authorship in the eighteenth and nineteenth centuries will recognize John Effingham's joking reference to anonymous and pseudonymous publication. Cooper himself wrote under the pseudonym A.B.C. in a series of newspaper articles from 1834 to 1836. By returning to AMS and reading with heightened attention, the editor corrected this error.

However, when AMS was the copy-text and a change in CAMAN conflicted with a change made in A, the editor often accepted the variant in A as the emendation, and rejected CAMAN, for reasons stated earlier. For example, at 115.12, Cooper wrote "his own indisposition" in AMS. He changed it to "his indisposition" in A, but to "an indisposition" in CAMAN. The editor accepted the variant in A as an emendation and rejected the variant in CAMAN/B. When a substantive change occurred in CAMAN and a different substantive change to the same word or phrase or sentence occurred in A, the editor's general rule was to accept the change in A as an emendation and reject the variant in CAMAN. Textual notes will explain any significant deviation from this rule.

First American Edition, Lea & Blanchard (A)

The first American edition of *Home as Found* was published by the Philadelphia firm Lea & Blanchard on 15 November 1838.[11] This was one of the first novels published by Lea & Blanchard, successor to the firm of Carey & Lea, which had been publishing Cooper's US editions since 1826. There is relatively little extant correspondence between Cooper and the firm in 1838, probably because Cooper visited Philadelphia a number of times over the course of the year and often talked to the publisher in person.

When AMS is extant, we can clearly see that Cooper made substantive changes somewhere between AMS and A, almost certainly on now-lost proof sheets. His emendations were often simple substitutions of words or phrases intended to sharpen a thought or image: trains that "fly" along a length of track become trains that "rattle" along a length (108.21), "may be" becomes "undoubtedly is" (129.7), "peculiar" becomes "anomalous" (143.16). He also moved clauses and changed tenses. The evidence revealed that at least for the portion of the first volume of the American edition where AMS is extant, he made substantive changes on the proof sheets but ones that would not demand extensive changes in typesetting.

As discussed already, on those occasions when an alteration made by Cooper in A was different from an alteration he made as CAMAN, the editor typically accepted as an emendation the variant in A. Having first written "neglect" at 123.39, to give another example, Cooper altered it to "grave neglect" in A and "serious neglect" in CAMAN. The editor accepted the variant in A as an emendation.

As noted, the compositor at A occasionally failed to read Cooper's handwriting accurately. At 164.37, Cooper wrote that Aristabulus was whispering "apart," and the compositor had him whispering "assent." At 134.35, Cooper wrote the word "any," and the compositor read it as "gay." By studying Cooper's handwriting carefully, the editor corrected a handful of compositorial errors in A. Knowing this to be true, the editor also corrected a handful of compositorial errors in A when AMS was not extant. For example, at 363.39, the compositor at A saw "a nominal" sin, where the amanuensis saw and B printed a "venial" sin. Based on the editor's experience in working with Cooper's handwriting, the amanuensis was almost certainly correct, and the editor corrected that mistake on his own authority, with AMAN as the source of the emendation.

When AMS was not extant, however, we cannot tell with assurance in A whether the compositor (or Cooper) made a particular change to the text. This was especially true at the level of accidentals. The editor assigned responsibility for most changes at the level of accidentals to the compositor, because we know that the publisher imposed house conventions on punctuation and style. But the editor assigned substantive changes to Cooper, under the theory that A's compositor did not have the freedom to make such changes, unlike the compositor at B who seemed in the case of *Home as Found* to have more freedom to alter the text than might normally be expected (as noted already, and see below). Textual evidence bears this out: the American edition hews closely to AMS, and when it deviates it does so through what the editor believes to be lost proof sheets marked by Cooper; the British edition consistently follows AMAN/CAMAN but repeatedly alters it at the level of accidentals and even substantives.

The editor made one very substantial and important change to A as copy-text. The editor moved a 503-word anecdote from its location in A at 254.25 to its appropriate location at 252.4. AMS is not extant at this point in the text, but AMAN/CAMAN demonstrated that Cooper wrote the anecdote as a second thought on a separate sheet of paper, certainly in AMAN and probably in AMS; he directed the compositor working with AMAN/CAMAN to insert it at 252.4. In fact, the amanuensis or Cooper did not include the anecdote in AMAN/CAMAN, or perhaps the compositor did not follow his directions, or perhaps the attached page was lost, because the anecdote was not printed in B. It was printed in A, but not in the location that Cooper had specified in his directive in CAMAN. The conversation between and actions taken by Captain Truck and the "Commodore" in that scene make more sense now that the anecdote is in its proper place.

The comparison of A and B revealed another very substantive difference between the two editions. Near the beginning of volume 2 of the American edition, at 192.7, AMAN and B have 623 words of text that are not printed in A. The editor presumed that Cooper authorized the deletion of these words in A. They are part of a conversation among John Effingham, Ned Effingham, Aristabulus Bragg, and Steadfast Dodge. It is possible that Cooper was already realizing that volume 2 was going to run long in the American edition (and it did), so he deleted them. It is more likely that he had second thoughts about the provocative nature of the conversation taking place at that point, decided to shorten it, and either intended the deletion to apply only to A or made it so late in the production process that B was unaffected. Scholars may wish to read the deleted material in the Rejected Readings list.

First British Edition, Richard Bentley (B)

Cooper mailed the final installment of the amanuensis copy of the novel to Bentley on 25 July 1838. Bentley published the novel on 28 November under the title *Eve Effingham; Or, Home*. It was set from the amanuensis copy, as abundant textual evidence demonstrated. As noted already, there was no evidence that Cooper read proof for this edition or had any hand in its preparation. Therefore, the Bentley edition is nonauthorial.

　　Cooper had used Bentley as his British publisher for more than a decade. At the time, he had been disappointed with Bentley's proofreading of his final volume of European travel writing, *Excursions in Italy* (1838; published in the United States as *Gleanings in Europe: Italy*). As early as summer 1837, Cooper was insisting that Bentley employ a more "vigilant proof-reader" on his works (*L&J* 3:269). While clearly following the amanuensis copy, however, B took many liberties with the text. Repeatedly, the punctuation was altered, phrases were altered or deleted, clauses were moved within sentences, and nouns like "public" were treated as plural. Many of these changes can be explained by Bentley's imposition of a house style and British conventions, but some cannot. Some were substantive changes made by Bentley and, based on all available evidence, not authorized by Cooper. For example, 172.9, Cooper wrote "mentioned" in AMS, and A printed that word; the amanuensis copied the word correctly, but Bentley changed it to "referred to" in B. When AMS is extant, B often altered AMAN/CAMAN in substantive ways: "medallions" became "brackets" (134.5), "put in" became "observed" (131.25), "truer" became "more consistent with truth" (130.14), and "own the property" became "can legally claim it" (184.12).

The editor typically accepted variants in the Bentley edition as emendations only in instances when the conventions of grammar, orthography, or logic dictated the necessity of doing so, and no other witness demonstrated the correct wording or punctuation. Any emendation based on a variant's appearance first in the Bentley edition was accepted as an emendation under the authority of the Cooper Edition. In a few cases, B is adduced as a more correct variant of an emendation authorized by CAMAN. At 170.13, for example, Cooper changed "when" in AMS to "more particularily when" in CAMAN; B printed "more particularly when," and the editor cited it as the first instance of Cooper's (corrected) intent. In that case, the existence of the manuscript witnesses permitted the editor to see that B was emending Cooper's own emendation of AMS in CAMAN. However as noted earlier (see note 9), the editor faced a dilemma in that portion of the text when only the two printed witnesses survive. There, when B deviated from A in substantive ways, the cause might well have been because Cooper authorized a change via CAMAN; but the cause might also have been because B altered the text on its own authority. In the first few chapters of the novel, when neither AMS nor AMAN/CAMAN is extant, the editor accepted a small handful of variants from B as emendations based on his familiarity as editor with Cooper's practices; but many were rejected as unauthorized.

Hinman Collation

According to his correspondence, Cooper contracted with Carey, Lea, and Blanchard in September 1838 to have the first edition of *Home as Found* stereotyped, with the publishing firm to own the plates and the copyright for two years, after which time they would revert to Cooper. His letter was addressed to "Carey, Lea, and Blanchard," but Carey had retired by that time. The firm was already publishing under the imprint of Lea & Blanchard. In the absence of a need for Cooper to authorize a second edition, one would expect to find no substantive variations in copies of *Home as Found* printed during the author's lifetime.

A copy of the first edition owned by Lance Schachterle served as a standard of collation. Two additional copies were collated. One was a copy donated to the American Antiquarian Society (AAS) by the estate of James Franklin Beard; it is cataloged at the AAS as G526 C777 Home 1838 ("Charles A. Taylor" owner). The other was a copy loaned to AAS by the Special Collections Department at the Michigan State University Library; it is cataloged there as PS 1407. H7 1838. No substantive variants in collation were discovered.

Any variants between copies of *Home as Found* may safely be attributed to the wear on the type of the normal printing procedures of the period; none suggests any authorial intervention in the press run of the edition.

Later Editions

Home as Found does not require a stemma. The first American edition published by Lea & Blanchard was stereotyped by J. Fagan, and no further editions were published in Cooper's lifetime. Stringer & Townsend published two "editions" soon after Cooper's death, one in 1852 and one in 1856. Although each was called a "New Edition," both were impressions from the same stereotyped plates created by Fagan. Even as late as 1871, Hurd & Houghton used the plates to create another impression. Townsend reset the novel for the Darley edition in 1860.

On the British side, the edition by Bentley was not reissued in Cooper's lifetime. In 1852, Bentley published a combined edition of *Homeward Bound* and *Home as Found*, under the title *Homeward Bound*. He erased all traces that the second novel was a sequel, keeping the thirty-four chapters of *Homeward Bound* intact, and then suturing to them eight chapters from *Home as Found*. The sutured chapters are focused solely on bringing the romance of Paul and Eve to its conclusion. The single edition was a manageable 404 pages in length.

There were two German translations of *Home as Found* in Cooper's lifetime (*Evchen Effingham, oder die Heimath: ein Fortsetzung "der Heimfahrt"*, Frankfurt: J. D. Sauerländer, 1839; and *Eve Effingham*, Stuttgart: Liesching, 1846), one French translation (*Eve Effingham*, Paris: Charles Gosselin, 1839), and one Dutch translation (*Eva Effingham, of Schetsen van Amerikaansche Zeden*, Zutphen: W. J. Thieme, 1841). An English edition was also published in France (Paris: Baudry's European Library, 1839), but there is no evidence in his correspondence that Cooper was involved in its production. The editor did not treat it as a witness.

Conclusion

The present edition of *Home as Found* is an eclectic text. Using the author's holograph manuscript as a copy-text when it exists, and elsewhere the first American edition, which Cooper read and emended in proof sheets, this edition corrects numerous errors introduced by the compositor at Lea & Blanchard and incorporates improvements that Cooper authorized as he proofed the amanuensis copy, including a substantial change to the placement of an anecdote in chapter XIX.

Collation of the witnesses revealed two important facts. Early in the novel, especially, when only A and B are extant, the substantial differences between the American and British editions stand in stark relief. In the first five or so chapters of the novel, before either of the handwritten witnesses is extant, there are nearly 700 substantive differences between the editions. Some are minor, like "contemplation" and "contemplations" at 13.33, but others are more substantial, as when either the amanuensis or the compositor in London left out what was probably an entire line of manuscript at 30.27–29. Throughout the novel, B's variants compared to A were caused by emendations made by Cooper to A, by nonauthorial mistranscriptions in AMAN, by authorial emendations in CAMAN, by mistakes made by the compositor at Bentley, and by substantive alterations made by someone at Bentley. But in the apparatus for this early section of the novel, the cause is unknown and irrelevant; one can simply see the difference between the two editions in the long list of rejected readings from B (and the much shorter list of emendations from B). Indeed, a few variants in B were accepted as emendations in the first five-plus chapters of the novel, when only A and B are extant, either to correct obvious errors or because it seemed likely that the compositor at A was mistaken or the editor felt confident that B's reading was more true to Cooper's intent. The editor provided a Textual Note where the logic was not obvious. To the many substantive differences between the published editions, we can add the fact that Bentley often changed Cooper's punctuation and spelling (at the level of accidentals, and thus those cases are not recorded as rejected readings), did not offer the reader a preface, and changed the title. In many ways, the American edition and the British edition are two very different texts, and present a messy but fascinating study in textual transmission in the Victorian period. Even as early as chapter I, this becomes a problem: in the American edition, the Effinghams' house in Manhattan is in Hudson Square, in the British edition it is on State Street, a dozen blocks farther south from Hudson Square. (See the Explanatory Note at 6.29.) It is impossible to tell whether Cooper finally preferred one over the other or whether he intended the location to be different in the two editions.

In collation, a second fact emerged most clearly when AMS is the copy-text and AMAN/CAMAN survive as witnesses. Here, one can see Cooper working quickly but efficiently. He wrote steadily and without a lot of false starts. He clearly had a large structure in mind and a concept of small-scale actions (dinner parties, conversations, the trip on the lake, etc.) that would propel his characters to the romantic resolution at the end of the novel. At one point in chapter XIX, probably after he had completed a first draft of the chapter (or section of that chapter), he interpolated a short fable into a conversation; we know this because he had to direct his amanuensis to interpolate it into her manuscript, meaning she had already written ahead to the end of the conversation. In the six-plus chapters for which AMS survives, that is only moment when Cooper substantially rethought his own first intention. He also checked his daughters' transcription in AMAN fairly carefully, though perhaps not as rigorously as he might have, correcting their work and tinkering with his own phrasing and emphasis. Prior to the publication of the first American edition, he also certainly emended the text on proof sheets from the printer in Philadelphia, again tinkering with phrasing and emphasis. What we can see very clearly in this section of the novel when all of the witnesses are extant is a remarkably confident writer who wished to make an argument about his country but nevertheless wanted to let the plot dictate the action. His substantive revisions sharpened and clarified ideas, but the "true picture" was substantially whole from the very beginning.

NOTES

1. James Franklin Beard, ed., *The Letters and Journals of James Fenimore Cooper*, 6 vols. (Cambridge: Belknap Press of Harvard University Press, 1960–68), 3:269. Cited parenthetically hereafter as *L&J*.

2. The two novels were *The Last of the Mohicans* (1826) and *The Prairie* (1827).

3. See the Historical Introduction for a discussion of the contemporary reception of the novel.

4. The extant correspondence tells us less about Cooper's negotiations with his US publisher because, as he wrote to the firm in August 1838, "we will settle . . . when I see you" in Philadelphia (*L&J* 3:335).

5. Robert E. Spiller and Philip C. Blackburn, *A Descriptive Bibliography of the Writings of James Fenimore Cooper* (New York: R. R. Bowker, 1934), 9.

6. Lea & Blanchard was the successor firm to Carey & Lea, which had published Cooper's US editions from 1826 to September 1838.

7. In 1838, Cooper's four daughters were between the ages of nineteen and twenty-five. They were almost certainly not paid for their work. The editor cannot tell which daughter transcribed which section of the text, although it is clear that four different hands were involved.

8. There is also a very short section in chapter IX where AMS is torn, and A serves as copy-text. See the Textual Note at 112.1–5.

9. It is important here to crystallize the editorial dilemma. In the first five-plus chapters of the text, we have been left with only Lea & Blanchard (A) and Bentley (B). There are nearly 700 substantive differences between the two editions in these chapters. Some variants can be attributed to compositors' mistakes, and some as just noted must be attributed to editorial changes made by Bentley and not specifically authorized by Cooper. However, judging by the evidence when all witnesses are extant, many are the product of a change made by Cooper as CAMAN (printed only in B) or on the lost proof sheets (thus printed only in A). Often, then, in these early chapters it is undecidable which variant to accept because both were authorized by Cooper. This problem can best be exemplified from examples when all the witnesses are extant. At 118.32, for example, Cooper wrote the word "suspicious" in AMS, then revised it to "suspicious circumstances" in CAMAN. Following AMS, Lea & Blanchard printed "suspicious"; following C/AMAN, Bentley printed "suspicious circumstances." The editor followed B in this case, accepting "suspicious circumstances" as Cooper's revision of his initial thought in AMS. If no witnesses were available, we would be forced to choose between A's "suspicious" and B's "suspicious circumstances" without knowing what Cooper initially or finally authorized; we would just know that he authorized both. To take another example, at 120.5, Cooper wrote "wish" in AMS and emended it to "desire" (via the lost proof sheets) in Lea & Blanchard. Without the manuscript witnesses, we would be forced to choose between A's "desire" and B's "wish." In this case, the editor followed A because Cooper's emendation on the lost proof sheet was his final thought, but we would have no way of knowing that without the witnesses. In general, the editor has taken a conservative approach in these early chapters when only A and B are extant, hewing closely to A as the copy-text and emending it only in the types of cases enumerated.

10. Following the editorial guidelines of the Cooper Edition, Cooper's citations for epigraphs in the copy-text were emended to identify author, title, and position of quotation in the work from which it derived.

11. The *Bibliography of American Literature*, 9 vols (New Haven: Yale University Press, 1955-1991), records two possible printings of the first edition. The compiler, Jacob Blanck, comments that one extant copy of the Lea & Blanchard first edition includes "a notice dated November, 1838, regarding the paper on which the book is printed" (item 3883, 2: 290). The editor was not able to locate and inspect an edition that includes that notice. However, it was almost certainly not a new printing. Cooper does not mention the need for a new printing in his correspondence, and sales were disappointing. The first edition was stereotyped, as noted on the copyright page; all reprintings in Cooper's lifetime were from those plates.

Textual Notes

6.29   The author's manuscript (AMS) and the Lea & Blanchard edition (A) locate the Effinghams' townhouse in Hudson Square in lower Manhattan, the Bentley edition (B) on State Street more than a dozen blocks farther south. See the explanatory note for information on those two neighborhoods in the 1830s. See the Textual Commentary for the dilemma presented by B, which contains many emendations clearly authorized by Cooper via his corrections to the amanuensis copy, but also many variants not authorized by him.

8.5   "Revival" is more accurate than "commencement" here. Their (former) intimacy commenced in childhood; it will be revived in this scene and in the rest of the novel. The Cooper Edition (CE) accepts the variant in B as an emendation. Here and elsewhere through 76.24, variants in B are accepted as emendations on the authority of CE.

8.12   CE follows A here, but it is a case where possibly the compositor at Lea & Blanchard or the amanuensis misread Cooper's manuscript. In his handwriting, "the natural" would have looked very similar to "their mutual."

10.6   Based on the logic of the conversation between Grace and Eve, CE accepts the variant in B as an emendation. Grace is picking up on Eve's observation that Americans like to "protest" their contempt for the opinions of travelers to the United States. It makes sense for her to say that we "protest our disdain [for those travelers' books] a little too strenuously." In that phrasing, "protest" is a transitive verb and "disdain" is the direct object. In the rejected phrasing in A, "protest" and "disdain" are both intransitive verbs, allowable for "protest" but not for "disdain." The editor believes the compositor at Lea & Blanchard misread Cooper's handwriting here ("and" for "our").

10.32   Both "two" and "too" make sense here. CE follows A.

11.9   The compositor at Lea & Blanchard no doubt intended to place a hyphen here, as "them" is the last word on page 14 of A and "selves" is the first word on page 15. But the hyphen is missing.

11.14   A has a comma after "quiet," B does not. Both make sense, because "quiet" can serve as a noun or as an adjective. Without the comma, Eve is saying that two things (quiet restraint and good tone) are preferred; with the comma, she is saying that three things (quiet, restraint, and good tone) are preferred.

12.17   The single quotation marks in B indicate correctly that Eve is reading from the manuscript book.

14.18   CE follows B here. The narrator is describing Bragg's unease around the more sophisticated Eve. Upon meeting him, she has immediately put him at a distance. Hoping to marry her, he recognizes that he will have to move carefully. This is tactful, not tasteful. The editor believes that the compositor at Lea & Blanchard misread Cooper's handwriting: "taste" for "a tact."

14.26   CE follows B here. Bragg's caution is being compared to the caution of a rebuked schoolgirl, which the variant in B makes clear.

14.33   This is a strange variant in B. The phrasing there suggests that in speech and in thought, Bragg is Eve's equal, whereas in A his thoughts are finished and clear but his "accents" are not. Cooper could well have written "refined and harmonious" in AMS; it is the sort of mistake he sometimes made in manuscript composition. The amanuensis might have overlooked his emendation of her copy, or he made the emendation on the proof sheets for A.

16.3   CE follows B here and in the next line. Bragg and Grace are both referring to Eve's comment that she did not know that the imitations (plural) of ancient architecture were owing to republicanism (singular). The pronouns that follow refer to imitations, not republicanism, as B makes clear.

17.20   This is the sort of emendation that Cooper would have made to AMS. The word "so" is repeated in the sentence, and the variant in B deletes the repetition and sharpens the language.

17.29   CE follows B here. Eve is saying that inexperienced travelers cannot know the value of what they see and that it would be ironic if they were the only ones who could "criticise" (or say). The compositor at Lea & Blanchard read "say" for "see." The two words probably looked quite similar in Cooper's handwriting.

19.25   Cooper and/or the compositor altered this sentence substantially in B. Here, the indefinite pronoun "one" in A might indeed cause readers some confusion. It seems at first glance to refer to Bragg, but in fact refers to "someone" or "anyone" or a "person" who could overlook Bragg's "prurient politeness." The meaning is clear enough when the reader takes "one" to be "someone" or "anyone." In B, the indefinite pronoun is changed to an "observer" (of Bragg). In this single sentence, there are five substantive variants between A and B. CE follows A in all of them. See the next sentence in the novel.

19.28   In A, the narrator's claim that "It is true" is followed by two noun clauses; the second noun clause begins with "that," the first does not. Cooper or the compositor at Bentley emended the sentence to make the clauses parallel. Here,

CE accepts the variant in B as an emendation, correcting a grammatical mistake in A.

22.5   B has a dropped "t" here, thus "he" instead of the intended "the."

23.39   CE follows B here. Bragg's metaphor implies that "entire" families uprooted themselves because of the desire to move west during the real estate speculation boom of the mid-1830s. In Cooper's handwriting, those two words probably looked quite similar.

24.38   Because the word is italicized, it presumably refers to the French word *naïveté*, which has both diacritical marks. CE follows B here. See also 39.36.

29.15   A has "desired" here, B "decided." This is probably a case in which the amanuensis misread Cooper's handwriting. The two words would have looked quite similar.

33.26   Eve uses the indefinite article for every other item in this extended comparison, so CE follows B here.

36.33   CE follows B here, clarifying that the narrator is referring to the "first two [of three] visits," rather than two first visits.

36.36   CE follows B here. The narrator seems to be referring in the singular to the plan ("project") to include Truck in the first two visits while excluding Bragg. That may be conceived as two different plans (and thus "projects"), but it seems more likely that the compositor or the amanuensis misread Cooper's handwriting.

46.4   The editor follows the spelling in A here because Cooper intended the name of the city to be mispronounced by Mrs. Jarvis.

46.11   The "l" was dropped in A.

48.9   In English, a native speaker might say "perforce." But the phrase is italicized in the A and B, meaning it is the French *par force*, or "by force."

51.1   The variant here and in the next line was almost certainly caused by Cooper's handwriting; "factious" and "faction" would have looked identical, as would "Fractious" and "Fractions." CE follows B. The two adjectives (factious/ Fractious) make better sense in the context of the conversation.

54.29   In A, the plural noun ("knowledge and cleverness") becomes singular ("It") in the next sentence. It seems likely that Cooper emended the two sentences, so CE follows B here.

59.18   Cooper likely revised this sentence to delete the awkward repetition of the word *but*.

73.40   CE follows B here. The context in the previous paragraph makes "distinction" a more likely word choice, perhaps a change that Cooper made to CAMAN but did not make to AMS.

75.3   CE follows B here. The sentence is not grammatically correct without the addition of "and."

76.28   CE follows A here, indicating that John Effingham is quoting someone. The editor could not locate a specific source. Cooper might have had Goethe or Kant in mind. In the amanuensis copy, a double quotation mark preceding "an intuitive perception of things in their real colours" is crossed out, and the sentence ends with the usual double quotation mark, indicating the end of John Effingham's explanation to Eve. The cross out may or may not be authorial. The fact that Cooper deleted the word "all" in A suggests that he approved the sentence as is.

81.32   Here and with "enrol" at 81.35, CE follows Cooper's use of spellings more common in England than in the

United States. Webster's 1828 *American Dictionary of the English Language* indicates that these words should be spelled "shyly" and "enroll." Cooper will sometimes adopt American usages, sometimes British. American English and culture were in transition, and his spellings—and many other elements of his novels—reflect that fact.

83.35   CE emends A here. The amanuensis transcribed the word as "permits," while the compositor at Lea & Blanchard set the word as "points." Both words make a certain amount of sense, and in Cooper's handwriting they would have looked quite similar. The editor takes Pith's point to be that he writes when the weather "allows him to" (permits), not when the weather "directs him to" (points). Interestingly, the compositor at B also set the word as "points," even though the amanuensis clearly wrote "permits."

84.10   In Cooper's handwriting, "rogue" might well look like "odist" (or "odeist"), but CE follows A here. Pindar *is* the writer of an occasional ode. See 81.18.

85.35   This is one of many places where two variants are authorial: "am apt to" in A and "commonly" in CAMAN. Because A is the copy-text here, CE follows it.

87.32   The amanuensis wrote "ponding" here, almost certainly a mis-transcription of "pondering." On AMAN, Cooper emended the mis-transcription to "pausing."

88.27   CE follows A here. The amanuensis left a blank spot at the end of a line here, big enough for one word, expecting that her father would fill in the correct word as he proofed her copy. "Byronic" may have been a word she could not decipher, or Cooper emended his original thought on the proof sheets.

93.29   B makes the verb plural here, but A and AMAN have it as singular. The list of three things can be considered collectively, as parts of a single phenomenon, so CE follows A.

96.2   CE follows A here. On CAMAN, Cooper made two changes at 96.1–2: he changed a comma after "friendly" to a period, and he added the clause "the time . . . proper home." He was either responding to a mistranscription of AMS by the amanuensis (who might have omitted the word "him"), which the compositor at Lea & Blanchard read correctly; or he emended AMS differently on the proof sheets.

97.29   CE follows A's "one pin knocked out of so frail and delicate a fabric." The image derives from weaving. The amanuensis wrote that the pin is "knocked over," and B followed. To knock "over" a pin is a bowling image, and it mixes the metaphor (bowling, fabric) in a way that does not seem authorial.

98.2   Both "flushes" and "flashes" make sense here. CE follows A, where "flushes" means "to become suddenly red; to glow" (Webster's 1828 *American Dictionary of the English Language*).

98.22   Today we might say that the flames were brought "under control," and the comma in A suggests that the sentence in AMS may have ended with another word like "control." But at the time the phrasal verb "get under" was used in reference to controlling a fire. CE follows AMAN.

98.29   CE follows AMAN (and B) here in reading the word as "insecurity." Both "insecurity" and "insanity" make a certain amount of sense, but the investors' sudden loss of wealth points most directly to its "insecurity." The amanuensis's handwriting is clear, and given Cooper's typically crabbed handwriting it seems probable that the compositor at Lea & Blanchard read "insanity" for Cooper's "insecurity."

99.21   The amanuensis wrote "home" instead of "hours," triggering Cooper's addition on AMAN of "their time at." That variant is rejected in favor of what was almost certainly Cooper's initial wording.

102.19   The amanuensis wrote "man, man" which is surely a mis-transcription of Cooper's "mammon." See 97.38. Because the amanuensis did not capitalize the initial *m*, the editor assumes that Cooper wrote the word without the initial capital. A no doubt capitalized the word to conform to their house style. CE rejects CAMAN's variant, "money merely," because Cooper was trying to fix the amanuensis's mis-transcription of his original intent.

104.36   There are three authorial variants here. The variant in A might well have been caused by the compositor's mis-transcription, since in AMS "a" looks a bit like "its." The amanuensis transcribed AMS correctly ("that a discussion"), and because the word "that" is then crossed out, CE follows CAMAN. All three variants are listed on the Emendations list for the sake of clarity.

105.12   The compositor at Lea & Blanchard misread Cooper's handwriting here.

106.17   CAMAN is the authority here, because Cooper added the clause in AMAN.

106.37   Cooper edited AMS here, changing "the same" to "quite as much." But he forgot to mark out "same," leaving "quite as much same." However, the amanuensis correctly transcribed "quite as much." Then Cooper emended the amanuensis' transcription to "just as much."

109.16   On AMS, Cooper lightly marked out the word "for" and inked a period heavily over his initial comma. The amanuensis and the compositor at Bentley read his intentions correctly, the compositor at Lea & Blanchard did not.

110.10   CE follows A here. The amanuensis mistranscribed the word "pure" in this sentence, which triggered Cooper's change on the amanuensis copy.

111.14   Often, in this section of the novel for which AMS is extant, CE accepts substantive variants in A under the theory that Cooper authorized emendations on now-lost proof sheets. Here, the compositor almost certainly misread AMS where "spot" was lightly marked out and "place" written above it. Cooper had noticed that he used the word "spot" twice in the same sentence.

111.20   Cooper's handwriting is difficult to decipher here: the compositor at Lea & Blanchard read "trial," the amanuensis read "toil." The latter makes better sense in this context.

112.1   AMS is torn at the bottom of a page, and A serves as the copy-text from 112.1 ("It is known") to 112.5 ("the eye").

112.5   A is the copy-text for a few lines here, and CE follows it. The amanuensis appears to have written that the view was even with "the eyes," not with "the eye" as in A. Cooper emended the apparent mis-transcription by changing it to "their eyes."

116.39   Cooper clearly emended "marred" on the amanuensis copy. It is not clear why he made what is essentially a visual change in the word.

118.27   Cooper's joke here has been lost to all readers of the novel until now, because the amanuensis and the compositor at Lea & Blanchard both read Cooper's "print" as "point." Those familiar with the conventions authorship in the eighteenth and nineteenth centuries would recognize John Effingham's joking reference here to anonymous and pseudonymous publication. Cooper himself wrote under the pseudonym "A.B.C." in a series of newspaper articles from 1834 to 1836.

119.29   The emendation made by Cooper on AMAN is noted on the Emendations list, but for the sake of clarity we also list the variant authorized by Cooper in A.

120.27   Cooper crossed out "little" on AMAN, but neglected to mark out the article "a." The compositor at B deleted the article. But see the Rejected Readings list here, as B went on to reverse the next two clauses.

120.34   Another case where Cooper altered both handwritten manuscripts but the changes are not identical. CE follows the change made in A.

121.18   The entry has been listed this way for the sake of clarity. Cooper added these two sentences to AMAN and thus has authorized them. But he made a small mistake in writing them ("But it was it a ruling trait") that B corrected; however B did not spell Aristabulus's name correctly. Thus the passage as a whole is emended on the authority of CE.

125.6   Lightly marked out on AMS and overlooked by the compositor at Lea & Blanchard.

127.13   It seems likely here that the compositor at Lea & Blanchard misread Cooper's handwriting.

134.4   The compositor at Lea & Blanchard misread Cooper's handwriting here, reading "gay" for "any."

138.27   The compositor at Lea & Blanchard misread Cooper's handwriting here, reading "would" for "could."

146.26   Cooper altered both manuscripts here, adding a clause above the line in each case ("to . . . its proper force"). However, the two changes were not identical: he wrote "feel" in AMS, "entertain" in CAMAN. CE follows AMS.

147.40   Cooper originally wrote "very" before "modest" in AMS, but then he crossed it out, no doubt because the word occurs in the next clause. The compositor at Lea & Blanchard missed his lightly marked deletion.

151.39   Another case in which Cooper made changes on both AMS and AMAN, but they were not identical.

153.37   With a different pen on AMS, Cooper interlined "in this country." The compositor at Lea & Blanchard ignored his emendation.

158.31   This seems like a curious omission in A and was probably not authorized by Cooper. Grace is looking through works convenient for a traveler to own; "books" is too general. The compositor overlooked the word "road" here, just has he missed the "ed" crossed out on "professed" a few lines earlier in AMS.

162.27   Cooper began to write "inhabitants" here, but only got as far as "inhab" before crossing it out and writing "tenants." The compositor at Lea & Blanchard read the word as "inhabitants."

164.37   The words "assent" and "apart" look similar in Cooper's handwriting. The compositor at Lea & Blanchard read "assent," but the context here suggests that Cooper intended "apart."

166.34   Cooper added the clause above the line in AMS, leaving two punctuation marks intact. Since "Ought" in the next sentence is capitalized, CE chooses to accept the dash rather than the comma. The other witnesses variously tried a comma, a colon, and a period.

172.17   In A, Cooper emended AMS by deleting "with vigorous arms." He also retained a clear subject and verb ("they soon urged the boat"). On AMAN, Cooper tinkered with the sentence as well, retaining "with vigorous arms," changing "and" to "when," and deleting the pronoun "they." The compositor at Bentley recognized a problem with the sentence as Cooper altered it, and made it clear that Paul and Templemore "urged" the boat from the shore. CE accepts the entire sentence as Cooper emended it in A, rather than trying to mix and match the variants from Cooper's two different attempts to alter the sentence. The rejected readings are listed with emendations for the sake of clarity.

173.7   The compositor at Lea & Blanchard did not notice that Cooper had crossed out the word "all" on AMS.

174.26   In AMS Cooper clearly has Eve respond to the commodore's "sogdollager" by saying "socdollager" with a "c." And the first "g" in sogdollager at 174.23 has been emphasized, as if Cooper traced the letter twice. The *Oxford English Dictionary* and the *Dictionary of American Regional English* cite both spellings in their entries on the word, as well as the spelling "sockdollager."

175.10   Cooper clearly wrote "surrended" here, and he actually corrected the amanuensis's transcription of "surrendered." "Surrend" was obsolete long before 1838, but the editor presumes that he intended the commodore to be speaking colloquially or archaically.

179.33   Twice in this paragraph, the compositor at Lea & Blanchard misread AMS, not seeing the crossed-out "and" here and, a few lines later, reading "falling" for "fearful."

185.37   This emendation is not authorized by any witnesses. Cooper apparently intended the word "always" (in quotation marks) to serve as a noun; it seems parallel to "time immemorial" in the next clause. The editor believes that he intended to say that to Americans, "always" is equivalent to a mere eighteen months, just as (to Americans) "time immemorial" is equivalent to the time since the last crisis in the market. In the sentence that he wrote, however, "Americans" is a noun, and "always" can be mistaken by the reader for an adverb modifying "means," even though the scare quotes are meant to call attention to "always" as a noun.

192.6   Here, AMAN (and thus B) includes more than 600 words of dialogue between John, Ned, Aristabulus, and Steadfast that are omitted from A. Since A is the copy-text at this point, that material is rejected under the assumption that for some reason Cooper authorized its deletion in A. See the discussion in Textual Commentary.

196.23   CE follows AMAN here because the context seems to call for the plural "rights." The compositor at Lea & Blanchard probably misread Cooper's handwriting.

208.31   Both "like" and "unlike" make sense here, because Noah sent the same dove out twice. The first time it returned with nothing, telling him that the dove could not find a place to land. The second time it returned with a green twig, telling him that the flood had receded enough for dry land to appear. CE follows A.

224.15   CE follows B here. Eve is referring to Captain Truck, in the singular.

230.37   Cooper tinkered with this exchange (229.26–231.29) on AMAN and (apparently) on the proof sheets of A. CE largely follows A. At 230.14, John reads the first letter and hands it to Paul. Paul glances "his eye over" it, and then sets it aside. John hands him letter two at 230.33, and Paul reads it at 230.37. Cooper was right in A to change the pronouns to the singular. Paul is reading letter two; he then lays it down, waiting "for the next," which must be a single letter ("which was," not "which were").

252.4   At this point in AMAN, a note in Cooper's hand instructs the amanuensis and printer to "(Insert here, (page 132 twice))." Cooper then emended the next sentence to say that the commodore started speaking again "as soon as he had recovered breath" (at 253.19). The editor believes the commodore must have "recovered" from his laughing fit at the end of the little fable that Cooper intended to move to this point in the manuscript. In AMS, he almost certainly wrote the fable after he completed the first draft of all or part of the chapter without it, adding a second page 132 ("page 132 twice") in his consecutively numbered sequence because the fable was an afterthought. Obviously, AMS is not extant at this point to verify this, but the internal evidence here is strong that he emended AMAN to include the fable at this point, not at 254.27 as in A. The problem was that the amanuensis did not transcribe the fable on the second page 132. Thus, for this section, A serves as the copy-text and there are no variants because the fable was not included in the amanuensis copy or in Bentley. However, the entire section 252.5–253.18 in A is also an emendation authorized by Cooper in the amanuensis copy, in the sense that it has been moved from its location in A (following "offer the ladies our homage" at 254.26) to its new location in CE following "lost all his awe of his companion." This is done on the authority of the directive in Cooper's hand on AMAN. Without AMS in hand, the editor theorizes that Cooper added the captain's fable to his narrative after the amanuensis had made her copy of the chapter, or even of the entire volume; that would explain why she (and the compositor at Bentley) did not include it. It is also possible that she copied it (also on a separate page) only to have it become separated from the manuscript at the typesetting stage in London.

254.26   See note at 252.4. Cooper's emendation here brings the chapter to a close, following his directive to move the anecdote. In A, the anecdote now follows after the word "homage." It is not recorded in its entirety on the list of rejected readings.

258.29   This seems to be a misreading by the compositor at Lea & Blanchard. Why would Grace shake her "hands and head" at this moment? No doubt, Cooper's handwriting made "handsome head" look like "hands and head."

258.40   Here, too, the compositor at Lea & Blanchard seems to have misread Cooper's handwriting. CE follows AMAN.

281.5   Cooper added the adjective "full" to "justice" on the amanuensis copy, apparently without noticing that the adverb "fully" soon follows. Bentley choose not to print the adjective.

289.3   The amanuensis correctly wrote "you" here. Truck is speaking to David, who might cross the Atlantic again someday (with Truck). Truck himself is planning to cross in a few weeks. The compositor may have misread the author's manuscript here.

300.39 The amanuensis began a new paragraph here, whereas the compositor at Lea & Blanchard did not. In AMS, Cooper did not always generously indent the first line of a paragraph. CE follows the amanuensis here, believing that the compositor overlooked an indentation that indicated that Cooper wanted a paragraph break.

305.6 Because this entire sentence in A is so different from the one in AMAN (see as well the rejected readings at 305.2 and 305.5), the editor follows the sentence in the copy-text in its entirety, rejecting this authorial variant.

349.29 Bentley tried to fix this clause, which is not grammatically correct. Cooper might have intended John's emotions to be reflected in his ungrammatical speech, or he might not have been writing or editing carefully. CE follows A.

356.30 From Cooper's crabbed handwriting, the amanuensis and the compositor at Lea & Blanchard made two different kinds of sense here. CE follows the amanuensis, whose transcription emphasizes the male and female gossips in small-town Templeton.

363.39 As at 356.30, the editor believes that the amanuensis read Cooper's handwriting correctly here.

372.10 The editor believes that the amanuensis read Cooper's handwriting correctly here.

375.24 "Aristabulus Dodge" is clearly a mistake in A. The amanuensis's transcription suggests that Cooper might have intended to place all three characters (Bragg, Dodge, and Mrs. Abbott) in the church and that the compositor at Lea & Blanchard simply overlooked the "Mr." in AMS. However, the next sentence refers to two characters ("neither"), not three. The editor assumes that Cooper intended to place Dodge at the church, since he mentions that "neither" of these two characters belonged to Eve's church and we know from chapter X that Aristabulus did belong to it.

382.4   In AMAN, Cooper corrected the amanuensis's (probably accurate) transcription of "Wenlock." At that point, Cooper was unsure of the name he had assigned to this character. He wrote "Wenham" on the amanuensis copy, and then to be sure added a note for the printer: "(put this name as it is in the former sheets)."

Emendations

The following list records all changes introduced to the copy-texts. The reading of the Cooper Edition (CE) appears to the left of the square bracket. The source for that reading appears to the right of the bracket, followed by a semicolon, the copy-text reading, and the copy-text symbol. If not listed, the readings of texts that fall between the copy-text and the source cited for the readings of the Cooper edition may be presumed to agree substantively with the copy-text reading. If an intervening reading does not agree substantively with the copy-text, that intervening reading and its symbol are recorded after the copy-text reading and its symbol.

Several conventions and sigla appear in the Emendations list of *Home as Found* for the reader's convenience and information. In an entry, the curved dash ~ represents the exact word that appears before the square bracket and is used in recording punctuation and paragraphing variants. A caret ^ to the right of the square bracket signals the absence of a mark of punctuation on the left. An asterisk * indicates that the reading is discussed in the Textual Notes.

The following texts of *Home as Found* are referred to:

A, Philadelphia: Lea & Blanchard, 1838
B, London: Bentley, 1838
AMS, Author's holograph manuscript (partial)
AMAN, Amanuensis copy of author's manuscript (partial)
CAMAN, Cooper's editorial changes to AMAN

Volume 1

Title page   "Thou art perfect." Prince Henry, *Henry IV, Part 1*, 2.4.35.]CE; *Pr. Hen.* "Thou art perfect." A

3.13	"Homeward Bound"]CE; 'Homeward Bound' A
5.7	coz."]B; coz. ^ A
5.10	*Much Ado About Nothing* 3.4.39–40.]CE; Shakspeare. A
6.33	*chère*]B; *chere* A
6.39	*chère*]B *chere* A
*8.5	revival]B; commencement A
9.39	by-ways]B; bye-ways A
*10.6	our disdain]B; and ~ A
10.13	the travellers]B; them A
10.23	by society you meant those unpleasant crowds]B; you meant those unpleasant crowds, by society A
11.2	'ulterior intentions']B; " ~ ~ " A
*11.9	themselves]B; them selves A
12.12	*Oui, Mademoiselle*]B; Oui, Mademoiselle A
*12.17	"'Mr. . . . estate.']B; "Mr. . . . estate." A
14.8	speaking first]B; first speaking A
*14.18	a tact]B; taste A
*14.26	as that with which a]B; as a A
*16.3	they]B; it A
16.4	these imitations are]B; it is A
17.1	likely to erect a complicated house]B; apt to cause a complicated house to be erected A
17.2	probable, have]B; likely, apt to have A
*17.20	desire that I should keep]B; show so much interest in my keeping A
*17.29	see]B; say A
19.8	'a has . . . 'a goes]CE; he ~ . . . he ~ A
19.10	*Much Ado About Nothing* 3.3.125–127.]CE; *Much Ado About Nothing.* A
*19.28	true, that he invited those near him to eat of everything he could reach, but he used his knife as a coal-heaver uses a shovel; the company he was in, however,]B; true, he asked every one near him to eat of every thing he could himself reach, and that he used knife as a coal-heaver uses a shovel; but the company he was in, A
19.40	the delay and dignity of this arrangement]B; there were a delay and a finish in this arrangement that A
20.16	an epitome]B; a sample epitome A
22.28	cities."]B; ~ . ^ A

23.25	laws did not actually prohibit]B; law did not actually punish A
*23.39	entire]B; active A
*24.38	*naïveté*]B; *naiveté* A
29.7	beautiful.]CE; ~ ! A
29.9	*A Midsummer Night's Dream* 3.1.148.]CE; Shakspeare. A
31.2	*La république*]CE; *Le republique* A, *La republique* B
32.10	Russell Squares]B; Russel ~ A
32.32	*américaines*]CE; *Americaines* A, *Américaines* B
*33.26	a history]B; history A
36.12	*coteries*]B; *côteries* A
*36.33	first two]B; two first A
*36.36	project]B; projects A
38.7	Ready." / "And I." / "And I." / "And I." / "Where]CE; Ready." / "And I." / "And I." / "Where A
38.16	*A Midsummer Night's Dream* 3.1.163.]CE; Midsummer-Night's Dream A
39.23	countrywomen how greatly the peace of mind of an American woman is endangered by transplanting her] B; countrywomen, the great hazards of destroying her peace of mind, that are incurred by transplanting an American woman A
39.36	*naïveté*]B; *naiveté* A
40.36	latter]B; latter's A
41.7	wife, on the other hand, not unfrequently expressed]B; wife expressed A
45.15	but as soon as she did she overwhelmed her]B; and even she was covered A
*46.11	nearly]B; near y A
46.20	"lion"]B; ' ~ ' A
46.21	"blue"]CE; ' ~ ' A
*48.9	*par*]B; *per* A
49.34	aged black servant]B; an aged black A
*51.1	factious]B; faction A
51.2	Fractious]B; Fractions A
*54.29	fancied Mrs. Bloomfield superior to those of her own sex whom she had so often admired abroad: for her knowledge and cleverness were untrammelled either]B; even fancied Mrs. Bloomfield's knowledge and cleverness

	superior to those which she had so often admired in her own sex abroad. It was untrammelled, equally A
56.7	out, / And never gives to truth and virtue that]CE; out; / And never gives to truth and virtue, that A
56.11	*Much Ado About Nothing* 3.1.68–70.]CE; Much Ado About Nothing. A
57.26	*chevaux*]B; *chevau* A
*59.18	We must not lose the precious moments, however,]B; but we will not waste the precious moments, A
59.22	*dites-moi*]B; *dîtes moi* A
62.21	"entertained"]B; ' ~ ' A
62.29	"entertained"]B; ' ~ ' A
64.9	than on]B; than A
64.36	"entertainees"]B; ' ~ ' A
65.3	already,]B; ~ ; A
65.13	recall]B; recal A
66.21	*présent*]B; *present* A
69.25	"make . . . shines;"]B; 'make . . . shines;' A
69.37	"under orders,"]B; 'under orders,' A
72.7	is *The most lamentable comedy and most cruel death of Pyramus and Thisby.*"]CE; is the most lamentable / Comedy, and most cruel death of Pyramus and / Thisby." A
72.10	*A Midsummer Night's Dream* 1.2.11–12.]CE; Peter Quince. A, B
72.22	everywhere met]CE; every where ~ A
*73.40	a distinction]B; an illustration A
74.5	to converse with in each of the dialects with which she was familiar]B; with whom to converse in each of her dialects A
*75.3	and every]B; every A
75.30	"Author . . . Tweedle,"]CE; 'Author . . . Tweedle', A

A remains the copy-text; AMAN/CAMAN are extant as additional witnesses from 76.24 to the end of the text.

78.20	*tenue*]AMAN; *tenu* A
79.11	company, in order that she might know their persons at least.]CAMAN; company. A
79.15	intellectual refinement and unequalled modesty]

	CAMAN; refinement and modesty A
81.16	here, but yourself,]CAMAN; here A
81.38	sentiment, in his time,]CAMAN; sentiment A; sentiment in his time B
82.13	among us like a green bay tree]CAMAN; like a bay tree among us A; among us like a bay tree AMAN
82.19	very longing]CAMAN; longing A
82.26	who, having]CAMAN; who ^ having A
82.29	corner, as I hope to be saved.]CAMAN; corner. A
82.38	person—"which is more than happens to every lion that is caged."]CAMAN; person. A
83.1	all I have done]CAMAN; all A
83.23	something equally clever]CAMAN; something A, AMAN; something clever B
83.29	*Injee*]CAMAN; Injee A
83.30	stun'-sails]CAMAN; stun'sails A
*83.35	permits]AMAN; points A
83.38	order of the day]CAMAN; order A
84.11	when he]CAMAN; and A
84.14	desire]CAMAN; wish A
84.33	old England]CAMAN; England AMAN, A
84.41	*us*]CAMAN; us A
85.22	and profiting]CAMAN; profiting AMAN, A
85.23	some]CAMAN; most A
85.33	S.R.P.]AMAN; J.R.P. A
87.7	very great]CAMAN; great A
87.21	present relief in killing as many as possible, even if they came to life, again, hereafter]CAMAN; relief in killing as many as possible A
87.31	Chateaubriand]AMAN, B; Chateaubriant A
88.25	his society]CAMAN; it A
89.8	four last]CAMAN; four A
90.8	the natures of the times deceas'd, / The which observ'd, a man may prophesy, / With a near aim, of the main chance of things / As]CE; the nature of the times deceased, / The which observed, a man may prophesy / With a near aim, of the main change of things, / As A
90.13	*2 Henry IV*, 3.1.80–84.]CE; King Henry VI. A, AMAN; King Henry IV. B

90.30	favor]CAMAN; behalf A; favour B
90.34	things]CAMAN; these things A
91.22	to which I am about to introduce you]CAMAN; which I am about to introduce you to A
91.40	one smallish]CAMAN; one A
92.25	sir—]CAMAN; sir; AMAN, A, B
92.31	inches, instead of acres.]CAMAN; inches. A
93.1	still higher point]CAMAN; point still higher A
94.33	it, at all.]CAMAN; it. A
94.34	intentions are good,]CAMAN; intentions, A
95.9	'there is no death']CAMAN; ^ ~ ~ ~ ~ ^ A
95.13	delusion]CAMAN; illusion A
96.29	short, narrow]CAMAN; short A
96.30	furnace]CAMAN; enemy A
97.7	stood near]CAMAN; stood A
97.28	losses, insurance,]CAMAN; losses, A
97.38	mammon]CAMAN; Mammon A; manners AMAN
98.3	still marked]CAMAN; marked A
98.7	soon]CAMAN; now A
98.22	have been got]CAMAN; be got A
*98.22	under.]AMAN; ~ , A
98.28	its possession]AMAN; their ~ A
*98.29	insecurity]AMAN; insanity A
99.9	*The Taming of the Shrew* 4.2.93.]CE; Shakspeare AMAN, A, B
99.14	preceding]AMAN; proceeding A
99.36	given,]AMAN; ~ ; A
100.2	in another]CAMAN; into another A
100.32	her]CAMAN; all her A
101.2	as Grace]CE; as Eve A; that Eve AMAN; that Grace B
101.15	or assuming that]CAMAN; ~ ~ the A; while the atmosphere was assuming that B
101.17	elements in winter.]CAMAN; elements. A
101.27	deemed]CAMAN; now ~ A
101.38	class of tastes]CAMAN; taste A, AMAN; class of taste B
*102.19	mammon]CE; Mammon A; man, man, AMAN; money merely CAMAN, B
102.32	and that, moreover,]CAMAN; and that A; and, moreover, that B

102.34	the last important]CAMAN; this important A, AMAN
103.10	Italian,]B; ~ ; AMAN, A
104.26	discriminating]CAMAN; ~ from necessity A

Copy-text shifts to AMS at 104.32.

*104.36	a discussion]CAMAN; that a discussion AMS; that its discussion A
104.37	sincere]A; honest AMS, AMAN, B
105.2	dreamy days]A; ~ , ~ AMS
105.5	Eve]A; Grace AMS, AMAN, B
105.10	head in disapprobation]CAMAN; head AMS
105.15	pretension]A; pretention AMS
105.22	remains a]A; ~ a a AMS; ~ of a AMAN, B
105.25	else.]CAMAN, A; else." AMS
105.32	true, Miss Effingham,]CAMAN; true AMS
106.14	two; on]CAMAN; two, and on AMS
106.16	years, and the other in possession for an eternity of the same period.]CAMAN; years. AMS
106.18	'always']A; " ~ " AMS
106.29	'*Les . . . tort*,']A; "*Les . . . tort*" AMS
*106.37	just as much]CAMAN; quite as much same AMS; quite as much A, AMAN
107.3	expressing her discontent]A; saying something, AMS
107.16	feelings,]AMAN, A; ~ ^ AMS
107.24	common-place]A, AMAN; common place AMS
107.39	closer too,]A; closer AMS
108.9	for]A; of AMS
108.16	*Amérique*]A; *Amerique* AMS
108.17	eyes, however,]CAMAN; eyes AMS
108.21	rattle]A; fly AMS
109.7	me where is fancy bred, / Or in the heart or in the head? / How begot, how nourished?"]CE; me, where is fancy bred," / "Or in the heart, or in the head?" / How begot, how nourished?" AMS
109.11	*The Merchant of Venice* 3.2.63–65.]CE; Song in Shakspeare AMS
109.23	pace.]AMAN, A; ~ ^ AMS
109.27	been]CAMAN; now been AMS
109.27	on one of]CAMAN; on AMS

109.28	routes]CAMAN; route AMS
109.34	meaning, in his own good time,]CAMAN; meaning, AMS
110.3	a secret, however]CAMAN; still a secret AMS
110.22	singularly]A; singularily AMS
110.27	dearest]A; dear AMS
110.31	such things existing]A; for such things exist AMS
110.37	excite]A; extort AMS
110.38	*forêt*]AMAN; *fôret* AMS
111.6	and to the left]CAMAN; and left AMS
111.7	them all]A; every one AMS
111.14	predecessors]A; predecessor's AMS
111.28	*coup d'œil*]A; view AMS
111.31	'Vision']A; " ~ " AMS
111.34	new]CAMAN; novel AMS
111.37	¶ That]CAMAN; ^ ~ AMS
111.39	first]A; now AMS
112.7	woods]A; forests AMS
112.12	valleys]A; vallies AMS
112.17	of England]AMAN, A; of ~ ~ AMS
112.17	England or Switzerland]CAMAN; England AMS
112.28	hill-tops]CAMAN; mountain-tops AMS
112.30	mountains]CAMAN; hills AMS
112.32	ascents]CAMAN; ~ of the mountains AMS
112.37	atmosphere]CAMAN; air AMS
112.37	did not seem so far]A; seemed much less AMS
113.9	region]CAMAN; country AMS
113.18	though a better]CAMAN, A; a better AMS
113.21	being, in this respect, as unlike a continental European town, south of the Rhine,]CAMAN; being as unlike a continental European town, south of the Rhine, in this respect AMS
113.29	great mass of their fellow creatures]CAMAN; *oi polloi* of the human race AMS
113.38	the dollars and cents of the neighborhood, will, by any practicable means,]CAMAN; dollars and cents will, by any process, AMS
113.40	suitable]A; suited AMS
114.2	or of a]CAMAN; or a AMS
114.6	monstrosities,]AMAN, A; ~ ^ AMS
114.6	tavern;]CAMAN; ~ , AMS

114.7	neighbors, including even the churches.]CE; neighbors, including, even the churches.]CAMAN; neighbors. AMS
114.8	*piazza'd*]CAMAN; piazzaed AMS
114.12	taste]CAMAN; taste, in the remoter ages of the region, AMS
114.14	had, since last presented to the reader, undergone material changes, that were directed by]CAMAN; had since undergone material changes, under AMS
114.21	and after the building had attracted their gaze, the whole party took seats on stumps and fallen trees, before a syllable was uttered.]CAMAN; and the whole party took seats on stumps and fallen trees, before a syllable was uttered, after the building had attracted their gaze. AMS
114.26	that of]AMAN, A; of that AMS
114.37	refer them confidently]CAMAN; refer all AMS
114.38	for explanations of which I shall be compelled to consult the higher authorities]CAMAN; for which I shall be compelled to consult the authorities for explanations AMS
115.1	eye, now,]A; eye, AMS
115.7	whistled, as a gentleman will sometimes whistle,] CAMAN; whistled, AMS
115.10	disposed]CAMAN; ~ , AMS
115.12	his indisposition]A; his own indisposition AMS; an indisposition CAMAN,B
115.15	in which]A; on ~ AMS
115.16	much, indeed, as his great predecessor,]CAMAN; much as his predecessor in the occupation, AMS
115.18	the appearance of your]CAMAN; your own AMS
115.20	neighbors']CE; neighbor's AMS; neighbours' A
115.21	uglier]CAMAN; worse off AMS
115.23	pass, unmolested by any very furious criticism.] CAMAN; pass unmolested. AMS
115.33	and of]CAMAN; and AMS
115.34	little too much]CAMAN; little AMS
115.36	rashly innovated]CAMAN; innovated AMS
115.37	Eve; "I]CAMAN; Eve, "for I AMS
116.1	unnecessarily alarmed]CAMAN; alarmed AMS
116.3	singularly]A; singularily AMS

116.9   whom or what]CAMAN; whom AMS
116.9   belong;]CAMAN; ~ , AMS
116.10   of most of]CAMAN; of AMS
116.13   'cloud-colour']A; " ~ " AMS
116.21   'the . . . thanks.'"]A; "the . . . thanks." AMS
116.24   athwart]AMAN, A; atwhart AMS
116.32   nationality.]AMAN, A; ~ ^ AMS
116.33   *Un si beau calme fait penser à l'éternité.*]CAMAN; *On pense à l'éternité, dans une telle calme!* AMS
116.36   coolly]AMAN, A; cooly AMS
116.37   the summer before for twenty.]CAMAN; for twenty, the summer before! AMS
*116.39   marr'd]CAMAN; marred AMS
117.6   True,]A; ~ ^ AMS
117.10   'Wigwam,'"]CE; "Wigwam," AMS; 'Wigwam?'" A, B
117.11   abode.]CAMAN, A; ~ ; AMS
117.23   look for a]CAMAN; expect him to AMS
117.26   another. "There]CAMAN; another, "there AMS
117.26   boat]CAMAN; boat out AMS
117.27   pass of luxury]CAMAN; pass AMS
117.30   it; the lake and mountains have been poetized, a dozen times, in the last ten years.]CAMAN; it. AMS
117.35   onward state]CAMAN; state AMS
117.39   sorts, sir,]CAMAN; sorts, AMS
118.7   of creatures]A; of here AMS; of living animals CAMAN, B
118.8   asked Eve, "that]CAMAN; Eve asked, "who AMS
118.28   names, now-a-days]CAMAN; names AMS
118.29   'Silent Pine,']A; " ~ ~ ," AMS
118.30   'Speaking Rocks,']A; " ~ ~ ," AMS
118.31   'Fairy Spring.'"]A; " ~ ~ ." AMS
118.32   suspicious circumstances]CAMAN; suspicious AMS
118.37   forenoon. He]CAMAN; ~ ; he AMS
119.3   there he is]AMAN, A; There is AMS
119.3   sinner!—]CAMAN; ~ ; AMS
119.7   half-rustic dress]CAMAN; dress AMS
119.10   prevailing wish]CAMAN; general desire AMS
119.10   possible.]CAMAN; possible, though it was sufficiently neat and simple AMS
119.12   the foot-paths]AMAN, A; ~ a ~ AMS
119.12   had]CAMAN; have AMS

119.16	hesitating]CAMAN; stopping AMS
119.20	hourly looked for, and indeed I waited]CAMAN; expected and indeed waited AMS
119.21	arrival;]CAMAN; ~ , AMS
119.27	soon cordially]CAMAN; cordially AMS
119.28	Powis]CAMAN; Mr ~ AMS
*119.29	feelings, and the meeting passed off, as one of mutual surprise and pleasure, without any exhibition of emotion to attract unusual comment.]CAMAN; emotions, and the meeting passed off, as one of mutual surprise and pleasure, without any exhibition of feeling to attract unusual comment. AMS; emotions, and the meeting passed off, as one of mutual surprise and pleasure, without any exhibition of unusual feeling to attract comment. A
119.34	between both]CAMAN; between AMS
119.38	could]A; would AMS
120.3	'Falls,']B; "~ , " AMS
120.5	particularly]AMAN, A; particularily AMS
120.5	desire]A; wish AMS
120.8	particularly]AMAN, A; particularily AMS
120.14	once more]CAMAN; again AMS
120.15	hands warmly]CAMAN; ~ , ~ AMS
120.18	man resumed]AMAN, A; ~ , ~ AMS
120.21	'the . . . clean']A; " ~ . . . ~ " AMS
120.26	of course]AMAN, A; of ~ ~ AMS
*120.27	annoyed B; a little annoyed AMS; a annoyed CAMAN
*120.34	We will defer the great pleasure that is in reserve]A; But we will defer the pleasure that is in reserve AMS; We will defer the pleasure of an explanation CAMAN, B
121.4	that lovely]A; the ~ AMS
121.4	paused, again and again,]CAMAN; paused AMS
121.14	so it be]A; so be it be AMS
121.14	legitimate verse]CAMAN; wholesome rhymes AMS
121.15	are, now,]CAMAN; are AMS
121.17	ceased, not knowing what excuse to make,]CAMAN; ceased, AMS
*121.18	light-hearted and laughing; Aristabulus being quite as merry as any of them, though he scarce knew why. But it was a ruling trait in the character of this

person, never to suffer himself to get behind the ages.]
CE; laughing and light hearted. AMS; light-hearted
and laughing; Aristabulus being quite as merry as any
of them, though he scarce knew why. But it was it a
ruling trait in the character of this person, never to
suffer himself to get behind the ages. CAMAN; light-
hearted and laughing; Aristobulus being quite as merry
as any of them, though he scarce knew why. But it was
in a ruling trait in the character of this person never
to suffer himself to get behind the age. B

122.5	Chapter X.]A; ~ Xth. AMS
122.7	spot I came to seek,—/ My father's ancient burial-place . . . / It is the spot,—I know it well—]CE; spot, I came to seek, / My father's ancient burial place—/ It is the spot—I know it well, AMS
122.12	William Cullen Bryant, "An Indian At the Burial Place of his Fathers," ll. 1–2, 5–6.]CE; Bryant. AMS
122.31	turpitude]CAMAN; unworthiness AMS
122.35	at seeing]A; in ~ AMS
123.29	preferment]CAMAN; success AMS
123.33	though,]CAMAN; ~ ∧ AMS
123.33	rank]CAMAN; one AMS
123.29	grave neglect]A; neglect AMS; serious neglect CAMAN, B
124.16	reached]CAMAN; got to AMS
124.33	my way, with so much luggage,]A; my, with so much luggage, way AMS
124.38	matter]CAMAN; ~ much longer AMS
*125.6	wishes to]AMS; wishes to avail himself of this opportunity to A
125.7	also. He]CAMAN; ~ ; he AMS
125.7	me, by letter,]CAMAN; ~ ∧ ~ ~ ∧ AMS
125.14	by the young man]CAMAN; to himself AMS
125.18	on the canal]CAMAN; to pass AMS
125.20	fortnight]A; forthnight AMS
125.21	sincere regrets]A; regrets AMS; regret B
125.34	solicitations.]AMAN; ~ ∧ AMS
125.37	the immediate escort]A; alone, by the side AMS
125.38	By this time, they had not only reached the highway, but had]CAMAN; The party, by this time, had not only reached the highway, but it had AMS

126.2	"modern enterprise;"]CE; 'modern enterprise;']AMS; ^ modern enterprise; ^ AMAN; a ^ modern enterprise; ^ A; ^ modern enterprise, ^ B
126.4	are time]A; is ~ AMS
126.12	seclusion.]CAMAN; seclusion, as they descended along a path as safe and convenient as a French *allée.* AMS
126.16	for A; and, ~ AMS
126.21	since]A; for AMS
126.22	find]A; found AMS
126.24	low?]A; low, then? AMS
126.34	'poetize the lake,']A; " ~ ~ ~ , " AMS
126.35	a couple]AMAN, A; a few couple AMS
127.3	Icaruses]A; Icaru's AMS; Icarius' AMAN; Icarus' CAMAN
127.5	was two]A; ~ in ~ AMS
127.6	condensed]CAMAN; so ~ AMS
127.19	'pride of Kings,']A; " ~ ~ ~ , " AMS
127.13	'people']AMAN; " ~ " AMS
127.23	reply]CAMAN; answer AMS
127.25	navy than that]A; ~ but ~ AMS; than that CAMAN, B
127.26	agreeably!]CAMAN; ~ , AMS
127.31	the smiling Paul]A; Paul, with emphasis AMS
127.33	*cousin Jack*]CAMAN; cousin Jack AMS
127.35	admit, yourself]CAMAN; admit AMS
127.37	am a sailor]A; am a sailor, now, AMS; am now a sailor B
128.2	uttered]A; had ~ AMS
128.31	interrogatories.]AMAN, A; ~ ; AMS
128.33	there are as]AMAN, A; there as AMS
128.36	bargain. You]CAMAN; ~ , for you AMS
128.37	and]A; besides AMS
128.38	regularly]B; regularily CAMAN; regular AMS
129.1	church;]CAMAN; ~ , AMS
129.5	hoarse. I dare say he will get over it, however] CAMAN; hoarse; but I dare say he will get over it AMS
129.7	undoubtedly is]A; may be AMS
129.15	particularly to]A; particularily AMS; particularily to CAMAN
129.15	to the windows]A, CAMAN; the windows AMS

129.19	them.]CAMAN; them, on every plan they can invent. AMS
129.23	Paul's]A; Pauls AMS
129.27	standard;]CAMAN; ~ , AMS
129.28	fortnight; change being so]CAMAN; forthnight, for change is AMS
129.34	hear that]CAMAN; ~ this AMS
129.38	the point]CAMAN; that ~ AMS
129.39	entirely]A; fairly AMS
130.1	the point]CAMAN; this ~ AMS
130.4	Paul's]A; Pauls AMS
130.15	believe, first and last,]CAMAN; believe, AMS
130.17	ancient gothic tower in green wood]CAMAN; gothic tower in wood AMS
130.22	denominations]A; denominations themselves AMS
130.25	'Many . . . minds']A; ^ ~ . . . ~ ^ AMS
130.35	he only]A, AMAN; he who only AMS
130.38	added]A; observed AMS
131.12	particular spot]CAMAN; spot AMS
131.14	even more]CAMAN; even AMS
131.28	one.]AMAN, A; one." AMS
131.34	finds it]A is apt to see AMS
131.37	When]A; While AMS
132.4	talents, in the house in question.]CAMAN; talents. AMS
132.5	certainly carrying]CAMAN; carrying AMS
132.9	Dear]A; Ah! AMS; Oh! AMAN, B
132.27	*Effinghamisé, si*]CAMAN; ~ ^ ~ AMS
132.27	*c'est un petit château.*]CAMAN; c'est un chateau. AMS; *c'est un château.* AMAN
132.34	a little]A; the ~ AMS
133.7	come. If I lose a scruple of this sport, let me be boil'd] CE; come; if I lose a scruple of this sport, let me be boiled AMS
133.10	*Twelfth Night* 2.5.2–3]CE; Shakspeare AMS
133.24	that]A; which AMS
133.26	Wigwam]A; wigwam AMS; "Wigwam" AMAN, B
133.28	she]A; that ~ AMS
133.31	described the interior of this house, in another work] A; had occasion, already, to describe the interior of this house AMS

133.37	regularly]A regularily AMS
134.1	Wigwam]AMAN, A; wigwam AMS
134.3	Venetian]AMAN, A; Venitian AMS
134.6	of]CAMAN; and ~ AMS
134.15	circumstance]A; feature AMS
134.23	too often]CAMAN; often AMS
134.25	particularly]A; particularily AMS
134.29	vestiges]A; vestige AMS
135.6	the table]CAMAN; table AMS
135.8	size]A; space AMS
135.10	kindly.]CAMAN; ~ ; AMS
135.17	Anne]AMAN; Ann A; Even Anne AMS
135.24	taste,]CAMAN; tastes," AMS
135.27	coolly]A; cooly AMS
135.34	*métier*]CE; AMS
135.34	*goût*]B; *gout* AMS
135.35	*impossibilités* AMAN, A; impossibilities AMS
136.19	risk]A; risked AMS
136.22	as a]AMAN, A; as ~ ~ AMS
136.37	the mistress of an American]A; an American mistress of a AMS
137.4	arches]A; archs AMS
137.22	residence. ⁊ "For," she added, "you]A; residence, for, she added— ⁊ "For," she added—"You AMS; residence. ⁊ "For," she added, "You CAMAN
137.23	*villeggiatura*]AMAN, A; *villagiatura* AMS
137.26	*villeggiatura*]AMAN, A; *villagiatura* AMS
137.30	nothing]A; for nothing AMS
138.7	cottage]A village tenement AMS
138.14	coolly]A; cooly AMS
138.36	downright]A; very AMS
139.7	apprentices']A; apprentice"s AMS; apprentice's AMAN
139.14	Wigwam]A; wigwam AMS
139.15	in unpacking]A; with unpacking his AMS
139.28	from]A; off of AMS; off AMAN, B
139.37	lose]A; will loose AMS
140.5	street.]CAMAN; ~ ; AMS
140.17	as at]A; at AMS
140.26	Aristabulus,]A; ~ — AMS
140.30	particularly]A; particularily AMS

140.37   things to a crisis]A; this, to a point AMS; them to a
            point AMAN, B
140.38   dahlias]AMAN, A; dahliahs AMS
141.3   actually]A; had ~ AMS
141.5   will]A; would AMS
141.7   other]AMAN, A; other' AMS
141.8   would]A; should AMS
141.9   warnts]CAMAN; wants AMS
141.22   the shop]A; his ~ AMS
141.28   Lather]CAMAN, A; Soap AMS
141.29   particularly]A; particularily AMS
141.30   propose]A; ~ to you AMS
141.34   so very]CAMAN, A; much too AMS
142.14   law on his side, but all]A; law of his side, but all of AMS
143.7   "In sooth, thou wast in very gracious fooling last night,
            when thou spok'st of Pigrogromitus, of the Vapians
            passing the equinoctial of Queubus. 'Twas very good, i'
            faith."]CE; In sooth, thou wast in very gracious fooling
            last night, when thou spokest of Pigrogromitus, of the
            Vapains passing the equinoctial of Queubus. AMS; "In
            sooth, thou wast in very gracious fooling last night,
            when thou spok'st of Pigrogromitus, of the Vapians
            passing the equinoctial of Queubus; 'twas very good, i'
            faith." A
143.11   *Twelfth Night* 2.3.22–25.]CE; Sir Andrew Ague-Cheek
            AMS
143.14   It has just been said, that the progress of society]
            CAMAN; The progress of society, it has just been said,
            AMS
143.15   anomalous]A; peculiar AMS
143.23   mark]CAMAN; marks AMS
143.32   secretly knows]A; well understands AMS
143.35   mental qualities]CAMAN; qualities AMS
144.14   condition]A; society AMS
144.18   commence]A; commences AMS
144.24   pretension and effort that so commonly accompany
            infant]A; pretention and effort that commonly
            accompanies all infant AMS; pretention that commonly
            accompanies all infant AMAN; pretention that
            notoriously accompanies infant CAMAN
144.27   *pêle mêle*]B; *pèle mèle* AMS

144.33   repress even]CAMAN; repress AMS
144.38   those older districts, that]CAMAN; its older districts,
            which AMS
145.1   singularly]A; singularily AMS
145.2   it these]CAMAN; it, its AMS
145.3   such elements there be]CAMAN; these, elements, be
            AMS
145.12   a division into castes, that is]CAMAN; the division
            into castes that are AMS
145.16   on its]A; ~ their AMS
145.20   advantage, however, in the]A; happiness, however, in
            their AMS
145.22   time between]CAMAN ~ , ~ AMS
145.24   more]A; longer AMS
145.38   their influence]CAMAN; the influence of the latter
            AMS
146.4   not, in a physical sense, been literally gathered to their
            fathers,]CAMAN; not been literally gathered to their
            fathers, in a physical sense AMS
146.15   sieges and scars]CAMAN; scars, and sieges AMS
146.17   familiarity]CAMAN; their ~ AMS
146.19   sincerely]CAMAN; the most ~ AMS
146.21   be found]AMAN, A; found AMS
146.34   singularly]A; singularily AMS
147.22   Howel]CAMAN, A; Howell AMS (*Also corrected at*
            147.24, 147.32, 148.3, 148.10, 148.25, 148.28, 148.30,
            148.36, 149.2, 149.7, 149.27, 150.25, 150.35, 151.7,
            151.11, 151.21, 151.38, 152.27, 153.4, 153.38, 154.13,
            and 154.16.)
147.40   he his]CAMAN; ~ that ~ AMS
148.2   treat as]CAMAN; think AMS
148.5   unavoidable]A; the very AMS
148.9   good]A; old AMS
148.15   honestest]A; gentlest and ~ AMS
148.22   really brought]CAMAN, A; actually ~ AMS
148.22   an Englishman into port.]A; into port an Englishman.
            AMS
148.23   predilections]CAMAN, A; predilection AMS
148.39   liked their]AMAN, A; liked AMS
149.6   we, who are]A; we are AMS
149.7   have]A; and have AMS

149.13	of the]A; ~ your AMS
149.23	particularly]A; particularily AMS
149.35	my dear young]CAMAN; young AMS
149.37	—Oliver . . . Eve –]CAMAN; , ~ . . . ~ ; AMS
150.1	doubt,]B; ~ ; AMS
150.6	set fire to Rome]CAMAN; lived AMS
150.9	Not]A; What, not AMS
150.29	was]CAMAN; were AMS
150.39	Peter's]A; Peters AMS
151.3	considered it]A; set it down as AMS
151.4	Paul's]AMAN, A; Pauls AMS
151.12	know when as boys]A; knew when boys, when AMS; know; when boys AMAN, B
*151.39	they are to your taste.]A; it is to your taste. AMS; they are to your liking? CAMAN, B
152.23	'we . . . hear']A; "we . . . hear" AMS
152.32	something, or who did not pass most of his time in England.]CAMAN; something. AMS
153.8	his]CAMAN, A; this AMS
153.13	men, in after life,]CAMAN; men, AMS
153.24	other person]CAMAN; other AMS
153.28	subjects.]CAMAN; subjects—AMS
153.31	than with what]A; than what AMS
153.33	word, perhaps;]CAMAN; word, AMS
153.36	*idéal*]AMAN, A; *ideál* AMS
153.40	issuing from a room in]CAMAN; coming from AMS
154.31	finest]CAMAN; finest-looking AMS
155.5	treaty]A; Congress AMS
155.28	yes,]A; ~ ; AMS
155.40	one]A; baron AMS
156.26	read]A; ~ all AMS
156.28	Howel]CAMAN, A; Howe AMS
157.2	father's]AMAN, A; fathers AMS
157.9	the pass to]CAMAN; to the pass in AMS
157.13	importance]CAMAN; moment AMS
158.9	*Henry VIII* 1.2.9.]CE; Queen Katherine AMS
158.12	regularly]A; regularily AMS
158.15	were]A; had been AMS
158.24	necessary manner]CAMAN; manner AMS
159.9	order, itself,]CAMAN; order AMS

159.23	'Senators' ladies']A; "Senators ladies" AMS
159.36	covered]A; covered, again, AMS
160.5	should]A; ought to AMS
160.15	singularly]A; singularily AMS
160.32	be—nay that it *ought* to be –]CAMAN; become, nay that it *ought* to be AMS
160.34	superior in her eyes, with the exception of those who actually ruled]CAMAN; superior, with the exception of those who actually ruled, in her eyes AMS
160.35	fact]A; alone AMS
160.40	courteous]A; corteous AMS
161.6	equals in station of any of their European associates,] A; equals of their European associates, in station, AMS
161.12	station]CAMAN; condition AMS
161.16	gentleman on earth]A; gentleman AMS
161.35	Sidley, earnestly,]CAMAN; Sidley, AMS
161.40	know that CAMAN; suppose AMS
162.13	to true happiness and respectability any where]A; to our true happiness and respectability AMS
162.16	calmly]A; carelessly AMS
162.34	those that]A; those AMS
162.37	feels]CAMAN; feel AMS
162.39	it probably feels]CAMAN; they probably feel AMS
162.40	its colonial]CAMAN; their ~ AMS
163.19	feeling—"]CAMAN; feeling that such is the theme—" AMS
163.27	little baron, or rag baron, as they call it in this country,]CAMAN; little baron, AMS
163.36	segar-smoking Capt.]CAMAN; Capt. AMS
163.39	present; we]A; present, and we AMS
163.39	will now]CAMAN; will AMS
164.1	completed]CAMAN; now ~ AMS
164.3	respectable-looking]A; respectably looking AMS
164.7	house; and, yet, all but one, wore their hats!]CAMAN; house, though all, but one, wore their hats. AMS
164.10	decency]A; others AMS
164.17	these three]CAMAN; the ~ AMS
164.18	really]A; actually AMS
164.40	Active]A; Free AMS

165.14	'good look-out,']B; " ~ ~ , " AMS
165.26	at it]A; on ~ AMS
165.27	allow, Miss]A, AMAN; ~ ∧ ~ AMS
165.33	solemnity]CAMAN; solemnity of manner AMS
165.34	self satisfied]CAMAN; self composed AMS
165.39	due emphasis on the adjectives.]A; an emphasis on the adjective. AMS
166.3	filled]CAMAN; ~ only AMS
166.5	Aristabulus, "that]AMAN, A; ~ ∧ ∧ ~ AMS
166.13	subject, and with his usual point.]CAMAN; subject. AMS
166.15	expressed]CAMAN; expressing AMS
166.16	singularly]A; singularily AMS
166.29	disgusted at]A; ~ with AMS
*166.34	tone—]CE; tone,—AMS
167.2	remember]CAMAN; remember the time AMS
167.10	'appearances.']CE; 'appearances ∧ ' AMS; ∧ appearances. ∧ AMAN, A
167.18	substance]A; essence AMS
167.22	stone pavement]A; stone pavements A; pavements AMAN, B
167.22	Desert, ready to receive the burthens of their masters;"—Mr. Dodge loved to draw his images from the different parts of the world he had seen—"not] CAMAN; Desert—" Mr Dodge loved to draw his images from the different parts of the world he had seen—"ready to receive the burthens of their masters;—not AMS
167.29	Active Inquirer," said Aristabulus.]A; Free Inquirer." said Aristabulus ∧ AMS
168.3	high-backed]A; high back AMS
168.10	new-school]AMAN, A; new school AMS
168.12	leaning]CAMAN; standing AMS
168.15	"Yes," observed Mr. Gouge, "give]A; "Yes, observed Mr Gouge, give AMS
168.16	A man]AMAN, A; "A ~ AMS
168.17	need of]CAMAN, A; ~ for AMS
169.5	Chapter XIV.]A; Chapter XIV ∧ AMS
169.7	Cade, we'll]CE; ~ — ~ AMS
169.9	*2 Henry VI* 4.8.33.]CE; Mob. AMS
169.13	on the subject of religious forms, appear to be

	peculiar]CAMAN; appear to be peculiar on the subject of religious forms AMS
169.19	Templemore.]AMAN, A; Templemore ^ AMS
169.20	particular sect which holds it in pious horror]CAMAN; sect which holds it in utter abomination AMS
169.21	worthy ancestors]CAMAN; pious ~ AMS
169.22	neophytes]A; all neophytes AMS
169.22	ran]A; run AMS
169.26	gnat]A; knat AMS
169.28	"worthy ancestors"]CE; "pious ancestors" AMS; 'worthy ancestors" CAMAN; pious ancestors A; worthy ancestors B
169.29	having been Americans]CAMAN; being American AMS
169.35	that church which she herself so deeply reverenced.] CAMAN; the same church as herself. AMS
169.37	so easily]A; easily AMS
169.40	use]CAMAN, A; uses AMS
170.2	the profession]CAMAN; a ~ AMS
170.4	know]A; know that AMS
170.9	peculiarly]AMAN, A; peculiarily AMS
170.13	more particularly when]B; when AMS; more particularily ~ CAMAN
170.17	had imbibed for such things,]CAMAN; imbibed on this subject AMS
170.18	think,]A; ~ ^ AMS
170.21	two]CAMAN; three AMS
170.25	worthy]CAMAN; pious AMS
170.31	exclaimed]A; exclaimed all AMS
170.32	Yea, literally, in every door, I might almost say; certainly in every]CAMAN; Yes, literally every door, I might almost say; certainly every AMS; Yea, in every door, I might almost say; certainly in every B
170.38	out to me]A; out AMS
171.1	eye on]A; eye at AMS
171.3	thought]CAMAN; thoughts AMS
171.4	on their thresholds.]CAMAN; on their very thresholds. AMS; as they term it, on their threshold. B
171.17	term,]AMAN, A; ~ . AMS
171.22	in the way]CAMAN; by way AMS
171.25	it]CAMAN; so indecent a blunder AMS

171.30   Powis," he remarked, "and it was not Roman. What]A;
           Powis;" he remarked, "and if it was not Roman; what AMS
171.33   hastily]CAMAN; eagerly AMS
171.36   bishops]AMAN, A; a bishops AMS
171.39   revolution. It was an English rather than an American
           church."]A; revolution; it was an English church, rather
           than an American." AMS; revolution; it was an English
           rather than an American church." B
172.8   little]A; little rude AMS
*172.17   and Paul and the Baronet taking the oars, they soon
           urged the boat from the shore.]A; and, Paul and the
           Baronet taking the oars, they soon urged the boat from
           the shore, with vigorous arms. AMS; when, Paul and
           the Baronet taking the oars, soon urged the boat from
           the shore with vigorous arms. CAMAN; when Paul
           and the baronet, taking the oars, by dint of vigorous
           exertion, soon urged the boat from the shore. B
172.19   The world is getting]A; This world is really getting
           AMS
172.22   cliffs, towards which the]CAMAN; cliffs of which, the
           AMS
172.34   amèricain]CE; Amèrican AMS, Americain A
172.35   one's self]A; oneself AMS
172.37   extraordinaire pour une Parisienne."]AMAN, A;
           extraordinaire pour une Parisienne ^ ^ AMS
172.40   this lake]A; our ~ AMS
173.9   said]A; cried AMS
173.11   morality]CAMAN; moralizing AMS
173.17   'Fairy Spring,']A; "Fairy Spring," AMS
173.24   a short]CAMAN; but ~ ~ AMS
173.24   advance]A; the advance AMS
173.29   'commodore.']A; " ~ . " AMS; "commodore. CAMAN
173.31   now]A; but, now AMS
173.32   or on the]CAMAN, A; or the AMS
173.38   then]A; now AMS
173.39   party through his spectacles]A; party AMS; party,
           through a pair of spectacles CAMAN, B
174.13   entirely round]A; quite ~ AMS; round B
174.16   lake bore its blossoms]A; water bore its blossoms AMS;
           the water had its blossoms like the plants CAMAN, B

174.19	for by those who have the knack]CAMAN; for, like potatoes AMS
174.20	draughts]A; draught AMS
174.30	and to the]CAMAN; and the AMS
174.32	Grant, when he was alive,]CAMAN; Grant AMS
174.39	on its legs]CAMAN; when slaughtered AMS
175.1	had]A; have had AMS
175.1	Effingham.]A; ~ ^ AMS
175.19	had]CAMAN; got AMS
175.26	affirm]A; say AMS
175.27	forest, and even with the trees.]CAMAN; forest. AMS
175.30	looking at]CAMAN; ~ on AMS
175.35	would]CAMAN; could AMS
175.38	though, I own,]CAMAN; though AMS
176.2	wish]A; now wish AMS
176.4	John,]A; ~ ; AMS
176.6	these echoes]CAMAN; the ~ AMS
176.6	often satisfied]CAMAN; satisfied AMS
176.7	but like]CAMAN; ~ they ~ AMS
176.8	Otsego water]CAMAN; Otsego AMS
176.9	paddled]A; ~ up AMS
176.11	way to]CAMAN; ~ quite ~ AMS
176.18	that there is no]A; there is no such thing as an AMS
176.21	our ignorance, and as a taunt for our]CAMAN; our AMS
176.24	as much as]CAMAN; as AMS
176.25	pine]A; tree AMS
176.29	of]A; of the mystery of AMS
177.2	half]CAMAN; half of AMS
177.4	the mysterious]A; those unintelligible AMS
177.5	vigorous]CAMAN; rich AMS
177.6	American wood]A; the American woods AMS
177.7	hemlocks]A; young ~ AMS
177.16	which he had used in steering]A; with which he had been steering AMS
177.22	higher than]CAMAN, A; above AMS
177.28	pride]CAMAN; nature and ~ AMS
177.34	fifteen feet]AMAN, A; fifteen AMS
177.35	enough]A; just ~ AMS
178.1	named,]B; ~ ^ AMS

178.1	it is]A, AMAN; it AMS
178.7	Otsego water]CAMAN; Otsego AMS
178.7	lay, like a]A; lay a AMS
178.13	the artificial]A; our ~ AMS
178.20	crest]A; little ~ AMS
178.23	that]A; ~ he AMS
178.25	for a minute or two at the]A; for a minute or two, intently at the AMS; intensely for a minute or two at the B
178.26	'that . . . sea!']A; "that . . . sea!" AMS
176.26	waved in]CAMAN; waved there, in AMS
176.28	eloquent]A; an eloquent tree AMS
178.32	probably]A; has ~ AMS
178.36	five]A; ten AMS
178.37	was pulled off in the lake]CAMAN; was off in the lake AMS; was pulled off into a situation B
179.3	in which the latter did not lose the minutest]CAMAN; which did not lose the minutest AMS; in which the latter did not lose the most minute B
179.9	kinsman; "I]CAMAN; kinsman, "for I AMS
179.15	most aptly]A; aptly AMS
179.17	he is a]A; his is, indeed, a AMS
179.22	house."]AMAN; ~ ^ " AMS
179.26	an organized]CAMAN; the ~ AMS
179.29	slumbering echoes]CAMAN; echoes AMS
179.32	reissued, and rolled]A; reissued, again, and passed rolling AMS; reissued, and passed, rolling B
179.36	western hills . . . eastern mountains]A; western mountains . . . eastern hills AMS
179.40	smiling]CAMAN; laughing AMS
180.1	A sheet of water like this]CAMAN; This sheet of water AMS
180.6	protested earnestly to the contrary,]CAMAN; made no answer; AMS
180.9	Pic-Nics,]A; ~ ^ AMS
180.9	place]A; point AMS
180.10	old]A; noble ~ AMS
180.18	cousin]A; cozen AMS; coz AMAN, B
180.18	learn that]A; learn AMS
180.23	among these]A; in ~ AMS
180.30	This can hardly be]CAMAN; Are you AMS

180.33	silent]CAMAN; almost silent AMS
180.35	just heard]CAMAN; heard AMS
180.39	John would]A; ~ , ~ AMS
181.6	greatly disliked]CAMAN; disliked AMS
181.28	that fact]CAMAN; the ~ AMS
181.31	fact. It]CAMAN, A; ~ ; ~ AMS
181.34	the Point]A; it AMS
182.7	He could not conceal from himself, moreover]CAMAN; Still, he could not conceal from himself AMS
182.18	absent for]A; absent AMS
182.22	insists that it owns the Point]A, CAMAN; insists that it owns the point AMS; insist that the Point is common property B
182.26	Point]CAMAN, A; point AMS (*Also corrected at* 184.20, 184.21, *and* 184.31.)
182.29	the public may discover, if it]CAMAN; the public will discover, if it AMS; will be shown, if the public B
183.4	coolly]A; cooly AMS
183.25	men under excitement are usually wrong]A; men under an excitement are usually wrong AMS; people acting under excited feelings are very liable to fall into error B
183.28	this fact]CAMAN; the ~ AMS
183.31	increasing wonder]CAMAN; wonder AMS
183.32	for effecting]A; of ~ AMS
183.34	existence]CAMAN; effects AMS; effect A
183.35	the affair]A; this ~ AMS
183.36	this very excitement]CAMAN; the excitement AMS
183.40	politico-pious]A; politically pious AMS
184.3	excesses and crimes]CAMAN; excesses AMS
184.11	more]A; the ~ AMS
184.12	many against one]A; one against many AMS
184.13	wrong]A; very ~ AMS
184.19	favor the]A; favor, as ~ AMS
184.32	use]CAMAN; user AMS
184.34	adds to]CAMAN; adds AMS
184.35	and increases]A; ~ it ~ AMS
184.36	may desire]CAMAN; desires AMS
184.38	public to hold the property]CAMAN; public to hold AMS; public AMAN
184.39	fact?]A; ~ . AMS
185.4	whole]A; entire AMS

185.5   more particularly]A; the ~ particularily AMS
185.6   'excitement.']B; "excitement." AMS
185.19   place]CAMAN; spot AMS
185.30   that could not easily be rebutted.]CAMAN; of weight."
            AMS
185.32   and these]A; ~ even ~ AMS
*185.37   that to an American]CE; that an American AMS
185.38   'always']A; " ~ " AMS
185.38   'time immemorial']A; " ~ ~ " AMS
186.6   such a]A; any such AMS
186.7   any.]CAMAN; any, indeed. AMS
186.19   or to give]CAMAN; or give AMS
186.24   a special]A; an especial AMS
186.25   Point,]CAMAN; "Point," AMS
186.29   patience]A; impatience AMS
186.39   make]CAMAN; leave AMS
187.2   have known]CAMAN; know AMS
187.21   had told]A; have ~ AMS
187.24   family]A; own ~ AMS
188.4   legal title]A; title in law AMS
188.22   or as a man]CAMAN; or a man AMS
188.24   had retired]CAMAN; retired AMS
189.7   "There shall be in England seven halfpenny loaves sold
            for a penny; the three-hoop'd pot shall have ten hoops,
            and I will make it felony to drink small beer. All the
            realm shall be in common, and in Cheapside shall my
            palfrey go to grass."]CE; There shall be, in England,
            / Seven half-penny loaves sold for a penny; the three
            hooped pot shall have teen hoops; and I will make
            it a felony to drink small beer: all the realm shall be
            in common, and, in Cheapside shall by palfrey go to
            grass." AMS
189.12   *2 Henry VI* 4.2.65–69.]CE; Jack Cade. AMS
189.30   a few days]CAMAN; the day AMS
190.11   was]A; ~ now AMS
190.13   night, agreeably to our arrangement, Mr. Effingham,"
            Aristabulus commenced,]CAMAN; night, Mr
            Effingham," Aristabulus commenced, "agreeably to our
            arrangement, AMS

Copy-text reverts to A at 190.23.

190.23   to take counsel]B; consult A, AMAN; to take council
CAMAN

190.34   Effingham,]B; ~ ; A

191.27   crises]B; crisises A

192.1   so profound a]CAMAN; a profound A

192.4   employer]CAMAN; employers A

193.7   in as]CAMAN; ~ so A

193.24   know nothing of that which]CAMAN; know every
thing that A; have hidden every thing that AMAN

193.25   century.]AMAN; ~ ^ A

194.21   different.]CAMAN; different in character. A

194.28   welfare, principles]B; welfare A; welfare principles
CAMAN

*196.23   rights]AMAN; right A

197.20   gross impiety]CAMAN; impiety A

198.2   quarter,]CE; ~ ; A

198.12   remark, which was teeming with truth, ended]
CAMAN; remark ended A

199.5   Chapter XVI.]CE; ~ II. A

199.7   palace, a Broad-street, / Where all heroic ample
thoughts did meet. / Where nature such a tenement
had ta'en, / That other's souls]CE; palace, a broad
street, / Where all heroic, ample thoughts did meet. /
Where nature such a tenement had ta'en, / That other
souls A

199.12   John Norton, "Dirge for the Tenth Muse," ll. 77–80.]
CE; John Norton. A

200.2   doing the cooking and the]CAMAN; cooking and A;
her duties of cooking and B

200.31   Orlando Furioso Samuel]CAMAN; Orlando Furioso A
(*Also corrected at* 200.38 *and* 201.2.)

201.30   bonnet, (this word by the way of brevity, Mrs Abbott
chose to call bunnet)—Take your bonnet,]CAMAN;
bonnet, A

201.40   beg her if she can lend me a watering pot, too]
CAMAN; ask her if she can lend me a watering-pot A;
beg her, if she can, to lend me a watering-pot B

202.7   for religion, even.]CAMAN; for them A; even for
religion B

202.26   Effingham herself,]CAMAN; Effingham A

202.31	"Not she, indeed! Though I]CAMAN; "I A
203.2	about it]CAMAN; at ~ A
203.11	ragged]AMAN; rugged A
203.12	bolted in]CAMAN; entered A
204.3	Ma' wants]B; Ma, wants A; Ma wants AMAN
204.30	Effinghamses]CAMAN; Effinghams A
204.34	months]CAMAN; so long A
205.9	man in her life]CAMAN; single man A
205.17	Abbot, much as a dog would snap at a bone.]CAMAN; Abbott. A
205.27	contemplated]CAMAN; thought of A
206.5	marm]CAMAN; ma'am A
206.5	always afraid]CAMAN; afraid A
206.9	sorts of ways]CAMAN; she could A
206.31	scenery]CAMAN; usages A
206.31	'our beautiful nature']CE; " ~ ~ ~ " A
207.32	lower.]AMAN; ~ . " A
208.1	more positively]CAMAN; positively A
208.2	marm]CAMAN; ma'am A
208.3	solitary, insignificant]CAMAN; solitary A
208.14	inconsistencies]CAMAN; contradictions A
208.28	marm]CAMAN; ma'am A
208.33	common]CAMAN; general A
209.16	usages, while it so unequivocally betrayed that it knew nothing of its spirit.]CAMAN; usages. A
209.20	ownership of the spot in dispute,]CAMAN; ownership, A
209.25	seek]CAMAN; find A
209.25	own conduct]CAMAN; conduct A
209.29	that what he had done, had been done in the mode he had adopted, although it was precisely the mode] CAMAN; that what he had done, had been done in precisely such a mode, although it was the mode A, AMAN; of the mode which he had adopted in doing what he had done, although it was precisely the one B
209.35	so well knew]CAMAN; knew A
209.38	and notwithstanding the high profession of liberty made by those implicated, they]CAMAN; notwithstanding the high profession of liberty made by

	those implicated; and they A
210.23	that]CAMAN; to the cap A
211.5	Chapter XVII.]CE; ~ III. A
211.10	William Lisle Bowles, "The Sanctuary: A Dramatic Sketch," ll. 51, 53.]CE; Shakspeare A
212.6	yonder bird]CAMAN; that ~ A
217.10	himself at the Wigwam]CAMAN; himself A
217.12	there]CAMAN; at the Wigwam A
218.21	get to be]CAMAN; get A
219.7	Mam'selle]CAMAN; Mamselle A
219.13	respect]CAMAN; way A
220.18	and to]CAMAN; and A
222.24	condition, yet,]CAMAN; condition, A
222.39	miserable week]CAMAN; week A
*224.15	guest]B; guests A
225.6	waiting]CAMAN; in waiting A
225.32	have changed]AMAN; change A
228.5	Chapter XVIII.]AMAN; ~ IV. A
228.12	William Cullen Bryant, "The Past," ll. 35–38.]CE; Bryant A, B, AMAN
229.4	*voilà tout!*]CAMAN; that is all. A
229.25	them]CAMAN; it A
230.19	"David Bright,"]AMAN; ' ~ ~ ; A
230.19	"Mrs. Jane Dowse."]AMAN; ' ~ ~ ~ ." A
230.25	might]CAMAN; should A
230.37	aside]CAMAN; down A
231.1	answer]CAMAN; answers A
231.39	"pet,"]AMAN; 'pet,' A
232.10	fact that]CAMAN; ~ , ~ A
232.25	that bundle]CAMAN; the ~ A
234.7	suffer]CAMAN; allow A
234.20	and with]CAMAN; and A
234.32	for one of]CAMAN; for A
235.8	sisters']B; sister's A; sisters AMAN
235.19	appeared]CAMAN; had met AMAN; met A
235.23	sisters']B; sister's A
235.35	in obedience to]CAMAN; by A
238.38	and more especially so in]CAMAN; in A
239.22	is so free, by law.]CAMAN; is, in one sense, free. A; is

	free, in one sense. AMAN
241.5	Chapter XIX.]CE; Chapter V. A
241.7	"Item, a capon . . . . . 2s. 2d. / Item, sauce . . . . . 4d. / Item, sack, two gallons . . . . . 5s. 8d. . . . / Item, bread . . . . . ob."]CE; "Item, a capon, 2s. 2d. / Item, sauce, 4d. / Item, sack, two gallons, 5s. 8d. / Item, bread, a half-penny." A
241.12	*Henry IV, Part 1* 2.4.535–537, 539.]CE; Shakspeare A, AMAN, B
241.17	given to]B; gaiven to]CAMAN; he gave A
241.29	were established]CAMAN; was ~ A
241.34	had been]CAMAN; was A
241.40	rowed]CAMAN; ~ out A
242.1	anchor, or to repair to the Point, for a pic nic, as you may determine."]CAMAN; anchor." A
242.28	his efforts]CAMAN; rowing A
243.7	in the family.]CAMAN; as it were, in the family. A; in the family, as it were AMAN
243.9	as well as I know this lake, sir]CAMAN; by heart, Captain Truck A
243.14	leave time]AMAN; have ~ A
243.23	'cable-rope.'"]CE; 'cable-rope." A; "cable ropes." AMAN; 'cable-rope.' B
243.27	That I can believe, for]CAMAN; Ay, Ay, A
243.27	strong fresh-water]CAMAN; fresh-water A
244.10	jerking uselessly]CAMAN; jerking A
245.29	his]CAMAN; all ~ A
246.14	may find in]CAMAN; see in such A; may find in such B
247.8	hand, furiously.]CAMAN; hand. A
248.15	But,]CAMAN; Only A
248.17	his fortune]CAMAN; use of his knowledge A
248.25	general. A tax on tobacco!]CAMAN; general; a tax on tobacco. A
248.28	raised to his lips a large silver punch bowl, which Pierre had furnished,]CAMAN; raised a large silver punch-bowl, which Pierre had furnished, to his lips, A
248.31	regarded him,]CAMAN; regarded, AMAN; regarded him ^ A
248.36	near a minute]CAMAN; some time A
248.37	moved so much as an]CAMAN; moved A

249.35   'Old Hickory.'"]CE; 'Old Hickory.' A; 'Old Hickory."
          AMAN; Old Hickory." B
249.39   it says a great deal]CAMAN; then it says so much A
250.1   to his lips a second time]CAMAN; a second time to
          his lips A
250.11   instant]CAMAN; time A
251.38   will, now,]CAMAN; will A
251.40   went]CAMAN; now went A
*252.4   companion. ⸿ "And so you have become a laker in
          your religion, my dear commodore," continued the
          general, between his teeth, while he smoked and
          squeezed a lemon at the same time, "and do your
          worshipping on the water?" ⸿ "Altogether of late,
          and more especially since my dream." ⸿ "Dream! My
          dear sir, I should think you altogether too innocent
          a man to dream." ⸿ "The best of us have our failings,
          general. I do sometimes dream, I own, as well as
          the greatest sinner of them all." ⸿ "And of what did
          you dream—the sogdollager?" ⸿ "I dreamt of death."
          ⸿ "Of slipping the cable!" cried the general, looking
          up suddenly. "Well, what was the drift?" ⸿ "Why, sir,
          having no wings, I went down below, and soon found
          myself in the presence of the old gentleman himself." ⸿
          "That was pleasant—had he a tail? I have always been
          curious to know whether he really has a tail or not."
          ⸿ "I saw none, sir, but then we stood face to face, like
          gentlemen, and I cannot describe what I did not see."
          ⸿ "Was he glad to see you, commodore?" ⸿ "Why, sir,
          he was civilly spoken, but his occupation prevented
          many compliments." ⸿ "Occupation!" ⸿ "Certainly, sir;
          he was cutting out shoes, for his imps to travel about
          in, in order to stir up mischief." ⸿ "And did he set you
          to work?—This is a sort of State-Prison affair, after
          all!" ⸿ "No sir, he was too much of a gentleman to
          set me at making shoes as soon as I arrived. He first
          inquired what part of the country I was from, and
          when I told him, he was curious to know what most of
          the people were about in our neighbourhood." ⸿ "You
          told him, of course, commodore?" ⸿ "Certainly, sir, I
          told him their chief occupation was quarrelling about

religion; making saints of themselves, and sinners of their neighbours. 'Hollo!' says the Devil, calling out to one of his imps, 'boy, run and catch my horse—I must be off, and have a finger in that pie. What denominations have you in that quarter, commodore? So I told him, general, that we had Baptists, and Quakers, and Universalists, and Episcopalians, and Presbyterians, old-lights, new-lights, and blue-lights; and Methodists—. 'Stop,' said the Devil, 'that's enough; you imp, be nimble with that horse.—Let me see, commodore, what part of the country did you say you came from?' I told him the name more distinctly this time—" ⁊ "The very spot?" ⁊ "Town and county." ⁊ "And what did the Devil say to that?" ⁊ "He called out to the imp, again—'Hollo, you boy, never mind that horse; *these* people will all be here before I can get there.'" ⁊ Here the commodore and the general began to laugh, until the arches of the forest rang with their merriment. Three times they stopped, and as often did they return to their glee, until, the punch being ready, each took a fresh draught, in order to ascertain if it were fit to be offered to the ladies. ⁊ "My]CAMAN; companion. ⁊ "My A

253.19   "My dear sir," said the commodore, as soon as he had recovered breath, "I am a thousand times sorry that you came from that river, for, to]CAMAN; "My dear sir," said the former, "I am a thousand times sorry you came from that river, for, to A; "My dear sir," said the latter, "I am a thousand times sorry you came from that river, for, to AMAN; "To B

254.7   commodore gravely]CAMAN; commodore A

254.8   if, by hook or crook, he can get farther west]CAMAN; if he can get farther west, by hook or crook A

*254.26   homage, and some punch."]CAMAN; homage. ⁊ And A

255.5   Chapter XX.]AMAN; Chapter VI. A

255.9   *Romeo and Juliet* 2.2.33.]CE; *Romeo and Juliet* A, B

256.17   cultivated]CAMAN; and highly cultivated A

256.20   all was]CAMAN; it was all A

257.20   them, indeed,]CAMAN; them, A

257.27   fatal-character]CAMAN; catastrophe-character A

257.32	cross readings]CAMAN; cross-eyed readings A
258.7	though neither observed]CAMAN; for neither perceived A
258.8	passed]CAMAN; both ~ A
*258.29	handsome head]AMAN; hands and head A
258.30	delusion . . . is . . . its charms]CAMAN; delusions . . . are . . . their charms A; delusion which . . . is . . . its charms B
*258.40	pent feelings]AMAN; first ~ A
260.3	delight]CAMAN; pleasure A
260.34	proffer]CAMAN; ~ of connecting herself for life, A
261.8	ever to]AMAN; even ~ A
261.11	sexes in]CAMAN; ~ , ~ A
261.14	Eve quietly]CAMAN; Eve A
261.20	precise question]CAMAN; question A
262.19	urgent. It is the privilege of your sex.]CAMAN; urgent. A
262.26	better picture of a rational passion]CAMAN; cooler picture of passion A
262.31	Eve, hastily,]CAMAN; Eve, A
263.20	proposal, as, however, it was rather supposed she might.]CAMAN; proposal. A
264.20	be now]CAMAN; be A
264.26	generally take her bias in such matters,]CAMAN; take her bias in such matters, generally A
265.28	ungrateful, inconsiderate]B; ~ ^ ~ CAMAN; ungrateful A
266.15	did open,—not the door—but]CAMAN; did, though it was not the door, but A
266.19	even remembered]CAMAN; remembered A
267.5	Chapter XXI.]CE; Chapter VII. A; Chapter 1st AMAN; Chapter I B
267.7	think / Has business]CE; thinks / He has business A
267.10	*Henry VIII* 5.4.74–75.]CE; King Henry VIIIth. CAMAN; King Henry VIII. A, B
267.31	*chère*]CE; chere A
268.19	Mademoiselle Viefville]CAMAN; Mademoiselle A
268.39	I wish]CAMAN; But ~ ~ A
269.38	admissable]CAMAN; admirable A
270.3	they made]CAMAN; made AMAN, B

270.5	one of the village churches having]CAMAN; for one of the village churches had A
270.10	having been]CAMAN; being A
270.12	wood; lived]CAMAN; wood, having lived A
270.22	cloaks, too,]CAMAN; cloaks A
272.7	else. He]CAMAN; else, and he A
272.7	great difference, therefore,]CAMAN; difference A
272.9	very much]CAMAN; so ~ A
272.29	"exercises"]AMAN; 'exercises' A
274.14	amusements. A balloon or two succeeded.]CAMAN; amusements. A
274.19	common yarn]CAMAN; rope yarns AMAN; rope-yarn A
275.1	*Américains*]AMAN; *Amêricains* A
275.33	do not]CAMAN; does ~ A
277.16	anything else]CAMAN; modesty A
278.5	Chapter XXII.]CE; Chapter VIII. A; Chapter 2 AMAN; Chapter II B
278.11	*Antony and Cleopatra* 3.4.20–22.]CE; Antony and Cleopatra. A
279.12	signal advantage]CAMAN; advantage A
279.29	Eve, hastily,]CAMAN; Eve, A
280.9	an irreparable misfortune, Mr. Powis; I]CAMAN; a misfortune Mr. Powis, and I A
280.15	country]CAMAN; one A
281.4	ever disposed]CAMAN; disposed A
282.1	said, pointedly, and as he thought with dignity,] CAMAN; said, A
285.26	But, here]CAMAN; Here A
286.20	but he has]CAMAN; but has A
286.23	'*à nous aborder*']B; " ~ ~ ~ " A
286.35	stood waiting their arrival]CAMAN; still stood A
287.33	plump]CAMAN; right A
287.35	dead]CAMAN; plump A
*289.3	you cross]AMAN; we ~ A
290.5	Chapter XXIII.]CE; Chapter IX. A; Chapter 3. AMAN; Chapter III. B
290.7	silver-sweet]CE; silver sweet A
290.10	*Romeo and Juliet* 2.2.165–166.]CE; Romeo and Juliet

	AMAN; *Romeo and Juliet* A, B
293.16	effects of one of the commonest and most popular features of the American state governments]CAMAN; utility of the vote by ballot A
293.18	to produce practical consequences, on his hearers."] CAMAN; produce a practical effect." A, AMAN; be productive of practical consequences to his hearers." B
294.7	a man]CAMAN; any ~ A
296.2	for, when there exists a real sympathy between the sexes, feeling responds to feeling as echo answers sound]CAMAN; for feeling responds to feeling, as the echo answers sound, when there exists a real sympathy between the sexes A
298.3	attachment]CAMAN; love A
*300.39	¶ Eve]AMAN; ^ ~ A
301.16	it bears]CAMAN; bears A; also bears B
301.28	indeed!]CAMAN; ~ , A
302.25	that person]CAMAN; he A
302.37	father's family]CAMAN; ~ relatives A
305.6	Half]CAMAN; There half A
306.5	Chapter XXIV.]CE; Chapter X. A; Chapter 4ᵗʰ AMAN; Chapter IV B
306.7	do marvell's wisely, good Reynaldo, / Before you visit him, to make inquire]CE; do marvelous wisely, good Reynaldo, / Before you visit him, to make inquiry A
306.11	*Hamlet* 2.1.3–5.]CE; *Hamlet* A
306.15	Anne]AMAN; Ann A (*Also corrected at* 306.25, 307.25, 307.36, 307.38, 309.9, 309.32, 375.12, 377.19, 377.39, 385.9, 386.24, 387.18, *and* 387.23.)
308.32	fervent]CAMAN; young A
309.39	a more miraculous]CAMAN; miraculous A
314.26	shoemaker, or his coachman]CAMAN; shoemaker A
314.37	compeers]CAMAN; Manhattanese A
315.9	I ascribed that part of the report, at once,]CAMAN; I, at once, ascribed that part of the report A
317.9	attachment]CAMAN; love A
317.16	least for]CAMAN; ~ , ~ A
317.18	drawing-room; until]CAMAN; ~ , and ~ A
318.5	Chapter XXV.]CE; Chapter XI. A; Chapter 5ᵗʰ AMAN;

Chapter V B

318.7	". . . to]CE; "—to A
318.10	*Hamlet* 3.2.22–24.]CE; Shakespeare. A
320.18	periodical, with him]CAMAN; periodical A
320.31	statement, or a positive]CAMAN; statement or A
320.40	or it expressly commands]CAMAN; or A; as it expressly commands B
323.8	abuse]CAMAN; species of ~ A
323.16	periodical in general]CAMAN; periodical A
325.37	even to]CAMAN; and least of all, A
329.5	Chapter XXVI.]CE; Chapter XII. A; Chapter 6th AMAN; Chapter VI. B
329.7	"Happily, when I shall wed, / That lord whose hand must take my plight shall]CE; "Haply, when I shall wed, / That lord, whose hand must take my plight, shall A
329.11	*King Lear* 1.1.100–102.]CE; *Cordelia.* A
329.30	woman. It]CAMAN; ~ , that A
329.31	and if it was tinctured with the more glowing imagination and ample faith of youth, it was]CAMAN; and which, if it was tinctured with the more glowing imagination and ample faith of youth, was A
329.33	high principles]CAMAN; her ~ A
329.36	leave a temporary]CAMAN; have ~ ~ A; have a tempory AMAN
330.39	"Proposals! Downright, *bonâ fide,* blushes-causing proposals!]CAMAN; "Proposals!" A
331.13	so often practiced]CAMAN; practised A
332.11	greatest]CAMAN; most A
334.30	time, however, to render a very]CAMAN; time to render my A
335.8	and again]CAMAN; again A
336.14	we have never]CAMAN; we never A
337.36	value]CAMAN; do A
340.11	open compartment]CAMAN; compartment A
340.30	rising involuntarily]CAMAN; rising A
340.35	both the pious ladies]CAMAN; both A
341.27	raised]CAMAN; took A

342.5	himself suddenly]CAMAN; himself A
344.5	Chapter XXVII.]CE; Chapter XIII. A; Chapter VII AMAN; Chapter VII. B
344.8	her?]CE; her. A
344.10	*Hamlet* 2.2.559–560.]CE; *Hamlet.* A
346.1	At]CAMAN; And at A
347.16	one]CAMAN; ~ , then A
350.2	reason]CAMAN; own ~ A
352.28	an exacting]CAMAN; exacting A
353.1	few]CAMAN; only A
353.28	long been]CAMAN; been A
354.15	Nescopeck]CAMAN; Bristol A
355.22	deception. The certificate and entry in the church books were both made some time after the marriage,] CAMAN; deception; this certificate was given after the death of my wife, A
355.24	they could not do harm]CAMAN; it could do no harm A
*356.30	or her]AMAN; other A
356.37	gladden a parent's heart, only.]CAMAN; alone gladden a parent's heart. A
357.5	Chapter XXVIII.]CE; Chapter XIV. A; Chapter VIII AMAN, B
357.7	when time shall serve, there shall be smiles—"]CE; when the time comes, there shall be smiles." A
357.10	*Henry V* 2.1.5–6.]CE; *Nym.* A
358.33	be to his]CAMAN; be his A
358.36	monstrous! And]CAMAN; monstrous disagreeable, and A
360.12	I]CAMAN; Well, ~ A
361.1	A. No. 1]CAMAN; A, No. 1 A
361.4	to be A. No. 1, or even No. 2; or have]CAMAN; to have A
361.29	ma'am?]CAMAN; ~ , A
361.35	experienced, or even been exercised.]CAMAN; experienced. A
362.2	cordially join]CAMAN; join A
362.29	Reels, jigs, and fiddle de di]B; Reels. Jigs and Fiddle de di CAMAN; Reels. Fiddle de di AMAN; Real fi diddle

de di A

362.33   my-aunty-and-sue-me-Anne]CAMAN; my-aunty-all-suit-me-Anne A

363.38   continued to the last]CAMAN; continued A

*363.39   the venial]AMAN; a nominal A

366.22   a hungry alligator]CAMAN; an alligator in Lent A, AMAN

367.40   harm with it]CAMAN; harm A

369.8   private, and for no other.]CAMAN; private. A

371.5   Chapter XXIX.]CE; Chapter XV. A; Chapter IX. AMAN, B

371.7   know my heart's dear love is set / On the fair daughter of rich Capulet. / As mine on hers, so hers is set on mine, / And all combin'd]CE; know, my heart's dear love is set / On the fair daughter of rich Capulet; / As mine on hers, so hers is set on mine; / And all combined A

371.13   *Romeo and Juliet* 2.3.57–61.]CE; *Romeo and Juliet* A

371.30   that class is]CAMAN; they are A

371.33   of provincial]CAMAN; of all provincial A; of all of provincial AMAN

*372.10   common failings]AMAN; commoner feelings A

373.23   Grace (for on both these heiresses had he entertained designs)]CAMAN; Grace, for on both these heiresses had he entertained designs, A

373.35   to keep]CAMAN; or ~ A

374.2   *learn*]CAMAN; *know* A

*375.24   Mr. Steadfast Dodge and]CE; Mr. Aristabulus Dodge and A; Aristabulus, Mr. Dodge, and AMAN, B

375.36   in removing]CAMAN; as it removes A

376.5   married at all]CAMAN; married. A

377.35   permission. She]CAMAN; permission; and she A

378.2   her to]CAMAN ~ of A

378.19   once more kissed]CAMAN; kissed A

380.6   time, I confess,]CAMAN; time, A

381.37   bright anticipations]CAMAN; anticipations A

382.30   usages]CAMAN; ways AMAN; usage A

383.6   since]CAMAN; that A

383.26   lost]AMAN; longest A

383.34   modesty, taste]CAMAN; taste A

384.3	husband]CAMAN; young ~ A
384.33	heart]CAMAN; noble ~ A
385.23	awkwardness]CAMAN; feeling A
386.21	to look]CAMAN; look A
386.22	fault; Paul released]CAMAN; fault, and Paul to release A
386.35	word]CAMAN; formidable word A

Rejected Readings

The following list records the substantive variant readings that appear in texts subsequent to the accepted reading and are rejected in the present edition. The reading accepted in the present edition appears to the left of the square bracket. The source for that reading appears to the right of the bracket, followed by a semicolon, the variant reading, and its source. All texts that contain rejected readings are cited to the right of the square bracket; texts that are subsequent to the source of the accepted reading and not cited may be presumed to agree with the accepted reading.

In an entry, the curved dash ~ represents the exact word that appears before the square bracket and is used in recording punctuation and paragraphing variants. A caret ^ to the right of the square bracket signals the absence of a mark of punctuation on the left. An asterisk * indicates that the reading is discussed in the Textual Notes.

Variants in punctuation, preferred British spellings (color-colour), and other spellings that do not affect pronunciation are not cited on this list.

The following texts are referred to:

A, Philadelphia: Lea & Blanchard, 1838
B, London: Bentley, 1838
AMS, Author's holograph manuscript (partial)
AMAN, Amanuensis copy of author's manuscript (partial)
CAMAN, Cooper's editorial changes to AMAN

5.16   a month or two in it, then to repair to Washington
            for a few weeks, at the close of its season, and]A; the
            winter in it, and B
5.28   contended]A; contends B

5.32	and then]A; ~ who would ~ B
5.35	wants]A; base B
5.35	A man]A; As a ~ B
5.36	and a]A; ~ as ~ B
6.3	so easy]A; such ~ B
6.6	demands]A; demand B
6.19	objected his years and affection, and the scheme]A; pleaded his years and his affection in opposition to the scheme, and it B
6.23	these two]A; the ~ B
6.28	apprehension]A; apprehensions B
*6.29	Hudson Square]A; State Street B
6.36	in]A; after B
7.7	meet]A; receive B
7.16	seen]A; beheld B
7.17	thoughts]A; idea B
7.19	with the]A; by ~ B
7.19	as with]A; ~ by B
7.29	struck]A; impressed B
7.30	during]A; in B
7.33	the meeting]A; that ~ ~ B
8.8	had rather were]A; would rather had been B
8.9	Effingham a]A; ~ had ~ B
8.11	Notwithstanding]A; ¶ ~ B
*8.12	the natural]A; their mutual B
8.18	got to understand something of]A; begun to understand B
8.35	is]A; happens to be B
9.5	it might]A; it B
9.10	at Paris]A; in ~ B
9.13	town]A; city B
9.14	that one never hears of]A; of whom one never hears B
9.15	those]A; the family B
9.21	very]A; a ~ B
9.24	the last suddenly exclaimed]A; suddenly exclaimed the last B
9.25	honestly, now]A; honestly B
9.28	find]A; think B
9.30	hear]A; know B
9.31	has struck]A; strikes B

10.3	cousin, and though]A; cousin. Though B
10.4	and the good]A; and good B
*10.32	two small]A; too ~ B
10.38	at Paris]A; in ~ B
11.6	and coupled with]A; and, with B
11.11	books.]A; ~ than formerly. B
*11.14	quiet, *retenue*]A; ~ ^ ~ B
11.16	it is]A; they are B
11.20	affection]A; affections B
12.9	another]A; any other B
12.17	¶ "Here]A; ^ "Here B
12.22	treats of]A; touches on B
12.23	'Mr.]A; ¶ 'Mr. B
12.28	justice's]A; justices B
12.30	it]A; ~ with *éclat* B
12.33–34	has nothing to lose, but wary and cautious in all things in which he has a real]A; has a real B
13.15	You]A; ¶ " ~ B
13.19	humility,]A; ~ , vulgarity, B
13.21	part]A; a ~ B
13.33	contemplation]A; contemplations B
13.34	card,]A; ~ intensely, B
14.7	eye]A; eyes B
14.9	in]A; within B
14.10	is to be expected]A; is expected B
14.24	his wife]A; Mrs. Aristobulus Bragg B
14.25	Mr. Effingham]A; ~ John ~ B
14.28	shrewd]A; ~ and observant B
14.31	approaches]A; approached B
*14.33	uncouth and provincial]A; refined and harmonious B
15.2	did not see]A; had not seen B
15.8	a great]A; great B
15.29	what]A; ~ , I believe, B
15.32	newer]A; new B
16.7	these]A; all ~ B
16.12	partly behind]A; behind B
16.22	but then]A; but B
16.26	it yourself]A; it B
16.27	merits]A; peculiar features B
16.31	that any]A; any B

16.33   different]A; somewhat ~ B
16.33   he]A; that ~ B
16.36   citizen]A; citizens B
16.38   one would]A; a person might B
16.39   use]A; display B
16.39   the man]A; a ~ B
17.11   in a manner]A; in such a manner as B
17.19   the disappointment]A; my ~ B
17.20   May]A; But may B
17.38   pride]A; feeling B
18.4   suppose]A; ~ that B
18.5   the category]A; this ~ B
18.6   expected to witness]A; expected B
18.12   dinner]A; dining B
18.13   announced]A; announced to them B
19.19   get]A; have B
19.20   as]A; so B
19.21   a dinner]A; dinner B
19.23   awkwardness would have betrayed him fifty
           times, before]A; he would have been betrayed by
           awkwardness fifty times before B
*19.25   one who overlooked]A; an observer, overlooking B
19.27   *oi polloi*]A; nameless crowd B
19.27   were it not for a peculiar management in the]A; had it
           not been for a certain remarkable management in his
           B
19.28   himself]A; ~ at the table B
19.32   the silver-forkisms]A; silver forkisms B
19.34   with the peculiarity already mentioned as an exception.
           This touch of deportment, (or management, perhaps,
           is the better word,) being characteristic of the man, it
           deserves to be mentioned a little in]A; the peculiarity
           already alluded to, which, being characteristic of the
           man, deserves to be mentioned a little more in B
19.37   service at Mr. Effingham's table was made in the quiet,
           but thorough]A; dinner at Mr. Effingham's table was
           served in the quiet and complete B
19.41   organ]A; organs B
20.3   that he had acquired]A; acquired B
20.6   or by]A; by B

20.7	foundation]A; foundations B
20.11	grasp. Of these he soon accumulated all]A; grasp: all these he soon accumulated B
20.12	by taxing]A; ~ means of ~ B
20.12	when]A; after which B
20.13	or wherever]A; wherever B
20.31	all the others at table]A; the rest of the company B
20.35	offered his own]A; presented his B
20.36	he had]A; that he had B
20.37	that, pointed like so many enemies' batteries, loaded with headaches and disordered stomachs, garnished sundry village bars of his acquaintance]A; that garnished sundry village bars of his acquaintance, pointed like so many enemies' batteries, loaded with headaches and disordered stomachs B
21.6	omnium-gatherum]A; *omnium gatherum* which he had never before witnessed B
21.8	was]A; had been B
21.9	compelled]A; now ~ B
21.10	and, such was his ordinary assiduity with the knife and fork, that,]A; and exercising his ordinary assiduity with his knife and fork, B
21.15	make]A; become B
21.17	the baronet]A; a ~ B
21.20	answering one of his own]A; replying to one of his B
21.22	about there being such]A; about such B
21.23	as it was unsalaried rank, he attached no great importance to it]A; to unsalaried rank he attached no great importance B
21.28	first appearance]A; *coup d'essai* B
21.32	a death]A; death B
21.35	much about refuting it; or what he now fancied to be an untruth]A; to rebuke what was untrue, or what he fancied to be so, without much ceremony B
*22.5	it was as *the*]A; you were *he* B
22.8	myself]A; of county clerk B
22.10	sir," pithily inquired Captain Truck, "to what preferment would you have risen by this time?"]A; sir, to what preferment would you have risen by this time?" pithily inquired Captain Truck. B

22.26	with most]A; of ~ B
22.30	distrusted]A; suspected B
22.34	conveniences]A; conveniencies B
23.1	have you]A; you have B
23.4	were offering]A; presented themselves B
23.5	sir," said Aristabulus,]A; sir,"— B
23.7	that were then]A; which then were B
23.10	town-trade—" ¶ "Mr.]A; town trade." ¶ "Town trade!" ¶ Mr. B
23.27	the lost]A; his ~ B
23.31	loved]A; love B
23.32	it being]A; which is B
24.3	population."]A; population also." B
24.23	recollections of ancestry, and to the solemn feelings]A; feelings of ancestry, and to the solemn ties B
24.24	tradition]A; traditions B
24.26	he]A; one B
24.33	he]A; that ~ B
24.34	wound]A; have wounded B
24.38	she had]A; had B
25.3	economists, and]A; economist," observed Mr. Bragg, "and B
25.10	confess to]A; confess B
25.11	put in]A; interposed B
25.20	attachments]A; attachment B
25.23	beautiful than]A; ~ in your eyes ~ B
25.29	think, in]A; think that in B
25.31	inquiry]A; ~ , then, B
25.32	others]A; others, I allow B
25.34	sawyers]A; sawyer B
26.9	home]A; house B
26.10	to get]A; if you had got B
26.11	would]A; would even B
26.15	flushed]A; ~ with feeling B
26.15	suddenly changed]A; changed B
26.30	table]A; the ~ B
26.35	testimonials]A; testimonies B
26.37	skill]A; your ~ B
26.40	you too]A; and ~ , ~ B
27.3	lords—retain them?]A; lords who retain such! B

27.8	emotions]A; emotion B
27.20	could]A; would B
27.20	a hundred]A; one ~ B
27.31	Those are]A; They come B
27.32	come nearer]A; get ~ B
27.34	as near]A; so ~ B
28.2	the same perilous scenes as those from which they had so lately escaped, in their good company again]A; again in their good company the same perilous scenes as those from which they had so lately escaped B
28.6	or by]A; and ~ B
28.12	Aristabulus again,]A; Aristobulus, B
28.17	bowl]A; vessel B
28.24	quite as]A; as B
28.27	at table but a few minutes longer, when they retired, Mr. Effingham having dropped into]A; only a few minutes longer at table, but Mr. Effingham followed B
29.15	in an aside]A; aside B
*29.15	desired consent]A; decided ~ B
29.23	But you do me injustice in]A; You do me injustice, however, in B
29.25	have]A; ~ also B
29.32	is quite]A; is B
29.33	in his way, it was ever my good fortune to meet with] A; it ever was my good fortune to meet B
29.35	while Pierre]A; Pierre B
29.36	much as]A; much B
29.41	ever attaining]A; attaining B
30.1	One cannot]A; I ~ B
30.14	because they know that perfection is hopeless, and because they]A; because, though they know perfection to be hopeless, they B
30.18	we]A; ~ confessedly B
30.25	the tastes]A; taste B
30.27	is faulty, or condemn that which their own experience tells them is relatively]A; is relatively B
30.40	is]A; ~ in B
31.13	moment]A; ~ at least B
31.28	proprieties.]A; proprieties to intimate that the mass of men have rights. B
31.31	reasons already]A; reason B

32.4	anticipating]A; remembering B
32.6	New-York.]A; New York, a little *mal adroitment*, perhaps. B
32.7	desirous]A; anxious B
32.13	for there were both novelty and excitement in having an intelligent foreigner question her]A; for it was a novel and exciting circumstance to be questioned by an intelligent foreigner B
32.16	allusion]A; allusions B
32.22	distinctions made, when the differences are not obvious,]A; more distinctions than obvious differences, B
32.34	quite impossible that *coteries* should not form]A; impossible that *côteries* should not be formed B
32.36	exactly even]A; even B
32.37	by opinion, by a silent consent, if not by positive ordinances, above another]A; above another by opinion, by silent consent, if not by positive ordinances B
32.39	that]A; the distinction B
32.40	found]A; met with B
33.1	getting to be]A; getting B
33.2	the others]A; others B
33.3	more]A; much ~ B
33.19	arisen]A; ~ then B
33.25	as Europeans under]A; as well as Europeans, under precisely B
33.28	another]A; the other B
33.30	on having]A; in ~ B
33.33	*celle*]A; *cette* B
34.10	with]A; as B
34.12	circumstance]A; circumstances B
34.13	a mind, as]A; one mind; for B
34.16	I now]A; now I B
34.25	but they]A; but B
34.27	them]A; ~ solely B
34.35	which]A; this B
34.37	laughing]A; warmly B
35.1	that, in its nature, must be, Grace,]A; which in its nature must be B
35.16	honour]A; advantage B

35.31   it out]A; out a Hajji B
35.36   of our own, and by]A; on our part, and B
35.38   answer]A; answers B
36.1   Surely, Eve, you would not wish]A; Surely you would
            not wish, Eve, B
36.6   upon it]A; ~ his doing so B
36.14   one can do any thing he or she pleases, any where that
            he or she likes, it is pretty safe to say that he or she is]
            A; persons can do anything they please, wherever they
            like, it may safely be said that they are B
36.18   Half the time, such things are]A; Such things are very
            frequently B
36.19   in requiring]A; to require B
36.20   without even]A; without B
36.25   most]A; more B
36.26   But]A; And B
36.29   our]A; the B
37.2   marks a European's notions of such matters]A;
            distinguishes a European notion on such matters, as
            they are connected with America B
38.21   as a whole they appear better]A; they appear better,
            upon the whole, B
38.23   high dress]A; full-dress B
39.2   was less finished in her manners than Eve, certainly]A;
            was, certainly, less finished in her breeding than Eve B
39.4   a shade]A; slightly B
39.6   under no circumstances, could ever]A; could never,
            under any circumstances, B
39.10   be]A; have been B
39.28   upon]A; on B
39.34   intuitive]A; instinctive B
40.20   wondered]A; ~ that B
40.23   while on the other hand, Sir George himself]A; Sir
            George, however, B
40.30   Mr. Jarvis]A; Mrs. ~ B
40.31   from the fact of their having been]A; from their being
            B
40.35   a family]A; of ~ ~ B
40.36   having gone]A; going B
40.37   symptoms]A; now ~ B

40.38	But no]A; No B
40.39	certain essentials]A; many respects B
41.1	an itching]A; a craving B
41.3	was, at least,]A; at least, was B
41.4	causes]A; the cause B
41.5	a feeling of envy, or unkindness of any sort, while]A; any feeling of envy or of unkindness, he was B
41.6	he quietly]A; and quietly B
41.9	the remark]A; a remark of this nature B
41.11	she gave]A; on which she entertained B
41.13	our *better*]A; better than ourselves B
41.16	did nothing but visit every one]A; visited everybody B
41.17	street]A; one ~ B
41.18	visiting the]A; ~ all ~ B
41.20	certain sort]A; same ~ B
41.22	will make an exception]A; would make exceptions B
41.22	of numbers]A; ~ number B
41.24	carmen should]A; cart-men were to B
41.26	through with]A; through B
41.31	insist on it,]A; insist B
41.34	himself, or herself, better than ourselves]A; himself better than we are B
42.3	and one that has]A; and has B
42.14	meaning]A; means B
42.20	ask is a claim]A; claim is B
42.30	carmen]A; cartmen B
42.32	carmen]A; cartmen B
43.23	Verse]A; Versa B
43.24	Dr. Prolix]A; Mr. ~ B
43.28	you.]A; ~, or to his cousin John Effingham either. B
43.31	house]A; ~ again B
43.36	do not]A; don't B
44.1	done]A; committed upon B
44.21	any thing]A; any B
44.25	*propriâ*]A; *in propria* B
44.27	The simple]A; "The ~ B
44.35	unsupported, as if she were out of leading-strings,]A; unsupported, B
44.38	there being]A; ~ actually ~ B
45.2	fully two]A; two B

45.3	of all]A; in ~ B
45.4	actually walking]A; walking B
45.9	in]A; of B
45.14	their]A; this B
45.14	had not recollected]A; did not at first recollect B
45.21	sincere]A; a ~ B
45.24	She]A; Eve B
45.25	when the former,]A; and he, after B
45.25	respect]A; respects B
*46.4	Nully]A; Neuilly B
46.6	prevent]A; suppress B
46.13	the most]A; more B
46.13	the best]A; better B
46.16	"delightful letters published in the Active Inquirer,"]A; "delightful letters" published in the "Free Inquirer," B
46.21	"blue"]CE; blue B
46.28	those remarks]A; these ~ B
46.29	do fall]A; fall B
46.33	Comments on its facts are generally esteemed by the people of a country,]A; People generally esteem comments on the facts of their country B
46.35	treat as freely as possible its]A; comment as freely as possible on B
46.37	among its other profundities, never seen]A; never, among its other profundities, thought B
46.39	would she]A; would B
47.2	do not even]A; usually themselves only B
47.3	so]A; such B
47.4	at seeing a man like her kinsman overlooked, in order that a man like Mr. Dodge should]A; that a man like her kinsman should be overlooked, and such a man as Mr. Dodge B
47.9	opinions]A; opinion B
47.11	judgments]A; judgment B
47.16	might]A; may B
47.17	what strikes me as being quite odd, under such circumstances,]A; yet it is remarkable that there is B
47.25	True]A; Now B
47.27	now see]A; see B

47.28	exceptions]A; ~ only B
47.29	appliances, and not much even in these.]A; appliances. B
47.31	as a]A; for B
47.33	shall not say that the taste would be merely fastidious, for much is wanting that would add to the grace and beauty of society, while much that is wanting would be missed only by the over-sophisticated.]A; will not call the taste merely fastidious, for while there is much that would be missed by the over-sophisticated, much is really wanting that would add to the grace and true beauty of society. B
47.37	as is]A; so ~ B
48.2	elsewhere]A; would be ~ B
48.5	an imitative people of necessity]A; of necessity an imitative people B
48.6	Then they are]A; They are also B
48.8	has got]A; has B
48.12	an approach near enough to get into]A; approaching near enough to learn B
48.23	saw the ladies into]A; escorted the ladies to B
48.30	Middle States]A; State of New York B
48.33	enjoyed, if there exists the least opportunity]A; had, if the least opportunity arises B
48.34	lights in]A; ~, and the appearance of things ~ B
48.35	collected]A; assembled B
48.37	families; she is childless, affluent, and universally respected where known, for her breeding, benevolence, good sense, and heart," said John Effingham, while the party was driving from one house to the other. "Were] A; families;" said John Effingham, as the party was driving from one house to the other. "She is childless, affluent, and universally respected where known, for her breeding, benevolence, good sense, and heart." Were B
49.8	vulgar and uninstructed finery]A; vulgar finery B
49.9	one]A; a person B
49.11	minds]A; mind B
49.12	observed]A; quietly ~ B

49.18	by]A; in B
49.20	more of her class than exist to-day, but certainly we once had them]A; a greater number of her class than we have at present, but certainly they were once B
49.25	attended.]A; ~, since it is founded in natural laws. B
49.33	carriages]A; carriage B
49.35	though even he]A; but did not B
49.35	while]A; as B
49.36	them, with respectful attention. Mrs.]A; them. With respectful attention, Mrs. B
50.3	the proper]A; proper B
50.6	better]A; more properly B
50.12	were]A; was B
50.19	now resumed]A; resumed B
50.20	any]A; her guests generally B
50.21	a way]A; any ~ B
50.23	would have been the case with Mrs. Jarvis,]A; Mrs. Jarvis would have done B
50.30	might almost]A; might B
50.37	in simple]A; simple B
50.39	suitable]A; ~ there B
51.14	we hear]A; one hears B
51.16	sufferings]A; suffering B
51.18	passed the crisis in which deception is not practised, I]A; arrived at the crisis in which deception is never practised, I do not B
51.30	to think I shall]A; to B
51.36	Might]A; May B
52.8	else]A; besides B
52.10	then]A; there B
52.19	one betrays a]A; a writer betrays B
52.22	wares . . . have]A; ware . . . has B
52.24	on them]A; ~ it B
52.25	but]A; and B
52.28	theories]A; speculation B
52.29	passes]A; ~ with us B
52.30	but a very general mistake, I believe,]A; but, I believe, a very general mistake B
52.31	in supposing]A; to suppose B
52.32	would]A; must B

52.38	entirely]A; altogether B
52.38	things]A; ~ that exists B
53.15	push]A; pursue B
53.22	saw the]A; perceived Sir George's B
53.23	its abuses, strongly]A; the abuses, she was strongly B
53.26	she was not]A; and was not, therefore, B
53.31	leave]A; make B
53.34	there is]A; that there is also B
53.38	'experiment']A; ^ ~ ^ B
53.40	changes]A; change B
53.41	forward]A; go forwards B
54.3	country, in one sense at least, is retrogressive, and the people, as they cannot]A; country is, however, in one sense, retrogressive; the people who do not B
54.7	gallowses are]A; the gallows is B
54.12	Bloomfield then changed her manner, and from using that light-hearted gaiety with which she often rendered her conversation *piquante*, and even occasionally brilliant,]A; Bloomfield's manner then changed from that light-hearted gaiety which often rendered her conversation *piquante*, and occasionally even brilliant, and B
54.15	subject soon turned to that]A; conversation soon turned upon the subject B
54.16	forcibly, on such a subject,]A forcibly, B
54.20	were]A; was B
54.21	in]A; by B
54.25	did contain]A; contained B
54.25	be ranked]A; rank B
54.26	circumstance]A; fact B
54.31	prejudices]A; ~ which are B
54.34	had so often]A; had B
54.36	lacked]A; lost B
54.41	houses]A; ~ as her's, B
55.4	houses]A; ~ as theirs B
55.10	us . . . us]A; one . . . one B
55.12	for]A; to be B
55.13	Eve,]A; ~, laughing, B
55.18	the house]A; her ~ B
55.19	put in]A; interposed B

55.19	will]A; would B
55.20	of]A; about the B
55.23	do!"]A; do myself; or even that Mr. Powis, who is a paragon in his way." B
55.25	carriages]A; ~, they B
55.26	visiting]A; to visit B
56.14	is termed]A; was ~ B
56.15	too]A; also B
56.15	though of one]A; though B
56.17	a few do]A; some persons yet B
56.18	indisputable]A; indispensable B
56.18	gentility; and as]A; gentility. As B
56.24	should]A; might B
56.25	forbear from]A; forbear B
56.39	not likely]A; more likely not B
56.41	live]A; ~ all B
57.12	hoped that]A; hoped B
57.14	much]A; ~ as B
57.15	explanations]A; explanation B
57.17	house]A; door B
57.17	the out-door part of the arrangements]A; this part of the arrangement B
57.20	to the usual feelings of competition and contention, added that particular feature of humility which is known]A; added to the usual feelings of competition and contention that distinguish the occupation the sentiment that is so well known B
57.24	which]A; that B
58.2	Effingham. "As]A; ~, in his dry manner; "as B
58.3	your ears now tell]A; one of your senses now tells B
58.11	American world]A; American B
58.14	got]A; received B
58.16	paid a]A; paid B
58.19	only staid . . . that]A; stayed . . . only that B
58.20	the opportunity]A; an ~ B
58.25	loved]A; liked B
58.28	find]A; found B
58.28	of somebodies]A; ~ a somebody B
58.29	may]A; might B
58.36	one wonders]A; it is surprising B

58.38	as rapidly]A; so ~ B
59.3	his]A; ~ own B
59.6	in London even]A; even in London B
59.6	fancy]A; think B
59.7	thinking]A; saying B
59.7	unknown]A; unseen B
59.9	do agree with you, in this particular, certainly, for]A; certainly agree with you in this particular; B
59.10	one]A; we B
59.10	houses]A; ~ that were B
59.11	England not having]A; for London has not B
59.13	agree with you entirely]A; perfectly agree with you B
59.15	as compact]A; so ~ B
59.17	quite]A; most B
60.1	likewise]A; it is true B
60.5	whom appeared]A; them evidently
60.12	or his]A; ~ to ~ B
60.18	shall]A; will B
60.19	neither]A; either B
60.29	that sofa]A; this ~ B
60.35	this]A; and ~ B
60.38	the scene]A; what passed B
60.39	think]A; not ~ B
60.40	quest]A; search B
61.2	Mrs. Houston's rooms this night]A; the rooms of Mrs. Houston to-night B
61.4	too]A; much ~ B
61.5	one]A; ~ else B
61.7	it]A; ~ all B
61.14	long]A; ~ ever B
61.20	surer]A; surest and promptest B
61.28	discussion]A; this public ~ B
61.32	her.]A; her. There would be no use in changing their seats, moreover, the whole action of the piece consisting principally of private opinions uttered in a public manner. B
61.39	you'll]A; you will B
61.40	more]A; worse B
62.15	would]A; should B
62.20	he now]A; he B

62.23	would]A; can B
62.28	literally nothing]A; nothing B
62.29	in]A; on B
62.30	mistaken]A; much ~ B
62.32	while]A; ~ she was B
62.33	*peux*]A; *veux* B
62.35	arrived, by any means.]A; arrived. B
62.40	a firm]A; her ~ B
63.4	that Eve was actually]A; the additional information that Eve was B
63.6	excessively]A; extremely B
63.8	her place]A; place B
63.11	society. 'Tis]A; society." ¶"'Tis B
63.23	seriously attacked myself by]A; attacked myself, seriously, with B
63.29	as intellectual as]A; so intellectual as that of B
63.36	with]A; by B
63.37	the circle]A; her ~ B
63.39	get]A; ~ together B
64.5	compared]A; unavoidably ~ B
64.12	be]A; ~ always B
64.19	countenance]A; ~ , also B
64.20	index, too,]A; index B
64.21	acts]A; actions B
64.22	reverse]A; opposite B
64.24	who]A; clenching his fist, for he B
64.25	listener]A; witness B
64.26	in]A; into B
64.33	compelled]A; induced B
64.33	obliged]A; compelled B
65.3	quietly]A; smiling B
65.4	in]A; ~ the code of B
65.4	those]A; these B
65.8	never . . . or]A; not . . . nor B
65.35	goodness]A; extreme ~ B
66.1	privileged.]A; ~ , and surprisingly bold. B
66.3	notwithstanding]A; however B
66.4	usages]A; ways B
66.6	It is]A; 'Tis B
66.25	near to]A; near B

66.27	twenty]A; seventeen B
66.34	knowledge]A; his ~ B
66.35	these persons having]A; for these persons have B
66.35	every]A; any B
67.10	and]A; ~ , of course, B
67.12	manner.]A; ~ , like another person. B
67.21	he had never seen any society that deserved the name before this very night]A; before this very night he had never seen any society that deserved the name B
67.37	now generally admitted]A; generally admitted now B
67.38	legs.]A; ~ , as a *sine qua non.* B
68.1	through]A; in B
68.11	picked]A; began to pick B
68.13	but]A; ~ only B
68.14	the school to which she belonged infinite credit]A; infinite credit to the school to which she belonged B
68.18	hope]A; I ~ B
68.27	river, and the captain cherished]A; river when the captain received B
68.29	expected that]A; expected B
68.30	although]A; ~ I was B
68.38	exclusion]A; exclusiveness B
69.1	lodge]A; cabin B
69.2	half as]A; ~ so B
69.7	no more could tell where Apsley House is]A; knew no more where Apsley House was B
69.8	than he knew]A; than B
69.13	and of]A; and B
69.16	was aware we are nearly on a level with]A; am aware we are not much below the level of B
69.18	a little inferior to that part of the world, yet.]A; yet a little inferior to that part of the world. B
69.20	Asia or Africa]A; Africa or Asia B
69.22	flattering]A; flattery B
69.27	although]A; though B
69.35	one that]A; one B
69.36	accuse]A; ever ~ B
69.38	aware]A; ~ that B
70.2	conversing]A; *conversationy* B
70.7	on duty]A; performing the offices B

70.24	must]A; might B
70.24	to know no]A; not to know any B
71.2	dream of the fragrance]A; dream B
72.17	pecuniary arrangements]A; arrangements B
72.20	the excellence of the genus]A; their excellence B
72.22	everywhere met]CE; met with everywhere B
72.25	seen ludicrously]A; ludicrously apparent B
72.27	told]A; ~ that B
72.27	duller]A; commoner B
72.29	hit]A; broke B
72.30	one of the occasions in question]A; such an occasion B
72.35	usually sat]A; was usually B
72.37	dinner]A; convivial ~ B
73.1	into]A; to B
73.2	while]A; though B
73.2	a European]A; an ~ B
73.4	quality of table]A; fare B
73.5	manliness of tone]A; tone of manners B
73.6	a simplicity]A; simplicity B
73.6	always found]A; found B
73.11	All]A; During B
73.11	baronet got to be more and more intimate in Hudson Square]A; baronet's intimacy in State Street was increasing B
73.15	Grace gradually]A; ~ as ~ B
73.16	and]A; ~ of B
73.18	most of the]A; the State Street B
73.23	general, erroneous]A; erroneous B
73.30	baffle]A; disappoint B
73.32	characters of their mind will show themselves]A; character of their minds will show itself B
73.37	with what]A; to ~ B
73.39	¶ The]A; ^ ~ B
74.7	*conversazioni*]A; *conversazioni*; or, as the honest captain called them, *conversationonys.* B
74.11	captain]A; baronet B
74.14	of the literary merits of the]A; of the B
74.17	our national]A; the ~ B
74.20	not of]A; not B
74.21	social character]A; vanity B

74.24	in a provincial town, than to succeed]A; than to succeed in a provincial town B
74.29	*Cavaliero*]A; *dei cavalieri* B
74.34	stop to dwell on]A; dwell upon B
74.40	rooms were]A; room was B
75.5	quite positively]A; decidedly B
75.8	display of talents]A; particular display of talent B
75.10	meant]A; commonly ~ B
75.15	besides]A; in addition to B
75.16	Monthly]A; Mouthly B (*Also rejected at* 82.16, 85.39, 87.16, *and* 88.9.)
75.21	of them]A; about ~ B
75.22	talents]A; talent B
75.29	as also]A; also B
75.33	besides]A; with B
75.34	talents]A; talent B
76.7	party from Hudson Square]A; State Street party B
76.8	heard]A; had ~ B
76.17	had]A; he ~ B
76.18	public mind]A; public B
76.19	that this]A; this B
76.22	better done]A; done better B
76.23	of the force of]A; of B

A remains the copy-text; AMAN/CAMAN are extant as additional witnesses from 76.24 to the end of the text.

*76.28	'an intuitive perception of things in their real colours."]A; ^ an intuitive perception of all things in their real colours." CAMAN, B
76.31	precise]A; very AMAN, B
76.32	run the gauntlet]A; " ~ ~ ~ " AMAN, B
76.38	*representation*]A; *a representation* B
77.4	the precedency]A; precedency B
77.10	a proper]A; proper B
77.15	place, or]A; ~ ^ and AMAN, B
77.16	an ardent desire to manifest a proper homage to]A; an ardent desire to manifest a homage to AMAN; a veneration for B
77.17	should be]A; was B

77.18	twenty]A; seventeen AMAN, B
77.21	called on]A; called AMAN, B
77.22	of the chase, of the wreck, and of]A; resulting from the chase, the wreck, and B
77.23	rapidly, but effectually,]A; gradually but rapidly AMAN, B
77.31	on the subject]AMAN; upon ~ ~ B
77.39	to]A; in B
78.7	commonly thought]A; thought AMAN, B
78.10	knew only]A; only knew AMAN, B
78.11	It was generally understood,]A; All that was generally understood was the fact AMAN, B
78.16	in]A; within AMAN, B
78.24	things that]A; things B
78.25	with]A; the task of B
78.36	through with]A; through B
79.1	talents]A; talent B
79.4	seen nor ever heard of a single being in the room, with the exception of Mr. Dodge and her own party, before this night,]A; before this night seen, or even heard of, a single being in the room, with the exception of Mr. Dodge and her own party, B
79.4	ever heard]A; even ~ AMAN
79.8	one half as]A; any half as AMAN; any half so B
79.9	Legend's]A; Legend AMAN, B
79.9	As it would not very well do, however,]A; As, however, it would not very well do B
79.13	Mrs. Legend taking]A; said Mrs. Legend, who took B
79.16	modesty at a glance]A; modesty B
79.17	distinguished]A; remarkable AMAN, B
79.35	about]A; in AMAN, B
80.18	are]A; is AMAN, B
80.26	have it, of]A; have of AMAN; have the line for B
80.31	scarce]A; scarcely B
81.5	God]A; Heaven B
81.6	age,' 'behind the age.'"]A; age! behind the age'!" AMAN; age! behind the age!" B
81.11	with]A; by AMAN, B
81.23	accosted]A; saluted AMAN, B
81.27	a moment]A; for ~ ~ B

81.28	nearer]A; near AMAN, B
*81.32	shily A; fearfully AMAN, B
81.33	a man]A; he was ~ ~ B
81.36	on]A; in B
81.39	ladies who were addicted to the same taste]A; ladies AMAN, B
82.3	three first]A; three B
82.10	writer of odes]A; odist AMAN; odeist B
82.13	who]A; that AMAN, B
82.15	see that]A; see AMAN, B
82.31	amusement]A; enjoyment AMAN, B
82.33	and rest]A; ~ to ~ B
83.15	talents]A; talent B
83.19	happy]A; ~ as B
83.20	pursuits]A; pursuit AMAN, B
83.32	written two novels in that way already]A; already written two novels in that way AMAN, B
84.3	*litterateur,"* Gray whispered to]A; *litterateur,* Gray," whispered AMAN, B
84.9	and]A; so I B
84.9	get]A; ~ at AMAN, B
*84.10	rogue]A; odist AMAN; odeist B
84.13	purpose]A; wish AMAN, B
84.13	honest old]A; old AMAN, B
84.14	Pith]A; Mr. Pith AMAN, B
84.31	put in]A; said B
84.32	dogmatical manner]A; dogmatical sentiment AMAN; ~ sentiment in his manner CAMAN, B
85.1	returned]A; said AMAN, B
85.3	process that is]A; process AMAN, B
85.6	now carried]A; carried AMAN, B
85.7	pulpits]A; pulpit AMAN, B
85.16	sentimental petticoats]A; petticoats AMAN, B
85.23	cigar;]A; segar, he added B
85.31	good deal]A; little AMAN, B
85.34	Guy-kee-oh-*ly*]A; Guy-kee-*oh*-ly AMAN, B
85.35	on how]A; upon ~ AMAN, B
*85.35	am apt to]A; ought to AMAN; commonly CAMAN, B
85.36	'oh-lee;' . . . 'oh-lie.']A; "oh!-lee!" . . . "*oh*-ly." AMAN, B
85.38	as crack]A; so ~ B

86.24	put in]A; remarked B
86.29	where]A; what AMAN, B
86.33	admit of]A; admit B
86.34	grounds]A; ground AMAN
86.38	Pindar whispered]A; whispered Pindar AMAN, B
86.38	whiff]A; but ~ AMAN, B
86.39	you'll]A; you will AMAN, B
87.4	near]A; nearly B
87.26	the coast]A; it AMAN, B
87.27	then have]A; have AMAN, B
*87.32	pondering]A; pausing CAMAN, B; ponding AMAN
87.33	had got]A; began B
87.36	whole-souled]A; whole soul AMAN, B
88.7	so used]A; roused B
88.22	agreeable]A; pleasant AMAN, B
*88.27	Byronic]A; [*blank*] AMAN; charming CAMAN, B
88.29	commemorated]A; sung AMAN, B
88.37	cabins]A; cabin AMAN, B
88.39	to make]A; and ~ AMAN, B
88.40	I am]A; I'm AMAN, B
89.1	until they were]A; until AMAN, B
89.7	a funnier]A; funnier AMAN, B
90.16	Hudson Square]A; State-Street AMAN, B
90.24	quarter]A; parts AMAN, B
90.25	is devoted]A; are appropriated B
90.27	although the distances were not great, the carriages were ordered,]A; the carriages were ordered, although the distances were not great, B
90.29	given up expecting]A; ceased to expect B
90.33	were]A; was B
90.39	as]A; ~ though it were B
91.5	these people]A; the ~ AMAN, B
91.6	Viefville, the conversation being in French, but which we shall render]A; Viefville. (The conversation was in French, but we shall render it B
91.7	reader.]A; ~ .) B
91.14	some who frequent]A; some frequent AMAN
91.17	and accompany]A; to ~AMAN, B
91.17	on their]A; in ~ AMAN, B
91.18	now]A; soon AMAN, B

91.30	Aristabulus]A; Mr. ~ AMAN, B
91.33	villa]A; ville AMAN, B
91.37	us]A; me AMAN, B
92.7	sons]A; son AMAN, B
92.15	look at]A; ~ upon AMAN, B
92.17	other]A; any ~ B
92.21	calculating]A; calculation AMAN, B
92.27	thing, in this market. Now]A; thing, in this market, now AMAN; thing; in this market, now B
92.34	of being]A; ~ its ~ AMAN, B
92.37	sales-room]A; sale's room AMAN; sale-room B
93.8	those]A; these AMAN, B
93.18	as gross, as wide-spread, and as]A; so gross, so widely spread, and so B
*93.29	has completely]A; have ~ B
93.30	got to be]A; become so B
93.31	few]A; you AMAN; they cease CAMAN; they cease to B
93.35	gain; national honour]A; ~ , and national power AMAN, B
93.41	exhilarating]A; exiliary AMAN; exciting CAMAN, B
94.12	infatuations]A; infatuation AMAN, B
94.28	opinions, in all their phases,]A; opinions, in all their faces, AMAN; opinions, B
95.7	gets to be]A; becomes B
95.18	and]A; ~ thus B
95.20	wants; and thus]A; wants. In this manner B
95.24	advances]A; advance AMAN, B
95.25	which]A; who AMAN, B
95.37	Hudson Square]A; State-street AMAN, B
96.1	friendly;]A; ~ , AMAN; ~ . CAMAN, B
*96.2	inviting him to visit him in the mountains in June.] A; invited him to visit the mountains in June. AMAN; invited him to visit the mountains in June, the time he had set for his own return to his proper home. CAMAN; invited him to visit the mountains in June, the time he had fixed on for his own return to his proper home. B
96.8	more]A; rather ~ AMAN, B
96.17	occurred only]A; occurred AMAN, B

96.21	streets]A; street AMAN, B
96.27	the conflagration]A; conflagration AMAN, B
96.36	these celebrated]A; the ~ AMAN, B
96.39	when]A; during which B
96.40	the most]A; most AMAN, B
97.2	resistance]A; assistance B
97.6	other horrors]A; horrors B
97.11	its narrowest]A; the ~ AMAN, B
97.13	their touch]A; the ~ AMAN, B
97.15	sound]A; the ~ AMAN, B
97.18	morning, and the]A; morning; the B
*97.29	out]A; over AMAN, B
97.38	sheeted]A; heated AMAN, B
97.39	tottering, or fallen. It lay]A; in a tottering condition, or having fallen down. It was situated B
97.40	was]A; were B
*98.2	flushes]A; flashes AMAN, B
98.6	destruction]A; impending ~ B
98.6	crackling]A; cracking AMAN, B
98.7	distant fast]A; quickly distant B
98.11	possessed of themselves, no]A; possessed themselves AMAN; did not possess of themselves CAMAN, B
98.12	flame]A; flames AMAN, B
98.17	house crumbled to pieces after house, under the dull explosions,]A; house crumbled to pieces after house, under the dull explosion, AMAN; house after house, crumbled to pieces under the explosion, B
98.39	wide-spread and corrupting,]A; widely spread and too corrupting B
98.40	by even]A; even by B
98.42	a vice]A; vice B
98.42	infallible]A; means of AMAN, B
99.16	parade, and leaves us little more to say of the events of the winter.]A; parade. B
*99.21	hours]A; home AMAN; their time at home CAMAN, B
99.22	venturing however,]A; venturing B
99.25	which we have just related]A; at which we have just hinted AMAN, B
99.27	enjoyments]A; engagements AMAN, B
99.33	of an American]A; of American AMAN; of America CAMAN, B

99.34	a town life]A; it B
99.36	*belles*, the struggles of an uninstructed taste, and a representation]A; of the struggles of an uninstructed taste, and of entertainments B
99.38	so seldom]A; seldom AMAN, B
99.38	elegance and convenience]A; elegances and conveniences AMAN, B
99.39	in which]A; wherein B
100.11	wharves]A; wharfs AMAN, B
100.13	respect]A; ~ , Grace AMAN, B
100.14	beheld]A; before ~ AMAN, B
100.21	the whole party, while it felt the justice of Eve's observation,]A; while the individuals who composed it felt the justice of Eve's observation, they B
100.29	had the advantage yet]A; yet had the advantage B
100.30	so much]A; all AMAN, B
100.37	smiling]A; with a smile AMAN, B
100.37	embarrassed]A; too ~ B
101.5	end of]A; end and of AMAN, B
101.7	Grace rejoined]A; rejoined Grace B
101.12	offers]A; offer B
101.15	atmosphere was already getting]A; earth was already tinted with B
101.18	well]A; to advantage B
101.20	adorned]A; adorn AMAN, B
101.20	bold]A; yet ~ B
101.22	great velocity]A; grand velocity AMAN; velocity B
101.23	the scene scarce finding time to pall on the eye; for]A; for there was not time for the scene to pall on the eye; B
102.9	a suitable]A; suitable AMAN, B
102.14	no domestic architecture]A; that of a domestic character B
102.16	respected]A; connected AMAN; consulted CAMAN, B
102.18	mushroom]A; unknown AMAN, B
102.21	much more]A; made more AMAN; more CAMAN, B
102.35	maintain,]A; maintain it B
103.9	Grace still]A; ~ was ~ B
103.20	question]A; a ~ AMAN, B
103.24	their surprises]A; the surprises they create B
103.34	water]A; waters AMAN, B
104.1	those]A; these B

104.4	place, and that seems insufficient.]A; place. B
104.7	the left]A; their ~ AMAN, B
104.8	the elevation of which]A; whose elevation AMAN, B
104.19	render]A; renders AMAN, B
104.28	At West Point they stopped]A; ¶ The party stopped at West Point B
104.32	an arm]A; her ~ B

Copy-text shifts to AMS at 104.32.

105.7	for few]AMS; few AMAN, B
*105.12	regular architects]AMS; vulgar ~ A
105.28	nation advancing as fast]AMS; nation, advancing fast CAMAN
105.30	the taste]AMS; taste AMAN, B
105.30	both things]AMS; both B
105.35	half]AMS; ~ of B
105.35	are new]AMS; is ~ B
105.36	half]AMS; ~ of B
105.38	an]AMS; and ~ B
105.39	moment, and even]AMS; moment. Even B
106.3	sentiments of man, afraid]AMS; sentiments, afraid CAMAN; sentiments, are afraid B
106.11	in which]AMS; which AMAN, B
*106.17	for an eternity]CAMAN; of ~ ~ B
106.26	owner?]AMS; ~ . A
107.22	tastes]AMS; taste B
107.23	conveniences]AMS; convenience AMAN, B
107.28	knew]AMS; know AMAN, B
107.36	a]AMS; there is ~ B
107.37	better]AMS; there is something ~ B
107.37	every thing that is elsewhere degraded to a respectable height]AMS; to a respectable height every thing that is elsewhere degraded B
107.38	there commences an attraction of gravitation]AMS; this height is attained an attraction of gravitation commences B
108.1	attractions and gravitations,]AMS; attraction and gravitation AMAN, B
108.2	this average]AMS; the ~ AMAN, B
108.6	the towns]AMS; towns B

108.13	purely]AMS; merely AMAN, B
108.24	the party had passed through]AMS; through which the party had passed B
108.27	of Mr Effingham's]AMS; belonging to Mr. Effingham B
109.14	ascending into]AMS; in ascending B
*109.16	sort. Mademoiselle]AMS; ~ , for ~ A
109.21	south]AMS; southward B
109.24	obedience to instructions]AMS; observance of instruction AMAN; observance of instructions B
109.35	other carriage]AMS; carriage B
*110.10	apparently by a pure]AMS; apparently by a mere AMAN; and this, apparently, by a mere CAMAN, B
110.28	scenes]AMS; scene AMAN, B
110.35	Heaven]AMS; heavens AMAN, B
*111.14	place]AMS; spot A
111.15	shoulder]AMS; shoulders AMAN, B
*111.20	toil]AMS; trial A
111.22	small circle]AMS; small opening circle AMAN; little circle CAMAN, B
111.27	and were well]AMS; and well AMAN; and they were well CAMAN, B
111.30	Now, indeed, do . . . and yonder is]AMS, CAMAN; Now do . . . and yonder, indeed, is A; Now do . . . and indeed yonder is AMAN; Now do . . . and yonder, indeed, is B
111.34	bursts]AMS; burst AMAN, B
111.37	causes]AMS; cause A
*112.1	¶ It]A; ^ AMAN, B
112.3	that]A; that one AMAN, B
*112.5	the eye]A; their eyes CAMAN, B; the eyes AMAN
112.5	Hundreds]A; ¶ Hundreds AMAN, B
112.8	water, tree tops that intercepted the view of the shores, and]AMS; water, and B
112.9	high . . . ground, limited the landscape.]AMS; the landscape was limited by high . . . ground. B
112.13	The contrast between the dark hues of the evergreens, with which all the heights near the water were shaded, was]AMS; The dark hues of the evergreens, with which all the heights near the water were shaded, were B
112.19	this shore]AMS; the ~ B
112.20	saw]AMS; was A

112.26	opposite to]AMS; opposite AMAN, B
112.28	ranges]AMS; range AMAN, B
112.29	places]AMS; certain ~ B
112.33	immediately on]AMS; on B
112.35	an air]AMS; a straight unbroken B
113.1	and the]AMS; ~ as ~ B
113.5	shoots]AMS; shoot AMAN, A, B
113.8	county town]AMS; country ~ AMAN, B
113.19	dwellings]AMS; buildings AMAN, B
113.26	and by]AMS; and A
114.3	customer, or client,]AMS; customer B
114.26	of disapprobation]AMS; otherwise B
114.32	county]AMS; country A
114.37	could]AMS; would B
115.4	quite]AMS; altogether B
115.15	rather more]AMS; more AMAN, B
115.19	answered]AMS; said AMAN, B
115.20	of perceiving]AMS; perceiving AMAN, B
115.29	call]AMS; will ~ B
115.38	*catism*]AMS; *cattism* A
115.38	objects]AMS; things AMAN, B
115.40	afflicted]AMS; affected A
116.4	all that]AMS; all AMAN, B
116.11	inventions]AMS; invention A
116.18	that, is]AMS; that ∧ is A; which ∧ ~ AMAN, B
116.31	Lungeren]AMS; Lungern AMAN, B
117.4	prey]AMS; preyed AMAN, B
117.18	our]AMS; your AMAN, B
117.25	and some]AMS; some AMAN, B
118.5	rhinocerosies]AMS; rhinoceroses AMAN, A, B
118.19	that we know]AMS; we know this much B
*118.27	in print]AMS; point AMAN; in point CAMAN, A, B
119.8	dress]AMS; ~ which B
119.12	following]AMS; and following CAMAN; and followed B
119.15	a party]AMS; another ~ AMAN, B
119.16	deem]AMS; think AMAN, B
119.18	person]AMS; figure B
119.24	warmth and number of the greetings]AMS; warmth of the greetings AMAN; warmth of the greetings that followed CAMAN, B

119.38	sir, you are not wrong;]AMS; you are not wrong AMAN; you are not wrong, dear sir; CAMAN, B
120.4	ship's]AMS; ship B
120.9	days.]AMS; ~ ? AMAN, A, B
120.11	you here so early]AMS; you so early AMAN; so early, it is true CAMAN, B
120.13	hope, I]AMS; hope, which I A, B
120.25	Aristabulus, for a novelty, was a little dashed.]AMS; Aristabulus, for a novelty, was a little daunted. AMAN; Aristobulus himself—a thing of unusual occurrence— was a little daunted. B
120.27	annoyed by the curiosity that is apt to haunt a village imagination, since his arrival in Templeton,] AMS; annoyed, since his arrival in Templeton, by the curiosity that is apt to haunt village imaginations, B
120.29	a beautiful]AMS; the beauties of B
120.31	there was more meant than was expressed]AMS; there more was meant than expressed CAMAN; more was meant than was expressed B
120.32	who]AMS; that B
120.36	to be]AMS; somewhat B
121.1	severer]AMS; more severe B
121.7	dark heads among these]AMS; heads among these AMAN; solemn summits among those CAMAN, B
121.15	even to speak]AMS; to speak even AMAN
122.21	arrived]AMS; when he arrived B
123.3	or accident might induce]AMS; might dictate, or accident offer B
123.13	had]AMS; have ~ AMAN, B
123.17	last]AMS; least A
123.29	on duty of interest]AMS; while engaged in the discharge of important duties B
124.12	scarce]AMS; scarcely B
124.26	a few days before we sailed]AMS; within a few days of our sailing B
124.29	follows]AMS; followed A
124.33	luggage]AMS, CAMAN; baggage B
124.37	all our generosity]AMS; the generosity of us all B
125.8	he will]AMS; ~ is to B
126.9	surface, and the]AMS; surface; the B

126.11   with its]AMS; in ~ B
126.13   altogether, they who were]AMS; they who were
            altogether B
126.14   praises]AMS; praise B
126.31   in Templeton]AMS; at ~ B
126.32   cast]AMS; caste B
127.5   was two lines of Pope's]AMS; was in two lines of Popes
            AMAN; was in two lines of Pope B
127.5   effectually AMS; completely B
127.11   in twenty]AMS; out of twenty B
*127.13   glowing]AMS; glorious A
127.16   pretending to look graver, than she felt,]AMS;
            assuming a look of seriousness not altogether in
            unison with her feelings, B
127.33   register]AMS; registers A; Register B
128.4   reached]AMS; arrived at B
128.8   minutest object distinct]AMS; most minute object
            distinctly visible B
128.14   avow]AMS; own A
129.16   off]AMS; far ~ B
129.18   methodism flourishing]AMS; as methodism has
            flourished B
129.30   so far as I have any, however,]AMS; as far as I have
            any however, AMAN; however, as far as I have any, B
129.31   regrets]AMS; regret B
129.32   gained a material advantage over us, in a very essential
            point, lately.]AMS; lately gained a material advantage
            over us in a very essential point. B
130.11   mean, really]AMS; really mean B
130.14   truer]AMS; more consistent with truth B
130.16   by]AMS; ~ people of B
130.19   the Baptists]AMS; belongs to ~ ~ B
130.31   the half]AMS; half AMAN, B
131.1   officers]AMS; offices A
131.1   religion]AMS; ~ is AMAN, B
131.9   think]AMS; have thought B
131.10   sects]AMS; sets AMAN, B
131.25   put in]AMS; observed B
131.27   invest]AMS; ~ his property B

131.28	in a place with but]AMS; where there is only B
131.22	eye]AMS; eyes AMAN, B
131.35	taverns]AMS; tavern AMAN, A, B
131.37	steps]AMS; step A
132.13	word]AMS; words A
132.14	Mr Bragg]AMS; Aristabulus AMAN; Aristobulus B
132.31	of Europe]AMS; in ~ AMAN, B
132.32	Parthenon]AMS; Pantheon AMAN, B
133.36	superstructure]AMS; superstructures AMAN, B
133.38	that]AMS; which B
133.40	in the way of appearance]AMS; in appearance B
*134.4	any]AMS; gay A
134.8	is peculiar]AMS; is B
134.17	the way of the arts, if not in the way of]AMS; arts, if not in B
134.35	medallions]AMS; brackets B
135.16	me with such a disgrace]AMS; to do so B
135.30	the hystericks]AMS; hystericks AMAN; hysterics A, B
135.39	Eve added]AMS; added Eve B
136.5	very right]AMS; right AMAN, B
136.5	John Effingham answered]AMS; answered John Effingham B
136.10	a proper]AMS; proper B
136.20	corderoys]AMS; *corderoys* AMAN; corduroys A; *corduroys* B
136.28	domestic architecture]AMS; domestic B
136.36	calamities of which you are fated to experience many, as the mistress of an American household.] A; calamities, many of which you, as an American mistress of a household, are fated to experience. B
137.9	the interest]AMS; an ~ AMAN, B
137.9	interest an]AMS; ~ which ~ B
137.28	other's countenance]AMS; others' countenances A
138.4	house]AMS; home AMAN, B
138.7	brick . . . brick]AMS; brick . . . bricks AMAN; bricks . . . bricks CAMAN, B
*138.27	could]AMS; would A
139.10	of a twelve]AMS; of twelve AMAN, B
139.14	Pierre]AMS; Pierce AMAN, B

139.20	interposed]AMS; interrupted AMAN, B
140.8	change, and so they recommenced their yells, their oaths, and their game. In the mean while,]AMS; change. Meanwhile AMAN, B
140.16	for the future as well as at the present moment,]A; at the present moment, as well as for the future, B
140.24	for the]AMS; the AMAN, A, B
141.16	and as]AMS; but ~ B
142.1	out of rule, or contrary to his own notions of propriety in what had passed,]AMS; in what had passed out of rule, or contrary to his own notions of propriety, B
142.7	an actual]AMS; the ~ AMAN, B
142.13	great decision]AMS; decision AMAN, B
142.18	liberty was]AMS; that liberty was B
143.18	hazards]AMS; hazard B
143.26	adventures]AMS; adventure AMAN, B
143.31	some]AMS; something B
143.31	claim]AMS; claims A
144.15	are]AMS; is B
144.28	more regulated]AMS; better ~ B
144.32	a superiority]AMS; superiority AMAN, B
144.35	What]AMS ¶ ~ A
145.4	effects]AMS; effect AMAN, B
145.9	general and regular]AMS; general AMAN, B
145.19	qualities]AMS; [*illegible, crossed out*] AMAN; qualities, perhaps CAMAN, B
145.20	advantage, however, in the pleasures of the time being; while,]A; happiness, so far as the pleasures of the time being are concerned; CAMAN, B
145.31	almost to live]AMS; to live almost AMAN, B
146.2	All of]AMS; All B
146.8	entered]AMS; had ~ B
146.8	young]AMS; early B
146.10	tradition]AMS; traditions AMAN, B
146.17	changes]AMS; change B
146.21	there was to be]AMAN, A; which could be B
*146.26	feel]AMS; entertain CAMAN, B
146.34	sentiments]AMS; sentiment A
146.35	did begin]AMS; began B
147.2	now ushered]AMS; ushered AMAN, B

147.2	will]AMS; shall AMAN, B
147.17	refutation]AMS; refutations AMAN
147.27	could be called]AMS; might be called either B
147.37	for]AMS; to indicate B
147.37	the mind]AMS; mind AMAN, B
*147.40	modest]AMS; very ~ A
148.4	discussion]AMS; discussions AMAN, B
148.4	limited in knowledge by the very circumstances, and disposed]AMS; so limited in knowledge, and so disposed B
148.6	first]AMS; former B
148.15	honestest]A; gentlest and honestest AMAN; most gentle and honest B
148.16	put in]AMS; added B
148.39	no more]AMS; not ~ AMAN, B
149.19	Eve answered]AMS; answered Eve B
149.28	convenient]AMS; conveniently situated B
150.7	can think]AMS; think AMAN, B
150.16	and worth]AMS; worth AMAN, B
150.22	spots and persons]AMS; spots AMAN, B
150.28	excellencies]AMS; excellences B
151.9	ever heard]AMS; heard AMAN, B
151.15	shared]AMS; have ~ AMAN, B
151.15	passage]AMS; voyage AMAN, B
151.28	have]AMS; ~ already AMAN, B
152.5	non-descript—original]AMS; non-descript—original AMAN; non-descript,—an original, CAMAN, B; nondescript-original A
152.8	hear]AMS; ~ you say AMAN, B
152.22	the torrent]A; this ~ AMAN, B
152.31	got to believe]AMS; believed B
153.2	had also]AMS; had AMAN, B
153.10	first]AMS; former B
153.12	excellencies]AMS; excellences B
153.14	ghosts]AMS; ghost AMAN, B
153.35	provincial education]AMS; education B
*153.37	imperfections in this country]AMS; imperfections A
154.3	of London]AMS; in ~ AMAN, B
154.7	Hebdomad]AMS; Hebdomadal B
154.17	binding]AMS; bindings AMAN, B

154.18	sentiments are concerned, or sound sense]AMS; sentiments or sound sense are concerned B
155.1	interposed]AMS; interrupted AMAN
155.35	despite]AMS; spite AMAN, B
156.7	European]AMS; Europeans AMAN, B
156.22	rejoin]AMS; join AMAN, B
156.33	sources]AMS; a source AMAN, B
156.34	so]AMS; such B
156.37	interests]AMS; events AMAN, B
157.21	peculiarities]AMS; peculiarity AMAN, B
158.15	labored]AMS; laborious AMAN, B
158.20	it, enjoying that peculiarly lady like luxury, which is to be found in the process of having another gently disposing of the hair. Annette wielded the comb, as]AMS; it at her toilette-table. Annette was in attendance as B
158.24	darling, even in this necessary manner, though so long accustomed to it,]CAMAN; darling, B
158.29	profess]AMS; professed A
*158.31	road books]AMS, CAMAN; new ~ AMAN; books A
158.34	Ah!]AMS; Oh! B
159.9	*can be very*]AMS; *can be very* AMAN; is *very* B
159.10	James 1st]AMS; James I A, B
159.11	1701]AMS; 1700 AMAN, B
159.14	are]AMS; can AMAN
159.17	1701]AMS; 1700 AMAN, B
160.3	for quite]AMS; for B
160.4	and she had been carefully taught, too]AMS; though she had been carefully taught B
160.10	notions]AMS; notion B
160.12	condemned, for their obstrusion and ignorance, and too often justly reproached and condemned,]AMS; condemned, AMAN; condemned, for their obtrusions and ignorance, CAMAN, B
160.29	real, and]AMS; real, B
160.30	truly respectable]AMS; respectable AMAN, B
160.31	Eve]AMS; ~ therefore B
161.39	on ourselves]AMS; upon ~ B
162.1	who]AMS; which AMAN, B
162.10	before a hundred lustres are past, we shall]AMS; we shall before long B

162.16	naturally]AMS; reasonably AMAN, B
162.22	three first]AMS; first three B
*162.27	tenants]AMS; inhabitants A
162.29	thinking. Political dependency, moreover, is much more easily thrown aside, than mental dependency. It] AMS; thinking. It AMAN, B
163.20	Baronet is noble]AMS; baronet *is* noble A; ~ is *noble* AMAN
163.21	that]AMS; of ~ B
163.22	quite recently]AMS; recently B
163.32	understood]AMS; learned from B
164.5	having]AMS; combining B
164.8	long]AMS; familiar B
164.9	and his]AMS; ~ this AMAN, B
164.10	to]AMS; that he should B
164.11	others]AMS; society B
164.14	taking the place of]AMS; superseding B
164.15	which habit]AMS; the origin of which B
164.15	has a part of its origin in]AMS; can be traced to certain B
164.17	stimulated by the arts of]AMS; generated by the arts of crafty B
164.20	or was doing more]AMS; indeed, they were doing nothing more B
164.25	sides]AMS; part B
164.29	Gouge]AMS; gogue AMAN; Mr Gouge CAMAN
*164.37	apart]AMS; assent A
164.38	getting]AMS beginning B
165.3	moustachies]AMS; mustachoes AMAN; moustachios A; mustachios B
165.7	rose]AMS; arose AMAN, B
165.19	equality. We]AMS; equality—to A
165.20	near]AMS; nearly B
165.39	due emphasis on the adjectives.]A; an emphasis on the adjective in both cases. CAMAN, B
166.11	"As secondary to the main object, the public convenience,]AMS; "For the public convenience also, as secondary to the main object, B
166.12	put in]AMS; observed B
166.14	turned]AMS; ~ round B

166.15	and his]AMS; while ~ B
167.7	mildly]AMS; smiling mildly AMAN; more mildly CAMAN, B
167.9	that part]AMS; the ~ A
167.13	not improved]AMS; improved A
167.16	proprieties]AMS; properties AMAN, B
167.19	extravagances]AMS; extravagancies A
167.32	remarks (I dare say they will be very worthless ones)] AMS; remarks, I dare say they will be very worthless ones, AMAN; remarks—I dare say they will be very worthless ones—CAMAN
168.8	the thanksgivings]AMS; thanksgivings AMAN, B
168.15	stirring]AMS; strong A
169.21	them]AMS; such worshippers B
169.33	excellencies]AMS; excellences B
169.36	ridiculous]AMS; so ~ AMAN, B
169.38	when]AMS; where A
170.1	there was not a single cross to]AMS; not a single cross could B
170.2	settled]AMS; inhabited B
170.7	the religious]AMS; religious B
170.27	meliorated with]AMS; ameliorated by B
170.35	back from]AMS; back B
170.35	crusades]AMS; crusade A
170.38	*croix* in the windows, which has]AMS; crosses in the windows, which have AMAN, B
171.14	her curiosity]AMS; curiosity AMAN, B
171.14	doors]AMS; door A
171.18	was surmounted]AMS; is ~ CAMAN, B
171.25	one exception]AMS; an ~ A
172.7	boat]AMS; boats AMAN
172.9	mentioned]AMS; referred to B
172.10	using him]AMS; requiring his services B
172.26	Australis]AMS; Australia AMAN, B
172.30	houses]AMS; homes A
172.31	with you]AMS; as you justly observe B
*173.7	must feel]AMS; ~ all ~ A
173.12	plentier]AMS; more plentiful B
173.25	of the oars]AMS; from ~ ~ B
173.30	times when, living]AMS; in a time, when being B

173.36	and movements that were quick as those of]AMS; yet in his movements as active as B
173.36	not glanced aside]AMS; scarcely glanced B
173.37	until]AMS; before B
173.37	in the]AMS; by ~ B
174.20	the fishes]AMS; fishes B
*174.26	socdollager]AMS; sogdollager AMAN, A, B
174.30	allusion]AMS; allusions AMAN, B
174.34	that have]AMS; which ~ B
175.4	day, and I]AMS; day. I AMAN, B
175.4	but]AMS; only for B
*175.10	surrended]AMS; surrendered A, B
175.20	near]AMS; nearly B
175.22	Eve. "With]AMS; Eve "with AMAN; Eve "and with CAMAN; Eve, "and with A, B
176.7	have]AMS; hear A
176.10	such]AMS; great B
176.15	her body, so as to face the old man, as]AMS; round so as to face the old man, while B
176.26	reaching seventeen, his]AMS; it reached seventeen, when his B
176.28	it]AMS; that ~ B
176.31	called out]AMS; exclaimed B
176.32	farther]AMS; further AMAN, B
176.36	adieus]AMS; adieu B
177.5	nature is governed]AMS; Nature governs all things B
177.8	contrasting admirably]AMS; contrasting AMAN, B
177.20	a tree]AMS; any ~ B
177.24	grow]AMS; grows A
177.25	its increase, for a thousand years, had been upward,]AMS; its increase, had been upwards, for a thousand years, AMAN; its size had been increasing for a thousand years, B
177.28	near]AMS; nearly B
177.31	ascending]AMS; when ~ B
177.35	infused]AMS; combined B
177.38	strong enough]AMS; sufficiently strong B
177.38	just possible]AMS; possible AMAN, B
178.4	whistled round]AMS; raged around B
178.4	top]AMS; tops A

178.9   last]AMS; least AMAN, B
178.13   excellencies]AMS; excellences B
178.22   poetry, who came under this tree," said John
             Effingham, "that he did not fall]AMS; poetry come
             under this tree," said John Effingham, "without falling
             B
178.31   misapplied]AMS; misplaced A
178.38   came at one glance into the view]AMS; was at one
             glance exposed to view B
179.1   back again, with a closeness of resemblance that
             actually startled the novice]AMS; back again, with
             a clearness of resemblance that actually startled the
             novices AMAN; back with such a marked resemblance
             and clearness of tone as actually startled the novices B
179.6   those do give]AMS; those give B
179.14   an undivided]AMS; our ~ B
179.18   he explained]AMS; explained B
179.24   field artillery]AMS; artillery AMAN, B
179.25   and even]AMS; even AMAN; or ~ CAMAN, B
179.28   look, momentarily, for]AMS; momentarily expect B
*179.33   cliff]AMS; and ~ A
179.36   echoing]AMS; re-echoing B
179.37   fearful]AMS; falling A
180.1   thunder, I]AMS; ~ which ~ B
180.3   And yet I]AMS; And I AMAN, B
180.10   rude]AMS; rudely constructed B
180.18   are yet]AMS; are AMAN, B
180.20   claim]AMS; claims AMAN, B
180.22   claim]AMS; claims AMAN, B
180.29   or it will get it]AMS; to prevent the attainment of it B
180.38   which she seemed so seriously to dread, possible.]
             AMS; as a possible occurrence which she seemed so
             seriously to dread. B
181.3   answered]AMS; appeared AMAN; answered the bell
             CAMAN, B
181.17   pretends]AMS; pretend B
181.19   its right]AMS; their ~ B
181.21   nothing is easier than that *you*]AMS; it is very possible
             that you B
181.21   confess]AMS; feel B

181.22	public has]AMS; ~ have B
181.22	its title]AMS; their ~ B
181.23	this spot]AMS; the ~ AMAN, A, B
181.32	country]AMS; county B
181.33	displeasure]AMS; ~ abroad B
182.10	these changes were quite sensibly]AMS; them were evidently B
182.12	held bold language, when it suited their purpose to intimidate]AMS; held bold language, when it suited their purposes to intimidate]AMAN; had recourse to bold language when their object was intimidation B
182.19	alone in the library, again,]AMS; again alone in the library B
182.23	is determined to maintain its]AMS; are determined to maintain their B
182.25	it is *not* the owner]AMS; they are *not* the owners B
182.35	proper]AMS; ~ that AMAN, B
183.4	public, which he himself as habitually deferred to,] AMS; public, to which he himself as habitually deferred B
183.5	as any]AMS; ~ an AMAN, B
183.7	as he viewed]AMS; for such he considered B
183.18	full]AMS; quite ~ B
183.19	gained an inkling of what had passed]AMS; acquired some knowledge of what had taken place B
183.22	excitements]AMS; sensations B
183.26	excitements]AMS; excitement A
183.34	own]AMS; admit B
183.38	vernacular]AMS; ~ language B
184.2	called]AMS; commonly ~ AMAN, B
184.9	exists]AMS; exist A
184.9	own]AMS; am the rightful owner of B
184.10	it]AMS; them B
184.12	own the property]AMS; can legally claim it B
184.17	an imagination that]AMS; his imagination, which B
184.18	the popular caprices]AMS; the popular caprice A; popular caprice B
184.18	it had got to deem]AMS; he ultimately considered B
184.20	say,]AMS; affirm that B
184.25	its title]AMS their ~ B

184.33	make]AMS; constitute a B
184.36	cease intruding,]AMS; abandon their intrusion B
185.9	unfolding]AMS; and proceeded to unfold B
185.11	pendant]AMS; appended B
185.12	titles]AMS; title deeds B
185.13	has a better, let it]AMS; are in possession of better, let them B
185.14	its claim]AMS; their ~ B
185.18	your parent gave this spot to the public]AMS; he voluntarily surrendered this spot to the community B
185.28	naming quite]AMS; naming B
185.32	never heard but three, and]AMS; have only heard of three, and even B
185.34	in]AMS; during B
185.35	but]AMS; only for B
186.6	titles, let them show better,]AMS; titles, let them show a better, AMAN; deeds; let them show a better title, B
186.20	looked among the papers a]AMS; examined the papers for a B
186.23	Mr Effingham said]AMS; said Mr. Effingham B
186.24	that he]AMS; he AMAN, B
186.27	evidence, I]AMS; ~ which ~ B
186.28	wandering]AMS; wondering A
186.35	left it without]AMS; there could be no B
186.39	seven]AMS; several AMAN, B
187.1	employers]AMS; employer AMAN, B
187.3	it ought, sir, before it]AMS; it ought, before it AMAN; they ought, before they B
187.4	it ought]AMS; they ~ B
187.7	has]AMS; have B
187.9	it, and to inform it that it does]AMS; them, and to inform them that they do B
187.12	printers, although I deny that there exists any such obligation.]AMS; printers. AMAN; printers, although I deny that there is any such obligation. CAMAN
187.27	best, nay the only]AMS; best AMAN, B
187.28	that has]AMS; which ~ B
187.40	malignancy]AMS; malignity B
189.16	many days]AMS; some time afterwards B
189.19	too, quite often,]AMS; too often B

189.23	he seemed]AMS; seemed B
189.29	Dodge, happily]AMS; Dodge B
189.33	to have seen]AMS; any stranger who had witnessed B
189.34	one who did not know them, might]AMS; might B
189.35	weight of the]AMS; weightiest matters of B
189.39	Effingham]AMS; Effinghams A
189.39	read the daily journals, that were received from town each morning, with a most provoking indifference.] AMS; read with a most provoking indifference the daily journals that were received from town each morning. B
190.3	in relation to]AMS; concerning B
190.4	be doing]AMS; unburthen their minds B
190.6	As the latter . . . the four]AMS; The latter . . . and the four B
190.18	acknowledgement for]AMS; acknowledging B
190.21	was]AMS; were B

Copy-text reverts to A at 190.23.

190.23	has]A; have B
190.23	on its]A; on their B
190.24	it may conceive itself]A; they may conceive themselves B
190.26	it would have consulted its own dignity more, had it] A; they would have better consulted their own dignity had they B
190.26	its own]A; their ~ B
190.31	conceive]A; form an adequate notion B
190.36	nature. "A]A; nature, "a AMAN; nature; "a B
190.38	Three cannot get]A; No three can AMAN, B
190.40	consequence]A; natural ~ AMAN, B
191.3	"But, sir, you do not yet know the nature of those resolutions!"]A; [*omitted*] AMAN; "But, sir, you do not yet know the nature of these resolutions!" CAMAN
191.15	destroy]A; quite ~ AMAN, B
191.19	the forbearance]A; their ~ B
191.20	this resolution, as to pass]A; the one resolution as B
191.22	public's is an awful power]A; power of the public is awful B

191.25   word, too,]A; word AMAN; favorite word CAMAN;
          favourite word B
191.29   it]A; they B
191.32   its power]A; their ~ B
191.33   It]A; They B
191.38   farther]A; further AMAN, B
191.39   notwithstanding the]A; ~ his AMAN, B
192.5   quietly waiting]A; waiting AMAN, B
*192.6   scruples. ¶ "They]A; scruples, and to speak plainly. ¶ "I
          am sorry to be obliged to add, Mr. Effingham," he said,
          "that the meeting resolved you had rendered yourself
          odious by your course in reference to the Point, and
          that it held you and your notice against trespasses
          in sovereign contempt." ¶ "If I am to be deemed
          odious, for claiming a right to control that which is
          my own," Mr. Effingham quietly remarked, "what is
          your publick to be deemed, for claiming to control
          that which is not its own?" ¶ "Men will certainly
          regard this resolution with different eyes. I ventured
          to hint to the meeting that there might possibly be
          some mistake; but—" ¶ It resolved, as usual, that it
          was infallible," interrupted John Effingham, who had,
          with difficulty, kept silence to that moment. "You may
          regard this affair, as you please, Ned, but in my eyes
          it is a deliberate perversion of truth, a violation of
          law, and a most indecent outrage on the rights of a
          citizen." ¶ "Good Heavens! Mr. John; you forget these
          were the resolves (Aristabulus was a Massachusetts
          man, and he preferred that Shakesperian term to the
          simpler word 'resolution,') of a public meeting! A
          sacred public meeting!" ¶ John Effingham was about to
          answer, with the cool contempt, he really entertained
          for such an abuse of terms, when a gesture from his
          cousin induced him to continue silent. ¶ "Will you
          have the goodness, Mr. Bragg," said the latter, "to
          give me some accurate notion of the composition of
          this meeting? Surely, Mr. Howel did not attend it?"
          ¶ Aristabulus was obliged to confess he did not. Mr.
          Effingham then named some twenty or thirty of the
          more respectable and intelligent inhabitants of the

village, including nearly every one who, by social
position, age or residence would have a right to be
active on any such a question, and he found that not
one of them all had been present. Surprised at the
result, after the parade with which Mr. Bragg had
introduced the subject of the meeting, he next inquired
the names of those who had actually been foremost in
the matter. By far the greater number, were composed
of that floating population which forms so large and so
unsettled a part of most American communities, and
some were actually residents of a month's standing. ¶
"These persons are mostly strangers to me," said Mr.
Effingham, "and by their years, or their residence, can
know little of the merits of the disputed question, and
absolutely nothing of my father, who has now been
dead near thirty years." ¶ "They are, notwithstanding,
the people, sir!" ¶ "No, sir, they are *not* the people;
and it is as impudent a pretention, on their part, to lay
claim to be so considered, as it is to lay claim to my
property." ¶ "It is enough that they consider themselves
the people," said John Effingham, "to pretend to do
anything. I trust, Ned, you do not mean to submit to
this outrage?" ¶ "What would you have me do, John,
but pity those who are so grossly ignorant of propriety,
as to set themselves up as judges in their own case?
Certainly, I shall maintain, to the letter, my legal rights,
and further than that, I do not see anything is required
of me. That much is now required, even in behalf of
the laws of our common country." ¶ "But they have
publickly expressed their contempt of you!" ¶ "The
surest possible sign they do not feel it. Contempt is a
silent quality, and is never paraded before the world.
No man is despised, when it is thought necessary to
make solemn and formal declarations to that effect.
I hope by my conduct, to show on which side the
contempt really exists." ¶ "They]AMAN; scruples, and
to speak plainly. ¶ "I am sorry to be obliged to add,
Mr. Effingham," he said, "that the meeting resolved
you had rendered yourself odious by your course in
reference to the Point, and that it held you and your

notice against trespasses in sovereign contempt." ¶
"If I am to be deemed odious for claiming a right
to control that which is my own," Mr. Effingham
quietly remarked, "what is your public to be deemed
for claiming to control that which is not their own?"
¶ "Men will certainly regard this resolution with
different eyes. I ventured to hint to the meeting that
there might possibly be some mistake; but—" ¶ They
resolved, as usual, that they were infallible," interrupted
John Effingham, who had, with difficulty, kept
silence to that moment. "You may regard this affair
as you please, Ned, but in my eyes it is a deliberate
perversion of truth, a violation of law, and a most
indecent outrage on the rights of a citizen." ¶ "Good
Heavens! Mr. John; you forget these were the resolves"
(Aristobulus was a Massachusets man, and he preferred
that Shaksperian term to the simpler word resolution,)
"of a public meeting! A sacred public meeting!" ¶
John Effingham was about to answer with the cool
contempt he really entertained for such an abuse of
terms, when a gesture from his cousin induced him
to continue silent. ¶ "Will you have the goodness,
Mr. Bragg," said the latter, "to give me some accurate
notion of the composition of this meeting? Surely, Mr.
Howel did not attend it?" ¶ Aristobulus was obliged to
confess he did not. Mr. Effingham then named some
twenty or thirty of the more respectable and intelligent
inhabitants of the village, including nearly every one
who, by social position, age, or residence, could have
a right to be active on such a question, and he found
that not one of them all had been present. Surprised at
the result, after the parade with which Mr. Bragg had
introduced the subject of the meeting, he next inquired
the names of those who had actually been foremost in
the matter. By far the greater number were composed
of that floating population which forms so large and
so unsettled a part of most American communities,
and some were actually residents of only a month's
standing. ¶ "These persons are mostly strangers to
me," said Mr. Effingham, "and by their years, or their
residence, can know little of the merits of the disputed

question, and absolutely nothing of my father, who has now been dead nearly thirty years." ¶ "They are, notwithstanding, the people, sir!" ¶ "No, sir, they are *not* the people; and it is as impudent a pretension on their part to lay claim to be so considered as it is to lay claim to my property." ¶ "It is enough that they consider themselves the people," said John Effingham, "to pretend to do anything. I trust, Ned, you do not mean to submit to this outrage?" ¶ "What would you have me do, John, but pity those who are so grossly ignorant of propriety as to set themselves up as judges in their own cause? Certainly, I shall maintain to the letter my legal rights, and further than that I do not see anything is required of me. That much is now required even in behalf of the laws of our common country." ¶ "But they have publicly expressed their contempt of you!" ¶ "The surest possible sign they do not feel it. Contempt is a silent quality, and is never paraded before the world. No man is despised when it is thought necessary to make solemn and formal declarations to that effect. I hope by my conduct, to show on which side the contempt really exists." ¶

	"They B
192.9	in the]A; for ~ B
192.11	for the opinions of those who have sufficiently demonstrated that their opinions are of no value, by the heedless manner in which they have]A; for opinions the worthlessness of which is so clearly demonstrated by the heedless manner in which those who avow them have B
192.12	are of]A; have AMAN
192.17	to tell]A; will ~ AMAN, B
192.19	laws]A; law AMAN, B
192.20	prosecute]A; persecute B
192.30	penalties]A; pains and ~ AMAN, B
192.32	character]A; characters AMAN, B
192.36	Aristabulus.]A; Aristabulus. It will make ill-blood, and an unpleasant neighborhood." AMAN; Aristobulus. "It will make ill-blood, and an unpleasant neighbourhood." B
192.38	no one]A; no man AMAN, B
192.39	thinks *itself*]A; thinks itself AMAN; think themselves B

192.39	affair]A; case AMAN, B
193.1	that cannot err, and know that the public has not]A; which must have thoroughly convinced you that the public have B
193.3	bit]A; point AMAN, B
193.13	that]A; because B
193.27	has more claims]A; have more claim B
193.28	it has fallen into error, it]A; they have fallen into error they B
193.31	county]A; country AMAN, B
193.32	pocket]A; pockets AMAN, B
193.33	with a view]A; in order AMAN; so B
194.1	its disposition]A; their ~ B
194.3	gave]A; he ~ AMAN, B
194.4	those]A; those the AMAN; those who were B
194.19	set]A; order B
194.19	came]A; comes AMAN, B
194.23	where]A; when AMAN, B
194.31	propinquity]A; propensity AMAN; approximation CAMAN
194.39	that fault]A; the ~ AMAN, B
195.3	public was]A; ~ were B
195.5	getting to be]A; becoming B
195.16	error]A; errors AMAN, B
195.23	rightly enough in the general signification of the term, they]A; they rightly enough, in the general signification of the term, AMAN, B
195.27	views]A; regards B
195.30	was greatly pained]A; felt greatly annoyed B
196.1	insist]A; am satisfied B
196.1	much altered]A; altered B
196.27	and have]A; ~ I ~ AMAN, B
196.33	can know]A; know AMAN, B
197.2	get to be]A; become B
197.4	recurrences . . . accustom]A; recurrence . . . accustoms B
197.8	barely becoming]A; not B
197.10	revere. In short, everything contributes to produce such a state of things, painful as it may be to all of any feeling, and little to oppose it."]A; revere." B

197.13	in being]A; when B
197.20	the government]A; government AMAN, B
198.2	quarter]A; question AMAN; respect CAMAN, B
198.7	parallel]A; a ~ AMAN, B
198.10	neglect the duties]A; neglect duties AMAN
198.10	is a little too apt to neglect the duties is ought to discharge, and to assume duties it has]A; are a little too apt to neglect duties they ought to discharge, and to assume duties they have B
199.16	it has]A; as ~ B
199.18	and which were dignified]A; dignified B
199.19	been also said]A; been said already AMAN; been said CAMAN, B
199.24	having]A; had B
199.28	small]A; some ~ AMAN, B
199.28	five children, and of]A; who had five children, and a B
199.36	and by no means an]A; but by no means a very AMAN, B
199.40	but]A; excepting B
200.1	they]A; she and her mistress B
200.8	being herself a late arrival in]A; being herself a late arrival of AMAN; having herself but lately arrived at B
200.11	about making]A; to make B
200.13	obtruding herself]A; obtruding AMAN, B
200.23	has used]A; have ~ B
200.26	opposite the parlour windows]A; opposite to the parlour window AMAN, B
200.38	Mrs. Abbott being]A; for Mrs. Abbott was B
201.1	got to be]A; become B
201.6	you. Hurry,]A; you, Fury, AMAN, B
201.19	Debby]A; Delby AMAN, B
201.24	their poor carrots]A; carrots to their poor B
201.28	this instant]A; instantly AMAN, B
201.38	Stop in]A; Step ~ B
202.3	put in]A; said B
202.22	off of]A; off B
202.24	lighten her concern, you think.]A; heighten her concern AMAN, B
202.33	hold of]A; ~ on AMAN, B
202.36	true that]A ~ whether AMAN, B

203.10	the point of salvation up]A; up the point of salvation B
203.11	Miss Abbott]A; Mrs. ~ B
203.14	Miss Abbott]A; Mrs. ~ B
203.17	name, however,]A; name B
203.19	*warnts*]A; *wants* AMAN, B
203.20	*warnt*]A; *want* AMAN, B
203.30	if standing in his way, as if he were its owner, should the door happen to be open.]A; if it stand in his way, like its owner, if the door happen to be open. AMAN; if stand in his way, like its owner, if the door happen to be open only an inch. CAMAN; if it stand in his way, like its owner, if the door happen to be open only an inch. B
203.39	folks]A; the ~ AMAN, B
204.3	Miss Abbott]A; Mrs. Abbot B
205.6	ailings even]A; ailings B
205.10	unqualifiedly]A; dreadfully AMAN, B
205.20	a widower's]A; widowers B
205.25	horror of]A; ~ at B
205.34	lady, who had lent her name to a neighbour,]A; lady B
205.36	in the head]A; on ~ ~ B
206.5	are as]A; as AMAN, B
206.24	to nigh]A; nigh to B
206.29	paintings]A; painting AMAN, B
206.31	'our beautiful nature']CE; ^ *our* beautiful nature ^ B
206.32	it, and, as]A; it; as B
206.33	backsliding]A; backslidings B
207.1	and things touching private interests, that I know she did and must understand, she always disdainfully refused to enter into.]A; and she always disdainfully refused to enter into things touching private interest, that I know she did and must understand. B
207.2	interests]A; interest AMAN
207.6	preaching was she sitting,]A; preaching, AMAN, B
207.9	regenerating, soul-reviving, spirit-groaning,]A; regenerating, AMAN, B
207.15	by *that* parson.]A; by the power. AMAN; by their power. B
207.29	to it]A; ~ *that* AMAN, B
207.34	county]A; country AMAN, B

207.37	has owned it. The public, moreover, says it owns it, and what the public says,]A; have owned it. They public, moreover, *say* they own it, and what the public say B
207.40	does]A; do B
208.1	It *does*]A; They *do* B
208.1	nameless]A; lady B
208.12	and was not]A; and not B
208.14	the vacuums]A; vacuums AMAN, B
208.18	activity]A; an ~ B
*208.31	unlike]A; like AMAN, B
208.32	hopes]A; gossip AMAN, B
208.35	the means]A; means B
208.35	corroboration]A; a ~ B
209.5	accounts]A; account AMAN, B
209.11	and when a sufficient time had elapsed to prove that these prurient denouncers of their fellow-citizens had taken wit in their anger, he]A; and after a time he B
209.22	it had]A; they ~ B
209.27	it]A; they B
209.31	every one]A; everybody B
209.33	insisting that]A; insisting AMAN, B
209.34	choose]A; ~ that B
210.10	will]A; does AMAN, B
210.15	nearly]A; closely AMAN, B
210.19	constantly]A; actually AMAN, B
210.20	being]A; their ~ B
210.21	have got to bow]A; bow B
211.18	gay buoyancy]A; buoyancy AMAN, B
211.19	anticipations]A; hopes AMAN, B
211.19	a country-house]A; an American country house AMAN, B
211.21	near]A; nearly AMAN, B
211.26	near]A; nearly B
211.27	land, moreover,]A; land, B
211.29	this rapid]A; such ~ AMAN, B
211.31	Eve]A; Grace AMAN
211.33	Mrs. Hawker]A; the first AMAN, B
212.6	prettily]A; gaily AMAN, B
212.9	and I]A; I AMAN, B
212.11	is but]A; is AMAN, B

212.15   as free]A; so ~ B
212.19   In no case, however,]A; But, in no case, AMAN
212.21   but, as for]A; for B
212.21   insist]A; maintain that B
212.30   in]A; but ~ AMAN; yet ~ B
212.32   In nothing, perhaps, did there exist no differences]A;
          Perhaps there is no difference more prominent than
          that which shows itself B
212.32   differences]A; difference AMAN
212.35   in their populations.]A; in their populations, in many
          essentials. AMAN; between their populations, in many
          essentials. CAMAN; between the habits and tastes of
          their respective populations. B
212.38   answered]A; said B
213.6   cause]A; causes B
213.9   is to be]A; is B
213.11   that]A; which B
213.13   that]A; which B
213.21   practical, and the practical qualities get to be imparted
          even to]A, CAMAN; piratical, and the guilty gets to
          be imparted to AMAN; practical, and the practical
          qualities are imparted even to B
214.3   devoutest]A, CAMAN; devoted AMAN; most devout B
214.3   get]A; become B
214.9   just]A; vivid AMAN, B
214.14   put in]A; said B
214.15   who had]A; had also B
214.19   Howel?" ¶ "Excellent, the best in the world, John
          Effingham."]A; Howel?" AMAN, B
214.23   polygamy, if it had a British]A; any usage of such an
          origin AMAN; any usage which can boast such an B
214.26   reproachfully. ¶ "That is a question I shall leave Mr.
          Howel himself to answer."]A; reproachfully. AMAN, B
214.30   prejudices.]A; prejudice AMAN, B
214.34   picture, France]A; picture is afforded by France, B
214.36   we]A; one AMAN, B
215.17   please]A; pleases B
215.29   few]A; as ~ B
215.30   of the greater distances is done by steam,]A; is
          accomplished by means of steam, think of B
215.34   this]A; that ~ AMAN, B

215.37	except]A; but AMAN
216.3	more than the expected number of guests was in the vehicle]A; the vehicle contained more than than the expected number of guests B
216.6	that]A; who AMAN, B
216.9	until]A; ~ after AMAN, B
216.9	done]A; performed B
216.10	profound was]A; ~ were B
216.11	got to supplant]A; supplanted B
216.21	reached]A; had ~ AMAN, B
216.23	boat]A; boats AMAN, B
216.35	than that of]A; than B
216.39	as much]A; so ~ B
217.1	gave him pleasure]A; gratified him exceedingly B
217.3	a tone of thought and breeding, moreover, that was as far removed as possible from any thing strained or artificial:]A; which was at the same time completely removed from anything of a strained or artificial character B
217.14	all: for the]A; all. The AMAN, B
217.18	of Paul Powis']A; to Paul Powis AMAN, B
217.18	act]A; correct AMAN
217.24	after all]A; when ~ AMAN, B
217.31	to his account]A; on that circumstance AMAN, B
217.37	were connected]A; are ~ B
218.7	was more rejoiced]A; rejoiced more sincerely B
218.8	his fate proved to be]A; was his fate AMAN, B
218.10	circumstance with me,]A; circumstance B
218.15	that]A; what AMAN, B
218.17	friend," taking]A; friend," said Mr. Effingham, taking B
218.31	room]A; absence B
218.33	truly loved you and your daughter, until both]A; really loved your daughter until she AMAN, B
219.18	must have been overworked in this way, lately,]A; have some notions of your own about these matters, AMAN, B
219.23	know each other regularly now]A; knew each other regularily AMAN; knew each other regularly B
219.24	going through the ceremony yourself]A; making them acquainted AMAN, B
219.25	you]A; yourself AMAN, B

220.6	acme]A; perfection B
220.11	old England]A; England AMAN, B
220.15	thick,]A; thick that B
220.28	in the world]A; under the sun AMAN, B
220.31	along in]A; in AMAN, B
220.38	discourse]A; discussion AMAN, B
220.38	ladies]A; ~ again AMAN, B
220.39	excellencies]A; excellences B
221.13	insisting]A; insisted AMAN, B
221.14	got to be]A; become B
221.14	or with]A; or AMAN; or through B
221.16	consider the entire country as things had been]A; form his opinion of the entire country from the aspect which things B
221.17	experience, in the vicinity of the docks]A; experience. AMAN; experience, near St. Catharine's Docks. CAMAN, B
221.19	Hawker]A; ~ pleasantly AMAN, B
221.20	really]A; do ~ AMAN, B
221.21	hazard]A; hazards AMAN, B
221.27	and Trinculos]A; Trinculos AMAN, B
221.31	person in the way of libations]A; person B
221.35	claims]A; claim B
221.37	wind;]A; wind, in such a subject, AMAN, B
222.7	praises]A; praise B
222.20	Eve, smiling,]A; Eve, AMAN, B
222.22	perfect gratitude]A; gratitude AMAN, B
222.23	lady]A; ~ pleasantly AMAN, B
222.25	my younger]A; any older AMAN, B
222.26	Eve, anxious to change the subject, for she saw that Paul was]A; Eve, laughing, and anxious to change the subject, for she saw Paul AMAN; Eve, laughing, but anxious to change the subject, for she saw Paul CAMAN, B
222.28	a decision]A; my ~ AMAN, B
222.30	no feeling involved in the]A; no feeling involved in her AMAN; no reason for her B
222.35	shall be made]A; must be AMAN, B
222.37	lady]A; lady's AMAN
223.3	pleasantry]A; trifling AMAN, B

223.6	improper]A; ~ intentionally AMAN, B
223.11	eyes]A; eye AMAN, B
223.17	before she answered in the negative, and this too in a way to give more meaning to her reply, although nothing could be farther from her intentions.]A; and this, too, in a way to give more meaning to her reply, although nothing could be further from her intentions before she answered in the negative. AMAN, B
223.22	blemish]A; trifling ~ AMAN, B
223.23	fifty]A; ~ , yet AMAN; ~ yet B
223.26	adroitly abandoned the subject]A; instantly abandoned the trifling AMAN, B
223.31	may, and the Truck lives another revolution of the sun!]A; may. B
223.33	retire soon]A; speedily retire B
224.1	caprices]A; caprice AMAN, B
224.4	can conceive of]A; understand B
224.5	scarcely of any direct declaration, that shall not]A; I feel assured that any direct declaration of yours must B
224.6	both these]A; ~ of ~ AMAN, B
224.7	profound]A; his ~ AMAN, B
224.8	observed]A; said AMAN; said, struggling not to betray herself CAMAN, B
224.11	thankful]A; thoughtful AMAN; grateful CAMAN, B
224.12	a friend]A; an old friend AMAN, B
224.25	charges]A; charge B
224.27	as at all became]A; as coolly became AMAN; as became CAMAN, B
224.27	quite a minute]A; for a brief period B
224.29	aroused]A; called AMAN, B
224.29	sustain him]A; restrain him AMAN; sustain the latter CAMAN, B
224.33	an unusual impatience of manner]A; an impatience of manner unusual to her AMAN; an impatience of manner and an abruptness unusual to her CAMAN, B
225.2	quite lately]A; lately B
225.5	was from]A; came from AMAN, B
225.8	Mr. Ducie kept this]A; This, Mr. Ducie kept AMAN
225.11	but I]A; and ~ B
225.16	tastes]A; taste B

225.18   have been]A; be B
225.20   neither—I should think he must be from the south.]
            A; either;—he must be from the south, I should think.
            AMAN, B
225.22   embarrassment]A; an awkward embarrassment AMAN;
            her feelings CAMAN, B
225.23   steadily answered]A; answered AMAN; answered
            simply CAMAN, B
225.27   have heard]A; heard AMAN; hear CAMAN, B
225.29   surely be]A; be AMAN, B
225.32   would gladly]A; could ~ AMAN
225.34   much gratified]A; gratified AMAN, B
225.35   has suddenly become]A; is AMAN, B
225.37   it all]A; he is AMAN, B
226.3   word]A; words AMAN, B
226.13   residences]A; residence B
226.17   were]A; became B
226.19   as he has subsequently been on]A; as, subsequently, on
            AMAN, B
226.28   not]A; ~ now AMAN, B
226.28   the honour]A; this ~ AMAN, B
226.31   with being]A; at ~ AMAN, B
226.37   how much he is pleased with her.]A; that he is pleased
            with her, AMAN; that he is happiest when permitted
            to be near my cousin. CAMAN, B
227.2   so openly]A; openly AMAN, B
228.16   the door]A; his ~ AMAN, B
228.17   opened]A; was ~ B
228.18   I left]A; left AMAN, B
228.22   the room]A; his ~ AMAN, B
228.27   a word]A; one ~ AMAN, B
228.32   know that]A; know B
229.1   though it may]A; but ~ will AMAN, B
229.8   his load]A; the article mentioned AMAN; the case
            CAMAN, B
229.9   the visit]A; he AMAN, B
229.11   any]A; any one B
229.16   are they]A; they are B
229.17   them]A; ~ for B
229.21   opposite]A; ~ to AMAN, B

229.22	and first]A; ~ of ~ AMAN, B
229.27	first read the paper]A; read the paper himself AMAN, B
228.28	in form, an unsealed letter; and it was addressed]A; addressed B
229.29	The certificate itself]A; This certificate AMAN; The certificate B
229.35	for which I know she has since been deeply repentant] A; that I know she has since been deeply sorry for AMAN, B
230.5	some time in]A; for some time in the mind of B
230.6	The latter]A; They AMAN, B
230.9	spoke]A; all ~ AMAN, B
230.22	freely professed]A; professed freely AMAN, B
230.25	was addressed]A; and ~ ~ AMAN, B
230.27	old]A; of old date AMAN, B
230.30	employed by]A; which actuated B
230.34	but]A; only B
230.34	he is evidently]A; evidently AMAN, B
*230.37	letter just named, and then he laid it]A; letters just named, and then he laid them AMAN, B
231.1	No. 1, and letter No. 2,]A; "No. 2," and letter "No. 3," CAMAN, B
231.3	Strongly]A; Strong AMAN, B
231.8	regret in]A; regrets in AMAN; regrets for CAMAN, B
231.14	got to be]A; become B
231.23	paper he had last]A; papers he had AMAN, B
231.26	the still more]A; their most AMAN; their more CAMAN, B
231.28	events]A; event AMAN, B
231.40	passed]A; had ~ B
232.1	later]A; latter AMAN, B
232.2	the annuity]A; an ~ AMAN, B
232.3	after]A; of AMAN, B
232.4	term]A; name AMAN, B
232.6	near]A; nearly B
232.7	consumed more than]A; consumed AMAN, B
232.9	had struck]A; struck AMAN, B
232.16	what was the precise injustice]A; precisely what injustice was B

232.24	secretary]A; secretaire B
232.25	that]A; which B
232.26	busied himself]A; was for some time employed B
232.28	we observed]A; were [*illegible*] AMAN; were observed CAMAN, B
232.29	the packet]A; his ~ AMAN, B
232.31	secretary]A; secretaire B
232.33	read]A; yet ~ AMAN, B
232.34	lights before you]A; light before us AMAN, B
232.37	secretary]A; secretaire B
232.38	contains]A; usually ~ AMAN, B
233.2	my secretary]A; that secretary of my own AMAN; that secretaire of my own B
233.3	precious effects]A; own property AMAN, B
233.5	It]A; That AMAN, B
233.5	the case]A; this ~ AMAN, B
233.9	countenance]A; manner and ~ AMAN, B
233.9	excited]A; ~ all AMAN, B
233.10	assent, and]A; assent; B
233.11	secretary]A; secretaire B
233.14	when]A; and AMAN, B
233.15	enough]A; ~ together AMAN, B
233.18	in wishing]A; by ~ AMAN
233.19	bestow;]A; bestow, and AMAN, B
233.21	in your]A; of ~ AMAN, B
233.28	for]A; to know AMAN, B
233.31	voices and looks]A; voice and look B
233.36	feel any curiosity]A; feel sufficient, interest AMAN; feel sufficient interest CAMAN; desire information B
233.36	desire]A; wish B
233.38	things]A; ~ that AMAN, B
233.39	interest]A; an ~ AMAN, B
234.1	and,]A; and being B
234.3	places]A; place B
234.5	who spoke huskily]A; with a melancholy smile AMAN, B
234.7	a single]A; one AMAN, B
234.15	given you.]A; given B
234.23	their young protector was left]A; he had left their young protector AMAN, B

234.36	the imperative]A; an ~ AMAN, B
234.37	resign]A; abandon my profession B
235.3	little skill in]A; skill in the AMAN, B
235.6	country]A; your ~ AMAN, B
235.7	a kinsman]A; your ~ AMAN, B
235.12	most favourable impression, on]A; most favorable impression in my favor on all AMAN; strongest impression in my favor on CAMAN, B
235.16	perhaps,]A; perhap, to any on board, AMAN, B
235.16	was no just ground]A; was no just grounds AMAN; were no just grounds CAMAN, B
235.27	imputations]A; of his ~ AMAN, B
235.28	between]A; and, as, AMAN, B
235.29	the humour]A; a ~ AMAN, B
235.33	suitable]A; a ~ AMAN, B
235.35	ordered to chase]A; he chased AMAN, B
235.37	to sail]A; sailing orders AMAN, B
236.1	away with him,]A; away B
236.4	got to be,]A; became B
236.5	when there have]A; where ~ has AMAN, B
236.6	character]A; characters AMAN, B
236.16	opinion]A; foreign ~ AMAN, B
236.16	respect]A; should ~ B
236.19	disposed]A; induced B
236.20	might otherwise have been the case]A; they might otherwise have been disposed to do B
236.28	surprise]A; ~ that B
236.28	deaths]A; death B
236.37	of the opposition]A; opposition AMAN, B
237.2	quietly]A; legally AMAN, B
237.6	expected]A; ~ that B
237.10	swaggers]A; even ~ AMAN, B
237.13	to have]A; in having B
237.16	a dog]A; the ~ AMAN, B
237.19	will one day]A; one day will AMAN, B
237.26	your pleasure]A; according to your own pleasure B
237.29	Mademoiselle]A; if ~ AMAN, B
237.32	question]A; a ~ AMAN, B
237.33	scarce]A; scarcely B
237.35	uncertainty]A; doubt AMAN, B

238.7	and dying, he]A; and B
238.8	artisan]A; founder B
238.14	for so many]A; for twenty AMAN; so many CAMAN, B
238.19	knew any thing]A; knew AMAN, B
238.25	repudiated]A; repudiates AMAN, B
238.26	and yet]A; yet AMAN, B
238.27	from which the offer came]A; which offered it AMAN; which made the offer CAMAN, B
238.33	in his turn]A; himself AMAN, B
238.34	largest]A; larger AMAN, B
238.35	commoner]A; common AMAN, B
238.36	as much]A; so much B
239.4	ever]A; had ~ AMAN, B
239.7	own mortifications]A; mortifications AMAN, B
239.9	man at least affects]A; men, at least, affect AMAN, B
239.10	merits]A; merit B
239.27	Americans, in a moral sense, pass]A; Americans pass, in a moral sense, at least, AMAN, B
239.30	mediums! It is]A; mediums is B
239.31	notions]A; notion B
239.35	the seals]A; our ~ B
239.36	yet, certainly, very promising]A; yet very promising AMAN; not very promising at present B
239.40	own room]A; room AMAN, B
240.1	renewed]A; repeated B
240.2	brilliantly handsome]A; handsome AMAN, B
241.28	etiquette,]A; etiquette, however, AMAN
241.29	soon settled]A; settled AMAN, B
241.30	the rest]A; most AMAN, B
241.31	lake, and to join them in the course of the afternoon.] A; lake in the course of the afternoon, if he had influence enough to induce them to accompany him. AMAN, B
242.7	tastes]A; taste B
242.12	conceal all]A; conceal AMAN, B
242.15	wish]A; you ~ B
242.24	ill]A; little AMAN, B
242.28	professional]A; little AMAN, B
242.35	due to]A; due AMAN

243.1	a ship]A; ship AMAN, B
243.2	sir, if]A; if AMAN, B
243.18	as did his grandfather before him.]A; as his grandfather before him did. AMAN, B
243.20	were none]A; are ~ B
243.21	better saints]A; better AMAN, B
243.26	these terms]A; such ~ AMAN, B
243.28	dropped]A; drop AMAN, B
243.33	hear]A; heard AMAN, B
243.34	'casting-anchors,']A; "casting anchor," AMAN, B
243.39	sail, too,]A; sail, AMAN, B
244.4	But seven]A; Only ~ B
244.9	rigging and modesty, both at the same time]A; mathematics and modesty, both at the same time AMAN; their grammar, as well as a little modesty, and both at the same time, too. CAMAN, B
244.23	Quite probably]A; Probably B
244.23	before heard]A; heard AMAN; even heard CAMAN, B
244.25	Notwithstanding]A; Now, not withstanding AMAN, B
244.28	in which he was now engaged]A; he was now engaged in AMAN, B
244.30	being]A; having been AMAN, B
244.34	remark]A; remarks AMAN, B
244.34	commodore's]A; commodore B
244.40	thrashing]A; threshing AMAN, B
245.14	earnestness]A; his ~ AMAN, B
245.15	A 'sogdollager' is a salmon trout, and not a species] A; The sogdollager is a salmon trout, and a species AMAN, B
245.19	in wasting]A; of ~ B
246.15	salmon trout]A; salmon AMAN, B
246.17	almost ready to believe]A; ready to believe almost AMAN, B
246.20	allude now. A]A; allude. Now a AMAN, B
246.22	those animals]A; these ~ AMAN, B
246.26	mountain]A; mountains AMAN, B
246.33	accompanies]A; generally ~ AMAN, B
246.34	pertain]A; pertained AMAN, B
246.34	land]A; law AMAN
246.35	larger]A; longer AMAN, B

246.37	duly impressing]A; impressing AMAN, B
246.38	mere fresh-water]A; fresh-water AMAN, B
247.6	the mountain]A; that ~ AMAN, B
247.22	as wide]A; so ~ B
247.29	peculiarity]A; ~ in this intercourse of a general nature AMAN
247.31	the courtesy of]A; of AMAN; the usages of CAMAN, B
247.36	where]A; when B
247.37	prepared a dinner]A; preparred dinner AMAN; prepared dinner CAMAN,B
248.5	venerable oaks]A; old ~ AMAN; fines ~ CAMAN; fine ~ B
248.6	general,]A; general, with his mouth half filled, AMAN, B
248.16	will give]A; gives AMAN, B
248.20	forms]A; form B
248.23	differs]A; different AMAN; is different CAMAN, B
248.25	new to me]A; new to AMAN; new too CAMAN, B
248.27	to many happy returns of]A; many happy returns to AMAN, B
248.30	a knarled]A; an knarled AMAN; a gnarled B
248.30	looked like a man who was taking an observation, for near a minute.]A; looked like a man who was intently taking an observation, for near a minute. AMAN; looked, for near a minute, like a man who was intently taking an observation. B
248.35	There is]A; That ~ AMAN, B
249.1	come]A ~ out B
249.13	with]A; in company ~ AMAN, B
249.15	of a]A; on ~ B
249.16	of a]A; on ~ B
249.20	strike]A; snap AMAN, B
249.23	Certain]A; Certainly B
249.25	I am]A; I'm AMAN, B
249.29	since they]A; as ~ B
249.30	would sometimes]A; would AMAN; *would* B
250.6	in the top]A; on ~ ~ B
250.27	If]A; Now, if AMAN, B

250.39	put in]A; said B
251.15	bottom]A; stand AMAN, B
251.16	When]A; As AMAN, B
251.17	cup]A; eyes AMAN, B
251.24	ground to them]A; ground B
251.41	in the course of mingling,]A; being mingled B
252.3	his awe]A; awe B
253.21	concealment,]A; concealment, my dear sir, B
253.31	with]A; ~ all AMAN, B
253.35	returning home]A; going back, AMAN; returning, CAMAN, B
254.2	is still]A; as it still is B
254.7	Depend on]A; ~ upon AMAN, B
254.25	get it ready]A; go AMAN, B
255.20	which covers]A; that ~ B
255.22	got]A; gotten AMAN, B
255.26	water]A; waters B
255.30	arena so lately in]A; spot so lately in AMAN; spot so recently the subject of B
255.34	public, his beloved public,]A; public, AMAN, B
256.1	delights]A; delight B
256.13	merry-making]A; merry-makings AMAN, B
256.14	tastes]A; taste B
256.26	companions, either,]A; companions, B
256.27	a humour that was]A; humour, B
256.29	world, that was]A; world
256.31	Grace, alone,]A; Grace B
256.40	duty]A; duties AMAN, B
256.40	was]A; this was B
257.1	has]A; had AMAN, B
257.15	tenderly]A; so ~ AMAN, B
257.19	witticisms]A; witticism AMAN, B
257.22	these outlandish dog-in-the-mangerisms.]A; such dog-in-the-mangerism. AMAN; such dog-in-the-mangerisms, that no one else could enjoy. CAMAN, B
257.27	Mrs.]A; my dear ~ AMAN, B
257.33	impute]A; impute it to B
257.37	true, however,]A; true B
257.37	haunts]A; courts AMAN, B

257.38	the education]A; his ~ AMAN, B
257.40	my foot]A; foot AMAN, B
258.4	separating naturally, they strolled in groups or pairs again]A; separating into groups or pairs, they again strolled B
258.6	the preparations]A; their ~ AMAN, B
258.9	view]A; sight AMAN, B
258.20	few causes]A; little cause AMAN, B
258.24	Not]A; Never AMAN, B
258.36	amusements]A; amusement AMAN, B
258.41	she even wrung]A; and she even wrung AMAN; and she wrung CAMAN, B
259.1	and in]A; in AMAN, B
259.12	merely what]A; what AMAN, B
259.13	signifies]A; means AMAN, B
259.32	what she knew]A; her knowledge B
259.33	not such another]A; no such other AMAN, B
259.35	perception]A; perfection AMAN, B
259.35	equal excellence]A; excellence AMAN, B
259.41	well knew]A knew AMAN, B
260.4	was forgotten]A; were ~ B
260.14	that sense is]A; sense is AMAN; sense CAMAN, B
260.15	beauty]A; beauty even AMAN; beauty alone B
260.17	to the feelings]A; on ~ ~ AMAN, B
260.31	another thought]A; a thought AMAN, B
261.15	astray]A; far ~ AMAN, B
261.19	lights.]A; lights, which are not the lights of reason. AMAN, B
261.21	more than once]A; half a dozen times AMAN, B
261.22	road]A; *train* AMAN, B
261.30	wife]A; partner AMAN, B
262.4	protecting]A; in ~ AMAN, B
262.5	father]A; excellent ~ AMAN, B
262.11	sacred]A; ~ of life AMAN, B
262.14	disposition]A; dispositions AMAN, B
262.29	though, as silence universally 'gives consent—'"]A; though "as silence gives consent—" AMAN; though 'as silence gives consent'—" B
262.33	with each other]A; to each, other AMAN; to each other's CAMAN; to each other B

262.34	to cause]A; to AMAN; for CAMAN, B
262.38	making me a very]A; making me very AMAN; making a very CAMAN, B
263.27	meant]A; means AMAN, B
263.28	the girl]A; that ~ AMAN, B
263.34	a boat]A; boat AMAN, B
263.35	suitable close]A; proper close AMAN; dignified close CAMAN, B
263.37	when the latter]A; who AMAN, B
263.39	host]A; latter AMAN, B
264.3	an intention]A; any ~ AMAN, B
264.15	fortune]A; fortunes AMAN
264.24	in her heart]A; in heart AMAN, B
264.38	the facts]A; facts AMAN, B
264.39	things, observation, as it usually happens]A; respects observation, as is usually the case AMAN, B
264.40	expose]A; detect AMAN, B
264.40	has been]A; had been AMAN, B
265.4	things. Perhaps you will think me selfish, but] A; things, but AMAN; things. At the risk of being thought selfish, CAMAN, B
265.20	a moment]A; for ~ ~ B
265.30	wrong]A; wrongly B
265.31	Wrong]A; Wrongly B
265.32	simple-hearted]A; simple minded AMAN, B
265.34	might]A; ought to AMAN, B
266.8	last in the secret]A; latest in the secret AMAN; last to know it CAMAN, B
266.9	believe]A; ~ that AMAN, B
266.11	strenuously endeavoured]A; endeavored AMAN; endeavoured B
266.17	fell, the young baronet was at hand to receive her. Instead]A; felt, the young baronet was at hand to receive her. Instead AMAN; felt the young baronet was at hand to receive her, instead B
267.16	fourth]A; 4th AMAN, B
267.19	a parade]A; the ~ AMAN, B
267.20	were consumed]A; was ~ AMAN, B
267.22	drinks]A; liquors B
267.25	festival of the nation]A; national festival B

267.26   in]A; decked ~ B
267.32   *la célébration de votre indépendance*]A; the celebration
            of your *indépendance* AMAN; the celebration *de votre*
            indépendance CAMAN, B
267.34   are made]A; have been making B
267.34   is to be]A; are to be AMAN
268.1   *et Monsieur Powis, même!"*]A; *même, Monsieur Powis?"*
            AMAN, B
268.7   mutes of]A; ~ attending B
268.20   put in]A; observed B
268.37   collisions]A; collision B
268.39   collisions]A; collision B
268.39   associations]A; associating AMAN, B
269.7   "Surely, sir,"—Eve never spoke to Mr. Bragg, now,
            without using a repelling politeness—"surely, sir,]A;
            "Surely, sir, AMAN, B
269.11   unpopular; nor do I see why the sports in a city"—
            Aristabulus was much too peculiar in his notions,
            to call any place that had a mayor and aldermen a
            town,—"should not be just as rustic as those of a
            village. The contrary supposition violates the principle
            of equality."]A; unpopular." AMAN; unpopular; nor do
            I see why the sports in a *city*"—Aristabulus was much
            too peculiar in his notions, to call any place that had a
            mayor and aldermen a *town*,—"should not be as rustic
            as those in a village. The contrary supposition violates
            the principle of equality." CAMAN; unpopular; nor do
            I see why sports in a *city*"—Aristabulus was much too
            peculiar in his notions, to call any place that had a
            mayor and alderman a *town*,—"should not be as rustic
            as those in a village. The contrary supposition violates
            the principle of equality." B
269.20   shoulders]A; shoulder AMAN, B
269.20   significant]A; silent AMAN, B
269.27   some]A; *des* AMAN, B
269.35   form]A; be formed B
270.1   ladies]A; three ~ AMAN, B
270.2   and, accordingly,]A; accordingly, and, AMAN, B
270.9   The academy]A; That ~ AMAN, B
270.11   town-meetings, and caucuses,]A; and town-meetings, B

270.14	appeared]A; appears CAMAN
270.19	thought to be the latest fashion]A; considered as such B
270.21	the more admitted bucks]A; those more openly acknowledged leaders of the public taste B
270.24	glanced her eye]A; cast a passing glance B
270.26	ago]A; before AMAN, B
270.28	as striking]A; so striking AMAN, B
270.36	the present assembly]A; this assembly AMAN, B
270.38	a pretty fair sample, too, of their appearance]A; a pretty fair average of their appearance AMAN; present a pretty fair specimen of their general appearance B
271.8	as respects your own sex]A; so far as your own sex are concerned B
271.9	mean]A; have mentioned B
271.10	truth]A; the truth B
271.11	the hands and the feet]A; the hands and feet AMAN; their hands and feet B
271.11	Those are]A; There ~ AMAN, B
271.16	are they]A; they are B
271.20	just]A; had ~ B
271.22	That of the occasion of which we write]A; That which was heard on the present occasion B
271.35	or a particular mode of signing complaints practised by seamen, in]A; or a communication AMAN; or a particular mode of signing letters, practised by seamen, in CAMAN, B
271.36	cannot tell which is]A; could not tell which was AMAN, B
272.18	time]A; times AMAN, B
272.21	largest investments in]A; largest inroads upon AMAN; most rapid advances towards B
272.26	further]A; farther B
272.33	how far, or it might be better to say, how high, ignorance reaches on such subjects, and how few men,] A; how few men AMAN, B
272.37	John Effingham]A; Mrs. Bloomfield AMAN, B
272.39	as an average information]A; taken as an average B
272.39	superior]A; far superior AMAN, B
273.1	notion]A; notions AMAN, B

273.1   common in]A; others with B
273.2   there can be but one truth in any thing, however]A;
            but there can be but one truth in any thing AMAN, B
273.7   their every-day]A; the every day AMAN; everyday B
273.8   institutions]A; institution B
273.9   regulated]A; governed AMAN, B
273.19   the possession]A; in the possession B
273.19   gain by party]A; reap the benefit B
273.21   as strong]A; so strong B
273.22   a government]A; legislation B
273.23   place]A; the place AMAN
273.32   Mademoiselle]A; ~ Viefville AMAN, B
273.34   time]A; of ~ AMAN, B
273.34   But]A; ¶ "But AMAN, B
273.37   all who honour it]A; "all who honour it" AMAN; 'all
            who honour it' B
273.39   and which]A; one ~ AMAN, B
274.5   adapted]A; well adapted B
274.7   topped]A; crowned B
274.16   it was]A; they were AMAN, B
274.23   at hand]A; commencing B
274.25   gleaming with glancing light]A; one mass of brilliancy
            B
274.31   all the back-ground of persons and faces]A; the
            background was thronged by persons and faces, who B
274.33   a human]A; the human B
274.37   changes from brightness to deep darkness]A; transition
            from vivid brightness to deep gloom B
274.38   made the beauty of the scene, which soon extorted
            admiration from]A; constituted the most beautiful
            feature of the scene, and excited the admiration of B
275.15   three, by way of maintaining the equilibrium.]A;
            two three, by way of maintaining the equilibrium.
            CAMAN; two also AMAN
275.27   but the]A; besides ~ B
276.6   Active Inquirer]A; Free Inquirer AMAN
276.15   proportion of those of]A; proportion of B
276.17   man, and, as]A; man, as AMAN; man,. As CAMAN
            man. As B
276.23   motive for surprise]A; reason for astonishment B
276.25   other nations]A; others B

276.31	rules]A; has domination B
276.32	judges that]A; judges who B
276.34	shares in]A; should participate B
276.35	gross]A; great AMAN, B
277.5	its other evils]A; other of its evil consequences AMAN, B
277.7	that are propagated]A; propagated B
277.12	Active Inquirer]A; Free Inquirer AMAN
277.14	had never]A; never had AMAN, B
277.31	of such]A; such B
277.34	wades through]A; mades through the brine of the ocean AMAN; makes its way through the brine of the ocean CAMAN, B
278.21	improvements]A; improvement AMAN; an improvement CAMAN, B
278.21	Effingham]A; Effingham's AMAN, B
278.23	the branch]A; a ~ AMAN, B
278.23	this country]A; the ~ AMAN, B
278.28	irregularities]A; inequalities AMAN, B
278.35	irregularities]A; inequalities AMAN, B
278.39	got to move]A; were moving B
279.4	profiting immediately]A; immediately profiting AMAN, B
279.10	honours that accompany]A; honor that accompany AMAN; honour which accompanies B
279.15	pointedly]A; archly AMAN, B
279.17	involuntary]A; involuntarily AMAN, B
279.20	concealments]A; secrecy B
279.30	felt an interest in you, quite naturally,]A; naturally felt an interest in you, B
279.31	out]A; out to be B
279.33	own]A; admit B
279.33	my]A; within the AMAN, B
279.35	perhaps, may,]A; may, perhaps, B
279.36	in our]A; on ~ B
279.38	that she]A; of which she B
279.35	odd]A; oddly B
280.5	arm,]A; arm, as they pursued their walk, AMAN, B
280.7	moment]A; moment which B
280.10	feel]A; have felt B
280.15	best loved]A; loved best AMAN, B

280.23	mother's]A; mother B
280.27	as artificial]A; so artificial B
280.30	exactly say as much]A; say exactly as much AMAN; say so much as that B
280.31	in that way]A; for possessing the feeling in a very strong degree B
280.35	gets to feel]A; feels B
280.40	so many additional ties]A; additional ties AMAN; so many ties in addition to those of blood CAMAN, B
281.2	elder]A; older B
*281.5	justice]A; full justice CAMAN
281.7	men]A; man AMAN, B
281.9	fate]A; feeling B
281.10	easily]A; may be ~ B
281.10	continued and exacting]A; continued B
281.17	the institutions]A; their institutions B
281.18	we may]A; I could wish we might AMAN, B
281.30	this county]A; all this country AMAN, B
281.33	of religious]A; in religious B
282.3	should]A; might B
283.4	elastic]A; healthy AMAN, B
282.5	shall be]A; should be B
282.7	more]A; for ~ B
282.7	gets to be]A; becomes B
282.18	father's]A; father B
282.21	taste . . . caprice]A; tastes . . . caprices AMAN
282.22	main object]A; great object AMAN, B
282.27	heartlessness]A; heartliness AMAN; heartlissness CAMAN
282.30	a step]A; an act B
282.35	Spirit's sustaining]A; Spirit in sustaining B
282.35	us in]A all B
282.37	by the means of]A; through B
282.39	witnessed]A; enacted B
282.39	in some]A; by some B
283.4	who, in furthering their objects, were so accustomed to "stirring people up,"]A; who were so accustomed to "stirring people up," in furthering their objects, AMAN, B
283.7	which first]A; who first B

283.10	is accustomed]A; accustomed AMAN; was accustomed B
283.15	provincial school of religious]A; school of provincial religious AMAN, B
283.15	so much in favour, in]A; favoured by a portion of B
283.19	queer mixture]A; strange mixture B
283.21	and of]A; and AMAN, B
283.21	meannesses]A; meanness AMAN, B
283.26	tastes]A; taste B
283.31	so high]A; such high B
283.36	little shoemaker's loo]A; "little shoemaker's loo" AMAN, B
284.1	sentiments to which they had just listened]A; sentiments they had just listened AMAN; sentiments they had just listened to B
284.8	friend]A; friends AMAN, B
284.13	of the family]A; of family B
284.16	good-mother]A; great mother AMAN, B
284.24	interests]A; acquisition B
284.25	cause Eve to]A; make Eve B
284.27	currents as strong]A; as strong currents AMAN, B
284.28	as many]A; so ~ B
284.29	seldom]A; frequently B
284.31	would]A; might AMAN, B
284.32	that]A; in order that B
285.4	exhibiting]A; to exhibit B
285.7	what]A; of what AMAN, B
285.12	Which,]A; Which, I fear, AMAN, B
285.16	to habit, and to the]A; for habit and the B
285.24	strong]A; plain AMAN, B
285.25	not often then beyond the plainest of its effects]A; even then the feeling is of a very ordinary character B
285.30	into the grounds]A; in the grounds AMAN, B
285.34	and he clearly]A; and clearly AMAN, B
285.35	persons of those]A; persons AMAN, B
285.36	none of whom he had stopped]A; to none of whom had he spoken AMAN, B
286.6	hauteur]A; ~ and distance AMAN, B
286.12	a moment]A; for a moment B
286.12	then he removed]A; then removed B

286.18	the next pair that approached would be they]A; they would be the next pair who approached B
286.21	liberty to]A; liberty, which has tempted him to B
286.25	with our]A; of our AMAN, B
286.32	passenger]A; passenger with his master AMAN, B
286.39	the obscurity rendering]A; for the obscurity rendered AMAN, B
287.1	for each]A; as each AMAN, B
287.8	Miss Eve Effinghams]A; Miss Effinghams AMAN, B
287.26	it could have happened]A; it happened AMAN, B
287.38	captain?" demanded the laughing Eve]A; captain, to prevent you?" demanded Eve AMAN, B
287.40	next, and she]A; after that; she AMAN, B
288.12	all of]A; about B
288.19	that is]A; that was AMAN, B
288.20	*cannot*]A; *could* not AMAN, B
288.27	should be]A; shall be AMAN; shall both be CAMAN, B
288.36	the other]A; the appearance of the other AMAN, B
288.36	Oh!]A; Ah! AMAN, B
289.2	Oh!]A; Ah! AMAN, B
289.6	Dowse]A; Dowe B
289.8	that had]A; had AMAN; who had CAMAN, B
289.11	about the soul]A; in soul AMAN, B
289.17	Dowse]A; Dowe B
290.39	know that my]A; know AMAN, B
291.4	in the bargain]A; into ~ ~ B
291.21	and was]A; and he was AMAN, B
291.22	earnest]A; devout AMAN, B
291.26	this country]A; the ~ AMAN, B
291.37	doubted of]A; doubted B
291.39	justness]A; fitness AMAN, B
292.2	than of]A; but of AMAN, B
292.9	that get to be]A; who become B
292.13	advantages]A; advantage AMAN, B
292.18	the substance]A; their ~ B
292.19	is not]A; are not AMAN, B
292.26	felt]A; possessed B
292.28	improvement]A; an ~ AMAN, B
292.31	pretension of]A; ~ to B
292.35	only too closely associated in ordinary minds]A; too

	closely associated in ordinary minds alone B
292.36	elegancies]A; elegances B
292.40	the tone]A; that ~ ~ AMAN, B
293.2	peculiarity]A; peculiarities AMAN, B
293.7	agent]A; public agent AMAN, B
293.15	utter]A; to ~ AMAN, B
293.20	all this]A; this AMAN, B
293.24	and the petty]A; and petty AMAN, B
293.27	that the]A; if the B
293.28	was no]A; is no B
293.31	as much]A; so much B
293.36	principles]A; principle AMAN, B
293.37	attainments]A; attainment B
293.39	great principles of the institutions]A; governing principles of the government AMAN; ruling principles of their government B
294.1	sides against his own country]A; sides against his own government AMAN; part against those principles B
294.1	informing that of]A; informing B
294.3	legislative part of the government]A; legislature of the country B
294.5	The presses that have]A; That portion of the public press which has B
294.6	indifference or levity]A; indifference AMAN, B
294.6	a few would]A; a few would be influenced to AMAN; a few would be induced to CAMAN; another might be induced to B
294.10	reason that]A; ~ why B
294.23	get along with]A; put up with B
294.25	but those]A; except those B
294.30	brains]A; brain AMAN, B
295.1	probable that]A; probable, B
295.13	manner]A; measure AMAN, B
295.15	any prejudice]A; any prejudices AMAN; prejudices B
295.18	louder]A; more loudly B
295.23	have]A; have had AMAN, B
295.28	As I told Mr. Howel, in your presence, that]A; As I have I have told Mr. Howel, in your presence, that that AMAN; I have told Mr. Howel in your presence that that B
295.38	a near]A; any ~ AMAN, B

296.8	himself.]A; himself to be. AMAN, B
296.38	speaking]A; talking B
296.38	forced]A; rather forced AMAN, B
296.39	rather than voluntary]A; than voluntarily spoken B
297.1	need a permission, being]A; need such a permission, as you are AMAN, B
297.11	perhaps]A; nor perhaps B
297.25	made]A; were B
297.28	superiority, her attainments,]A; superiority of attainment, AMAN, B
297.30	did you possess]A; you possessed B
297.33	near]A; over and near AMAN, B
297.35	enabled]A; sufficed to permit AMAN, B
297.39	she said]A; said she B
298.6	but little]A; little AMAN, B
298.18	intentions]A; intention B
298.19	to exaggerate]A; exaggerate AMAN, B
299.2	as well as]A; and AMAN, B
299.12	an imperious duty]A; a duty AMAN, B
299.13	observed]A; the case AMAN, B
299.17	and Paul, endeavouring]A; while Paul was endeavouring B
299.24	earthly]A; all earthly AMAN, B
299.31	dwelling]A; to dwell B
299.35	which can]A; can AMAN, B
299.38	when a mere child]A; at my birth AMAN; when I was a mere child CAMAN, B
300.3	and removed]A; and, at once, removed AMAN, B
300.6	into]A; upon B
300.18	father, you will remember.]A; father. AMAN, B
300.19	"I am an unworthy confidant, to have forgotten this so soon. Poor Powis, you were, indeed, unhappy!"]A; "Not know your father!" exclaimed Eve, the tones of her voice betraying powerful sympathy with the privations of the orphan, however, rather than any vulgar or common place surprise. AMAN, B
300.23	interest sufficient to excite]A; sufficient interest for AMAN; interest enough to excite CAMAN, B
300.26	reserves]A; reserve B
300.31	disappointments]A; disappointment AMAN, B
300.32	a clear expression]A; an expression AMAN, B

300.35	again prove]A; prove AMAN, B
300.39	second time]A; first ~ AMAN, B
301.1	by the]A; in ~ AMAN, B
301.7	minded]A; obeyed B
301.14	letter]A; last ~ AMAN, B
301.15	only a month]A; but ~ ~ AMAN, B
301.19	another gentle]A; a ~ AMAN, B
301.22	precious]A; precious, though trifling, AMAN, B
301.27	that]A; this AMAN, B
301.32	that caused feelings, keen as mine naturally were on such a subject, to]A; that feelings, as keen as mine would naturally be on such a subject, led me to AMAN; that feelings, so keen as mine would naturally be on such a subject, led me to B
301.35	motive of deception and dishonesty.]A; avenue of deception and dishonesty on this delicate subject. AMAN, B
302.3	Paul]A; Paul's arm AMAN, B
302.13	But, you are in an error,]A; I now perceive your error AMAN, B
302.33	arduous]A; long AMAN, B
302.38	relatives]A; relations AMAN, B
303.12	inclined]A; had led AMAN, B
303.14	But from]A; ~ of B
303.17	cruelly]A; much AMAN, B
303.27	is usual]A; was usual AMAN, B
303.29	"Miss]A; "Ah! Miss AMAN, B
303.35	virtually without]A; without AMAN, B
303.40	face bathed in tears, and flushed]A; face flushed AMAN, B
304.1	even heightened her loveliness]A; rendered her loveliness doubly winning AMAN, B
304.22	be at]A; have AMAN, B
304.26	beyond them]A; alone AMAN, B
304.27	that]A; that at length AMAN, B
304.38	but releasing]A; releasing AMAN, B
304.39	and found]A; but AMAN, B
305.2	perceiving that the occasion was favourable to a private conversation with his accepted son-in-law, and quite as unfavourable]A; saw that the occasion, on all accounts, was favourable to a private conversation between

	himself and his accepted son-in-law, and unfavorable AMAN, B
305.5	quietly took]A; took AMAN, B
*305.6	arm,]A; arm, therefore, CAMAN, B
306.22	remained]A; sat AMAN, B
306.22	still suffused]A; suffused AMAN, B
306.23	her hands lying before her folded]A; her folded hands lying before her AMAN, B
306.27	child]A; old charge AMAN, B
306.36	gush]A; display AMAN, B
306.37	one of the other's regulated mind]A; a mind so well regulated as that of Eve B
306.39	no; as far]A; now; far AMAN; no; far, as far CAMAN, B
307.6	claim, on]A; claim, to AMAN, B
307.13	beam]A; look AMAN, B
307.17	said Eve]A; Eve said AMAN, B
307.25	does Anne Sidley think]CE; does Ann Sidley think A; would Anne Sidley say AMAN, B
307.38	In all that related to physical wants]A; As regards the care of her infancy B
308.16	perfect purity]A; a perfect purity AMAN, B
308.21	existence]A; thinking AMAN, B
308.27	answer be]A; answer to be AMAN, B
308.31	demanded Eve]A; Eve demanded AMAN, B
308.35	and often]A; and often and often AMAN, B
309.3	But surely, the mere circumstance that he had]A; I admit that the mere circumstance of his having B
309.8	a particular]A; one ~ AMAN, B
309.13	so great]A; a ~ AMAN, B
309.23	thus overshadowed]A; overshadowed AMAN, B
309.24	affections. "It is, truly, as you say."]A; affections. AMAN; affections; "it is, truly, as you say." CAMAN, B
309.28	old nurse]A; darling old nurse AMAN, B
309.30	circumstance]A; circumstances AMAN, B
309.36	ironical]A; so ironical AMAN, B
310.9	serpent's]A; serpent B
310.15	so composed in manner]A; with a manner so composed AMAN, B
310.22	character]A; odious character AMAN, B

310.25	his ardent declarations]A; his ardent declamation AMAN; their ardent declamations B
310.29	countenance]A; sweet countenance AMAN, B
310.29	shone]A; shown AMAN, B
310.29	the room]A; from the garden AMAN, B
310.36	star-gazing]A; passing AMAN, B
311.8	friendly]A; winning AMAN, B
311.31	taught]A; first taught AMAN, B
311.39	the unpleasant]A; this ~ AMAN, B
311.41	speech]A; words AMAN, B
312.1	like words of doom]A; like a doom AMAN; like those of doom CAMAN, B
312.8	repair]A; undo AMAN, B
312.16	make]A; makes AMAN, B
312.17	got to be]A; become B
312.25	do not]A; dare ~ AMAN, B
312.27	that you ought at least]A; that, at least, you ought AMAN; that at least you ought B
312.30	occasion]A; an occasion B
312.38	reserves]A; reserve B
312.39	suitor]A; suitor for my hand AMAN, B
313.7	Assheton."]A; Assheton," Eve answered, after a moment's hesitation. AMAN, B
313.22	to our]A; towards our B
313.23	own]A; own sex B
313.24	were there]A; were B
313.29	uttered]A; given AMAN, B
313.35	effort]A; effect AMAN, B
313.37	drawing-rooms, human]A; drawing-room human AMAN
314.1	or in that of Sir George, or in]A; or that of Sir George himself, or of AMAN; or in that of Sir George himself, or in B
314.16	low associations]A; a low association AMAN, B
314.17	there be]A; there can be AMAN, B
314.21	to that which]A; to what AMAN, B
314.29	none]A; no one AMAN, B
314.30	to having]A; at ~ AMAN, B
314.39	gotten to associate]A; associated B
314.40	pictures]A; thoughts AMAN, B

315.1	much the most]A; the most AMAN, B
315.6	other suitor, infinitely the]A; other the AMAN, B
315.26	with the]A; ~ all ~ AMAN, B
315.27	gotten the mastery of]A; acquired the mastery over B
315.31	when they]A; where they AMAN, B
315.36	think]A; thought AMAN, B
315.39	am grateful]A; feel ~ AMAN, B
316.22	very]A; very, ~ AMAN, B
316.29	of feelings]A; of the feelings AMAN, B
316.30	confidences]A; confidence AMAN, B
317.8	such essential]A; essential B
317.9	under]A; only under AMAN, B
318.14	assembled.]A; assembled in it. AMAN, B
318.20	were in]A; were engaged in B
318.27	more]A; a more obstinate AMAN, B
318.32	hopes]A; hope B
318.35	have gotten a]A; have got a AMAN; have a B
319.20	political systems]A; systems AMAN, B
319.26	in a work]A; of a work AMAN; for a work B
320.2	once, that]A; once, or that CAMAN, B
320.3	I am glad]A; ¶ "I am glad AMAN, B
320.4	hands, Mrs. Bloomfield, and]A; hands," said Mrs. Bloomfield, "and B
320.16	mystification]A; mystifications AMAN, B
320.29	at all times]A; at times AMAN, B
320.33	it really is]A; they really are AMAN
320.39	provision of the law is]A; provisions of the law are B
321.1	than of]A; than B
321.6	the country]A; that country AMAN, B
321.8	believe that]A; believe this AMAN, B
321.10	his opinion]A; ~ opinions AMAN, B
321.13	Bunker Hill]A; Bunker's Hill B
321.13	Cowpens]A; Monmouth AMAN, B
321.16	into the country]A; in the country AMAN; through the country B
321.20	admission]A; admissions AMAN, B
321.27	article]A; articles AMAN, B
321.27	commences]A; commenced AMAN, B
321.40	the passage]A; that passage AMAN, B
322.10	that it]A; that which it B

322.22	this?" ¶"Why does not the author reviewed expose this?" ¶"Why does not a gentleman wrangle with a detected pick-pocket?"]A; this?" AMAN, B
322.25	literary]A; literally AMAN, B
322.30	late date]A; ~ day AMAN, B
322.38	you,]A; you that AMAN
323.7	It strikes]A; They strike AMAN, B
323.33	a dog]A; the dog AMAN, B
324.5	put in]A; said B
324.13	&c. &c. &c.]A; &c. B
324.14	should]A; should certainly B
324.28	getting to be]A; becoming B
325.4	astonishing the four quarters of the world. I]A; astonishing; in the four quarters of the world, I B
325.6	these two]A; those two AMAN, B
325.7	all other]A; all the other AMAN, B
325.9	acute learned]A; acute and learned B
325.15	put in]A; interposed B
325.17	than]A; than on AMAN, B
326.6	that all]A; why ~ B
326.9	at last]A; ~ least AMAN, B
326.9	credit]A; order AMAN; odour CAMAN, B
327.1	remark]A; remarks AMAN, B
327.21	discussions]A; discussion AMAN, B
328.6	homes]A; houses AMAN, B
328.20	to do]A; as if to do AMAN, B
329.17	and the]A; ~ with ~ B
330.1	got to be]A; become B
330.3	goes]A; is AMAN, B
330.6	pure of]A; ~ in B
330.12	received her cousin]A; receives her father's cousin AMAN, B
330.22	matter]A; question AMAN, B
330.25	he shall not]A; not AMAN; he may not CAMAN, B
330.27	promoted]A; permitted AMAN; admitted CAMAN, B
331.4	"every]A; "for every AMAN, B
331.16	not as]A; ~ so B
331.39	more]A; now AMAN, B
331.40	first]A; now first AMAN, B
331.41	mutually]A; naturally AMAN, B

332.7	Dearest sir!]A; Father! AMAN, B
332.9	at home]A; either ~ ~ AMAN, B
332.19	Father!]A; Sir! AMAN, B
332.24	family connections]A; family or connections AMAN; family or connexions B
332.30	an American marriage, where]A; American marriages, when AMAN, B
332.32	carried, necessarily, into associations for which their habits have given them too much and too good tastes to enter into]A; carried, necessarily, into associations for which their habits have given them too much and too good tastes to indulge in AMAN; carried into associations repugnant to their taste and habits B
332.35	if really]A; if she be really B
332.38	connections]A; connexion B
332.39	communications]A; communication B
333.2	knew]A; know AMAN, B
333.23	fidelity]A; felicity AMAN, B
333.29	attachments]A; attachment B
333.30	did]A; then did AMAN, B
334.19	the whole time]A all the time AMAN, B
334.21	Jack]A; our cousin AMAN, B
334.33	last person who]A; last who AMAN, B
334.36	Is it even so?]A; It is even so; AMAN, B
335.17	you were]A; we ~ AMAN, B
335.26	friend]A; patron AMAN, B
335.32	relation]A; relative AMAN, B
335.33	disappointed]A; disappointed in this expectation AMAN, B
335.34	more than]A; but AMAN, B
336.5	relative]A; relation AMAN, B
336.12	there are . . . we know]A; there were . . . we knew AMAN, B
337.16	arose]A; arrive AMAN; arrose CAMAN
337.17	in your favour twenty years ago]A; twenty years ago, in your favour AMAN; twenty years ago, in your favor, too CAMAN, B
337.21	that this]A; this AMAN, B
337.29	as discrete and as]A; so discrete and B
338.5	Do so]A; Do AMAN, B

338.7	ten]A; near ten AMAN, B
338.21	join]A; come to AMAN, B
338.25	happy]A; truly happy AMAN, B
338.35	thought so once,]A; once thought he cherished a passion for her, B
339.10	had committed]A; committed B
339.25	first]A; one first AMAN, B
339.27	produced]A; made AMAN, B
339.30	believing that]A; believing AMAN, B
339.31	fashion having undergone no very striking revolution in]A; for fashion has undergone no very striking revolutions in AMAN; for fashion has undergone no very striking revolutions during B
340.2	came from]A; come ~ AMAN, B
340.6	heightened than lessened]A; heightened AMAN, B
340.10	feeling]A; emotion AMAN, B
340.12	dressing-box]A; dressing case AMAN; dressing-case B
340.12	supposing that]A; supposing AMAN, B
340.14	and opened the lid with a view to replace the picture of Eve's mother, with a species of pious reverence.] A; and, with a sort of pious reverence, opened the lid intending to replace the picture of Eve's mother. B
340.16	that now]A; which now AMAN, B
340.33	the missing]A; your ~ AMAN, B
341.3	as to the countenance, or the]A; in the countenance, or in the AMAN; in the countenance or in the B
341.7	almost livid]A; livid AMAN, B
341.15	very picture]A; picture AMAN, B
341.19	hoarsely, as he]A; hoarsely; he AMAN, B
341.24	yet I]A; yet do I AMAN, B
341.28	Powis]A; Paul AMAN, B
341.37	have been]A; be AMAN, B
342.3	his eyes]A; eye AMAN; his eye CAMAN, B
342.3	appears to be]A; appears AMAN, B
342.9	'I have taken the child with me to get the picture from the jeweller, who has mended the ring, and the little urchin knew it at a glance.'"]A; *I have taken the child with me to get the picture from the jeweller, who has mended the ring, and the little urchin knew it at a glance.*" AMAN, B

342.13	knows]A; knew AMAN, B
342.15	ever retained]A; always ~ AMAN, B
342.35	an apprehension]A; his ~ AMAN, B
342.40	gentlemanlike]A; gentlemanly AMAN, B
343.1	caused his countenance to appear]A; made his countenance appear AMAN, B
344.15	of the confidential]A; ~ all ~ ~ AMAN, B
344.17	sensations]A; emotions AMAN, B
344.20	look]A; glances AMAN; looks CAMAN, B
344.22	the conversation]A; their ~ AMAN, B
344.29	honest heart]A; heart AMAN, B
345.3	novelty]A; sake AMAN, B
345.7	ought you]A; you ought AMAN, B
345.14	known that]A known AMAN, B
345.17	quest]A; search AMAN, B
345.20	by means]A; by the means AMAN, B
345.23	the word]A; that ~ AMAN, B
345.23	in]A; to these AMAN, B
345.25	treasures]A; treasure AMAN, B
345.30	passed.]A; passed between us. AMAN, B
345.31	offer, Mr.—that]A; offer, that Mr.—that AMAN; offer, B
345.39	cousin]A; *our* cousin AMAN, B
346.2	Paul]A; dearest ~ AMAN, B
346.5	will remain]A; may ~ AMAN, B
346.8	the bloom which happiness had left]A; health or happiness had left the bloom AMAN, B
346.17	so]A; so that AMAN, B
346.19	for]CAMAN; from AMAN
346.26	child?]A; son? AMAN, B
346.26	the solemn]A; his ~ AMAN, B
346.27	almost a]A; an almost AMAN, B
346.32	your mother blameless]A; you his lawful child. AMAN; you the child of a blameless mother CAMAN, B
246.39	that in its exhibition caused]A; that caused, in its exhibition, AMAN, B
346.40	these young]A; their ~ AMAN, B
347.1	pure was]A; pure AMAN, B
347.2	feeling]A; the other's feelings AMAN, B
347.13	sort of]A; kind of AMAN, B

347.13	weighed]A; weighed heavily AMAN, B
347.13	if not on the comforts]A; and comfort AMAN, B
347.17	concerned with]A; concerned in AMAN, B
347.19	perfect liberty]A; liberty AMAN, B
347.25	him]A; them B
347.30	got to be]A; become B
347.30	and]A; for AMAN, B
347.33	were his own views than those of]A; his own views were than those of most of AMAN, B
347.35	or as to]A; or AMAN, B
347.38	for principles]A; principles AMAN, B
348.5	consequences]A; the consequences AMAN, B
348.6	avoid perceiving]A; fail to detect AMAN, B
348.9	very frame]A; frame AMAN, B
348.13	heralds]A; herald AMAN, B
348.14	while]A; though AMAN, B
348.17	broke]A; at last broke AMAN, B
348.20	letter]A; letters AMAN, B
348.26	listen—]A; listen to— AMAN; listen to. B
348.28	herself precipitately]A; herself AMAN, B
348.29	sufficient]A; sufficient to us AMAN; sufficient for us CAMAN
348.30	to know]A; ~ hear AMAN, B
348.37	your own sense of]A; your sense AMAN; your sense of B
348.37	dear father]A; my ~ AMAN, B
349.3	to be]A; will be AMAN, B
349.4	facts. My tale will be very short, and I crave your patience, Ned, while I expose my former weakness to these young people."]A; facts." AMAN, B
349.7	then he]A; and then AMAN; and then he CAMAN, B
349.19	as eccentric and violent]A; as violent and eccentric AMAN; so violent and eccentric B
349.24	as entirely]A; so entirely B
349.26	learn that your father was accepted, (though the marriage was deferred two years in consideration for my feelings,)]A; watch the marriage of your parents, AMAN; learn that my kinsman was accepted, (though the marriage was kindly deferred two years, in consideration for my feelings,) CAMAN, B

349.28	a resentment]A; and a resentment B
349.29	that was]A; which was AMAN, B
*349.29	parents,]A; parents, were alike contending, B
349.30	home]A; them AMAN, B
349.31	own]A; acknowledge B
349.32	lurked]CAMAN, A; looked AMAN
349.35	arrangements to]A; arrangements, even to B
349.38	sad blot]A; blot AMAN, B
350.2	feared]A; trembled B
350.6	was, itself, a]A; was a AMAN; was truly a CAMAN, B
350.14	were anger]A; produce ~ B
350.29	had got to be]A; became B
350.33	explanations]A; explanation B
350.33	there being no bans or license necessary]A; no banns nor license being necessary AMAN, B
350.34	only being]A; being only AMAN, B
350.35	so unmindful]A; so far unmindful AMAN, B
351.6	believe that]A; believe AMAN, B
351.17	passed]A; been passed AMAN, B
351.23	any untruth]A; an ~ AMAN, B
351.23	one would think you]A; you AMAN, B
351.27	extorted]A; exacted AMAN, B
351.33	hurrying]A; hastening AMAN, B
352.5	reunited]A; ~ to her AMAN, B
352.11	poor wife]A; wife AMAN, B
352.12	innocently demanded]A; demanded AMAN, B
352.21	can suppose]A; would ~ AMAN, B
352.23	Paul asked]A; said Paul AMAN; asked Paul CAMAN, B
352.25	course was taken]A; was the course adopted AMAN, B
352.31	to me were then]A; to me were AMAN; then were CAMAN, B
353.5	this person]A; him AMAN, B
353.17	about]A; concerning AMAN, B
353.21	married after]A; married Mabel Warrender, after AMAN, B
353.31	that, in 1829, during our late visit to the old world, I ascended the Nile with General Ducie for a]A; that during our late visit to the other hemisphere, I ascended the Nile, in 1829, with General Ducie as a AMAN, B
353.39	very verge]A; verge AMAN, B

354.22	certainly had]A; had certainly AMAN, B
354.32	little doubt]A; no ~ AMAN, B
354.39	until, in his fourth year, she yielded him to Mr. Powis,] A; until she yielded him to Mr. Powis, in his fourth year, AMAN, B
354.40	trouble]A; the ~ B
355.2	latter]A; letter B
355.7	after the fainting fit of the latter, as soon as his]A; as soon after the fainting fit of the latter as his AMAN, B
355.10	would settle]A; settle AMAN; will settle CAMAN, B
355.17	the endorsement]A; an ~ AMAN, B
355.20	energy]A; emphasis AMAN, B
355.21	child. He was innocent]A; child, for he was ignorant AMAN; child, for he was innocent CAMAN, B
356.9	of his]A; of all his AMAN, B
356.32	hope,]A; hope, therefore, AMAM, B
357.16	that]A; which B
357.16	different causes]A; a different cause AMAN, B
357.17	first]A; former B
357.34	gentlemanlike]A; gentlemanly AMAN, B
357.36	their rights]A; themselves AMAN, B
357.39	criticisms]A; criticism AMAN, B
358.1	stands]A; stand AMAN, B
358.2	being a topic of never-ending]A; is the topic of principal AMAN; being the topic of principal CAMAN, B
358.8	nobleman, as a matter of course, to]A; nobleman, was, as a matter of course, ascribed to B
358.30	feelings impetuous as hers seldom waiting]A; for feelings impetuous as hers seldom waited AMAN, B
359.3	foreign]A; foreignified AMAN, B
359.8	the public]A; that the public was AMAN, B
359.26	by the]A; ~ all ~ AMAN, B
360.4	superiority]A; ascendancy AMAN, B
360.4	with]A; with the results of AMAN, B
360.7	has attended]A; have attended B
360.8	has certainly]A; have certainly B
360.9	the prevalent]A; that prevalent AMAN, B
360.10	is the]A; ~ in ~ B
360.15	vital religion]A; morality AMAN, B
360.15	goes]A; go AMAN, B

360.17	I beg you will call to them]A; do call to them AMAN; do call them B
360.22	those]A; the two AMAN, B
360.25	bustle]A; little ~ AMAN, B
360.31	neither]A; only AMAN, B
360.36	be really]A; be B
360.38	happen to know]A; know AMAN, B
360.40	introduced to him]A; introduced AMAN, B
361.12	Eve Effingham]A; Effingham AMAN, B
361.21	Merely]A; I understand—merely AMAN, B
361.24	existed]A; existed such a confusion AMAN, B
361.26	that neither]A; ~ she ~ B
361.35	Ah,]A; Oh, AMAN, B
362.3	meant]A; merely meant AMAN, B
362.7	put in]A; said B
362.7	"but that merely shows they have some education; it is done every where."]A; "but all who do not hold on to the platform do that." AMAN, B
362.12	letters]A; a reader AMAN, B
362.17	queens," said the Captain. "Why]A; queens. Why AMAN, B
362.18	sin,]A; sin, Mrs. Abbott, AMAN, B
362.30	put in]A; observed B
363.1	hope ever]A; hope AMAN, B
363.5	grace, either]A; beauty AMAN, B
363.23	gotten to be]A; become B
363.27	cards]A; all fours AMAN; all-fours B
363.27	happens]A; happened AMAN, B
363.34	without regard to rank]A; all together AMAN; altogether B
363.37	that disputant]A; the ~ AMAN, B
363.37	while]A; though AMAN, B
363.39	though]A; albeit B
363.39	doubt,]A; doubt that AMAN
364.2	the Christian]A; christian AMAN; Christian B
364.8	Truck found]A; ~ now ~ AMAN, B
364.29	her]A; her full AMAN, B
364.33	Abbott, shaking both hands,—"awful—awful—awful!]A; Abbot, "awful, awful! AMAN, B
364.36	captain,]A; captain, coolly, AMAN, B

364.40	cross,]A; cross, indeed, AMAN, B
365.8	evidence]A; evidences AMAN, B
365.12	thorough-working]A; thoroughly working AMAN, B
365.13	in a]A; with a AMAN, B
365.22	presence of the odious cards]A; odious presence of the cards AMAN, B
366.10	down comes all that rests on it, again.]A; down all that rests on it comes again. AMAN, B
366.22	that transaction]A; the action AMAN, B; the transaction CAMAN
367.7	us in]A; in in AMAN; me in B
367.18	fish]A; the ~ AMAN, B
368.37	a ray]A; ray B
369.12	as learned]A; learned AMAN, B
369.20	John]A; Mr. John AMAN, B
369.33	should fall to their share]A; an equal chance AMAN, B
369.41	answered, in]A; answered on AMAN, B
370.3	but is]A; ~ it ~ B
370.10	too lenient]A; lenient AMAN, B
370.11	be an unhappy]A; not be a happy AMAN, B
370.12	to Eve]A; and ~ B
370.13	Here both]A; Here B
370.13	the nip]A; their ~ B
370.14	soon got to be]A; to be AMAN; got to be CAMAN; became B
371.31	had the usual tournure]A; had the usual *tournure* AMAN; possessed the usual *tournure* B
371.34	soon]A; had soon AMAN, B
371.36	fashion, being of]A; fashion, and, being of AMAN; and, being composed of CAMAN, B
371.37	and of]A; of AMAN; was of B
371.38	is not without its]A; has unusual AMAN, B
372.3	the bridal]A; its ~ AMAN, B
372.3	While]A; As AMAN, B
372.7	bore with]A; bore B
372.31	certain]A; many AMAN, B
372.32	did look at]A; did look on AMAN; looked on B
372.39	will marry]A; shall ~ AMAN, B
373.1	perfectly mute with astonishment]A; mute with astonishment for a short time AMAN, B

373.2	often seen]A; seen AMAN, B
373.7	own maid]A; maid B
373.7	than that which the reader]A; than the reader's AMAN; than the reader B
373.9	has just]A; has B
373.12	to seek this consummation to]A; to this consummation to AMAN; to this consummation of all CAMAN, B
373.16	came from]A; come from AMAN, B
373.21	turned]A; had turned AMAN, B
373.26	piquancy]A; poignancy AMAN, B
373.27	her proposals and been]A; his proposals and been AMAN; his proposals and had been CAMAN, B
373.30	*un avocat*]A; an *avocat* AMAN, B
373.32	The plan]A; Their plan AMAN, B
373.35	trader,]A; trader, to keep tavern, AMAN, B
374.11	enacted]A; clenched AMAN, B
374.14	a month's warning]A; a month's notice AMAN; a regular notice CAMAN, B
374.16	on a hint]A; at a hint AMAN, B
374.17	the engagement]A; his time AMAN, B
374.26	are brought]A; were ever brought AMAN, B
374.26	similar occasions]A; a similar occasion AMAN, B
374.28	in honest pride, and in an]A; in an honest pride and an AMAN; in an honest pride and B
375.6	trust]A; ~ to AMAN, B
375.9	of their]A; in ~ B
375.14	around]A; round AMAN, B
375.15	the wedding]A; their wedding AMAN, B
375.15	whole]A; whole of the AMAN, B
375.18	blending, from many points, with the gayer trees in the grounds of the former]A; blending with the gayer trees of the grounds of the former, from many points AMAN, B
375.24	delay]A; any ~ AMAN, B
375.27	that morning]A; this morning AMAN, B
375.28	scruples]A; scruple AMAN, B
375.30	that publicity-principle]A; the ~ AMAN; the publicity principle B
375.32	of curiosity]A; of their curiosity AMAN; of their rabid curiosity CAMAN, B

375.33	because the]A; ~ a AMAN, B
375.40	When]A; As AMAN, B
376.2	eagerly]A; sagely AMAN, B
376.7	lying in]A; being AMAN, B
376.9	the class]A; that ~ AMAN, B
376.10	wrongs]A; as wrongs AMAN; as a wrong B
376.12	That is]A; It is AMAN, B
376.12	which]A; that which AMAN, B
376.22	them]A; them both AMAN, B
376.24	obtrusive]A; intrusive AMAN, B
376.26	proceed]A; proceed swiftly AMAN, B
376.27	half]A; a quarter of AMAN, B
376.28	was]A; were B
376.31	while]A; as AMAN, B
376.32	the unbidden tears falling]A; while the unbidden tears fell AMAN, B
377.8	feeling; we will]A; feeling, but we will AMAN; feelings, but we will B
377.10	new]A; now AMAN, B
377.11	heart, too, dear]A; heart. Dear AMAN, B
377.20	the honest and affectionate creature being much too] A; for the honest and affectionate creature was too AMAN, B
377.22	emotions]A; affections AMAN, B
377.26	said Eve, taking]A; and Eve took AMAN, B
377.29	prove happy]A; prove happy ones AMAN, B
377.30	I do—I do—I do -]A; I do—I do—B
377.37	mother before her]A; mother B
378.2	contrary with her own tongue]A; contrary B
378.3	to have assurance made]A; to make assurance AMAN, B
378.14	will all]A; shall all AMAN, B
378.32	moment, was startled]A; moment startled AMAN, B
378.39	is possibly]A; may be AMAN, B
378.40	affections were another's before]A; heart was another's long before AMAN, B
379.1	Eve]A; coz AMAN, B
379.6	wedding-day]A; wedding-days AMAN, B
379.8	conscious]A; heartfelt AMAN, B
379.18	grounds]A; ground B

379.24	Messrs. Effinghams]A; Messr. Effingham AMAN; Mr. Effinghams B
379.26	saying that]A; saying AMAN, B
379.26	now persuade]A; persuade AMAN, B
380.4	Ah!]A; Oh! AMAN, B
380.5	shaking his head]A; plaintively AMAN, B
380.21	genteelest]A; gentlest AMAN, B
380.24	suppose]A; ~ that AMAN, B
380.31	Third]A; Third in AMAN, B
380.38	much more]A; more AMAN, B
380.39	honour]A; favor AMAN; favour B
380.39	passage]A; passages AMAN, B
381.9	indeed, Mam'selle]A; indeed, AMAN, B
381.20	proceeded in his enumeration of wonders.]A; proceeded. AMAN, B
381.21	seeing]A; having seen AMAN, B
381.22	Dogs, now,]A; Dogs, AMAN, B
381.29	as polished]A; so ~ B
381.38	repay one]A; repay AMAN, B
382.2	supreme]A; extreme AMAN, B
382.3	got to be]A; become B
*382.4	Wenham will]A; Wenlock may not AMAN; Wenham may CAMAN, B
382.6	representative]A; representation B
382.16	was so,]A; was AMAN, B
382.18	can move in manhood]A; can now move, in full manhood AMAN; can now move with in full manhood B
382.21	as blind]A; as bland AMAN; so bland B
382.24	weaknesses]A; weakness AMAN, B
383.13	when used understandingly]A; when judiciously used B
383.13	so infallibly]A; as infallibly AMAN, B
383.14	circumstances, while her attire]A; circumstances. Her morning attire AMAN, B
383.15	its customary]A; the customary AMAN, B
383.24	the exquisite]A; and the exquisite AMAN, B
383.26	nearly]A; almost AMAN, B
383.38	sight painful]A; painful sight AMAN, B
383.40	and he]A; as ~ AMAN, B
384.8	her hands]A; both her eyes AMAN, B

384.8	her]A; her a moment AMAN, B
384.11	which had]A; which B
384.21	pensive]A; gentle AMAN, B
384.22	first]A; at first AMAN, B
384.36	perfect]A; noble AMAN, B
384.40	often,]A; often, dear Paul, AMAN, B
384.40	lies]A; is AMAN, B
385.4	my father—my dear]A; my dear B
385.7	kind, excellent]A; excellent B
385.9	worthy]A; the ~ B
385.13	understandingly]A; confidently B
386.5	You possess]A; Thou possest AMAN
386.5	duty; of]A; duty, and of AMAN, B
386.7	you are]A; thou art AMAN, B
386.8	you]A; thee AMAN, B
386.15	same way]A; unprofitable task AMAN, B
386.17	innocent]A; as ~ AMAN, B
386.17	crimson tinge covered]A; crimson tinged AMAN, B
386.18	who is]A; that ~ AMAN, B
386.23	the brief]A; their ~ AMAN, B
386.40	always safe]A; safe B
387.1	the kingdoms]A; their ~ AMAN, B
387.10	wishes]A; wishes, like AMAN; wishes like B
387.25	now I]A; I now AMAN, B
387.32	but]A; and AMAN, B
387.34	Paul resumed, when his swelling heart permitted him to speak.]A; Paul when he could speak. AMAN; Paul continued when he could speak. CAMAN, B
388.2	great pain]A; pain B
388.9	who *quits* it last.]A; the superior that quits it first. AMAN, B
388.14	dearest]A; beloved AMAN, B
388.18	is commencing under auspices so favourable as to seem almost providential.]A; may be said to commence. AMAN, B

Word Division

List A records compounds hyphenated at the end of the line in the copy-texts and resolved as hyphenated or unhyphenated as listed below. If the word occurs elsewhere in the copy-texts or if Cooper's other manuscripts of the period consistently followed one practice respecting this particular compound, the resolution was made on that basis. Otherwise, first editions of his works of this period were used as guides. List B is a guide to transcription of compounds hyphenated at the end of the line in the Cooper Edition: compounds recorded here should be transcribed as given; words divided at the end of the line and not listed should be transcribed as one word.

List A

3.32	fellow-creatures
9.39	highways
12.38	town-clerk
13.20	drawing-room
19.25	overlooked
21.9	forthwith
26.32	punch-bowl
27.34	nobody
29.19	drawing-room
32.28	gentlemen
40.40	painstaking
42.12	anti-republican
45.2	New-England
45.11	outbreaking
45.30	self-respect
49.11	overshadowed
50.33	to-night

53.9	sometimes
65.38	twelvemonth
66.38	grandfather
77.27	quarter-deck
80.30	gentleman
85.34	Gwy-ky-o-*lee*?
87.31	Chateaubriand
88.17	oyster-supper
96.11	New-York
98.9	seamen
102.38	New-Haven
106.40	highway
116.24	noontide
124.18	Yorkshire
129.28	fort[h]night
140.31	blackguard
168.10	new-school
172.9	boatman
173.22	overhanging
194.4	forthwith
195.29	Clear-headed
199.27	village-fashion
203.11	bare-footed
205.19	fortnight
206.5	close-mouthed
211.40	countrywomen
214.13	pork-barrel
215.18	stagecoach
215.20	rail-roads
220.16	flying-jib-boom
220.36	never-dying
221.3	twenty-four
222.5	packet-training
237.20	countrymen
242.39	cable-rope
244.12	tiller-rope
248.28	punch-bowl
249.28	ship-masters
251.11	ship-masters
256.39	self-denial

264.11	countrymen
272.1	French-looking
277.20	fellow-creatures
279.32	countryman
283.22	self-reliance
308.14	single-hearted
309.23	overshadowed
310.36	star-gazing
321.12	twenty-eight
333.11	kinsman
340.12	dressing-box
345.20	money-yielding
346.35	breakfast-bell
351.32	south-western
357.34	gentlemanlike
362.40	skipping-rope
364.17	rope-jumper
367.37	clear-sighted
369.28	well-regulated
375.18	church-yard
379.37	wedding-feast
381.13	East-Cheap

List B

8.29	New-York
13.3	law-honesty
14.13	self-command
24.17	fire-side
25.8	tomb-stone
28.29	drawing-room
39.18	Quick-sighted
40.13	drawing-room
40.15	land-agent
40.24	uncalled-for
47.35	over-sophisticated
49.15	common-place
56.14	New-York
59.7	New-York

60.34	ear-shot
61.23	good-looking
63.24	*New-York*
64.22	half-affected
68.13	self-possession
79.14	grand-looking
92.9	twenty-five
109.15	wheel-track
133.21	community-character
137.11	paper-hangings
150.11	great-great
167.3	old-school
168.10	new-school
179.39	melo-dramatick
180.27	law-breaking
196.12	unheard-of
202.34	Rinaldo-Rinaldini
207.9	soul-reviving
211.34	lady-like
220.30	hang-dog
224.35	fellow-passenger
226.22	dinner-bell
236.27	heirs-general
242.4	Otsego-water
242.22	fresh-water
246.30	weather-beaten
246.38	fresh-water
248.25	law-makers
250.25	salt-water
257.11	self-abasement
257.27	fatal-character
264.16	ill-assorted
267.28	breakfast-table
272.15	horse-chestnut
273.7	every-day
278.20	well-known
283.22	self-reliance
288.37	left-hand
308.14	single-hearted
318.30	way-side

322.23	pick-pocket
324.27	New-York
327.17	quick-minded
330.33	straight-forward
342.26	self-possessed
345.14	great-grandson
348.41	self-respect
353.22	brother-in
362.34	aunty-Anne
365.37	jack-screw
366.19	Blunt-Powis
367.1	to-morrow
367.34	fresh-water
369.36	weak-minded
370.5	to-morrow
372.8	self-command
376.27	drawing-room
381.17	good-natured

CPSIA information can be obtained
at www.ICGtesting.com
Printed in the USA
BVHW081138300123
657433BV00007B/166